THE DROW HATH SENT THEE

GOTH DROW™ BOOK FIVE

MARTHA CARR

MICHAEL ANDERLE

LMBPN Publishing
PMB 196, 2540 South Maryland Pkwy
Las Vegas, NV 89109

First US Edition, October, 2020
eBook ISBN: 978-1-64971-212-7
Print ISBN: 978-1-64971-213-4

THE DROW HATH
SENT THEE

THE DROW HATH SENT THEE TEAM

Thanks to the JIT Readers

Peter Manis
Diane L. Smith
Veronica Stephan-Miller
Deb Mader
Paul Westman
Kerry Mortimer
Angel LaVey
Jackey Hankard-Brodie
Larry Omans
John Ashmore

If we've missed anyone, please let us know!

Editor
The Skyhunter Editing Team

DEDICATIONS

From Martha

To everyone who still believes in magic
and all the possibilities that holds.
To all the readers who make this
entire ride so much fun.
And to my son, Louie and so many wonderful friends who remind me
all the time of what
really matters and how wonderful
life can be in any given moment.

From Michael

To Family, Friends and
Those Who Love
To Read.
May We All Enjoy Grace
To Live The Life We Are
Called.

CHAPTER ONE

"The Crown! The Crown!"

Fists and swords pounded against chests and plate mail in harsh, echoing rhythm with the chant.

Cheyenne Summerlin stood in the center of all of it and could only focus on the pain lancing through her chest just below both shoulders. Worse than that was the searing agony bursting over and over through her hip. She gritted her teeth and let Ember hold her upright a little longer in the center of the Heart's courtyard. *This is either ghost pain from that bullet, or something's seriously wrong.*

"You okay?" Ember muttered, hovering beside her friend as every magical in the courtyard knelt, thumped, and chanted their allegiance to the new O'gúl Crown.

"Yeah, Em." With a grimace, Cheyenne met her *Nós Aní's* gaze. "Any chance you could whip up some quick healing for me? Can't really make my first and last decree as Crown if I can't think straight."

Ember gazed at the magicals staring fervently up at them both. They growled their chant, some of the orc guards hissing and snarling as they said it, but she thought she saw them smiling now and then around their thick yellowed tusks. "Uh-huh. Hang tight."

"If I hang on any tighter, I'm gonna end up crushing you." Cheyenne looked at Maleshi and Corian, who both remained on their knees and stared at her with wide, glowing silver eyes. Seeing that feral grin of victory on both nightstalkers' faces made this whole thing that much weirder. *Without L'zar present, they're the craziest-looking ones here. How enlightening.*

She sucked in a sharp breath when Ember settled her free hand over one of the deep, thick holes Ba'rael's purple darts had left in the new Crown's flesh. A soft golden light bloomed beneath the fae girl's palm, and warmth instantly spread up and over Cheyenne's shoulder. It was gone the next second, and Cheyenne snarled at the new flare of intensified pain bursting through her shoulder. It almost knocked her sideways, but Ember kept a firm grip on her friend's arm and steadied Cheyenne as she staggered.

"What?" The fae's unnaturally wide luminous violet eyes grew even wider. "What's wrong?"

"That wasn't supposed to make it feel worse, was it?"

"It feels worse?" Ember peeled the shredded fabric of Cheyenne's shirt away from her shoulder and winced. "Kinda looks worse too."

The black streaks in the half-drow's flesh that had appeared almost instantly with the wound were darker now, snaking away from the thick hole trickling blood and moving up across Cheyenne's collarbone and farther across her chest.

"Awesome." Cheyenne swayed, her eyelids fluttering, and tried to shake off the dizziness. "I don't wanna be the one to say there's something up with your healing, Em."

"There's nothing wrong with my healing."

"So, I'll go with the shitty poison that bitch pelted into me."

"Hey, I healed the real blight right out of a raug chief, okay?" Ember nodded and gave her friend's arm a reassuring squeeze. "I'll figure out how to heal you too."

"I know you will." Having so many O'gúleesh gazes centered directly on her made Cheyenne's skin tingle. *Didn't wanna be the center of this kind of attention, but whatever. That's gonna change right now.* "Okay. I'm gonna walk on my own for this."

"I'm right behind you." Ember nodded and released her grip on her friend's arm.

"Cool." Cheyenne faced the magicals kneeling in front of her and tried to roll her shoulders back. The pain intensified, and she gave up any attempt to straighten out of her slump before she staggered toward the much smaller group of L'zar's rebels and the members of the Four-Pointed Star. She stopped in front of Persh'al, who grinned up at her and dipped his head. "Persh'al."

"Cheyenne."

Kneeling beside him, Elarit looked the new Crown over from head to toe and dipped her head too. A small, close-lipped smile bloomed on her lips beneath the delicate silver chains draping from ear to ear across her cheekbones and the bridge of her nose.

Yeah, sure. Now she's happy to see me.

Cheyenne swallowed and forced herself not to fall right on top of the troll couple. "Dude, you gotta stand up for this."

Persh'al blinked. "What?"

"I'm not having this conversation with you while you're on your knees, man. Come on." She gestured weakly for him to stand and spared a brief glance at the other kneeling magicals surrounding them. *Give 'em a show, right? Not sure they'll love it, but they'll have to suck it up and deal.*

The blue troll glanced at his long-distance girlfriend, and Elarit gave him a barely perceptible shrug. Frowning, Persh'al finally cocked his head. "You okay, kid?"

"We can talk about that later. This is a little more important."

"Okay."

Maleshi glanced at the new drow Crown and the blue troll, then pushed to her feet and thrust her hand in the air. A bolt of crackling silver lightning raced from her outstretched fingers straight up through the center of the courtyard, past the nonexistent ceiling, and into the dull gray sky over Hangivol. "Silence! The Crown speaks!"

The general's shout echoed against the stone walls of the courtyard. The banging on metal and stone stopped instantly, and the Heart fell eerily silent.

Cheyenne raised an eyebrow at the general, who grinned again and dipped her head in a small bow.

"Right." Trying to ignore the countless pairs of eyes settled intently on her, Cheyenne clenched her fists at her sides against the growing agony in her shoulders and hip and returned her attention to Persh'al. "I can think of a million reasons right now why it's a good thing L'zar couldn't be here for my weirdly anticlimactic victory. If we can even call it that."

Persh'al grinned, oblivious to what was coming next.

Cheyenne cocked her head. "Number one on my list, though, is this. You want the job, or what?"

"Huh?" The blue troll's yellow eyes widened, then he burst out laughing. The sound of it raced across the courtyard, bringing confused sniggers and chuckles from some of the other gathered O'gúleesh.

She let him have his moment and slowly turned her head to look at both nightstalkers beside her. Maleshi's small smile faded, and Corian stood abruptly as he realized what was happening.

"Cheyenne." He approached her for more of a private conversation, and the stern curiosity on his face cut Persh'al's laughter short. "Are you sure?"

"You just won, kid," Maleshi added as she joined them. "All this is yours. There's no rush. Plus, you look like you're hurtin' a little."

Corian scratched behind his pointy, tufted ear. "We haven't even had a chance to set everything in motion yet. Make it official."

Persh'al's orange mohawk wobbled as he looked quickly at the halfling and the nightstalkers acting as her advisors. "Wait, you're serious?"

"Come on." Cheyenne tried to shrug, and the pain flaring beneath her shoulders made her hiss. "Look, we all knew I was coming into this with no desire whatsoever to be the Crown over here. I don't want it, and there's no point in me keeping it longer than this."

"Whoa, whoa." Persh'al slapped a hand against the shaved side of his orange-speckled head. "You want me to take the..." He gulped and couldn't finish.

Cheyenne looked him dead in the eye and nodded. "Yeah."

The blue troll blustered and fidgeted before stepping away from her and turning mutely toward Elarit. The troll woman raised an eyebrow before looking at Cheyenne again with a whole new appreciation.

"Still needs a vote, though," Corian muttered.

"Sure." Cheyenne peered around the troll at the Four-Pointed Star rebels and raised her voice as much as she could. Quickening pulses of searing heat radiated through her shoulders and across her hip. "That's what we're doing right here right now. I choose Persh'al

Tenishi as the new O'gúl Crown. To turn his cycle after mine, or whatever."

Maleshi snorted.

"Anyone opposed?"

L'zar's band of rebels against the old Crown got slowly to their feet. When Nu'ek rose, her massive hirsute body blocked most of the kneeling orc guards behind her. The Golra jerked her chin at Cheyenne and snorted. "Tell us, then."

Cheyenne absently reached for her blazing hip, snarling and immediately withdrawing her hand when it brushed the purple dart still protruding from her flesh and pants. "Tell you what?"

"Tell us why." The ogre Sakrit nodded. "Explain your choice."

"Right." Clenching her eyes shut against the pain, Cheyenne took a deep breath. *They better make a damn decision soon. I can't keep standing here like this.* "Persh'al's the best choice, and yeah, I honestly believe that."

The blue troll grinned at her and folded his arms.

"He knows his way around, and I don't just mean in Hangivol. We spent a lot of time in the Outers, and he knows how to deal with O'gúleesh everywhere. Even when we made the crossing Earthside, he didn't give a shit about fighting off those things in the in-between on his own. All he cared about was getting a dozen refugees safely across the Border, because that was what they wanted, and they couldn't do it alone." Cheyenne nodded at Persh'al. "You like to make plans. Good ones. And you know how the system works over here, all the tech and the rewriting history in the walls, or whatever the hell that's supposed to be."

The courtyard was quiet as everyone hung on the new Crown's words.

Cheyenne wracked her brain for anything else that would get her point across. *I shouldn't have to defend my choice. If he wants it, it's his.*

She weakly cleared her throat. "Persh'al hasn't once strayed from doing his part to get us here, even when he hated what he had to do. We've all made sacrifices, right? Some of us more than others. This troll made sacrifices too, and now he's here. He's not half-bad in a fight, either."

Persh'al chuckled. "You're kinda startin' to grow on me, kid."

Trying to smile back at him, Cheyenne swallowed and immediately corrected herself when she started swaying on her feet again. "Don't worry. I'm sure I'll do something to screw that up."

"Not after this."

The magical made of swarming black specks coalesced into his humanoid, black-cloaked form and fixed his glowing red eyes on her from the center of his seemingly empty hood. "I can't speak for the others, Cheyenne, but I will say I prefer the Black Flame on the throne."

A murmur of assent passed through the other members of the Four-Pointed Star. Nu'ek, Sakrit, Elarit, and of course Persh'al were among those who didn't openly agree with the swarming magical's sentiment.

Cheyenne bit her lip to bring her focus away from her hip. *Someone could stab me in the back right now, and I wouldn't feel it over this bullshit.* "You know what? I'm only going by what I prefer right now, and this troll's a damn good replacement."

Maleshi chuckled and raised an eyebrow as she surveyed the rebels' reactions.

With a rolling growl, Nu'ek took one giant step forward, the click of her claws on the stone floor of the courtyard echoing sharply around them. "I stand by the Crown's decision."

"Yep." Sakrit stepped forward and thumped a fist on his chest. "A new Cycle turns."

The swarming magical burst into millions of black specks and rematerialized on the other side of Persh'al. "If the Black Flame commands it."

Cheyenne blinked heavily. "I'm pretty sure I do, yeah."

One by one, the rest of L'zar's underground rebels stepped forward to show their support for Persh'al Tenishi. Maleshi and Corian turned away from Cheyenne to face the blue troll and thumped their fists on their chests.

"Shit." Persh'al let out a high-pitched chuckle and shook his head. "You can't be serious about this."

"Look at this." Cheyenne pointed to her face, trying to hold herself together even as her eyelids fluttered again. *I'm either gonna puke or pass out.* "This is my serious face, troll. Suck it up and give your answer already."

"L'zar's not gonna like this, kid."

"The only magical who has to deal with L'zar anymore is L'zar. Make your own damn decisions now, huh?"

Maleshi's silver eyes narrowed. "You good, kid?"

"I want a goddamn yes or no."

"Like I have an answer?" Persh'al tossed his hands in the air. "You couldn't have warned me? This was the last thing on my mind!" He paused and turned toward Elarit with wide eyes when she placed a hand on his shoulder.

The troll woman dipped her head. "On a silver platter, *ma gairín.*"

"A silver…" He swallowed and looked everywhere but at Cheyenne's face until his yellow eyes finally settled on her golden ones. "Yeah. I mean, hell, yeah. Shit, Cheyenne. I'll do it."

"Great." Cheyenne grimaced and started to turn away. "Got that taken care of. Now I can—"

Her knees buckled, and her eyes rolled back in her head as she dropped.

Ember took the split-second distraction as her final opportunity and yanked the purple thorn from her friend's hip. Blood sprayed in a wide arc across the black stone floor of the courtyard, then Cheyenne crumpled to the ground and didn't move.

"Gotcha." The fae girl looked at Ba'rael's last magically poisoned dart and tossed it behind her shoulder. When she looked back, she found every magical in the Heart staring at her. "Hey, she was already going down. I pulled this thing out after her eyes rolled back."

Maleshi glanced at Cheyenne's unconscious form on the ground and raised her eyebrows, then turned toward Persh'al. "By order of the Black Flame, brothers. Ambar'ogúl's new Crown!"

The orc guards leaped to their feet and started banging on shields and chest plates all over again. The Four-Pointed Star rebels joined in, and Persh'al looked like he was about to bolt.

"Hey." Elarit grabbed his wrist, and he stared at her.

"I have no idea what I'm—"

She slapped him across the cheek, then pulled him roughly into an embrace for a wild, painful-looking kiss.

The magicals in the courtyard roared in approval and pounded on whatever metal they had on hand.

Ember floated backward away from them, her lips twitching as she decided whether to be concerned about that slap or just forget it and be happy for them. Corian finally lifted his gaze from Cheyenne, rubbed the back of his neck, and smirked at Persh'al. "A fell-damn troll on the throne. Never thought I'd live to see the day."

Maleshi leaned toward him and muttered, "Never thought we'd live, period."

"Bullshit." Shooting her a sidelong glance, Corian stepped through the ring of O'gúl guards encircling the courtyard and slapped a hand on the black stone wall. A burst of silver lightning crackled up the stone, and two seconds later, blazing lights in every color shimmered over the walls before the entire courtyard was illuminated by flashes of magical light. They raced all the way up the high walls and exploded into the sky, taking the magic built into the very foundation of Hangivol with them.

The air above the capital of Ambar'ogúl crackled and sparked with magical energy, alerting everyone in the city and beyond that a new Cycle had turned. Even the O'gúleesh beyond the more civilized cities where the inner ring ended and the Outers began could feel the change, though most of them did not see the magical burst rise from the center of Hangivol. Ba'rael Verdys was finished, Cheyenne the Black Flame had abdicated her birthright, at least in Ambar'ogúl, and Persh'al Tenishi ruled as the world's first troll Crown.

Persh'al laughed when Elarit finally released him and stepped away, tossing her coiled scarlet braids away from her face. "Hey, General."

Maleshi turned slowly toward him and spread her arms. "Here we are, right?"

"Apparently." He jerked his chin at her and bounced a little on the balls of his feet. "So, what's my cool name, huh?"

The general blinked quickly and forced back a laugh.

Byrd barked out a laugh and slugged the new troll Crown in the shoulder. "Whatever it is, man, there's no way you're gettin' anythin' better than the Black Flame."

Lumil sniggered. "I kinda like the sound of Blue Freak."

Persh'al jerked his hand toward the goblins, twisting his fingers into the O'gúl equivalent of flipping the middle finger. Byrd and Lumil cracked up and fell all over each other, which inevitably turned into a shoving match five seconds later.

Maleshi clasped her hands behind her back and nodded at the troll. "We'll think of something."

Ember rose from where she'd hover-crouched beside Cheyenne's body and clapped her hands once. "I know it's crazy exciting, but can someone tell me where the hell I'm supposed to take the drow who made all this possible?"

Nu'ek stepped forward, sending both the orc guards and the rebels scattering to get clear of her hulking form. "Plenty of empty rooms, fae. I'll show you."

"That'd be great." Ember watched as the huge Golra bent to scoop Cheyenne into her arms. "Whoa, hey. Just be careful, all right?"

Nu'ek's red eyes flashed at the fae girl. "Just because I could crush her in one fist, it doesn't mean I will."

"Right." Ember lifted both hands in front of her and floated backward. "I know that."

The Golra tossed her wild red curls away from her face, her leather vest creaking as she carried Cheyenne in both arms like a sleeping baby. "I like you, fae, but you should work on not being such a mouse. You're still the Black Flame's *Nós Ani*, are you not?"

"Yeah. As far as I know."

Nu'ek grunted and stomped across the courtyard toward the curved arch on the opposite side. Her wings stretched wide across her back with a gust of air, then folded back into place again as she ducked and squeezed her massive form through the arch.

Ember frowned and glided across the courtyard after her.

Corian caught up with the fae girl and walked beside her. "What happened to her?"

"What, you didn't see the darts go through like bullets?"

He shook his head. "Cheyenne doesn't just pass out when something hurts a little."

"I don't think it was a little, Corian. Honestly, it looked a lot like the blight."

"But not exactly."

"Nope. We get her in a bed or something like one, and I'll have a chance to look her over without her threatening to break me over her knee if I poke her the wrong way."

The nightstalker snorted. "I have nothing but faith in your abilities, Ember."

"Well, thanks."

"Make it as fast as you can, though, huh?"

Ember shot him a sidelong glance as they approached the archway and stepped into the darkened hall. "You think I'm gonna just take my sweet time with it and keep her in pain for fun?"

He ignored the sarcasm and nodded at the tips of Nu'ek's wings disappearing around the corner. "She's not the O'gúl Crown anymore, not technically, but she still has responsibilities to both worlds. Mostly Earth at this point."

"Like what, exactly?"

"She didn't tell you?"

Ember gave him a pointed smile. "She tells me everything, nightstalker. I just wanna hear it from you."

Corian studied her profile for a moment, then clasped his hands behind his back and waited for her to turn down the next corridor after Nu'ek. "It was either ruling from the Heart here, or taking her place as Earthside royalty. Guess she chose to rule on Earth."

"Huh." Ember cocked her head. "Not sure why you're telling me, though. I just follow her back and forth across the Border."

The nightstalker pressed his lips together and stared straight ahead. "Very funny. You two really are the perfect team."

"Yeah, I know."

CHAPTER TWO

Lying on the king-sized bed in her estate in Henry County, Bianca Summerlin lurched out of her three-day magical coma and gasped. Her eyes flew open, and she stared in shock at the opposite wall and the closed French doors of her bedroom.

"Oh!" Eleanor hopped away from the ice water when the glass slipped from her hand and fell on the Persian rug. The glass didn't break, but it rolled and left a trail of cold water seeping into the fibers. "Bianca?"

For the first time since taking up employment at the Summerlin estate, Eleanor ignored the spill and rushed toward Bianca's bedside instead.

"Can you hear me? Oh, my God, I can't believe it. Bianca?" She waved a hand in front of her employer and friend's face, timidly bending forward to search for any expression. "If you can hear me, blink twice and...oh!"

She jumped again when Bianca stiffly turned her head to meet the other woman's gaze. "I'm not a performing circus animal, Eleanor."

"Well, it took you long enough to answer me." The housekeeper pressed the back of her hand against Bianca's forehead, then grabbed the woman's face and turned her head from side to side.

"What exactly are you looking for?" Bianca asked, then took a deep breath through her nose.

"That's a good point. I wouldn't know."

"Then please unhand my face."

Eleanor jerked her hands away and stepped back. "Sorry. I'm sorry. How do you feel?"

"Smothered, to be perfectly honest."

"Oh." The housekeeper took another step back. "Any side effects?"

"Eleanor, I have no idea what I've just woken from or to. I do, however, intend to find out." Bianca shifted closer to the edge of the bed and paused. Her head tilted slightly, and she frowned as she reached up to scratch an itch on her collarbone. "When was the last time the sheets were changed?"

"Nothing wrong with the sheets." Eleanor stepped forward again and reached toward her employer. "But I wouldn't start scratching."

Bianca sucked in a sharp breath when the pain beneath the itch she'd meant to scratch flared along her collarbone and her chest. "What in the world?"

She carefully peeled down the collar of her silk pajama shirt and stared at the raw red mark burned into her flesh. The edge of another peeked out at her from beneath the fabric, and she slowly undid the first four buttons to see an entire swath of healing burns on her chest and shoulders. A quick test of her forearms confirmed those hadn't been spared, either.

"Eleanor!"

"You know, I'd like to say I can explain, but I'm not sure that's true."

"Do your best, please." Without looking at her housekeeper, Bianca rebuttoned her blouse and sat stiffly on the mattress, staring straight ahead at the French doors. "Starting with how I went from standing in my own backyard at the end of a particularly trying day to lying in my bed in nightclothes."

"Oh. Well, to start, I can tell you I'm the only one who touched your clothes. Took me a minute to get you changed, but I wanted to make you comfortable." Eleanor bit her lip to stifle the onset of tears.

"Thank you." Bianca turned to meet the other woman's gaze and nodded. "Take a seat and try to be as detailed as possible. Concise."

"Right." Glancing around the room, the housekeeper returned to the armchair she'd occupied for the last few days at Bianca's beside and sat tensely. "Well, those men were here. The ones in black who were supposed to keep an eye on those rocks."

"Yes, I remember that part. Let's move on."

"The obstacle in the yard did something to you."

Bianca dipped her head and blinked. "Go on."

"You were frozen, Bianca. Unresponsive, and no one could get you to move. Not even Cheyenne."

After a brief pause, Bianca frowned. "I find it difficult to believe that Cheyenne would have an issue moving anything, let alone me."

Eleanor scoffed. "Well, it's not because you're too heavy, I can tell you that much." Her employer's deepening frown wiped the smile off her lips. "It was something unnatural if you get my drift."

"Yes, Eleanor. I understand the type of unnatural phenomenon we've unfortunately been dealing with on the property lately." Bianca's nostrils flared, which was the only visible sign of her distaste for anything that had to do with that other world. Her daughter's other world. Her hand lifted on its own toward a burning itch on the opposite shoulder, but she stopped herself with a small, resigned grimace. "So if it was impossible to move me—"

"Something happened. I don't entirely understand it." Eleanor wrung her hands in her lap. "That structure was destroyed. Or it destroyed itself. Then you fainted."

"I did no such thing." Bianca barely shook her head, a warning and a plea for her friend to drop the matter and leave it at that.

"Well, Cheyenne was here when it happened. She brought you to your bed, and that was the end of it."

Bianca slowly licked her lips and spread her arms, gesturing at the raw symbols that could be seen above the collar of her nightshirt. "And these?"

"That happened while you were asleep. I have no idea what they are or why they're there."

Taking a deep breath, Bianca fastened the top button on her shirt, closing it around her unusual new scars as much as it would go, and nodded. "If there's anything else you remember that might be of importance, Eleanor, I'm sure you understand how strongly I wish to hear it."

"Well," the housekeeper said as she shrugged and smoothed the tops of her pant legs, "if I could wrap my head around any more of it—"

Bianca stood abruptly. "That's fine."

"W-what are you doing?" Eleanor leaped to her feet and raced toward her employer. "Bianca, you can't—"

"I'm standing. And yes, I can."

"But you need rest."

"How long was I in bed?"

Eleanor paused. "Three days."

Bianca's eyebrows twitched up, then settled in their normal place again. "Then it seems I've had plenty of rest. Thank you."

She headed toward the French doors on slightly shaky legs but willed her body to obey.

"But we don't know what that thing did to you." The housekeeper bustled after her. "You could have permanent damage."

"Yes. Permanent damage in the form of scars." Bianca pulled the French doors toward her and threw them aside. "That is hardly a reason to sequester me in my bedroom now that I'm awake."

Eleanor asked, "Where are you going?"

"You said it was destroyed, Eleanor. I want to see that insufferable eyesore for myself." Bianca moved swiftly down the hall toward the wide staircase. "Are those surly men in black uniforms still on the lawn?"

"No. No, everyone left when the stones fell down."

"That will be all, Eleanor. You know how much I appreciate your dedication, and in this instance, your devotion to caring for me while I was indisposed." Bianca almost dropped on the staircase as she descended the first step, but she steadied herself on the cherrywood railing and regained her balance enough to head down to the main floor.

"Of course." The housekeeper followed her with a worried frown. "That hasn't disappeared now that you're awake."

"I relieve you of the burden." Bianca didn't turn around or pause on the stairs. Her gaze was focused intently on the glistening hardwood floor in the foyer at the foot of the stairs. "And do stop hovering."

Eleanor was halfway to catching up with the other woman but paused and muttered, "I'm not hovering."

Bianca ignored her in lieu of concentrating on the bottom of the staircase. Refusing to let anything stop her, she paused on the landing, smoothed a few stray hairs away from her face, and turned to head for the back of the house.

"Oh, my goodness." Trying not to run down the stairs, the housekeeper picked up the pace as much as she could. "Bianca? Bianca, listen to me. I really don't think going out there right now is the best choice. As I said, I don't know nearly enough about what happened to feel safe about it. Why would you go right back out to the thing that did this to you?"

She rounded the staircase and caught the last of Bianca's fluttering jade silk pant leg disappearing beneath the staircase and past the dining table.

"Of course, I'm not going to lock you up in your room, but at the very least, please come back upstairs. I'll make us a light lunch. How does that sound? We'll take it in the breakfast room, and you can stare at the remains of that ghastly pile of rock all you want. I promised I'd look after you, Bianca, and that includes when stuff like this happens and I have no idea what it is."

Eleanor stopped on the other side of the dining table and stared at her employer.

Bianca stood at the open French doors that led to the veranda, her back rigidly straight and one hand tightly gripping the door handle.

Eleanor took two more tentative steps forward and peered around her employer's stiff figure to see their most unexpected visitor standing at the balcony railing in Bianca's favorite spot. "Oh my."

Bianca swallowed her rage at the sight of him in his true form and held her ground. *I'm not going anywhere, and he knows it.*

L'zar turned around to face her and leaned against the railing. His golden eyes looked her up and down, and that cocksure smile returned to his inhumanly gray lips. "I always knew you were unstoppable."

She forced herself to release her death grip on the door handle, mostly to hide that both her hands were trembling, and lifted her chin. "I thought I made things perfectly clear the last time you and I saw each other."

"Oh, yes. You did."

Bianca raised an eyebrow, her eyes narrowing as she fought back the urge to scream and slap the bane of her existence on the other cheek. "Then do enlighten me as to why the hell you're on my property."

L'zar grinned, his eyes blazing with triumph. "She did it, Bianca. Everything I knew she could do, she did."

For a moment, she didn't say anything and opted for simply glaring at the man—or whatever he was—who'd single-handedly changed the course of her entire life. *Cheyenne. He's talking about Cheyenne, and he wouldn't be smiling like that if she wasn't safe.*

"I have no interest whatsoever in your world," she said, her strength and conviction returning now that she knew her daughter no longer faced whatever threat she'd gone off to face with this man. "You'd be a fool to think otherwise."

"Naturally." L'zar looked her over again, his gaze lingering briefly on the edge of the red rune scar peeking out from beneath the collar of her silk top. "We won't talk about my world."

"We certainly will not."

The drow thief dipped his head, smiling the whole time, and never took his gaze off his daughter's mother as he strolled casually across the veranda and sat in one of the iron patio chairs. "Now that the immediate danger's out of the way, I wanted to take this opportunity to speak to you. If you'll allow it, of course. We have a lot to discuss concerning our daughter's future, and I'd much rather involve you in the process this time around."

Bianca swallowed thickly, fighting the urge to clench her jaw. *I should tell him to go fuck himself. It's the least he deserves.*

She felt Eleanor creeping slowly up behind her. Fortunately, the housekeeper remained silent while Bianca Summerlin weighed the pros and cons of every possible next move she could make when it came to the most appalling person she'd met in her life.

But he's not a person, is he? Just a monster who fathered my child.

A breeze blew in from the mountains on the other side of the valley, whistling between the iron rungs of the balustrade and wafting Bianca's unpinned hair away from her face. L'zar's grin returned, and he gestured at the empty patio chair across the table.

"Eleanor."

"Yes?"

Bianca blinked and rolled her shoulders back, glaring unflinchingly at the drow on her veranda. "Bring out the good scotch, please. Only one glass."

The housekeeper glanced sharply at her, then dipped her head and scampered toward Bianca's office to retrieve the requested bottle.

L'zar clicked his tongue and nodded. "Good thinking. It's probably for the best not to drink right after recovering from a drow curse."

"Oh, you mean the one sitting at my table uninvited?"

He chuckled softly through his nose and spread his arms. "I suppose I deserve that. I do hope it is good scotch."

Bianca stepped lightly onto the veranda, entirely composed again now that she'd regained control of the situation. A small, closed-lipped smile graced her mouth, the type of smile others thought inviting and polite but which always felt bitter. "You still underestimate me, L'zar. That glass is not for you."

CHAPTER THREE

*W*hat the hell?

Cheyenne tried to roll over so she could get her cheek away from whatever scratchy, wiry thing that was pressed roughly against it. Her hip screamed at her like it had the one and only time she'd been shot with a bullet instead of magic.

If I'm chained up to a fake hospital bed again, heads are gonna roll.

With a groan of effort, she managed to push herself off the scratchy blanket and ease over onto her back. "Fuck!"

Both shoulders burned, and her hip radiated agony up her side and down her leg into her feet. Black spots danced in her vision until she finally closed her eyes and quit trying.

A muffled explosion sounded somewhere outside the room, followed by the muted cheers of hundreds of voices at once. More small explosions followed, like bursting fireworks, and she slowly tried to open her eyes again.

"Well, look who decided to finally wake up." Ember floated into Cheyenne's field of vision, grinning and raising her eyebrows at her friend laid out on the bed.

Cheyenne grunted and turned her head to see the rest of the enormous bed, most of it stretching out beside her. She took up maybe a fifth of it. "Big beds in Hangivol too, huh? And I don't remember going to sleep."

"Well, that's because you didn't."

"So?"

"You passed out." Ember spread her arms. "I got that last dart, though."

"Jesus." Cheyenne closed her eyes and tried to steady her breathing against the pain. "Thanks for waiting 'til I was out."

"Well, yeah. I wasn't about to try it again while you were conscious. How you feelin'?"

"Like shit, Em."

"Huh. He said it would last longer. Hold on."

"What?" Cheyenne tried to push herself up onto her forearms but dropped back down again at the blazing protests of the wounds in her shoulder. Instead, she peeled her shirt away from one of the dart holes and tried to focus her blurry vision on the dark crater in her flesh and the black streaks growing away from it. "These are smaller now, aren't they?"

"They better be." Ember returned to the bedside with a thick metal canister. "Took a little trial and error, but we figured out a few things. Narrowed down to how to keep those black streaks from growing and, well, I guess how not to wake you up after you fainted."

Cheyenne paused. "How long have I been lying here, exactly?"

"I'm guessing something like twelve hours. Whatever constitutes as twelve hours in this world, anyway. You went down hard, halfling. We had plenty of time to test a few things out."

Twelve hours? Well, I guess it's better than three days chained to a FRoE bed.

"You keep saying 'we,' Em. Wasn't cute with Neros. Definitely doesn't work with you."

"Very funny. I mean 'we' because I had some help. Couldn't heal you with my own magic, so I had to get creative. Think outside the solo healer box, ya know?"

More explosions came from outside the room, and this time, a bellowing roar dampened by layers of stone walls followed. "Can you hear that?"

"The explosions? Not unless I'm standing out in the hall."

"What's going on out there?"

"I think it's like a giant New Year's Eve party. A New Cycle party, I guess. Pretty sure this celebration is gonna last a lot longer than the last one."

"With riots and everything, huh?" Cheyenne glanced at the metal canister in her friend's hand. "No way that's hairspray."

"Nope. Hold still."

"What? Are you gonna…ah!"

Ember pressed a hand firmly on the center of Cheyenne's collarbone, then jammed the end of the metal canister against the wound in the halfling's left shoulder. A sharp thunk and a hiss came from the metal tube, then Ember pulled away and raised both hands.

"What the hell?" Cheyenne lifted a tentative finger toward her shoulder.

"Huh." Ember grinned. "How do you feel now?"

"Like I just got out of a bath."

"That doesn't make sense, but I guess it doesn't have to."

"What did you do to me, Em?" Cheyenne blinked heavily and lifted her left hand. "No pain in my shoulder, but my head's spinning."

"That, my halfling friend, is a painkiller that works on drow." Ember set the canister down on a squat table beside the bed, then folded her arms. "You're welcome."

"Pshh." Chuckling, Cheyenne turned her hand back and forth. "That doesn't exist."

"Yeah, tell that to your pain-free shoulder and your spinning head. And your seriously goofy smile."

Cheyenne pursed her lips, then had to wiggle her jaw around to make sure it was still there. "That stuff is intense."

"Just give it a minute. It's not supposed to make you high all day."

"At this point, Em, I wouldn't have a problem with that."

"Ha-ha. I can think of a few magicals who'd have a problem with you being hopped up on darktongue serum."

"Wait, what?" The warm, fuzzy, floaty feeling was sucked out Cheyenne's head all at once, and she propped herself up on her elbows to stare at her friend. "You put that nasty-smelling salve into an aerosol can and injected me with it?"

"Hey, see? You're back to your normal pissed-off self." Ember grinned and folded her arms. "Relax, okay? First of all, not an aerosol can."

"That's the least important thing right now."

"And second, I didn't shoot you up with salve. That would be," Ember said, frowning and glancing at the ceiling, "highly irresponsible and probably life-threatening. I know that's nothing new for you, but I've stepped into this whole healer role with both feet."

Cheyenne cocked her head and gave her friend a deadpan stare. "I'm waiting for you to stop telling me what it isn't, Em."

"Right. Darktongue serum. Didn't I say that?"

"Yeah."

"Oil, Cheyenne. Extracted from the plant and mixed up with…I don't know what. He wasn't clear on that part, but I'm pretty sure it was water."

"He?"

Ember grimaced. "Yep. Venga put as much as I did into figuring out how to make this work for you. Turns out the necromancer's something of an alchemist, too, which is really weird to say. Like, alchemy is totally a real thing over here."

Cheyenne blinked. "Ember."

"Yeah."

"You let the necromancer who created the blight touch open wounds on my body?"

"What? No." Ember scoffed and rolled her eyes. "He didn't touch you. Promise. But I spent a lot of time watching that scaleback at work, and I gotta say the guy knows what he's doing."

"Uh-huh."

"No, really. What he does isn't that different from the kind of healing I do. I mean, think about it. Put healing and death magic together, and you get ways to heal death magic. Case in point, your thirty seconds of loony-drow painkillers."

"Wow." Cheyenne shook her head and closed her eyes. "I can't envision you and the lizard-dude working right next to each other, but I guess it's better than you still hating his guts while we're all here."

"Oh, don't get me wrong. He's still an asshole, and weirdly neurotic about some things. Totally pissed off that he didn't get a chance to fuck with Ba'rael as much as he wanted before she disappeared." Ember shrugged. "But yeah. I guess he's not that bad."

"And he said to inject darktongue oil into me because that's what heals the blight?" Cheyenne gingerly touched the hole in her left shoulder again, which was redder now after having been jabbed with the injection canister but didn't offer more than a brief ache when she touched it.

"That's not the blight per se." Ember peered at the faded black streaks on Cheyenne's shoulder. "No way to know if Ba'rael meant to do that when she used you as a dartboard, but her magic and whatever else kinda made the blight go rogue in her hands, I guess."

"So, this is something new." Sighing heavily, Cheyenne closed her eyes. *You can't shoot the messenger, especially if she's your best friend.* "And now we have to figure out how to heal the real blight and a mutant strain?"

"I don't think so." Ember straightened again and nodded. "I'm pretty sure Venga can already."

The fae girl's eyes widened, and a vacant expression passed over her face.

"Em? Hello?" Cheyenne waved a hand in front of Ember's face, and her friend blinked.

"What? Sorry."

"What was all that about?"

"I'll tell you in a sec." Ember pointed at her. "I was about to say the necromancer can explain it a lot better than I can, but we're pretty sure this version of the pseudo-blight is specific to you."

"Oh, great. She tailored a plague to her own niece."

Ember stuck a hand on her hip. "Are you really surprised?"

"No. You know what does surprise me, though?"

"That's impossible to guess."

"The fact that none of us has any idea what happened to Ba'rael."

Ember nodded slowly. "Yeah. What an exit, though, right?"

"I'm serious, Em."

"I know. Just trying to keep things light 'cause, like, you still have three magical dart holes in your body."

"Well, thanks to you and your serum, I can ignore those a little longer." Cheyenne slowly pushed herself up the rest of the way to sit on the side of the massive bed. She took a long, slow breath and nodded. "And now I'm remembering things."

"I sure hope so. Didn't think those darts had built-in amnesia, too."

"I mean, what happened in the courtyard. Neros swooped in and took out her magic with his own."

"And then hugged her." Ember wrinkled her nose. "Hell of a way to take down the worst drow Crown in O'gúleesh history, huh?"

"Yeah, but where did they go?"

The fae girl shrugged. "To the final deathflame, perhaps?"

They looked at each other and sniggered. "That sounds weird coming out of your mouth."

"I know. Just trying a few sayings on for size. What do you think, though? You think the Spider's gone for good?"

Cheyenne frowned and glanced at the huge bed and the door. "I don't know. I get this feeling that the answer's no. Can't say why."

"Well, I've learned to trust your feelings." Ember smiled. "The responsible-drow-magical feelings, not the pissed-off-goth-halfling feelings. Just to be clear."

"Oh, thanks. Glad you made a distinction."

"So, what? You think Ba'rael Verdys is living the life back in Nor'ieth with the creepily pale son she sent away forever like a smelly pair of shoes?"

"Interesting comparison." They both snorted, and Cheyenne tried to run a hand through her bone-white hair, got her fingers stuck in the tangled mess, and gave up. "Wouldn't that be the ultimate reward for the old Crown, though, huh? Spending eternity in a hidden realm where she's the least powerful magical, can't bend any of the Olfarím to her will, and doesn't have what it takes to get herself back out."

"The last two of the Verdys line banished indefinitely." Ember's chuckle cut off abruptly when she saw her friend's darkening frown. "Yeah, and I meant it. You're not a Verdys drow, Cheyenne. I don't give a shit who your dad is. Everything L'zar and Ba'rael screwed up in either world is over now 'cause you ended it."

"That's what I'm hoping for, Em. Not sure how well that's gonna go over when I—"

The door to the giant bedroom swung open and bashed against the wall. Corian, Maleshi, Persh'al, and Elarit headed quickly through the doorway single-file, and Elarit closed the door swiftly and silently behind her until it settled into place with a click.

Persh'al threw both hands in the air. "She lives!"

Cheyenne raised her eyebrows and stared at each of her visitors. "Uh-huh. And she's wondering why all four of you came busting in here without so much as a knock."

Maleshi grinned at Ember. "You didn't tell her we were coming."

"No." The fae girl shrugged. "We got carried away with, like, at least three different conversations we almost got to finish."

"We kinda booked it from the main hall," Persh'al muttered. "Lotta hyped up O'gúleesh wanting to burst in here without so much as a knock and get to see you up close and personal, kid. Honestly, I wouldn't be surprised if that included a bunch of worship chanting and trying to cut off a lock of your hair or something."

Cheyenne wrinkled her nose. "What?"

"Everyone's excited, kid." Corian folded his arms and shot Persh'al a quick sidelong glance. "You did the unthinkable. Ba'rael's gone, and you turned a new Cycle twice in two weeks."

"Technically, it's still the same Cycle." Maleshi lifted a finger and nodded at the halfling. "But we can get into the details later."

"Don't worry." Ember leaned toward her friend and gave her an exaggerated wink. "I left specific instructions for who comes in and out of this room until you're ready to leave it."

Cheyenne snorted. "So, what, you posted a bulletin?"

"It's all over the system, kid." Persh'al pointed at the ceiling. "And I might've rigged up a few leftover machines to make sure nobody tries to get cute and sneak in here against your *Nós Aní's* orders."

"You're giving orders now." The halfling turned slowly toward Ember again and cocked her head. "That's new."

"So is this." Ember slightly turned her head and pointed at the glistening silver-white bar of a new activator behind her ear. "Nice, right?"

"Upgrades always are." Cheyenne cracked a smile. "You tapped into the system with that thing to keep everyone away from me?"

"Well, yeah. Come on, Cheyenne. I might not be the world's best tech master and hacker of everything. Okay, the best in both worlds." Ember folded her arms. "But I didn't think you'd forget that we used to be in the same classes."

"I didn't forget, Em." Cheyenne flashed her friend a winning grin and nodded. "Glad you're figuring out how to do more than keep a crawler from throwing you down the stairs."

"That was my magic working like shit. It's back."

Elarit studied the activator behind Ember's ear and shrugged. "It's not as intricate as the one I gave you, but that happens with short-notice custom orders. The way I've heard it, you could make a first-generation sync work as well as anything that counts as top-of-the-line in this city."

Cheyenne tried to smile at the troll woman but couldn't quite get there. *There's no way she doesn't remember biting my head off. What does she want?* "That might be stretching it, but thanks."

Ember grinned. "She made it for me, Cheyenne. I'm still trying to get that through my head."

"Just don't practice with synced spells before I have a chance to get out of this bed, okay?"

"Got it. For now, I'm good with tapping into the freakin' walls and sending messages. So cool."

The room lapsed into a slightly tense silence, and Cheyenne glanced from face to face. *If they're waiting for me to say something profound, they came to the wrong drow.*

CHAPTER FOUR

"So." Cheyenne slapped her hands on her thighs, bringing a momentary twinge into her doubly wounded hip, and looked at Persh'al. "I already made my one-and-done first declaration as Crown. What about you?"

"Well," the troll said with a chuckle, "I'm not really expecting you to jump on the bandwagon with this or anything."

Cheyenne closed her eyes. "Please don't tell me you changed your mind."

"What? No way. Are you kidding? I wouldn't give this up for all the gourmet *angarfat* in Hangivol. And I never thanked you for, you know, picking me. I know I wasn't your first choice, kid, but I'm happy to have made it onto the list."

"Sure. You were in the right courtyard at the right time."

Persh'al's nervous smile faded. "You mean, like a random—"

"No." Cheyenne laughed. "I'm screwing with you, man. Of course, I picked you, and I meant everything I said to the Four-Pointed Star, by the way. Sorry I didn't put the pieces together sooner. I could have asked you in private without all the pressure."

"Right." His eyes widened, and he stared at her like she'd asked him to take the job all over again. "You're killin' me, kid. You know that?"

She grinned and pointed at him. "And you're stalling."

"What?"

"First order of business, Crown. What was it?"

"Well, it…"

Elarit and Maleshi exchanged knowing glances before the general cleared her throat. "He ordered a *myrein*."

Cheyenne tried to choke back a laugh, but it spewed out of her anyway.

Persh'al frowned. "It's not that funny."

Corian chuckled softly. "It is when you're the only one not laughing about it."

"I'm not the only one." The blue troll turned toward Elarit, but she was in the process of trying to cover up her soft laughter too. "Oh, come on! If it's so hilarious, why'd you agree to it?"

The troll woman slipped her arm through his and raised her eyebrows. "Can't I be impressed and amused at the same time?"

"I guess you can."

Ember spread her arms. "Somebody wanna tell me what a *myrein* is?"

"O'gúleesh wedding, Em."

The fae girl leaned toward her friend in surprise, then turned her head to squint at Persh'al. "Who's getting married?"

Elarit lifted a purple finger. "That would be us."

Ember's eyes widened. "Oh. You're the secret girlfriend."

"Secret?" Corian shot Persh'al a questioning frown. "Not what I heard."

"You didn't hear shit, nightstalker."

"Oh, I hear plenty." Corian's lips split into his intensely feral grin. "Doesn't mean I don't know how to keep my mouth shut."

Persh'al froze. "Wait, you knew?"

"If you're talking about your refusal to follow one of L'zar's less insane but still stupid orders," Maleshi added, "specifically the one to abandon Elarit to her fate without you, then yes, Persh'al. We both knew."

The blue troll's mouth opened and closed without sound, and he turned his shocked gaze on Cheyenne.

"Hey, don't look at me. I didn't say a word."

"I don't get it."

The general shrugged. "Well, it wasn't getting in the way, and telling L'zar would've turned it into something that did."

Ember snorted. "And it would've made them serious hypocrites if they snitched on you."

Both nightstalkers turned slowly to give her matching warning glances.

"What?" She spread her arms. "I figured this was confession time. All secrets out in the open, 'cause L'zar's not coming back, right?"

"That's hardly a secret, Ember." Persh'al pointed at Maleshi and Corian. "But hey, good to know I'm not the only one who thinks half of L'zar's orders are bullshit."

Corian's smile faded. "Careful."

"Or what? L'zar's gonna lose it when he hears about what's happening today, and he can't do a fell-damn thing about it, 'cause guess who's the O'gúl Crown now?" Persh'al rolled his shoulders back and covered the back of Elarit's hand, which was wrapped around his forearm, with his. "So it doesn't matter. No more secrets, but thanks for having my back, I guess."

Maleshi elbowed Corian in the side. He rolled his eyes and muttered, "We're all on the same side, troll."

"You know, that's what I thought." Grinning, Persh'al pointed at Cheyenne. "So how 'bout it, kid? You gonna be there, or what?"

"Be where?"

"At the ceremony."

"When is it?"

"Three hours."

"Jesus." Cheyenne laughed and almost tried running a hand through her hair again before remembering how impossible it was. "Why?"

"First royal decree, kid. You don't drag out something like that."

Elarit's beaming smile faded slightly when she met Cheyenne's gaze. "And we've waited long enough."

"No, right. Sure. I've never been to a wedding, so I don't even know what I'm supposed to do, or whatever."

Maleshi cocked her head. "Are you kidding?"

"Nope." The bitter smile she gave the general brought on a small, ignorable headache. "You think Bianca Summerlin wanted to drag her little halfling kid along and run the risk of me blowing up the bride and groom 'cause I couldn't have a second piece of cake?"

Ember snorted. "That does sound like something you'd have done as a kid."

"Very funny."

"It's not like a human wedding, kid," Corian added. "In any culture."

Cheyenne frowned at the new troll Crown, then shrugged. "Then I guess I'm starting with a blank slate."

Persh'al's eyes lit up. "That's a yes, right? Sounds like a yes."

"Yeah, fine." She tossed a dismissive hand toward him but couldn't quite hide a small smile. "I'll be there to watch or whatever."

"Right on, kid."

"It'll be a little more than watching," Corian added and folded his arms. "At least for you, Cheyenne."

"No, he asked me to be there, not to participate."

"It's a simple process, but it has to be done. As far as Ambar'ogúl is concerned, and I do mean the world and not its inhabitants, you're still the Crown."

"No, I'm not."

"Old laws, kid." Maleshi shrugged.

"You can't use that as an excuse for everything."

"Except for when it applies to everything." Corian nodded at her, then turned to the door. "I'll walk you through it when we get to that point. And after the *myrein*, we still have a lot of plans to make. Loopholes to find in the old laws so we can make this possible, and nailing down how we're gonna put everything back together."

Cheyenne spread her arms. "And yet, we're getting ready for an O'gúleesh wedding twelve hours after our greatest victory."

After opening the door, he looked at her over his shoulder and smiled. "We did what we came here to do. That's worth celebrating."

"Right."

Persh'al and Elarit turned to leave the room. The troll man pointed at her again. "We'll see you there. I'm serious, Cheyenne. We better see you there."

"Yeah, okay."

Maleshi winked at the halfling and followed everyone else into the hall without a word. Then it was just Cheyenne and Ember.

"Well, that was a surprise." Ember stared at the closed door. "No one bothered to tell me what all the celebrating was about. I just made an apparently uneducated guess."

"New Cycle party isn't technically wrong, Em. They just decided to tack an O'gúleesh wedding onto it for fun."

"You think it'll be fun?"

"No idea. After what we've seen here, I'd bet on the fighting pits being part of it."

"Then yeah." Ember nodded vigorously. "Sounds like loads of fun."

"I still don't get how you're so into those fights, Em. Especially as a healer."

"Hey, I'm pureblooded O'gúleesh through and through." The fae girl spread her arms. "Just spent my whole life Earthside until a couple of weeks ago. Lemme tell ya, I had no idea what I was missing."

"Glad you're finding ways to stay entertained." Cheyenne rolled her neck from one shoulder to the other, then arched her back as far as it would go before her darktongue-numbed shoulders protested with more than a few twinges. "I'm still trying to wrap my head around what's next."

"A serious party is what's next, halfling."

"Apparently, yeah. I'm talking about all the other stuff that I left unfinished Earthside before we came back to storm the fortress. My mom's still in a magical coma, and I'm gonna have to come up with a way to do justice to this whole 'drow royalty on Earth' thing."

Ember pointed at her. "So, you didn't forget."

"I don't generally forget anything as big as that, Em."

"No, I mean, Corian tried to shove those same reminders down my throat, like he thinks everything you know disappeared into thin air when you passed out."

Cheyenne snorted. "That's Corian for you. No, L'zar made it perfectly, annoyingly clear that if I gave up the throne here, I'd be taking on something like it Earthside. Not sure why that's a thing when there hasn't been anyone ruling magicals on the other side of the Border, but I have a feeling anyone I ask would tell me something about the old laws and that I have to deal with it."

"Couldn't have said it better myself."

"Right. I don't know, I have a feeling I'll be starting with the FRoE when I step into my Earthside-royalty boots. And yeah, Em, I'm talkin' huge, heavy, lace-up black combat boots. That's the only thing that works."

Laughing, Ember shook her head and floated away from the door. "If anyone can rock 'em, you can."

"I know, right?" Cheyenne watched her friend with a tired smile, and when Ember reached the bedroom door, she added, "For some reason, I'm thinking you probably wanna stay on this side a little longer this time, right?"

Ember turned around with a small frown. "What makes you say that?"

"Just a feeling. The responsible-drow-magical kind, anyway."

"Oh. I mean, yeah. There's a lotta work to do here. Helping Venga figure out how to reverse the blight is kinda high on the list, too."

"I know. I'd stick around longer too, but I gotta get back to crash that meeting between Colonel Thomas and the loyalists over there. You'll come back with me for that, at least, right?"

Ember wrinkled her nose, smiling in confusion. "Duh. I like it here, Cheyenne, but Earth's my home. And I already told Corian I'm the one who follows you back and forth across the border, so it's not like I can go back on that and still have magicals take me seriously around here."

"Cool."

"Get a little more rest before this giant-ass party, okay?" Ember pointed at the injection canister on the table by the bed. "If things start to feel weird, pop another one of those suckers in wherever feels like a good spot. If you can inject it in the wounds, though, that's the most effective."

"I probably won't. Kinda starting to think I have an Achilles hip."

Ember chuckled and opened the door. "You do you, halfling. Oh, hey, and if you need anything…" She gave Cheyenne a goofy grin and tapped the activator behind her ear. "Like texting but a million times better."

"Yeah, I know. Hey, this feels kinda familiar, doesn't it?"

"I know you're not talking about both of us having activators."

"No." Cheyenne scooted herself back along the bed so she could rest against the wall. "I mean one of us laid up recovering from something, and the other one rushing out the door with reminders to call or text if anything happens."

Ember's eyes widened with exaggerated realization as she nodded. "Yeah! Now you know how annoying it is, huh?"

"Okay, get out."

CHAPTER FIVE

Two hours after Ember left Cheyenne's temporary recovery room somewhere in the Crown's fortress, the halfling reached for the injection canister and jammed it into the flesh above her hip. The warm wave of euphoria washed over her, and she sank back into the pillows to stare at the ceiling with a dazed smile.

You'd think I would've built up a tolerance to darktongue by now. But holy shit, this stuff works.

It took another ten minutes for the buzz to settle out of her system, but the pain in her shoulders and hips was almost nonexistent.

She didn't know how much longer she lay sprawled out on the bed before someone knocked on the door. "Yeah?"

The door creaked open, and Lumil slunk into the room. For the first time since they'd met, the goblin woman looked genuinely embarrassed as she stepped forward with a pile of cream-colored cloth with O'gúleesh runes embroidered in bright-orange on the trim. She wore the same clothes.

Cheyenne propped herself up on her elbows and snorted. "What the hell are you *wearing*?"

"It's tradition, okay? For the whole *myrein* shebang." Lumil extended her arms and looked down with wide yellow eyes at the folded outfit resting there. "And these are for you."

"Very funny." Cheyenne pushed herself all the way up and scooted toward the edge of the bed. "I'll give you credit for going all-in on this one, but I'm not buying it."

"I'm serious." Lumil scowled. "Everybody's wearin' these things today."

"Not me." The halfling eyed the flowing light-colored fabric and wrinkled her nose. "Not today or ever."

"Just take the fell-damn clothes already, will ya?"

"Nope."

The goblin woman's lower jaw jutted out in frustration as she aimed one of Cheyenne's deadpan stares right back at her. "You have to."

"Wrong again. I don't dress up in white."

"Hey, I'm not asking you to change your whole fell-damn style, kid. It's one day."

"Look, if Bianca Summerlin couldn't get me to ditch the black dress for an all-white-attire summer gala, your chances are a hell of a lot lower. And I'm sure an exception can be made for the former O'gúl Crown who stepped down to run things Earthside. Don't you think?"

"Whatever." Lumil tossed the clothes unceremoniously on the table beside the bed. The injection canister toppled onto the floor and rolled beneath the elevated mattress. The goblin woman's eyes widened. "Looks like you got the party started in here a little early."

"The party's been going on for hours already, but nice try." Cheyenne pushed herself off the bed, gritting her teeth as she knelt and felt around beneath the bed for the canister. When she found it, she stood again with a grunt and shook the canister at Lumil. "This thing's for medicinal purposes only, by the way."

"Uh-huh. That's what they all say." The goblin woman folded her arms and watched Cheyenne collect her new black trenchcoat from the foot of the bed. "Don't let me catch you using that thing every twenty minutes."

With a snort, Cheyenne gingerly shrugged on her trenchcoat, then slipped the canister into one of the large, deep pockets. Her fingers quickly found the silver coil of her activator in the other pocket, and she nodded. "Not even remotely what I'm into, but if I was, do you really think you'd be able to stop me?"

Lumil unfolded her arms, her green hands clenching into fists as she stared at Cheyenne from beneath the tuft of yellow hair falling into her eyes. "I think your brief moment of O'gúl rule is startin' to go to your head. What are you doing?"

Cheyenne's eyes were wide, her cheeks puffing out slightly as she pressed her lips together and held back a laugh.

"What's wrong?" Lumil looked her up and down. "You gonna hurl or something? I'm trying to have a serious conversation here!"

The halfling laughed and dropped back onto the edge of the bed. "I can't…"

"You know what? Hand over the can of idiot juice." The goblin woman thrust out a hand and waited. "Right now."

Cheyenne forced her laughter back down. "Lumil, I'm sorry, okay?" Another laugh bubbled up inside her. "I can't take you seriously in that getup!"

Lumil spread her arms and glanced down at the flowing, cream-colored tunic and pants. "It's tradition!"

"You look like you dressed up as a yogi for Halloween."

"You're a real pain in my ass right now, you know that?"

"But you're missing some mala beads and henna." Lumil scoffed, and Cheyenne stood again and pulled out the darktongue canister again, tipping it toward the goblin woman. "This might help with the pain in your ass, though."

Lumil stared at the canister and couldn't help but chuckle at the joke. "Screw you, halfling."

"Yeah, yeah." Cheyenne stuck the thing back in her pocket and spread her arms. "I'm guessing you're supposed to take me wherever we're going after I joined the cult and put on the new getup, right?"

"Fucking come on, then." Rolling her eyes, the goblin woman trudged across the room and jerked open the door. "You're gonna feel like a real asshole when we get there and you're the only one not showing respect like everyone else."

"Well, good thing I'm used to people judging me for looking different, right?" Cheyenne followed her apparent guide out of the bedroom and into the hall. "And I know how to show respect without trying to look like something I'm not. That's the real disrespect right there, faking it."

She stopped as soon as she closed the door behind her and looked at the hall.

"Whoa."

"Still feelin' like yourself?" Lumil sniggered and stared at the halfling as Cheyenne's gaze passed over the walls and the high ceiling of the corridor.

"I'm not what's different around here. When did this happen?"

"Come on, kid. You knew the system was rewriting itself."

"Yeah. Didn't think the system would literally rewrite the walls."

Lumil took off down the hall with a snort and waved for Cheyenne to follow her. "You're the one who can see all the way to the core with that beefed-up activator. Don't tell me you can't figure out how this kinda reprogramming works."

Cheyenne slipped the activator out of her pocket and lifted it slowly toward her ear. "The reprogramming I know doesn't change the physical hardware. What happened to all the black stone?"

"Like you're not about to figure that out. Hurry up, will ya? Everybody's waiting, and we can't get started without you."

When the activator attached behind her ear, Cheyenne's eyelids fluttered briefly, and she widened her eyes at all the new information syncing with her magic. Flashing lines of code in green and blue scrolling across her vision brought up new information, programming for rearranging the look and feel, and even some of the city's structural layout. She only had to think about finding what had changed the black stone walls of every corridor in the Crown's fortress to a nearly white gray. The coded lines translated from O'gúleesh to English brought up an answer she hadn't expected:

System **rewrite in progress. Program access design under Cycle II recalibrating. Source Order: Ironbreak. Estimated time to completion 25 hours 17 minutes.**

The numbers counted down in real-time, and Cheyenne couldn't help a small laugh. "Persh'al chose all this, huh?"

"Yeah, the troll likes to think he's all badass, but I'm pretty sure the doom and gloom were startin' to get to him." Lumil turned around and pointed at the halfling. "Bet you wouldn't've changed a thing if you decided to stick around as Crown on this side, huh?"

"Well, maybe not as much as this. He got rid of the psycho-drow-murderer look, so that's a plus."

They went around the next corner, and Cheyenne found herself pausing to study the lines of new code that were rewriting the histories and commands of the entire system throughout Hangivol. Then she'd come back to the present and hurry after Lumil, who didn't stop once to wait for her.

"So the whole city changes into whatever Persh'al wants it to be."

The goblin woman shrugged. "Sure. I don't know. My skillsets revolve around something a little more physical, know what I'm sayin'?"

"Like your fists."

"Yeah, halfling. Like my fists. Need a demonstration?"

Cheyenne ignored the goblin woman's attempt to act pissed off and studied the walls. "Guess he brushed up on his knowledge of all the tech over here."

"I mean, he got to choose a few things, but the rest of it's pretty much out of his hands."

"Who controls the rest of it?"

Lumil turned around with a raised eyebrow. "Is that a real question?" When Cheyenne folded her arms and waited, the goblin woman gave her an answer. "Not any of us, kid. No magical runs the system in Hangivol or anywhere else in this whole ass-backward world. Ambar'ogúl's running the show on this one."

Cheyenne cocked her head. "A world full of magicals is in charge of maintenance for a tech system those magicals had to create."

"Yep."

"How does that even work?"

"You're asking the wrong goblin, kid." Lumil tossed a dismissive hand in the air and continued down the corridor. "Hell, any goblin's off the list of experts on the subject."

"So, this place is sentient. Like, inherently and then with the tech, yeah?"

"You lost me at 'sentient,' kid."

Cheyenne couldn't take her eyes off the constantly updating elements flashing and scrolling across the newly lightened walls that only looked like stone. "I mean it thinks for itself. Heals itself with the deathflame in the pits and rewrites an entire system whenever there's a new Crown."

"Dude, seriously?" Lumil shook her head and walked faster to put more room between her and Cheyenne. "Bother somebody else with this shit, okay? You're making my head hurt."

Cheyenne flicked her fingers and turned down the brightness of the scrolling code lines so she could focus on something else as she followed Lumil around two more turns in the labyrinth of corridors. *No one's gonna be able to answer* these *questions for me. That's something I'll have to tap into when all this is over.*

After descending two flights of stairs and making another right turn, they entered a narrow vestibule, where the members of the Four-Pointed Star were waiting for them.

Ember looked Cheyenne over from head to toe and cocked her head. "Lumil was supposed to bring you a change of clothes."

"Yeah, they're on the table by that giant-ass bed."

"Come on, Cheyenne. That's part of the ceremony."

"Hey, I'm here to be a part of it, okay? But I'm not putting on all that." The halfling choked back a laugh. "Looks pretty decent on you, though."

"Stupid fae and their stupid, good-looking…" Byrd scratched his armpit through the flowy material of his white and orange-embroidered tunic, scowling. "This isn't a one-size-fits-all kinda thing."

Lumil punched him in the shoulder. "Shut up. No one wants to hear about your discomfort, okay? There's plenty of that going around." She jerked the waistband of her loose pants left and right, pulled them down along her hips, then hiked them back up again and gave up.

Maleshi approached Cheyenne and Ember with a small smile. "Told you."

Ember rolled her eyes at the general. "Okay, fine. General Hi'et gets one point. I have at least a hundred, so keep at it."

Cheyenne shoved her hands into the pockets of her trenchcoat and looked back and forth between them. "Points for what, Em?"

The fae girl stared at the double doors leading out of the vestibule and shook her head, a small smile playing on her lips.

"Your *Nós Aní* assumed your relief at having found someone to take the throne for you would be enough to get you into the monkey suit."

Maleshi jerked on the embroidered collar of her own tunic and shrugged. "I knew you wouldn't do it."

"Huh." Cheyenne eyed the general's uniform, slightly different from what every other magical now wore. "And you got the fancy upgrade."

"Well, I haven't made any official promises." Maleshi shot her a sidelong glance, her silver eyes flashing beneath the artificial lights glowing in sconces along the walls. "But General Hi'et took a place of honor during more ceremonies than you can imagine, kid."

"Yeah, and General Hi'et shouldn't talk about herself in third-person. Like, ever."

"Cute."

A sharp crack came from behind them as Foltr thumped the end of his staff on the light-gray stone floor. He wore the same material as everyone else, though his ceremonial dress came in the form of a long robe that stopped above his ankles and exposed his crooked red-clawed feet. The old raug came forward, scrutinizing the other rebels in their appropriate attire. He stopped when he saw Cheyenne and frowned. "Should've expected this from you."

"Sorry to disappoint." She shrugged. "But I'm here. With all due respect. Ready to watch two trolls get married?"

Foltr grunted and thumped his staff again to continue his approach. "If you aren't aware of the nuances, *hinya*, you're in no position to refuse tradition. That includes the drapes."

He whacked the thick, hanging fabric of Cheyenne's trenchcoat with his staff.

"Hey." She stepped back, trying not to laugh. "This could be a designer coat, Grandfather. You don't know."

"Designed by a human and bought by a magical with no respect for the old laws."

Tilting her head, Cheyenne pursed her lips and stared the old raug down. "Now you're gonna tell me the old laws apply to a dress code too?"

"Doesn't matter what I say, *hinya*. Something tells me you won't listen anyway." Foltr stopped, rested both hands on the gnarled knot at the top of his staff, and glared at her.

She waited for him to back down, but he didn't. *The old dude has balls, I'll give him that. Guess that's what surviving a million years in this world gets you.* She gave him a genuine smile and leaned closer. "Any chance you wanna tell me what '*hinya*' means? You're not the first magical to call me that. Or the first raug, even."

Foltr smacked his lips. "Well, I can't call you *Aranél* anymore, can I? You gave that away at the drop of a hat."

"I have a name, though."

He blinked slowly at her, then rolled his eyes and moved through the gathered crowd of white-garbed rebels toward the double doors.

"Oh, come on." Cheyenne gestured at him and looked at Maleshi. "That was friendly conversation."

"With some things, kid, it's the same here as it is Earthside." The general glanced briefly at the old raug's back and shrugged. "Generation gap."

Ember snorted. "It's gotta be worse here. How long is a generation?"

"Few thousand years. Give or take."

"Yeah, that'll leave a lotta room for differences of opinion."

Cheyenne gazed around the vestibule and couldn't let go of her curiosity. "Seriously, though. *Hinya?*"

The double doors creaked slowly open into the room beyond, and the dressed-up magicals moved forward in a wave.

"It means, 'child.'" Maleshi pursed her lips and stared straight ahead as she took off after the others.

Cheyenne blinked.

"Ha." Ember elbowed her friend in the side and gave her a mocking grimace. "Kinda sounds like you've been demoted."

"Uh-huh." They walked in at the end of the group heading through the doors, and Cheyenne laughed in surprise. "Still a hell of a lot better than being the Crown."

CHAPTER SIX

I t took her a few seconds to recognize the room when they finally entered behind the others. The courtyard at the center of the Heart looked different with the lighter walls, the cracks and crumbling slabs repaired. The banister around the second-story walkway gleamed bright copper, and all the once-dark forbidding arches leading into the courtyard now had the same double doors, each of them engraved with O'gúleesh runes and intricate detailing.

Cheyenne didn't have the time to translate the runes with her activator, her focus on the streamers and thin strips of glistening silver hanging from the upper-story balcony. These were draped across the lowest branches of the Nimlothar tree too, which was the only proof that they were in the Heart again and not some ballroom she hadn't seen.

"Nobody told me we'd be coming right back here," she muttered, gazing around.

"Not surprising, though, right?" Ember grinned as the gathered magicals spread out through the courtyard, creating a path straight ahead that led toward the base of the Nimlothar. "Pretty much everything that means anything around here happens in front of that tree."

"I don't see why. Persh'al's not a drow."

Ember opened her mouth for another quick reply, then frowned. "True."

Persh'al, Elarit, and Corian were already waiting at the base of the tree, each of them wearing a uniform that would've fit right in at an ashram or temple but seemed wildly out of place in the violent, chaotic capital city of Ambar'ogúl.

Blood and honor, right? I hope no one's trying to keep those frocks clean through the rest of the night.

The new troll Crown jerked his chin at Cheyenne and waved her forward. Elarit glanced at him from the corner of her eye. Corian frowned when he saw Cheyenne in her usual all-black, and even Maleshi couldn't get him to lighten up about it when she leaned toward him and muttered something under her breath.

"You stepped in it," Ember said.

"They'll be fine." Cheyenne slowly trailed her gaze up the twisted, knotted trunk of the last Nimlothar. It had even fewer leaves now, though they still pulsed rhythmically with pale violet light. *All the decorations and celebrations in the world couldn't hide how sick this thing is. That's what we* should *be focusing on now—making sure it doesn't die on us while we're in party mode.*

Scowling at her in his flowing off-white tunic with a collar like Maleshi's, Corian gestured for Cheyenne and Ember to take their places on his left. When they did, he leaned toward her and growled. "You're not off to a very good start, Cheyenne."

"But I'm here."

"I have half a mind to send you back. We've waited long enough to get to this point. What's another ten minutes?"

"Hey, brother, it's fine." Persh'al nodded and winked at Cheyenne. "She's here, we're all here, and I'm about to swear the hell into this thing officially. If she doesn't wanna change, man, really don't care."

Corian's glowing silver eyes never left the halfling's face. "That's not the point."

Elarit cleared her throat. "The point, *vae shra'ni*, is that we've come this far against all the odds. Maybe *you* don't mind waiting another ten minutes just to prove your point, which may or may not be useless, but I've spent all day preparing for this to happen. I'd like to spend as little time in this courtyard as possible."

The nightstalker finally pulled his eyes off Cheyenne to look at Persh'al and Elarit, both of whom smiled expectantly at him and waited. Corian closed his eyes and stepped back. "As you wish."

The troll woman nodded and lifted her chin. "Thank you."

Corian grunted and gazed around the courtyard, waiting for the other magicals who'd bothered to be present to find their places and settle their conversations enough to hear him when he addressed them. A quarter of the orc guards who'd come to watch Cheyenne's slightly-less-than-epic showdown with her psychotic aunt were present now, and they watched the gathered officials and the new Crown at the base of the Nimlothar with eager anticipation.

I wonder how many of them hated to see Ba'rael go and how many are just hiding 'cause they feel like morons.

Maleshi leaned toward Cheyenne and muttered, "Fair warning beforehand, kid. To keep things from getting awkward when you inevitably interrupt the process."

The halfling frowned and looked over her shoulder. "Why would I do that?"

"Well, you won't now 'cause I'm about to tell you what's up." The general glanced at Corian, but the nightstalker gazed straight ahead with his hands clasped behind his back. "We found the loopholes we were looking for. The right path to take that'll keep any dumbshit with a death wish from challenging your choice of replacement."

"Okay. They'd be challenging Persh'al at that point, though, wouldn't they? He can handle it."

"Yes, but not the way the old laws dictate. Those are just about the only things that haven't rewritten themselves in the last twelve hours." Maleshi tilted her head from side to side, scanning the small groups of magicals, who were all dressed the same for the occasion and passing the time by conversing in low tones. "The troll needs more than your word and a few announcements from us to solidify his new position."

"I told you I'm not staying."

"No one's asking you to. We *are* asking you to bind yourself to the Nimlothar and receive its blessing for Persh'al as the Crown and Elarit as his mate."

Cheyenne turned fully around to face the general. "Okay, when you say bind myself, that doesn't sound like something I can do and then go home."

"I know it doesn't sound like that, but you're free to do whatever you want after this. I promise."

"Then what the hell does 'bind myself to the Nimlothar' mean?"

Corian cleared his throat and looked at her plaster-dusted black shirt, complete with bloodstains and shredded holes from Ba'rael's darts, instead of at Cheyenne's face. "It's basically the same thing you did with the seed, Cheyenne. That kind of binding."

"I'm not eating a branch."

Finally, the nightstalker met her gaze and raised an unamused eyebrow. "It's a fairly simple spell. I'll talk you through it. This is the only way Ambar'ogúl will accept your decision. The roots Hangivol put down over the hundreds of centuries with a drow on the throne, they're not giving up their hold anytime soon. You'll be the bridge."

"To what?"

"To putting a troll on the throne." Corian rolled his shoulders back, trying to hide his discomfort with this topic. "You can go home, but technically, whenever you make the crossing to this side, you'll still be Crown."

"No."

"Trust me, kid," Maleshi added, "you won't have to lift a finger if you don't want to. Persh'al's swearing in as your steward, more or less. He runs the show when you're gone, and he can still run the show while you're here if that's what you want. You'll be the only one he has to answer to."

"What I want is to be done with all this Crown bullshit," Cheyenne hissed.

Corian glanced at the growing crowd of witnesses as the last of them trickled in through the open doors on the opposite side of the courtyard. "It's a formality. An entirely necessary formality, or anything we do from here on out isn't going to stick. If it makes you feel better, we'll make a new law that anyone who sees the Black Flame walking through the city streets has to flip you off instead of bowing."

She snorted. "That's a good start."

"And this will only solidify your position Earthside." The aggravation melted away from Corian's face as he patiently waited for her to absorb the new technicality. "I know your head's in the right place, Cheyenne. You've done everything that was asked of you without knowing exactly what it was. We're only standing here right now because you chose not to walk away."

"Yeah, but that was always the plan."

"You don't want to rule from the Heart. I get it." Corian dipped his head toward her. "But you won't choose walking away over everything else we both know you care about. We still have a lot of work to do here and Earthside. This will help, and Persh'al deserves to be backed by the only drow, the only magical, who can make any of this possible."

Persh'al's neon-orange mohawk appeared over Corian's shoulder as the blue troll inserted himself into the conversation with a grin. "Thanks, brother."

Corian held Cheyenne's gaze and clenched his jaw. "Can't do it without you, and there's no point in trying to hide that anymore."

She stared right back at him and breathed slowly through her nose. *First, the legacy box wouldn't leave me alone, and now this goddamn throne won't let me walk away.*

Persh'al leaned to the side and circled his finger in the air. "Can we get crackin' on this thing? I'm about to start sweating through this getup, and it's not gonna be pretty."

"Fine." Cheyenne cocked her head. "Let's do it, then."

"Excellent." The blue troll's mohawk disappeared as he returned to Elarit's side.

Corian nodded. "Thank you."

"I mean it, though." She pointed at him. "No bowing or groveling or waiting on me hand and foot. And if I'm gonna make trips over here to hang around for longer than a day, I'm not staying in this fortress. Just not happening."

The nightstalker's lips twitched into a tiny smile, and he turned around again to face the audience for Persh'al's O'gúl coronation and the *myrein* he'd always wanted. "We'll find you an apartment."

"Better be a good one," Ember added.

Cheyenne shot her friend a sidelong glance and frowned. "Did you know about this whole loophole thing?"

"Nope. Feels like I'm in the secret club, but only, like, halfway."

"That makes two of us, Em."

Corian spread his arms wide and sent a burst of shimmering silver light out of both hands. His magic crackled along the opposite walls of the courtyard before smoothing out into waves of light that quickly disappeared.

Cheyenne thought, Looks like the place is rewriting itself not to be torn apart by crashing magic, either. Another point for upgrades.

The center of the Heart fell silent. All the gathered magicals—Four-Pointed Star rebels, citizens off the streets of the inner city, and orc guards alike, all wearing one variation or another of the ceremonial uniform—turned their attention to the small party at the base of the last Nimlothar.

"This is quite the day." Corian didn't quite shout, but his voice echoed against the walls just the same. A cheer rose from the crowd, interspersed with laughter and the occasional stomping of feet. The nightstalker's silver eyes widened, and he stuck on a brilliant smile that didn't quite match the intensity of his feral grin.

No, he saves that for when he's kicking someone's ass, like mine. Cheyenne pressed her lips together to keep from smiling and glanced at Persh'al and Elarit. The troll couple stood tall and proud on the other side of Corian, soaking it all in. *They deserve this.*

"We're here, as the old laws command," the nightstalker continued, "to bring in the turn of a new Cycle, no longer crushed beneath the Spider's darkening sway."

Roars of approval and excited shouts and more stomping rose in reply.

Corian lowered his arms by his sides again, and the strangely eclectic audience of mostly strangers quieted down again. "Persh'al Tenishi is one of a kind, isn't he?"

The few magicals who knew the new troll Crown chuckled. Lumil cupped a hand around her mouth and shouted, "May the blue…ah!"

Byrd elbowed her in the ribs, shook his head, and whispered harshly, "Not your day, man."

"I know it's not my day, assface. The guy doesn't have a title yet, for cryin' out loud."

The goblin man folded his arms and smiled at the group beneath the

Nimlothar tree, muttering through his tight grin, "Not your job to come up with one, either. Shut the hell up."

"You know what? You can suck it, you little—"

Corian cleared his throat and talked over them, graciously ignoring the bickering goblins in their natural state. "Persh'al Tenishi, the first troll to sit the O'gúl throne in Hangivol, accepts his duty and our pride today. He accepts the O'gúl Crown as his own, and the old laws of our world receive the new Cycle very well."

More cheers, more laughter and stomping, and Persh'al stood tall, albeit a little awkwardly, with his hands clasped behind his back as he rocked from heel to toe.

"Beneath the ever-watchful eye of the last Nimlothar," Corian continued, "we bind Persh'al to his name and his honor, and to those who went before him."

Cheyenne was too busy staring at the blue troll's slightly uncomfortable fidgeting to notice Corian turning toward her. Ember nudged her with a shoulder and nodded at the nightstalker, who bowed and gestured toward the Nimlothar when Cheyenne blinked at him.

"After you, Cheyenne."

"Right now?"

He raised his eyebrows and stepped toward the twisted bark of the gnarled tree behind her.

I seriously need to work on preparing for shit like this.

She moved stiffly toward him, her hands still jammed into her coat pockets, and tried to smile at Persh'al when he joined them.

"You're gonna have to tell me what's up, kid." The troll chuckled and warily eyed the tree. "I don't know how this thing works."

"You think *I've* done this before?" They looked at each other and waited for Corian to take the lead once more.

"O'gúl rule hasn't been handed down like this for quite some time." It wasn't a direct address to the onlookers, but it wasn't meant to be private, either. "This is a new age for all of us, thanks to the two of you. May it last as long as the old age, if not longer, hmm?"

Persh'al said, "Maybe if I came at this a few thousand years younger."

Maleshi barked a laugh, and the magicals closest to the tree who'd heard the troll chuckled and nodded, staring intently at their new Crown and the last piece of his official coronation.

"All right." Corian dipped his head toward Cheyenne. "Place your hand on the tree, kid. Both of you."

"Yep." Persh'al smacked his hand on the rough bark and grimaced when a fleck of ancient, dried wood scraped off beneath his touch. "Shit. Sorry."

Corian closed his eyes but didn't say anything.

Cheyenne slowly lifted her hand to the Nimlothar's twisted trunk and pressed her palm against it. A flash of warm energy pulsed beneath it and raced halfway up her arm. She gritted her teeth and tried to focus on that instead of the undertones of the tree's pain that came with it. *It's dying, and it's still giving whatever it has left to make this happen. How do I even know that?*

"Whoa." Persh'al let out a self-conscious chuckle and widened his eyes at her. "You feel that, right?"

"Oh, yeah." *Way more than he does, I bet.*

The bark beneath their hands pulsed with pale violet light, then the tree lit up. Wave after wave of the same light raced from their hands to the center of the tree and streaked up to the branches, illuminating the few dozen leaves still clinging to their source. The Nimlothar groaned and seemed to lean toward the blue troll and the drow halfling sharing its energy.

Corian nodded in satisfaction, then turned around again to address the crowd. "A new Cycle turns, and Ambar'ogúl answers! The Nimlothar answers! May the Ironbreak rein!"

"May the Ironbreak reign!" The gathered magicals chanted it over and over, stomping their feet and banging on their chests and the metal doors now installed within every archway around the courtyard.

"Stay like that a little longer, Cheyenne," Corian muttered before turning to Persh'al and pounding his own fist against his chest. "Here we are."

The blue troll chuckled. "Never thought I'd see you swearing allegiance to me, of all magicals, *vae shra'ni*."

"It's a surprise for all of us. A good one." The nightstalker bowed his head, then looked slyly up at his friend. "You weren't expecting me to fall to my knees, were you?"

"Man." Persh'al scoffed and removed his hand from the tree as he turned back toward Maleshi and Elarit, who were standing six feet in front of them.

Neither of them noticed the cold shiver that ran down Cheyenne's spine when the Nimlothar pulsed with a brighter light the second the troll's hand left the ancient wood. *It knows the difference between us, that he's a troll, not a drow.* Another wave of cold energy shot down her spine. *What does this thing want from me?*

CHAPTER SEVEN

"Look at this," Maleshi called to the crowd as Persh'al rejoined her and Elarit. "We have a binding to the Crown and a *myrein* all in the same day. Lucky us."

Corian grinned at the general, now putting on her own show for everyone, and stepped close to the tree, where Cheyenne's hand rested against it. "Like I said, kid. This is pretty much the same thing as what you worked on with the Nimlothar seed for your trials."

"I don't think so." She eyed the pulsing streaks of violet light shooting up the tree and into the branches, over and over. *Like a heartbeat.* "There's something else going on here."

"That's a bunch of magic older than anyone in this courtyard." He sniggered. "Yes, including Foltr. Try to focus and do the best you can, all right?"

"Sure." Cheyenne closed her eyes and took a deep breath. *And once again, I'm taking pointers in drow magic from a nightstalker. What could possibly go wrong?*

"Two O'gúleesh together at the Heart's doorstep," Maleshi shouted. "Persh'al Tenishi, the Ironbreak Crown of Ambar'ogúl, and Elarit Masharun, the best spark-setter in Hangivol. I don't think I have to say more about either one of them."

Harsh, unabashed laughter echoed through the courtyard.

"You can connect with the seed to reach the tree, if that helps," Corian muttered. "It fell from these very branches when the tree still blossomed."

"Okay. Connect and do what?"

"Bind yourself, Cheyenne. The Nimlothar wants a promise. It may tell you what that is, though I wouldn't be surprised if its voice has grown too quiet for you to hear. If that's the case, tell it you'll be a part of what happens next in this world. Show your commitment."

She cracked open one eye and settled it on his face. "Next you're gonna tell me to start hugging trees, huh?"

He took a deep breath and shook his head. "Just do it."

Shutting her eye again, Cheyenne pressed her hand more firmly against the rough bark and focused on the pulse of magic flaring beneath her touch. *Talk to the tree. Make a promise. Well, tree, if you're still capable of telling me what you want, now's the time to share.*

"Bound by the old laws and carried into a new dawn." Persh'al's and Elarit's voices echoed the appropriate response for their *myrein* ritual.

Maleshi grinned at them and stepped back to retrieve something from a metal box at her feet. When she stood with a small green orb in her hand, the crowd erupted in bellowing cheers and roars of approval. "Now to bring your promise to life, eh?"

Corian leaned so close to Cheyenne's ear, she could feel his body heat when he whispered, "Anything yet?"

"I'm working on it." *Promises from everyone. And I'm trying to hear what a tree has to say to me. This is ridiculous.*

"Let it come to you, kid. When it happens, you'll know."

"Yeah? You have personal experience talking to drow trees?"

"Focus whatever's in that drow head of yours on the Nimlothar, not me."

Cheyenne whispered, "Then stop talking."

"The fire that unites us all," the general shouted, "now uniting two in their first step together toward the final flame."

A flash of silver light erupted in her hand, and the green orb cracked before bursting into green flames. The O'gúleesh in attendance went wild, stomping their feet and pounding on anything within reach.

Cheyenne could hardly think with all the noise and the shuddering tremble of the stone floors beneath her feet. *What do you want from me?*

The small ceremonial deathflame leaped from Maleshi's hand, splitting in half to settle first in Elarit's open palm and then Persh'al's. The troll woman sucked in a sharp breath when the flames touched her violet flesh.

"Now you carry the deathflame as one." Maleshi stepped back behind the troll couple and spread her arms. "And you'll face it as one."

Grinning at each other, Persh'al and Elarit stepped closer and clasped each other's wrists. The green fire sparked and hissed and raced up their arms, growing and spreading across both their bodies as they stared at each other and fought not to let go.

Cheyenne frowned, her eyes still closed in concentration. *Okay, maybe this isn't gonna happen. So, tree, I'll make my own promise.*

A burst of searing heat jolted violently through her hand and into her entire body. She tried to pull her hand away but couldn't; tried to open her eyes, and instead found herself looking at the Nimlothar tree but without anything else in the courtyard.

The vision was so much like the last one she'd had of this tree, every branch and twisted spiral of ancient bark consumed by black flames. Her body was on fire too, and the lilting song coming from the Nimlothar rose into a grating screech of pain and sorrow. Somewhere far away, another voice wailed in mourning. More voices joined it, wordlessly crying out. Then Cheyenne was standing in the destroyed Nimlothar forest outside the Sorren Gán's fiery lair, feeling every one of the decimated trees calling out to her, begging, pleading, sharing their pain.

The last Nimlothar in her vision dipped its branches toward her and brushed them over her face, her hair, her clothes, creaking and groaning.

In the Heart's courtyard full of celebrating magicals, Elarit and Persh'al shouted in their effort to keep a firm hold on each other's forearms. The deathflame consuming them flared brighter, stretching feet above their heads toward the open sky, and a deafening crack split the air.

Cheyenne gave a searing gasp and finally opened her eyes. Corian turned toward her in surprise, but she stared blankly at the Nimlothar's glowing violet light, which was growing steadily brighter beneath her hand. *Okay. Okay, I get it. I promise I'll do everything I can to make it right.*

The tree's purple light blazed with a second-long intensity, momentarily blinding every pair of magical eyes in the courtyard.

When the light faded from the tree and didn't return, the deathflame fire around Persh'al and Elarit snuffed out. The troll couple fell to their knees together, still gripping each other's forearms as trails of dark-green smoke rose from their arms and shoulders.

"Well." Maleshi chuckled in surprise and spared the Nimlothar and Cheyenne a quick glance. "Seems like a pretty unanimous approval to me."

The magicals who'd gathered to witness both ceremonies one right after the other recovered from their shock and erupted into cheers and roars, snarling and throwing fists in the air as they chanted for the Ironbreak and now his mate.

Persh'al bowed his head toward Elarit and laughed weakly. "Not as bad as I expected."

Breathing heavily, the troll woman looked at him with a crooked smile, the thin silver chains settling across the bridge of her nose. "You were screaming like a pup."

"Come on. If anyone's gonna make me scream, it's you."

Maleshi snorted, then cleared her throat. "Time for the real party now! Let's get the hell outta here!"

The Four-Pointed-Star members lifted another cheer for their new Crown, and the random citizens and O'gúl guards echoed it as they shoved and jostled each other on their way toward the double doors at the end of the courtyard.

The troll couple stood, still recovering from their shared pass through the deathflame.

"Look at you!" Byrd shoved Persh'al in the shoulder and winked. "Tied to the ol' ball and chain now, ain'tcha?"

Elarit narrowed her eyes at him. "What's that supposed to mean?"

"It's a useless Earthside saying," Persh'al muttered. "Doesn't mean shit."

Byrd's grin faded as he glanced at the trolls. "For real? Aw, come on! Lighten up a little."

"You can explain it to me once we're through those doors. How 'bout that?" Elarit gestured at the dwindling crowd surging through the courtyard's exit.

"Not until I've had at least an entire bottle of Bloodshine," Persh'al muttered, wrinkling his nose at the streaks of burnt cloth along his arms.

"Even better." Elarit grabbed his hand and tugged him forward, shoving Byrd out of the way to follow the magicals partying in their names.

"Hey, wait up!" Byrd turned in a quick circle, his eyes wide. "Where the hell's Lumil?"

A crash and explosion of red light flared in the corridor on the other side of the double doors, followed by Lumil's cackling laughter and someone else's furious roar.

Maleshi gestured at the doors with a pert smile. "There you go."

"Damnit! She can't sit still for two seconds." Byrd took off across the courtyard, shoving random magicals out of the way and slipping past as they snarled and tried to engage him in fights.

Cheyenne watched the procession leaving the Heart's courtyard with wide eyes, trying to breathe steadily so her heart would quit rattling around in her chest.

Corian tilted his head until his ear almost touched his shoulder and studied her. "You heard something."

"Yeah." She glanced up at him, then had to look away. "Saw something too."

"And your promise?"

"I sure as hell made it." *And now there's one more thing on my list of impossible magical fixes.* "I need a minute to work this one out in my head."

Maleshi approached them and clapped a hand on the halfling's shoulder. "Well done, kid. If we gave out medals for this kinda thing, you'd have all of 'em right now."

Cheyenne shrugged away from the general's hand and shook her head. "Where do I go to get a drink?"

"Pretty much anywhere in the city today." Maleshi eyed her with a confused smile. "You okay?"

"I will be after a few tankards of grog."

Corian chuckled and headed after the last of the ceremonies' witnesses. "It's about time we made that a priority."

Maleshi gave Cheyenne a final once-over, then shrugged and hurried to catch up with him.

"Seriously, though." Ember floated up behind Cheyenne and dipped her head. "You look like you saw a ghost or something."

"I don't know, Em. The ghosts of trees, maybe."

The fae girl choked back a laugh. "What?"

"Nothing." Cheyenne placed her hand gently on the Nimlothar again, but the tree didn't have anything else to show her and didn't respond. "I'll probably be more coherent with a good buzz on."

"Or at least less moody." Ember bumped her shoulder against her friend's and floated across the courtyard. "I bet Vedrosha's packed right now. What do you think?"

"The fighting pits right after a new Crown steps up and a wedding by deathflame?" Cheyenne snorted and hurried to catch up with her *Nós Aní*, shoving her hands deep into her pockets again. "Sounds just like the kinda thing that happens around here."

"I know, right?" Ember grinned. "So awesome."

"Meh. Say that again when I'm spilling grog foam all over the place."

"You've got yourself a deal."

CHAPTER EIGHT

The party took to the streets of Hangivol like it had when Cheyenne placed her drow *marandúr* coin on the altar eleven days ago, only this time, L'zar Verdys wasn't here to dampen the celebration with his presence. The O'gúlccsh dancing and carousing through the glittering metallic labyrinth of the capital's lower levels made that perfectly clear. There wasn't a snarling, scowling face in sight, except for the magicals starting brawls outside storefronts, which lasted only as long as it took to get in a few good punches before barrels of grog and sealed bottles of fellwine and Bloodshine were cracked open and poured all around.

Ember stopped short as a skaxen woman leaped from behind a display table outside a produce shop. The magical shrieked and darted across Ember and Cheyenne's path, blasting a sickly yellow burst of magic at an orc roaring with laughter. His laughter cut off abruptly beneath the skaxen's attack, and he swept a meaty green arm against the rat-like skaxen's shoulder to knock her backward before offering her a bottle of fellwine in return.

"This is even crazier than the last time," Ember muttered.

Cheyenne stalked past her after the group of cheering, roaring magicals dressed in the ceremonial flowing cream-colored uniforms. "Even more of a reason this time to get crazy, right?"

"More of a reason?" The fae girl floated quickly forward to catch up with her friend. "What's better than the long-lost drow heir returning to claim her birthright from the worst Crown this world's ever had?"

"Half-drow, Em."

Ember scoffed. "Yeah, like that even matters. And you didn't answer my question."

"What's better?" Cheyenne shrugged. "Probably that L'zar isn't here to screw it all up somehow."

"You're giving him way too much credit. You know that?"

"Maybe." Cheyenne scanned the city streets filled with dancing, brawling, laughing, drinking O'gúleesh. Up ahead, Nu'ek roared something unintelligible and sent a scrawny goblin flying away from the *myrein* procession on their way to the fighting pits.

Persh'al laughed and raised a fist into the air, throwing up a burst of blue sparks. "No holding back today, brothers! Vedrosha calls to all of us!"

Cheers and stomping, metal-banging approval rose at the new Crown's cry, and the procession picked up the pace toward the outskirts of the city and the newly re-opened fighting pits.

Cheyenne cocked her head. "Or maybe they're happy not to follow a drow anymore."

"A Crown of the people, huh?" Ember looked at a group of six floating metal orbs passing overhead, swooping low to follow the procession. "Whoa."

"What?"

"Is this what you see with your activator?" Ember pointed at the orbs. "I can read everything those orbs are picking up. They're like O'gúl GoPros built into drones."

Cheyenne barked a laugh. "Yeah, I guess they are."

Ember shot her friend a sidelong glance, her eyebrows flickering together. "But that's not everything you see, is it?"

"Not everything, no." The scrolling lines of code racing across the city streets and walls of every building and alley still flashed across Cheyenne's vision in muted colors. *And I'll leave it that way for now. There's way too much going on to try to pick apart the way this system works right now.*

"What else, then?" Ember playfully slapped her friend's shoulder with the back of a hand and laughed. "Go on, spit it out. I wanna see how much I can pick up on my own."

"It's a lot, Em."

"Yeah, that's what everyone keeps saying, but no one's said why you're better at all this tech stuff, other than playing with transport trains and taking your activator back with you across the Border." Ember's excited smile faded. "Shit. I can't take mine with me, huh?"

"I mean, you could try."

"Nope. Not gonna risk it. Hey, I wonder if Persh'al Tenishi the Iron-break would do a fae a solid and hold onto it for me when we're Earthside."

Cheyenne leaned away from the roaring crowds gathering around the fighting pits as the procession stepped out onto the glistening metal grounds of Vedrosha. Her activator responded immediately with an option to turn down the background noise that was threatening to become the only noise, and she quickly accepted.

"You okay?"

"What? Yeah." Cheyenne gave her friend a crooked smile. "Got a little loud, but I took care of it."

Ember frowned. "Took care of it?"

The halfling tapped her pointed gray ear poking out from beneath her bone-white hair. "Turned down the volume."

"For real?" The fae girl's luminous eyes widened. "You can do that?"

"Yeah." Apparently, that was not a basic activator feature.

"Holy shit."

Cheyenne laughed. "*That's* the thing that surprises you?"

"You know what? I'm sure it's not the most impressive thing you can do with that little silver coil, but that's about all I needed to hear."

"An extra perk, I think. But hey. If Elarit made yours, I bet you'll be cruising around and finding a bunch of new things you can do too."

"Yeah, all while I have to listen to this noise at actual levels." As if the celebrating O'gúleesh responded directly to Ember's comment, the procession of *myrein* witnesses and the citizens of Hangivol gave another roaring cheer, stomping on the metal ground and shoving each other in excitement as Persh'al and Elarit stopped in front of the largest fighting pit. "I guess it's worse for you, huh? Drow hearing and all."

Cheyenne shrugged. "I can handle it."

"Ironbreak!" Lumil shouted, thrusting a fist glowing with her spinning red runes in the air. "Into the pit!"

Byrd immediately took up the cry, and the magicals around them echoed the name of their new Crown. Elarit's high, ringing laughter rose through the chanting, and Persh'al pushed up the sleeves of his flowing tunic. "Shall we, then?"

"With pleasure."

Both trolls jumped down onto the sand covering the bottom of the pit, and the troll Crown's loyal subjects went wild with primal excitement.

"Jesus." Cheyenne shook her head. "I can't stay here to watch this again."

"Seriously?" Ember leaned forward, trying to peer through the crowded magicals in front of her to get a good look at the pit. "This is better than MMA and rugby combined."

"Rugby?"

"Yeah. Like football without pads, kinda. Those guys get smashed."

Cheyenne folded her arms. "Didn't know you were a fan of watching fights, Em."

"Please. I'm a fan of watching a little bit of everything, except for maybe the Hallmark channel. You know what? Never mind." Ember pumped a fist in the air. "Ironbreak!"

Cheyenne scanned the pit grounds. Grog and fellwine had made its way out here by the crateload, and O'gúleesh gathered around the various stations to grab what they could before returning their attention to the fight between the newly *myrein*-wedded couple.

She was about to head toward the closest barrel of grog spouting sloshing amber liquid and spattering foam all over the open metal ground, but the activator lit up a brighter flash of yellow light in her vision. She followed the source of the new code and paused. *More like an incoming message or a summons.*

Scanning for the coded pathway, Cheyenne found the yellow light growing stronger toward the northern edge of the city and the multi-colored flames spewing into the sky.

"Hey." She nudged Ember and nodded at the other side of the city. "I'm gonna go check that out."

Grinning eagerly, Ember turned away from the excitement of the first pit fight under Persh'al's rule and settled her gaze on the flames flickering along Hangivol's outer wall. Her smile disappeared. "I know I don't have to tell you what's over there, Cheyenne."

"Nope. Wanna come?"

"You want me to come with you to check out the Sorren Gán. At the fellfire pits."

Cheyenne shrugged. "I mean, you don't have to. I wanna see how the cleanup by magical feasting went."

"You know what I think?" Ember blinked. "I think you're a masochist."

"I mean, you're not wrong. It's better than watching friends slit each other's throats in the sand so they can burn each other with the death-flame and call it their duty."

"Ha. Yeah."

"Up to you, Em. I need a break from crowds and shouting." Cheyenne nodded at her friend, then pushed her way toward the north end of Vedrosha and Hangivol's outer wall.

Ember glanced longingly at the fighting pit, then back at her retreating friend and sighed. "Fine."

"Cheyenne!" Lumil shouted, pointing at the halfling moving away from the pits. "You and me in the pit after this. I call first dibs."

The halfling turned halfway around and raised an eyebrow at the grinning goblin woman. "I don't wanna hurt you."

"Aw, come on!"

"Get Byrd in there with you. Maybe you can finally work a few things out."

Lumil's smile morphed into a scowl of disappointment as Cheyenne disappeared into the crowd, Ember floating along quickly behind her.

"Fuck yeah, I'll fight you." Byrd punched her in the shoulder. "I'll put *veréle* down on that pit right over there."

"Man, you know I'll rip you apart."

"No way. Come on." The goblin man raised both fists in preparation, bouncing back and forth. "I can take a hit."

"Not when I'm trying."

Behind them, Corian folded his arms and glanced down at the squabbling goblins. "I think it's an excellent idea."

"Yeah, I bet you do." Lumil waved him off.

"Then how about this? I'll put *veréle* down on that pit for the two of you to jump down. Or one of you can fight me instead."

The goblin woman's eyes widened, and she exchanged surprised glances with Byrd before turning around to leer up at the nightstalker. "Putting your *veréle* where your furry mouth is, huh?"

"If it gets you to shut up longer than five minutes, absolutely."

"You're on, nightstalker." Lumil punched Byrd in the gut, making him stagger sideways as he doubled over. "You hear that?"

He grunted. "What the hell's wrong with you?"

"Dumbest question you've ever asked. You and me, dumbass. Then the winner takes on Mr. High-and-Mighty over here, and we double the pot."

Byrd rolled his eyes as Lumil and Corian shook firmly. The nightstalker's silver eyes flashed, and he broke into a wide, feral grin. "Deal."

CHAPTER NINE

Once Cheyenne and Ember reached the north end of Vedrosha's open ground, which was teeming with bloodthirsty, intoxicated, fight-crazed O'gúleesh, the outer wall of the city was a lot easier to reach. They stopped at the high wall, and Ember wrinkled her nose. "Guess we went the wrong way, huh?"

"Nope."

"But it's solid." The fae girl knocked on the wall and received a metallic clang in return. "Either we missed the way out, or it's somewhere up there. What? Why are you looking at me like that?"

Cheyenne tried to wipe the smile off her lips and shook her head. "No reason."

"That's the same look you had when you handed me that illusion charm. What am I missing?"

The halfling scanned the code scrolling over the metal surface until she found the command to let them out. Her finger swiped quickly across the metal wall, and the tiny square segments composing every inch of Hangivol's metal surfaces folded back and peeled away from each other. Five seconds later, an open doorway materialized, and Cheyenne gestured at it. "After you."

"Damn." Ember frowned at the doorway, then glanced quickly at her friend. "Activator?"

"It's a safe bet to assume that anything I do over here is activator-related, Em. Unless it's drow magic spewing out of my hands."

Ember floated slowly through the thick metal wall and down the short tunnel to the walkway on the other side. "I don't see anything in here."

"No code on the walls?"

"I mean, there's like a map of the city. Level names. Where we are right now. That's about it."

"Huh." Cheyenne followed her friend out of the short tunnel and onto the walkway, which closed behind them on its own without her having to prompt it. "I guess that's one more thing to stick on the list."

"The list of all the things Cheyenne Summerlin can do better than everyone else? Didn't know we were making a list."

"I mean, you asked, Em."

"Yeah, I know. How silly of me."

They made their way north along the curving walkway outside the city wall toward leaping, hissing flames in every color. The Sorren Gán came into view long before they reached the fellfire pits, the blazing orange flames of its body sending up thick clouds of black smoke into the darkening sky.

"Damn." Ember fell behind Cheyenne when she stopped to take in the sight. "That's what you tried to fight in that cave?"

"Pretty much the only thing in either world I couldn't blast away even a little. I don't even think it felt my magic, honestly."

"Looks like that thing Gandalf fought in *Lord of the Rings*."

Cheyenne turned around to frown at her friend. "Come again?"

"Never mind."

The walkway dipped into another tunnel leading out onto the fellfire grounds. When they emerged on the other side, Ember shook her head and gazed around. "What is this place again?"

"Fellfire pits."

"You say that like I'm supposed to know what those are."

"Like a smithy. Kinda."

Ember snorted. "We're going renaissance now?"

"It's where they make the metal, Em. First time I came here, that's what they were doing. All the tech, all the walls and floors, and every-thing metal, made in those huge pits that—" The closest pit beside them burst in a roaring column of green flames shooting a dozen feet into the air before quickly sputtering out again. "Okay, like that."

"Looks like a giant deathflame to me."

"I have no idea what the difference is. Just that there is one, apparently."

Ember snuck another glance at the Sorren Gán, who was lying on its back in a crater of earth beyond the edge of the fellfire pits. The crater flickered and shimmered with purple and silver flames all moving together like ripples in a pond. "And that thing came here to feast on magic?"

"Yeah. I kinda released it all out here before the city blew up last time."

"Oh, right. How could I forget the exploding capital?" The fae girl snorted. "I think I'll stay right here."

"What?"

"No, seriously. You go ahead. I'm having flashbacks of you and L'zar flying out of that cave on fire, and it's not really something I'm looking forward to experiencing."

Cheyenne studied her friend's determined grimace and shrugged. "I mean, I wasn't gonna talk to it or anything. Just wanted to see how things got cleaned up."

"Well, it looks like the Sorren Gán's in a food coma." Ember started to turn on the wide path back toward the sloping tunnel. "Now we know. Maybe we can find a bottle of Bloodshine."

The flames around the Sorren Gán flared higher as the creature stirred in its pool of liquid fire. It snorted a burst of blue flame from its charred, fiery nostrils, and two blazing red eyes flickering with more fire opened in the thing's massive head. It rolled sideways in the pool, its black and gray belly distended, and growled.

"You are braver than your father, little drow." Multi-colored flames rose and fell, flickering across the crater as the Sorren Gán's thunderous voice made the ground tremble.

Cheyenne squared her footing and stopped, holding her ground as the earth's shaking subsided again.

"Great." Ember stared at the creature. "We woke it up."

"Come closer," the Sorren Gán rumbled. "I am sated, and even one so small as you would be too much. Come."

Cheyenne sighed. "You threw me into a lake of fire last time, so I'll stay right here, thanks."

Thick black smoke belched from the creature, and it rolled farther onto its side in the pool of fire to fix its fiery eyes on her. "You may be smarter than your father as well, which he should have anticipated. Where *is* L'zar?"

Just when I thought he was out of the picture. Cheyenne stared at the orange and red flames flickering in the Sorren Gán's eyesockets. "He's not here, and I don't think he's coming back."

A rolling, grating laugh bellowed from the creature's throat. "He thinks he's found his missing piece, has he? This is not the first time I've been told L'zar would never return, but he cannot help it. He is bound to me."

Ember floated forward and stopped beside Cheyenne to mutter, "Think it knows about the curse?"

"I'm not gonna give up that information, Em. Let it think whatever it wants."

If the Sorren Gán heard their conversation, it didn't react. One fiery black-ribbed wing fanned out from the massive creature's back and pointed straight at the sky, trailing smoke. Something like a roaring yawn escaped the gaping black mouth, and the pool of multi-colored fire rippled again. "The new Cycle turned for you today, did it not, little drow?"

"New Cycle, sure. Not for me."

"Interesting."

They stared at each other for so long, Cheyenne was about to call it and head back to the tunnel. Then the Sorren Gán puffed a stream of bright-purple flames across the barren, kicked-up earth between them. The fire reached out like tendrils toward the halfling's face. When she felt the cool, tingling energy of the creature's magic, she forced herself not to step away from it.

"I have feasted on the Spider's greed." Glistening silver smoke belched from the fiery black mouth. "I have more than enough magic to last me a thousand years, so I will give you what you seek in approaching me here."

Cheyenne frowned at the creature and waited. She wasn't seeking anything, but okay. This crazy-ass fire-beast wanted to give her something. Not sure she wanted it.

"I don't want what L'zar wanted," she said. "And I'm definitely not getting on my knees for you like he did."

The Sorren Gán roared with laughter. The crater filled with liquid fire and the scattered pools of multi-colored flame rose higher at the sound. The creature rose slowly off its side, spewing drops of liquid fire, and sat upright in the bed it had made itself after gorging on the excess of Ba'rael's stolen magic. "You are not your sire, little drow. There is nothing I desire that you could give me."

"We both know you don't give things away for free."

"Not free. Are you not the one who released this feast for me beyond the city?"

Cheyenne shrugged. "Yeah, that was me."

"Then cease your attempts to battle me with ingratitude," the creature hissed. "And listen."

After shooting a quick glance at Ember, Cheyenne cocked her head.

"You sure this is a good idea?"

"Nope. But if it doesn't want anything from me, what's the worst that could happen?"

The Sorren Gán released another puff of thick, acrid black smoke. The temperature around them rose by at least ten degrees, and shimmering light grew within the black cloud that hovered like a veil between the halfling and the fiery creature who feasted on magic and her father's race.

"Your work is yet unfinished, daughter of L'zar." The Sorren Gán's voice radiated around the fellfire pits. Lights rippled in the cloud with every syllable as if this woven magic here were speaking instead of the creature rendered immobile by its own gluttony. "Ambar'ogúl still burns beneath the Spider's filth. The streams run as black as the heart, and the blade unwielded grows dull."

Oh, great. Another fucking prophecy.

"Find the vessel. For what must come next, the vessel is of you but not you, one piece of the whole and still fragmented. Separate. When you mend that fragment, little drow, the sword that cut out the heart will gleam anew, tempered by the flames I have given you."

The shimmering cloud of black smoke disappeared, leaving a foul stench behind and the still-warming temperatures around the Sorren Gán's feasting grounds.

"What the hell was that?" Ember muttered out of the corner of her mouth.

Cheyenne shook her head.

The Sorren Gán grunted and fell back into its fiery crater. Puffs of liquid flame spouted around it and rained down on the empty earth beyond the pits. "That is all, little drow."

"It's Cheyenne."

The creature rumbled out a dark, echoing chuckle. "I know. Now leave my sight before my appetite returns."

"What's the vessel?"

The Sorren Gán gave no reply as it closed its flaming eyes.

"Come on." Ember grabbed the halfling's arm and pulled her back toward the tunnel. "I don't think it was joking about the appetite thing."

Another erupting column of fellfire from a pit directly in front of them cut off Cheyenne's line of sight to the Sorren Gán, and she turned around with a scowl. "I'm sick of everybody giving me vague-ass riddles and calling them gifts. How the hell is any of that supposed to help?"

"No clue, but hey, the other prophecies kinda worked out, right?

"Yeah, but they only made sense after the fact." They stepped back onto the walkway lining Hangivol's outer wall. "If that's the way prophecies are supposed to work, I'm good not hearing any of it. It only pisses me off."

Ember smirked. "You're handling it really well for being pissed off."

"I'm learning."

Cheyenne stopped at a different section of the wall and slid her finger down the column of activating code in the wall to open the door again. When the square segments peeled away to reveal another short entrance tunnel, Ember sighed. "You can do that anywhere, can't you?"

"Everywhere with a command written in the wall to make an opening, yeah." They walked through the tunnel back into the city, and Cheyenne rolled her eyes. "L'zar could do it without an activator."

"He sees all the magic, though. That's totally different. And for real, can you picture him using any of this tech?"

That made the halfling chuckle. "He'd break it before he could figure out how to use it."

"Exactly. You've always had that to dangle over his head."

"Not something I'm trying to keep going, though, Em. I'm over L'zar. He's done everything useful he can possibly do, and he can't even come back to this side. The drow thief is finally obsolete."

"But not the drow halfling."

"Sometimes I wish I were."

Ember shook her head. "No, you don't."

"Kinda. Once we get the blight back under control over here, I don't know if I'll even have a reason to come back."

"Oh, come on. Not even to visit all your new friends? And what about the parties?"

Cheyenne shot her friend a playful frown. "What *about* the parties?"

"Nothing Earthside even comes close to an O'gúl rager."

"Ha. So that's your favorite part."

The fae girl shrugged. "Hey, now that I'm not watching from the sidelines in a wheelchair anymore, yeah. I think that's my favorite part."

They both laughed and passed through an alley between high metal buildings that was dark beneath the now-black sky. "After we clean up the shitstorm Ba'rael left behind, Em, sure, we can come back for the O'gúl ragers."

"Nice."

As soon as they emerged from the alley into the artificial light cast by glowing lamps jutting from the metal walls, a swarm of floating silver orbs swooped toward them. Blue and yellow lights flashed as the orbs' multiple segments spun.

Ember peered up at the floating pieces of tech and frowned. "Somebody's trying to get a better look at the ex-Crown."

"Well, somebody's gonna be disappointed." Cheyenne raised her hand toward the closest bobbing orb and struck it with a telekinetic wave. The orb hurtled backward, and with the activator's help, she disassembled some high-society magical's spy drone into a hundred glistening pieces. Then she scattered them across the street.

The other orbs whirred and spun madly, lights flashing as if the tech machines were as surprised as whoever controlled them from their high towers in Upper Tech.

Ember snorted and folded her arms. "Yeah. Really disappointed."

Cheyenne glared at the other orbs, targeting each of them with her activator and locking on. *Nah. Better to send a message than say nothing, right?*

"Okay, I might be co-ruling with Persh'al Tenishi, or whatever we wanna call it," she said, making sure it came out loud enough for the orbs to pick up, "but I'm not a circus act. Mind your own business. Got it?"

One of the orbs slowly dipped away from the others and toward her.

Cheyenne summoned a crackling sphere of black energy in one hand and let it flare a little larger than normal. "Get lost."

The orbs whirred and bobbed away down the street, their owners clearly having picked up on the message.

"You think someone's gonna charge you for the damage?" Ember asked.

"They can try." Cheyenne laughed in surprise and spread her arms. "I might be the poorest magical in Hangivol, though."

"And one of the richest trust-fund babies in Virginia. What a way to keep the drow co-Crown humble, right?"

Both girls burst out laughing and headed through the lower-level streets toward the unceasing roar of the celebrating O'gúleesh echoing toward them from the fighting pits. They stopped when a larger and darker metal sphere rounded the corner of the next building up ahead. The thing clicked and whirred slowly, with far fewer flashing lights than the others.

"Seriously, with everything running through this giant system, it shouldn't be that hard to get the damn point across."

Ember pointed at it. "That one looks old."

"Older generation." Cheyenne studied the simplified code swirling around the orb and summoned another black energy sphere. "Easier to take out, I'm guessing."

The floating dark orb clicked twice. "A message for the Black Flame."

The voice was tinny and spoke through a thin buzz of static.

Cheyenne snuffed out her attack. "Right."

Grinning, Ember cocked her head at the orb and nudged her friend's arm. "I still can't get over how cool that name is."

"I mean, it's better than 'princess.'" Cheyenne folded her arms and nodded at the messenger orb. "Go ahead, then. What's the message?"

"Your new quarters are waiting for you in the inner ring. Do you wish to see them?"

"New quarters?" Ember turned slowly to look at her friend and raised her eyebrows. "Fancy."

"In the drow level, too." Cheyenne waved at the messenger orb. "Sure. We'll check 'em out."

"Follow." Two green lights flashed on the orb's middle segment, then it took off past them and floated down the narrow side street.

"Look at that. Personal tech escort to your new quarters in Hangivol." Ember laughed. "You're gonna get real comfy here, aren't you?"

"We can hang out for a few days, at least." They turned the corner after the orb, which led them around a knot of magicals dancing and drinking and punching each other in the face when the side street widened into one of the lower level's main avenues. "Jeeze. Might as well be a mosh pit out here."

"You ever been to a real one?" Ember asked, staring at an orc woman and an ogre man, thin by ogre standards, crashing their tankards into each other's shoulders and laughing at the foam spilling all over both of them.

"Really?"

"Yeah, I don't know. Seems like your kinda scene."

"Oh, sure. A bunch of people jumping around in a packed venue, shoving me from behind and elbowing me in the face. The whole world would know I was there after that."

Ember snorted. "Hey, you've gotten a lot better at keeping your drow explosions under control."

"And when the hell have I had the time to go to a concert since I learned how to do that?"

"Well, here's your chance."

"I wanna check out my quarters first. Hey, watch it!" Cheyenne stepped out of the way and raised a shimmering black shield beside her when an empty bottle of dark green glass sailed end over end toward them. It thunked into her shield and shattered when it hit the ground, followed by an explosion of laughter.

"No one touches the Black Flame of Hangivol!"

"Throw it back, drow!"

"She's gonna rip off your head, Moxley."

Cheyenne kept walking after the orb. "You know what? If my new apartment or whatever fits our standards, I'm good to hang out there for a while. If not, I might come back here and join the party."

"You mean, join the street brawl and rip off a few heads?"

"That's a healthy emotional outlet over here, Em."

"To the new Crown!" A goblin man stumbled toward them, sloshing his drink as he spread his arms and reached toward Ember to pull her into the party.

She zapped the tankard out of his dripping purple hand and sent it skittering across the ground beneath the stomping feet in the crowd, and he hobbled off after it with a snarl.

"Yeah, I'm down for a night in too."

CHAPTER TEN

The orb led them by the quickest route through Upper Tech, which gave Cheyenne and Ember only a moment to look at the raging party in the posh upper level's glittering silver streets. A group of ridiculously dressed skaxen stared at them before the messenger orb opened a new tunnel and disappeared through it.

"High-society skaxen in bird costumes." Ember waved enthusiastically at them before darting through the newly opened tunnel, which took them up a flight of stairs. "You can't make this stuff up here, can you?"

"Upper Tech's weird." The tunnel door closed behind them, and up ahead, the messenger orb activated lines of soft white light along either side of the ceiling. "Feathers might be a step up from a sequined cape."

"On a skaxen?"

"Yeah. And glitter."

"Ew."

When they reached the uppermost level of Hangivol surrounding the Crown's fortress, the echoing celebrations on every other level of the city had died to a low murmur far below.

"Wow." Ember looked around with raised eyebrows, nodding at the drow in the streets, who stood in small groups and talked in low voices. "This is how drow party, huh? All calm and regal."

Cheyenne pointed at a group of drow tossing shimmering metal disks in the air and seeing how many blurred, speedy punches they could get in on their opponents before catching the disks again. "Not sure I'd call that regal."

Blood sprayed from a drow woman's mouth when her opponent clocked her in the jaw. With a low chuckle, she grinned and burst into enhanced speed. The next second, she was behind the drow man who'd punched her, with an arm around his neck and one of the metal disks held to his throat. The disk clicked and pushed out four serrated blade tips that pressed against his flesh. The drow man laughed and raised his arms, and the others gathered around them laughed.

Ember shrugged. "I mean, royalty were all drow before this, so yeah. Kinda regal."

"It's fucking each other up for fun, Em." Cheyenne caught the glowing silver gazes of three drow women holding small silver cups of fellwine that illuminated their faces in an eerie green glow as they stood in the doorway of a squat metal building. They raised their glasses, and she gave them a half-nod of acknowledgment. "I mean, I get that this is how things work over here, but I'm not that into it."

"For real? You, the Goth drow who's always been into this kinda dark shit?"

"Okay, can you picture us bashing each other's brains in for fun?"

"We'd have some ice cream afterward and call it good." They laughed, and Ember shook her head. "No. I'll slap you in the face when you need a good reminder of how stupid you get when you're pissed, but that's about it. Don't get me wrong, though—I enjoy it. A little."

"I probably would too if I were you, but I'm not gonna hit you for fun."

"You're scared of the fae magic."

"Uh-huh."

The orb stopped at an immensely tall metal building visible from the outer rooms of the Crown's fortress and flashed another green light. "Twelfth floor."

"Oh, good. We get to take it from here."

With another grating click that sounded like old mechanisms sticking on each other, the messenger orb opened a panel on its underbelly and tossed a black metal square at the halfling. She caught it and glanced at the O'gúl rune etched on one side. Her activator translated it into a room number, 1242.

"Coded for your convenience. If the Black Flame desires additional features, she will find the design panel inside the door." The thing took off for the walls of the fortress and disappeared through an open window. A thin metal panel slid into place behind it with a bang.

"I seriously wish they'd use my name already."

"I mean, that *is* your name now, right?"

"Not really." Cheyenne grabbed the gleaming door handle and opened the door for Ember to float inside. "But if it gets me my own quarters outside the fortress, I guess I can deal with it."

The hallway inside was lit by soft yellow lights along walls that led back to a round black metal platform on the opposite side. Cheyenne's activator lit the access pathways when they mounted the platform, and she swiped her hand and the black room chip across the wall.

"Whoa." Ember spun when the black dais lifted them off the bottom floor and through a circular tube climbing up the back of the building. Lines of soft light flashed up and down as they passed the lower stories and headed to the twelfth floor. "They have elevators here."

Cheyenne shoved her hands in her pockets and looked up. "They have everything here, only better."

The platform stopped, and they stepped off into a wide hallway lit by the same soft lights set in the walls on either side.

"Okay, now this is kinda creepy." Ember floated slowly forward, scrutinizing every aspect of the hallway. "Drow apartment buildings taking Victorian décor straight from Earth."

"Kinda makes you wonder which one came first, right?"

"Well there's no way a human made the crossing over here, saw the style, and figured, 'Hey, I'm gonna take this back to Earth and make it a thing.'"

"Yeah, but a magical could have."

"Huh." Ember wrinkled her nose. "The portals go back that far, don't they? Makes my head hurt thinking about it."

Cheyenne snorted. "Then stop thinking about it."

She stopped in front of the black door with the same rune as on the black metal square. The door was covered in intricately etched designs that hinted at tree shapes and vines. *Too many trees. Like all the dead Nimlothar. I gotta stop thinking about that too.*

"Oh, hey. I see how to get in." Ember reached toward the door and slid her finger along the flashing yellow square Cheyenne saw through her activator. The door clicked and let off a flash of orange light. Ember hissed and jerked her hand back, shaking it out. "Okay, ow."

"Maybe you're not the right drow, huh?" Cheyenne swiped her finger across the same yellow square, and the door clicked again and slid into the wall with a soft hiss.

Ember scowled at the door. "Would've been nice to have a little warning for that."

"Keeps curious magicals from breaking into the drow zone."

"Whatever."

The room beyond illuminated automatically as soon as they stepped inside, and the door slid back into place silently.

"Hey." Cheyenne nodded, her smile growing. "So far, so good."

"They went Victorian in the hall and Minimalist in the rooms, huh?" Ember looked around with an approving nod. "Okay."

"You're really into this whole design thing, huh?"

"Are you forgetting who furnished our entire apartment?"

"Nope, and my fae designer did an excellent job if you ask me." Cheyenne turned around with a conceding shrug. "I like our place better, Em, but this isn't half bad."

"Can't argue with that. It's huge."

Their O'gúl apartment lacked windows and natural lighting, though Cheyenne figured she could create a window by giving the walls a few commands. *Not sure I wanna look outside and see this crazy city anyway, but it's an option.*

The gray walls were bare, and the only furniture was in the middle of the room—a black couch that looked like spray-painted cardboard boxes and two matching black chairs. No tables, no decoration, no sign that this was an apartment, not a waiting room.

"Okay, wait." Ember turned slowly, eyeing the bare walls. "Where's the kitchen?"

"You're assuming O'gúl houses have kitchens, Em."

"With all this technology, they can't make a place to cook their own meals?"

Cheyenne studied the lines of code scrolling through the walls; there weren't nearly as many here as in the exterior makeup of the building and the public areas in the city. *Because everyone wants to control their space.* "Over there."

"What?" Ember spun to stare at where the halfling pointed.

"Go check it out."

The fae girl floated toward the left front corner of the apartment's main room and stared at the walls. "No way. I feel like we're in a sci-fi movie."

"You asked about kitchens." Cheyenne joined her, studied the activation lines. "Pretty much anything we want, right? I mean, by O'gúleesh standards, at least."

Ember's hand flashed purple when she ran her fingers across the blank walls. Blue lines zigzagged across the metal away from her touch, and she frowned. "It's not working."

"Are you getting command prompts?"

"Jesus Christ, are you shitting me?" Ember backed away from the wall. "No, I don't get command prompts. I see options and what I want to do. You're telling me you get a full-on instruction manual?"

Cheyenne reached toward the scrolling code flashing yellow in her vision. "More like a choose-your-own adventure, honestly."

"Well, you can choose your own ass-kicking." The fae girl folded her arms. "I can't believe this. Elarit just handed over that top-line activator, no questions asked, huh?"

"Okay, so maybe not everything's the activator." Cheyenne selected the options for two cups, and the system pulled up the available drink selection. "I guess the prompts are me."

"Damn. No wonder everybody's been gushing about your tech knowledge."

"I guess."

"Kinda makes a lot more sense when you think about L'zar wigging out all the time if he sees the magical version of command prompts floating around him everywhere he goes."

"I'm done talking about L'zar, okay?" Cheyenne slid her finger across the wall, twisted her hand to the right, and stepped aside.

With a loud hiss, the seamless metal wall, which looked like concrete, opened two panels, and a heavy drawer shot toward them.

Ember yelped and darted to the side, then peered curiously into it. She looked at Cheyenne and narrowed her violet fae eyes. "You did that on purpose, didn't you?"

"Opened the minibar? Yeah, I thought that's what you wanted."

"I mean, open it and try to hit me."

Cheyenne forced back a laugh. "I can't tell if you're serious right now."

"I don't know what I am." Scoffing, Ember reached into the metal drawer and snatched the copper cup and the bottle of Bloodshine. "Fucking command prompts."

"I didn't think it would get to you like this."

"Neither did I!" Ember sped across the room with another flash of purple light and dropped onto the boxy couch. "Get the hell over here and drink this with me before I down the whole thing myself."

"Yep. Just a sec." Cheyenne scanned the rows of options on the pseudo-kitchen's system. "I'm guessing you're hungry."

"Only because I'd rather not wake up tomorrow in as much pain as you woke up today." The cork popped out of the Bloodshine bottle and bounced across the room. Ember said as she poured herself a tall glass of the bubbling gold booze, "Okay. Yeah, food sounds good. Sorry, I'm being a dick."

Cheyenne finished choosing the closest thing to recognizable food, set the command to prepare their meal, and grabbed the second copper cup. The now-empty drawer clanged back into place, and the seams between the panels disappeared again. "Totally okay. Kinda hard to compete with me in that arena, so I won't hold it against you."

"Very funny." Ember lifted the bottle and looked around the room. "I seriously hope nobody lived here before you. Where the hell did they put things?"

"Uh, do you want me to show you how to do it?"

The fae girl's only reply was to chug down half her cup.

And I thought I *was the one feeling out of place here.* Cheyenne took the closest black boxy-looking armchair and leaned down to reach for the line of code she wanted that was scrolling across the metal floor. *Or I could try it with magic instead.*

She sat back in the chair and flicked her finger at the floor beside the couch. Her activator lit up the spell prompt, and a yellow dart of light struck the place she would have touched. The segmented pieces of metal unfolded and built upon themselves until a sleek, round black table formed beside the couch.

By the time Ember lowered her copper cup from her lips, the new furnishing was firmly in place. The bottle of Bloodshine in her hand clinked against the edge of the table, and she jumped in surprise and stared at it. "Did you make that?"

"Yep."

"From where you're sitting?"

"Mmhmm."

Ember leaned forward without looking away from the table to hand the bottle to her friend. "My brain is melting."

"Takes some getting used to, I guess." Cheyenne took the bottle and filled her cup before standing to set it down on the table.

"You're loving this, aren't you?"

"You know what? I love that I can tell this place to make me furniture." The halfling sat again and lifted the copper cup to her lips. "Not so sure I love grumpy Ember."

They stared at each other for a moment, then the fae girl sighed. "Sorry. Again. I think reality might finally be setting in."

Cheyenne took a small sip of the fizzy alcohol, and this time, she enjoyed the cool tingle of boozy energy racing up through her nose and into her head. "Well, if you wanna talk about it, I'm all ears."

Ember's violet eyes flicked toward her friend's pointed purple-gray ears, and they both laughed. "You're taking that a lot more in stride these days than you used to."

"Guess I'm finally growing into 'em."

"I like it." With another quick scowl at the table, Ember refilled her cup and held it in both hands on her lap.

"For real, though, Em. Something on your mind?"

"Too much, maybe. And I'm guessing this is how you feel a lot more than I do, so I'm getting a whole different perspective on what I used to think were your attitude problems."

Cheyenne snorted.

"So here's my deal. It was cool to get to watch Venga working his death-magic whatever to make that serum for you. Working with a version of the blight, I guess. And I'm willing to put aside the fact that he made the blight, 'cause he obviously has a weird set of skills with healing, or at least cleaning up after something he created."

"But you don't like him."

"I don't like anyone who worked with that much enthusiasm for Ba'rael."

Cheyenne cocked her head. "That include Maleshi?"

"What? No. Okay, maybe I just don't like the scaleback necromancer. Fair enough."

"Do you think he'll be able to figure out how to clean this place up?"

Ember shook her head. "I don't know. He wouldn't talk about it, so I figured we were focusing on taking care of you while you were out. How are they, by the way?"

"The magical dart holes?" Cheyenne picked her shirt away from her shoulder to study the still-fading black lines of drow-tailored blight stretching away from the wounds. "They look a little better. Might have to give them an extra boost again before the night's up."

"Go ahead. I was told there's pretty much no way you could take too much, and I don't think any of us wanna see you and your dart holes get any worse right now."

"Yeah, maybe later." Cheyenne sat back in the armchair and shifted around. "Just gonna put it out there; our furniture at home is way comfier than this."

"Right?" Ember elbowed the back of the couch. "Maybe it's an O'gúleesh thing, huh? Get too comfortable, and you lose the urge to fuck shit up and get in fights."

They laughed and raised their copper cups toward each other in a wordless toast.

"Anything else on your mind?"

"Just everything else." Ember shrugged and drank again. "No big deal."

"Well, if it helps, I'm not even a little worried about taking care of Colonel Thomas and the rest of the Bull's Head scumbags when we go back Earthside." Cheyenne took a deep breath. "It'll be like the first time I crashed a FRoE sting, only this time I know what I'm getting into."

"You want me there for that?"

"Only if you wanna be."

Ember wrinkled her nose. "I'll think about it."

"Sure. We still have a few days." Leaning back fully in the armchair, Cheyenne dangled her copper cup over the armrest and stared at the ceiling. *The recliners are way better too.* "I definitely want you there when I go check on my mom, though. If you don't have anything better to do."

"I'm your *Nós Aní*, right? Bound to serve and all that crap." Ember almost snorted bubbly Bloodshine all over herself with her next sip. "Of course I'll be there."

"Thanks. 'Cause once I'm done taking care of the loyalists and cutting Colonel Thomas out of the FRoE, I need to focus on getting her out from under that curse. Which I don't even understand."

"You seem to be doing an awful lot of figurative cutting these days."

"Yeah, yeah. The heart. The rot. The curse. Oh, hey. You think a necromancer knows anything about curses?"

Ember blinked at the floor and cocked her head. "First time I've ever known anything about a necromancer, and I'm not about to assume anything. Venga's like a mad scientist with a conscience. Maybe."

"I wanna go talk to him tomorrow. See what he's figured out so far about healing the blight."

"Sure." A sudden grin flashed across the fae girl's face, and her eyes widened. "Hey, something I can do that you can't."

"Oh, yeah?"

Ember pointed at the activator behind her ear. "I did put his room on a map in this thing. That has to be the only way magicals don't get lost in the fortress. That place is a freakin' maze."

"Well, then there you go." Cheyenne raised her cup toward her friend one more time. "Something you know that I don't, Em. I totally need you to be my guide."

"Good thing you kept me around, huh?" Ember drank again, and that seemed to ease the rest of her short-lived frustration.

I don't need to tell her I could find Venga in the system anyway. Or pull that map right out of her activator if I wanted.

A low buzz and a flash of blue light came from the corner behind them, and Ember asked, "Are we calling that the kitchen?"

"I guess."

Another pulse of light raced across the wall, streaking down the metal toward their side of the room. "What's that supposed to be?"

"The O'gúl version of a microwave timer." Cheyenne quickly stood and went to the kitchen wall as a shorter, wider drawer opened to present two metal plates covered in steaming food with a name she couldn't even pretend to know how to pronounce. *Smells kinda like pizza, if you ignore the pit-sweat undertones.*

"Oh, my God." Ember stared at their plates of food and took another long drink. "We have our own replicator."

"Huh?"

"It's a *Star Trek* thing. Never mind."

CHAPTER ELEVEN

One O'gúleesh meal and three-quarters of a bottle of Bloodshine later, Ember floated up off the couch and gingerly set down her cup. "I need to sleep."

Cheyenne chuckled. "Hey, don't stay up to make me feel better."

"Didn't even cross my mind." With a crooked smile, Ember looked at the one other door on the right side of the room, then turned to study the door on the left. "Which room's mine?"

"Beats me. You choose."

The fae girl blinked heavily and belched. Gold sparks fizzled out of her mouth before disappearing again, and she swallowed. "Closer. I feel a lot better, by the way. That's good stuff."

"Glad you're here, Em. Goodnight."

"Good-fucking-night, halfling." Ember floated in a not-so-straight path toward the door on Cheyenne's left. "Tomorrow, we'll tackle the necromange…necaroms…shit. You know what I mean."

She slapped her hand on the door, which opened beneath her touch and closed quickly again behind her.

Cheyenne stared at the door with the ghost of a smile. *Lucky smack, I guess.* She waited for a moment longer, listening to the soft creak of whatever bed was in her friend's room. When the apartment fell silent again but for Ember's snores sneaking through the door, the halfling set her empty cup on the side table and headed for the other room. *There better be a bed in this one too. No way am I sleeping in one of those chairs.*

She tested the activator's ability to sync with her magic again when it prompted her with a command to wave the door aside, grinning when it worked. *My spellwork might be shit, but I've got this activator thing nailed down on both sides of the Border.*

It was definitely another bedroom, though the only piece of furniture in it was a bed built on a platform jutting from the opposite wall. Sitting on the edge of it was her backpack. Cheyenne cocked her head with a chuckle, then climbed the two metal steps like stacked boxes and sat on the mattress. *Okay, softer than the couch.*

She kicked off her black Vans and let them drop to the floor before lying back and staring at the ceiling. Even when she dimmed the illuminated streams of code endlessly moving over every metal surface, closed her eyes, and focused on breathing, her body fought with her to keep moving.

Finally, she sat up again. "I already got twelve hours of sleep today. Not passing out anytime soon."

She hopped off the bed and walked in a slow, curious circle, pulling the system up in her vision again to take a look at her options. "So, if I'm working with synced magic now, guess this is the time to practice." *And here's hoping I don't blow anything up again.*

Rubbing her hands together, she stepped toward the left-hand wall and chose the path she wanted based on what the activator gave her. *Sure. A window. Why not?*

Her fingers reached toward the wall; she didn't even realize her hands were moving with some memory she didn't have until she was halfway through casting the spell. Then her gaze dropped to her gesturing fingers, and she stifled a surprised laugh. "Holy shit."

The wall responded the way she wanted it to, panel after segmented panel folding back and disappearing within the rest of the metal until a perfect square had opened for her.

If this wasn't so cool, I'd be freaking out about my hands being possessed.

Cheyenne dropped her hands to her sides again and stepped toward the newly created window to peer at the city below. Floating lights bobbed slowly back and forth across the streets of the inner circle inhabited only by drow, and one fae *Nós Aní*, illuminating the dark figures who all looked like L'zar's halfling daughter. Beyond that, the lower levels glinted with lights of their own and flashing magical bursts. The buzz of celebration still raging through Hangivol's streets and alleyways came through the window in a muted blur.

Should be louder.

She reached toward the window, and when her finger should have gone straight through into open air, it met a slight resistance. The paneless window flashed blue light that spread across the open square, then her hand was through. She turned it back and forth in the cool night air. "Interesting."

Then she poked her head through and leaned over the edge of the window. *Bet I can do more than this, though.*

Craning her neck, she studied the front of her new O'gúleesh apartment building. As soon as she decided what was possible, her activator lit a series of pathways to do what she wanted. "Oh, yeah."

With one hand steadying her against the inside wall, Cheyenne leaned around the side of the window, pressed her hand against the outer wall, and flicked her fingers in the offered pattern up the side of the building. The system code scrolling across the walls flashed in succession, climbing toward the roof. The segmented panels did what she wanted, letting out a series of clicks and whirs and sending a small vibration along the entire wall until…

Cheyenne grinned. "I built myself a staircase. Hell, yes."

It took a little more effort than she expected to pull her body through the energetic film covering the window instead of glass, but then she was standing on the ledge jutting from the building's outer wall. A light wind twisted her white hair in front of her face, and she brushed it away before taking the first high step onto the next platform.

She must have climbed at least ten stories up the thick metal ledges before stepping lightly onto the rooftop. Her trenchcoat flapped around her calves in the breeze as she turned to study Hangivol below her. *I've seen enough of Ember's favorite movies to know this is as close to superhero-y as I'll probably ever get.*

She took a moment to view the bobbing lights of the capital's lower levels, catching the scent of whatever the citizens were cooking as the partying carried on as fervently as it had started. Then a prickling tingle of energy raced up the back of her neck and spread across her shoulders. *Haven't felt that in a minute.*

The whisper of a soft footstep behind her caught her attention, and she whirled with a black energy sphere bursting to life in her hand.

"What do you think you're doing?" She froze and cocked her head, frowning at the drow child standing in the center of the rooftop and staring at her. The kid's eyes flickered toward her crackling black and purple magic, but she didn't move. "Oh."

Cheyenne snuffed out the spell and rubbed her hands down the sides of her coat before shoving them in her pockets.

"What are *you* doing?" The girl asked more out of curiosity than fear.

Not even a little fear. Of course not.

"You mean, up here on the roof? I could ask you the same question."

The kid jerked her chin at the halfling, her white hair drawn back in a loose bun the way Cheyenne had first seen L'zar wearing it. "You first."

Cheyenne snorted. "Kinda obvious, isn't it? I'm up here watching the city."

"Not a lot to watch. Just a bunch of O'gúleesh drinking and fighting."

"Sound like you're pretty used to that, huh?"

The girl shrugged and looked the halfling up and down. "Nice coat."

"Yeah, thanks." With a chuckle, Cheyenne turned toward the edge of the roof and sat, letting her legs dangle over the side. "I still think it's a good view."

The girl didn't try to sneak up on the older drow again as she headed toward Cheyenne. The next second, she was sitting beside the halfling, her much shorter legs dangling over the edge the same way. When she leaned forward to look down at the platforms the halfling had cast out of the wall, Cheyenne almost reached out to keep the girl from falling over. The drow kid straightened again and looked up to study her face. "Did you do that?"

"Yeah. Pretty cool, right?"

"I guess." The girl looked at the star-studded sky and gripped the edge of the roof with both hands like they were sitting on a bench.

Cheyenne thought, *First drow kid I've seen other than me, and she gives just as many fucks as I did.* "How'd you get up here?"

The kid shrugged again. "There's a ladder sequence at the back of the building. I use it all the time."

"You come up here all the time?"

"Yeah. How else would I know the city hasn't changed?"

Cheyenne barked a laugh and nodded. "Fair enough. What's your name?"

"Ki'zi."

"Nice to meet you, Ki'zi. I'm Cheyenne." She reached out, and the girl glanced at her hand briefly before turning back to look out over the glistening city.

Jeeze. Talk about a dose of my own medicine. Fighting back another laugh, Cheyenne stuck her hands in her lap and stared in silence with this much smaller drow who could've been her ten years ago.

"You're the Black Flame, aren't you?"

"Well, I guess that works, seeing as most O'gúleesh don't bother to learn my name. But I told you, so you can call me Cheyenne."

Ki'zi hunched her shoulders. "My parents say you killed the Spider and turned the Cycle."

"Ha. Your parents must be catching a lotta rumors, kid. I didn't kill anyone."

"But you tried to."

"Yeah, I guess."

"If the Spider didn't meet the final deathflame, where is she? Did you chain her up? Throw her to the bloodletters? There's a Sorren Gán outside the city. Did you know that? I bet that's what happened. You fed her to that thing, huh? I wish I was there to see it."

"Whoa, okay. Hold on a minute." Cheyenne rubbed her mouth to keep another laugh at bay and turned to study the girl. "First of all, the Sorren Gán's not eating any drow anytime soon, so you don't have to worry about that part."

Ki'zi's glowing golden eyes bored into Cheyenne's. "I'm not worried."

"Of course not."

When the pause lasted longer than normal conversation warranted, the girl shook her head. "And second?"

"Huh?"

"You said first of all."

"Oh. What's a bloodletter?"

Ki'zi frowned up at her, then wrinkled her nose with a skeptical laugh and looked away again. "Nobody said anything about you being funny."

"Right." Cheyenne ran a hand through her hair. *Because of* course *an O'gúleesh drow would know what a bloodletter is, and nobody knows what I really am.* "I guess I have my moments like anyone else."

"Can you teach me?"

"How to be funny?"

Ki'zi rolled her eyes and pointed sharply at the platforms jutting from the side of the building below them. "How to do stuff like that."

"Hey, if you can figure out how to activate a ladder to get up here, you'll figure that out on your own. I can already tell you're smart."

The girl scoffed. "A ladder's easy. I wanna do something no one else can. Except for you, maybe."

"Gotcha." Nodding slowly, Cheyenne watched a small group of laughing drow cross the main avenue of the inner circle before disappearing inside a lit storefront. More laughter and shouts of welcome rose from the open door and faded again into the buzz of partying filling the air above Hangivol. "To tell you the truth, I'm still learning how to do this kinda thing too."

Ki'zi briefly shook her head. "You don't have to lie to me. I'm a hundred and twenty-four, okay? I can handle it."

Cheyenne almost choked and stared at the sharp, angular features of the girl's profile. "Yeah, that's old enough for the truth." *I had to wait more than long enough to get that from everyone else.*

"I know." Ki'zi raised an eyebrow. "So, will you teach me something or not?"

Words failed Cheyenne as she pursed her lips in an amused smile. "Why don't you show me what you got?"

"My magic?"

"Sure."

Ki'zi rubbed her hands on her loose dark trousers, then snapped her fingers. A pale silver light bloomed in her palm when she opened her hand, and she flicked her wrist and hurled the light down into the street. It crashed into the main avenue with a bang like exploding fireworks and sent a rippling jolt of energy across the ground toward the buildings on either side.

"*Tyey!*" A drow woman stuck her head out of the lit storefront and stared up and down the street.

Ki'zi burst out laughing, her high voice ringing out above the revelry, and the drow woman looked at the rooftop. The girl's laughter died abruptly, and she pointed at Cheyenne.

"Hey, wait a minute." The halfling laughed, then spread her arms and shouted at the drow below, "My bad."

When the drow woman recognized Hangivol's Black Flame, she raised an eyebrow and gave them both a dismissive wave before retreating into the shop again.

"Low blow, kid."

Ki'zi shrugged. "Nobody will punish you for practicing your magic."

The smile on Cheyenne's lips faded a little. "But they punish you, huh?"

Leaning back and propping herself up with both hands behind her, the girl looked at the starlit sky. "They say it's to keep me safe."

"Your parents."

"I'm a fast learner. Father told me if I kept at it the way I started, I'd spark up my *Cuil Aní* and have to face the trials early."

Drow trials. A hundred and twenty-four or ten, she's still just a kid. Cheyenne raised her eyebrows and had to look away so the girl wouldn't see her frown. "That's pretty early."

"No, it's not, but they told me not to keep practicing because the Spider would call me into the Heart and make me show her too."

"Beside the last Nimlothar. Yeah, I know."

"You've seen it, right? You had to. Everything happens in the Heart."

"I've seen it. Spoke to it, too."

Ki'zi shifted to face Cheyenne head-on and stared at her with wide eyes. "Did it answer?"

"Yep. I mean, not with actual words."

"Tell me what you saw." A slow smile crept across Ki'zi's face. "I want to know."

Cheyenne wrinkled her nose. "Just asked me for a favor, kid, and I promised to do my best. That's all." *I don't care how old she is. I'm not talking about visions of dead and dying trees and the black fire taking out the last one left.*

Ki'zi scowled and scooted away from her. "You're just like everyone else."

"Why, because I won't tell you about a conversation I had with the last drow tree in Ambar'ogúl? Come on, Ki'zi. Kind of a private thing, don't you think?"

"That's the problem. Everyone's private. Nobody wants to teach me or let me learn on my own or do anything more than launch energy at the street." The girl pushed to her feet and spun to storm off across the rooftop. "I thought you'd be different."

"Sorry to disappoint." Cheyenne stared across the other rooftops of the high buildings in the inner circle. *Shit, she's exactly like me. I thought all this was a product of being a halfling and having two seriously abnormal parents. Looks like a lot of it is a drow thing. Still.* "Okay, hold on."

When she turned around, Ki'zi was standing rigid in the center of the rooftop with her fists clenched at her sides. The breeze lifted loose locks of white hair away from her shoulders and trailed them sideways like streamers.

"I'll teach you something. Not anything huge, 'cause I have a feeling I'll get a visit from your parents if I do that, and I'm not trying to make those kinds of friends, okay?"

Slowly, the girl turned around again and studied the halfling with narrowed eyes. "I don't want to learn tricks. I want something real."

"Yeah, I bet you do." With a short laugh, Cheyenne pushed to her feet and joined the drow child who was technically five times her age in the center of the rooftop. "You have an activator, right?"

Ki'zi made an insulted face.

"Of course you do, and you used it to build a ladder. What am I thinking?" The halfling spread her arms, shrugging to adjust the shoulders of her trenchcoat, and wracked her brain for a good non-trick in drow magic to teach a kid. "All right. So, would you say you're better with spellcasting or syncing with the tech?"

The girl scrunched her face and snapped her fingers repeatedly, created a spray of silver sparks each time. "Tech. Definitely."

It's like they fucking cloned me. "Yeah, me too. Okay, a piece of advice, then. If you can tap into the activator far enough, it stops doing what you want for you and starts feeling more like your hand, right?"

"I can't take off my hand."

"No, I know." Cheyenne sighed. "You're giving me a real run for my money, aren't you?"

"Money?"

"Just something I picked up Earthside. Doesn't matter. Look." Cheyenne stepped back and scanned the code moving across the rooftop between them. *Don't make it cheesy, Cheyenne. Make your point.* "You ever do any meditating?"

Ki'zi's golden eyes widened, and she lifted her chin. "All the time."

"Really?" Cheyenne grinned. "I didn't expect that answer. You've got a leg up on me, and that's very cool. It's like meditating or tapping into your drow powers, yeah? I can't imagine a kid like you wouldn't have the latest tech."

"Finished building this one before you showed up and put your *marandúr* on the altar."

The halfling shook her head with a low chuckle. "Totally not surprising. If you can tap into that, the thing starts working like your own mind. Like a part of you that yes, you can take off if you have to, which is kinda the beauty of it. It does whatever you want when you want it, just like your hands or your feet."

Reaching toward the rooftop between them with both hands, Cheyenne flicked her fingers toward herself. The activator illuminated the threaded segments of nonessential metal making up the rooftop, and she selected as many of them as she thought she'd need. Various panels spread out to make up for the tiny square holes left by the pieces she pulled from the roof and lifted into the air between her and Ki'zi. The girl grinned, captured by the floating metal chips glinting in the starlight.

First time in my life, I feel like I'm putting on a magic show. It's for a good cause.

Cheyenne selected command after command, prompted by the activator with no lag between what she wanted to do and what it offered her. The tiny metal chips morphed and bent into shape as she pulled them together, her fingers twisting and curving in the casting of a spell she couldn't name and didn't have to. The last piece settled into place with a faint pulse of violet light, and a four-pointed star the size of a golf ball spun slowly in the air between them. The seams between the metal chips sealed themselves, and Cheyenne nodded. "Go ahead."

Ki'zi gently plucked the metal piece in the shape of Cheyenne's magical signature, the same as L'zar's and Neros' and probably Ba'rael's too out of the air. "This is you."

"Yeah. In a way, I guess it is."

The girl turned the trinket over in her hands, frowning as she tried to figure out the mechanics of making something like that despite the tiny, amused smile playing on her lips. "How did you do this?"

"Like I said, kid. Don't separate yourself from what you can do. That includes the activator, right? It can be a part of you. Then you do it."

"Right." Ki'zi slipped the four-pointed star into her pocket. "I'll do it."

"Good." Cheyenne pulled the apartment chip the messenger orb had spewed at her from her pocket and turned the rune side so the girl could see. "This is me too. When you make your own version of what you stuck in your pocket, and I have no doubt you will, come find me."

Ki'zi nodded at the chip, then spun and darted across the rooftop toward the back of the building. She skidded to a stop at the edge and whirled again. "Cheyenne!"

"Ki'zi."

"Thank you."

"No problem. Thanks for the company."

Ki'zi snorted and slipped over the side of the rooftop. Her hands and feet clanged on the metal rungs, the sound steadily fading as she climbed down toward whatever level of their shared building she lived on.

Cheyenne chuckled. "Now I know how everyone felt, meeting me. That was weird."

She gave herself another minute to look out over Hangivol and the O'gúl parties still raging on every level of the city. The multicolored flames of the Sorren Gán's newest camp-out flickered beyond the northern edge of the capital's outer wall. *There's no way I'll make the crossing Earthside and stay there, even if we didn't have a blight to heal and a necromancer to whip into shape. If I'm gonna play drow royalty on Earth, it's gotta be for everyone, not just the O'gúleesh over there.*

With a deep breath, she stepped off the edge of the rooftop and made the climb back down her conjured steps to the open window in her new bedroom in Ambar'ogúl. *A drow kid can't practice her magic in her own home out of fear. Yeah, sounds familiar. That has to change too.*

CHAPTER TWELVE

Cheyenne's hip was back at half-agony by the time she sealed the window in her room and climbed into bed. She took the injection canister out of her pocket before shrugging out of the trenchcoat and dropping it on the floor, then she pulled down the waistline of her black pants and grimaced at the raw red hole in her hip and the faint black lines still trailing away from it.

Better if I jam this thing right into the source, huh? Damnit, Em. You're too good of a healer for me not to take your word for it.

She put the bottom hem of her shirt into her mouth to keep it out of the way and pulled the top of her pants down a little farther. Then she sucked it up and pushed the canister against the dart wound in her hip.

Maybe she screamed, but it was muffled by the wad of shirt in her mouth. Cheyenne jerked away from the pain and found herself on her back as the canister toppled from her hand to the floor. Sucking raw breaths through the shirt in her teeth and her flaring nostrils, she stared at the black spots dancing in her vision until the darktongue serum did its job.

Her mouth went dry despite the pain seeping out of her, along with her immediate ability to think straight. She tried to spit out her shirt, but it clung to her lips, and she had to try three times with a heavy, floating hand before she could get it all out. Blinking heavily, Cheyenne let her hand drop to the bed and let out a dazed chuckle. "Eh, okay. I've had worse."

She drifted off to sleep with a crooked smile as the black lines around her wounds slowly faded.

That night, she had another dream. Cheyenne would have called it a nightmare if she'd had the awareness to know it for what it was.

The first thing she saw was Ba'rael Verdys' face frozen in a silent scream within a veil of dark, shimmering light. The dethroned O'gúl Crown hung suspended in mid-air, her arms outstretched in the same position in which she'd left Hangivol and the Heart's center courtyard at the hands of her own son. Despite the fact that she didn't move—couldn't move—and made no sound, her golden eyes pulsed with an inner light.

Cheyenne stared at her aunt and felt the warm shiver that only came in dreams race up her spine. *She can see me. Whatever this is, she knows I'm here.*

"Cheyenne."

She didn't have to turn or look for whoever had called her name. One second she was alone with Ba'rael, and the next, she stood face to face with Neros. Her cousin's abnormally pale skin stood out in contrast to the veil of dark light encompassing his mother. His washed-out golden eyes widened as he stepped toward her.

Cheyenne wanted to step away but couldn't move. *Personal space, Neros. It's a real thing.*

"You are not finished yet, cousin." Neros' white hair whipped around his head, and from somewhere far away in this dreamscape, a cold wind howled toward them. "Do not let what is required of you fall away beneath what you have already accomplished. I did what I could to clear the path, and now you must walk it."

Ba'rael's eyes flashed even brighter, and Cheyenne thought she heard someone screaming from very far away.

What the hell else am I supposed to do?

Neros replied to her thoughts as if he could hear them, though she couldn't tell if she was speaking out loud. "The vessel still waits to be filled, Cheyenne. To sharpen the blade and burn away the remnants of the blackness and the rot. Find the vessel, restore it, and you restore Ambar'ogúl and the world I see in you through the Weave."

Where are you? What happened?

"Do not stop, cousin. Your purpose is not fulfilled!"

The faraway screaming, one continuous, shrieking wail, grew louder. Ba'rael's frozen eyes flared with brilliant golden light and drowned out everything else, filling Cheyenne with a searing flare of her own magic erupting inside her.

Cheyenne jolted awake with a shout and flopped around on the bed, kicking and punching the thin coverlet she'd twisted around herself in sleep. "Goddammit, these fucking dreams!"

When she finally had the blankets off, she rolled onto her back, breathing heavily, and wiped the sweat off her face. *Never just a dream, is it? It's all prophecy and truth and what's actually happening. This whole thing has hijacked my damn brain.*

"Cheyenne?"

"Yeah."

"You okay?"

The halfling wiped her face again, pulling sweat-sticky strands of white hair away from it and her neck. "Fuck if I know, Em."

Without thinking, she tossed her hand toward the door, and the activator still synced with her magic slid the door aside into the wall to reveal Ember. The fae frowned and gazed around the room. "Whoa. Yeah, I might not have an answer for that either if I were you."

"What?" Cheyenne pushed herself up onto her forearms, grimacing at the pain pulsing in the wounded flesh below her shoulders, and looked around. "Shit."

Dark patches of singed metallic craters decorated the walls and ceiling of her new bedroom, and a small stream of smoke rose from the newest hole in the wall to Cheyenne's right where she'd opened the window the night before. She glanced down at her hand, which obviously hadn't been damaged although she'd apparently blasted spells left and right while she was unconscious.

"Okay." Ember grimaced. "Remind me to never walk into your room while you're sleeping."

"You don't do that anyway, do you?"

"Well, no. This is another reason not to."

Cheyenne pushed all the way up and scooted forward to sit on the edge of the elevated platform bed. "I didn't even know I was doing that."

"Of course not. Nobody knows they're sleepwalking or talking in their sleep or sleep-fighting when they're doing it." Ember stayed safely in the doorway and gave her friend a sympathetic frown. "Another nightmare?"

"I guess we can call it that, but they're never just nightmares. More vague bullshit." Cheyenne ran a hand through her tangled hair, then shook her head. "I don't even know what I'm supposed to do with this shit."

"Wanna start by talking about it?"

For a moment, the halfling merely stared at her *Nós Aní*, her eyes wide and unblinking. "More vessel crap."

"Like what the Sorren Gán said in its weird-ass gift?"

"Yeah. How benevolent, right?"

"Yeesh." Ember wrinkled her nose. "If I had that thing coming to me in my dream…"

"No, it wasn't the Sorren Gán. Honestly, I think I'd be a lot more pissed off if it were."

"So, who was it?"

"Ba'rael at first. Just frozen like she was in the Heart," Cheyenne said. "Like a fucking spider caught in amber."

"Huh. And she told you all this?"

"No. I've heard her in dreams before, Em, when she was trying to find me or whatever. Neros was there too."

"Oh." Ember nodded slowly, then frowned and shook her head instead. "I feel like I'm missing something."

"Join the club." Cheyenne pushed off the edge of the bed, foregoing the blocky steps, and landed barefoot on the floor with a grimace. Her hip flared with pain, and she grabbed the edge of the platform to keep from going down.

"Whoa, hey." Ember floated swiftly into the room to help the halfling but stopped when Cheyenne got back on her feet and shook her head. "Okay, let me see."

"See what?" Cheyenne grunted against the pain and stared at the rumpled bedding to focus again.

"Your hip. Obviously, there's an issue."

"Yeah, your darktongue serum doesn't do shit."

Ember folded her arms and cocked her head, waiting for her friend to come back down from her high-flying rage.

Turning her head slowly to meet the girl's gaze, Cheyenne grimaced. "Sorry, Em. I didn't really mean that."

"I know."

"I'm used to darktongue healing every wound, no problem. Maybe the serum's better at giving me a buzz."

"Or maybe the poison Ba'rael shot into you doesn't heal, even with the strongest magical medicine. Did you think of that?"

"Huh." Cheyenne finally released the platform and straightened. "I guess not."

"And that's why I'm here, to think about the stuff you don't have any room in your head to think about." Ember's disapproving frown melted, and she let out a wry chuckle. "I never got a good look at the darktongue salve. You always slathered it on in private."

"Because it fucking hurts, and nobody needs to see that."

"Okay, but I'm like ninety-nine-percent sure that the serum in that canister is at least sixty percent stronger." Ember shrugged. "That's what Venga said."

Wrinkling her nose, Cheyenne took two unsteady steps away from the bed, finally confident she wouldn't topple over beneath the pain in her hip again. *Not looking for a repeat of flopping around on the floor like the last time my hip took me out.* "You know, normally, I wouldn't put any stock in what Venga knows about darktongue or healing, but the salve was made Earthside. I have a feeling even the stuff you can pick up in Peridosh isn't as strong as what we could find here."

"Maybe. You said the trolls gave it to you?"

"Yeah. Yadje. I guess she makes it for fun. Or money. I don't know."

Ember said, "Sounds like you had a healer friend way before I figured out what I could do."

"Maybe. That family's a little out of touch. Why are we even talking about them?"

"Because it calms you down." Ember gave a half-hearted shrug and floated toward the bed, stooping to retrieve the injection canister from the floor beneath the platform. "I'm not about to start having serious conversations with you when you're still in fuck-it mode."

"Ha." Cheyenne tried to roll her shoulders back, but the pain in her unhealed wounds made it impossible. "Hip and shoulders. It's always the hip and shoulders."

"Not always." Ember straightened with the canister in hand and pointed it at her friend. "Just the really bad ones, I guess."

"Right."

"So suck it up already and let me see."

Cheyenne gave the fae a deadpan stare, then rolled her eyes and stared at the far corner of the ceiling as she peeled down the waistband of her pants.

Ember floated quickly toward her. "Jesus Christ. What did you do?"

"What?" When the halfling looked down at her wounded hip, her eyes widened. "Fuck. It got worse."

"No, it was made worse. Cheyenne, it looks like you bashed yourself with a baseball bat and tossed yourself off the side of the building."

Cheyenne snorted. "There's an image."

"I'm serious. That's the biggest bruise I've ever seen. Okay, not including on me after surgery, but damn. We shouldn't even be able to see a bruise when your skin's already bruise-colored." Ember's luminous violet eyes flicked toward her friend's and bored into Cheyenne. "What. Did. You. Do?"

"What you told me." The halfling nodded at the canister. "Inject it right into the wound."

"That's not an injection site, Cheyenne. That's internal bleeding from blunt-force trauma."

"Hey." Cheyenne gave her a crooked smile. "Now you sound like a doctor."

"Because I learned enough about what shit does to the body when a bullet went through mine. I did not tell you to try breaking your own hip with this thing." Closing her eyes, Ember let out a long sigh. "Okay. I'm down to forget you went super-drow stupid on yourself if you'll let me try to heal whatever the hell you pulled."

"Yeah, sure." Holding down the waistband of her pants with one hand and lifting the hem of her shirt with the other, Cheyenne stared at the corner of the ceiling again while Ember placed a hand over the massive bruise swelling the halfling's hip and up into her stomach.

Gold and violet light blossomed beneath Ember's palm, and a warm wave of energy made its way deep into Cheyenne's hip before spreading up and down that side of her body.

"Fuck."

"This hurts?"

"Everything hurts, Em." Cheyenne closed her eyes, and the warm energy faded. It took some of the pain with it, but not all of it. "Any chance your fae healing kicked up a notch and you finally figured out how to…"

Ember gingerly prodded the skin beside the gaping dart hole in her friend's hip, and Cheyenne snarled through clenched teeth. "Nope. Sorry."

Cheyenne swallowed thickly. "It's fine. I guess we already knew that wasn't a thing."

"Neither is letting you handle this canister by yourself. Hold still."

"Em, I don't need—"

The canister pressed into the halfling's belly above her hip and let out a sharp hiss as the darktongue serum injected into her.

"Jesus." Cheyenne's eyelids fluttered. "You need to work on your bedside manner."

Ember floated toward her friend again when the halfling staggered sideways. She grabbed Cheyenne around the waist and held her upright until the halfling could hold herself up. "Manners? Yeah, I figure those aren't at the top of your priority list. They're a waste of time when you're trying to heal a thick-headed drow who doesn't know the difference between healing and self-flagellation."

Cheyenne barked a laugh, surprising them both, then sucked in a huge breath and trailed her unfocused gaze across the room. "Self-flagellation. Not something I've tried."

"Don't even think about it. I am not saving your ass if you do this to yourself on purpose."

"Em." Cheyenne let out a low, buzzed hum as she lazily turned her gaze on her friend. "Come on. I'm not that fucked up."

"You mean, physically or psychologically?"

They both laughed, and the warm tingle spreading through Cheyenne's body like a towel pulled out of the dryer faded enough for her to stand upright and stop smiling like an idiot. *An idiot who can't figure out how to be gentle with her own damn self.*

"Both probably."

Ember floated around her friend to face her head-on and studied Cheyenne's eyes. "Okay. You're starting to come back, huh?"

"Maybe. Thanks."

"Uh-huh. Let me look at your shoulders too. And yeah, I promise I won't poke them." The fae didn't wait for an answer before she pulled the collar of Cheyenne's shirt away to study first one dart wound, then the other. "At least *they* don't look worse."

"That's a start."

"Can I say I really love it that you thank me for surprise-injecting you and calling you a masochist and slapping you in the face when I have to?"

"You didn't call me a masochist."

"I didn't?" Ember's eyes widened, and she released her friend's shirt before floating backward. "Huh. Well, I was thinking it."

"Don't hold back."

"Trust me, Cheyenne, I'm not." After looking her friend over one more time, Ember nodded and cracked a small smile. "Feel better now?"

"Yeah."

"Good. Now get your ass out to the kitchen-not-kitchen and show me how the hell to work that instant microwave or whatever. I'm starving." The fae spun and drifted quickly into the main room of their Hangivol apartment.

Cheyenne hissed a laugh and paused to study the charred metal craters in the walls and ceiling. The activator blinked in her vision, pulling up what she wanted before her fingers moved of their own accord in a series of quick gestures to complete the spell. The metal in the walls responded instantly, shifting and rearranging itself to get rid of the drow-magic craters and the burn marks in a matter of seconds.

Nodding in satisfaction, Cheyenne stepped out of the bedroom and waved a hand behind her to close the door. *Shit spellwork, huh? Not anymore.*

CHAPTER THIRTEEN

"I don't want anything weird, okay?" Ember folded her arms and watched her friend intently as Cheyenne scanned the options their new kitchen system presented. "You told me once about Jell-O with eyes, and now I can't help thinking about it every time I know there's food coming in this place."

"That was supposed to be a delicacy, Em. I'm pretty sure whoever stocked this place didn't make sure we had Upper Tech five-star meals in our fridge, or whatever the version of that is over here."

"Really? No five-star gourmet meals for the Black Flame?"

"Ugh. Stop calling me that."

"You said it was badass."

"Yeah, it is." Cheyenne swiped her finger across the wall, searching for anything on the menu that seemed remotely familiar, but the O'gúleesh-to-English translations only made it harder. They had English words for food that didn't exist Earthside. "It's a badass name, but I'm not the Crown."

"Kinda."

"Nope. Persh'al Tenishi the Ironbreak rules Ambar'ogúl. I'm just backup."

"Okay, you can tell yourself that all you want, but that doesn't change what happened."

Cheyenne looked at her friend over her shoulder and raised an eyebrow. "You sure you don't want Jell-O with eyes?"

Ember pointed at her. "See, you're making threats, but I can tell when they're empty."

Laughing, Cheyenne returned her attention to the scrolling pseudo-menu in the kitchen's system. "You can see this, right?"

"A menu with a bunch of O'gúleesh words I've never heard? Yeah."

"Okay. Give me a sec." Stepping back, Cheyenne eyed the code scrolling across this section of the wall, used solely for the purpose of ordering whatever food was behind the wall, then searched through her activator's prompts until she found three different commands for analysis, visuals, and user-friendly selections. She pressed one hand on the command frame and swiped three other lines of code down toward it along the wall until they combined. "There."

Ember laughed. "Let me guess, O'gúleesh kitchens don't come standard with images of pantry inventory."

"I don't think that was an option until now."

"So, you can read the Weave with O'gúl tech, and now you're rewriting the systems." Ember folded her arms. "I hit the jackpot when I sat down next to you in the Student Center freshman year."

"Right. 'Cause you knew we'd end up here five years later."

"Of course." Ember stepped toward the wall and scanned the images of food options scrolling across the frame. "I became your friend because of your potential."

Cheyenne snorted. "That's the biggest load of bullshit I've heard from you so far."

"Believe it, don't believe it, whatever." Ember shrugged, then pressed the image for what could have been a fruit salad, if any of the apparent fruit was the right shape and color. "I knew you were different the first time I saw you get pissed off about your drow ears creeping out of your Goth-chick hair."

The wall flashed, and a series of whirs and clicks emanated from behind it, followed by the sound of heavy chopping.

"Anyone would know I'm different by seeing that, and I'm sure nobody looks at a halfling and thinks, 'Hey, there's some potential right there. She doesn't belong to either world.'"

"Okay, admittedly, I didn't know you'd be the drow halfling born with a Sorren Gán's black fire who was supposed to fulfill a shitload of O'gúleesh prophecies and take the throne of the entire world." The chopping sound behind the wall stopped, and two panels slid aside before a metal tray protruded from the wall with a bang. Ember eyed the large metal bowl of whatever fruit salad she'd selected and shrugged. "But the potential to debunk the myth of halflings as reality? Yeah, I was way on board with that one."

"You've put a lot of thought into this."

"Not really." Ember picked up the bowl, gave it a quick sniff, and turned around to head to the boxy couch. "I'm making it up as I go along. Taking a lotta pages out of your book, honestly."

"Oh, good. The fae healer's trying to follow in the drow halfling's footsteps. This'll be fun."

They sat together on the couch to pick out the pieces of O'gúleesh produce that didn't, at the very least, smell like meat.

"I can't tell if that's mold or peach fuzz on steroids."

Cheyenne grabbed a slice of deep-purple fruit quartered like an orange and popped it into her mouth. *Frosting. Fruit that tastes like frosting. Not my thing.* "Well, if it bothers you to try it, I won't hold it against you for not clearing your plate."

"Ooh, but I like these." Ember lifted a sprig of small, round black berries and shook off the other pieces of maybe-fruit. "These are good."

"And you know this how?"

"Well, I mean, technically, the Olfarím dosed them with some kinda magical drug, but that's pretty unlikely here, right?" Without waiting for Cheyenne's opinion, Ember stripped off a handful of berries and popped them into her mouth. "Oh, man. Even better than I remembered."

"I'm really hoping you don't start tripping out on me in the next few minutes." Cheyenne eyed her friend with an uncertain smile and grabbed a section of what could have been a pomegranate if the seeds weren't neon-green and three times the regular size. "I still need you around to check me when I get pissed and stupid."

"Don't worry. I'm not gonna start." Ember froze, her eyes wide, and Cheyenne almost leaped from the couch in surprise before the fae let out a huge belch. "Whew."

"Jesus, Em. You can't talk about psychedelic fruit and then make a face like that as you're eating it."

"It's not, it's not." Ember waved her off. "Totally fine. I think I've figured out what my favorite food is over here."

With a snort, Cheyenne shook her head and bit into the neon-green mega-pomegranate. "Most of this stuff isn't half bad."

"Some of it I'm not touching for anything. What are we supposed to do with the trash?"

They both gazed around the room, looking for the coded sign of a trash receptacle or something that worked at least to get rid of waste. "I got nothing, Em, and now I realize there aren't any bathrooms."

"Oh, that was easy." Ember pointed at the closed door to her bedroom. "That pulls out of the walls and floor too."

"Of course it does. Shower?"

"Does it look like I showered?"

"Nope." Cheyenne finished the last bite of her whatever-fruit and tossed the rind back into the bowl. "I'm gonna go check it out."

"Sure. I'll be here eating the rest of whatever this is and hoping you don't bash yourself into the disappearing bathroom walls."

"Your confidence is the only thing that keeps me going sometimes. You know that?"

Ember crammed her mouth full of berries again. "Yeah, me too."

Half an hour later, Cheyenne stepped out of her bedroom again, fully washed and dried but wearing the same tattered clothes. Ember turned away from the wall beside her bedroom when she heard her friend's door open and shut behind her and frowned. "I heard something in there, but somehow, you don't look very refreshed."

"Oh, thanks." Cheyenne headed back to the couch and flopped down on it, then grimaced. "I really miss our couch."

"Yeah, this stuff doesn't scream comfort, does it? So, shower?"

"Self-cleaning and self-deconstructing." Cheyenne tried to toss her arm over the back of the couch, but her throbbing shoulder made it impossible. "Same kinda film around it like the windows and a built-in dryer. Now all I need is a new wardrobe for when we inevitably come back here to hang out for a few days."

"What windows?"

"Oh. I opened one in the wall last night. Climbed up to the roof and had a weirdly enlightening chat with a drow kid."

Ember folded her arms. "Okay, why wasn't that the first thing we talked about this morning?"

"Nightmares. Prophecies. Seeing my maybe-dead, maybe-still-alive aunt and cousin in my head while I tried to bring my bedroom down on top of me in my sleep." Cheyenne shrugged. "Seemed a little more important."

"A drow kid."

"Yeah. It was like meeting myself, only she's a hundred and twenty-four years old and obviously full-blooded drow.

"Obviously." Ember grinned. "You're making friends."

"I didn't say that."

"You're making friends with little drow girls who look up to you. Holy shit, that's the cutest thing ever."

"Okay, you can stop."

"Ha! For real, though. The Cheyenne Summerlin who crushed a beer bottle in her hand and stormed out of Gnarly's two months ago would've thrown a kid across the room instead of talking to her."

"Wow. That's what you think of me, huh?"

"Well, not anymore."

They laughed, and Cheyenne ran her fingers through her hair she hadn't brushed but had somehow been untangled by the high-tech shower in her bedroom.

A soft alarm bell chimed, followed by a flash of orange light on the wall beside the front door.

Ember cocked her head. "Is that a doorbell?"

"I think the general mode of letting someone else know you're at their door on this side is to either knock as loud as you can or bash the whole thing in." Cheyenne stood from the couch and headed toward the door, scrutinizing the lines of flashing orange code. "Oh. Come check this out."

Ember joined her, and Cheyenne pointed at the flashing line:

Incoming Message

"Message?" The fae folded her arms. "So, it's a mailbox."

"I don't know." Cheyenne swiped her hand along the command for accepting the message, and a small panel fell open from the wall like a glove compartment. The metal screen there flashed a few times, then the message appeared in lines across the surface, accompanied by a recording of a deep, metallic voice neither of them recognized.

"The necromancer Venga Qhrall summons you to his laboratory for initial testing. Your immediate presence is mandatory."

"Are you kidding me?" Ember snorted. "Well, I guess it's time for you to go."

"Both fae and drow are expected to attend."

"Shit."

The message screen sent a map of Venga's location to both girls' activators, then the entire written transcript disappeared, and the metal box folded back up into the wall. The seams sealed again as if the device had never existed.

Cheyenne cocked her head. "That's not his voice."

"Nope. You think he has an assistant to record his messages for him?"

"You've spent more time with him than I have, Em. Did you see any assistants?"

"Well, no."

"Then it's probably a voice the system uses." Cheyenne turned around and headed back to her room to grab her shoes.

"What? You mean, I've been listening to Alexa talk like a robot who just discovered inflection when I could've been listening to someone who sounds like Morgan Freeman?"

Cheyenne laughed. "What?"

"I mean, a little."

"You better not be using Alexa at our place."

"No way. Had one in my old apartment, though." Ember turned to look at her friend and shrugged sheepishly. "One of the things you blasted to pieces when you were fighting whoever."

"Oh. Well, normally I'd say sorry, but I'm not a huge fan of voice services. They're not as smart as everyone thinks."

"You think those things are gonna spy on you."

"Well, if they did, Em, would you blame me for not wanting one around?" Cheyenne waved at her bedroom door and disappeared into the other room when it opened at her command.

Ember tossed her violet-streaked hair out of her eyes and scoffed. "No, I couldn't blame you. Doesn't mean I don't think they're awesome. This, on the other hand?" she said, turning to glare at the wall where the message box had disappeared. "This is creepy."

"What are you talking about?" Cheyenne returned to the main room, still shoving her feet into her black Vans and gingerly shrugging on her trenchcoat before waving the door shut behind her.

"A summons from a necromancer popped out of a box in our apartment. All this tech everywhere, and there's no damn privacy in this world. Anyone could find where you live, open up a box into random magicals' apartments, and send them messages."

"Wow." Cheyenne chuckled and headed toward the front door. "You know that's pretty much the same thing as the internet, right?"

"Cheyenne, I don't have the internet built into the walls of my apartment. That's what's creepy."

"Come on, Em. The walls in Upper Tech were swallowing magicals whole a few weeks ago. This is a courtesy in comparison."

"Summoning someone doesn't sound like much of a courtesy."

"Yeah, the robot guy said our presence was mandatory, but it's not like we don't have a choice. What's the scaleback gonna do, hunt us down and give us a lecture?"

"Or a blast of extra blight just for fun." Ember folded her arms. "No, I don't think he'd do that, but I don't like being summoned."

"We seem to be experiencing role reversal, here." Cheyenne patted her friend's shoulder and nodded. "No one's making us do anything, Em, but this is about the blight. Necromancer or not, we need to check it out."

"Well, I know that." Ember rolled her eyes but couldn't hide a small smile. "I wasn't gonna say no and just stay here."

"You thought that message was just for me."

"It's technically your apartment. I'm just mooching."

"Ha-ha. Come on."

CHAPTER FOURTEEN

The wide main avenue of the drow-inhabited inner circle was the only thing they had to cross to get to the Crown's fortress. Small pockets of drow citizens were up and going about their business for the day, moving slowly and precisely and casting small smiles and curious glances at the halfling ex-Crown and her fae *Nós Ani*. In some of the open doorways and storefronts, a number of drow hadn't finished their celebration of Persh'al's coronation, though most of them now slumped on the ground against walls or sprawled in uncomfortable-looking metal lounge chairs.

The loud, obnoxious partying in the rest of the capital had died down quite a bit since the night before. There was the occasional shout from the lower levels or a stray burst of magic from some drunk O'gúleesh who didn't know when to call it quits, but for the most part, Hangivol had fallen quiet in the throes of a morning recovery.

Cheyenne waved her hand at the huge, heavy iron double doors leading into the armory, and they stepped inside to find the same scene with the Crown's orc guards. Many of them were sprawled across the room, which was filled with metal tables and benches. Some had even passed out on the tables, their weapons hanging loosely from unconscious hands or on the ground beside them.

"Huh." Ember leaned toward her friend and muttered, "Looks like the guards' loyalty didn't run as deep as Ba'rael thought."

"Or everyone in this city was itching for something to celebrate so they could finally loosen the hell up."

One orc grunted and staggered toward a table on the far side of the armory, carrying a huge barrel in his meaty arms. The barrel clanked down on the table, and the orc dropped to his knees to lower his open mouth beneath the spigot as he opened it. Pale green water spewed into his mouth and all over his face, and he guzzled it down like he hadn't had a drink in days.

"Hair of the dog?"

"Hangover cure." Cheyenne shrugged as they walked down the center aisle between the rows of tables and the passed-out guards. "Or both. I didn't touch the stuff. Smells like blood and sewer water."

"Yeah, I don't need drow super-smell to pick that up."

As they reached the far side of the room, the only conscious orc turned off the barrel's spigot and stood, shaking himself from head to toe like a wet dog and spraying green liquid all over his unconscious fellows. Then he looked at Cheyenne and Ember and thumped a fist weakly on his chest. "May the Black Flame reign."

"I'm not ruling anything."

He thumped his chest again, nodded curtly, and growled.

"Never mind. Not having this conversation with a hungover orc." She pushed open the doors in front of them and stepped into the corridor.

Ember hung back for a moment and nodded at the orc, pointing at the metal barrel on the table. "That stuff really work?"

"Only if you can stomach the taste." His belch echoed explosively around the armory, making some of the other passed-out guards stir, and thumped his fist to his chest again.

"Right." Ember grimaced and left him to it.

Cheyenne almost pulled up the map their message from Venga had given them but stopped herself. "So, you're still leading the way, right?"

"Yeah. I don't know why he sent us a map. I went back and forth from his little study or whatever to your room a million times yesterday while you were out. It's this way."

Cheyenne let her friend navigate the twisting, forking, labyrinthine corridors of the Crown's fortress. "Looks like the place is still rewriting itself," she said, studying the walls. Most of the metal surfaces designed to look like stone had taken on a lighter hue, while others still showed mottled patches halfway between pitch-black and silver-gray.

"Kind of cliché, don't you think?" Ember touched a patch of black on the mostly light wall, and the dark tint shivered beneath her finger.

"Redecorating after the last resident tortured and killed and stole magic from her not-so-loyal subjects?"

"No, I get that. I mean going from black to white. Yeah, sure, most people think of black being bad and white being good, but Persh'al was the tech guy in L'zar's weird little group, wasn't he?"

"Uh-huh." Cheyenne shot her friend a playful frown. "Not sure what you're getting at."

"I'm wondering why he didn't choose something cooler. If he knows how to reprogram the way this place looks, he could've done anything. Hell, made the place blue with orange spots like him."

"Oh, right. Then I'm wondering why you didn't make your room at home pink and purple."

"Very funny. I mean, it's weird that he chose light gray for everything. For real, if I could've decorated our apartment by programming a few lines of code without having to touch a can of paint, I would've gone crazy with it."

"You have magic, Em."

"Shit. Yeah, I guess that's a thing."

The farther they went, the more magicals they passed as Hangivol's citizens finally rose from their celebratory stupor. One room held a dozen skaxen shaking themselves off and blasting bursts of sickly orange magic across the room to wake each other up. One of them caught sight of Cheyenne and Ember staring at them through the open doorway and snarled weakly before gesturing at the wall. The door slid into place with an echoing bang.

"Looks like there are still a few assholes who don't want you here," Ember muttered.

"Or everyone's sick and tired of seeing a drow walking around like they own the place. Ba'rael, L'zar, me."

"Then Persh'al already has a leg up."

"That's what I was thinking when I picked him, yeah."

The next vestibule Ember led them through looked more like a tailor's shop than anything, with swaths of dark fabric hanging over the edges of two massive metal tables in the center. A tall, spindly machine with a pair of shears on one of its retractable arms cut through a piece of fabric at the end of the table, clicking and whirring and blinking with white and yellow lights as it worked.

"See, that's the right way to put those things to work. Who needs servants when you have high-tech machines?" Ember ran a hand over the dangling fabric beside her. The machine stopped, the blinking lights switching from yellow to dark orange. She pulled her hand back, and the machine took up its cutting again. "Yet somehow, I still feel like it's judging me."

"Or waiting for a command." Cheyenne nodded at the other side of the room. "You're still leading the way."

"Yeah, yeah. I'm going. It's right through here."

When they stepped through the next set of doors, they entered a wide circular chamber, much like the one in which Cheyenne had sent the emergency message to the Four-Pointed Star under L'zar's guidance the first time she'd entered the fortress. Only this one was filled with at least three dozen orc guards sitting at low square tables or on the floor propped up against the walls. They all turned to view the newcomers, and when they recognized Cheyenne, every one of them stood.

"May the Black Flame reign." The first orc to say it pounded his chest and bowed his head, followed by an echoing repeat as the other guards did the same.

"Whoa, whoa, okay. Come on." Cheyenne waved them off with a grimace. "You can cut it out with that whole thing, okay? I'm not gonna bite anyone's head off for not doing that. I might if you keep doing it, though." *So much for Corian following through with that order to flip me the bird instead.*

"It's our duty," the first orc growled, his hairless brow scrunching together. While it was almost impossible for an orc to close their mouth around the huge tusks protruding from their lips, this one almost looked like he was gaping in surprise. "We are pledged to the O'gúl Crown and nothing else."

"I'm not the Crown, okay?" Cheyenne spread her arms and let out a wry laugh. "How many of you were in the Heart yesterday when all that went down?"

The orcs stared at her, shifting uncomfortably from foot to foot. All of them nodded.

"Okay, then I don't get what's so hard to grasp. Persh'al Tenishi is your Crown, okay? Blue troll. Kinda hard to miss. Not me."

"You turned the Cycle, Black Fla—"

"Cheyenne. My name is Cheyenne. Let's leave it at that."

"Cheyenne." Her name whispered through the orc's thick tusks. "You turned the Cycle. The Spider is erased from this world. Persh'al Tenishi did not do this."

"Yeah, but I gave him the throne. You saw him take the oath."

"But you swore it with him."

Cheyenne sighed heavily. "Sure, you got me on a technicality. But seriously, I'm not here to rule, and I'm not going to be the Black Flame and have everybody argue with me about who's got what job."

"There is no argument." An orc with a puckered wad of scarred flesh where his left eye used to be pounded his chest again. "We answer to you."

"I appreciate that. Really. Okay, I'm ordering you to call me Cheyenne, not the Black Flame. And I'll order you not to bring this up again if I happen to stumble into your little meeting in this..." She turned toward Ember. "Where are we?"

"Where's Venga?" Ember stared around the room. "Where's all his stuff? He was here yesterday."

"The necromancer relocated." The one-eyed orc narrowed his eye at the fae. "What do you want with the scaleback?"

"What's it to you?"

"Whoa. Okay." Cheyenne wrapped her arm around Ember's shoulder and all but pushed her friend across the circular room toward the other side. "We're passing through, soldiers. As you were. Or whatever."

The first orc snarled at Ember. "If you're friends with the necromancer, tell him he has more than enough to answer for. Exile does not forgive."

"I wouldn't call us friends." Ember looked at the orc over her shoulder. "And I don't know why you're snarling at me, okay?"

"All right!" Cheyenne waved at the door, and it opened for both of them. "Maybe you guys didn't pick up on this. Fae *Nós Aní* over here, okay? Mine. So just dial it down a notch."

The gathering of orcs looked at each other, scowls and snarling forgotten, and all dropped to one knee to thump fists on chests again. "Forgive us."

"Yeah, yeah, we're good." Cheyenne pulled Ember through the open doors and nodded at the kneeling guards. "Come on, guys. Just act normal, huh? Everything's fine."

The one-eyed guard looked at her in confusion, like he didn't understand what the phrase "Everything's fine" meant.

A short, mottled gray-green orc thrust his fist in the air and shouted, "Blood and honor, Cheyenne!"

"Ha! Yeah, okay. I can get behind that one. Blood and honor."

The other orcs' shouts of the same erupted behind her even as she waved the door closed again. She looked at Ember, shaking her head.

"You know, I almost preferred it when everyone hated me because I walked through this place with L'zar. I can handle dirty looks, but the bowing is awkward."

"He moved his whole setup and didn't even bother to tell me." Ember stared down the next hall stretching ahead of them and gritted her teeth. "If he wants my fucking help, the least he can do is let me know he's not where he said he'd be."

"I mean, he sent us a map."

"That's not the point." Ember glared up at her. "I said I knew how to find him, and this is fucking embarrassing."

Cheyenne pressed her lips together and nodded. *If anyone knows feeling pissed-off and betrayed, I sure as hell do. Here's another reason to work on keeping my own shit in check.* "I know, Em. Not your fault."

"He would've told you if he was moving."

"Nah, I doubt it. Nobody tells me anything, and I don't think Venga likes me."

"Why not?"

"I mean, if everyone else credits me for wiping Ba'rael off the face of this plane, at least, he definitely blames me for screwing up his revenge plot."

"Huh." Floating away from the halfling, Ember stared at the light-colored walls around them and shrugged. "So, he's a douche."

"Yeah, I figured that out the second L'zar opened the guy's sensory-deprivation cell. Necromancy and douchebaggery go hand in hand, don't you think?"

"I guess." Ember blinked, then stared blankly at the wall for five seconds before nodding. "Okay, I pulled up the new map."

"Great."

"Wanna try again?"

"We *have* been summoned, after all."

Ember snorted and nodded down the hall. "Then keep up."

CHAPTER FIFTEEN

Cheyenne had pulled the map up with her activator just in case and decided not to say anything about it. By the time they reached the end of the corridor and the last turn leading to Venga's new workshop, the hair on the back of her neck prickled and started to rise. "This feels familiar."

"I was starting to think the same thing." Ember turned around to look back the way they'd come and wrinkled her nose. "Why?"

"Beats me, Em. I can't tell a single part of this place from the next, except for the courtyard. And yeah, I'm pretty sure I'd recognize it if we ended up in the basement torture chamber again."

They turned the corner and stared down the next long hall. At the end were two huge reinforced metal doors, and those Cheyenne definitely recognized. "No way."

Ember clenched her fists. "He took the fucking black-goo room?"

"Is that what we're calling it?"

"Well, what the hell else would you call it? Another torture chamber? The magic-stealing room? A mad scientist's murder lab? We watched those magicals die in that shit, Cheyenne, and that fucking four-armed lizard thinks it's funny to take over and play 'bad necromancer turned not-so-bad and trying to save the world' in there? No.

Uh-uh." Ember floated at a furious speed down the hallway, purple light flashing around her clenched fists.

Cheyenne silently followed her. *I can only imagine how much it would suck right now not to be able to stomp down this hall.*

Ember flung her hands toward the double doors and smashed them with a burst of purple light. The doors crashed open and swung back into place a second after the two slipped inside.

That would've felt good.

"What the hell are you thinking?" Ember shouted. "You summon us, and don't say a word about having moved!"

"I sent you a map," Venga growled.

"You can't work in here!" Ember floated toward a workbench built into the wall and started grabbing handfuls of vials and bottles and tubes to shove them into a metal crate on the far end. "This whole room needs to be destroyed. Wiped off the map. Taken out of the fortress. I'll fucking blow it up."

Venga fixed Cheyenne with wide eyes, his scaly lips pulled back in a snarl. "Do something."

The halfling folded her arms. "Yeah, you definitely did."

With a growl, the four-armed scaleback stomped across the room toward Ember. "Put that down, fae. No one told you to pack for me."

"No one told you it was okay to set up blight-experiment shop in here, either!" Ember stopped her angry packing when Venga snatched her wrist with one arm and removed the half-packed crate with two more to get it out of her reach.

"This is the only room in the whole fell-damn city with even a modicum of usefulness to me, and I still don't have what I need."

She jerked her wrist out of his scaly, black-clawed grasp. "Well, maybe you'd find what you need if you weren't working in a death chamber."

"Death?" Venga stepped back, cradling the crate under one arm, and scratched his head with the second arm on the same side. He looked around the room, then chuckled darkly. "You think it's wise to lecture me on death?"

"Just because that's the kind of magic you use, it doesn't mean it's all fun and games for everyone else." Ember glared at the necromancer and tossed a hand toward Cheyenne. "Come on, tell him."

"What? I'm not part of this."

"Cheyenne!"

The halfling stuck her hands in her pockets and shrugged. "I mean, yeah. It's kinda like taking a shit on someone else's grave."

Ember whirled and glared at her. "That's how you back me up?"

Cheyenne glanced at her friend and then the now-clearly-amused necromancer. "It just came out, Em. I didn't know we were ganging up on him together."

"So, you don't think there's a serious issue with setting up a workshop for healing the blight in the same room where this asshole's magic stole the power from innocent O'gúleesh and killed them?"

"No, yeah. Serious issue."

"There." Ember folded her arms and returned to glaring at Venga. "You heard it from the Black Flame herself. Move your shit out of here, then I'm ripping this room out by the walls."

"Em."

"What?"

"You just gave a command for me."

"No, I didn't. You said…" Ember clenched her jaw and closed her eyes. "Shit."

"I mean, I get it. You're pissed, and you have every right to be. We were all pissed the last time we walked through these doors. Or charged through what was left of them, anyway." Cheyenne looked over her shoulder at the perfectly intact doors. "Which seem to have put themselves back together pretty well. But whatever. Maybe we should give Venga a chance to explain why this has to be done here. Might be a good idea to hear all the facts before we start the demolition, right?"

Ember looked at the necromancer and scowled. "Why are you smiling at me?"

The scaleback blinked at her and set the metal crate back down on the workbench. "You can tell it's a smile, can you? Most O'gúleesh think this is the expression I make when I'm ready to tear them limb from limb."

"You're not building a very strong case for yourself."

"I am not under any obligation to explain myself to you, fae. If you wish to return with the Ironbreak at your side so he can order me to pack my things, by all means. Try."

The room fell awkwardly silent, then Ember lifted her chin toward the necromancer and muttered, "So, why this room?"

Venga turned from the right-hand wall and headed across the room toward the other side. Ember stared after him, and Cheyenne stood there with her hands in her pockets. *That was a lot.*

"This is where I created the blight." Venga reached the workbench on the opposite side and started unpacking the vials and tubes and ingredients, his four arms pumping up and down as he rearranged his supplies. One arm lifted to point straight up at the glass bubble suspended from the hole in the center of the ceiling, though his gaze never left his work. "I created that chamber specifically to channel the procedures Ba'rael wished to perform in this place."

"You mean, torture and siphoning magic and murdering her victims."

"You keep speaking about death, angry little fae."

"Yeah, because that's what happened." Ember slapped a hand on the metal walls of the pool that was once filled with black sludge and magicals in cages but was now empty and dry. The clang echoed around the room. "Right here. That bitch chained them up and sucked the magic right out of them while they screamed and begged for it to stop."

"You have quite the imagination." Venga chuckled. "Those chambers were built to siphon magic, yes, but not at that capacity."

"How would you know? You've been locked in a tank for the last five years."

The necromancer whirled around and hissed at her, his four arms spread wide with a different implement clenched in each hand. "Because I designed it!"

"Hey!" Both the fae and the scaleback turned to look at Cheyenne. "Let's cut it out with the arguing for just a second, 'cause I don't think we're all on the same page. We saw it with our own eyes, Venga. The day L'zar and I showed up to turn the new Cycle with my coin on the altar. We came right through this room, and believe me, those pools were full of the same sludge running in rivers through the Outers."

"Impossible." Venga slowly shook his head. "This wasn't built to siphon magic at that capacity."

"Yeah, you said that already." Cheyenne nodded at the ceiling. "That little bubble thing wasn't meant to hold magic at that capacity, either.

Neither was the city, and it almost blew itself up after how much the Spider overloaded it. No bullshit, Venga. She filled those pools with the blight and used them as dunk tanks for magicals who didn't deserve to die the way they did. No one does."

"Except for the Spider," Ember muttered. "Let's be honest."

Cheyenne ignored her friend's anger and raised an eyebrow at the necromancer.

"I did not build this place to take life, Cheyenne," he growled. "Merely to offer an alternative."

"An alternative to life?" Ember scoffed. "Yeah, that's called death, genius, and I watched those magicals die in cages. Right here."

Venga's scaly upper lip curled up in a warning snarl, but the confidence had seeped out of him. When his all-black eyes flickered toward Cheyenne and he turned his head her way, she nodded.

"We all saw it. General Hi'et can confirm that story if you feel like you need a second opinion."

The necromancer trembled, his face twitching in rage. Then he let out a startling roar and whirled around, hurling his glass implements against the wall of shelving beside the back wall of the room that had also repaired itself in the last two weeks. Shards of glass flew in every direction and pelted his stash of instruments. Cheyenne raised a shimmering black shield in front of Ember and another in front of herself, shattered glass and small pieces of metal pinging off them before clattering to the floor. She left the necromancer to fend for himself.

Venga hissed and ducked when a piece of glass whipped across his face and lodged beneath the scales of his cheek. More fragments rained off his hunched shoulders as he picked gingerly at the glass shard and removed it with more dexterity than his thick black claws looked like they could handle. "I wish you had not disposed of the Spider as quickly as you did, drow."

"Yeah, I know." Cheyenne waved down the shields. "You wanted to make her pay. So did I, honestly, and now neither of us has the satisfaction of having done that. Her son gets the credit for that part."

"You fought her in the Heart."

"And almost died." She gave him a weak smile and pointed at her opposite shoulder and the still unhealed wound from her aunt's poisoned magical darts. "Although you could've stuck me a million other times with shattered glass, I'm gonna thank you for the dark-tongue serum. It works. Sort of. Now the three of us need to work together to figure out how to get this shit out of my body so I don't have to go through the rest of this as a walking wound or a host for whatever new strain of the blight Ba'rael had in her magic."

Venga grunted and turned slowly toward Ember before flicking the shard of glass across the room, where it pinged against the wall. "You told her about that."

"We tell each other everything, yeah."

"And the serum hasn't alleviated the issue?"

"They're definitely an issue," Cheyenne said. "But let's call them what they are, huh? Unhealable wounds, which I've dealt with before, but these ones are about to make me permanently dependent on that darktongue serum if we don't find something that works."

"I may have discovered a solution." Venga turned toward the shelves along the back wall, the contents of which were now scattered. He swept a pile of shattered glass onto the floor and picked through his supplies.

"I mean, if I have to keep injecting myself a few times a day so I won't get worse, fine." Cheyenne took one step across the glass-littered floor and peered at the shelving. "We haven't found a way to keep the blight from spreading any closer to Hangivol or the rest of the major cities here. That's more important to stop first."

"The solutions to your poisoned wounds and this poisoned land are one and the same." Venga lifted a vial each in two of his hands, one of dark-green glass and the other clear with a blood-red liquid inside, and turned toward the workbench again. "You will heal first, Cheyenne. Then we'll heal the sickness of the Spider's dark web."

"Cool."

Ember watched them both with a clenched jaw. "You still haven't told us why we need to do this here."

Venga snorted and busied himself with mixing the ingredients he'd selected, his four arms moving quickly to uncork more vials and take pinches of powdered substances from small boxes. "Did it ever occur to you to ask why Hangivol was built here, in this part of Ambar'ogúl?"

"I don't know." Ember shrugged. "Undeveloped real estate?"

Cheyenne snorted and smiled sheepishly when Ember frowned at her. "Totally something I would've said."

"Hangivol rests atop a major vein of lifeforce magic flowing through Ambar'ogúl. The first drow knew this, though most have forgotten."

"Sylra Nightflame," Cheyenne muttered. "Yeah, we know what he did."

"Then you know why I built my study here centuries ago and not anywhere else." Venga kept working, the sounds of metal clicking and liquids being poured and vials being uncorked filling the room. "The Nimlothar within the heart grew from a sapling, already tapped into that lifeforce vein. That may be the only reason it still stands after everything the Spider thrust upon it. And a stronger convergence runs beneath our feet." He pointed again toward the glass bubble. "Straight up and down through the center of Ambar'ogúl, with the Heart and the Nimlothar just on the other side of this wall."

"And you can't work your magic without being right in the center of it, huh?" Ember met Cheyenne's gaze and shook her head in disbelief.

"Don't be obtuse." Venga didn't bother to return the glare he could feel on the back of his head. "My magic works anywhere I please. But I assume you want me working on diminishing the Undoing where my magic is at its strongest, powered by the lifeforce vein, yes? Or what little of it the Spider left behind for the rest of us."

"Yeah," Ember said, "Definitely want you at your best. As long as you can reverse this thing."

"I told you I would try. Leave it at that."

"You know where magic's even stronger than standing on top of a lifeforce vein?"

Cheyenne stared at her friend and slowly shook her head. *Not the time to go there, Em.*

"Nowhere has stronger magic," Venga grumbled. "Not since the Nimlothar forests were destroyed."

"Except for Nor'ieth."

Cheyenne closed her eyes, and she went there. *He's not gonna take us seriously after this.*

Venga froze, his scaly sides heaving beneath his jacket, then turned halfway toward the center of the room to look first at Ember, then

Cheyenne. "I believe your *Nós Aní* has lost her mind under the pressure."

"You're the necromancer," Ember shot back. "Anyone who chooses to work in death magic is crazier than I could ever be."

"We don't need to get into this." Cheyenne shrugged. "Focus on your work, Venga."

"And I'm not crazy," Ember added.

The scaleback chuckled. "Of course not."

Ember widened her eyes at Cheyenne and nodded at the necromancer.

Yeah, I have to back her up. Wrinkling her nose, Cheyenne bit the bullet. "And Nor'ieth does exist, by the way."

"I didn't summon you here to play games, Cheyenne. I find them highly unamusing."

"So, you haven't spent any time wondering where the pale, washed-out drow riding a *luré* came from when he ripped open a portal and snatched Ba'rael right out from under us?"

Venga let out a low growl and kept working. "We can discuss this at another time. For now, I believe we've reached our long-sought—"

His heavy iron crucible exploded with a clang and a balloon of thick, acrid scarlet smoke bloomed around the necromancer, letting off spiraling sparks and sending most of his other implements on the workbench to the floor.

The necromancer roared and slammed his lower two fists on the workbench while fanning away the red smoke with the other two. "The Blood of Yelv'iyt can fester in this fell-damn shithole for all the good it does me now!"

Cheyenne stepped back across the broken glass and choked back a cough as the scents of blood and burning metal mixed with something she didn't even want to try naming made her nose burn. "Like, actual blood?"

"Yes. The useless blood of a useless god!" Venga uncorked another vial and emptied it into the smoking, sparking bowl. The ingredients hissed, the smoke turned from red to a more natural gray, and he swept an arm across the workbench to send the whole crucible flying against the wall to spill his failed attempt all over the floor. "I need flesh-setter hide."

Ember blinked and waved her hand in front of her face. "Not more blood of a god, I hope."

"Don't be ridiculous. The gods are dead and gone from this world." Venga whirled and snarled at them. "Go into the lower city and buy me two wrapped coils of flesh-setter hide."

The fae leaned away and looked him up and down. "Get it yourself."

"If we want this done, I don't have time to go shopping, fae." He shoved a clawed hand into his pocket, pulled out a metal case the size and shape as a deck of playing cards, and tossed it at her. "Get it for me, and we will return to our work after I draw up a new plan!"

Ember caught the case, turned it over, and raised her eyebrows at Cheyenne.

The halfling shrugged. "Whatever it costs?"

"Yes, whatever it costs! You have my *veréle*, so go out and spend it." When neither of the girls moved, Venga roared again and lunged toward them. A flash of scarlet light illuminated at the tips of his claws, then Ember and Cheyenne found themselves pulled across the glass-littered floor toward the double doors, which were opening on their own. "Now!"

"Hey!" Cheyenne twisted around and launched an arc of purple sparks at the clawed hand controlling her from across the room. She had time to see her magic connect with his palm before she and Ember skidded out into the hall and the doors slammed shut. Venga hissed and threw something else across the room, then his lifeforce-connected lab fell silent.

Ember hissed at the closed doors, then smoothed down the front of her shirt. "You should've hit him with something stronger."

"I was making a point, Em, not trying to injure the only magical who knows more than we do about the blight."

"Still."

"Yeah, maybe." Cheyenne rolled her eyes and turned away from the door. "If he tries it again, I'll hit him harder."

"He thinks he's untouchable, bossing around the Crown and throwing us both out."

Stopping to look at her friend, Cheyenne shook her head. "Not you too."

"What?"

"I'm the *ex*-Crown, Em."

"Same thing."

"No, it's not." The halfling couldn't help but laugh in disbelief as she ran a hand through her hair. "Why is everybody making this so complicated? I was the Crown for maybe twenty minutes. Then I made Persh'al the Crown, and now I'm just Cheyenne again. Totally simple. Way easy to understand."

"Yeah, tell that to the Nimlothar that accepted him only because you were there to swear in with him and make some promise you conveniently forgot to tell me about." They headed down the hall, and Ember stared at her friend. "So? Are you gonna tell me what the last drow tree had to say?"

"Sure." Cheyenne shoved her hands into her pockets again. "To be clear, the tree didn't talk to me."

"Good. That'd be weird."

They both chuckled, the tension diffused now that they were out of Venga's death-magic vault and heading out to run errands for him.

Cheyenne took a deep breath and studied the light-gray floor beneath her feet. "It wants me to heal the forest, Em."

"The forest. Like, just a forest?"

"The Nimlothar forest. The one we passed on the way to the Sorren Gán."

"What?" Ember frowned, a confused smile lifting the corners of her mouth. "What did you tell it?"

Cheyenne shrugged. "I promised to do whatever I could to make it happen. To make it right."

"Look, however weird it is to talk about you talking to a tree, I'll go ahead and say that that tree is gonna be seriously disappointed."

"Oh, thanks."

"No, not because I doubt you." Ember shook her head, frowning at the end of the hall as they kept moving. "Because the Nimlothar forest is dead, Cheyenne. I'm pretty sure even a necromancer can't bring a tree back to life without making it something it's not supposed to be."

"Yeah. That's the thing, though, Em. They're not dead."

Ember stopped short and stared at Cheyenne until the halfling realized it and turned around to look at her. "We walked through that forest together. Those were dead trees."

"Nope."

"Then what the hell are they?"

Cheyenne shrugged. "Not alive. Beyond that, I got nothing."

"Shit." Ember started floating down the hall again, scrunching her face as she tried to process the revelation. "I seriously hope the Nimlothar didn't give you a time limit or something before it calls off the whole 'sharing the throne with Persh'al' thing."

"No time limit, at least not as far as I know. We have to heal the blight first, Em, then hope there's still enough time to heal the forest."

"Okay." Ember nodded slowly, then choked back a laugh.

"I know you're not laughing at me, but it kinda feels that way."

"No, not at you." The fae grinned. "I mean, here you are talking to trees and sharing magic with them, and you just made a promise to save the forest."

"So?"

"It's funny. Kinda sounds like you've gone from Goth to hippie."

Cheyenne cracked a smile. "Fuck off."

CHAPTER SIXTEEN

Fortunately, when they passed back through the fortress and into the drow inner circle via a more direct route, Cheyenne didn't have to deal with anyone else bowing or shouting out to the Black Flame or pledging their undying allegiance. Mostly, that was because they didn't see anyone else on their way out.

"So." Ember tossed the metal case Venga had chucked at her over and over in her hand. "Any idea where we're supposed to find flesh-setter hide?"

"Even if I knew what that was, why would I know where to get it?"

"I don't know. You got more tours of the city than I did."

Cheyenne laughed. "Yeah. The first was doing Persh'al's weird-ass version of reconnaissance, and the second was following L'zar around to see the grossest Oracle in all of existence before he tried to stop me from saving the city. You know, when it started to explode."

"Just thought I'd ask." Ember tossed the metal case again and cocked her head. "What is this, anyway?"

"A money case." Cheyenne studied it and shrugged. "No money over here, though. They call it *veréle*, and it's like…I don't know. See-through metal?"

"Of course it is. Everything's metal, or stone." They made their way down the main avenue of the inner circle, and while Cheyenne raised her eyebrows and nodded a few times at some of the drow standing in doorways and grinning that weirdly feral drow grin at her, Ember struggled to undo the latch on the case. "Jeeze. He really shut this thing up tight."

"Careful. If you open it wrong, it'll be like fifty-two-card-pickup, only with O'gúleesh money."

"I'm not gonna spill Venga's fortune all over the place."

"Well, look who decided to come out of hiding."

"Ah!" The case in Ember's hand popped open when she jumped in surprise, and she fumbled to keep the thin, laminated *veréle* cards from spilling all over the street. She gave up and frowned at Maleshi, who was standing two feet in front of her. "Where did you come from?"

The general pointed at the alley right beside them. "Probably a good idea to open a remarkably full case of veréle in private, Ember. Focus on where you're heading instead."

"Oh, yeah. Thanks. Gonna tell me to look both ways before I cross the street, too?"

When Ember bent to pick up the scattered cards, Maleshi raised a questioning eyebrow at Cheyenne.

The halfling shrugged and shook her head. "Just one of those days."

"Uh-huh. Doesn't have anything to do with having one of those nights last night, does it?"

"What's that supposed to mean?" Ember straightened again and shoved the *veréle* back into place, then clicked the case shut and stuck it in her pocket beside the bulge of Cheyenne's injection canister. "'One of those nights?'"

"The same kind of night every magical in Hangivol had last night. That's all." Maleshi clasped her hands behind her back. "I'm assuming there was drinking involved on your end."

"Yeah, and we can both hold our liquor." Ember realized how short she was being and sighed. "Sorry. Like Cheyenne said, just one of those days."

"I'm sure." The general glanced at them, smiling expectantly.

Cheyenne looked across the street and back. "What?"

"Oh, nothing. I thought you might—"

"I swear on the Crown's head, you pilfering *radag,* if you ever step foot in my establishment again, I'll have your disgusting hide stripped from your bones." A drow woman launched a golden-brown burst of light at a magical in a dark hood, who staggered backward out of a doorway opening into the alley and thumped against the opposite wall.

"I wasn't trying to steal from you, Alo'thi."

"I don't care." Another burst of light cracked against the alley wall beside the hooded magical's head. "Do not let me see you again."

The door slammed shut with a clang, and the magical peeled himself off the alley wall before staggering into the street. The edge of a clenched jaw and a wrinkled nose covered in mottled pink-and-gray flesh poked out of the darkness of the magical's hood. He stopped beside Maleshi and waved at the alley. "You told me she wouldn't be a problem."

"She's not." The general smiled down at him. "Looks like the problem was you."

"That's ridiculous. Why would I—" The magical stopped and turned slowly to face Cheyenne and Ember, though his black hood still obscured most of his face. "You."

Cheyenne and Ember exchanged glances, then the halfling shrugged. "Me. And you are?"

"This is Mirl." Maleshi gestured at the magical and dipped her head. "An old friend."

"You do like to mince words, don't you?"

"Oh, come on. Don't tell me there isn't something like friendship buried deep down in there beneath all the rest."

Mirl snorted within the darkness of the hood and indicated Ember with a crooked pink-and-gray splotched hand poking out from the folds of his cloak. "Who's the fae?"

"Ember." The girl dipped her head to get a better look beneath the hood. "Sorry, it's kinda hard to meet someone when you can't see their face."

"Yeah, tell me about it." Mirl whipped the hood back to reveal himself, cocking his head to the side and flashing a grin displaying stunted, brown-stained teeth in Ember's general direction.

Cheyenne tried to keep a straight face. *Dude looks like a pig and a baby mouse all smooshed into one.*

Mirl's filmy white eyes stared at nothing, his head tilting from side to side as he leaned closer to Ember. "But you can see me now, can't you?"

"Yeah." Ember blinked quickly. "Nice to meet you."

"Uh-huh. Nobody says that to me and means it." He jerked the hood back over his head until only his mottled jaw and the bottom of his grotesque snout were visible. "So, can we get moving on this, General, or do I have to force you into something neither of us wants?"

"You can try," Maleshi replied, "I'd like to see that very much."

"Well, now I'm out of ideas. No thanks to you."

The general stared at him and didn't say a thing until Mirl started tittering inside the darkness of his hood.

"What are you guys up to?" Cheyenne asked.

Maleshi looked away from her old friend and blinked at the halfling. "That's none of your business, kid. What are *you* doing?"

Cheyenne snorted. "Wondering how that's not a hypocritical question."

"Venga sent us out on a shopping spree." Ember patted her pocket. "On his dime."

"Hmm." Maleshi glanced at Mirl, who fumbled with something beneath the folds of his cloak and muttered unintelligibly. "Any progress?"

She doesn't wanna talk about it in front of this guy. Who the hell is he? Cheyenne and Ember shared a knowing glance. "Kind of."

Ember scoffed and folded her arms. "Progress in making me want to wring his scaly neck."

Maleshi chuckled. "You're not the first to feel that way about the necromancer, Ember. I'm sure you won't be the last."

"But I might be the one who does it. Now he says he needs flesh-setter hide for whatever he's trying next."

"Ah. That's interesting."

Cheyenne forced herself to look up from the cloaked Mirl, who was intermittently grunting and hitting himself on the side of the head. "Why?"

The general let out a wry chuckle. "Because I have absolutely no idea what it's for."

"Any idea where we can get it?" Cheyenne looked quickly at Mirl when he shouted and furiously banged the heel of his palm against his temple, making himself stagger away from the general.

Ember's eyes widened. "Are you okay?"

"Who are you talking to?" Mirl growled.

Maleshi clasped her hands behind her back again and looked at the pale sky. "That would be you, *radag*."

With a final blow to his head, Mirl hurled himself sideways. Pink light burst from the side of his hood, followed by two small, glinting golden orbs buzzing through the air. His short, stubby fingers tipped in gray claws moved incredibly fast to snatch the orbs from the air, and they disappeared into the folds of his cloak. Mirl vigorously rubbed the side of his hood where his ear would be and shook his head. "These fell-damn things. Now don't get me wrong. I'm as much a fan of a good time as the next magical, it's the tickling I can't stand."

"The tickling?" Ember wrinkled her nose. "You know, I don't even wanna know."

"Suit yourself." Mirl hocked up a noisy ball of phlegm and spat across the avenue. "Messes with my sinuses too."

"No kidding." Cheyenne grimaced and looked at Maleshi.

The general chuckled. "Maybe Mirl can help."

Ember forced herself not to look at the thick, splattered gob five feet away from the cloaked magical and swallowed. "Nope. I think he's helped enough."

Mirl thrust a stubby finger in the air, his squashed mouth opening in another stained, reeking grin. "Do *you* know where to find the best flesh-setter hide in Hangivol? Or any flesh-setter hide, now that I think about it."

Cheyenne shrugged. "Guess you got us between a rock and a hard place, man."

"Eh?" The magical cocked his head toward her, his bright-pink tongue hanging halfway out of his mouth in concentration.

"Never mind."

"Go ahead and take 'em." Maleshi clapped a hand on the guy's cloaked shoulder. "I don't think the drow here are going to appreciate you soiling their streets in the middle of the morning."

"I'll soil whatever I want, thank you very much."

"I'll meet you outside the Heart when you're finished."

"You're gonna sit there all day and wait for me, are you?"

The general smiled. "I would never. But I do know how long it takes you to get down to the lower levels and back up again."

"Pah. You think I'm so predictable." Mirl turned and hurried away down the avenue, waving for Cheyenne and Ember to follow. "Keep up, you two. Once we get below, I might not be able to hear you if you fall behind."

"Wait." Ember looked at Maleshi. "You're sending us with him?"

"You can do whatever you want. I hooked you up with an excellent guide."

"And I'm shit at picking faces out of a crowd!" Mirl let out a shrieking cackle, doubling over as he moved and shaking his head beneath the dark hood.

"Have fun." Maleshi wiggled her fingers at them and headed toward the fortress. "Try not to spend all your *veréle* in one place."

"Not ours." Ember patted her pocket again and floated slowly after Mirl. "Venga's."

"Oh." Turning around to dip her head at Cheyenne, the general gave her a small smile and widened her silver eyes. "Then never mind."

She didn't look at them a second time before disappearing inside the outer walls of the fortress, which were starting to take on the lighter hues of the interior.

"Come on, Em." Cheyenne nodded at the magical scuttling quickly down the avenue. The drow coming out of their homes and storefronts at the end of a very quiet morning in Hangivol glared at Mirl, some even stepping back inside and shutting their doors again to keep him out.

"I'm usually not very picky," Ember muttered, "but I'm not sure I'm a fan of that guy as a guide."

"Most magicals aren't," Mirl called, startling them both because he heard their conversation yards behind him. "But if you don't wanna get lost or kidnapped or mugged or drugged in the darkseller bazaar, your best bet is to follow someone who looks like me. Heh. Or so I'm told."

He disappeared around the corner into another alley, and Ember frowned. "He's blind, right?"

"That's what it seems like, yeah."

"So how did he know I'm fae?"

Cheyenne said, "Same way everyone knew you were fae before you looked like one."

Ember grimaced and lowered her voice. "He can fucking smell me too?"

"I think he did the same with me."

"Yeah, but he didn't call you 'drow.' Just 'you.'"

"Good point. That'd make it sound like recognition even if it wasn't." Cheyenne tried to hold back a laugh. "Maybe he knew it was me because I'm the only drow who would be hanging out with a fae."

"Ew." Ember shivered. "I don't like that he can smell me."

They rounded the corner and found Mirl waiting for them at the end of the short alley with a mottled hand pressed to the wall. "You're gonna have to grow a stronger stomach if you wanna make it out of the bazaar in one piece, fae. The darksellers can smell fear too, I swear. It's how they fund their trade."

His fingers crawled along the wall like thick, hairless caterpillars as he tilted his head up toward the sky. The hood fell back a little more to reveal the rest of his wrinkled snout and one filmy white eye staring blankly at nothing.

"Ah. Every time, am I right?" He swiped quickly along the wall in three different directions, and a new doorway opened to reveal a tunnel heading down toward the lower levels. "You have maybe thirty seconds before this closes. Don't be dumb."

Then he took off into the tunnel, his shuffling gait echoing behind him.

Ember closed her eyes, then floated through the doorway behind him. Cheyenne glanced back at the mouth of the alley, which was fortunately empty. *No one's gonna be spying on the* radag *they all wanna stay away from. Won't* this *be fun?*

"Hey, by the way," Ember whispered, though they were both sure Mirl could hear them in the silence of the tunnel, "what's a darkseller bazaar?"

"O'gúleesh black market, Em."

"I should've handed you Venga's money case and stuck with Maleshi."

"You'll be fine. No one's gonna mess with us."

"But I wouldn't be surprised if they tried," Mirl called over his shoulder. "Lotta magicals willing to pay a claw and a tentacle to get either on fresh fae blood. Almost as much as they'd cough up to find a nightstalker in their greedy little grasps." He cackled again, occasionally reaching out to brush a hand against the tunnel wall.

Ember pressed her lips together. "And that right there is why Maleshi sent us off with him alone."

"We'll be in and out of there with the flesh-setter hide in no time, Em."

"Uh-huh. Hopefully, with all our internal organs intact."

Cheyenne snorted. "Fingers crossed."

CHAPTER SEVENTEEN

irl led them down two more tunnels, both of which they accessed through back alleys with only the occasional curse spat his way. The magicals who recognized him stared in disbelief when they also recognized the Black Flame of Ambar'ogúl and her fae *Nós Aní* traveling with the unsavory *radag*. Those who didn't recognize him recognized Cheyenne, if not Ember, and chose to stay away just the same.

At least no one's groveling at my feet. Maybe we should keep the guy around all the time.

By the time they reached the lower level of the capital, the place was bustling with its usual crowds of lower-class magicals going about their day after last night's raucous party. Most of them looked about as rough as Cheyenne expected. A small number of them thumped fists on chests when they saw her, but no one had enough time to even consider speaking to her before Mirl ducked down a dirtier, grittier alley and somehow managed to open a new doorway in the metal walls he couldn't see.

"How does he know?"

"Normally, I'd have no idea." Cheyenne didn't bother to turn around and see who was watching them this time before following Mirl through another secret tunnel. "But I'm guessing it's the same way you can get up and move around without walking."

"Oh, I see." Ember folded her arms and shot her friend a sidelong glance as the wall closed behind them. "All disabilities are the same on this side because we all have magic, huh?"

"I mean, I didn't say that."

"But you were thinking it."

"Okay, sorry. It was the first answer that came to mind."

"Well, you know what?" Ember cocked her head and wrinkled her nose. "You might be right about that."

"Quit the chitchat, young'uns." Mirl stopped at the newest tunnel's dead-end and turned to face them, pulling back his hood one more time with a grin. "If you talk too much, somebody's gonna end up using it against you."

"Shut up and follow you, huh?" Ember nodded. "Got it."

"I didn't say that. You *don't* talk, and those necrotic parasites will have you eating right outta their hands."

Ember shook her head when Cheyenne frowned at her in concern.

"So stay close, huh?" Mirl twisted his hand on the blank wall in front of him. "And don't touch anything, or you'll end up looking like me."

He cackled and stepped back as the wall unfolded into an incredibly narrow doorway. Thick white smoke trailed out of it from the space beyond, and Cheyenne and Ember hurried to catch up with their guide as he disappeared through the smog.

The darkseller bazaar seemed as crowded as the public marketplace on the lower level, though there was a lot less shouting and brawling and haggling and a lot more brooding.

Cheyenne glanced at a troll woman with such dark purple skin she could have passed for a drow if it weren't for the scarlet hair and eyes. The troll stared right back at her, not bothering to look down at her work as she scraped a wickedly sharp curved blade against a whetstone with a thick, repetitive motion. Behind her hung a string of what looked like a butcher's inventory until Cheyenne realized the stringy parts dangling from the bottom was scarlet hair trailing from dangling troll heads.

Still a butcher, I guess. I seriously hope they were dead before she added them to that collection.

The thick smoke cleared away past the first few tables and booths, and it was easy to keep an eye on Mirl's cloaked figure ahead of them and take a quick look around at the same time.

The smoke, as it turned out, came from a massive Goldsmile den on their right, where a metal fan whirled incessantly and pumped the haze out of the shop and into the far end of the bazaar. Someone inside cackled, and Cheyenne caught a glimpse of narrowed eyes in various colors glowing through the fog.

"A trinket for your mother, drow?" An old skaxen with dull brown-orange skin drooping in folds off his frame lurched away from his table to approach her. "Made from the bones of the giant *ulundo.*"

Cheyenne glanced at the dangling loops of a necklace the skaxen presented to her, made of bones with a few bits of flesh and hair still dangling from them, and pretended to consider the offer. "Nope. My mother would strangle me in my sleep before she thanked me for a gift like that."

The skaxen chuckled, and they saw that all but one of his short, pointy teeth was missing. "Sounds like a drow after my own heart."

"Yeah, good luck." She stepped past the end of his table without turning back and shook her head.

"Okay." Ember nudged her friend's arm and leaned toward her. "While you're yucking it up about your mom with the creeper back there, I'm starting to feel like this was a really, really bad idea."

"What?"

"Ten o'clock. Three o'clock. One o'clock. Shit, Cheyenne. Every fucking o'clock."

Cheyenne cast quick glances at the long metal tables and storefronts built into the walls of the bazaar. *Guess I know which part of the city Peridosh was modeled after.*

Gnarled, hunched, unwashed, sneering magicals huddled in dark recesses and in dimly lit doorways, staring not at Cheyenne but at the fae floating alongside her. A magical with black and red skin and short brown horns protruding from his bald head chuckled when they passed. A black tongue darted out of his grinning mouth to lick his fingers, which were covered in a rust-colored substance like mud, then he lifted his fingers to his horns and stared unblinkingly at Ember.

"Gross. Creepy. It stinks down here." Ember eyed a magical of indeterminate gender who looked like a giant walking-stick bug, cringing as it pried thick gray fingernails from someone else's severed fingers one at a time and tossed them into a metal tin. "And I'm starting to think I might be claustrophobic."

"Don't go there, Em. Just keep moving, and keep your eyes to yourself, huh?"

"And look where? At the back of Mirl's head?"

"I mean, it's not a pretty picture, but at least it's not looking at you like you're on the magical auction block."

"Christ."

Mirl stopped abruptly, cocked his head upward to sniff the air, then pointed at the shop to his left. "There you go."

The girls stopped behind him, and Ember swallowed. "Those are bones."

"Better than hanging a bell on the door, eh?" Mirl tittered. "You can find your way back out. I have other business to take care of down here, but you didn't hear that from me." He hobbled away from them, then stopped again and shot them another wide grin. "And don't go searching around all wide-eyed for someone to help you. That's like blood in the water. R'leer'll come to you when he's ready."

"How long does that usually take?" Ember asked, her voice coming out in a hoarse whisper.

"As long as he wants." Mirl pointed at her, though his stubby clawed finger aimed more toward her thigh, and snickered before bustling away and disappearing into the eerily quiet crowd.

"You know what?" Ember swallowed thickly. "I prefer fighting back the blight at your mom's house to this."

"Shouldn't take nearly as much effort, though."

"Shouldn't it? Great."

Cheyenne nodded at the curtain of bones strung on thin metal wires hanging from the shop's doorway. They rustled and clacked as she brushed them aside to duck through the door. *Sounds like voices.*

"Oh, fuck." Ember batted the bone strands aside with both hands like she'd walked through a cobweb and spun to glare at them. "They talk."

"You heard it too, huh?" Cheyenne gazed around the shop and found four other magicals staring at her from various dark recesses behind stuffed shelves and through another string of bones and dried flowers dangling from the ceiling.

"I am not down for this."

"Keep it together, Em." Cheyenne leaned toward her friend and whispered, "They're watching us, and I don't wanna start anything down here."

Ember stiffened, her violet eyes widening even more than usual. "Are you telling me you're freaked out too? 'Cause we can leave."

"I'm kinda diggin' the vibe."

The fae girl blanched a light, washed-out shade of pink. "You're kidding."

"I said kinda. I wanna see what's up in this place, okay? Mirl said this R'leer guy would come to us, so let's take a look around and pretend we know what we're doing."

"Easy for you to say." A small shiver ran down Ember's back, but she stopped it halfway down and pulled herself together. "I should've known this was your jam."

"If they're not hurting somebody for no reason, then yeah, maybe it is." Cheyenne widened her eyes at her friend, then turned to stroll casually down the row of shelves lining the wall beside the door.

Ember's gaze darted around, barely touching the growing number of creepy magicals emerging from the shop's shadows, and floated quickly after the halfling.

The farther they made their way into the shop, the stranger the items became. Shrunken heads and three-foot wings pried off some unknown creature with bits of flesh and feathers still attached, others with dried-out gossamer membranes that had lost their sheen. Tails and eyes and unrecognizable body parts floating in jars of amber liquid, moving on their own. A metal tub of small black tiles carved with O'gúleesh runes that morphed in and out of faces and whispered to the darkness like the strings of bones in the doorway.

Cheyenne did a double-take at these and raised an eyebrow. *Those are bones. Cool.*

She kept walking with Ember close behind her, ignoring the stares she could feel on her skin like fingers and tried to look for anything in here she could pick up with the activator. Two thin lines of code scrolled across the tops of the walls, but they were only to keep the shop intact, telling her the place stretched farther back into the walls of Hangivol's undercity than she could see from here. That was it.

Guess advanced tech and super-dark magic don't have a lot in common. Good to know.

A bird with maroon and scarlet feathers hung from the ceiling by a thin wire wrapped around its neck. Ember grimaced as she peered up at it. "I wonder how long these things keep in a place like this?"

"It could literally be forever," Cheyenne muttered.

Ember reached slowly toward the bird. "Yeah, but why would—"

The bird's wings darted away from its dangling body, its eyes popping open before rolling back in its head. A strangled croak spilled from its sharp black beak, which opened and snapped shut.

"Jesus." Ember jerked her hand away and stared in horror at the creature, which was now spinning slowly as it hung. The thing's wings were tucked against its body again, and it closed its eyes when its sharp-taloned legs finally stopped twitching. "This totally counts as hurting someone for no reason."

"Em, Mirl said not to touch anything."

"Screw what he said. This thing's alive." Ember reached toward the bird again with both hands, and the thing let out another strangled squawk as it kicked and flapped its wings.

"If you touch that starjaw, I'll have to charge you for it."

Both girls jumped at the slow, calm voice right behind them and spun around.

A drow man who looked to be around Cheyenne's age, if she'd aged like full-blooded drow set his fingers gently on the counter serving as a center display island and glanced up at the fluttering bird dangling by its neck. "And somehow, I doubt a fae has any use for a starjaw's many properties."

Ember's mouth opened and closed as she stared at the bird continuously strangling itself. "It's still alive."

"Of course it is." The drow man's white eyebrows flickered briefly toward his hairline and the wreath of tiny bones, stringy feathers, and metal beads encircling his head. He whistled sharply, and a massive shape moved toward them from the other side of the shop.

When the giant ogre woman's scowling features came into view, Ember raised both hands and floated backward to bump against the center counter. "Hey, I didn't touch anything, okay? You don't have to get aggressive about it."

The ogre woman reached toward the struggling bird and gripped its black talons in one meaty hand while stroking her finger down the creature's feathered breast. It fell still with a shuddering coo and could have passed for a dead bird once more. With a grunt, the ogre looked down at Ember and put a hand to her throat. "It calms her. Don't touch."

Ember stared after the ogre woman lumbering away into the shadows, her mouth open in shock. "Strangling? Strangling calms the bird?"

"Starjaws have an attitude when they're not handled appropriately." The drow man cocked his head, strands of bones and beads clacking as they fell over his shoulder with his long white hair and eyed the still bird one more time. "Gyla has a gentle touch when it counts."

"I don't even…" Ember put a hand to her throat and swallowed. "This place."

The drow man turned his gaze to Cheyenne and looked her slowly up and down. His golden eyes blazed in contrast with the dark kohl smeared across his eyelids and beneath his lower lashes, and a line of white paint ran down the center of both his dark-gray lips. "I don't imagine you do, though."

Cheyenne snorted. "Excuse me?"

"Have a gentle touch." He bit his bottom lip, and the white paint stayed where it was. "I prefer something a little rougher."

Okay, am I imagining it, or is the drow Captain Jack Sparrow coming onto me right now? Cheyenne eyed him sideways. "Look, whatever you're trying to do, it's not gonna work."

He tilted his head to the other side, his gaze roaming all over her face. "What am I trying to do?"

She narrowed her eyes at him. "I have no idea, or I'd make you cut it out."

"Too bad. I would have enjoyed that."

Despite the weirdness of his gaze on her, Cheyenne couldn't help a tiny smirk. *Lamest pickup lines ever, but he's not even smiling. Can't say I'm not a little into it.*

"Uh-huh." She looked him over in turn and jerked her chin at him as she turned away. "We have browsing to do."

"What do you seek?" He glanced quickly at Ember, who'd watched the entire interaction with a grimace of disgust.

"We can find it ourselves, thanks." Cheyenne raised her eyebrows and stepped past him, looking at the piles of darkseller oddities without a single clue as to what any of it was. *Don't touch anything, and don't ask for help. I've screwed up enough times to know not to go against advice like that.*

"Or you could accept my assistance when I give it." The drow man turned slowly after her but stayed where he was. "And perhaps a lowered price. Depending on what it is, of course."

Ember blinked. "This is your shop."

"Occasionally." He tapped his fingers on the center counter and turned his head toward the fae girl, though his eyes never left Cheyenne, even as she kept her back turned to him. "R'leer."

Cheyenne thought, *Look at that.*

"Well." She turned back to him and folded her arms. "Where's your flesh-setter hide, then?"

R'leer moved slowly toward her, the bone strings swaying with his hair and clacking against the rings of metal and leather wrapped around his throat. He stopped inches in front of Cheyenne and leaned toward her, staring at her lips. He reached around her, barely brushing her folded arms, and felt through the items on the counter behind her before slowly lifting a coil of something between them.

Cheyenne raised an eyebrow. "I need two."

The drow man's eyes narrowed slightly, and he invaded her personal space one more time to retrieve a second. Then he held both coils between them and took a long, slow inhale.

Dude's all up in my bubble, staring at me and smelling me like Neros did, and I'm okay with it. What the fuck is happening right now?

"Anything else?" R'leer whispered.

"No." The corner of her mouth twitched. "That's it."

"Forty-five *veréle* for both." He finally stepped back to look her up and down again. "Normally, I charge thirty for just the one."

"Gotta love a half-off sale." *For the first time, someone's making me pay for magical ingredients. If he knows who I am, he doesn't give a shit.*

Behind the weirdly intriguing drow shop-owner, Ember snorted and tried to cover it with a forced cough. R'leer tilted his head at Cheyenne and waited for her to hand over the payment.

She couldn't look away from the golden eyes locked on hers. *Or maybe I don't want to.* "Em."

"Huh? Yeah?"

"You have the *veréle.*"

"Right." Ember pulled Venga's *veréle* case out of her pocket and struggled again to open the latch.

R'leer turned slowly away from Cheyenne to study the fae, tilting the two coils of flesh-setter hide up and down in his hand.

"Need some help?" Cheyenne asked.

"No, Cheyenne." The case popped open. "I got it." Ember squinted at the thin cards of O'gúleesh money and let her activator translate the runes so she knew how much to pull out. "Okay. He said forty-five?"

"I did." R'leer turned to eye Cheyenne again, biting down one more time on his bottom lip.

Could be a tattoo. You never know over here. Cheyenne studied the drow man's morbid headdress and the swooping strands of bones and multiple leather-like loose collars around his neck. When she glanced at the flesh-setter hide in his hand, she almost cracked a smile at his black-painted nails. *Well, look at that.*

"Here you go." Ember floated awkwardly forward and thrust a handful of the plastic-looking *veréle* toward R'leer. "Forty-five."

He didn't look away from Cheyenne but held out his other hand. As his fingers closed slowly around the stack, he handed the flesh-setter hides to Cheyenne and tilted his head. She'd seen that look before the day she'd met L'zar face to face, her drow-thief father behind bars and her shoulder burning from the unhealing wound of a skaxen dipshit's black-magic sludge.

Like a hungry dog looking at a steak. Big difference between what L'zar wanted from me and what I bet this drow would do.

She took the coils of flesh-setter hide, lifted them in front of her, and dipped her head. "Thanks."

"Any time. I'll see you soon."

Those words broke the tension, and Cheyenne gave a wry laugh. "Yeah, we'll see."

She stepped past him, holding his gaze until he was behind her. "Come on, Em. Time to go."

"Uh-huh." Ember glanced between her friend and the creepy drow man staring after Cheyenne like she was a rare item he could acquire and put on display in his darkseller shop. She shoved the *veréle* case back into her pocket and turned to follow the halfling toward the door. When she glanced over her shoulder one last time, he was still there, the fingertips of one hand pressed lightly on the center countertop. R'leer widened his eyes at her, and she slapped at the curtain of strung bones to hurry through them after Cheyenne.

R'leer turned his head toward where the drow woman Cheyenne had stood against his shelves and sniffed the air. *In my shop. Interesting.*

He waited beside the center counter piled high with displays of rare and in some cities illegal items he'd procured over the last three hundred years in case she decided to return. She didn't, and after a quick scan of the dark windows lining the front of his shop, R'leer headed toward one of the darker recesses in the back.

The magicals he employed to keep the place running for him and who dealt with the unsavory clients he didn't want dirtying his hands met his gaze and nodded as he passed. Gyla grunted and lowered herself onto the worn, ratty fabric of the armchair that had become something of a throne for the ogre woman in this establishment. She closed her eyes and didn't say a word as R'leer passed her and turned into a dark, smoke-filled alcove.

Sitting on a pile of rank, dusty pillows, the Oracle crone Ur'syth puffed on a pipe hose, the other end of it attached to a burning bowl of Goldsmile R'leer had personally acquired for her. The crone's black-painted face scrunched in on itself as she looked at him, then she blew a stream of thick white smoke and nodded toward the front of the shop.

"You know who she is, Darkchild?"

R'leer nodded and turned to lean against the outer wall of the alcove beside the crone's hiding place. "L'zar's daughter."

Ur'syth took another long drag from the pipe, then turned her wrinkled face to the ceiling and opened her blood-red mouth. She puffed four bursts of smoke into the air above her, which coalesced a four-pointed star rising to the ceiling before the shape disappeared.

"Stay away from that one." White smoke puffed around the crone's toothless gums, filtering out of her wrinkled, black-painted lips as she spoke. "She's got the Weave all over her and can't even see it."

R'leer glanced briefly down at the burning dish of Goldsmile nestled in the Oracle's lap. Then he returned his gaze to the front of his shop to scan the passing shapes of Hangivol's more darkly inclined magicals passing by in the narrow avenue of the bazaar. "I know."

CHAPTER EIGHTEEN

Cheyenne and Ember hurried out of the bazaar. The wall beside the Goldsmile den emitting puffs of hazy white smoke unfolded at a wave of the halfling's hand, then they were in the tunnel again. The low murmur of the darksellers inviting O'gúleesh into their shops of black magic and macabre supplies cut off as soon as the door sealed behind them, and Cheyenne burst out laughing.

Ember stared at her with wide eyes. "I don't get it."

"Don't get what, Em?" The halfling's activator lit the shortest path through the city's lower levels and back to the fortress since she knew where she wanted to go. She stuck the flesh-setter hides in her coat pocket and stared straight ahead.

"Whatever that was." Now that they were out of the bazaar, Ember finally loosened up and cracked a smile. "I mean, I get it. Everyone's intrigued by the ex-Crown Black Flame, but come on. That drow took it way too far."

"He didn't do anything."

"Oh, but he wanted to." Ember laughed. "And you didn't do shit to stop him."

"Nothing to stop, Em."

"Uh-huh." The fae folded her arms and followed her friend to the first turn in the tunnel. "Or maybe you didn't want to stop him."

"Whatever."

"Oh, my God. Cheyenne Summerlin has a crush on a bone drow dressed up like some kind of witch doctor."

Cheyenne cast her friend a sidelong glance, trying to look annoyed, but a tiny smile crept through. "Okay. You have to admit all the bones were weirdly hot."

"No." Laughing again in surprise, Ember shook her head. "No, I don't have to. You do. The guy was wearing makeup, Cheyenne."

"So?"

"And he got all up in your personal space. You stood there staring at him, and I thought the world was ending."

Cheyenne scoffed. "What?"

"Look, if anyone else had looked at you like that and practically pressed you up against a counter, you would've splattered their brains all over the wall."

"Whoa. Jeeze. To be clear, I've never splattered anyone's brains anywhere."

Ember pointed at her. "Not for lack of trying, right?"

Cheyenne shook her head but couldn't wipe the smile off her face. "We needed the flesh-setter hide. That's it. I wasn't about to jeopardize that because one drow got a little too close."

"One creepy-hot drow. Your words, not mine."

"I said, 'weirdly,' Em."

"Yeah, well, he creeped me the fuck out. So did you, playing right into his dark vibe."

"I didn't play into anything except for getting what Venga sent us to get. That's it."

"Uh-huh." Ember looked her friend up and down and chuckled. "It's totally fine, Cheyenne. Just admit it. You went all melty for a drow darkseller wrapped in bones and feathers."

"Going melty, whatever the hell that's supposed to mean, isn't on my priority list right now." Cheyenne stuck her hands in her pockets and ran her fingers over the coils of flesh-setter hide. "He got my attention, that's it. And now we're out here."

Ember narrowed her eyes as she stared at the halfling's profile. "You're thinking about going back, aren't you?"

"Come on. You're making way too big a deal out of this."

"No, I don't think I am. Hey." The fae grabbed Cheyenne's shoulder, and they stopped in the empty, dimly lit tunnel. "Promise me you won't go back there by yourself to flirt with the bone drow."

"That wasn't flirting."

"Right. Like you know anything about how drow flirt." Ember's crooked smile grew, then quickly faded again. "I'm serious. Promise?"

"Yeah, Em."

"Say it."

"I promise." *I won't go back there to flirt with R'leer. But if I happen to need something else only a darkseller with my kinda style has in his shop...* Cheyenne nodded at the end of the tunnel. "Now, can we drop this and get back to the necromancer? We're not gonna heal the blight by standing here philosophizing about drow courting rituals, okay?"

Ember barked a laugh and took her hand off Cheyenne's shoulder and they continued up the tunnel. "You say that like we're talking about exotic birds, or…" She swallowed thickly. "Fuck. That bird."

"He had some weird shit in there, that's for sure."

"What kind of living thing calms down by being strung up with a wire around its neck?"

"A starjaw, apparently." Cheyenne shrugged. "I mean, I kinda get it."

Ember choked in surprise and stared at her friend. "Please don't tell me you're into the whole strangulation thing. I don't think I could handle that."

"No! I'm just saying everybody has their own thing. Like for me, I'm in my happy place when I'm either hacking into a system that doesn't want me there or bashing loyalist faces in trying to get their shit off the streets. It's all relative."

"Different strokes. Is that what you're saying?"

"Yeah. And that bird just wants to be hung by the neck and stroked down its belly."

They both laughed, and Cheyenne's activator lit a doorway on their left for a potential shortcut from the lower level toward the center of the city.

"This way."

"Right into the wall, huh?"

"Come on, Em." Cheyenne flicked her fingers at the illuminated code on the wall, and it rearranged itself to open onto an ascending staircase. "That shouldn't surprise you by now."

Ember studied the open doorway even as the halfling stepped through to climb the stairs. "It does when I still can't see half the damn doors before you open them."

"Well, then hurry up before it closes."

With a jolt, Ember floated quickly up the stairs, slipping through the doorway before it folded back into place and sealed up without a trace behind her.

They made quick time back up through the city toward the Crown's fortress. Most of the passages lit by Cheyenne's activator were empty, though they passed two different groups of magicals huddling in the dark recesses for private conversations and transactions they didn't want anyone to see. Some of them thumped fists to chests when they recognized the Black Flame, but no one said anything.

Cheyenne wouldn't have noticed anyway. She was too busy thinking about R'leer and the way he'd looked at her. What he'd said.

"I don't imagine you do, though. Have a gentle touch. I prefer something a little rougher."

The next tunnel let them out in a different alley between high buildings in the inner circle, and Cheyenne ran a hand through her hair, ignoring the stares and knowing smiles cast her way by Hangivol's resident drow. *Flirting or not, R'leer was after something. It's one thing to make a sale. That's his job, and I'd bet everything I have that he knows who I am and that I wasn't the Crown for more than twenty minutes. So if he's not going after the power I don't really have, what the hell does he want? What else does he know?*

She moved on autopilot through the twisting halls of the fortress, vaguely aware that Ember was talking to her. R'leer's gaze and the way he'd studied her took up the forefront of her mind and wouldn't leave her alone.

"Hey. Hello?" Ember stopped and stuck her hands on her hips. "Cheyenne."

"What?" Blinking, the halfling glanced around and found her friend six feet behind her. "What's up?"

"Have you been off in your own world this whole time?"

She shrugged with a small, sheepish smile. "Maybe."

"Yeah, I could tell."

"Sorry, Em. Just turning over a bunch of stuff, you know?"

"Uh-huh." Ember pointed at the doors into Venga's lab at the end of the hall. "Think you can get your head back in the game before we head into the necromancer's lair again?"

"Lair." Cheyenne snorted, then wiped the smile off her face and nodded. "Yep. I'm good. We're in blight-healing mode."

"Okay, good." Ember glanced at her as she floated past and pointed to her own mouth. "You're drooling a little, by the way."

"What? No, I'm not." Cheyenne quickly wiped the corner of her mouth, but there was nothing there. Her friend's laughter echoed down the corridor. "Yeah, very funny."

"Just trying to keep you on your toes." Ember waited for the halfling to join her, then they pushed open the doors and stepped inside.

Venga hovered over the same workbench on the left-hand wall as if they hadn't left. He didn't turn to look at them as he mixed and poured with two hands and cast a long, complicated spell with a third. He reached his fourth hand toward the girls and grunted. "Do tell me you returned with what I asked for."

"Yep." Ember handed the necromancer's *veréle* case to Cheyenne, and the halfling stepped forward to place that and the two coils of flesh-setter hide into Venga's open palm.

He stopped working and stepped away from the table, thrusting the case back into his jacket pocket as he studied the flesh-setter hide. "Hmm."

"What's wrong?" Cheyenne folded her arms. *If that drow handed me something I didn't ask for to get me to come back, I'm done playing nice.*

"Nothing." Venga slipped a sharp black claw beneath the copper coils wrapped around the first coil of flesh-setter hide and sliced neatly through them. "These are fresh. Far more potent than I expected."

The flesh-setter hide crumbled in his hand when he crushed it violently. A sharp, bitter tang filled the air, and Cheyenne wrinkled her nose. "That's a good thing, right?"

"It means you bought more than we needed. If this trial isn't successful, though I'm certain it will be, you won't have to return and waste any more of our time."

"Hey, we didn't waste anything," Ember said. "We were in and out of there."

"Of course." Venga sifted the handful of crushed hide in his hand into a large crucible in front of him. A thick bubbling sound filled the air, the stink of the flesh-setter hide intensified, and Cheyenne felt herself growing dizzy. The scaleback necromancer thrust a black claw at Cheyenne without turning away from his work. "But she would have loved to stay."

Ember barked a laugh and clapped a hand over her mouth. She shot her friend a quick glance and cleared her throat. "What makes you say that?"

"It's her nature."

"No." Cheyenne's nostrils flared, and she exhaled sharply against the stink of Venga's new concoction burning up her nose. "I might be related to both L'zar and Ba'rael, but I'm not into the dark shit. As far as magic's concerned, anyway."

Ember gave her friend a once-over.

"First you force me to defend my position with this room, now you're arguing against the very fabric of what makes you who you are," Venga hissed, his four arms darting out and in and pumping wildly as he grabbed ingredients and stirred and cast brief bursts of spells. "Must I explain your own heritage to you?"

Cheyenne folded her arms. "Whatever you think you know, my heritage doesn't include black magic."

Venga snorted and stepped aside to reach for another vial of a viscous yellow liquid from the shelf on his right. "How you got this far knowing as little as you do defies all logic."

"Yeah, I've been the exception to a lot of rules." Cheyenne frowned at him. "That doesn't include sitting back and letting someone else insult me."

"That was a compliment. Take it or leave it."

"I'll leave it, thanks."

The necromancer stopped his furious work and turned around to look her over. "Drow were the original darksellers, Cheyenne.

Purveyors of necessary goods too unsavory for the rest of us to dirty our hands with, not practitioners of dark magic."

"Oh." She rubbed a hand under her burning nose and shrugged. "So, you're telling me I should want to go back down there to play personal assistant with your shopping list?"

"More or less. I'm surprised you didn't take longer."

Ember's chuckle escaped through her nose even as she pressed her lips together. "Well, she wanted to."

Cheyenne flashed her a quick warning glance, then rolled her eyes and fought back another smile.

Venga cracked a thin metal tube against the edge of the workbench, splitting it neatly in half, then pulled the two ends apart and dumped tiny glistening silver beads into his concoction. Another burst of smoke ballooned from the crucible, flashing purple and black and green this time, and he stuck one end of the broken tube into the mixture, stirring and pulling it out to check it like an engine dipstick.

Cheyenne leaned sideways, attempting to look around the necromancer's bulky, scaley form. "What's the flesh-setter hide for?"

"I need silence. Surely you can appreciate the sentiment."

She frowned and exchanged confused glances with Ember. *What the hell's that supposed to mean?*

A hissing whisper filled the room as Venga cast an unintelligible spell. All four hands moved in different gestures, pulsing every few seconds with red and black light. Another puff of smoke rose from the crucible, followed by a loud, crackling groan like a lakebed freezing over. Then the necromancer fell silent and dipped his head toward his work. "Ah."

"Is that a good 'ah' or a bad 'ah?'" Ember asked.

He ignored her and grabbed what looked like a metal ladle from the shelf, though the bowl at the end of the handle was long and narrow with a lip at the end for precise pouring. His other hand snatched a round metal tin the size of a two-liter bottle cap, then he dipped the weird ladle into the crucible and poured the silver-green sludge into the tin. Silver sparks flew from the small, round piece of metal, but the substance settled quickly. Despite the necromancer's huge hands and the black claws at the tips of his fingers, he handled the tiny tin with delicate care and didn't spill a drop.

The ladle plunked back into the giant crucible, and Venga leaned down to blow lightly on the silver-green substance cooling rapidly in its new casing. He grunted and watched his creation intently, waving a brusque hand toward Cheyenne. "The black fire."

She frowned and drew her head back. "What about it?"

"Summon it, *hinya*."

"I mean, if you want to risk something happening to your—"

"Do it!" Venga's four shoulders hunched over the workbench. "We're running out of time."

"Yeah, okay. Jeeze. No pressure or anything." Shaking her head, Cheyenne closed her eyes and took a deep breath. *Not a fan of pulling up my single most destructive ability on command to humor a necromancer, but whatever. Here we go.*

She thought of the Nimlothar seed that had made itself a part of her and felt the pulse of her magic strengthen and flare to life. Though she was already in drow mode and had been for the last two days, the intensity of her magic jolted up the base of her spine, burning all the way up until she couldn't contain it any longer.

Black fire erupted, racing up her purple-gray hands and along her arms, neck, and chest. A halo of dark flames whipped around her bone-white hair, tongues of it flickering from the corners of her eyes and filling them with black light when she opened them. *If I have to stand here like this much longer, I'm gonna need a target for this.*

She gritted her teeth against the immense power racing through her. The black-lined wounds in her shoulders and hip burned fiercely.

"Whatever you're doing, make it quick." Her voice filled the lab in a dark, eerie growl in multiple tones as she stared at the far wall.

"That is the plan." Venga stepped toward her, his black eyes wide as he looked her over. Then he lunged at the halfling, drawing a muscular arm back before slapping his hand on the center of her chest.

Cheyenne stumbled backward. "What the fuck?"

"Hey!" Ember darted forward. "What the hell are you doing?"

The black fire racing across Cheyenne's body snuffed out on its own, and a pulse of agony spread from her chest where the necromancer had hit her. She screamed and doubled over, slapping her chest to find the metal bottlecap-sized tin stuck to her flesh. "Fuck! Get this fucking thing off me!"

She clawed at the tin, and a burst of heat unlike anything she'd experienced with her drow magic pulsed through her chest. Cheyenne staggered and dropped to one knee with another scream as she doubled over, forgetting her attempts to remove the device.

Ember raced toward her friend, but a crackling burst of blood-red magic seared through the air in front of her face and made her stop. She glared at Venga as Cheyenne screamed again. "Are you serious?"

"Wait." Though he pointed at her with a claw engulfed in another sparking crimson spell, his black eyes remained fixed on the halfling doubled over on the floor. "Just wait."

"Fuck you." Ember approached her friend, her legs and hands flashing with purple light as she knelt beside Cheyenne, her knees and shins still hovering an inch off the ground. "Cheyenne? Hey."

The small metal tin dislodged from the halfling's chest and pinged on the floor, wobbling as it rolled on its side, hit Venga's boot, and toppled over.

Cheyenne's knuckles pressed painfully into the stone floor to keep her from falling flat on her face, but she'd stopped screaming. Breathing heavily, she fought to gain control of her body again and swallowed. "I'm good, Em."

"Bullshit."

"Really." The halfling pushed to her feet, gratefully accepting Ember's help up when the fae grabbed her arm to steady her. Cheyenne looked down at her shirt and the disappearing wisps of smoke coming from the perfectly round hole burned through the fabric. The skin beneath was a darker shade of her purple-gray flesh, but that faded quickly into its normal color. "Well, this shirt's fucked."

Ember gave a sigh of relief. "It kind of already was. You sure you're okay?"

"No, but I don't feel like I'm getting cut open anymore, so there's that." Cheyenne lifted her glowing golden eyes to Venga's face and sneered at him. "Low blow, necromancer."

"I could have gone much lower." He kicked aside the empty metal tin, sending it clattering across the room. "But the chest is a good place to start."

Ember whirled toward him, her fists clenched at her sides. "You can't just slap a whatever-the-fuck-that-was onto someone without their permission or even a goddamn warning!"

"I just did." Venga's four hands opened and closed in anticipation as he stared at Cheyenne's chest.

Cheyenne rubbed her chest, then her hand moved absently to her shoulder to scratch the burning itch there. "Doesn't make it okay, asshole. Do that again, and I don't give a shit how much you know about the blight."

"It doesn't matter now, does it?" Venga pointed at her shoulder, where her unconscious itching had pulled down the shredded fabric of her shirt to reveal the unhealed wound there. "Look."

Cheyenne stopped itching and glanced quickly down at her shoulder. The black streaks kept at bay by the darktongue serum faded rapidly, shrinking back into themselves toward the crusted edge of the wound that still wouldn't close up. She quickly pulled down the other side of her shirt to find the same thing on the opposite shoulder.

"Oh, my God." Ember's eyes widened, and she nodded at Cheyenne's hip.

"Yeah." Cheyenne jerked down the waistband of her pants, hiking up her shirt to get a good look at the last of the black streaks disappearing from the perfectly round hole there too. "Damn. It worked."

Venga spread all four arms and dipped his scaly head, exposing his sharp teeth in a leering grin. "A success, one might call it."

"Sure." Cheyenne dropped her shirt and hiked up her pants. "Thanks, I guess. For the healing. Not the rest of it."

"My pleasure, Cheyenne."

"So, this is it, then." Ember stopped staring at the slowly closing wounds through Cheyenne's shirt and looked at the necromancer. "We found the antidote, at least the one that works for Cheyenne, right?"

"I told you what healed the Black Flame would also heal this world, did I not?" Venga turned toward his workbench again and fiddled with the rest of the silver-green sludge in the large crucible.

Cheyenne's mouth went dry, and she drew her tongue between her upper lip and her teeth, trying to get everything unstuck.

"And we did not find anything," Venga continued with a dismissive wave. "I will credit you with procuring the flesh-setter hide, but let us not forget who engineered this so-called antidote."

"Oh, sure. That's what you're the most concerned about, huh?" Ember glanced at Cheyenne and shook her head. "Taking credit."

Cheyenne's gaze dropped to the floor, and she blinked against the shifting, undulating lines of code in her vision. *They're not supposed to move like that.*

"We will heal Ambar'ogúl at its core, Ember. I worked for Ba'rael in good faith, and she betrayed me and my reputation. I wish to clear my name."

"I didn't think necromancers could clear their names. Death magic and all."

"Death and life are two sides of the same coin, fae. Perhaps you will realize this as your experience increases."

Wiping sweat from her forehead with the back of her forearm, Cheyenne said, "Something's wrong."

"What?"

"It will pass." Venga waved them both off and kept working, though his urgency had faded and his hands now moved slower. "Healing takes its toll, just as destruction does."

"No, I mean something's really wrong." Cheyenne lurched forward, her vision swimming. A tight, burning knot of nausea clenched in her stomach.

"Hey, what's going on?" Ember asked, leaning forward to meet her friend's gaze as she set a hand on Cheyenne's upper back.

Cheyenne heaved and stumbled forward, not sure where the hell she meant to go but feeling the need to get away from the scaleback and his reeking potions. She took three lurching steps, and the pain in her hip made her leg wobble. Her knee buckled, and she threw herself against the edge of the closest empty chamber that had been filled with magic-siphoning black sludge two weeks before. Her body did the rest all on its own, and she vomited black and silver tinted with green into the empty basin.

CHAPTER NINETEEN

"Shit." Ember darted toward Cheyenne and couldn't think of anything to do but pull her friend's hair away from her face and hold it there. "Venga, this doesn't look right."

"I said it will pass," he hissed. "If you expect this process to be quick and easy and comfortable, you will be disappointed."

Cheyenne heaved and vomited again, then kicked the metal wall of the basin. She groaned and sagged over the edge, giving herself a second to catch her breath. "I don't think this is part of the process."

"You good?" Ember stared at her, and the halfling nodded. "Here."

The fae pulled a hair tie off her wrist and handed it over.

"Thanks, Em." Cheyenne tied her hair back in a sloppy mess just in case, then turned stiffly and sank to the ground with her back against the basin. Her hip flared in protest, and her shoulders echoed the sentiment and made her grimace. With a trembling hand, she peeled away the top of her shirt, then dropped her hand into her lap and thumped her head back against the basin. "Fuck."

"No." Ember pulled her friend's shirt away to take a look for herself. The black streaks had returned, only darker this time and spread almost as far as they'd reached before her first darktongue injection. "Damnit. Definitely not a success, necromancer."

"If you don't have the capacity for patience in my presence, I suggest you both leave and worry over the outcome elsewhere."

"It didn't work!" Ember straightened and pointed at Cheyenne. "You made it worse."

Venga whirled away from the workbench, one hand knocking aside a vial and sending it crashing to the floor. "Worse?"

"Yeah. Black streaks are back. Darker. Longer. Look at her. She's shaking."

"I'm not shaking, Em," Cheyenne protested in a raw croak.

"Well, I'm not handing you any sharp implements or a martini glass. Those are impossible to carry with a steady hand."

The necromancer stomped toward them across the broken glass he hadn't bothered to clean up. "Show me."

Cheyenne's head felt too heavy to lift, but she raised a hand to her shoulder and pulled the shredded over collar down with one finger. "Feels worse. Looks worse. I'm guessing it's worse."

Venga stared at her with unblinking all-black eyes. His lips peeled back in a snarl before he spun again and roared in outrage. "Not enough!"

He stormed across his lab, throwing crimson sparks at anything in reach. Clay jars shattered on the shelves, spewing powders and knocking over metal boxes and tools. His pounded two fists on the top of the workbench, then roared again and slammed all four hands on the underside of the bench. Metal screeched as the top of his workspace buckled upward, throwing even more tools and ingredients onto the floor. "I can't do the work if I don't have all the pieces!"

"Hey, we brought you what you asked for, okay?" Cheyenne closed her eyes and tried to breathe steadily through the nausea churning in her gut, though it wasn't nearly as intense. "You made the wrong potion."

Venga hissed and swept a hand across the undented side of the workbench, tossing everything on the floor with an obnoxiously loud crash and clatter of metal. "It's not the potion, drow. It's the vessel!"

Cheyenne's eyes flew open. "The what?"

"Vessel. Don't tell me you don't possess a working knowledge of your own fell-damn language."

"Well, that stupid metal cap thing's right over there." She pointed weakly at the rubble of smashed instruments and tools on the floor. "I mean, I guess this technically counts as a vessel too."

Her fist thumped the wall of the huge metal tank behind her with a clang.

Ember shook her head. "You can't be sick and not still be a smartass, can you?"

Cheyenne shrugged and grimaced at the newly awakened pain in her shoulders.

Another roar of frustration burst from the necromancer, but instead of continuing to destroy his lab, he stomped toward the shelves and tossed random objects over his shoulder until he found what he wanted. "You two are insufferable."

Cheyenne lifted her head enough to watch him storm toward them. "Hey, thanks."

"This isn't an issue of my tools or my potions." Venga glared at them, then stepped around the curve of the basin and bent over the side. "There must be something wrong with *you*."

"Ha. You mean all the dart holes and my own special strain of the blight you made? Yeah, I was starting to think the same thing."

"Undoing, drow! It's called 'the Undoing!'" The scaleback's lower arm punched the side of the basin even as his upper body leaned over the edge.

"You can call me Cheyenne anytime."

"Get out!"

Ember rose and turned to see the necromancer scooping up the startlingly large amount of silver-black vomit streaked with green from the basin floor. "What are you doing?"

"What must be done." When Venga was satisfied with the amount of putrid bile in the large glass vial gripped tightly in his hand, he straightened up and went back to his destroyed workspace. He flicked his hand and sent a spray of Cheyenne's puke across the room to join the glass and broken instruments on the floor.

"Jesus, what's wrong with you?"

"I will study it, and I will find the answer." He thumped the vial down on the bench and paused, his chest heaving. "There's obviously something wrong with her. This is where the issue lies. When I find it, I will manipulate the root cause, and we'll have our antidote."

Cheyenne didn't know why that made her laugh, though it came out as a weak choke. "Why do you need me for this? Obviously, not for the poison inside me right now, but for the whole Undoing. They're not the same thing."

"Did you really think you could turn a new Cycle after the Spider, your own flesh and blood, and not be part of this after the fact?"

Of course. It's always Cheyenne Summerlin being the damn chosen one for every little thing. This is bullshit. She cracked a humorless smile. "I mean, that's kinda what I was hoping for, yeah."

Venga thrust a clawed finger toward the door. "If you do not extricate yourselves from this room immediately, I assure you, you will not enjoy the alternative."

"Mad-fucking-scientist." Ember glared at his back, then stooped to wrap one of Cheyenne's arms around her shoulders and help the halfling to her feet. "Good luck with your puke experiment, asshole."

"Luck is for those without skill. Get out!" Venga pounded the huge bulge in the workbench and popped most of the dent back into place.

"Come on." Ember supported a staggering Cheyenne toward the doors, pausing briefly to reach for one of the handles.

Cheyenne waved a hand at the doors instead, and they opened at her command. Storming out wasn't an option at this point, but they hurried into the hall. Venga roared and waved the door shut behind them with a bang.

"Fuck him," Ember muttered. "I'm *this close* to blasting another hole in the wall and shoving him off the balcony."

"I bet he'd like it." Cheyenne swallowed thickly, then cleared her throat. "Working right next to the Nimlothar and all."

"Not after I'm done with him."

"I'm okay, Em."

"I don't care. Who does that asshole think he is? Slamming surprise potions into you and saying you're the problem. It's the other way around!"

"No." Cheyenne slowly drew her arm from around Ember's shoulders, paused, and slowly straightened. "I mean, I'm okay. Right now. Just gotta walk this off."

"Oh." Ember studied her friend as the halfling took slow steps down the hall, reaching out to steady herself with a hand against the wall. "You sure?"

"Yeah. The more I move, the easier it gets, and I'm pretty sure I'm done puking."

"That was seriously messed up."

"Yeah, I don't even know how that potion went from my chest to my stomach in under a minute."

The fae said, "That was weird, but I'm still talking about the necromancer."

"Right." Cheyenne's strength returned enough for her body to handle its weight on its own, and she took her hand off the wall. "Yeah. Messed up, but he's still the best chance we have of getting rid of the blight the right way. Or at all."

"I don't get how you can do that."

"What?"

"Just ignore the shit he pulled with you in the name of the greater good." Ember floated cautiously beside her friend, looking for any sign that Cheyenne might need her again. "I mean, yeah, healing the blight is a big deal. Especially since it's spilling out through the portals, and there aren't a bunch of fae stationed at every single one of them to fight it back.

"You thought I'd get all pissed and stupid and try to fight the guy without thinking it through?"

Ember blinked rapidly. "Well, yeah. I guess I kinda did. No offense."

"Not offended, Em. Not even surprised, honestly." Cheyenne gently stuck her hands in her coat pockets, trying not to tug too hard and make her shoulder wounds even worse. "I guess I'm getting better at seeing the bigger picture."

"Right. We'll call it that."

Cheyenne let out a weak chuckle as they moved through the fortress' corridors. "So, now what?"

"Until we hear from the crazy asshole about what's wrong with you?" Ember shrugged. "No clue. I mean, I guess we could try to find the others. Not Persh'al and Elarit. Newlyweds and everything."

The halfling wrinkled her nose. "Not an image I needed."

Ember snorted and gazed at the walls. "Or we could keep wandering around this place. I don't think I've seen even a tenth of it."

"More than I've seen. I bet we could find something that would be worth the time to look."

"I'm not stepping into another torture chamber." The fae shook her head. "I've seen enough of that shit, and even if everything's been cleaned up and put away, I can still feel what happened in places like that, you know?"

"Not from experience, but I get it. Hold on a sec." Cheyenne stopped and leaned against the wall to focus on searching through her activator.

"What are you doing?"

"Seeing if I can find anything good before we pick a direction." Her fingers flicked at her side as she pulled up a map of the fortress' layout. She scanned the rooms that came with their own names in the system: the Heart, the Sacrificial Chamber, the servants' corridor, the armory, the machine vault, the Spider's quarters. "Whoa."

Ember folded her arms and glanced down the hall. "What?"

"I wouldn't exactly call it cool, but I'm definitely interested."

"Cheyenne, I can't read your mind."

"Right." Cheyenne pushed off the wall and gestured down the hallway. "Pulled up a map of the fortress, and there's a section labeled 'the Spider's quarters.'"

"Oh." Ember wrinkled her nose. "You really wanna go after that? She's gone. No more Ba'rael Verdys terrorizing Ambar'ogúl."

"Yeah, but it's not like she had any time to pack her stuff before she took the fastest transport out of the city." Cheyenne met her friend's gaze and widened her eyes. "I bet her rooms have some seriously weird shit."

"Shit that could make a lot of things go wrong if we mess with it."

"Or shit that might have answers for us. We just have to look at it the right way, Em. Think of it as getting to know our enemy, okay? Sure, Ba'rael's gone, but this whole shitstorm came straight from her. If she was hiding anything in her quarters…"

"It was probably for a really good reason, Cheyenne."

The halfling looked at the next branching series of corridors and pointed to the left. "This way."

Ember sighed. "I'm not gonna get you to change your mind about this, am I?"

"Nope. It's good to have you around, though."

"Fine." The fae hurried after her friend down the next corridor, scanning the walls with her activator but only seeing half of what Cheyenne could read in the system's code. "We're leaving her clothes alone."

Cheyenne laughed. "What?"

"It's a thing I have, okay? I don't like looking through other people's clothes. Creeps me out."

"Interesting."

"Don't say it all judgy like that."

Cheyenne put on a mock-stern frown and stroked her chin. "Interesting."

"Okay, that's worse."

CHAPTER TWENTY

"There's no way this won't be creepier than walking into that darkseller shop." Ember stared at the narrow fourteen-foot-high door of black metal in front of them. Engraved on the surface was a giant spider with a massively swollen abdomen stretched across etched lines of a web. Daggers and thorny vines like barbed wire decorated the frame. She shivered. "No way."

"That's what makes this worth checking out, Em." Cheyenne stepped toward the door, her activator lighting up a command to open it with her magic. "So let's find out."

"Five minutes."

"Ha. That's not nearly enough time."

"That's all the time I'm willing to spend on the other side of the door, and she didn't even try to kill me."

"Okay, fine. Unless we find something you're really into, five minutes."

"Thank you."

Cheyenne waved a hand at the door, flicking her fingers and accepting the activator's prompted command. The door stayed firmly shut. "Huh."

"What, is it locked?"

"Very funny. I never have a problem with locks." Cheyenne stepped away from the door to look the whole thing over. "Must be a sequence I missed."

"Okay." Ember folded her arms and looked cautiously up and down the hall. "What if someone sees us here?"

"Then they thump a fist on their chest and move on. If everyone says I'm the one who got rid of Ba'rael, I don't think they're gonna care that we're breaking into her old room."

"I bet someone would."

"Then we'll deal with it." Cheyenne waved her hand at the door again, but still nothing. "This is weird." *First time I can see the answer right in front of me and can't use it.*

"Well, maybe we should go then."

"You sound scared, Em."

"Fuck yeah, I am."

Cheyenne shot her a sidelong glance. "Don't be."

"Oh, yeah. Sure. Now that you've said it, piece of cake."

Stepping close to the door again, Cheyenne swiped her fingers across the code scrolling over the engraved surface. The activator told her she'd gone through the correct sequences, but the door stayed where it was. *There must be something else, an extra step that doesn't have anything to do with tech or magic.*

Her hand passed over the thick legs of the spider, complete with tiny hairs, and over the base of the thing's swollen abdomen. Something in the door clicked, and a tiny needle shot from the metal to prick her finger before retracting again.

"Ow." She pulled her hand back and looked at the tiny bead of blood on her fingertip.

"Shit." Ember's eyes widened. "Let me see it."

"Em, it's a prick on my finger."

"Yeah, from the goddamn Spider's bedroom door. Maybe you don't think it's a big deal, but my brain is exploding with all the different kinds of poison she could've put on that thing. Or maybe you triggered a trap. Ever think of that?"

The door clicked and whirred, small gears and levers they couldn't see activating behind the surface. A silver light flashed across the engraved spider's body, and the door swung slowly inward with a groan.

Cheyenne slowly looked over her shoulder at her friend and raised her eyebrows. "Or the Verdys DNA was the missing piece."

Ember scowled and snatched the halfling's hand. "Not taking any more chances."

"What are you doing?" Laughing, Cheyenne tried to pull her hand away, but Ember held on long enough to let off a burst of gold light and send a rush of warm energy up the halfling's finger.

"There." Ember let go of her and gestured at the door. "Now we *both* know you're fine."

"Well, thanks." With another glance at her finger, Cheyenne turned back to the open door and stepped into Ba'rael Verdys' personal chambers. The room beyond was pitch-black. She scanned the darkness, looking for lines of code that didn't exist on the walls, floors, or ceiling. "She cut herself off from everything."

"Huh." Ember floated slowly into the room. "That must've taken a lot of extra work."

"Probably, yeah." Cheyenne checked her activator for possible light spells, but Ember beat her to it.

A flash of soft white light darted from the fae's outstretched hand and drifted up to the incredibly high ceiling. It stopped and hovered there as a long, narrow bar illuminated the room.

"Okay, one more point for the fae."

Ember grinned. "Just a spell I knew. Don't worry, I'm not taking your place as the fastest on the draw with an activator."

"I wasn't worried." Cheyenne glanced around the massive room and frowned. "Just confused now."

Ba'rael's private quarters were practically empty. A large, plain metal armoire rested against the far wall, the doors open to reveal two black robes and nothing else. Against the right-hand wall was a thin, uncomfortable-looking pallet on the floor. No draping curtains. No luxurious pillows or exotic bedding. A large, plain metal scrying bowl, now empty, sat on the floor between the pallet and the wall opposite the armoire, which held only a full-length frameless mirror.

"Yeah, this is creepy, all right." Ember floated past Cheyenne to get a better look at the room. "It's like no one lived in here."

"Well, to be honest, it wouldn't surprise me if she didn't. The Spider didn't strike me as someone who'd put a lot of time and effort into creating cozy spaces."

"What about her *Nós Aní*? The other drow?"

"Ruuv'i?" Cheyenne headed toward the pallet, searching for anything other than the spartan furniture and clearly unused scrying bowl. "I think they're married, or whatever the O'gúleesh version of that is."

"Right. This doesn't make sense." Ember approached the armoire and grabbed the handle of the closest open door, swinging it out to check behind it. "Not that I give a shit about what those two did in the privacy of their own room, but this is a whole lot of nothing for two drow rulers to call home."

"Maybe they just used it for sleeping."

"So then why the extra blood wards on the door?"

Cheyenne shrugged. "Maybe Ba'rael really valued undisturbed rest. Hard to imagine her sleeping."

"Might've been the only way for her to unwind after a long day of an entire world hating her guts and waiting for someone to show up and force her off the throne. You know, locking herself in here with nothing else."

"Yeah, maybe." Cheyenne stepped in front of the full-length mirror and studied her reflection: wild white hair, darker than normal circles under her eyes, tattered holes in her shirt and at her hip. *Not a good look, Cheyenne. Next time I make the crossing, I gotta stock up on extra clothes.*

She lifted a hand toward her shoulder, meaning to look at the worsening black lines in the dart wound. The other open door of the armoire creaked closed under Ember's touch.

"Whoa. You need to see this."

"What?" Cheyenne dropped her hand and turned around.

Ember stood in front of the armoire, the doors closed with two inches of space still between them, and gestured at a low metal table stashed in the corner.

"What is it?"

"I'm not gonna try to guess." Ember frowned at the low table and swallowed. "But it's not good."

Cheyenne stepped onto the pallet and off again to cross the room.

When the low table's contents grew clearer under Ember's magical light, the halfling stopped. "What the fuck?"

"Right?"

Dropping to her knees in front of the table, Cheyenne snatched one of only two items arranged intentionally on the metal surface. The stand of the picture frame clacked into place when she lifted it for a closer look. It was one of only three pictures Cheyenne had framed and set on the shelves in her old, run-down apartment. This one captured a moment from five years before: Cheyenne in human form, already years into her Goth self-expression, standing beside Bianca Summerlin on their veranda and holding the high school diploma she'd received from online schooling two years before any of her peers. Bianca's small, closed-lipped smile looked a lot more mocking now than it had seemed back then, even beside Cheyenne's sixteen-year-old deadpan stare at the camera, her head slightly tilted as she bore all the attention her mother never gave but had almost been made up for by Eleanor.

Cheyenne forced herself to look away from the picture and turned her attention to the only other item on the table, a pair of the brightly colored, comically decorated underwear her old troll neighbors had given her as an awkward thank you for bagging an orc asshole in their living room.

"What the fuck are these doing here?"

Ember couldn't think of anything to say and kept quiet.

"What is this? Looks like some kinda sick altar." Cheyenne dropped the underwear and hurled the metal table against the wall. There was nothing underneath. "I don't get it."

"You think she was using those to track you?" Ember asked. "You know, before you passed the trials?"

"I have no fucking idea. It's like she wanted me to find this." The halfling's eyes widened. "Or he did."

"Who did?" Ember floated over to the armoire when Cheyenne launched to her feet, the picture frame clenched in her hand.

"Ruuv'i." Cheyenne stormed across the room toward the open door. "Did you see what happened to him after Ba'rael and Neros disappeared?"

Chasing her friend, Ember frowned and tried to remember. "No, I don't think so. We were all pretty focused on you being a drow dartboard and becoming the new Crown at the same time."

"Shit. Yeah, it had to be him."

"You think he set up a shrine to you with an old picture and a pair of underwear?"

Cheyenne stormed through the open door and into the hall. "Either Ba'rael was using these for something, or Ruuv'i left it as a warning."

"Of what?"

"Em, these things came from my old apartment. I still pay for the place. It's in my name. I doubt he'd make the crossing to grab these, but someone brought them here and handed them over for that bitch to do whatever the fuck she wanted."

"But she's gone!"

"Look! This is me and Bianca." Cheyenne shoved the picture frame toward her friend. "I knew the Bull's Head had found my apartment when they painted blood on the door, but now they know about Bianca. They know her face. It doesn't take someone with half my skills more than an hour to run a search for her."

Ember stared at the picture as the realization sank in. "You think somcone's going to go after your mom?"

Cheyenne snarled and smashed the picture frame against the wall. Shattered glass hit the tops of her black Vans and she stepped back, peeling the photograph out of the frame before dropping it. She stuffed the picture into her pocket and stormed off. "Maybe they were gonna leave her alone before all this, but since Ruuv'i saw me take Ba'rael's place and snuck out of here without anyone seeing him? Yeah, he'll send someone after Bianca just to make us even."

"We don't know anything about the guy."

"We know he bonded to Ba'rael and agreed to be the bitch's yes-man for the rest of his life. That's enough to know I don't want him or anyone who answers to him anywhere near my mom. Not even in the same fucking world."

"Your old neighbors too." Ember picked up the pace until she floated alongside Cheyenne's furious, urgent strides. "Ruuv'i probably knows about them by now."

"Even if he doesn't know who they are, he knows I have O'gúleesh friends close by. Or at least close to my old apartment. Jesus, I hope they keep their head down over there."

"We're making the crossing again, aren't we?"

"Yeah, Em. Ruuv'i has at least a twenty-four-hour head start. I swear, if he touches her, I'm stepping up as Crown to take him down. Bring the whole fucking army across the Border with me if I have to."

Ember stared down the hall and gave Cheyenne the space she needed to process her anger uninterrupted.

Cheyenne swept through command after command on her activator to find Maleshi and Corian. She hadn't known she could do that, but just like her erupting drow magic burning through and bringing new strength despite the poisoned wounds still open in her flesh, her anger dampened her surprise.

At least they're in the same room. She only had to think about the message, and the activator sent it through Hangivol's massive system.

Stay where you are. I found something.

Ten seconds later, she got a reply.

We'll wait.

Good. That's about all the time for waiting we have left. Shit, I knew I shouldn't have stayed over here this long.

CHAPTER TWENTY-ONE

The activator pinged the nightstalkers' locations to her until Cheyenne and Ember reached a small alcove off one of the archways into the Heart's center courtyard. There were low couches and lounge chairs and tables filling what now served as a small meeting room.

Byrd and Lumil looked over the backs of the matching chairs they inhabited when they heard Cheyenne's stomping footsteps.

"Hey, kid!" Lumil's grin faded instantly. "Whoa. You look like shit."

Maleshi and Corian stood when they saw the fury in the drow halfling's eyes. Corian glanced at Ember. "What happened?"

"Okay, a lot of stuff."

"Did anyone think to look for Ruuv'i after I passed out yesterday?" Cheyenne interrupted.

The nightstalkers exchanged a quick glance. "We've had our eyes open, kid. Haven't found him yet, but we will."

"Better make that a top priority." Cheyenne ripped the folded photograph of her and Bianca out of her pocket and thrust it at him.

"What's this?"

"I found it in their room."

Maleshi's eyes narrowed. "Whose room?"

"Fucking Ba'rael's and Ruuv'i's room! Who else's?"

Corian unfolded the photograph and couldn't hide the widening of his eyes. "Huh."

"That's all you have to say?"

"It's an exclamation of surprise, Cheyenne."

"Yeah, I was pretty damn surprised too. What the hell were they doing with a picture of my mom?"

"Trying to tap into finding you, I imagine." Maleshi glanced at the photograph, then dipped her chin toward Cheyenne. "Wanna take a step back and breathe a little before we continue discussing this?"

"No, I don't want to take a step back. I just got pumped with a necromancer's nasty-ass potion that made me feel like I was being turned inside out and fucked up what little healing I had with these." She jerked down the side of her shirt to show one of the dart wounds and let go again without waiting for a response. "Then I find some kind of fucked-up altar in Ba'rael's bedroom with my stuff on it!"

"Anything with magical properties?"

"What? No. It was this and a pair of underwear."

The nightstalkers frowned at Ember, who shrugged. "Gift from her old neighbors. Trolls."

"Ah." However Maleshi managed to put two and two together, Cheyenne wasn't waiting around to ask about it.

"Which means those two fucking drow had direct access to my apartment, and now they know who my mom is."

Corian calmly handed the photograph back toward her. "Is there a request in here somewhere? Because *we* certainly didn't bring these across as a special delivery."

Cheyenne snatched the picture from him and jammed it back into her pocket. "I need to go back."

The general clasped her hands. "I thought you were staying until tomorrow? Hopefully through the rest of the day."

"Yeah, I know I said I'd stick around that long, but that was before I found an underwear-stalker altar dedicated to Bianca and me. I'm leaving."

"No, Cheyenne, you need to stay here." Corian studied her with his glowing silver eyes. "Venga said he's making progress on reversing the blight."

Ember snorted. "That's bullshit."

"And we still have a lot of work to do with getting Persh'al acclimated to his new role. Some of which includes guiding him in ways only you can, seeing as they require a drow to perform."

Cheyenne shook her head, her anger subsiding now that she'd let her discovery out in the open and cemented her decision to leave. "You know enough about drow magic to fill in for me. Whatever else needs to happen can wait until I come back."

"We don't have time to wait until whenever you decide to come back."

"I'm not asking for permission, Corian." She glared at him. "I'm telling you I'm leaving today. Right now, as soon as we're done here, whether you like it or not. And somebody needs to double up the search for Ruuv'i before he does something to fuck up whatever plans you already have. Because he will."

The nightstalker frowned, his tufted ears twitching above his feline features. "I don't disagree with you about that."

"Great. We're on the same page with something."

"I'll go with you, kid," Maleshi said.

Corian, Ember, and Cheyenne looked at her in surprise. The nightstalker let out a low growl. "Finished with your role already?"

The general shrugged. "There's only so much I can do in a few days, *vae shra'ni*, and if there's an issue when we're Earthside, at least Cheyenne will have someone there to back her up. I also have a pretend-human life to keep running smoothly despite all these brief disappearances from Maddie Bergmann's regular haunts."

Corian closed his eyes. "Fine. I'll handle what I can from here. Any estimate as to when you'll return?"

Cheyenne shook her head. "No, I don't know. I have a huge pain in my ass to take care of with the FRoE on Monday. Depending on how long that takes, I might have a little free time to pop in for another visit."

He looked at her with a raised eyebrow. "Your mastery of sarcasm is astounding."

"Yeah, you too."

Corian looked over his shoulder at the goblins and nodded. "Go with them."

"What?" Byrd scowled. "Come on, man. I was starting to get comfy over here."

Lumil lifted a tankard. "Yeah, and the booze hasn't stopped flowing since last night. They'll be fine."

The nightstalker glared at the goblins until they shifted uncomfortably in the armchairs. "Go. With. Them."

Byrd scoffed and spread his arms.

"I want you two to stay with Cheyenne until she decides to return."

Cheyenne grimaced. "They don't have to do that."

"If anyone's coming after Bianca, they're after the best way to find you, kid." Corian pointed at her. "Maleshi can't be with you every second."

"Neither can they."

"But they can shadow you while the general tends to her pretend-human affairs. I want eyes on you, and now that Persh'al's over here for the foreseeable few thousand years, you need someone."

"Yeah, whatever." Lumil waved him off and slumped in her chair. "We'll be your tails, kid."

Cheyenne glared at the nightstalker.

He gave her an apathetic shrug. "Sorry the most useful of us are a bit busy over here."

"Hey." Byrd slammed the armrest. "Way to instill confidence, asshole."

Everyone ignored him, even Lumil, who turned her attention back to her tankard.

"Well." Maleshi clapped her hands. "Looks like we'd better get a move on."

"One moment." Corian set a hand on her back, and she stopped. Then he raised his eyebrows at Cheyenne. "It won't take long. I need a few minutes of the general's time."

Maleshi looked at him with a confused frown.

"Okay." Cheyenne said, "A few minutes, then I'm out of here."

Corian nodded and nodded for Maleshi to walk with him through another doorway out of the makeshift meeting room, guiding her that way with his hand still on her back.

When they disappeared into the dark room beyond, Ember nudged Cheyenne lightly with her elbow. "You okay?"

"Not really, but they waited a few thousand years for me to show up. I can give 'em ten minutes."

Byrd snorted. "Bet they only need four. Nightstalkers can get a lot done in four minutes when the pressure's on. Know what I'm sayin'?"

Lumil snorted into her tankard.

Twenty minutes later, Cheyenne, Ember, Maleshi, and the goblins headed down the main avenue of the drow inner circle, making their way to the lower levels of the city.

Maleshi watched the halfling stalking ahead of her. "It does look remarkably like you know where you're going, and I'm not saying I doubt your intuition."

"Great. Don't start now."

"I wasn't planning on it, kid. But I would love to know which portal you've chosen for us to take back across."

Cheyenne slowed down a little and looked at Ember. "I haven't yet."

"Oh. Good thing I said something."

"Okay, fine. Which portals are the closest?"

"Well, there's one out in Ki'uali. Assuming the transport still runs that way and the blight hasn't sucked all the magic out of the air by now."

Cheyenne glanced at the general over her shoulder. "That's not helping."

"I'm trying to be practical, Cheyenne. I know you're worried about your mom, and I know you're putting everything else on the back burner until you confirm there's nothing to worry about."

"Yeah, making sure the Bull's Head hasn't shown up at her house is a nice extra helping of 'at least it's not worse,' but that won't make me stop worrying about her. She's still asleep under Ba'rael's curse, and that hasn't been made a priority on this side, either."

"It can be. Or we may stumble upon the solution when we get there. But first, we need to decide—"

"On a portal. Yeah, I get it." Cheyenne stopped and turned around to face the goblins, who dragged their feet across the avenue and looked highly disappointed to be leaving. "Any suggestions?"

Byrd shrugged. "Karu Ga'abil isn't that much farther than Ki'uali."

Lumil snarled at him. "Fuck you. I'm not going back to that shithole of a city even if Cheyenne gave me a royal-assed command. Nothing against you, kid. I have a thing with Karu Ga'abil, and they might have a bigger thing with me."

"Yeah. You're afraid they'll finish the job that fell-damn noose started."

Cheyenne rolled her eyes. "Okay, stop. Seriously."

The goblins shoved each other and finally gave up to pay attention to her instead.

"Really? There aren't any Border portals between here and the Outers?"

"Not since the Spider broke the extra one in the dungeon."

Ember folded her arms. "You mean the slaughterhouse."

Cheyenne closed her eyes. "Okay, give me a minute."

"You feelin' okay, kid?" Byrd asked. "I mean, I get it. You're a tough drow cookie and all that, but you look like you could use another long-ass nap. Or a drink."

"I'm fine." Cheyenne looked down at the system code rolling across the avenue beneath all their feet and nodded. "Does Hangivol's system keep records of the active portals?"

Maleshi cocked her head in acknowledgment. "Interesting Plan B. I honestly never thought to look."

"Okay, well, I did." Cheyenne frowned at the ground when a light buzz rose in the center of her chest. She lurched forward, and Ember was at her side immediately.

"You gonna hurl again?"

Lumil laughed. "Partied that hard last night, huh?"

"What?" Ember shook her head at the goblin woman. "Not everyone drinks like you."

"Well, excuse me."

Cheyenne lifted a hand to ward Ember away and glanced around the avenue. "I'm not gonna puke again, Em. This is different."

Maleshi watched her intently. "Well, now I'm intrigued."

"Yeah, tell me about it." Cheyenne scanned the avenue, waiting for the activator to pull up any warnings or possible explanation for the sharp, not-entirely-unpleasant tug she felt again at the center of her chest. She stepped to the side to follow the pull, and the feeling intensified.

"You're kinda freaking me out."

The halfling glanced quickly at Ember and shrugged. "Not trying to."

Cheyenne's legs moved beneath her on their own, propelling her across the avenue and into the second alley coming up on her left.

"What the hell?" Ember raced after her. "Cheyenne!"

Cheyenne laughed and spread her arms as she turned around. When she stopped to wait for the others to catch up with her, the tug at her core was almost unbearable. "Sorry. I can feel this… don't know. My guess is somebody or something wants me to follow it."

"Follow what?" Lumil entered the alley next with an amused smile, followed quickly by Byrd and Maleshi.

The tug repeated, and Cheyenne spun to head in the direction it pulled her. "If I knew, I'd say something that didn't make me sound crazy."

Ember turned back toward Maleshi. "What is it?"

"It's probably not the most accurate explanation, but I'd call it intuition."

"Yeah, she doesn't do this."

"Drow intuition, maybe?"

They caught up with the halfling just as Cheyenne finished waving open a new door in the inner circle's outer wall.

"Look at that." Maleshi nodded. "Cheyenne cast a spell."

"Yeah, that's a thing now." The halfling grinned at her and waved them forward. "Seriously, keep up. I don't wanna lose you guys following this." She lurched into the tunnel.

"Like a puppet." Byrd snorted and shook his head. "Whoever's doing that to her has serious balls."

Ember ignored him and raced into the tunnel.

"I'm sure we'll figure out what it is when she reaches the end of that invisible line," Maleshi said.

"So you do know what it is."

"No. That was an extraordinarily appropriate figure of speech."

CHAPTER TWENTY-TWO

The buzzing tingle and sharp tugs on Cheyenne's chest grew stronger the deeper she led them into Hangivol's lower levels. *Somebody needs to build a damn elevator in this place. I've walked at least ten miles today.*

"Any idea where we're going?" Maleshi called.

"Okay, that's number five." Cheyenne stopped at the end of another alley on the lower level and glanced both ways before the pull returned and jerked her to the right. "The answer hasn't changed, so you guys can stop asking."

Ember tried to ignore the gazes of the other magicals filling the busy street, who all noticed the strange, jerking motions of the Black Flame moving through the crowd. "It's weird that you're so calm about this."

"Doesn't feel like something I should be freaking out about, Em." Cheyenne opened another door when they reached the city's outer wall and shrugged. "So I'm going with it."

"I could go for another drink." Lumil paused at the opening of the short, temporary tunnel through the hall and bent over, propping her hands on her thighs. "Didn't have nearly enough spirithead this morning to not be hurting right now."

"I think the answer to that is to drink less." Byrd thumped her on the back and laughed as he followed Cheyenne and Ember toward the walkway on the other side.

"Bite me, asshole."

"Maybe if you catch up."

Maleshi didn't wait for the goblin woman to recover but gestured toward the open exit as she stepped through. "This is temporary."

"Yeah, yeah. Shit." Lumil straightened and jogged after the general, barely squeezing through before the city's outer wall sealed back up.

"This is crazy." Ember scanned the bleak, dry expanse of the grasslands surrounding Hangivol and the steep hill rising up into the closest mountain range on her right. "Can you slow down a little?"

Cheyenne chuckled. "Not really, Em. I think I'm close."

"Yeah, but to what? I'm not a fan of not knowing what's on the other side."

The halfling stumbled forward when the sharp tug nearly pulled her off her feet, and she picked up the pace around the curving walkway. "Whatever it is, it's gotta be…"

When the flickering, multi-colored flames of the Sorren Gán's makeshift bed and the creature's flaming form came into view beyond the fellfire pits, she forced herself to stop, fighting the continuous pull.

"Shit."

The Sorren Gán sat in the center of the massive crater it had made for itself, eyes closed, wings stretched wide and pumping columns of black smoke into the sky. Both of its giant flame-covered hands were extended, each of them emitting a stream of silver light tipped with more flames into the crushed earth in front of it.

Ember, Maleshi, and the goblins caught up with Cheyenne and saw the drow-eating creature.

The general hummed in calm surprise. "Looks like it's had its fill of the overflow."

"Damn." Byrd rubbed his bald green head. "Never thought I'd see one of those things in real life. That's one ugly bastard."

Trying to bring her heavy breathing back under control, Cheyenne stepped slowly down the walkway, keeping her eyes on the Sorren Gán. *There's no way.*

"Cheyenne," Ember hissed, trying to keep her voice low. "What are you doing?"

The fiery creature's glowing red eyes flew open, and the pull on Cheyenne's core that had led her through the entire city disappeared. She staggered forward under the release of pressure.

A dark, gaping hole in the shape of a giant grin split across the Sorren Gán's smoking face. "I am rarely surprised, even for my kind. But you, little drow, have managed to surprise me twice in the same century."

"Try the same month," Ember muttered.

"I didn't do anything," Cheyenne called.

"But you could have." The creature's smoking head turned slowly to follow Cheyenne as she stormed down the walkway to the tunnel leading to the fellfire pits.

"What did you do?" she shouted. "To me?"

"A mere experiment. I was curious after our riveting conversation last night."

Maleshi glanced at Ember. "You guys came to talk to this thing last night?"

The fae shrugged. "I mean, that's one kinda party, right?"

Cheyenne stopped at the top of the tunnel and faced the Sorren Gán. "Experimenting on me." *Seems to be a pattern of that lately.*

"A simple plucking of the threads, little drow." The creature chuckled, streams of smoke emanating from its nostrils. "Knowing what I do of your abilities, I was curious as to which parts of you I could pull through the Weave to my own ends. L'zar was generous in giving you the best parts of himself, wasn't he?"

"I wouldn't say that. I'm not sure L'zar has any best parts, and he definitely isn't generous." She folded her arms and stared across the empty fellfire pits. "Not cool to drag a drow across a city to see if she'll respond to your summons."

"I simply wished to see the common threads for myself, and now I have." The Sorren Gán pushed to its feet, sending the multi-colored flames surrounding it in the crater crashing to the ground. "My time here is at an end, little drow."

"Great."

The creature stretched its wings wide with a gust of air and swirling black smoke. Then it pointed with one clawed hand at the crater full of liquid fire as it stomped south toward the mountain range where it had built its lair. "Take a dive and go home, Cheyenne. It is no different from the others."

The thing's barb-tipped tail flicked back and forth as it walked. The ground shook beneath every step, hissing and sparking as pools of multi-colored flames fell from its massive body in a watery trail.

"Wait, what?" Cheyenne frowned at the crater that had become another lake of liquid fire. "What is this?"

The Sorren Gán didn't reply as it disappeared behind the screen of thick black smoke left in its wake.

Maleshi stepped up behind her and set a hand on the halfling's shoulder. "I think that's our ticket Earthside, kid."

"No way."

"Jump in and go home? Yeah, sounds like a new portal to me."

"Looks like one too. Shit." Lumil stared at the crater until she reached the mouth of the downward-sloping tunnel and headed into it.

Ember floated toward the halfling and the general as Byrd followed Lumil. "I didn't know there was a way to see what a portal looks like."

"It's a developed skill. Takes a few decades of walking past portal after portal to notice the nuances." Maleshi winked at the fae and gestured at the tunnel. "Shall we?"

She didn't wait for either of them to respond before stepping down. Ember cast Cheyenne a sidelong glance and shrugged. "So I know it's shitty to be dragged here against your will by the creature who broke your dad, but the thing kinda made up for it by giving you your own portal."

"Doesn't make up for it." Cheyenne grimaced and took a deep breath, gazing after the Sorren Gán's massive form, which was diminishing in the distance. "But I'm not about to turn away from it, either."

"That's what I figured."

By the time they exited the tunnel and made their way across the fellfire pits, Maleshi and the goblins had reached the side of the shimmering, fiery lake.

"Where does this thing even go?" Byrd hunkered at the edge of the crater and peered into the multi-colored flames.

"Who the fuck knows, man?" Lumil took a sideways step toward him. "But we can be pretty damn sure it's not a Border rez. None of those set up wherever this thing leads to Earthside."

He cocked his head. "True."

"So we're taking another jump then, huh?" Ember sighed. "Guess we gotta get used to this sooner or later."

"Just be ready." Maleshi grinned and rubbed her hands together. "To tell you the truth, it's been a really long time since I've jumped into anything new. It's exciting."

"That's one way to look at it." Cheyenne gritted her teeth against the pain that was steadily growing in her open wounds. "Em?"

"Way ahead of you." The fae pulled the injection canister from her jacket pocket and pointed it at her friend. "This time, I'm asking permission. And no, that doesn't include sticking you in the dart holes."

"Yeah." Cheyenne moved her trenchcoat out of the way and lifted her shirt on the side opposite her injured hip. "Like somewhere on my back or something, right?"

"Sure." Ember jammed the canister against the halfling's lower back, and the injection was administered with a hiss.

"Okay." Cheyenne raised an eyebrow and slowly closed her eyes. "Doesn't hurt nearly as bad like that."

Byrd and Lumil turned around. "Wow. That's a heavy-duty medcan you got there, Ember."

The fae stuck the canister back in her pocket. "She's got heavy-duty medical needs."

Cheyenne swayed a little and blinked against the rush.

Maleshi tapped her on the shoulder. "Can you make this crossing, kid?"

"What? Yeah, totally. I need, like, two minutes to be relatively functioning." She looked at the general with a crooked smile. "Better than this, anyway."

"Uh-huh." Maleshi studied the lake of fire and shook her head. "Three brand-new portals since you stepped up to the plate to finish this drawn-out story, kid. Can't help but wonder what else is gonna show up before everything's said and done."

"I think the same thing ten times a day."

The group stood there until Cheyenne felt the strongest of the dark-tongue serum's woozy effects fade into something resembling her normal state. "Okay. We're good to go."

"Yeah?" Lumil turned to look at her with an eager grin. "We're all jumping in?"

"Why the hell not?"

"Fuck, yeah." The goblin woman pounded her fist on Byrd's back and sent him stumbling into the colored flames. He shouted in surprise, dropped, and disappeared. "That's how you test a new portal, fucker."

Cackling, the goblin woman leaped into the flames, the red swirling runes exploding around her fists a second before she disappeared.

"Corian's really pissed at me for leaving, isn't he?" Cheyenne looked at Maleshi with a blank expression.

"Because he sent those two to join us?" the general replied. "I imagine he is."

"Great."

"Oh, here." Ember removed the activator from behind her ear and handed it over. "I really wanna keep this. Mind holding onto it for me?"

"Sure. Can't guarantee it'll make it, though."

"Well, you're the only shot at that happening."

"I'll do my best." After sticking the other activator in her pocket, Cheyenne took a deep breath and leaped over the edge of the crater. Maleshi and Ember followed her through Ambar'ogúl's newest portal into the in-between.

CHAPTER TWENTY-THREE

The sensation of falling into the crater and then sideways through the portal added to her discomfort when Cheyenne entered the in-between. Her lungs burned in her chest under the pressure, and she coughed for air behind Lumil and Byrd, who were getting their bearings. Maleshi and Ember recovered behind her, and the group gave themselves another moment to get oriented.

Cheyenne quickly caught her breath and wiped her hair out of her eyes. *Taking a shot of darktongue really helps with slipping in and out of here.*

Lumil grimaced and looked slowly around. "If I didn't already know shit was whack in this place, I'd say we ended up somewhere we're not supposed to be."

"This is definitely the in-between," Maleshi muttered. "Where it's been overrun by the blight."

Ember snorted. "How nice."

Lumil grimaced at the looming figures of the in-between monsters undulating in the thick, molasses-like substance that had replaced the black smoke. It bogged everything down, including the five magicals trying to make the crossing. "Man, that ruins all the fun. Look at those things. They can't even move."

"I'm gonna take that as a plus." Ember shrank away from a tentacle moving slowly through the syrupy fog toward her. The monster it belonged to didn't try much harder than that to touch her, and as soon as she was out of the way, the tentacle disappeared into the darkness.

"If it helps us cross that much faster, I have no problem with it." Cheyenne gritted her teeth and pushed herself to move faster across the invisible ground that sucked at her shoes like thick, squelching mud. "Except for the part where we're not moving any faster, either."

"Just go straight," Maleshi said. "You all know how this works."

They moved forward together, fighting the stickiness the in-between had become.

Byrd sneered at a darkening shadow moving slowly beside him through the haze of smog. "You really think this is the blight spilling over?"

"An educated guess," the general replied.

"So, are we all gonna come outta this infected?" The goblin man grunted and had to tug twice on his leg before his foot came loose and he could take the next step.

"If that were to happen in here, Byrd, we'd already be infected." Maleshi glanced briefly down at her hand and turned it over a few times. "Which I don't see at the moment. I'd say we're in the clear."

Cheyenne covertly pulled down the top of her shirt to check on one of her shoulder wounds. *Not any worse in here. Not any better, either, but at least it doesn't still hurt like a bitch.*

They slogged through the syrupy fog and the dark, dank heaviness of the in-between. It turned out to be a shorter trip than most of Cheyenne's crossings so far.

"That looks like the doorway, right?" Ember pointed up ahead at the vague outline of a rectangular patch of light twenty feet ahead.

It was hard to see through the smog and so much shadow, but nothing else in this place had the same shape.

"Yep." Cheyenne almost lost her shoe with her next step and growled as she shoved her foot back into it and tried again. "This is worse than having to fight off all the monsters at once."

"See?" Lumil stumbled forward when her foot popped free of the sludge. "That's what I'm saying."

"What's the plan once we cross through?" Ember asked.

Byrd scoffed. "Keep moving. What else?"

"No, I mean because we have no idea where this place leads."

Maleshi's silver eyes were firmly fixed on the pale glow of the doorway. "We assess the new location and respond accordingly. Unless there's a whole contingent of Bull's Head loyalists waiting for us on the other side, which I seriously doubt, I don't wanna see anyone charging anywhere with spells flying. Got it? Magic stays put until we figure out where we are."

"Yeah, yeah." Lumil waved her off. "I hope those assholes *are* waiting for us."

"You would." Byrd's shoe slurped out of the ground again, and he kicked off a sticky gob of black sludge. "I want out of here."

"Almost there."

They forced themselves to keep moving. Lumil was the first to reach the doorway, and she waited impatiently for the others to catch up. "We all gonna go through this thing at once?"

"Do I need to call for a single-file evacuation?" Maleshi growled, her patience growing thin with not being able to move as quickly as she was used to. "Just wait 'til we're standing next to you, okay?"

"Fine. Sure. Jeeze."

When they'd all reached the doorway, the stickiness thinned out enough that none of their party had to push or launch themselves to get a leg through the door. They stumbled through one at a time into warm air that stank of manure and hay.

Byrd groaned and picked up his foot. "Shit."

"Literally, by the smell of it." Lumil cracked up and thumped him on the shoulder as he shook a smelly glob of a different kind off his shoe.

Cheyenne narrowed her eyes and looked around. "A farm. That asshole sent us to a farm."

Maleshi chuckled and stepped carefully across the open-sided stable that hadn't been mucked out yet for the day. "Well, there are certainly worse places."

"Guys?" Ember pointed across the dirt road outside the stable. "The portals can't send us back in time, right?"

"Not in all the thousands of years I've known how they work. Relatively speaking." Maleshi turned to look in the direction Ember pointed and cocked her head. "But that does look remarkably like a century that's been over and done with for quite some time."

Cheyenne turned too and saw the barn's open door on the other side of the road. Inside, a woman who had to be in her mid-twenties sat on a small wooden stool beside a milking cow, one hand on the pail beneath the cow's belly and the other squeezing a teat below the animal's swollen udder. She stared at the five magicals who'd suddenly appeared, her mouth hanging open.

The cow, who didn't care about portals and magic but wanted to be milked, stomped a hoof into the hay lining the barn and mooed impatiently. The woman dropped her hand but didn't move.

"Yeah, that definitely looks like an 1800s getup." Cheyenne cocked her head. "Maybe 1700s if we're stretchin' it."

Before anyone else could say a thing, a group of almost a dozen humans rounded the building.

"The barn and stables are one of the most important hubs of modern living." A man wearing a full eighteenth-century costume, homespun cotton shirt, knee breeches, buckle shoes, and everything, gestured at the stables, oblivious to the five magicals staring at his tour group like wild animals caught in the headlights.

Almost as if one of them had shouted a reminder, the goblins, Maleshi, and Ember quickly cast their illusion charms before any of the strictly twenty first century visitors could aim their smartphones and cameras. Cheyenne fumbled with the thick metal cuff on her wrist, wrenched it off, and slipped out of drow mode. When the tourists' fingers pressed the buttons, all of them captured a surly-looking Goth chick standing in a barn beside a black-haired woman with green eyes, sandy-blond-haired Byrd and Lumil, who were dressed as twins, and a wide-eyed human-looking Ember.

Cheyenne glanced at her friend. Someone's bound to notice her feet don't touch the ground.

"Hey," one woman called, lowering her phone and sticking a hand on her hip. "Aren't you people supposed to be in character all the time?"

The tour guide turned around, his eyes widening when he saw the intruders. "You know these tours run every half hour," he hissed. "Get into the main house and get in costume!"

"Yep." Maleshi spread her arms, grinned at the tourists, and ushered their party out of the barn and around the corner. "Enjoy a glimpse of real life, people. You've got it so much better these days."

"I don't think that's helping," Cheyenne muttered, looking over her shoulder. "We just ruined his day."

"Over here." Maleshi darted behind the stable, glanced quickly around, then cast a portal straight into Persh'al's warehouse. The goblins darted through first, followed by Cheyenne and Ember. The general took a final look around at the mostly accurate setup of eighteenth-century colonial life in Virginia and chuckled. "Okay."

The portal closed with a soft pop behind her when she joined the others in the warehouse. Ember spun toward her and frowned. "That was Colonial Williamsburg, wasn't it?"

"It did have a certain 'nostalgia for tourism's sake' feel to it, yeah." Maleshi chuckled again. "For a second, I considered offering them a few pointers for improvement." She clicked her tongue. "But that would've been rude."

Cheyenne laughed. "I almost thought we went back in time too, Em. Milking cows?"

"Way more accessible than any of the rez portals." Lumil dusted off her hands and grimaced at Byrd when he lifted his shit-stained shoe again. "And it goes right back to the fellfire pits."

"Yeah." Cheyenne ran a hand through her hair. "But if that portal starts freaking out like the others and spilling Ba'rael's leftover shit, we're gonna have an issue. Pretty sure people didn't know about magic in the 1700s either."

Maleshi pointed at her. "They also didn't walk around with smartphones, intent on capturing the banalities of everyday rural life."

"Fair enough."

Byrd scraped his foot across the warehouse's concrete floor and stared nervously at the boxy room in the back. "Why'd you bring us here?"

"This is your stop. Welcome home." Maleshi opened another portal, and the dark circle of light grew in the air before illuminating a window into Cheyenne and Ember's apartment.

"Wait, what?" Lumil widened her eyes at the general. "No. No way, man." She stepped forward and lowered her voice. "I do not wanna be left alone in this warehouse with L'zar."

"Yeah, me neither." Byrd gestured at L'zar's cramped makeshift room. "Whatever he's doing in there, he can do it by himself. And Corian told us to stay with Cheyenne."

"Well, Corian's not here." Cheyenne glanced at the goblins. "Even if we had room for you at our place, I think you're safer staying right here."

Lumil frowned. "Why would we need to be safer?"

"So I don't kill you guys when you inevitably start nagging each other while I'm trying to focus on important stuff." The halfling pointed at them and stepped through the portal. "I'll text you if anything comes up."

"You don't have our numbers, kid!"

"I do." Maleshi grinned at them and offered a mocking bow before disappearing through the portal.

Ember stared at the goblins, shrugged apologetically, and followed.

The portal popped closed again, and Lumil smacked a fist into her hand. "This is bullshit."

"This is what happens when you can't keep your fists to yourself, asshole."

"Don't blame me." The goblin woman lunged at Byrd, but he leaped out of the way and scowled at her. "You're the one always pissing me off."

"Oh, yeah. Sure. Blame everyone else for your anger-management issues."

Lumil balled her fists and almost summoned the spinning red runes before remembering who else was sharing Persh'al's private warehouse with them, without Persh'al. She glanced at the door to L'zar's room and lowered her voice. "Let's take this outside."

Byrd shot L'zar's door a sidelong glance and cleared his throat. "Yeah, good idea."

CHAPTER TWENTY-FOUR

In their Pellerville Gables apartment, Cheyenne cocked her head at Maleshi and gave her a pert smile. "Thanks for the backup."

"Are you kidding me? Corian likes to toss orders around whenever he gets the chance. Honestly, I'm a little surprised he didn't consider your Crown offer for longer than a few seconds. That doesn't mean every order he gives is worth listening to."

"So, you don't think we're in any danger?" Ember asked, flopping onto the couch with a burst of violet fae magic.

"Eh. Maybe, maybe not. You two have pretty much everything you need at this point to figure out what's worth your time." The general opened another portal into her own house and nodded at Cheyenne. "I'll text you the contact info for Thing One and Thing Two. Don't forget to loop me into the group text or whatever."

"Thanks." Cheyenne headed for one of their black leather recliners, then stopped. "Oh, hey. You'd mentioned getting back to normal human life, and seeing as we both missed our classes yesterday, any pointers on how to cover my ass for missed time?"

The general winked at her and clicked her tongue. "I got you, kid. Already taken care of."

"What? Really?"

"You bet. Look, I wish I had more time to chat about it, but I'll fill you in later. Right now, I have a giant jacuzzi tub in my master bathroom singing my name. Stay in touch, got it?"

"Right. Thanks."

"You deserve it, Cheyenne, and a lot more than that, but hey. Baby steps." Maleshi stepped through the portal, tossing her hand over her shoulder in a goodbye wave without turning around to look at either of them.

The portal popped shut, and Cheyenne slowly lowered herself into the recliner. "Holy shit."

"I know, right?" Ember gave her friend a lazy smile and leaned back against the couch cushion. "Only two days without our own furniture, and it feels like two years."

"You did a really good job on these, Em."

"Yeah. You're welcome."

They sat there in silence, enjoying the comfort of being home, then Cheyenne shifted and pulled her phone out of the back pocket of her black jeans. "Of course my phone's dead."

"Zapped by the in-between. Hey, phones don't work on the other side, right? I never bothered to check mine."

"Nope. Even with a full battery, they just shut off." Cheyenne tested that by holding the power button, and the screen lit up. "Okay. I guess I don't need a charge."

Her phone buzzed eight times in quick succession, pulling up one notification after another of missed call, voicemail, missed call, voicemail.

"Jesus."

"What's up?" Ember raised her eyebrows, though her eyes were already closed as she lay sprawled on the couch.

"Eleanor made a lot of calls in the last thirty-six hours. Well, I guess just three. Huh. And a voicemail from Rhynehart."

Ember sat up and frowned. "He does not seem like the kinda guy who wants his voice recorded on someone else's phone."

Cheyenne snorted. "Very true. It's the first time he's left one for me."

"Well? Fucking listen to it." Ember slumped back onto the couch. "You can put it on speaker if you want. I don't mind."

With a muffled laugh, Cheyenne did that and played Rhynehart's message:

"Cheyenne, I want you to call me when you figure out what's happening with Colonel T." He paused and muttered something unintelligible, and a door closed softly in the background. Then he cleared his throat. "Assuming you found something. It's kinda hard to believe you won't. Anyway, let me know. I want in."

The message ended, and Cheyenne cocked her head at her phone's screen. "He wants in."

"I'd say that's a good sign, but you don't sound happy about it."

"I mean, the least he could've done was add a please to the end of it."

Ember laughed. "Right. To reciprocate for all the times you used courtesy and your surprisingly well-honed manners. When you wanna use them."

"Hey, I'm not shutting him out for not being polite. I'm just saying it'd be nice, okay? After all the shit he pulled on me, I still helped him out with turning over the new portal at my mom's place. Shit, I've solved every single shitty puzzle the FRoE couldn't handle on their own for them, and I could've just not told him about Colonel Les Thomas stinkin' up the FRoE men in black from the inside out."

"True." Ember stretched both arms far behind her head over the armrest. "But he did help you break a giant-sized, four-armed lizard necromancer without his magic out of Chateau D'rahl."

Cheyenne slumped back. Her phone dropped into her lap, and she almost laughed when her shoulders let off only a small twinge of discomfort. *Go, darktongue serum. Hopefully, it lasts a little longer this time.*

"Whatever. I'm not keeping score of who's done more favors, Em."

"Sure, you aren't."

"Rhynehart can wait a little longer to hear about the colonel's meetup with the Bull's Head. Oh, man, he's really not gonna like what I get to send his way about that one."

With a small chuckle, Ember snuggled farther into the soft couch cushions. "He doesn't like anything you send his way."

"Probably 'cause I always end up being right."

"Okay. The halfling's getting a big head, and we haven't even been Earthside for ten minutes."

"That's why I keep you around, Em. Didn't you know? Go ahead and add shrinking my head to the list of your most redeeming qualities while I figure out what's going on with Bianca." Cheyenne picked up her phone again, blinking quickly and frowning at the screen as she pulled up all three voicemails her mom's housekeeper had left since yesterday morning.

"Don't redeeming qualities need something to be redeemed from?"

"Yeah, that makes a lot more sense." Her finger hovered over the play button on Eleanor's first message, but she tapped the woman's name instead to start a call and put it on speakerphone again.

"Cutting right to the chase, huh?"

"Yeah, I figure it'll be easier if I can ask her questions in real-time. More often than not, her messages don't make sense."

The phone rang four times and got through half a fifth before the line was picked up. "Cheyenne!"

"Hey, Eleanor."

"Is everything okay? I left you three messages, didn't get a reply. You know, if you're too busy to pick up the phone, you can text me. I do have a cell phone."

"I know. Sorry, I was out of range. You know, different world and everything."

"Out of service? Cheyenne, I've never known you to stay away from cell or internet service for more than twelve hours at a time."

Ember snorted and covered her mouth.

Cheyenne forced herself not to laugh. "Yeah, Eleanor, cell phones and the internet aren't a thing over there."

"Over where…oh. *Oh!*" Eleanor chuckled in embarrassment, and a thick rustling came over the phone. "You know, I didn't stop to think about that. Of course, there's no cell service in a different world full of… Well, you know what I'm talking about.'

"Sure do."

"Wait, they don't have phones at all, right?"

Ember turned her head into the couch cushion to muffle her laughter. Cheyenne took the phone off speaker and lifted it to her ear. "No. No phones."

"Good. That's a very hard thing to imagine."

"How's Mom doing?"

"Well, she's fine. Didn't you listen to my voicemails?"

"Nope. Sorry. I figured I'd call you and get the details straight from the source."

Eleanor hummed in consideration, and the sound of ice clinking into more than one glass came over the line. "Bianca's doing as well as can be expected, sweetheart. Better even, in some ways."

I hope she's not making both of those drinks for herself. "Better how?"

"Oh. She woke up."

"What?" Cheyenne lurched forward in the recliner. "She woke up?"

Ember rolled over on her other side and raised her eyebrows. The halfling shrugged, turned the phone back on speaker for her friend's benefit, and listened intently.

"Yes. Yesterday morning at around ten-thirty. It wasn't that long after you and your friends left."

My friends. I guess everybody's my friend now. "And she's okay?"

"Yes, Cheyenne. She can walk, talk, eat, and dress, as long as it doesn't take her longer than ten minutes. You know, all these years, and I didn't realize until now how much she doesn't ask me to do for her. I've probably dropped five pounds in the last two days running around the house for every little thing."

"She's lucky to have you, Eleanor. Thank you."

"Of course. Even if it weren't my job, sweetheart, I'd still be here doing all the heavy lifting. That's mostly figurative these days. You should come up to see us if you can. I think it would really improve her mood."

"She's pissed about the whole thing, isn't she?"

Eleanor hummed into the phone again. "To put it bluntly, yes. But she's processing it all in classic, effortless Bianca Summerlin style."

"So, she's trying to pretend it never happened and won't talk about it."

"Well, it's only been two days. Seeing you might help. It certainly couldn't hurt."

"Yeah, I'll come up later tonight. Got a few things I have to take care of in town, but then I'll be there."

"Wonderful. Oh, and bring Ember too. Having her up here with us is always so nice. Make sure she's not, you know, pink and purple."

Cheyenne raised her eyebrows at Ember, who grinned at the cell phone. "Yeah, she'll be there too. I'll call again in a few hours, okay?"

"Thank you. See you soon." Eleanor hung up, and Cheyenne set the phone in her lap, blinking in surprise.

"Bianca's awake."

Ember pushed herself up to sit on the couch again. "So I heard. I'm surprised you didn't ask how."

"I mean, it doesn't really matter at this point. No more curse-coma. But I know she's gonna be all tense and angry when we get there." She returned the phone to her back pocket and shrugged. "I don't know how Eleanor's put up with her for more than two decades."

Ember feigned a contemplative frown. "Yeah. I can't imagine what it would be like to stick around with someone who can be so difficult to deal with on a day-to-day basis."

"Ha." Cheyenne pointed at her friend. "I see what you did there."

"Oh, good. I wasn't trying to be subtle."

"Whatever." With a soft chuckle, Cheyenne stood and headed toward her bedroom on the far end of the apartment past the mini loft. "I'm finally gonna change out of these clothes, then I have to go check out the old apartment. Can't leave that troll family hanging if anyone working for Ruuv'i gets even a whiff of them knowing me, and I've been in their apartment plenty of times."

"Yeah, no problem." Ember dropped back against the couch and closed her eyes. "I'll be here, drowning myself in gratitude for really fantastic upholstery."

"Yeah, okay. Don't get too comfy. I'd hate to see what you might do to me if I got between you and your beauty sleep."

With a snort, Ember flipped the halfling the bird.

CHAPTER TWENTY-FIVE

An hour later, Cheyenne and Ember stepped out of the halfling's Porsche Panamera and headed across the parking lot toward her old apartment building. The old man who had the apartment below hers returned to his front door on the ground floor, his dog trotting obediently at his side and panting in satisfaction. He glanced at Cheyenne, did a double-take, and stared as she and Ember hurried up the staircase in the open-air hallway.

"Hey, man." Cheyenne nodded at him. "Been a while."

"I wondered what happened to you."

"Just been doing a lot of traveling lately. Came by to check on my apartment before I head off again."

"Uh-huh." The older man followed them with his gaze as they moved up the open staircase, his hand clenched around the doorknob on his half-open door. "Safe travels."

When they reached Cheyenne's floor, Ember muffled a laugh and leaned toward the halfling. "He was looking at you like he thought you were dead or something."

"Wouldn't that be great? If there was a way for me to fake my death over here without losing the trust, I'd probably give it a shot."

"Hey, I'm already spending your money. You could just sign it all over to me."

"Not without getting raped by taxes, Em, but I see how it is."

Ember sniggered. "Yep. I've only been friends with you for five years and agreed to be your *Nós Ani* groupie and go with you back and forth across the border just to get at your Summerlin fortune."

"I knew it."

They reached her old apartment, and Cheyenne didn't even bother to take her keys out of her pocket. She gestured at the cracked-open door and grimaced. "Look at this shit. They broke the lock. The doorknob's ready to fall out."

She jiggled the knob to demonstrate, then dropped it again.

Ember shook her head. "No respect. No respect at all."

"Yeah, okay, Rodney." Cheyenne snorted and pushed open the door.

"Oh, okay. You didn't know a single Marvel character before you met me, but now you're calling out Rodney Dangerfield quotes?"

"I had a thing for standup in high school, okay?"

"Uh-huh."

They stepped into the apartment together and froze. Most of the small living room was covered in graffiti. The heavy wood executive desk she hadn't gotten around to moving into the new apartment tilted precariously after having had two of its legs hacked off. Her executive leather desk chair was gone, and what little else she'd kept in the place, dishes, silverware, packets of ramen noodles, and the clothes she hadn't taken with her were strewn everywhere. The bashed-in bedroom door she'd neglected to fix after her first attempt at spellcasting now rested against the wall instead of on its hinges.

"Well, shit." Cheyenne shoved her hands in her pockets and turned around. "I mean, I'm diggin' the artwork."

"You didn't leave anything valuable in here, did you?" Ember ran a hand over her hair.

"Nope. I mean, except for the chair, but that's already gone. I need a new one anyway."

"Damn. Three weeks. That's all it took, and you're still paying for this place."

"It's whatever, Em." Cheyenne peered into her bedroom and found the same disarray inside, complete with a graffitied hand raising the middle finger next to the anarchy symbol in dripping black paint that had long since dried. "At least somebody's been having a good time with this place. More than I ever did."

"Oh, my God." Ember burst out laughing, and when Cheyenne hurried out of the hallway again, she found the fae doubled over and pointing at a large basket on the floor beside the counter.

"What?"

"The fucking underwear." Ember floated backward across the floor to give Cheyenne a better view and cracked up again. "Nobody… I mean, there's still…"

Stepping closer, Cheyenne peered into the basket to see every single pair of brightly colored underwear, courtesy of Yadje and R'mahr's tailoring skills, still inside. *Except for the one I found on Ba'rael's creepy-ass altar.*

The halfling snorted. "Can't blame 'em, right?"

Ember's laughter finally calmed down, and she ran a hand over her illusioned brown hair. "That's just sad."

"It's the thought that counts." Cheyenne's smile faded. "I bet whoever grabbed the picture and a pair of that freaky underwear got a real kick out of leaving the door wide open when they left."

"It's not like you were coming back anytime soon."

"Yeah, I'm not worried about this, but I do wanna check on the trolls."

Ember sniggered at the basket of underwear again and turned to follow the halfling back into the hall. "I finally get to meet the weirdest O'gúleesh family this side of the Border, huh?"

"Oh, they'll love you." Cheyenne lowered her voice and eyed the troll family's front door two apartments down. "Don't say anything about the underwear. It was a big thing the last time."

The fae mimed zipping her lips and tossing away a key.

The smell of pancakes and buttered asparagus wafted from beneath the door, and Cheyenne frowned with her raised fist poised to knock. "Just expect weirdness and some awkward misinterpretations."

Ember wrinkled her nose. "Including their cooking, huh?"

"Oh, yeah."

Cheyenne knocked firmly on the door and pounding feet scurried across the apartment, followed by a quick shout of, "I got it!"

Three deadbolts and a chain slid out of their locks, then the door creaked open.

"Cheyenne!" Bryl flung the door aside, not bothering to keep it from banging against the wall, and grinned at the halfling. "You're back!"

"Hey, kid." Cheyenne nodded at the young troll girl and peered inside the apartment. "I'm not sticking around for very long. Just came by to check on a few things. Your parents are home, right?"

"Yeah. Come in." Bryl stepped aside and waved them into the apartment. "Who are you?"

Ember laughed.

"Oh, yeah. Bryl, this is Ember. Ember, Bryl."

"Nice to meet you, kid."

The troll girl stared at Ember with wide scarlet eyes. "What are you?"

Ember shut the door behind her, then twisted her fingers and dropped her illusion charm to reveal her faeness.

"Wow." Bryl grinned. "I didn't know you had fae friends."

"Yeah, well, I guess I just get along with everyone." The halfling and her *Nós Ani* tried harder than they should have to not to laugh.

"*Maji!*" Bryl shouted, leaning back to peer around the corner into the kitchen. "It's Cheyenne!"

"Ah!" A pot lid clanged on the stove, and Yadje came bustling into the living room with a startled grin. "Would you look at that? She's back."

"Not permanently, Yadje. Just stopping by."

"Oh, Cheyenne." The troll woman wiped her hands on a stained apron and glanced nervously at the front door. "Have you been to your apartment yet?"

"Yeah."

"It's terrible, that's what it is! I'm so sorry. R'mahr tried the first few nights to chase those good-for-nothing…Bryl, what's the word?"

"Assholes."

"Assho…no!" Yadje frowned at her daughter, who grinned and bit her lower lip in a poor attempt to hide it. "Who's giving you these words, eh? You read them in your books?"

"Someone at the market said it."

Yadje clicked her tongue and flapped a hand at the back hallway.

"Go bring your da out. He'll keel over if he knows Cheyenne came by and we never told him."

Still grinning, the troll girl raced down the hall, shouting loud enough for their neighbors on either side to hear that Cheyenne was in their living room.

"That child." Yadje shook her head, then looked at Cheyenne. "R'mahr tried to chase them off, Cheyenne. They did not want to leave, and more kept coming, so we put extra locks on our door instead."

"Yeah, I saw that. I'm glad you guys were able to stay safe with all that happening. I'm sorry you had to deal with it."

"No, no, we are sorry. Not enough time in the day to watch two apartments. Hardly enough time to watch one girl."

Cheyenne smiled and shook her head. "It's really okay. I didn't expect you guys to watch my stuff for me, let alone protect it. There wasn't anything worth protecting anyway."

"That is fortunate." The troll woman finally seemed to notice the fae standing inside her door and jumped. "I have no manners. Yadje."

Ember took the troll woman's hand for a firm shake. "Ember. Nice to meet you."

"Yes! Yes, indeed. A fae. Ha. Welcome to our apartment. Nothing like what I'm sure you're used to back home, but it suits us for now."

"Oh." Ember shrugged. "Well, I was born Earthside, so this looks pretty much like home to me."

"Ah! Born Earthside." Yadje clicked her tongue. "A *phér móre* and an Earthborn fae standing in my life room."

"Living room, *Maji*." Bryl rolled her eyes as she headed back down the hall, her father following quickly behind. "It's called the living room."

"It means the same thing, yes?" Yadje grinned at her guests.

Her daughter walked toward the couch and plopped down on it, then picked up her newest book, and whispered, "No, it doesn't."

"Cheyenne, Cheyenne!" A grinning R'mahr joined them by the door and reached out with both hands to clasp one of hers. He pumped her hand vigorously, his scarlet eyes twinkling. "So good to see you again. I wondered if we would. About your apartment…"

"Don't even worry about it. I'm not upset. I'm glad you guys are safe."

"Yes. Yes, we are. No more thugs knocking on our door, trying to squeeze us for what we don't have, thanks to you." The troll man chuckled. "Though I did think it rather odd to see so many different visitors at your place while you were gone."

Yadje scoffed and smacked his arm with the back of her hand. "Don't call them visitors. They were…"

"Assholes?" Bryl muttered.

"Ha!" R'mahr turned around to point at his daughter. "Exactly."

His wife's scarlet eyes grew wide in exasperation as she glanced at Cheyenne and Ember. "You hush and read your book, *hinya.*"

Ember laughed, covered her mouth, and shook her head. "Sorry. I shouldn't laugh at that."

"You laugh all you want." R'mahr frowned and leaned toward her before breaking into another eager grin. "Who are you?"

"Ember. Cheyenne's friend."

"And fae. We are blessed by Earthside opportunities, eh? Ha!" He shook her hand fervently, then patted his belly. "Yes. This is good."

"Hey, I'm curious," Cheyenne started. "Did you guys see anyone else break into other apartments here? Maybe the same people who got into mine?"

Yadje shook her head. "No."

"That is what I mean by odd, Cheyenne." R'mahr thrust a finger in the air. "Only you and your apartment. I do not think it's that special."

"Stop." His wife smacked him again, and he chuckled, flinching playfully away from her.

"No, it's really not." Cheyenne smiled at them. "I'm glad my place was the only target." *So far, and I need to make sure it stays that way. Short-term and long-term.*

"So." R'mahr smoothed the front of his baggy sweater, which was two sizes too big for him, and nodded. "Where have you been?"

"Well, I've taken a few trips across the Border since the last time we talked."

"What?" The troll man clapped both hands to his head, his jaw dropping in disbelief. "Why would you go back?"

Ember shot Cheyenne a sidelong glance. "We had some business to take care of over there, I guess you could say. In the capital."

"Ack." Yadje swiped her pinky across her forehead, then flicked it aside. "Curse Hangivol and everything that foul place has a hand in. Cheyenne, you know why we made the crossing to come here."

"Yeah, I do." Cheyenne gave her a sympathetic smile. "You guys picked the right time to leave, honestly. It's a lot worse over there now."

"Which we're working on fixing," Ember added with an encouraging nod. "And we will."

"You?" R'mahr chuckled. "What can you do?"

Cheyenne dipped her head. "You'd be surprised."

"*Maji*, the kitchen's smoking."

"Oh!" Yadje leaped toward the kitchen, followed by muttered curses and pot lids banging around. "I always forget about this stove cooking."

"It has a timer," Bryl offered.

"Timer. Timer. You keep saying this thing, and I don't know what it is!"

"Need any help in there?" Ember called.

"No! No, I've got it. Thank you." More items clanged, the gas stove clicked a few times, the sound of emitting gas cut off, and Yadje emerged from the kitchen again. "I'll finish that later."

R'mahr raised his eyebrows and rocked forward on his toes. "She's making waffles."

Ember frowned above a confused smile. "On the stove?"

"It's called a skillet, yes?" Yadje mimed tossing the handle of a pan. "To cook with."

"Yeah." Cheyenne nodded. "Or a pot or pan. Normally not for waffles, though."

"Yes, but it works. I just can't seem to find how to get those little squares into the big square."

Bryl snorted. "Pancakes. She's making pancakes."

"No, the container says waffle mix." Yadje shook her head and smiled at the girls in her tiny entryway. "These ideas of hers. I don't know where they come from."

"Well, it smells good either way," Cheyenne offered. *Minus the asparagus part.*

"Well, come in." R'mahr stepped back and waved them forward. "Come sit. Are you hungry? And what news from home, eh?"

"Shush." Yadje waved him off. "There is nothing I want to hear about it. That's that."

"You must be a little curious."

"No." The troll woman pointed sharply toward the kitchen. "Get them water, R'mahr. They don't want to sit here answering all your questions. Cheyenne's had enough of that."

"Yadje, we can't stay." Cheyenne shrugged and smiled, hoping to let the troll family down easy. "Like I said, this was just a quick stop, but it's really good to see you guys."

"Oh. Yes, of course. You too."

Bryl looked up from her book. "When are you coming back?"

"I don't know, kid. I'll try not to make it too long, okay?"

"Cheyenne. Tuesday." R'mahr pointed at her. "We'll be in Peridosh. Our weekly trip, remember?"

"Yeah, I remember."

"Come with us. It was so much fun the last time."

Cheyenne opened her mouth to protest and paused. Yeah, loads of fun, including a few assholes almost running them all over in the main avenue. "I'll think about it."

"Yes, yes. And after you think about it, you'll come." R'mahr grinned.

"Will you stop pressuring her?" Yadje shot him a warning glance. "She has enough to deal with without you pushing, pushing, pushing."

Her husband raised his hands and dipped his head, taking a small step backward. "No pushing. I've said what I wanted to."

"If I can make it," Cheyenne said, "I'll be there."

"Any room for a fae?" Ember asked.

"Yes!" Bryl shouted, leaping off the couch. "All the time."

"Awesome. Maybe we'll see you Tuesday." Cheyenne turned to open the door, and R'mahr leaped toward her.

"Wait. Cheyenne. If there is anything you can tell us, any news from Ambar'ogúl… We chose to leave, and we are finding our way here, but it's still home to us, yes?"

The halfling glanced at Yadje, who'd turned toward the kitchen but stared at Cheyenne with expectant scarlet eyes. "Honestly, a lot has changed in the last few weeks."

"Yes?"

"The Spider's gone."

Yadje turned fully to face her guests. "Gone?"

"Yeah, there's a new Crown now. Just happened yesterday."

"Ha!" R'mahr clapped his hands together and leaned forward. "Must have a massive pair of balls to get that job done."

Cheyenne snorted. "Kinda."

For the first time, Yadje ignored her husband's odd sayings, far more interested in hearing more from the halfling standing in her doorway. "Who is it?"

"A troll."

"For real?" Bryl shouted and raced toward her parents. "A troll like us?"

"Didn't know there was any other kind, kid." Cheyenne winked at her.

R'mahr slowly wrapped his arm around his wife, both of them staring at the halfling in shock. Tears swam in Yadje's eyes, and she swallowed thickly, trying to hide her emotions.

"I don't know if the name Persh'al Tenishi rings a bell, but now you know."

"Ha! A troll." R'mahr's lips quivered as he smiled at the half-drow and the fae. "Thank you. Thank you, Cheyenne. That is wonderful news."

"No problem. I'll see you soon, huh?" She smiled at the awe-stricken family, then gently closed the door behind her.

Ember said as they walked down the hall toward the front staircase again, "You really are set on giving Persh'al all the credit for everything, aren't you?"

"Not everything, Em." Cheyenne shrugged. "Those trolls already think I'm the greatest thing since anything invented on Earth that they've never seen before. I don't need to make their brains explode by telling them anything else. And yeah, Persh'al deserves a lot of credit. He's the only one who had the balls to step up to the plate."

"After you."

"Well, yeah. But he's already been the Crown, like, a hundred times longer than I was."

"R'mahr did say something about a huge pair of balls."

"Fuck." Cheyenne snorted, and Ember's laughter rang down the hall. "First and last time we broach that topic, 'kay?"

"Sure. Until the next time you visit the bone drow's secret lair."

"Careful. I'm in a good position to shove you down these stairs."

"And I can float over the ground. Remember?"

Cheyenne rolled her eyes and headed quickly down the staircase toward the ground floor. "I can't wait 'til your legs heal themselves all the way."

"Aw, thanks."

CHAPTER TWENTY-SIX

An hour and a half later, Cheyenne's Panamera crunched down the gravel drive of the Summerlin estate and rolled to a stop in front of the curved stone steps leading up to the front door. "Here we go."

Ember got out after Cheyenne and gently closed her door. "You okay?"

"What? Yeah. Why wouldn't I be?" The halfling's black Vans made very little sound on the gravel.

"Oh, I don't know. 'Cause your mom's awake after being unconscious for three days under a curse meant for L'zar. And let's be honest. We both know those scars aren't going away anytime soon."

"Or ever, probably. Okay, sure. I'm a little tense."

"She won't blame you, Cheyenne. She can't. That would be ridiculous." Ember floated up the steps after her friend, and Cheyenne paused in front of the huge front door to her childhood home.

"It would be if she came right out and said this was all my fault, but Bianca Summerlin doesn't point fingers." Cheyenne took a deep breath. "She calmly works around the whole situation until you end up pointing the finger at yourself."

"Well, if I see that happening, I promise to slap your hand away. How's that?"

Cheyenne nodded slowly. "Thanks, Em."

"You're welcome."

The halfling grabbed the door handle and pushed it open. She stepped slowly inside, gazing around, and moved out of the way so Ember could join her. *Okay, everything looks normal.* "Eleanor? Mom?"

As soon as Cheyenne shut the front door behind her, a crash of metal came from the kitchen, followed by the housekeeper's exclamation of surprise. Then the swinging door to the industrial kitchen on the right burst open, and Eleanor bustled toward the foyer, wiping her hands vigorously on the white apron tied around her torso. "Oh! You're here. Good."

"Hey, Eleanor." Cheyenne opened her arms for a quick hug when the woman reached her.

Eleanor let her go quickly, then smiled at Ember and pulled the fae in for a tight hug as well. "It's so good to see you two." She took a deep breath, opened her mouth, then frowned, blinking rapidly. "Hmm."

Cheyenne and Ember exchanged glances. "Everything okay?"

"Oh, yes!" The housekeeper nodded.

"Okay. You seem a little confused."

"Well, everything's confusing these days, isn't it?" Eleanor let out a nervous chuckle.

Ember smiled at the woman. "We have that conversation all the time. I think it's pretty normal."

"Normal." Eleanor laughed, then pressed a hand to her chest and scowled like she'd insulted herself.

Weird. Maybe she hadn't gotten enough sleep. She seemed totally fine on the phone. "Is Mom upstairs?"

"Hmm? Ah. Yes. Bianca's up in the master of ceremonies."

"What?" Ember and Cheyenne said together.

"What? Oh." Eleanor cleared her throat and tried again. "Up in the master key. No. The master in chief." With a distressed moan, she thrust her finger in the air and pointed at the right side of the second floor.

"Master bedroom?" Cheyenne offered.

The housekeeper opened her mouth, but nothing came out. She tried two more times, then swallowed thickly and gestured toward the kitchen. "I'm sorry. I seem to have forgotten how…what was I saying?"

The halfling stepped toward the only other parental figure she'd had besides Bianca and gently touched Eleanor's arm. "Did something happen?"

"Of course, sweetheart. Your mother's awake. I'd call that something."

"Okay." *Something's definitely wrong.* "I'm gonna go up and see her, all right?"

"Cheyenne, I don't think…" Eleanor drew her shoulders back and turned to the kitchen again. "I'm not feeling well, so I think I'll go lie down. Excuse me."

The housekeeper turned swiftly on her heel and raced back down the wide hall.

Ember floated after her but stopped. "Eleanor, can I help with anything?"

Eleanor shook her head vigorously and didn't turn around before she barreled through the door and disappeared.

"That was weird."

"Yeah." Cheyenne ran a hand through her hair, now High-Voltage-Raven-dyed black in her human form, and stared at the kitchen door until it settled back into place and stopped swinging. "She's really good at keeping it together. Most of the time."

"Well, maybe now that your mom's up, Eleanor doesn't have to keep it together anymore. You know, for both of them."

"Maybe. Maybe my mom has a better idea about what's going on, at least with Eleanor." When it came to everything else, the last thing Bianca Summerlin wanted was an explanation of what happened to her. Not if it had anything to do with magic. Or L'zar.

The girls moved quickly and quietly up the wide staircase that rose through the center of the Summerlin estate. Cheyenne cast a brief glance through the open French doors into the breakfast room. From where she stood at the top of the stairs, only the top half of the destroyed Border portal in her mom's backyard was visible, now nothing more than a pile of black stone rubble and cracked earth. *Nothing weird about that, either. And I'm sure destroyed portals don't pick themselves back up and carry on.*

She turned right and right again with Ember behind her, moving down the second-story hallway stretching toward the front of the house. Cheyenne stopped in front of the closed doors to the master bedroom and gritted her teeth. *Just keep reassuring her you'll take care of it. Because you will, Cheyenne. That's what you do.*

Ember's fingers lightly brushed her friend's arm as she whispered, "You got this." Cheyenne nodded at her with a small, uncertain smile, then softly knocked three times on the door. "Mom?"

She heard the rustling of sheets and a slight creak of the usually silent box spring. Cheyenne's drow hearing picked up the gentle pat of her mom's hands on the bedspread and the swipe of Bianca's fingers across either her face or her neck. *She's definitely awake.*

Cheyenne opened her mouth to call out again, but Bianca beat her to it.

"Come in." The woman's voice was as calm, low, and even-keeled as it was burned into her daughter's mind.

The halfling cranked down on the door handle and pushed open only one of the doors before stepping tentatively inside. "Hi, Mom."

"Cheyenne." Bianca Summerlin was on the right-hand side of her king-sized bed, her side, despite the other half of the bed having always been empty. She was propped against a massive pile of all the pillows that usually decorated the pristinely made bed in the early evening, even on a Saturday. The woman lifted her chin, showing no emotion although she was still in bed, her loose brown curls tied back neatly but without their usual sleek look. She was in turquoise silk pajamas, which made her look that much paler and surprisingly exhausted.

When her mom didn't say anything else, Cheyenne gestured at the open door behind her. "Ember's here too."

"Yes, I see that. Hello, Ember."

Ember smiled. "Hi, Bianca."

The woman's lips twitched into what couldn't remotely be called a real smile, even for her.

"Is it okay if she's here?" Cheyenne asked.

"I don't mind staying out here if you'd rather be alone."

"Alone." Bianca let out a quick hum of bitter amusement and gestured at the inside of her room. "Ember, I very much appreciate you accompanying my daughter to our home, whether it's in support of her or me or most likely both. You're welcome to join us."

"Okay, thanks." Ember floated through the doorway and shot Cheyenne a small, unsure smile of her own. "How are you feeling?"

Bianca glanced down at the one-inch space between the soles of Ember's shoes and the massive antique area rug. "I was going to say I'm doing as well as the circumstances warrant. But now, Ember, seeing you out of that wheelchair in such a short amount of time brings a certain unexpected optimism."

"Oh." Ember glanced quickly down at her hovering feet.

"Don't bother mincing words on my account. I was already aware of your involvement in Cheyenne's personal endeavors. I didn't realize quite how far that extended."

"Right." Ember nodded. "I didn't know this was possible either until the last time we saw each other."

The small, genuine smile Bianca gave the fae was a rare sight Cheyenne remembered being aimed at her maybe five times in her life. "I'm happy for you, Ember. Truly. Most people with similar experiences have to re-learn to navigate their life from an entirely new perspective. You've reached a highly coveted success against all odds."

"Thank you." Ember let out a soft, self-conscious chuckle. "I didn't do it all on my own, though, so I can't take all the credit."

"Indeed." Bianca's dark eyes shifted toward her daughter, then back to the human-illusioned fae. "But I will credit you for humility."

I've gotta be dreaming. Cheyenne stared at her mom, who was gazing in admiration at Ember. *If she knew the odds I've been up against, I'm not sure she'd be congratulating me at all. At least someone has her full approval. I stopped needing it anyway.*

"I know you're probably really confused," Cheyenne started. "And angry."

"Oh." Bianca let out an unamused chuckle. "Angry is a rather simplistic catch-all, Cheyenne."

"Mom, I'm sorry."

"Be that as it may, I am grateful to be conscious and capable of continuing through this situation fully of my own volition." When the woman tilted her head, the collar of her tightly buttoned silk nightshirt shifted slightly away from her collarbone. A half-inch of the highest scar magically burned into her flesh peeked out from beneath the fabric. Bianca caught her daughter staring but didn't try to hide the evidence. "If I had two armchairs in my bedroom, I'd offer you both a seat."

"That's okay." Ember shook her head with a patient smile. "Sitting and standing are pretty much the same thing for me at this point."

"Hmm."

Cheyenne swallowed. *I'm not gonna take the chair and make Ember stand. And there's no way Mom's inviting me to sit at the edge of her bed for a cozy heart-to-heart.* "Did Eleanor say anything about what happened that might've helped you wake up?"

"No, Cheyenne. Eleanor's explanation, though perfectly well-intentioned, was about as useful to me as a spoon is for carving a ham."

Ember choked back a small laugh.

Cheyenne nodded. "She did really well, all things considered."

"Oh, I have no doubt. And she'll continue to do well after the fact."

Ember jerked her thumb toward the open door behind them. "She did seem a little out of it when we got here."

Bianca blinked, her face expressionless again, and gave them a tense nod. "Yes, I suppose the last five days would take their toll on anyone. In varying degrees, of course."

The three women glanced around, everyone trying to be polite without stepping on any toes. Cheyenne badly wanted to clench her fists and walk out of the bedroom, to come back later when Bianca Summerlin wasn't so freshly out of a magical three-day coma. *We need to get this the fuck over with.*

She stepped forward. "Do you want to know what happened?"

Bianca slowly tilted her head. "Will knowing change anything about my current situation?"

Seriously? Cheyenne slowly shook her head. "No."

"Then I have no desire to hear the tale of how I came to wake up in my own bed with certain physical alterations." The woman blinked twice and swallowed.

"I wish I had an explanation."

"I didn't ask for an explanation, Cheyenne. I didn't ask for any of this, but here we are." She looked her daughter up and down and took a long, slow breath. "Nor do I blame you. I want to make that perfectly clear."

"Okay." Cheyenne nodded stiffly. "Thanks for saying it, at least."

"You know I wouldn't if I didn't believe you had little to no direct hand in it." Bianca stretched her arm out to the side and beckoned her daughter forward with a quick flick of her hand. "I'd come to you, but I seem to have spent my limited energy before two o'clock today."

Moving slowly, Cheyenne approached her mother's bed, forcing herself not to break Bianca's gaze. *This feels like the time I blew up the oak tree out front, only now I'm fifteen years older and bigger than her, and she's incapacitated in her bed. You're an adult, Cheyenne. Act like it.* She stopped in front of Bianca's outstretched arm, and her mom settled her hand gracefully back in her lap beneath the comforter.

"Well, sit down. It's difficult for me to keep my neck bent like this for very long." As if to drive her point home, Bianca lowered her chin and stared pointedly at the empty space at the edge of the bed beside her outstretched legs.

Wow. I was wrong about the cozy heart-to-heart. Cheyenne sat stiffly, and a heavy sigh of relief escaped her when Bianca leaned forward and set a hand on her daughter's thigh.

"Cheyenne, I won't lie to you." The woman lowered her voice and leaned closer. "You don't deserve it, and I'm no longer in a position to assume I can protect you from anything. Even my opinions."

"Okay."

"I find no satisfaction whatsoever in my personal situation." Bianca gave her daughter's thigh a brief, gentle squeeze. "But I can't put into words how relieved and grateful I am to see you here after the last time we parted ways. Healthy and well and in one piece."

Her gaze drifted from Cheyenne's face to take in the rest of her. She paused, removed her hand from her daughter's thigh, and pointed cautiously at the tips of the thick black lines streaking across Cheyenne's chest from beneath her black t-shirt.

"Did I speak too soon?"

"What?" Cheyenne looked down at her neckline and quickly tugged her shirt up over the poison lines. "No, Mom. I'm fine. Promise."

"Let me see."

"You don't need to. Really. "

"If you promise me you're fine and mean it, Cheyenne, I see no reason why you insist on hiding whatever that is." Bianca's eyes bored into her daughter's, and Cheyenne didn't have it in her to fight back on this one, not when she'd spent three days wondering if her mom would wake up from Ba'rael's curse.

Cheyenne glanced at the wall behind her mom and tilted her head. "Fine. Go ahead."

Bianca didn't hesitate to reach out and pull Cheyenne's shirt away from her neck and toward her shoulder. Her eyes widened and she stretched the shirt away from the open dart wound a little more, then lowered her hand into her lap. "What is that?"

"I got into a fight yesterday." *And we can leave it at that because if I say anything else, this moment is over.*

"A fight." Bianca blinked at her daughter and pursed her lips. "Do I want to know the details?"

"Nope. Other than that, I'm fine."

"She didn't start it," Ember added. She ran her hands down the sides of her pants and nodded.

Bianca glanced briefly at the fae, then scanned Cheyenne again. "I hope you finished it, too."

"More or less, yeah."

"You need to have that looked at." Bianca nodded at her daughter's shoulder. "It's festering."

"I know, Mom. Ember's one of the best healers pretty much anywhere for these kinds of wounds. They're a lot better than they were yesterday."

"They?" Her mom's eyebrows lifted. "There's more than one?"

"Yeah, but it's okay. I'm fine."

"Cheyenne, that does not look 'fine.'"

"I know, but it's not the worst thing that's happened to me, and I can still function. So I'm fine." The halfling's voice rose at the end of her statement, not of her volition. It surprised them both, and Bianca stared at her daughter until she finally gave in and dipped her head.

"If you believe you have this taken care of, I'll defer to your under-standing. I'm not too proud to admit that mine is remarkably limited."

Jesus, she's pulling out all the stops today. Bianca Summerlin doesn't back down.

Cheyenne opened her mouth to try reassuring her mom again in a gentler way, but she stopped when a prickling tingle of magical energy raced across the back of her neck and shoulders. It didn't fade but pulsed continuously. She rolled her shoulders back.

"What is it?"

"Nothing, Mom. I just remembered something I need to take care of." She shook her head and gave her mom a small, dismissive smile. *Someone's here. Right now, in her room, watching us. And it's not Ember.*

"Well, don't let me keep you from taking care of it." Bianca settled back against the pillows again and nodded.

I'm being dismissed. Cheyenne set her hand on her mom's shin beneath the comforter, then removed it and stood. "Call me if you need anything, okay?"

"I won't, Cheyenne, but I appreciate the sentiment." Bianca watched her daughter stand and cross the room to rejoin Ember. "Thank you for coming to see me—both of you. Feel free to stay through dinner or longer if you like. I'm still taking my meals up here for the time being, but Eleanor would be grateful for the additional company, I'm sure."

"Thank you." Ember smiled at the woman, but it faded when she saw the dark frown Cheyenne hid from her mom.

When the halfling looked at her friend, she shook her head only enough for Ember to see. *If Bianca knows there's someone else in here, she wouldn't say anything about it out in the open. I should've figured that out when Eleanor couldn't say "master bedroom."*

Cheyenne reached the open door and turned around to face her mom again. It was a longshot, but there was no way Bianca had forgotten their code phrase. *She came up with it so her halfling kid wouldn't have to tell her in public she was about to magically explode, and now I'm gonna use it in her bedroom. Jesus.*

The sharp, buzzing tingle raced continuously along the back of her neck and shoulders. "Mom?"

Bianca opened her eyes and settled them on her daughter.

"Do you guys have cherries in the house?"

Her mom blinked faster than usual but recovered quickly and lifted her chin. "No, Cheyenne. No cherries."

"I can get some for you if you want. Just say the word."

"I've lost my taste for cherries, but thank you. Do come to say goodbye before you leave, whenever that is."

"Okay." Cheyenne forced a smile, then turned back and nodded for Ember to step with her into the hall. *She might not have picked up on someone else in the room. She hadn't looked surprised that I brought it up. She's lying.*

"Good to see you, Bianca," Ember called over her shoulder.

"Thank you, Ember. I always enjoy your visits."

Cheyenne nodded at her mom, grabbed the door handle, and slowly closed the door with a gentle click. Then she stepped back and took a slow, deep breath, making as little sound as possible.

Ember frowned at her.

Cheyenne quickly lifted a finger to her lips, shook her head, then pointed at the closed French doors and mouthed, "Someone's here."

Ember's eyes widened, and she floated soundlessly toward the banister surrounding the second-floor landing without a word.

CHAPTER TWENTY-SEVEN

Cheyenne scanned the bare walls and the pristinely dusted French doors of her mom's bedroom. *Whoever it is won't hang around now that they've seen me here. All I have to do is wait.*

She counted silently to a full sixty seconds, then a humanoid shimmer of opalescent light materialized in the wall right in front of her. Black shoes and ironed black slacks moved through the wall first, followed by a button-down black shirt and L'zar Verdys' slate-gray skin and white hair.

The drow thief phased through the wall, looking over his shoulder and grinning at what he thought was a successful attempt at walking out of there without being caught. He was still grinning when Cheyenne pounced on him, grabbed two fistfuls of his button-down shirt, and slammed him against the now-solid wall.

"What the fuck are you doing?" she hissed.

L'zar's surprise faded and he blinked at his daughter. "Cheyenne. What a lovely surprise."

"Don't pull that shit with me, L'zar. You were in there the whole time!" She thumped him against the wall again, and he didn't even try to fight back. "You better start talking right now."

"Wait, wait. Easy, okay?" He let out a short chuckle and lifted both hands in surrender. "It's not what it looks like."

"Oh, yeah? So you weren't spying on my conversation with Bianca and decided to sneak out when you figured Ember and I were gone. 'Cause that's what it fucking looks like."

"Well, that part of it does have some truth to it." His smile faded when she growled at him. "I'm not hurting her, Cheyenne. She knows I'm here."

"What?" She jerked her hands away from his shirt and stepped back.

"You heard me." With a mocking frown, he readjusted his shirt and stepped away from the wall. "We were having a rather amicable conversation before the two of you arrived, and we thought it would be best if you didn't know I was here. For now."

"What the fuck!"

L'zar pursed his lips. "I realize this might be difficult for you to understand."

"Don't." Cheyenne pointed at him. "Don't even start with the 'let me explain this complicated matter to you' bullshit."

"I would like to explain, though."

"No. Everything that comes out of your mouth is bullshit and poison." Cheyenne summoned a crackling black energy orb in one hand and cocked her head at her father. "I swear to god, L'zar, if you've done anything to hurt her—"

"Really, now. Why would I want to do that?"

"You already did!"

One of the French doors creaked open. Drow father and daughter turned at the same time to see Bianca step cautiously into the hall, steadying herself with one hand on the closed door. She looked at Cheyenne, then Ember, and her face remained aggravatingly impassive even when she met L'zar's gaze. "It seems your plan had more holes in it than you realized."

L'zar scoffed. "Well, I never said I was perfect."

Bianca glanced at the crackling energy sphere in her daughter's hand and blinked slowly. "This isn't the place or time, Cheyenne. Put it away."

The black and purple orb snuffed out, and Cheyenne stepped forward. "Mom, are you seriously going along with this?"

"I'm not going along with anything." While the rest of Bianca was calm, composed, and perfectly in control despite being barefoot and in pajamas, the ligaments on the hand tightly gripping the closed door betrayed the effort she was putting into staying on her feet. "I won't say I particularly enjoy this man's presence in my home, especially looking the way he does, but I agreed to let him stay temporarily."

L'zar clapped his hands and grinned, staring at his daughter and her mother. "We're finally all together with nowhere to be and no other pressing issues. Isn't it wonderful?"

Cheyenne and Bianca gave him matching blank stares.

"Oh, come on." He chuckled. "You have to see what a fortunate sliver of synchronicity this is. After all this time, here we are. Our own little family reunion moment."

"The fuck it is." Cheyenne summoned a new energy sphere and ignored the pointed glance Bianca shot her way.

L'zar narrowed his eyes and glanced at them. "But we *are* a family."

"No." Cheyenne and her mother said it at the same time.

"Oh." L'zar dropped his arms to his sides and shrugged. "And here I was, thinking the word had a literal definition."

Bianca ignored him and met her daughter's gaze. "We've been talking, Cheyenne. Since I regained consciousness yesterday morning."

"About what?"

"About you and everything that lies both behind you and in front of you." Bianca dipped her head.

She already knows what happened to her. Ba'rael's curse, L'zar's part in it, everything. "I can't believe this."

"That's all it's been, Cheyenne." L'zar clasped his hands behind his back, his composure back now that she wasn't trying to kill him and his familial proposal had been outright rejected. "Bianca and I were merely talking. Quite civilly, I might add."

"Yeah, right."

"I think right now, while emotions are running high," Bianca added, "we should table this discussion. Go our separate ways and approach this in the morning."

"Emotions running high." Cheyenne studied her mom and the woman's composed posture. Bianca raised an eyebrow, and that sealed the deal. "Right. I'll go take some time to cool off, shall I?"

She snuffed out the second energy sphere she never got to send into L'zar's face and gave her mom a challenging look.

"This is real, Cheyenne." L'zar reached out and brushed his hand against her shoulder. "We only want what's best for you."

"Fuck off." She shrugged away from him and stormed down the hall. "You want what's best for yourself."

Bianca watched her daughter stomp toward the top of the stairs before jogging down them to the main floor, but she didn't say a word. "Hmm. I think your powers of persuasion have diminished a good deal in the last twenty-one years."

L'zar chuckled. "She'll come around. We had the opportunity to get to know each other quite well during our time on the other side."

Bianca turned toward him and raised an eyebrow. "Then she's even less likely to forgive you."

He grinned and stepped toward her. "What about you, Bianca? Are you any more inclined to warm to me again now that you see the full scope of things?"

She tilted her head back to look up at him as he brushed the backs of his fingers against the turquoise satin of her nightshirt. "Not so far."

"Ah." L'zar glanced at his hand, removed it from her arm, and dropped it at his side again. "We have time, and I hope I've made it clear I'm not going anywhere anytime soon."

"You can congratulate yourself all you want for staying in my presence longer than four consecutive hours, but don't mistake my prioritizing Cheyenne's wellbeing for forgiveness or even acceptance."

"No. Of course not." L'zar clasped his hands behind his back and dipped his head toward her in a shallow bow. "Take all the time you need. Can I bring you anything?"

Bianca eyed him, then stepped back into her room, grabbing the handle of the open door. "The last thing I want right now is to see your face. Go skulk somewhere else."

She closed the door firmly in his face.

"Hmm." L'zar chuckled and straightened from where he'd bent toward Bianca Summerlin. Then he turned and locked eyes with Ember, who still stood by the rail surrounding the second-floor landing, her eyes wide. "I think that went rather well, don't you?"

She shook her head and lifted both hands. "Don't try to drag me into this, man."

"Well, then why are you still standing there?"

"You guys were blocking the hall." Ember shrugged and floated past him, staring at the open doors of the breakfast room until she turned at the top of the stairs.

"Talk to her, will you?" he asked. "She listens to you."

"Sorry." Ember gestured at him and floated quickly down the staircase. "Whatever the hell that was, L'zar, you're on your own."

He watched her until she headed beneath the stairs off the foyer. With a final glance at Bianca's closed bedroom doors, he turned toward the front of the house and strolled casually down the hall. "They'll come around."

L'zar's body shimmered in the air, and he disappeared.

<hr>

Ember could hear Cheyenne rooting around in the wet bar beneath the stairs before she rounded the corner into the dining area. The halfling knelt in front of the liquor cabinet, pulling out bottle after bottle until she found the one she wanted and stood. "You okay?"

"No." The bottle popped when Cheyenne jerked off the lid, and she poured four fingers of dark-amber bourbon into a rocks glass. "And I don't wanna talk about it."

"Okay, well, you want any ice in that?"

Cheyenne lifted the glass and set the bottle on the top of the wet bar with a clink of glass on glass. "Also no, Em, but I definitely wouldn't mind the company. You want one?"

"Yeah, sure. Half of what you're drinking and a lot more ice."

The halfling quickly turned back to snatch another rocks glass off the cabinet's top shelf. The lid of the ice drawer slammed aside, and ice plinked violently into the glass before she filled it as full as her own.

Ember's eyes widened when her friend handed her the drink. "I said half as much as you."

"That is half, Em. Blame the ice." Cheyenne knocked back a huge gulp of bourbon and closed her eyes. "I can't believe this. The two of them getting together behind my back like some kind of co-parenting team. Are you fucking kidding me?"

Ember sipped her drink.

"There's no way she believes the crap spewing out of his mouth, right? She has to know how full of shit he is." The halfling took another large gulp and gritted her teeth, staring at the floor. "He's not here because he cares about her. There's something else he wants out of this."

She tapped a finger against her glass, frowning as her gaze flickered across the hardwood.

Ember tilted her head. "You do wanna talk about it?"

"No." Cheyenne looked at her friend, a tense smile plastered onto her lips. "I wanna get shitfaced, Em, and talk about literally anything else until I'm passed out on the floor. 'Kay?"

Ember floated slowly forward, raised her glass, and clinked it against Cheyenne's. "That's what friends are for."

"Damn straight."

CHAPTER TWENTY-EIGHT

"You know what really gets me?" Cheyenne Summerlin slumped against the armrest of the loveseat in the sitting area of her mom's house, her glass of bourbon sloshing around in her hand as she propped her arm up on the expensive upholstery.

Ember stared into her gin and tonic. She'd switched to that after the first bourbon. "I'm afraid to ask."

"I'm so fucking sick of the games, you know?" Cheyenne paused to take another huge gulp of her second drink in the last half hour. It wouldn't be long until she went back for a third. "Like, everyone thinks this is something we can get out of in the end. If it works out, great. If it doesn't, no problem. It's not like it affects us."

The fae squinted at her friend, then eyed Cheyenne's nearly empty glass. "You're still talking about L'zar and Bianca, aren't you?"

"No." Cheyenne looked down at her drink too. "Maybe. I think I'm venting about everyone else, and I probably haven't had this much bourbon in an hour since the first time I raided that wet bar."

Ember snorted. "You know what really gets me?"

"What?"

"The fact that human booze gets you all loosened up like this when the hardcore medical stuff doesn't do shit."

Cheyenne said, "Did I tell you about when I broke my arm as a kid? Doctors kept upping the anesthesia."

"And couldn't knock you out with a dose big enough for a full-grown man? Yeah, you told me."

"Oh."

Ember sipped her drink, then shrugged. "Honestly, I'm more concerned that any doctor would pump that amount of drugs into a little girl."

"Yeah, well, most doctors don't see little girls who can change the color of their skin and grow pointy ears when they're in a hell of a lot of pain. At least, it hurt a lot back then, anyway."

"Well, yeah. You were a kid."

"With a high tolerance for pain and all the tolerance for narcotics. Too bad no one tried to get me wasted first and then take me in for surgery."

Ember wrinkled her nose. "I don't think alcohol and invasive surgery are a good idea. Blood thinner and everything, right?"

"Yeah, Em. I know. I'm just sayin'." After knocking back the rest of her drink, Cheyenne sighed, slapped the armrest, and kicked off her black Vans, letting them fall wherever they landed on the area rug in the sitting area. *I don't think Mom's gonna give a shit where I leave my shoes right now. She's got a bigger mess upstairs. If L'zar even is still upstairs.*

She craned her neck to glare at the underside of the huge central staircase and the hallway where she'd left both her parents staring tensely after her. *He can go fuck himself.*

"Okay. Time for another." She stood from the loveseat and gestured at Ember with her empty glass. "You want more?"

"I just made this one."

Cheyenne shrugged. "Yeah, okay. Sure. We're both goin' at our own pace."

"Uh-huh. And mine stops when I reach that line between being here for you while you angry-drink and joining you in the land of I Don't Give a Fuck."

The halfling's rocks glass clinked down on the glass surface of the wet bar before the dwindling bottle of bourbon opened in her hands again with a pop. "I'm allowed a night of drinking myself into that land,

Em. Especially after all the shit upstairs I'm trying to burn out of my memory with good booze."

"Fair enough. I'm not trying to stop you. Just callin' it like I see it."

"Fine. I don't want you to feel like you have to chaperone me in my mom's house. I can handle it."

"I know." Ember sat back against the pillows on the chaise and muttered into her glass, "I'm wondering about everyone else."

Cheyenne poured herself another four-finger glass of bourbon, no ice, pretending she hadn't heard her friend's most-likely-private comment. *I grew up in a house where you drink instead of talking about your feelings. Guess this apple rolled back to the tree on that one.*

She took a sip, let herself imagine she still tasted it as much as the first glass, and walked slowly back to the loveseat.

Ember chuckled. "You look like you sat on a cactus."

"What?"

"You feelin' okay?"

Cheyenne reached into her back pocket to pull out her buzzing cell phone. "Jeeze. Spend a couple of days in Ambar'ogúl, and you forget all about smartphones. They are a pain in the ass compared to activators. Am I right?"

"Not nearly as convenient." Ember raised her eyebrows. "You gonna answer that, drunk drow?"

"Highly buzzed, thank you very much." Cheyenne finally glanced at the name pulled up on her screen and wrinkled her nose. "Serious pain in my ass. It's Rhynehart."

"Yeah, you should put that on speaker too. You know, for fun."

"Right." With a snort, the halfling answered the call and put it on speaker for her *Nós Aní's* benefit. "What's up, Rhynehart?"

"Were you planning on calling me back, kid? Or did I slip your mind entirely?"

She took a long drink and made sure the slurp was extra-loud. "Kinda had a few things come up. Got your voicemail, though. That was a fun surprise."

"Glad you enjoyed it. Now I'm following up."

"Sweet." She slurped again. "About what?"

A long pause on the other line was his response. Then the agent cleared his throat. "You know, I've spent a long time hearing the differences over the phone and learning when not to ask, but I can't help it right now. Are you drunk?"

Ember laughed and quickly cut it off by taking a sip of her drink.

"Highly buzzed, Rhynehart. There's a serious difference. And yes, I promise I'll remember this conversation in the morning. So go."

"Uh-huh." He sighed heavily. "Well, first, I guess I could take this chance to thank you for the career change. Seeing as you played such a huge part in it."

Cheyenne frowned. *Why does he think I give a shit?* "Yeah, congratulations. We should talk about this thing with your superior's superior, yeah? You said you wanted in, so now I wanna know what you can do on base and with your clearance level to help us get ready for this thing on Monday. If I feel like letting you all the way in on it."

Ember widened her eyes at her friend's highly buzzed attitude, and Cheyenne took another gulp of bourbon in response. *I only told him about Colonel Thomas meeting with the Bull's Head assholes. Didn't invite him in yet.*

Rhynehart let out another sigh. "Nothing."

"Nothing what?"

"Nothing, as in I can't do shit on base and with my clearance level, seeing as it's non-existent now."

"What?" Cheyenne looked at Ember again, and the fae leaned over her lap to get closer to the phone.

"I got canned, kid," Rhynehart muttered, his low voice bordering on exploding with anger. "Thirteen fucking years at this gig and they stripped me of the whole thing the day a certain scaly inmate broke out of that prison."

"Shit." She took another drink.

"Yeah. Straight from my superior's superior, if that's the way we're skirtin' around the details. He thinks he's onto me. He probably thinks the same thing about you, seeing as every guard in the front of the building saw us walk in together with the new recruits."

He's still not gonna risk calling out Colonel Thomas by name or say what we were doing there over the phone.

"Well, shit, Rhynehart. Definitely didn't see that one coming."

"Yeah, me neither. Anyway, he knows what we know?"

"I seriously doubt it." Cheyenne sipped on her drink and sat back in the loveseat. "If you got sacked the day of, I would've seen something then. Had a meeting with him and everything."

Rhynehart paused. "In person?"

"Yeah, in person. That's how I know what I know, and I'm assuming that's why you called. Again. You want in?"

"Fuck yeah, I do. I've got nothing to lose."

Cheyenne smiled. "I know the feeling."

"Then I'll get everything together. Grab a team. Gear up."

"How are you gonna do that without your precious security clearance?"

He snorted. "Please. Being off the books doesn't mean I can't still get shit done. Off the books. So, when are we doing this?"

"You know, I don't think I've heard you this excited about anything."

"The fuckers tossed me out with the trash, Cheyenne! Like the last thirteen years never happened. Why wouldn't I wanna crush that asshole into the ground?"

"I like your attitude." She looked at Ember and raised her eyebrows over a small, satisfied smile. "But you're gonna have to wait. We'll do this on Monday, so you have about forty-eight hours."

"We should move that up."

"Nope. You're gonna have to wait, and I'll fill you in on the rest of the details later. I'm a little busy right now gettin' my bourbon on, so I'm gonna let you go."

"Cheyenne, hold on a minute."

She ended the call and dropped her phone on the plush loveseat cushion beside her.

Ember chuckled. "You enjoyed that, didn't you?"

"You mean the first conversation where I'm calling all the shots and the FRoE agent who fucked me over more than a few times couldn't say shit about it? Me? Enjoying that? Come on." Cheyenne lifted her glass to her lips again, grinning.

"Ex-FRoE agent."

"Doesn't fucking matter, Em. I'll be running a team through the first FRoE rebellion in twenty-one years."

"I thought it's only been around for twenty-one years."

"Even better." Leaning forward, Cheyenne stretched her drink out toward her friend, and they clinked glasses. "Maybe this is turning into a celebration."

"Okay." Ember took her first long drink, then stared at her glass as the ice swirled around in her gin and tonic. "Then I guess I'll switch to celebrating with you."

Cheyenne drank until she could barely taste the bourbon. Staggering up the wide staircase at the end of the night hadn't been in her plans, but neither she nor Ember was in a state to make the hour-long drive back to Richmond. The thought that L'zar might still be upstairs, hovering around Bianca as the woman recovered from the curse that had taken her out for the last three days, only briefly entered her swirling mind. She didn't really give a shit.

The next thing she knew, she was lying face-down on the bed she hated in the room she hated. Ember's muttered conversation to herself floated down the hall from the open door of the guest room. The whole world spun around the halfling, made worse when she closed her eyes.

Everything that's happened over the last few months, and this is the first time I get full-on shitfaced. Fairly sure I deserve it.

She was sure she'd deserve everything she felt the next morning, too.

CHAPTER TWENTY-NINE

Neros returned to her in her scattered dreams, flickering in and out of clarity. No Ba'rael Verdys hanging suspended in a tomb of dark light, but Cheyenne's cousin wasn't any less insistent in her mind.

"Don't stop, Cheyenne. Find the vessel. Use it the way it was meant to be used. You cannot do this alone, and Ambar'ogúl will not survive without you. The vessel, Cheyenne. Cheyenne!"

She bolted awake again with a raw, gasping breath. Pain and nauseating dizziness burst through her head when she sat up way faster than she should have. "Oh, fuck."

Thumping back down on the bed, she rolled over on her side, fully intending to curl up in the fetal position and sleep through what was sure to be a twelve-hour hangover at least. But as her eyelids fluttered closed, she couldn't ignore the bright silver light strobing with growing intensity on the floor. *What?*

Cheyenne slowly opened her eyes again, grimacing at the blaze inside the pile of her trenchcoat still where she'd shrugged out of it the night before. *No way I'm getting back to sleep with whatever the hell that is shining in my face.*

With a grunt, Cheyenne pushed over to the edge of the bed and slapped the floor, trying to grab her trenchcoat without leaving the mattress. Her finger finally snagged in the thick folds of black fabric, and she tugged the whole thing up onto the bed with her. The violent silver flashing continued until she snarled and all but ripped her coat apart to get to the source. "Fucking stop already!"

She finally found the pocket, shoved her hand inside, and felt the cold, metallic exterior of the Darkglass with Neros' four-pointed star inside. The second she pulled the container free from her pocket, the silver light flashing around her cousin's manifested magic cut out. And at the same second, in the master bedroom on the other side of the second floor, Bianca Summerlin screamed.

It wasn't so much a scream as a shout of surprise and pain and outrage, but it was as close to a scream as Cheyenne's mom got.

The halfling forgot all about the Darkglass and her coat and leaped off the bed. She'd almost forgotten about her hangover too until the first jarring steps across her childhood bedroom reminded her of the poor decision she'd made last night. *One poor decision and you're useless.*

She nearly barreled into Ember, who came out of the guestroom, her purple-streaked hair frazzled and sticking out in all directions. They glanced briefly at each other in surprise, then Ember cast her human-illusion charm, and they took off around the top of the wide main staircase, past the breakfast room, and finally to the closed doors of Bianca's bedroom.

The woman's surprised shouting had died down, but she'd started yelling her daughter's name from behind closed doors. "Cheyenne! I need you in here!"

Cheyenne jerked down on both door handles and threw the doors open at the same time. "Mom, what's going on?"

Bianca lay on her back, slightly propped up by pillows with her arms lying straight and rigid at her sides. Her chest heaved, and she looked up at her daughter with wide eyes. "I wish I could say."

"Oh, man." Racing toward her mom's bedside, Cheyenne looked Bianca over, grimacing both at the dizzying pain in her head and the painful-looking rune burns all over her mom's flesh. Every single one of them glowed with bright orange light coming from within the marks, and the skin around each O'gúl rune looked red and raw and very painful.

"What is this?" Bianca panted, then closed her eyes and let out a slow sigh. "Besides highly uncomfortable."

"I don't know. Mom, I'm sorry. I don't know."

"Don't apologize, Cheyenne. Get me a glass of water and some ibuprofen at the very least."

"Yeah, sure."

"You can stay here," L'zar said as he materialized in the room as if walking through a portal.

Cheyenne jumped and spun around. "Where the hell did you come from?"

"I've been in this house for forty-eight hours, Cheyenne. Hardly a difficult concept to grasp." The drow thief brushed past her to stop at Bianca's bedside and frowned down at her in concern. His golden gaze swept across her body, moving quickly back and forth. "Where does it hurt?"

Bianca let out a bitter laugh. "Everywhere, you idiot. Where do you think?"

A low hum escaped him. "The most."

She sighed, blinking quickly at the ceiling. "Here."

Bianca grimaced when his fingers brushed the raw, glowing flesh in the center of her chest beneath her silk nightshirt.

L'zar reached for her shirt, but she slapped his hand away.

"Don't touch me."

"I need to see."

"Then ask me to show you." She waved his hand away and glared at the open doors on the opposite side of the room. "I'm bedridden and weak, not unconscious."

A tiny smile crept across the drow's face. "Please, Bianca. Show me."

Pursing her lips, Cheyenne's mom reached for the collar of her nightshirt one more time and pulled it aside. "That's the worst of it. Right here."

"Hmm." L'zar bent down until his face was a mere six inches from her chest, ignoring her burning glare. "I believe that's because it's new."

"What?" Cheyenne stepped over to them and tried to get a better look at the newest rune burning itself into her mom's skin. "I thought that part of the curse was done."

"Apparently not." He straightened and shot his daughter a quick sidelong glance. "Smells like you had quite the night."

"Shut up."

Bianca let out a shuddering sigh as she fought to control her reaction to the pain blazing across her skin. "I'm not a fan of you knowing which injuries were already on my chest and which were not."

L'zar shrugged. "I cataloged them for the purpose of discerning a pattern, but if you'd rather I didn't monitor either the improvement or the decline of your personal health, Bianca, say the word, and I'll take my leave."

"No." She shut her eyes and let out another long, slow, forced breath. "I don't know the first or last thing about any of this."

"As I suspected." He dipped his head and waited for her to keep going.

"Don't leave yet." Bianca didn't look at him; couldn't look at the drow man who'd turned her life on its head twice in two decades as she asked him to stay without really asking. That was painful enough.

"So, why is this still happening?" Cheyenne asked.

L'zar tapped a finger on his lips and stared at the new rune on Bianca's chest. "I imagine it's a message. Information leftover from Ba'rael's curse when it formed the other runes."

Bianca cleared her throat, her mouth dry when she opened it. "I want knowledge and facts, not imagination. Especially not yours."

He dipped his head to her, though she still hadn't opened her eyes. "Then we'll call it an educated guess."

"What does it mean?" Cheyenne gestured at her mom's chest. "The new one. I can't read this stuff."

"Not even with your activator?"

The halfling glared at her father, her head pounding. "Not when it's written in flesh, L'zar."

"Interesting. That new one means 'vessel.'"

She blinked in disbelief, then cocked her head and kept staring at the rune. "Are you fucking kidding me?"

"Cheyenne, watch your fucking language!"

The bedroom fell silent at Bianca's uncharacteristic outburst.

Cheyenne swallowed and stepped away from the bed. "Sorry."

"Stop apologizing," her mom muttered. "I'm enough of a hypocrite as it is."

Turning to shoot Ember a glance, Cheyenne shrugged and removed herself from the vicinity of the bed. *I'm gonna make her blow up like that again, and then I'll go off too.* She rubbed her forehead, forcing herself to stay here instead of retreating to her bedroom to sleep off her hangover.

"You okay?" Ember muttered as L'zar and Bianca held a private conversation in hushed voices Cheyenne couldn't even pretend to be interested in right now.

"I hit the booze way too hard last night, Em, and now I'm feelin' it."

"Oh." Ember chuckled and floated behind her friend to place both hands on Cheyenne's shoulders. "I'm a total dick for not doing this sooner."

"Not doing what?" Cheyenne's eyes widened as a blazing warmth trickled from Ember's hands through the halfling's entire body. Something like an electric jolt and a chill raced through her and raised goosebumps on her arms, then the pain in her head subsided, her nausea disappeared, and she didn't feel like curling up in the corner anymore. "Holy shit," she whispered, making sure only Ember could hear it this time.

"You're welcome." Ember gave her friend a firm slap on the back. "Pretty neat, huh?"

"For sure. Thanks." Cheyenne smiled at her, then frowned. "How'd you know you could cure a hangover?"

"Because I drank almost as much as you did last night and woke up fresh as a daisy." The fae shot a quick glance in Bianca's direction. "Given the circumstances."

"So, you healed yourself of a drunken stupor, is that it?"

"Yeah, without even trying. I knew it would work on you. A fae thing, I guess."

"Uh-huh. Well, I'm a grateful halfling either way." *And I need to figure out what the hell's going on with all this "vessel" bullshit now that I can think.* "L'zar."

He stiffened where he stood hunched over Bianca's bedside. "Cheyenne."

"Tell me about the vessel."

With his hands clasped behind his back, L'zar straightened and looked at her over his shoulder. "I don't know what you mean."

"Try again." She folded her arms and walked over to him. "If everyone's been coming to me about this vessel, whatever it is, I have a hard time believing you don't know anything about it."

"Define 'everyone.'"

"I really have to get into it? Okay, fine." Cheyenne counted on her fingers. "Venga and his backfiring potion. Two dreams of Neros now. The Sorren Gán." Her father's eyes widened at that last one like she knew they would. "And now it's showing up on my mother's skin. So what's going on?"

"Well." L'zar turned back to Bianca and eyed her. She was breathing steadily again now, her eyes still closed, and almost looked asleep if it weren't for her fists clenched tightly around handfuls of the bedspread at her side. "As intrigued as I am to hear about all this, I can't answer that question."

Cheyenne cocked her head at him. "That's strike two."

A small chuckle escaped him as he shrugged. From anyone else, it would've sounded nervous. From L'zar, it sounded careless. "Then I suppose I'll be striking off."

"Out," she corrected. "Striking out."

"You don't watch baseball, do you?" Ember asked.

Bianca sighed. "How is any of this relevant to the current situation?"

"Sorry." The fae clasped her hands in front of her. "It's not."

"She doesn't have anything to do with all this other stuff." Cheyenne gestured at her mom and glared at her dad. "So why is it showing up on her skin?"

L'zar cleared his throat. "Strike three, I suppose."

"Whew." Eleanor pushed a stainless-steel cart into the room and shook her head. "I don't know what's been wrong with me the last few days. Forget trying to talk."

The woman stopped when she looked up and saw three magicals standing in her employer's bedroom and Bianca lying motionless in bed.

Eleanor's mouth dropped open and closed two more times without any sound. Her eyes widened when she looked at L'zar, and the drow thief grinned at her.

"I see you've brought breakfast. Excellent."

CHAPTER THIRTY

"This isn't time for Christmas lights!" Eleanor blurted. She clapped both hands over her mouth and breathed heavily through her nose.

L'zar chuckled. "Certainly not for another few months."

Cheyenne studied the housekeeper with narrowed eyes. "Still not feeling any better, huh?"

Eleanor cocked her head. "I can't remember which key goes in the pizza."

Ember and Cheyenne exchanged a confused glance. "Eleanor, maybe you should sit down for a second."

"I don't know why everyone's punching the sleeping bag." Furiously shaking her head, Eleanor stared at the prepared tray of Bianca's breakfast resting on the cart and pushed it all at the bed. She glared at L'zar, then lifted the serving lid from the tray and stuck it on the cart's lower shelf.

"Ah." L'zar leaned forward to sniff at the still-steaming scrambled eggs, sautéed spinach, and granola-filled yogurt. "I don't see anything wrong with your cooking."

"No!" The housekeeper batted at L'zar's face until he straightened and stepped away from the cart, chuckling.

"Eleanor." Bianca had opened her eyes and now gazed intently at her friend. "What is the matter?"

"I'm not inclined to blow bubbles," the woman muttered, her head shaking in quick, trembling jerks as she stared right back at her employer.

Then Bianca's gaze slowly shifted to L'zar. "I want an explanation for this."

"For what?"

Cheyenne set a hand on Eleanor's rigid shoulder, trying to reassure the woman who clearly wasn't herself. "Yeah, I was thinking the same thing."

"Oh, come on." The drow spread his arms. "It's not fair to gang up on a guest."

"What did you do to her?"

"Nothing." He glanced from Cheyenne to the housekeeper and back again. "Of consequence."

"L'zar."

"It's just a small charm." He chuckled and stepped away, walking and talking himself into a corner beneath the unamused stares of all four women in the room. "I wanted a little privacy. You know, in case the wrong kind of person found their way into this house looking for the right drow if you catch my drift."

"Not cool."

"It's nothing harmful."

Cheyenne slowly shook her head. "You don't need a privacy charm to keep Eleanor from making any sense when she opens her mouth. Take it off."

L'zar rolled his eyes and flicked his fingers at the housekeeper.

Eleanor let out a surprised squeak, covered her mouth with both hands again, and flushed a bright red. Her anger pushed her even farther into finally speaking her mind. "You asshole!"

"Yes, thank you. I've heard that one before. Many times."

The housekeeper skirted past the breakfast cart, glaring at L'zar the whole time, and sent a swift, powerfully angry kick into his shins.

"Ow." He hunched over and stepped away from her, then glanced down at her shoes. "Those don't look like steel-toed boots."

"No. They're Danskos. And you're the worst sort of villain I've ever met." Turning swiftly with her nose turned up, Eleanor grabbed the handle of the cart and stepped backward to bring it all the way up to Bianca's bedside. Cheyenne moved back, but when L'zar didn't budge because he was too busy smirking at her boiling frustration, she smacked him in the chest and stomach. "Out of my way. You shouldn't even be here. Bianca needs rest, and you're the last thing to aid anyone's healing."

L'zar dipped his head. "Also not a new predicament for me."

"Move!"

He finally stepped aside, and Eleanor shot him another scathing glare before situating the cart beside Bianca and offering the woman a glass of orange juice.

"At the very least, drink this."

"Thank you, Eleanor." Bianca slowly sat up and pulled herself up the bed to lean against all the pillows again. She accepted the orange juice with as much decorum as if she weren't in excruciating pain from remnants of a drow curse and her housekeeper hadn't been charmed into idiocy by that same drow. "Breakfast looks lovely. I hate to ask you for one more thing."

"Whatever you need." Eleanor nodded, shot L'zar a quick scowl, then gave Bianca a tight smile.

"Ibuprofen, please. Something stronger if we have it."

"I'll see what we have. There's a bottle of champagne in the cellar."

"Not this morning, Eleanor. Thank you."

"Of course." The housekeeper spun around again, snorted in disgust at L'zar. "And don't even think about laying a hand on that food. Do you hear me? I'll sweep you right out with the trash." Without waiting for a reply, she bustled through the room to the open doors. When she met Cheyenne's gaze, Eleanor rolled her eyes and didn't say another word as she left.

L'zar stared after her and tilted his head. "With a broom, do you suppose?"

"Do not mistake my allowing your presence in this house as full permission for you to do whatever you please." Bianca's voice was low, authoritative, and carried as much weight in its warning as every time she'd used it with Cheyenne.

Been a long time since I've heard that. And I'm so glad to see it's not directed at me this time.

L'zar spread his arms. "I was merely—"

"There was no 'mere' anything about what you did." The woman didn't have to shout to get the same effect. "If you think I'll allow this grotesque invasion of personal autonomy to continue—with Eleanor, with me, with Cheyenne or Ember—I will rescind any amount of good-will you've received thus far, however little that may be."

"Don't be angry with me."

"I'm beyond anger at this point." She stared at him with the undrunk glass of orange juice in her hand until L'zar stepped back and dipped his head again.

This time, though, he was frowning. "I apologize."

"That's a start."

"Mom." Cheyenne seized the chance to interrupt the tension a little and steer the conversation back to where it needed to be. She gestured at her own chest. "Can I take a look at that?"

"I don't see what for."

"To see if I recognize anything."

"Don't bother yourself, Cheyenne," L'zar cut in. "I've already examined those runes closely enough for the both of us."

"Oh, sure. I'd say forgive me for not taking your word for it, but I don't really care." She stepped past him and sidled around the breakfast cart to get to her mother.

He watched them for a moment, then lowered his voice and leaned toward them. "I may be able to find an alternative solution to this."

"Don't bother yourself, L'zar." Cheyenne glared up at him and shook her head. "You've already done enough."

He took a sharp breath. "Be that as it may, I still feel compelled to offer what little knowledge I do possess in this matter."

"Nope."

"Cheyenne, I can help. I *want* to help."

"No. You're done playing wannabe drow hero. You're out of the picture now, remember? You gave it all up. I did my job, you were cursed and exiled, and nobody needs you anymore. You knew this would happen."

Her father straightened, the concerned frown gone from his face in an instant as he lifted his chin and gazed at her over his long, aquiline nose. The corners of L'zar's mouth twitched into a subdued sneer. "As you wish."

He took off across the room, swerving around the edge of the breakfast cart without missing a beat. Cheyenne stared at the bedspread in front of her until she heard his footsteps, light even in anger, fade down the staircase and into the foyer.

She took a deep breath, let it out slowly, and looked at her mom. "Bad idea to let him stay here."

Bianca blinked quickly, then leaned back against the pillows to peer around her daughter. "Ember, would you kindly give Cheyenne and me a few minutes alone, please?"

"Oh." Ember's eyes widened, and she pointed at the open doors. "Uh, sure. Yeah."

"Thank you. And close the doors behind you if you would."

"No problem." When the fae glanced at Cheyenne on her way out, the halfling could only give her an apologetic shrug.

"Maybe Eleanor made something else for breakfast. You can go check if you want."

"Yep. I'll see you downstairs." Ember grabbed both door handles and pulled the doors swiftly shut behind her, slowing before they met in the middle with a soft click.

Cheyenne turned back to her mom and raised her eyebrows. *Totally weird to be shut up here alone. It's not like there are any secrets left in this house anymore. I hope.*

Bianca sighed heavily and swatted the breakfast cart blocking her daughter from the bedside. "Get this thing out of the way, will you? The thought of food is making me nauseous."

Cheyenne gently pushed the cart out of the way and let it roll to a stop on the area rug. Bianca finally took a long drink of orange juice, staring at her daughter as she did so before glancing pointedly at the comforter beside her legs. Cheyenne didn't have to be told to sit. *She's wishing she'd said yes to the champagne, I bet. I'm surprised she didn't ask for tequila.*

With her drink now almost empty, Bianca set it delicately on the nightstand, took another deep breath, then folded her hands in her lap and met her daughter's gaze. "First of all, Cheyenne, I don't want you to have the wrong impression of the situation."

The halfling glanced quickly around the room as if someone might appear out of thin air at any second to interrupt them. *L'zar can, so there's always that possibility.* "Which situation, Mom? The one where you're lying in bed with burns all over your body after being cursed, or the one where you wouldn't talk to me about him for twenty-one years but are suddenly cool with letting him camp out in your house?"

Bianca dipped her head, acknowledging her daughter's anger. Her hesitant swallow betrayed her discomfort better than anything in her nearly composed expression. "Seeing as I don't quite know what the correct impression would be for the former, I am referring to the latter."

"Right. What impression do you think I have?"

"Listen to me, Cheyenne. I am in no way comfortable with that man being here. Well, he's not a man. His presence brings me no satisfaction, no joy, and certainly no additional comfort in my present position, namely lying in bed, as you put it. Your father is insufferably inscrutable and persistent. He speaks in riddles."

Cheyenne snorted. "Yep."

"And he can't sit still for longer than thirty seconds at a time."

"Huh." The halfling tilted her head. "That's a new one."

"It's infuriating."

"Yeah, I bet." *No meditating and lying around with his hands behind his head. Sounds like the Weaver's not as comfortable here as he wants everyone to think.*

"I don't want him here. If I had the choice, if I knew I could snap my fingers, make a call, and have him dragged off this property forever, I'd do it."

"I know, Mom."

Bianca let out a bitter chuckle, then winced when she shifted her position on the bed.

Cheyenne stared at her. Bianca Summerlin didn't fidget. Not even when she was in pain.

"Despite all that, I haven't told him to leave."

"Oh." Cheyenne slowly turned her head away from her mom,

though she couldn't look away. *Why do I have a feeling she's about to say something I don't wanna hear?* "Why not?"

"Because honestly, Cheyenne, I'm frightened." The woman said it with no hesitation, no embarrassment, and no attempt to soften the blow of a revelation like that.

Her daughter closed her eyes in confusion. "Wait, what?"

"I don't know what's been done to me," Bianca continued matter-of-factly, "and I certainly have no inkling as to what lies ahead or how to alleviate the symptoms, or if it's even possible. I'm at a complete loss as to what comes next or to whom I should turn for any aspect of the circumstances."

"Mom, I'll take care of this, okay? You don't have to."

"I know you will." Bianca set a hand on her daughter's knee and nodded slowly. "You haven't let me down so far when you say you'll take care of something, and I have full faith in your ability to do that again. But let him help."

Cheyenne stared at her mom's hand on her knee. "You want me to let L'zar help me clean up his mess."

"Well, if you choose to see it that way, I can't stop you." Bianca's hand slid back into her own lap. "However you see it, that's what I'm requesting of you. Let him help. And if he fails, of which I suspect there is a very high chance, we'll get rid of him together."

It took a moment for that to sink in, then Cheyenne looked quickly up at her mom with raised eyebrows. "Get rid of him."

"That's what I said, Cheyenne. Together. You and I."

A soft laugh of disbelief escaped the halfling. "You know, most of the time these days, the phrase 'get rid of him' means something a little different. What do you mean by that?"

Despite her discomfort and all the unknown surrounding her, Bianca graced her daughter with a small, knowing smile. "Use your imagination. You've always been quite good at that."

Cheyenne sighed. "Okay. I guess. I'll let him help."

"Good."

And I seriously hope he does, 'cause I don't think even Mom has the resources to get rid of L'zar Verdys. Does she?

As Cheyenne stared at the wall beside the headboard, mulling over her confusion at her mom's request, Bianca pressed herself farther into the pile of pillows and closed her eyes. "That will be all for now. Being ripped out of sleep by my skin catching fire doesn't leave room for high energy levels."

"Got it." Cheyenne patted her mom's leg and considered leaning down to hug her, but Bianca didn't open her eyes again or show any indication that she wanted to be touched. *Probably not, if her skin's on fire.* So she turned slowly and headed for the doors.

"And remind Eleanor about the ibuprofen," Bianca muttered.

"Or something stronger, right?"

Her mom took a long, deep breath and didn't move. "Or something stronger. Thank you."

Cheyenne slipped quietly through the doors and closed them gently behind her. Then she turned to the staircase and paused. *What the fuck does "get rid of him" mean? If she thinks we're taking this into patricide, she's worse than I thought.*

CHAPTER THIRTY-ONE

Once she got downstairs, Cheyenne poked her head through the swinging door into the industrial kitchen and found Eleanor plating two servings of eggs, bacon, and hash browns. "Eleanor?"

"Oh!" The housekeeper jumped and grabbed the skillet handle with both hands to keep from dropping it. "You almost gave me a heart attack, Cheyenne."

"Sorry. I'm not trying to sneak up on you."

"I should hope not. We've already had enough of that around here as it is." Eleanor waved in the general direction of the rest of the house.

"Asshole?" Cheyenne offered.

"Ha. Well, I was trying to expand my vocabulary, but that's the only word that feels right at the moment."

"Yeah, I know the feeling. Hey, you still keep the medicine cabinet in the same place, right?"

"What? Oh." The skillet clanged back down on the range stovetop, and Eleanor vigorously wiped her hands on her apron. "I forgot the ibuprofen."

"I can take it to her if you want."

"No, no. I moved the whole medicine cabinet last spring. Had a new one built, and it's a little tricky to… No, I'll get it." Eleanor set a fork on each plate, then picked up the dishes and carried them over to

Cheyenne. "For you and Ember. I'm sorry I didn't have anything ready for you earlier than this."

"Eleanor."

"Yes?" The woman stopped right in front of Cheyenne.

"All that's on L'zar, okay? Don't apologize for what he did to you."

"Well. I'm not in the habit of shrugging responsibility off on someone else, but in this case, I'll make an exception. So I take it back."

"Good." Cheyenne took the breakfast plates, and the housekeeper pointed at her.

"And we never talk about it again."

"Deal. And thanks for breakfast. This is perfect."

"Well, it's the least I can do. Help yourself to anything else if I missed something. I know I don't have to tell you, but that includes the liquor cabinet."

"What?"

Eleanor waved off the halfling's surprise and gave her a pointed look. "I caught a glimpse of you stumbling into your room last night, sweetheart. I've never heard you make so much noise just walking." She looked at Cheyenne and frowned. "Honestly, I'm surprised you look as well as you do this morning. You're not drinking that much as a regular thing these days, are you?"

Cheyenne laughed. "Nope. The perks of having a fae for a best friend."

"Well. Lucky you." With a chuckle, Eleanor hurried off to bring Bianca that ibuprofen. Cheyenne pressed her back against the swinging kitchen door with her hands full of breakfast and found Ember sitting in what had apparently become her usual spot on the chaise in the sitting area down the hall.

The fae perked up when she saw the plates piled high with eggs and bacon and floated effortlessly to her feet. "That looks awesome."

"If Eleanor made it, it will be."

They moved to the dining table beneath the staircase with an epic view of the veranda at the back of the house and the huge back lawn surrounded by forest. The crumbled mess of the destroyed portal ridge was barely visible from the dining area, but Cheyenne took a seat with her back to the entire wall of windows anyway. *I don't wanna think about that shit while I'm eating.*

They dug into their eggs in silence. When Ember finally slowed down enough to leave room for conversation, she looked up at Cheyenne. "So. Bianca, huh?"

"You know, I'd ask what about her, but it's pretty much everything at this point."

"Yeah. It's pretty weird." Ember stuck another forkful of eggs in her mouth and chewed thoughtfully. "Especially the whole vessel thing, right?"

"Whatever the hell that is, I need to figure out how to keep it away from her." The bacon crunched beneath Cheyenne's next violent bite. "She didn't do anything to deserve this."

"For sure." Nodding slowly, Ember pushed the last of her eggs around on her plate and considered the bacon. But her mind was somewhere else. "Okay, this might sound crazy."

Cheyenne snorted. "As crazy as everything else right now? I think that might make it normal at this point."

"Maybe. I mean, it's too close to home for this to be an actual coincidence. What if Bianca has something to do with healing the blight?"

The halfling's fork clattered onto her plate, and she stared at her friend. Cheyenne barked out a bitter laugh. "Nice try."

"Hear me out, though. You're hearing all this stuff about the vessel, whatever the hell that is. The Sorren Gán brought it up with some vague-ass prophecy shit. Didn't it say something about you being part of some greater whole or something like that?"

"Honestly, Em, I was paying more attention to whether it looked hungry enough to try eating me and the fact that I fucking hate prophecies."

"Okay, sure. Then what about Venga?"

Cheyenne picked up her fork again and gave her friend a blank stare. "What about him?"

"'There's something wrong with the vessel.' That's what he said."

"Okay. Now you're putting stock in what a necromancer said after surprise-injecting me with what was supposed to heal me and obviously didn't even come close." The halfling hooked a finger through the top of her shirt and glanced down at the wound on her shoulder. "Made it worse."

"I think he was talking about you as a vessel." Ember lifted a strip of crispy bacon to her mouth, trying to play it casual as she gauged Cheyenne's reaction. "What if Bianca's, like, the other vessel?"

Cheyenne stared at her half-eaten plate, slowly pushed it away from her, and sat back in her chair. "No."

"So? She just happens to have the rune for 'vessel' branded on her chest now? For fun?"

"She's got a lot of other runes on her skin too, Em. Does that make her everything else those runes mean too?"

Ember shrugged. "I wasn't saying that. I'm trying to put the pieces together."

"Yeah, well, maybe all the pieces we have don't even go to the same puzzle." *Except that everything is connected right now, and it all centers around me. It's also bullshit.* "Bianca's already got enough on her plate. A portal in her backyard, L'zar holing up in her house like he owns the place, and Ba'rael's curse using her as a human chalkboard. No way is she getting any more involved in this because the pieces might fit. That's ridiculous. I mean, yeah, she's my mom, but she's human, and she doesn't want anything to do with this."

"You didn't either, Cheyenne." Ember raised an eyebrow. "She's already part of it."

"And that's on me." Cheyenne blinked at the shiny surface of the table. "I should've done more to make sure that didn't happen."

She stood quickly, her chair screeching as it scooted back across the hardwood floor, and grabbed her plate.

"Hey, none of this is your fault." Ember floated off her chair too. "You can't blame yourself for this."

"I didn't say it was my fault, Em, but I sure as hell didn't pull out all the stops, either. My mom got way too close to all this when that portal ridge showed up on her property, and I should've stopped it all right there. Put her up somewhere else until it was safe again instead of letting her stay here because she wanted to. None of this would've happened."

Ember grabbed her plate and followed her friend down the hall to the kitchen. "You think you would've been able to get her out of here?"

"In case you haven't noticed, Em, I'm strong enough to carry three Biancas at the same time. I could've taken her somewhere way out of the line of fire before she even knew what happened."

"True. And I'm sure she would've obediently stayed wherever you put her because you're her daughter, and you happen to be L'zar's daughter too."

Cheyenne paused in front of the kitchen door and looked over her shoulder. Then she pressed her side against the swinging door and headed into the kitchen. "Okay, fair enough."

"You did everything you could've done, and no one knew Ba'rael's curse would make it through that portal and hit your mom. None of us could know. This isn't on you."

"Fine, Em. Not my fault. I get that. It's L'zar's."

Ember snorted. "Not everything is the drow's fault."

"Sure. Just most of it." Cheyenne turned from the industrial-sized sink to grab Ember's plate. The fae snatched the last few strips of bacon before handing it over. "And now I have to figure out what the hell's happening to Bianca so I can stop it. Then we'll focus on this vessel bullshit."

The dishes clanged into the sink, and Cheyenne gave them a brief, careless rinse with the spray hose dangling above the faucet. "But I can't put either of those things first until after we take down Colonel Thomas at that meeting tomorrow. Feels like all these steps are backward, but whatever."

"You know I'm here to help you with all of it."

"Yeah, Em. I know."

They stood there in the kitchen, Cheyenne glaring at the floor with her arms folded and Ember watching for signs that she needed to slap some sense back into her best friend. Again. Fortunately, the signs didn't pop up. "So, until we crash that meeting tomorrow night."

"Yeah, it sucks having to wait around for the right time to show up."

"I was thinking more along the lines of what's happening here."

"Oh." Cheyenne looked at her friend and shrugged. "I mean, Bianca's staying here, and I guess, so is L'zar."

"Really?" Ember turned to follow Cheyenne back out of the kitchen. "She's totally cool with it?"

"Not totally." This time, Cheyenne held the kitchen door open until the fae floated through into the wide hall. "But she's down to let him help. At least when it comes to getting the rest of this magic out of her to make sure something like this doesn't happen again. And I guess I'm gonna let him."

"Because she wants you to."

"Yeah. That's pretty much the only reason. I'll figure out why this is happening to her, but I'm not gonna rely on L'zar for anything anymore. Especially when it comes to my mom." Cheyenne stopped at the bottom of the staircase and folded her arms as she looked up at the second floor. "I don't need him anymore, either."

"I don't think you ever really did." Ember floated closer to the halfling, scanning the large, seemingly empty house before she whispered, "And I think he knows that."

Cheyenne shot her friend a sidelong glance. "Why are we whispering?"

"Because the guy literally moves through walls and makes himself invisible. He could be anywhere."

"Well, he's not down here." With a deep breath, Cheyenne nodded up the staircase. "I'm ready to get outta here, though. It's too weird being in the middle of all this right now."

"Sure. I need a shower and a change of clothes anyway."

They headed up the stairs with the low mutter of voices from inside Bianca's bedroom growing louder. Cheyenne knocked on the doors, and Eleanor opened them this time. "Everything okay?"

"Yeah." Cheyenne tried to peer around the housekeeper to get a look at her mom. "We're gonna head out."

"Come in, Cheyenne," Bianca called as she slowly pushed herself up off the bed.

Eleanor frowned at the woman as she opened the door the rest of the way. "Do you think you should be getting out of bed right now?"

"You pumped me full of orange juice and eggs, Eleanor."

"And I still see some on your plate." Eleanor nodded at the tray on the breakfast cart, and Bianca waved her off as she stood and took a slow step forward.

Cheyenne pressed her lips together to keep from laughing. Perfectly clear who had the mothering instincts here, even without having her own kids.

"Thanks for letting us crash here," Ember said, slipping through the open door behind Cheyenne. "And for breakfast."

"I hope I don't have to keep reminding you that you're always welcome here," Bianca replied, her voice tenser and lower than usual, though she'd molded her expression into its usual composure. Then she glanced at Cheyenne. "Both of you."

Eleanor cleared her throat and returned to the breakfast cart, fiddling nervously with the utensils and dishes and the tray lid. "Any idea when you'll be coming back?"

"Well, we've got some things to take care of in the next couple of days, but after that, if it's okay with you guys, I'll come back up here. Maybe Tuesday or Wednesday, to check in."

"Well, don't ask me." The housekeeper let out a nervous chuckle and shook her head. "I'm not the one making the schedule."

"Except that you are." Bianca gave her friend a brief glance, then nodded. "Tuesday or Wednesday is fine, Cheyenne. Call before you head up."

"I will." Cheyenne approached her mom and dipped her head, trying to make the conversation a little more private in a space that didn't offer much privacy. "Are you sure you'll be okay for the next few days?"

"If I had an issue with you leaving, I would have said so."

"I know. I have to make sure. You know, with everything else going on right now."

"I'll manage." Bianca offered a tight, closed-lipped smile. "And so will you, I have no doubt."

They stared at each other, and Cheyenne couldn't think of anything else to say that hadn't already been said. Bianca blinked in discomfort and leaned slowly forward. *Is she about to hug me right now?*

L'zar appeared in the doorway and slapped a hand on the closed door, jarring everyone out of the moment. "And I'm not setting foot out of this house until we find a solution, Cheyenne. That's a promise. You don't have anything to worry about."

Grimacing, the halfling stepped away from her mom but couldn't quite bring herself to look at her father. "Except for that."

"Would it make you feel better if I told you I won't leave your mother's side until she's safe?"

"No." Mother and daughter said it at the same time with equal force.

The Weaver shrugged and stepped into the bedroom anyway. "It's a figure of speech. The part about not leaving her side, not the part about staying in the house."

Cheyenne took a deep breath and forced her irritation down into a tiny box before she looked back at her mom. "You can tell him to leave."

"As long as he stays out of my way, I'm willing to submit myself to the aggravation."

Eleanor snorted, still fiddling with the breakfast cart. "And out of my kitchen. You hear me? That's off-limits."

L'zar spread his arms. "There are ground rules. I understand."

Yeah, like he ever gave a shit about rules or personal boundaries. Cheyenne placed a hand gently on her mom's upper arm and nodded. A hug at this point would've been awkward for many reasons. "Call me if you need anything."

"Cheyenne, I'm not an invalid. And Eleanor handles anything I could possibly need."

The housekeeper let out a squeak that was half laughter, half nervous surprise. "Business as usual around here."

"I mean, if you need anything Eleanor can't handle."

"I'll be here, Cheyenne." L'zar cocked his head. "I can handle it."

"Yeah, sorry for not having full faith in your ability to handle anything right now." Cheyenne raised an eyebrow at him. "Wait. I'm not sorry about that."

The Weaver grinned at his daughter. "Point taken."

"But if you're gonna play drow protector here, you have to stick to the plan. Got it?"

"Of course." He glanced around the room and frowned. "And that plan is?"

"If you think of anything connected to those runes or something new shows up, if anything changes or looks different, if Bianca even sneezes in a way that doesn't sound right, you call me. No exceptions."

"Really, Cheyenne." Bianca let out a heavy sigh. "A sneeze?"

"I'm serious. I don't want to leave any of this up to chance, and who knows what might happen?"

"I'll be fine."

Cheyenne widened her eyes at her mom. "I know. And I still want to hear about it. I'm only good with L'zar staying here if he promises to hold up his end of the deal, which is telling me about anything the second it happens." She turned back to the drow thief and folded her arms. "And when I say promise, I don't mean the kind you only keep when you feel like it."

"I have no problem alerting you to any changes around the estate, Cheyenne."

"Say it."

L'zar clasped his hands behind his back and dipped his head. "Fine. I promise. Though I do have one minor request as far as the terms of upholding that promise are concerned."

Cheyenne rolled her eyes. "Of course you do. What is it?"

"I'd rather not have to use a phone if that's possible."

"What?"

He shrugged. "They're not my thing, modern Earthside technology being what it is. You understand."

"Not really."

A sharp laugh burst out of Ember, and she clapped a hand over her mouth before turning away to compose herself.

"The deal is you call me, L'zar."

"Why does it matter how I communicate with you?"

"Because I don't trust any other crazy way you might come up with. That's why."

A small frown creased the drow thief's eyebrows. "The Don'adurr Thread is just as reliable."

"It's really not. I don't want you popping up in my head whenever you feel like, so you get to pick up a phone, dial my number, and wait for me to answer. That's how this works."

"It's not my preference."

"I don't care. Why is this such a big deal for you?"

Blinking quickly, L'zar looked at the ceiling and sucked in an aggravated breath through his teeth. "I don't understand the nuances."

"Of cell phones?"

He closed his eyes and tilted his head in a barely perceptible nod.

Eleanor burst out laughing. Bianca shot her a stern look tinged with her own amusement, and that only made the housekeeper laugh even harder.

"I don't see the humor in this," L'zar muttered. "Nor do I appreciate your amusement at my expense."

Bianca turned her calculating gaze on the drow thief, and when she smiled, the composure she showed when she knew she had the upper hand, which was almost always, returned with it. "A good dose of humiliation now and again does wonders for one's commitment to self-improvement. Wouldn't you agree?"

L'zar glanced at her and said nothing.

Jesus, this is one of the weirdest conversations I've been sucked into in a while. "Look, L'zar. You're out of prison, and now you're stuck in this world forever. Figure out how to use a cell phone at the very least, or you'll be obsolete before they are."

A low growl escaped him, and he grimaced with flaring nostrils as he dipped his head to his daughter one more time. "Fine. Should the occasion arise, I will call you."

"Good." Cheyenne shared a knowing glance with her mom. "I'll see you in a few days."

"I look forward to it."

"Oh, no." Eleanor slammed the silver lid back down on the breakfast tray and hurried around the cart. "Don't think you can slip out of this house without a proper goodbye. Come here."

She opened her arms and drew Cheyenne in for a crushing hug that lasted a little longer than usual.

Cheyenne laughed and hugged the woman back, ignoring the flaring pain in her shoulders. "Same goes for you. Call me if anything changes."

"That's been my first priority since all this started." Eleanor released her and patted the outsides of Cheyenne's arms. "As long as you're in cell-phone range, if you know what I mean."

"I'm not going out of range again anytime soon, Eleanor. I promise."

"Good. It's strange enough to think about you being wherever that is. Ember." Eleanor practically threw herself at the fae to dole out another of her signature hugs. Ember laughed. "Always good to see you. And I know you'll keep an eye on this one while she heads out to save the world, won't you?"

Ember laughed, her eyes widening under the strength of the house-keeper's embrace. "I will. It's kind of my job, anyway."

"Sweetheart, if anyone understands how that works, I do." Eleanor reached up to pat Ember's cheek, then turned back to the cart. "Don't let us keep you. Be safe."

With a nod at each of them, the housekeeper grabbed the breakfast cart's handle and wheeled it out of the room, pausing only to shoot L'zar a disapproving scowl before she disappeared through the bedroom doors.

Then it was Ember, Cheyenne, and both the halfling's parents standing quietly in the bedroom. L'zar gestured at the open doors. "Better get to it, then."

Cheyenne glared at him. "Really? The drow squatter's telling me to leave."

"Well, you said you had business to take care of."

She looked at her mom again and fought back the urge to blast L'zar through the far wall. "See you soon, Mom."

Bianca nodded and slowly lowered herself onto the edge of the bed. "Drive safely."

"Yeah, we will." Cheyenne turned and headed out of the bedroom without looking at L'zar.

Ember followed her and glanced at the drow thief before lifting her hand to her ear, thumb and pinky finger extended in the shape of a phone, and mouthed, 'You better call her.' L'zar merely raised an eyebrow and stared after them as the girls headed down the hall.

Cheyenne ducked into her childhood bedroom to grab her trench-coat, then she and Ember headed down the stairs to the foyer and the front door. *Weird way to leave things here. Bianca and L'zar in her bedroom, hanging out.*

"I don't have the energy or patience for this right now." Bianca's voice drifted through the open door of her bedroom. "Close the door on your way out."

The halfling opened the front door and stepped into the crisp mid-morning air. *At least she doesn't make an exception for him when it comes to saying exactly what she's thinking. She'll be fine. She can handle him. As long as he doesn't pull any more stupid drow tricks.*

CHAPTER THIRTY-TWO

On their drive back to Richmond from the Summerlin estate in Henry County, Cheyenne connected her phone to the Panamera's Bluetooth and pulled up Maleshi's number. Ember looked at her but didn't say anything as the ringtone filled the car.

The general picked up on the second ring. "Well, good morning."

"I've had better." Cheyenne shrugged and stared at the road. "You busy right now?"

"Just talking to you, kid. What's up?"

"I have a few questions about what's going on with my mom. Not one of those things I wanna talk about over the phone, so I was hoping we could stop by in about an hour and talk it over in person."

"We?"

Ember sat back in the passenger seat. "Hey, Maleshi."

The general chuckled. "For a minute there, I had a vision of both your parents in my living room, Cheyenne. Gotta say it was hard to fully visualize, with your mom's condition and everything."

"Well, she's awake now," Cheyenne replied. "And she doesn't ever leave the house. She definitely wouldn't go anywhere with him."

"Can't blame her. If it's just you and Ember, sure. I'll see you in an hour."

"Thanks."

The call ended, and Cheyenne gripped the steering wheel even tighter.

"Didn't know we were making a detour to visit the general," Ember said.

"She might know something, Em. Or at least the next place to start looking for someone who might know something."

"About the curse on Bianca?"

"Yeah. And why she's been pulled into this, if there even is a reason."

"What happens if there is?"

Cheyenne cast her friend another quick glance and shrugged. "Then I'll figure out what it is and how to separate Bianca from everything else going on right now. I'm not gonna let her get dragged into this any further than she already is."

"Right. Find the loopholes."

The halfling took a deep breath. "Guess that runs on the drow side of the family too."

Less than an hour later, Maleshi Hi'et opened the front door of her house and stepped aside to let Ember and Cheyenne in. "You two are lookin' a little rough."

"Yeah, good to see you too." Cheyenne closed the door behind her as Maleshi walked down the entry hall to her living room on the left.

"Callin' it like I see it, kid. Hey, I made mimosas. Anybody want some?"

Cheyenne and Ember shared a confused glance as they followed the general around the staircase and into the kitchen. "You drink mimosas?"

"Sunday Funday and all that, right?"

Ember laughed. "Like, the real kind made with champagne, or did you stash Bloodshine around here somewhere?"

Maleshi stopped at the center island in her small kitchen and gestured at the bottle of champagne, a carton of orange juice, and the pitcher in which she'd mixed them. "The real kind. I wouldn't mix orange juice with Bloodshine if my life depended on it. That's disgusting."

"Yeah, okay." Ember shrugged. "I'll have one."

"Excellent." The general pulled two champagne flutes out of the cabinet, then looked at Cheyenne. "What about you?"

"I'm good."

"Hair of the dog is a thing, you know."

"Yeah, so is a fae healing the hangover right out of me. I'm not in the mood."

Maleshi glanced at Ember with raised eyebrows, the corners of her mouth turned up in approval. "I'm impressed."

"Thank you." Ember grinned when Maleshi poured the drinks and handed her a glass.

They clinked their flutes together, then the general took a slow sip and gestured at the kitchen table on the far side of the island. "Wanna take a seat?"

"Yeah." Cheyenne headed that way, gazing around at the potted plants hanging from the ceiling, vines trailing over the sides, and the blooming orchids lining the half-wall between the kitchen and the family room. "Didn't know you had such a green thumb."

"Oh. Well, I've had a few centuries to sort out the kinks in not killing every living thing I touch."

Ember snorted as she pulled out a chair at the table. "Plants and magicals are two totally different things."

Maleshi lowered herself into a chair across from Cheyenne. "I meant killing plants, Ember. But yeah, I can see where there might be some confusing overlap. So what's going on with your mom, kid?"

Cheyenne leaned back in her chair and stuck her hands in her lap. "Like I said, she's awake. So that's a plus, at least."

"Any idea how that happened?"

"Nope."

"But assuming the time of day was the same here and on the other side," Ember added, "it sounds like she woke up at the same time Ba'rael disappeared and Cheyenne had her fifteen minutes of ruling."

Maleshi's eyes widened. "Really?"

The halfling frowned at her friend. "Yeah. I wasn't even thinking about that part."

Ember shrugged. "I'm just making observations."

"Good ones too." Maleshi raised her glass to Ember and nodded. "That's an interesting development."

"But it's not what I need help with," Cheyenne said. "You saw the runes on my mom when she was still passed out, I guess."

"Yep."

"Well, she got another one this morning."

Maleshi cocked her head. "Another one?"

"Rune. A new one burned into her skin right here." The halfling tapped the center of her own chest. "L'zar said it's the symbol for 'vessel.'"

"So that's where he is." The general chuckled. "I was wondering what he decided to do with his suddenly wide-open schedule. It seemed a little odd the goblins were calling me from the warehouse asking about him."

"Yeah, he's filling it with hovering over my mom and terrorizing Eleanor." At Maleshi's confused frown, Cheyenne added, "The housekeeper."

"Ah." Maleshi sipped her mimosa, and the table fell silent again.

"You might wanna tell her about the whole vessel thing," Ember prompted.

The halfling said, "Everyone's talking about this stupid vessel, whatever it is. The Sorren Gán when we went to see it the other night. Venga was raving about it like a lunatic."

"As he does." Maleshi lifted her glass again.

"And I've had a few dreams with Neros in them."

The general's eyes widened. "Your cousin."

"Yeah."

"What were these dreams about?"

Cheyenne let out a heavy sigh and glanced at Ember as the fae took a long sip of her drink. "Basically, Neros looking almost as crazy as he did when he tried to get me to stay with him in Nor'ieth, only he was talking about the vessel too. That my work's not done, and I can't stop until I find the vessel and use it the way it's supposed to be used. More jumbled prophetic bullshit in a dream, honestly. Nothing new."

"And then the symbol appeared on your mom."

"Right."

Maleshi frowned in thought and nodded slowly. "Definitely sounds like it's all connected."

"That's what I said." Ember shrugged. "She doesn't wanna hear it."

"I didn't say that." Cheyenne shook her head. "I'm not gonna dive right into this, automatically thinking my mom's way more involved than she has any right to be. Not because she has one new symbol burned into her that means the same thing I've been hearing from everyone else for the last couple days."

The general studied her a moment and dipped her head. "It's good to stay neutral about it, at the very least."

"Any idea where I'm supposed to go from here?"

"Sorry, kid. I'm drawing a blank."

"Right. Do you know anyone over here who might have an answer for me?"

"I mean, there's always Gúrdu."

Cheyenne rolled her eyes. "Fuck Gúrdu. I'm done with Oracles."

"A sentiment I can get behind." Maleshi raised her champagne flute to the halfling and took another sip.

"I need to find someone who specializes in curses or something, right? Know anyone like that?"

"Cheyenne, I came Earthside for a specific reason, and that was to cut myself off from my old life. Including fraternizing with other magicals over here. Gúrdu found me back in 1804 when I was… Well, that doesn't matter. I'm the wrong magical to ask for a referral on this one."

"Shit." Cheyenne wrinkled her nose. "Maybe I can find someone in Peridosh."

"That might be the best place to start."

"What about Byrd and Lumil?" Ember asked. "Would they know anybody?"

The general snorted. "Those two wouldn't know a bane-breaker from a healer. I highly doubt they'd be useful in finding anyone with the kind of specialty you're looking for."

"Yeah, I didn't think so."

"So, we're starting from scratch with this one, huh?" Cheyenne folded her arms and shook her head, staring at the table. "I guess I'll have to make the crossing again in a few days and ask around Hangivol."

"Venga might have some answers."

"I'm not going to the scaleback necromancer who basically poisoned me to ask for advice on curing my mom."

Maleshi blinked in surprise. "Poison."

When Cheyenne pulled down the side of her shirt collar to reveal the unhealed dart wound and the black blight streaks, now twice as long as they used to be stretching across her skin, the general grimaced.

"I see. Then no, I wouldn't go to him either unless it was the last option."

"It's definitely the last option. I haven't run through all the others yet."

"Sorry, I'm basically useless to you on this one."

Cheyenne smiled. "Surprising, but I don't blame you. I've got a lotta shit piling up on my plate all at the same time."

"You know what always helps with a growing pile of shit on one's plate?" Maleshi lifted her drink to her lips again and grinned. "Day-drinking. The offer still stands."

"I went that route last night, Maleshi. Didn't give me any answer, either. But thanks."

"Any time."

"Okay." The halfling smacked her hands down on the table and pushed herself to her feet. "We'll leave you to your Sunday fun."

"Funday." Ember frowned playfully. "You've never heard that one before?"

"I'm not a huge brunch person, I guess."

"Fair enough." The fae downed the rest of her drink, set it on the table, and floated out of the chair. "Thanks for the mimosa."

"Always happy to drink with friends." Maleshi stood too and nodded at the front of the house. "I'll walk you out."

By the time they reached the door, the general had cast her human-illusion again, replacing black fur and silver eyes with black curls, green eyes, and olive skin. She held open the door for her visitors to step out onto the front porch. "Thanks for stopping by. If you end up with any questions a little more specific than, 'What do I do now?,' give me a call."

"Yeah. Thanks."

The general walked with them down the driveway to Cheyenne's car at the curb, her champagne flute raised at her side. She tilted her head to study the heavy scratches and unignorable dents on the Panamera's side and front bumper and grimaced. "Your ride's looking as beat up as you do."

"Wow." Cheyenne turned around to face her. "Did you forget what happened to it?"

Maleshi gave her a blank look, then sucked in a quick, surprised breath. "Right. It was me. I happened to your car."

"You obviously care as much as you did the last time it was brought up."

"Sorry, kid." The general shrugged. "Still not on my priority list."

"Uh-huh." With a final glance at the dings on the Panamera's shiny black body, Cheyenne shook her head and headed around the front of the car to the driver's side door. "Oh, hey. We're going after the colonel tomorrow. You want in on that?"

"Hmm. Tempting." Maleshi raised her glass. "I'll see how I feel about it tomorrow. How's that?"

"Yeah. Sure." Cheyenne opened the door and slid behind the wheel. *I don't get how she's so blah about everything when we're looking at taking out a huge chunk of the Bull's Head in this world, but whatever.*

"See ya," Ember called before slipping into the passenger seat. Maleshi smiled and nodded and waved them off with her mimosa in her hand like a suburban mom waving goodbye to her kids heading off to school in the carpool. On a Sunday.

CHAPTER THIRTY-THREE

Back at their apartment, Cheyenne stepped out of her bedroom and headed for one of the black leather recliners. Ember sat on the couch and pored through the loose-leaf stack of Maleshi Hi'et's spellbook. "What are you looking for in there?"

"Huh?" Ember blinked and looked up from the pages. "Oh. Figured I'd learn some new spells. And it couldn't hurt to look for something about removing curses, right?"

Cheyenne flopped into the recliner and cranked the handle until her feet were propped up in front of her. "I'm pretty sure she would've told us to go through her book if it was in there."

"Really? You think she's got enough space in her brain to remember everything she unloaded in a handwritten spellbook?"

"Fair point. I'll cross my fingers, then."

"Yeah, me too."

Cheyenne pulled her cell phone from her back pocket and stared at the card in her hand.

"What's that?"

"Card from that Lee guy I met at Union Hill. The auto restoration guy."

Ember's eyes widened. "Oh, yeah. You think he fixes nightstalker damage?"

"Ha. I'm gonna find out." Cheyenne dialed the number on the card for Blast from the Past Auto Restoration, then lifted the phone to her ear. *At the very least, I can leave a message and hope he'll call me back when he's open again.*

She didn't expect the line to click after the third ring or to hear the man's voice on the other end.

"Lee McDurn."

"Oh. Uh, hi."

A soft chuckle came through the line. "Hi."

"Sorry. I didn't expect you to be open on a Sunday."

"Ah, yes. Well, I keep my cell phone on me seven days a week. How can I help you?"

"Oh. Sorry to bother you."

"Not a bother. It's my business line too, so don't worry about it. One of the perks of being technically retired, you know. I get to work all day every day if I want and answer incoming calls. No harm done."

He put his cell number on his business card? Not the most legit way to do things, and I'm not making this conversation any less awkward. Cheyenne cleared her throat. "Okay. Uh, my name's Cheyenne. Not sure if you remember me, but we met at Union Hill a few weeks ago, and you gave me your card. You had the '37 Packard, and I had—"

"The brand-new Panamera. Yeah." The man's smile came through loud and clear in his voice. "Nice to hear from you, Cheyenne. How you doin'?"

"I'm all right. I was hoping you could help me out with some body-work. The Panamera got a little dinged-up."

"Ouch. Accident?"

"Yeah, accidentally trusting a friend of mine to take care of it for me when I was out of town for a few days."

Lee sucked in a sharp breath, and she could practically see him grimacing in her mind's eye. "One of the worst kinds of accidents. Sorry to hear that."

"Yeah, thanks."

"I'll tell you what, Cheyenne. If you're not busy today, why don't you head on over and we'll take a look?"

"Today?"

"Sure. I'm putzin' around up here with a few other projects. Nothing serious. I'd love to see that car."

"Yeah, okay. Thanks." She flipped the business card over. "You don't have an address on the card. Should I just Google it?"

"No, no. Don't bother with all that." Lee chuckled again. "I don't mind handing out my phone number, but putting my home address out there for every knucklehead to find me didn't seem like such a great idea."

"Home address."

"Yes, ma'am. Work outta one of my garages on the property. I promise it's all legit."

Cheyenne fought back a laugh. *I'm taking my car to a hobbyist. Guess we'll see how this pans out.* "All right. I can't get there without the address, though."

"Well, of course not. You callin' from a cell phone?"

"Yeah."

"Good. I'll text it to you. Don't worry about droppin' everything and rushin' out here on my account. As long as you show up before seven, it's all good. Any later, and you'll have to turn around and come back tomorrow."

She snorted. *So I have eight hours to get there.* "Not a problem."

"Excellent. Lookin' forward to seein' you and that Porsche."

"Yeah, thanks."

Lee hung up, and she got a text less than a minute later with an address. *Not too far away.*

"You know," Ember said as she studied Maleshi's spellbook, "you always miss half a conversation when someone's on the phone, but that one sounded weird."

Cheyenne flicked the business card before leaning forward to toss it onto the coffee table. "Kinda, yeah. The dude works out of his own garage, apparently. No business setup beyond a name on a business card."

"Huh. And you're still gonna go there instead of taking the car to an actual shop?"

The halfling gave her friend a playful frown. "That seems weird to you too?"

"I know how much you love the thing."

"Yeah, I think I'll give the guy a shot. He basically drooled over my car when we met, and he had this way-cool Packard with him that day. Purple. Chrome everywhere. The kinda stuff only people who love what they do put on cars that old."

"Whatever." Ember shook her head. "Car stuff goes right over my head."

"Well, I have a feeling the guy knows what he's doing, and he was cool. Didn't look at me weird or say a single thing about my piercings, so I won't have to deal with that bullshit, either."

"Yeah, go with the car enthusiast who doesn't judge a drow book by her Goth cover. Good plan."

Playfully rolling her eyes, Cheyenne pushed the recliner's footrest back into place and stood. "I think I'll head out there. You good here? Need anything?"

Ember raised an eyebrow but didn't look up from the stack of paper on her lap. "Go fix your ride, Cheyenne."

"Yeah, okay." Cheyenne stepped to the side of her couch to grab the trenchcoat she'd draped over the armrest. *Maybe this'll take my mind off how much I hate waiting. It's the little things, right?* "See you in a few hours."

"Yep."

As the halfling headed for the door, someone out in the hall beat her to it. A loud, hasty knock came on the door, and Cheyenne opened it abruptly. Their neighbor Matthew Thomas stood on the other side, frowning and looking ridiculously uncomfortable as he shoved his hands into his pockets.

"If this is about your alarm system and somebody hacking into your uncle's computer, man, you're beating a dead horse."

Matthew blinked. "What?"

"I didn't do it."

"No, that's not it." He cleared his throat and tried to peer around her for a glance inside her apartment. "Can I come in?"

"Why?"

"It's kind of important and fairly personal, and I don't wanna have that kind of conversation in the hall." Matthew glanced quickly up the hall at the elevators, but there wasn't anyone else there.

"You worried about somebody accidentally taking the elevator all the way up here and overhearing us?"

"It happens. Sometimes." Running a hand through his hair, Matthew shifted nervously from foot to foot and caught a glimpse of Ember inside. "Ember, please."

"Take it up with Cheyenne." The fae didn't look up from the spellbook.

He sighed. "Please. I won't take up a lot of time, but I need some help, okay?"

Cheyenne raised an eyebrow, stepped back, and swung the door open.

"Thanks." Matthew hurried into their apartment, and the door shut a lot harder than it had to behind him.

Cheyenne turned around and leaned back against the door, folding her arms. "Make it fast, okay? I've got an appointment."

He frowned at her, then shook his head. "Yeah, okay. Look, I don't know what's going on—all this crap with my uncle. I didn't wanna believe what you were telling me. I admit that. But I did some digging on my own."

"Oh, interesting. Find anything good?"

Matthew took a deep breath, his eyes growing wide. "No. That's the part that's freaking me out."

Ember dropped the stack of paper into her lap and finally looked at him. "What did you find?"

"Nothing. I mean, it's practically nothing, anyway. A superficial paper trail, and it's clean. Normal. Shows him clocking in every day for the last fifteen years at a nine-to-five in Hillcrest. I thought I was done, but then I found some numbers that didn't add up, and an extra bank account I couldn't get into, plus a backup system on the server I built for his home computer."

Cheyenne cocked her head. "You built your uncle his own personal server for home use?"

"Like you're one to talk." Matthew pointed at the mini loft. "You've got enough up there to power a whole company."

"Who told you that?"

"My security system when it pinged me with your IP address. No, I didn't hack into your stuff, but I saw enough to know you built your own server for home use too, okay? Not that weird of a thing for people like us."

Yeah, except for I use mine to hack into places most people don't even know exist. "Whatever, man. Why is this our problem?"

"Well, to start, I didn't build him a backup system, not the one he has. And I couldn't get into it."

Cheyenne shrugged. "Looks like you're too good at your job."

"No, I mean someone used what I built him to double-down and make that backup server, and whatever they did, it was done with knowledge about the way I program to specifically keep me out."

"Huh." Ember folded her arms. "Sounds like your uncle didn't want his cyber-security-whiz nephew spying on him."

"Yeah, and it doesn't add up. My uncle gave me full access to all his accounts, everything on his system, you name it, so I could build something better and integrate everything. I don't know why he's trying to hide it all from me now, and that extra bank account threw me off. I was hoping you could help me."

Cheyenne raised her eyebrows and studied him for a moment, letting the guy fidget and squirm a little before she popped the question. "Help you with what?"

"Come on, Cheyenne." Matthew couldn't look at her as he gestured at the mini loft where she kept Glen and her server setup again. "Why else would I ask you for a favor?"

"I don't know, Matthew. Seems a little presumptuous of you, don't you think?"

"What?"

Ember shook her head. "You weren't exactly jumping up and down to help us with a favor."

"Yeah, but that was different."

"Twice, right?" Cheyenne looked at Ember for confirmation.

The fae raised her hand and stuck up three fingers. "Three times."

Matthew sighed. "Okay, that was different. That was before I knew what you guys are."

"Oh, really?" Ember folded her arms again and cocked her head. "What are we?"

"You know, magic and stuff." He grimaced at the weak points of his nonexistent argument. "Look, I didn't know what was happening before. I mean, I still don't, but you showed me enough to know that I have no idea what I'm getting into. All I'm asking is that you take a look,

Cheyenne, okay? I'll give you access to my uncle's server, or at least the parts of it he didn't have someone else copy and build on. You can go in, take a look around, answer a few questions for me, and then I'll leave you alone."

She pursed her lips. "Sorry. Can't do it."

"Please, Cheyenne. I can't let this go. I thought I knew the guy, and now I'm finding all this stuff that doesn't add up, and I need to know what he's doing. Why he's keeping it from me. I fucking hate it, but I can't figure it out on my own."

"Yeah, that's frustrating."

Matthew aimed his pleas at Ember instead. "Do you guys know what he's up to? What he's hiding?"

"I don't know why you think I have anything to do with this." Ember draped an arm over the couch's armrest behind her. "If Cheyenne says she can't do it, Matthew, I'm not gonna turn around and tell you, 'No problem.'"

"Jesus." He pressed both hands to his head and turned around in a tight circle. "I'm never gonna live this down, am I?"

"Only if you keep freaking out like that." Cheyenne kicked away from the door and stepped over to him, spreading her arms. "Look, your timing's perfectly shitty, okay?"

"My timing?"

"Yeah. I know a few things that would blow your mind if I told you."

"Whatever. That's fine. Tell me. I can handle it."

"All right, slow down." She stuck her hands in the pockets of her trenchcoat and exchanged knowing glances with Ember. *I can't tell him anything until after this meeting tomorrow. Something tells me he's more likely to blow the whole thing for us than sit tight and keep a secret.* "We can talk about it again after tomorrow night."

Matthew glanced between Cheyenne and Ember, his frazzled panic intensifying. "Why? What's going on tomorrow night?"

"Yeah, if I wanted to tell you now, I wouldn't have said wait until after tomorrow night."

"Come on. What am I supposed to do until then, huh?"

She nodded curtly and slapped a hand on his back before guiding him with a little more force than necessary toward the door. "It's tough to have to wait around. Trust me, I get it, but that's what you're gonna have to do. Come back in a couple of days, and I'll explain what I can."

"I can't just do nothing."

"You'll be fine." She opened the door and nodded at the hall. "Find a few good movies or something."

Matthew turned around to look at Ember again. "Ember…"

She shook her head.

"Okay, how about this? Whatever happens tomorrow night, I'll make sure none of it blows back on you, okay?"

"You will?" Ember asked.

At the same time, Matthew asked, "Why would it blow back on me?"

Cheyenne nodded at Ember. "Yeah, I will." Then she turned to their neighbor. "Because of the shit you programmed and sold to O'gúl loyalists intent on carrying out orders they got from a leader they don't even know isn't in power anymore."

"I don't understand any of that."

"I know." She gestured at the hallway, more forcefully this time. "But I'll keep you out of it, okay?"

Matthew glanced at Ember, then frowned at the halfling. "I didn't think you liked me enough to protect me from whatever this is."

"Yeah, well, I don't, not really. But if you seriously had no idea what you were getting into at the beginning and you don't know now, I can't blame you for it. If I find out down the road that you're funding or working on anything for these assholes, if you're still even remotely involved, I'll bring you down. That's a promise." Cheyenne straightened her arm and pointed into the hall.

"Deal. I'm not taking a job like that one ever again."

"Great. Now you can go home."

"Ember." Matthew turned away from the open door and approached the couch.

"Jesus Christ," Cheyenne muttered. Shaking her head, she propped a hand on the doorframe and glared at him. *It's not like he can't take a hint. I wasn't fucking hinting.*

"Give me a minute," Matthew said, whether he was talking to Cheyenne or Ember or both of them. "Can I sit?"

Ember shook her head. "Not a good idea."

"Okay, sure. Yeah." He set his hands on the back of the couch instead and smiled weakly down at her. "I want to tell you I'm sorry."

"Well, thanks. And you've already said that. More than once."

"Yeah, I know. I mean it, though. You believe me, right?"

"I believe that you want me to believe it. Other than that, I don't really. What are you looking for?"

"What?" Matthew looked down at her again after scanning the living room. "Sorry, it's still weird to see you out of your wheelchair. I guess that's what I'm looking for."

"Well, you won't find it, 'cause it's not here."

His eyes widened. "What happened?"

"Magic, Matthew. Magic happened, and that's what's going on right now."

He let out a nervous chuckle and rubbed the back of his neck. "I guess I'm still getting used to that."

"I think you still need to get used to the fact that I'm not ready to have that conversation with you right now. Or anytime soon. At least until after Monday night, but that still feels like pushing it."

"So you're a part of whatever she's doing too?" Matthew gestured at Cheyenne, who was seconds away from grabbing him by the back of his button-down shirt and tossing him out of their apartment.

"I said, I'm not ready." Ember raised her eyebrows and shrugged. "It's too close to home. Literally, in this case."

Cheyenne tapped her fingers on the doorframe. "I'd take that as your cue to head on out, neighbor."

Ember picked up the stack of loose spellbook pages and got back to reading.

With a sigh, Matthew turned slowly around and headed for the door.

Oh, sure. I point into the hall, but it's the cold shoulder that gets the point across. This guy's got it bad for the fae, wheelchair, or no wheelchair.

"So, I can come back Monday night, and you'll tell me what's going on?"

Cheyenne wrinkled her nose. "Eh, better make it Tuesday morning. Late morning. There's a recovery period."

He stopped in front of the door and gave her a panicked frown. "A what?"

Rolling her eyes, Cheyenne leaned forward, grabbed his wrist, and hauled him through the doorway. He stumbled out, his mouth opening and closing when he realized how strong she had to be to pull him out after her like that. Cheyenne leaned back inside to grab the door handle. "Later, Em."

"Yep."

The door was finally shut with Cheyenne and their clueless neighbor on the other side, and the halfling pointed at Matthew's front door. "Go home. Have a drink, watch something, write a program, I don't know. Whatever gets you to calm the hell down. I have somewhere to be. And give it a rest with Ember, okay? Whatever you're trying to make happen, you're not doing yourself any favors right now."

He stared at her, then glanced at the wall behind her and nodded. "Yeah."

"Okay. See ya." Without giving him time to say anything else, she turned away and headed quickly down the hall. *The dude doesn't give up. Useful quality, I guess, just not with this.*

Before she reached the elevator, she heard Matthew Thomas' front door open and shut again. *At least he's learning.*

CHAPTER THIRTY-FOUR

It took her almost thirty minutes to get to the address Lee had texted her. Cheyenne slowed her car on the long gravel drive toward a property wall and an open gate with the house number mounted in huge, black iron letters on the side. *That's the one thing Mom didn't bother to put in on the estate, but everything else sure looks damn familiar.*

By the time she passed through the gate, the front of Lee McDurn's personal property came into view. There were sweeping manicured lawns, a wide, three-story mansion at the end of a circular drive with a fountain in the center, and two long, squat buildings on the west side of the property turned inward to face the main house. Cheyenne frowned at the house and took her car around the circular drive before stopping halfway between the four-car garage attached to the house and the two outbuildings.

"He said out of one of his garages." She pulled out her phone and was about to call him when the front door opened and the man stepped outside, waving excitedly at her as he jogged down the front steps, waxed handlebar mustache, cream-colored Stetson and all.

"Hey!" Lee reached the gravel drive and hurried to the driver's side door.

Cheyenne rolled down the window. "You got a lot of garages."

"Ha. Yeah, I've been thinking about putting up a sign. Never quite got around to it. Pull on up to the first one, yeah?"

"Sure."

Lee stepped away from the Panamera, gave it a once-over, and let out a low whistle. "Still looks good."

"I want it to look like somebody didn't drive it through the woods."

"You came to the right place." Lee nodded at the first outbuilding as he walked backward, then turned around to hurry toward the bay door, casting quick glances over his shoulder.

Cheyenne pulled the car around and headed to the opening bay door as it slid back into place along the ceiling of the garage. Lee stopped in front of the entrance and grinned at her with his hands in his pockets as she pulled up and parked. "Want me to keep going?"

"Nope. You're fine right there. I'll pull her in later on. Come on. I'll show you around."

She turned off the engine and left the keys in the center console before getting out to join him. "So when you said one of your garages, you meant one of your hangars, huh?"

Lee laughed and stuck out his hand for a brief shake. She took it and glanced around the inside of the garage. "Yeah, it's a little bigger than most garages in town."

She snorted. "Just a little."

"You won't find stuff like this at any of the body shops in Richmond. Hell, I don't know anyone within four states keeping this kinda inventory. I don't care what size garage they have." The man nodded and hooked his thumbs through his belt loops. "You wanna see this."

"I probably do."

Lee led her into the garage, which looked a lot larger on the inside, probably due to the half-dozen cars parked side by side down the length of the building.

"Wow."

"This is the workshop. I've got the finished collection in the other garage. Check this out. You ever see one of these?" He pointed at the racing-green Eagle E-Type Speedster at the front of the line. "This guy wanted a new paint job. Wouldn't have picked the color myself, but he insisted. Switched out a few parts on the interior, too. The seats had a few holes, leather peeling up off the steering wheel, stuff like that."

Cheyenne leaned over to peer inside. "Looks pretty good."

He laughed. "Yeah, pretty good. Then we got the 1937 Packard 120. You saw that one already. And this one here?" Lee gently patted the hood of a boxy-looking sedan in slate-gray with flecks of blue in the shimmering paint. "2006 Lexus LS430."

"See, this is the kinda car I expected you to drive away in when we met."

"Yeah. Yeah." The man grinned and readjusted his Stetson. "Definitely looks like an old-man car."

"That's not what I said."

"Ha. But you were thinkin' it. That's fine. I thought it too, but lemme tell you something about this car. Don't get me wrong, your Panamera's a piece of art on its own, but this? This is the wallflower of luxury sedans when it comes to looks, but it's got all the personality, I tell you what."

Cheyenne scanned the cream-leather interior and the wood panels on the steering wheel, doors, dashboard, and gearshift. "Doesn't look very fast."

"Hey, speed isn't everything. She can hold up, but the real kicker is the ride." Lee whistled and swept his hand away from him. "Best suspension of any car I've gotten to drive, and that's sayin' something. Hell, when I drove this baby up that gravel drive, couldn't feel a thing. Not a single bump."

"Nice."

He chuckled. "Uh-huh. Nice. Got it off a woman in Illinois who had absolutely no idea what she was sittin' on. She wanted it off her hands, and I was more than happy to help her out. These things go fast, if and when they show up on the market. They don't make 'em like this anymore."

"And you get one more ride in your collection."

"Yes, indeed. Working on updating the stereo system. That thing was top-of-the-line with all the bells and whistles back in the day, but no one uses cassette tapes and CDs anymore. Putting in a better nav system too. Then she'll be like brand-new. The Bluebook value on this thing is fifteen thousand. A damn steal if you ask me."

"Well done." Cheyenne stuck her hands in her coat pockets and looked into the back seat. *Less than a quarter of what I paid for mine, but whatever.*

"You don't even know, Cheyenne. Reclining back seats with vibrating massagers. There's a damn fridge in the back. Craziest thing I've ever seen."

"Even out of all the cars you've worked on?"

"Of course not." Lee nodded at the Lexus and grinned. "But all that comes stock with this baby."

"Huh."

"Yep." He led her down the line of cars, pointing out the Chevy Bel Air, the Alfa Romeo GTA-R, and the Range Rover Classic and laying out his favorite qualities of each. "I tell you what, it's a great way for an old man to put all his free time to good use. I find cars, buy 'em, fix 'em up. Sometimes I sell 'em, sometimes I don't, but it's all about the thrill of the hunt and being able to show 'em off in the end, you know?" He winked at her and gestured at the far end of the garage again. "So now that you've humored an old man geeking out about his cars, let's go take a look at yours."

"Sounds good." She followed him back down the line of cars, briefly scanning her warped reflection in each of the pristinely painted and detailed bodies as she passed. *Gotta humor him, right? I'd probably get this giddy too if anyone seemed remotely interested in seeing what I did with Glen.*

"All right. You got a few dings. Scratches." Lee rubbed his lip beneath his waxed mustache. "The driver's side headlight's gonna need replacing."

"Yep."

"How're the tires?"

"I mean, I bought the thing brand new. Shouldn't be anything wrong with them."

"All right. I'll take a closer look when I get up here under the wheel well. You got a bent rim too, you know that?"

"Yeah, I saw."

The man grinned at her as he straightened from studying the tires. "I'm assuming you want this patched up ASAP, huh?"

"The sooner, the better. If I have to pay you more for rush service, that's not a problem."

"Oh." Lee raised his eyebrows at her. "Always nice to hear."

She shrugged. "I just want my car back to normal."

"I hear ya. Come on, I'll write up an estimate, not that we have to stick to it. If it takes less time, I'm not gonna charge you for more. But I gotta keep track of what I'm doin' somehow, you know?"

"Sure." She followed him back into the garage toward a long, low desk against the back wall.

"Oh, hey. Help yourself to anything in the fridge. Mostly Fresca and water, I think. Maybe a few beers." Lee stepped behind the desk and opened a drawer to pull out a huge spiral-bound notebook of perforated pages with carbon copies. "This won't take me more than a few minutes."

"Yeah, thanks." Cheyenne grabbed a bottled water from the mini-fridge, then stood and scanned the shelves higher up on the wall. They were crammed with tools, old license plates, and three-ring binders. As she took a long drink of water, a framed photograph caught her eye. Lee and a woman in her late twenties stood side by side, their arms around each other's waists, laughing at the camera with the ocean in the background. "Where was this taken?"

"Hmm? Oh." A slow, lazy smile spread across Lee's face when he noticed the picture. "Yeah, that's Sandbridge six, maybe seven years ago. My daughter and I drove this sweet little cruise down there into Norfolk a few months before I sold the thing. Caroline. Right about the time she moved to Charleston, I think it was."

"Sounds like a fun trip." *The kind Bianca would shut down in a heartbeat if I so much as thought about taking a trip with her.* "Is she still in Charleston?"

The man's smile faded, and he looked back down at his binder of estimates. "You know, I'm not sure where she is these days."

Cheyenne shot him a quick glance, but he focused on writing out the estimate and shrugged. *That's the sound of a stranger crossing the line into personal-history territory.*

Lee kept talking. "Not that I wouldn't love to know, mind you. I can't get her to pick up the phone. Honestly, I don't even know if she has the same number. I could be calling a complete stranger, for all I know. You'd think I'd be able to tell whose number I'm calling, but she's not real big on recording voicemail messages. There's always a chance some poor bastard's been listening to my messages for years and laughing at me on the other end of it."

She wrinkled her nose and turned away from the shelf. "Sorry."

"What are you gonna do, right? Keep on keepin' on, I guess. Things change. People change. Sometimes, we turn out to be the complete opposite of who we thought we were, and it makes our kids turn against us."

"I wouldn't know."

"Why would you?" Lee glanced up at her briefly with a small smile. "You have any kids?"

Cheyenne snorted. "Definitely not."

"I see. Hell, even when you do have kids, you never know what you're doing. Who you are. All you know is that you do your best, even if it's not enough for them, and hope they don't hold all your shortcomings against you."

I wonder if he'd be saying the same thing if he knew about any of L'zar's shortcomings.

"You have a good relationship with your parents?" Lee asked.

Cheyenne cocked her head and walked slowly along the back wall, scanning the shelves but not really seeing anything on them. "With my mom, kinda. My dad, though, that's a totally different thing."

"You still talk?"

She looked at the man with a tiny frown. *I don't even know why I'm having this conversation with a guy I've only met twice.* "Well, we didn't for a long time. But yeah. We're talking now. Not exactly my favorite part of the day, though."

"Ah. But I bet you it's his favorite part." Lee pointed at her with his pen, then looked at the picture of him and his daughter again. "I tell you what, Cheyenne. Not a day goes by where I don't think about my daughter. What I could've done differently. What I'd give now to be able to spend a day with her like the day we had when that picture was taken. But hey, those are the regrets of an old man who's lived long enough to have few things left but regrets, right?"

"At least you have regrets."

Lee laughed and returned his pen to the notebook, shaking his head. "That's not something you hear every day."

"I mean, the ability to realize you were wrong and wanna make up for it, you know? Something my dad has a real issue with." Cheyenne took another quick drink of water. "I promise you haven't done anything close to what my dad's done. And I saw him this morning."

"Hmm. He must've done something right in raising you, then."

She snorted. "No, my mom gets the credit for that." *I doubt L'zar even thinks twice about what might happen if he crosses the line and I cut him out. He probably wouldn't even care. Not like Lee's daughter was meant to lead a coup and overthrow a magical dictator, but still.*

"Well. If you asked for my advice, I'd tell you one thing to remember and take with you." The man scribbled his signature at the bottom of the paper and dropped the pen on the desk. "It's hard enough to live with your own mistakes. But when our screwups are responsible for the mistakes the people we care about start makin' all on their own, that's when it's time to take a serious look at ourselves. Forgiveness and change. Taking responsibility and movin' on the best way we know how. Hopefully, our kids or whoever are willing to notice the change and eventually forgive us too. Who knows, right?"

Screwing the lid back onto her bottled water, Cheyenne nodded. "I hope she notices."

"Ha. Yeah, me too. All right." Lee slapped a hand on the estimate and quickly tore it off along the perforated edge. "Here we go. Estimated cost. Like I said, subject to change, but very rarely do I go over."

"Even if you did, I wouldn't have an issue with it." She joined him at the desk and took the pen he offered. "Seriously. Whatever you think needs to be done to get my car looking like it just came off the lot again, this is me giving you the all-clear to do it."

"I like the sound of that. Look that over and sign at the bottom if it's all good."

"Yep." Cheyenne put her signature right next to his and nodded. "Thanks, Lee."

"You betcha. Give me twenty-four hours, and you'll have your ride back home looking brand-spanking-new."

"Twenty-four hours?" Cheyenne took the carbon copy of his estimate and stuck it in her pocket without looking. "That's fast."

"Yeah, I know. But I like you. You listened to an old man's sob story, and the rest of this stuff I'm tinkering with doesn't have any set timeline to stick to."

"Cool. Thanks."

"You're welcome. You need a ride home?"

"No, I'm good. I'll call an Uber."

"You sure? I'm happy to take you into town."

She shook her head. "I'll be fine. Thanks." She pulled her phone out of her back pocket and pretended to pull up the Uber app she didn't have to find a ride.

"Okay. Well, if you change your mind, let me know."

"I'm good. Car should be here in ten minutes. I'll have them meet me at the end of the gravel." Cheyenne stopped when a glint of copper beads caught her eye on the shelf almost directly behind Lee's head. No way. She narrowed her eyes and gestured at the beads with a charm identical to those she'd seen in Peridosh. "What's that?"

"Hmm? Oh, a thank-you gift. People leave me the weirdest stuff all the time, and I guess I've grown something of a collection over the years. Bunch of random stuff that's neat to look at but not any more useful than that."

"I think you might be wrong about that. Do you know what it means?"

Lee's eyes widened, and he cocked his head, his smile growing by the second. "Do you?"

There isn't a set protocol for how to figure out whether or not someone knows about magic. She nodded. "I'm pretty sure I do, yeah. Comes from a whole different world, right?"

"Well, would you look at that!" Lee readjusted his Stetson one more time and chuckled. "How much do you know about this other world, huh?"

Cheyenne slipped into drow mode long enough for the man to get a good look at her. "You could say I've got a foot in the door."

"Ha!"

She slipped back into her Goth-human form and shrugged.

"And here I was, thinking you were a regular young woman with good taste in cars."

"I thought you were a car enthusiast who patches up the occasional accident."

"Very clever." Lee shook a finger at her, grinning. "Sorry to disappoint you, Cheyenne, but what you see with me is what you get."

"Huh. I've been telling people the same thing for a long time."

He laughed and slapped a hand on the desk. "No, I mean nothing non-human about this car enthusiast, but I've made a few friends over the years who have at least one foot in the door. Like you. I've always thought it a little funny that magicals still drive cars around."

"Well, unless you know a nightstalker, that's pretty much the only way to get around. With a few exceptions."

"Boy, my day's full of surprises. Don't worry. Your secret's safe with me."

Nodding, Cheyenne glanced at the copper beads and charm on the shelf again. "I trust you, but I do have a question that might seem a little weird."

"Oh, yeah? Hell, when you know about magic and magicals running around looking like regular people, not a whole lot sounds all that weird. Ask away."

She tilted her head and looked slowly back at him. *I'm taking a chance with this one, but it's not like I have anything to lose.* "You wouldn't happen to know anybody who deals with or at least knows more than the average magical about curses, would you?"

"Wow." Lee folded his arms and nodded. "You know, I might."

"Seriously?"

"I couldn't make this stuff up even if I wanted to. Serendipity at its finest."

"Tell me about it."

He opened another drawer in his desk and rummaged around. "Give me a minute. I know I've got one. Yep. Here you go."

Cheyenne took the thin, plain business card he handed her and flipped it over. "Awesome. Thank you."

"You bet. Don't make a call after nine p.m. or on weekends. That's a whole different mess you don't even wanna get into."

"Sure, okay." She stuck the business card in her pocket. "Hey, I appreciate this."

"Don't mention it. It's not like it took me a lotta time and effort to get you a number. I hope it's helpful."

"Yeah, me too."

"You should probably get goin' if you wanna meet that driver on time."

"Oh." Cheyenne chuckled and glanced at the garage's high ceiling. "Yeah, there's no Uber coming."

"Huh. So how're you gettin' home?"

"I'm one of those magicals who doesn't need a car or a nightstalker to get around." She stepped out of the warehouse and turned halfway around to raise her hand in farewell. "I'll wait to hear from you tomorrow, yeah?"

Hooking his thumbs through his belt loops again, Lee followed her out of the garage with a curious smile. "I'll call you when she's ready for you to pick her up."

"Thanks. Have a good one."

"Yeah, you too."

Cheyenne slipped into her drow form and into drow speed before the man could finish his sentence. The air crackled around her as she darted down the gravel drive in a blur of black and gray and white.

Lee stumbled forward, pulled by the shockwave trailing after her, and managed to catch his hat when the wind snatched it off his head. Chuckling, he set the Stetson back in place, adjusted the brim up and back down again, then dusted off his hands. "Well, I'll be damned."

CHAPTER THIRTY-FIVE

Ember had just finished making herself a chicken salad sandwich when Cheyenne burst through the front door of their apartment, grinning. "That was fast."

"Yeah." The halfling headed for the wrought-iron stairs leading to the mini loft. "And way more helpful than I expected."

Ember finished cutting her sandwich and lifted one half to her mouth. "So the old guy who fixes up old cars for fun is legit, then."

"I'm not talking about the car, Em." Cheyenne's feet pounded up the metal stairs. "I mean, yeah. He's legit. Said he'll be done tomorrow. But you know what's even better?"

Swallowing the bite of her sandwich, Ember picked up her plate and floated from the kitchen to the living room to stare up at her friend, who plopped down in the desk chair. "I've stopped trying to guess."

The halfling scooted closer to her desk, then leaned sideways to meet Ember's gaze through the iron bars with wide eyes. "He's a human with magical friends, Em. Who happened to have a card with a name and number of someone he thinks might know about curses."

"No shit?"

"No shit." Cheyenne forced herself not to punch a hole through Glen in her excitement when she powered on her system and waited for everything to boot up.

"How'd you find all that out?"

"A random necklace on his shelf, believe it or not. I recognized it, and he's officially the first human to not freak out when they see what I am for the first time."

"Weird." Ember dropped onto the couch with her plate in her lap and took another huge bite of her sandwich. "And kinda cool."

"I know."

"So why are you up there at the computer instead of calling this curse-magical whoever-it-is?"

"Well, it came with a warning. No phone calls on the weekends or after nine at night, which is fine. We have to deal with Colonel Thomas before anything else, and I'm not about to risk that by going to see a stranger who deals with curses."

"Right." Ember nodded. "So many things could go wrong in that scenario."

"Yeah, thanks." Cheyenne logged onto her desktop and pulled up her VPN to get ready for another dive into the dark web. "So for now, I'm gonna see what I can find out about this Inolu guy." She pulled the new card from her pocket and turned it over.

"Cool. Glad you found something." Ember grabbed the remote off the coffee table and aimed it at the entryway table by the front door. The apartment filled with the hum of Cheyenne's computer and of the flatscreen TV rising slowly out of the table. "You do your thing, and I'll do mine."

"Sweet. Hey, Matthew didn't try to come back and talk to you after I left, did he?"

"What? No." Ember scoffed. "I'd like to say he's smarter than that, but I really don't know anymore. Why?"

"Just curious. I wasn't sure if he took us seriously."

"Well, if he doesn't, I'll give him a reason to. And we can stop talking about him now if it's all the same to you. 'Cause you know he's gonna be breaking down our door first thing Tuesday morning looking for answers."

"No problem. I won't bring him up again." Cheyenne logged into her VPN and pulled up the browser for the dark web. *I'll be way too distracted to think about Matthew Thomas.*

"Thank you." With a flash of violet light, Ember's legs lifted onto the couch so she could sprawl out and lean back against the armrest in her usual position. "I'm gonna watch something awesome."

Cheyenne was already too involved to hear what her friend said as she clicked on *Third Quarter Projections* and made her way into the Borderlands Forum. *Making a name for himself with a human is one thing, but if this Inolu rings a bell with Earthside O'gúleesh, I'll know I'm on the right track.*

She drew up a new topic thread to post to the forum and made it simple, short, and direct, the best way to get anything done if she wanted it done right.

New Topic Posted Nov 4, 2021 at 3:17 p.m.; Original Topic Thread opened by User ShyHand71

Topic: Anyone Know Inolu?

I'm trying to find a little more information on Inolu Rosh. Honest opinions requested, and if you haven't dealt with this magical in person, please don't jump on here and start throwing out hearsay. I'm trying to get a clearer picture of what I might be getting into if I decide to make this call.

TIA.

Then she sat back and waited for the comments to roll in. Which they did. Quickly.

AlpacaLipsMeow: You forgot to add 'Asking for a friend.' I went to Inolu a couple years ago for a "skin issue." No regrets. Little bit on the pricey side, but I'd say absolutely worth it.

2BorFU: Are you kidding me? @ShyHand71 This is what you spend your time doing on a Sunday? Seriously, you're either wasted or in some serious trouble. Whatever it is, don't debase yourself by going to someone like Inolu Rosh for help. Better yet, don't debase the rest of us by posting this kinda shitstorm topic in the first place.

Laird4Quad: @ShyHand71 Whatever you're dealing with, I'm sure you can find someone who can help you way more than that shitty excuse for a magical. Maybe even someone on this forum. There's a reason Inolu is on this side of the Border, and I'm pretty sure it wasn't by choice. #makegoodchoices

orcsOVERwives: @2BorFU obviously had a bad experience with Inolu. 'Cause I don't think anyone else is this riled up about you asking the question, @ShyHand71. It's better to look for opinions

than set up a meeting with someone like Inolu and go in blind. To be fair, I also think you have better options than Inolu. At least I hope. But without knowing what you're looking for, it's hard to say. I wasn't very impressed, but that's me. You can make your own decision.

PWNpalACE420: @AlpacaLipsMeow No regrets, huh? Totally doesn't surprise me that you of all magicals would go to Inolu for a "skin problem." You need to get your head out of your ass. No bane-breaker can fix ugly. Or stupid. If it was possible, I guess you would've realized you got robbed.

B@dTimeCrossing: @ShyHand71 In a way, I'm with @orcsOVERwives on this one. There are probably better options if you're not sure exactly what you're looking for. But I will say that Inolu is completely worth it if you're trying to get something done but don't want to get your hands dirty in the process. I was completely satisfied with my experience. Let me just say I got a promotion and a new house two months after the fact, and we'll leave it at that. PM me if you want more details.

2BorFU: @AlpacaLipsMeow and @B@dTimeCrossing You two deserve each other. You can't even give real examples, and the less discerning among us are in serious danger of being misled by your false claims! And @orcsOVERwives, you don't know anything about me or my situation, so don't get all high-and-mighty on me about overreacting to a "bad experience." You're all fucking morons if you think going to a bane-breaker is even an option on this side. That's the kinda shit we made the crossing to get away from.

orcsOVERwives: @2BorFU Sounds like you need to see someone for those anger issues, dude.

2BorFU: @orcsOVERwives I don't have anger issues. Who the fuck are you to say I have anger issues? I'm pissed because you guys are giving @ShyHand71 the wrong information.

B@dTimeCrossing: @2BorFU The OP asked for honest opinions about personal experience. I don't think they meant that includes your honest opinion of other magicals' personal experiences. Let the OP make their own decision and go have a drink or something. You've been exploding all over the Borderlands the last few days. Give it a rest.

AlpacaLipsMeow: @2BorFU Bite me.

TuskTown11: Interesting thread. Weird comments. Sounds like @2BorFU just needs to get laid.

Cheyenne shook her head and took a deep breath. *This is like scrolling through random comments on Facebook. This is magicals-only with some seriously messed-up issues. What the hell is a "skin problem?"*

She snorted and scrolled through the rest of the quickly posted comments. *So Inolu is a good option if I don't wanna get my hands dirty. Well, I'm already neck-deep in magical dirt, but at least no one said Inolu is a phony. Worth a shot, right?*

"Sounds like you found something fun," Ember muttered as she stared at the TV screen.

"Sure, it's always fun to watch anonymous magicals on the dark web tear each other apart over a difference of opinion."

"So now you're starting a virtual war too, huh?"

Cheyenne scooted her chair back and frowned down at her friend in the living room. "What do you mean, too? I didn't start any war."

"No, I know. I meant another war in general. Never mind."

"No virtual wars, Em. Everybody has an opinion."

"Well, that's a given."

Focusing on her computer again, Cheyenne skimmed through a few more comments affirming what she already figured about Inolu: that this was the magical to go to for what she needed, whether or not anyone else thought it was a good idea. *I'll make the call tomorrow. Now I can get ready for this meeting with Colonel Thomas and the Bull's Head with a clear conscience.*

Slipping into drow mode so her activator would pull up everything she wanted, Cheyenne selected the command to download all the information she'd taken from Colonel Les Thomas' computer in his FRoE office days before and stuck it into the Bunker program to keep prying virtual eyes out.

The last thing I need is for Matthew to stumble on a backdoor into my system and find all this shit right out in the open. Even though he apparently thinks I can do whatever he can't.

With the colonel's files still in her homemade cyber bomb-shelter, she wrapped it all up in a more complex version of the encryption Maleshi, AKA Professor Maddie Bergmann, had assigned her Advanced

Programming class to create at the beginning of the year. *Ironic, right? The code that got her attention is the same thing I'm wrapping around classified FRoE information to send to a scorned ex-agent with a vendetta. I like it.*

When the encryption finished writing itself around the colonel's files, she created a new download link on her server, dropped the encrypted files there, then pulled up a new email to Rhynehart.

Subject: What You've Been Waiting For

Email: "GoRookieorGoHome701k49@C1"

Below that, she pasted the link for the file package and hit send.

There. Now he has everything. Piece of cake.

Her cell phone buzzed in her back pocket, and when she took it out, she frowned at Rhynehart's number on the screen. Or not.

She accepted the call and pressed the phone to her ear. "Something wrong?"

"What the hell is this shit?"

"What you've been waiting for, Rhynehart. I thought I made that pretty obvious."

The agent sighed. "There's nothing obvious about what you sent me. How the hell am I supposed to know what to do with this?"

"So, I have to explain how emails work too?"

"Yeah. Pretend I was born yesterday."

"With a full head of hair and everything, huh?"

"Cheyenne."

She spun away from her desk in the chair, stretching both legs out in front of her and propping one ankle across the other. "Yeah, okay. See that long string of letters and numbers underlined in blue? That's a hyperlink."

"Fuck you. I know what a link is. It doesn't pull up shit."

"Wrong. See the little popup with the text box?"

"And?"

Cheyenne bit back a laugh. "Login box, Rhynehart. Requires a password. Think you can figure out what that is?"

"Not if you don't fucking tell me. Oh. The email."

"There you go."

"Seriously, how was I supposed to know that? It's not like you sent instructions."

"I didn't think I had to."

Rhynehart cleared his throat. "Shit, I don't know. It could've been like a virus or something, right? Some asshole trying to steal all my personal info."

"Well, yeah, it's possible someone might want to do that. But no one's gonna send you a virus on my personal email set up through my private server, man. Thanks for the confidence in my security."

"Whatever." The sound of hard typing came over the line, followed by a short pause. "Okay. I'm in."

"Awesome."

"Holy shit, halfling!"

Cheyenne swiveled back and forth in her chair. "Yep."

"Fuck. I'm hanging up. I can't talk to you and look at all this at the same time."

"Okay."

"Damn. This is some seriously deep shit you stepped in." Rhynehart cleared his throat. "You sure no one else is gonna find this? I mean, you can find anything on the internet, right?"

"Not if it's encrypted like that and only two people have the key. Make sure you permanently delete that email when you're done, yeah?"

"Sure. I'll fucking shred it. Jesus Christ."

"Okay. I'll leave you to it. If you still want in on this afterward, meet me at Hard Times Café in Alexandria tomorrow. Two o'clock."

"Why two?"

She pressed her lips together to hold back another laugh and cocked her head. "Well, I would ask what time works best for you, but I know your schedule's been cleared for the foreseeable future. Two o'clock feels right."

"Fine."

"And feel free to bring a few of your guys if you want. At the very least, we won't look like two rogues moving in to deal with personal issues. Make sure they're agents you trust who wanna pull this asshole out by the roots as much as we do."

Rhynehart snorted into the phone and let out a long, slow sigh. "For something like this, Cheyenne, the only agents I trust are the ones you trust. I'll pull the team who went into Operation Free Lizard with us."

"That's cute. Did you make that up just now?"

"Discretion, halfling. That's what I'm going for over the phone. See you tomorrow."

"Yep."

"Jesus fucking—" The line went dead before Rhynehart could finish cursing in surprise.

Cheyenne finally let herself chuckle and spun her chair back to her desk and monitor. *He's gonna owe me big time after this. And now he can't use the chain of command as an excuse not to pay up.*

CHAPTER THIRTY-SIX

Cheyenne powered down her computer and stood from the desk chair. Her hip flared with renewed pain, and she sucked in a sharp breath before peeling down the waistband of her pants to take a look.

"Fuck."

"Most of the time, I can tell the difference between a good 'fuck' and a bad 'fuck,'" Ember called from the couch. "That one's taking up a gray area."

"Not a good 'fuck,' Em." Gritting her teeth, Cheyenne gingerly covered the dart wound in her hip and took a peek at her shoulder next. "Yeah, not even remotely."

Ember paused her TV show and floated off the couch. "What happened?"

"They're getting worse." Cheyenne let go of her shirt and trudged down the stairs to the living room.

"Still have that canister?"

"Yeah. I was hoping not to have to use it again right now."

"In your coat?"

"Yep."

Ember grabbed her friend's trenchcoat off the armrest of the couch and jerked the fabric all over the place, trying to find the pockets. She reached into one, then the other, and pulled out the long silver injection canister. By the time Cheyenne reached her, the fae pointed at her friend with the canister and raised an eyebrow. "Let me see."

"Or we could use it first and examine wounds later."

"You know, despite how awesome it is that you managed to bring this across with you, no. I want to see what those holes look like first."

Cheyenne snorted, rolled her eyes, and pulled down the other side of her shirt collar this time.

Ember grimaced. "Shit."

"Oh, yeah. Very reassuring. Thanks, Healer."

"Please. You wouldn't want me lying to you about something like that."

"No, but you could try improving your bedside manner." They looked at each other and laughed. "Okay, Em. Just get it over with."

"Yep." Ember floated around her friend, lifted the back of Cheyenne's shirt, and pressed the injection canister against the halfling's flesh.

Cheyenne grimaced and cocked her head in discomfort when the darktongue serum flooded her system with a low hiss from the canister. "Feels about as great as the first time."

"Well, it isn't the worst-feeling thing that's happened to you. I didn't slam a potion into your chest, either."

"True." The halfling blinked slowly, the warm blanket of drow-effective painkiller doing its job as quickly and efficiently as ever. "I gotta say, there are certain parts I'm growing fond of."

Ember handed over the canister, then turned and lowered herself onto the couch again. "Keep an eye on those, okay? If they keep getting worse even with the darktongue serum, we're not gonna be able to stay over here much longer."

"Why?" Cheyenne tossed the canister, caught it, and sank down into the black leather recliner. "Because Venga's the only…whew. This stuff is strong today."

"Or you've been gritting your teeth and bearing the pain longer than you realized." Ember folded her arms and watched her friend as the darktongue euphoria settled in. "And no. I'm not saying we'll have to make the crossing again because Venga's the only one who can help you. So far, he seems to be the only one who's made things worse for you."

"Oh, really?" Cheyenne's head bobbed a little when she shot Ember a crooked smile. "I hadn't noticed."

Ember ignored the dazed comment. "But he is the only one who knows as much as he does about the blight. And about what might get that poison out of you."

Cheyenne thumped her elbow down onto the armrest and propped her chin up on a fist. "Don't you mean the Undoing?"

"I feel like we should finish this conversation when you're not high."

"I'm not high." The halfling grinned and rolled her eyes. "Okay, I'm high. Give it two more minutes, Em. Then it'll float away."

"As long as you don't float away with it."

Cheyenne leaned her head back and closed her eyes, blowing out a long breath and puffing out her cheeks. *I won't float away, not that I mind the way this feels every once in a while. Which is why I need to stop needing this.*

When she opened her eyes again, the room wasn't spinning nearly as much. Ember came back into focus, her eyebrow lifting when Cheyenne's gaze settled on her friend's face.

"Better?"

"Yeah." Cheyenne blinked, sat up straighter in the chair, and cleared her throat. "Yep. Awkward buzz heading out right now. And the pain went with it."

"What about the black streaks?"

Cheyenne checked both shoulders and shrugged. "Maybe slightly less. Really, though, it's all starting to look the same. Just fucked up."

Ember sighed and swiped the loose hair away from her face. "I don't know if we'll be able to find what we need to heal you Earthside. That's all I'm saying."

"Maybe. Maybe not. But I can't afford to spend a whole lot of time hanging out in Hangivol and hoping Venga or anyone else stumbles across the solution." Cheyenne tapped the injection canister against her thigh, then paused. "But I could make quick trips and bring everything back with me."

"Like what?"

"Literally anything." The halfling raised the canister and pointed it at

Ember. "First the activator, now this. I mean, we already know it's the tech that doesn't make it across the Border. Unless it's on me, apparently. If we have to go back for another trial run with shitty necromancer potions that may or may not make this poison even worse, I can bring it all back here."

Ember's eyes narrowed. "That's kind of a risk, isn't it? Bringing over that much magic at one time? I mean, if anyone finds out what you're doing, I wouldn't be surprised if magicals started talking about Cheyenne Summerlin as the new dark-magic mule carrying heavy-duty necromancer shit across the Border."

"Who's gonna know?" Cheyenne spread her arms. "If we don't advertise it, nobody will. It's a way bigger risk to take all the time we need on the other side when Bianca still can't stand for longer than twenty minutes at a time and keeps getting burned with new O'gúl runes."

"You won't be able to help her if your own personal blight strain takes you down first."

"Come on, Em. I can do both. It'll take some thinking outside the box."

"Uh-huh."

"Yeah, you don't look all that convinced."

"Well, I'm not." Ember leaned back and slung an arm over the couch's armrest. "But I guess I'll have to watch and wait for you to prove me wrong."

"We'll figure it out." Cheyenne took a deep breath and ran a hand through her hair. "We have to be careful with how we move forward. It's one step at a time. First, we take down Colonel Thomas and get the Bull's Head out of the way. No more war machines. No more idiots who don't even know Ba'rael's gone coming after me. Then I meet up with the bane-breaker."

"Bane-breaker?"

"Yeah. Apparently, that's what he's called. The Inolu guy Lee referred me to."

"Huh. Okay, so he's next."

"Hey, if we wrap up this whole FRoE-traitor thing fast enough, I might even be able to call the guy tomorrow night. If not, then at least Tuesday. See where that leads me in getting the rest of this curse away from Bianca, and then we can head back to Ambar'ogúl and help Venga or whoever figure out what the hell has to happen to heal me and the blight."

"Hmm." Ember licked her lips in hesitation, opened her mouth, then frowned at the coffee table. "I'm gonna put it out there."

"Uh-huh."

"If your mom has more to do with this than you think."

"She doesn't." Cheyenne shook her head. "Sorry, Em. I can't even entertain that thought."

"Really? It doesn't feel remotely possible to you?"

"I don't care what it feels like. I'm not gonna let it happen. Bianca Summerlin stays out of this. Bottom line."

Ember stared at her friend for a moment, then shrugged. "You know, you're getting a lot better at hiding your 'pissed and stupid' habit."

Cheyenne snorted.

"But I can still tell you're pissed, and that's keeping you from seeing this a different way."

"I don't wanna see it a different way."

"Isn't that kind of your job?"

"Nope." Cheyenne dropped the injection canister into her lap and slumped back against the recliner. "My job is to keep my mom safe. Take down the colonel. Heal the blight. And then take on whatever I'm supposed to take on with this whole drow-royalty-on-Earth thing. Which I think might be easier than I thought."

Ember said, "Do go on."

"No, I'm serious. I mean, I'll have to test it out with a few different things. See how much I can bring back with me. But when I find out what the limits are, I could bring O'gúl tech over here and start handing it over to magicals on this side who could seriously benefit from it."

"With one minor issue, though." Ember stuck a finger in the air. "You're the only one who can bring advanced tech through the crossing, yeah. You're also the only magical who can use it on this side."

"Right." Cheyenne rubbed her chin and glanced at the ceiling in mock-contemplation. "But didn't we see crates upon crates of old-school tech smuggled across the Border and used to build war machines?"

"A bunch of metal chips and the activator coil Elarit built you are not the same thing."

"Clearly." Meeting her friend's gaze again, Cheyenne grinned. "But, and correct me if I'm wrong, I'm pretty sure we know someone who's figured out how to power O'gúl tech with human systems."

Ember's eyes widened, and she blinked. "No."

"Why the hell not?" the halfling asked. "If our dazed-and-confused neighbor wants to redeem himself, the only answer he'll have when I ask him to do this is, 'Fuck yeah, Cheyenne. I'll make you whatever you want. Thanks for not tearing me limb from limb.'"

The fae burst out laughing. "It's gonna be hard to get those exact words out of him on the first go."

"Eh, it's the intention behind it that counts."

"You seriously want to pull him into building programs for O'gúl tech again? How is that any better than what his uncle and the Bull's Head did?"

"Because Matthew Thomas and Combined Reality, Inc. won't be writing programs for war machines meant to seek and destroy and pave the way for a drow dictator's inter-world war. Obviously."

"So, what? You're gonna hand out activators to any magical who feels like they want one?" Ember leaned forward when the lightbulb of inspiration struck. "Holy shit. You could make a fortune on that."

"Right, like that's at the top of my list. It's not even *on* my list." With a surprised laugh, Cheyenne shook her head. "And that's not the point. If I'm gonna take this whole Earthside royalty thing seriously, and I don't even wanna think about all the things that could go wrong if I don't, it's not about money."

"Well, yeah. I know. I was just saying."

"Yeah, someone could make a fortune doing this. I'm the only one who can, so I won't be charging refugees for the one thing that can help their entire lives over here be less of a shitstorm and more like living. At least at first."

"Okay." Ember frowned. "Walk me through it, though. 'Cause all I'm seeing right now is like a popup lemonade stand on a Border rez with you sitting behind a cardboard sign that reads, 'Free activator. Don't be dumb, just take one.'"

Cheyenne gave her friend a deadpan stare, then they both cracked up. "I wanna ask how that's the first thing you come up with, but something tells me hopping into your head would be scarier than making the crossing on a bad day."

"Ooh. Ouch."

"Whatever."

"I'm serious, though. How would you even do that with a bunch of activators fresh from Hangivol and pumped up with Matthew's program? Assuming he agrees to do it for you in this hypothetical situation."

"I don't think it's that hypothetical, Em. And he'll agree." Cheyenne grabbed the handle on the side of the recliner and jerked it up to lie almost flat on her back in the chair. Then she folded both arms behind her head and studied the high ceiling of their apartment. "Funny. Now that I look at it, it's almost like all the pieces were written down beforehand."

"Oh, okay. Like a prophecy?"

The halfling scoffed. "Like this was all meant to play out this way. We take down Colonel Thomas and lay out everything he's been doing for the last five years right there for everyone to see, and I'm not just wiping out the rest of the Bull's Head and a high-ranking dude getting his hands dirty. The entire FRoE is gonna owe me one after that big time, and what better way to turn in those chips than by rewriting the way they operate on the reservations?"

"You think they're gonna step back and let you drive the whole FRoE ship?"

"Well, yeah. 'Cause their system's totally broken, and I'm the one who figured it out. Plus, the whole drow royalty thing gives me a leg up with the Earthborn magicals working as agents. They'll want to know about where they came from and all the shit they're missing out on by not being able to make the crossing because that's their job. Give the magical agents activators. Hand them out to the refugees coming fresh into this world after making the crossing. Show them how to use the tech, 'cause it'll obviously be different with a human program running the show. Probably won't be as good as what I've got, but it's something, and it's a hell of a lot more than any magical, O'gúleesh or Earthborn, has been getting from the top down. Not when Colonel Thomas has been at the top and playing footsie with fucking O'gúl loyalists for the last five years."

"Or longer."

"Yeah. Or longer."

Ember folded her arms and tilted her head, studying her friend's growing smile as Cheyenne envisioned the whole thing. "I'm surprised you're a lot more into this than being the O'gúl Crown."

"Why?"

"I mean, 'cause it's the Crown."

Cheyenne waved her off. "Anyone can be the Crown, Em. Obviously. Persh'al will do a hell of a lot better job than I would. He knows that world. And I know this one. Plus, there's no one else who can do what I can do over here. As far as the old laws go, however the hell they work, I'm still L'zar's daughter and heir to the throne. I still have a connection or whatever with the last Nimlothar. And I'm a halfling. Doesn't matter if it's the halfling part or because I'm the drow heir who broke L'zar's 'all your kids will die' prophecy, I'm still the only magical who can bring advanced tech across the Border. I'm the only halfling with L'zar's blood and the extra burst of Sorren Gán magic that came with it."

"And you can see the Weave in tech."

Quickly lifting her head, Cheyenne met her friend's gaze and laughed. "Yeah, I can see the Weave in tech. More like I can see the Matrix, right?"

Ember wrinkled her nose. "Yeah, I don't think so. I mean, you get points for having seen those movies, only the Matrix isn't real. Magic is."

"Whatever. I'll figure out what to call it eventually."

"Oh, you mean something like, 'you can see the Weave in tech?'"

"Nope." Cheyenne thumped her head back down on the headrest. "The Weave is L'zar's deal, and I'm not trying to walk anywhere close to his footsteps. I'll think of something."

"Maybe it'll come to you when you stage your second coup in a month and overthrow the leaders of the FRoE. You know, rewriting things again from the inside out, only on this side of the Border."

"Maybe. It's gonna happen, though, Em. I think I've figured out what I'm supposed to do. Like my place, or whatever. Helping out the

O'gúleesh who come over here and think the FRoE is the be-all-end-all on this side, except the FRoE was started by dumbasses like Sir, who don't even know how magic works. I get to change that."

"Good thing you're used to having your work cut out for you."

"Ha. For real."

CHAPTER THIRTY-SEVEN

Cheyenne woke the next morning with her regular scowl and the memory of dreams that made her skin crawl. She tossed the thick purple velvet comforter off and sat up with a groan. *I take it back. Prophecy dreams are way better than whatever the fuck that was.*

As she reached for her cell phone on the nightstand, the image of Bianca and L'zar in the master bedroom on the Summerlin estate came back to her from her dream. She shook her head vigorously and snatched up her phone. *Out of my head. That's it.*

At 7:05, she had almost three and a half hours until she had to be on the VCU campus to teach her undergrad class. No, she didn't have to rush through the morning, but now she had three hours for this damn dream to keep floating around in her head.

The smell of freshly brewing coffee tugged her out of bed, and she shuffled out of her room and toward the kitchen, scratching her head and mussing her already perfect bedhead. "Coffee ready?"

"Hey. Morning." Ember turned away from the kitchen counter and froze when she saw the halfling lumbering across the living room. "Rough night?"

"Just the part where I'm apparently dreaming about L'zar and Bianca."

"Doing what?"

Cheyenne shot her friend a pointed glare and raised an eyebrow.

"Oh. Oh, ew." Ember shook her head and turned back to the cabinets. Purple light flashed from her fingertip and around a second coffee mug before she directed the cup down on the counter beside the coffeemaker. "That's not right."

"Like I don't already know that." Cheyenne stopped at the kitchen island and dropped her forearms onto the granite countertop, leaning sleepily forward. "That kinda shit doesn't leave any room for a good night's sleep."

"I bet." Ember grabbed the coffee pot and filled a mug for each of them. The coffeemaker hissed and gurgled when she returned the pot, then she spun around and offered Cheyenne a cup.

The halfling took the coffee and couldn't force the grimace off her face even as she took the first steaming sip.

"You want anything in that?"

"Nope." Cheyenne stared at the coffee. *Nothing's gonna cover up the bad taste of dreaming about my parents like that.*

"Did you pick up on that kinda vibe between them?" Ember tossed a hand at the fridge, and the door opened and the bottle of flavored creamer sailed into her hand with a flash of violet light. "I mean, when we were there."

"Are you kidding? No. No way. The only thing between them now is that one night twenty-one years ago and the fact that I'm their kid. That's it. This dream doesn't mean shit."

"I mean, at the very least, now you know how totally uncool you'd be with it if they…you know."

"Stop. I can't think about this anymore."

"Sure." Ember stirred her coffee and stared at her friend. "Caffeine'll help."

"Probably not." *And why the hell am I having this kind of dream in the first place? Must be something seriously wrong with me, beyond the usual.* The halfling sipped the hot, bitter coffee again and scowled at the granite countertop. *I have way more important shit to think about today.*

After breakfast, a quick shower, and finding something to wear that didn't rub the black streaks around her unhealing wounds in unbearable ways, Cheyenne went through her backpack to double-check that whatever she might need was there. *I spend two days in Ambar'ogúl, and everything feels out of place over here when I get back.*

"So." Ember tied her purple-streaked hair up in a loose bun and sank onto the couch. "Anything you need me to handle while you're out playing Goth grad student?"

"The whole point is that I'm trying not to play anything, Em."

"Yeah, I know. Keeping all your options open. Doesn't it seem a little weird, though? That you're still going back and forth, trying to juggle both?"

Cheyenne zipped up her backpack with two quick jerks. "Maleshi's doing it."

"Maleshi's been here for a few thousand years, trying to keep up a human routine. And she's not the drow halfling heir who has frenemies in the FRoE and can bring O'gúl tech across the border."

"None of which is gonna help me down the road when all this settles down."

"Oh. Because you'll totally need a job once your philanthropy with O'gúleesh refugees is over and done with."

Cheyenne dropped her backpack on the couch and frowned at her friend. "Why is this bothering you?"

"I don't know." Ember shrugged. "I know that I'm a lot happier without having to juggle a spinal injury, being your *Nós Aní*, going to grad school full time, and trying to be a magical Earthside where the majority of the population doesn't even know we exist. I mean, sure, I'm only dealing with two outta four right now, but it's kinda nice knowing I don't have to split up my time. Also, yes, thanks to you. 'Cause it's not like I need a job, either."

"I don't care about the money, Em."

"I know."

"I don't wanna be relying on my perceived reputation as L'zar's daughter or the Black Flame or the halfling whatever for the rest of my life."

"And going through grad school where you know more about

computers and cybersecurity and programming than any of the faculty is gonna get you something more reliable than that?"

"Maybe." Cheyenne paused and let out a heavy sigh. "Probably not."

"Good. You're finally being honest."

"Look, I don't know what going through grad school is gonna get me at this point, okay? It seemed like the best idea before everything with L'zar and the FRoE fell into my lap."

Ember dug into the box of crackers in her lap before popping one in her mouth with a crunch. "I think *you* fell into *their* laps."

"Whatever. It hasn't even been two months. I get it. And it's not like it's all day every day. Four and a half hours a week. It's a joke."

"But the joke's important enough to keep doing it?"

"Maybe. I don't know, but I can't drop out to clear my time for the rest of this."

"Why not?"

"Because I don't do that."

Ember tilted her head. "I'm confused."

"I don't quit shit I start, Em. That's not what I do."

"Even if it's giving you absolutely no benefit?"

"It's a means to an end."

"What end?"

"Will you stop?" It came out louder than Cheyenne intended, and she stared at Ember with wide eyes, half in irritation, half in shock.

Ember returned the stare, then shrugged and stuck another cracker in her mouth. "Trying to get some perspective."

"I think I'm the only one who needs perspective about my choices. At least the ones that don't have the fate of two entire worlds and everyone living in them on the line."

"Sure. You want a normal, boring, slightly-more-than-advanced graduate experience to balance out all the weird shit." Ember grinned. "You could've started with that."

Despite her irritation, Cheyenne laughed. "If I'd realized that's what this was, I would've started with that, yeah."

"Then you learned something, so it's a conversation worth having."

"Yeah, okay." Shaking her head, Cheyenne lifted her backpack and strapped it over her shoulders. She grimaced at the added pressure on the dart wounds beneath the straps and pulled them away from her chest. "Backpack's not such a great idea."

"Do you need it?"

"Computer, wallet, phone, jar of darktongue salve, and the injection canister just in case. Yeah, I kinda need the backpack. I'm not buying a fucking purse."

Ember snorted. "Okay, then."

"Okay, so I'll be back at like noon, probably. You want me to grab anything while I'm out?"

"Nope. I'll hang out here, like every day. Doin' my own thing."

Cheyenne glanced at the door. *She doesn't sound all that happy about it.* "Okay."

"Oh, hey. Here's an idea." Ember sat up straighter. "Maybe I need my own car."

"Like, right now? Or are you talking about when your legs finish healing?"

The fae snorted. "Come on. I know I can't technically press on the pedals, but that never stopped magic from doing what it's supposed to do."

"Huh. I wonder how many magicals use spells to drive cars on this side? No activators for that, Em."

"Well, yeah, but still. I can make coffee with magic. Driving a car shouldn't be that much different."

Cheyenne snorted. "Foolproof logic, Em. You know, if you want me to buy you a car, come out and say it."

Ember's eyes widened. "Seriously? Would you buy me a car?"

"I don't know." Cheyenne shrugged before turning to the door. "It's a thought, though."

"Oh, sure. In this instance, I don't think it's the thought that counts."

"See you in a few hours, Em."

Ember's laughter spilled through the door and followed Cheyenne down the hall to the elevator.

Once the elevator doors closed behind her to take her down to the apartment building's lobby, Cheyenne reached into her pocket for her car keys and stopped. *Shit. The car's with Lee.* She pulled her activator from her pocket and stuck it behind her ear before slipping into drow mode. A short, simple thought brought up three different options for the spell she wanted.

Yes. Human illusion. Thank you.

Cheyenne flicked her fingers to select the command, and a surge of drow magic flowed up her spine and through her fingers as she cast the spell with gestures she didn't understand. She didn't even need words. The purple-gray flesh of her hand shimmered with silver light before fading into her human-pale tone. She turned her hand over a few times and smiled. *I love this thing.*

The elevator doors opened, and she stepped out into the perpetually empty lobby at the Pellerville Gables Apartments complex in full drow mode without looking full drow. Her black Vans made little noise on the marble floors, and as soon as she stepped through the glass front doors, she turned the corner and headed around to the back of the building. *Sure, it might be weird to enter drow speed looking like Cheyenne the Goth grad student, but hey, it's the same blur, just in reverse.*

She smiled at her intensely pale skin and stopped at the back of the building in front of the pressure-washed white-brick wall surrounding the dumpster. *And I don't have to worry about anybody seeing a drow face at the wrong second. Here we go.*

The air crackled around her when she slipped into enhanced speed and darted away from the apartment complex on the far north end of Richmond. A gust of dry, fallen leaves and loose pebbles on the asphalt kicked up behind her and pelted the wall around the dumpster, but no one was there to see the Goth girl disappear in a blur of black and white.

CHAPTER THIRTY-EIGHT

Cheyenne dropped out of drow speed behind the computer sciences building on the VCU campus, which happened to be on the north end. The shockwave of her sudden stop pulled more leaves and bits of dry grass and a Taco Bell wrapper toward her, as well as whipping her black hair around her face. She turned around to make sure she hadn't missed any unsuspecting witnesses, but no one else was hanging out behind the building.

That was awesome. She grinned and smoothed the hair away from her face. *I didn't even have to stop once. Getting better at this every day.*

Taking a quick scan of the parking lot with her activator, which didn't bring up anything, war machines, or otherwise, she shrugged and stepped between the computer sciences building and its neighbor. *So far, so good. I know I can't keep relying on this thing forever. Officially learning spells is on the to-do list—after I take care of everything else on my plate.*

The sound of low conversation drifted to her on the breeze whistling between the buildings, but it sounded off somehow. Subdued. *It's Monday. I get it. But Mondays are usually a lot louder.*

As soon as she stepped out of the narrow alley, Cheyenne stopped and scanned the quad stretching in front of the computer sciences building. The quad was packed with as many students as usual for 10:20 a.m. on any day of the week, but they all moved slowly, awkwardly, turning around to stare at the other students walking toward or away from them or glancing at the sky like there was something important up there they'd forgotten.

"Okay." Frowning, Cheyenne walked around the building to the front doors. She swept her gaze across the quad one more time and finally found the problem. "Oh, shit."

The newly sprouted portal ridge she'd managed to close a few weeks before while Maleshi helped shred up the attacking war machines was no longer manned by a bunch of Sir's FRoE agents dressed as emergency response team members. Someone on the VCU grounds crew had done their best to patch the giant rift in the grass, and all that remained of the portal that had never quite opened was a mound of new bright-green sod standing out from the darker-green grass of the quad starting to brown a little with the autumn chill. The new sod didn't do a thing to keep the dark, smoky wisps of black light from seeping out of the closed portal and into the air.

Grimacing, Cheyenne selected her activator's command prompt for zooming in on that brighter mound of grass to take a closer look. *Damn.*

The thin, smoky tendrils had pale O'gúl symbols that scrolled up and down before the smoke eventually dissipated in the air. *But it's not disappearing.*

As if to prove her point, a kid wearing a giant puffy jacket, a scarf, and a thick woolen beanie walked down the path cutting through the quad. His eyes were clear as he hurried to his next class, but the closer he got to the invisibly leaking Border portal, the more he slowed down. He stopped directly across from the mound of new grass spewing left-over blight and in-between crap into the air and blinked.

"Hey!" Cheyenne whistled loudly, and the kid turned his head to her in a daze. "You have a class to get to?"

"I think so?" The kid tilted his head at her and frowned, then spun slowly around to look for his answer behind him.

"Maybe hurry up," she called, studying anything and everything the activator could pull up for her about the leaking portal that was supposed to be dead. *Just more fucking blight spilling over into Earth, and now it's in the air.* She shoved her hands into her pockets and trudged down the sidewalk to the building's front entrance. *And apparently, it does weird shit to humans.*

The front hall inside held its usual number of students leaving their last classes or approaching their next, but all of them walked with a syrupy sluggishness. Cheyenne caught snippets of conversation here and there, most of which stopped halfway through a sentence without anyone asking for the rest of it. Some of the students looked up from their dazed staring to watch her as she moved quickly down the hall, but the Goth girl was quickly forgotten in the fog.

Cheyenne picked up the pace to her undergrad classroom, scanning the blank faces and slow movements around her. *Hell of a way to weed out the magicals from the humans. Now my normal speed is enhanced speed.*

The classroom was empty when she stepped through the door three minutes before her 10:30 class. She flipped on the lights and headed down the aisle to her desk at the front of the room. The activator didn't pull up anything in her vision, no traces of floating airborne blight and definitely no spying war machines. "I guess we're good for now."

She gingerly shrugged off her backpack and set it on the desk. Fortunately, her open wounds weren't giving her much trouble right now. *Maybe that's because the blight in the air is a bigger problem right now.*

With a sigh, Cheyenne pulled out the chair behind the desk and waited for her students to show up.

At 10:35, only one short, dark-haired girl had wandered into the room, and it took her another three minutes to choose her seat. By 10:45, only half the class had shown up, all of them looking confused and like they forgot every other minute where they were and what they were doing here. Five minutes after that, Cheyenne cleared her throat and stood.

One of the kids in the back, who'd resorted to picking his nose in the absence of regular mental functioning, started when she moved. "Ow. Shit." He pulled his finger out of his nose and stared at it.

"Okay." Cheyenne clapped her hands. "So, it looks like this is what we're working with today."

"With what?" The kid who wore all the puka-shell necklaces cocked his head, his mouth hanging open.

Well, at least he managed to show up. "With class. Which is where you are, by the way."

"I hope your mom's okay," the short dark-haired girl said in a breathy drawl.

Cheyenne looked sharply at her. "What?"

"Your mom. That sucks."

How the fuck does she know shit about that? "Look, I don't know what you think is going on."

"Oh, yeah." A larger guy with thick, round glasses slowly bobbed his head. "Because you weren't here on Friday. Right? Wait, was I here on Friday?"

"Not sure." Cheyenne stuck her hands in her pockets and frowned as she scanned the quarter-full classroom and only half of her students. "I wasn't."

"Yeah, 'cause of your mom. That email you sent us made me sad." The dark-haired girl stuck out her lower lip and nodded at Cheyenne, her eyes wide and glistening. "So, tell her good luck from me."

"Right. Thanks." Cheyenne took a deep breath. Maleshi had said she'd taken care of it. Pre-emptive mom issues for the win. *I had no idea my mom would need more help when I was in a different world fighting Ba'rael on Friday.*

"So, when do we get to…" The puka-shell kid's voice trailed off as he developed a sudden interest in the overhead lights.

"All right. You know what?" Cheyenne thumped a fist on the desk, and her students jumped in their seats. "It's your lucky day. I think we've all got a case of the Mondays, am I right?"

No one said a thing, and only half the students who'd bothered to show up even looked in her direction.

I can't believe I said that. Hopefully, nobody remembers.

"All right. I'll send out an email about this assignment too so nobody forgets, which seems likely right now. Go find whatever kind of job you're hoping to get after college with a major in Computer Sciences and bring back all the info about it on Wednesday."

"That's our homework?"

"Yeah. Class is over early today."

"Wait, what's our homework?"

"The thing she just said. Didn't you hear her say we have to, uh… what do we have to do?"

"Jesus." Cheyenne closed her eyes and took a deep breath. "Go home and check your emails tonight, okay? I'll send it out to everybody. Simple assignment. Time to leave."

The undergrad students took five times longer than normal to get out of their seats and figure out where the door was. With a sigh, Cheyenne pointed at the back of the room and waited as they all slowly filtered out. Then she stared at the open doorway after the last of them had gone and rubbed her mouth. *There's no way I'm passing my first year of grad school when shit like this keeps getting in the way. I just gave them a fifth grader's homework.*

She grabbed her backpack off the desk and carried it by the top strap instead of slipping it over her shoulders. The lights clicked off when she slapped the light switch, and she walked quickly down the hall to where she knew Maleshi was teaching her class right now. She only passed two other people in the hall, a student staring blankly at a crack in the wall and a faculty member walking faster than anyone else she'd seen today but mumbling incoherently to himself and blinking.

I guess everyone's affected by brain fog differently. This is bad.

When she reached Maleshi's current classroom, a quick peek through the narrow rectangular window showed no difference in her human students. Maleshi was slumped in her chair at the front of the room, her eyes closed as she rubbed her forehead in aggravation. "No, Damien. This isn't personal hygiene class. I don't think that's even offered at this university, but if that's your biggest concern right now, I think it's time for you to change disciplines."

Cheyenne dropped her backpack against the wall and folded her arms, peering through the window as she tried to get a better look at the students. *You'd think there'd be one or two magicals enrolled here who aren't getting their brains blight-scrambled, right? Everyone's human, and everyone close to that portal is screwed.*

After five minutes of another irritatingly useless attempt to get her students to pay attention, Maleshi finally looked at the door and saw Cheyenne staring at her through the window. The general spread her arms and shook her head.

Cheyenne shrugged. *Yeah, I don't know, either, but we need to talk this over.*

Fortunately, "Professor Bergmann's" class got out at 11:15, so Cheyenne didn't have to wait long for the opportunity to have that discussion. She didn't think she had the willpower to stand at the open door while Maleshi's students meandered out into the hall, starting and stopping random conversations without finishing a thought. One girl turned around to look at her professor and opened her mouth to say something. She forgot what it was, and Maleshi headed to the door to chase her out.

"Keep moving, kid." She waved at the girl. "Whatever it is can wait 'til the next class."

"But it was important. I think."

"I know. Look, I've got somewhere to be, and as much as I don't wanna be there, it's kinda my job. Go splash some water on your face or something, and I'll see you Wednesday."

"Water? I'm not thirsty."

"Go, go, go." Maleshi came as close as she could to pushing the girl into the hall without touching her.

Cheyenne frowned after the dazed, wandering students, then grabbed her backpack and stepped into the empty classroom with the general. "This is nuts."

"Yeah, you're telling me." Maleshi folded her arms and stared at the slow river of students moving through the hall. Under her human illusion, she somehow managed to pull off looking concerned and amused at the same time. "Like there's something in the water."

"It's in the air."

"What?"

Cheyenne closed the classroom door behind her and gave the general a pointed look. "Literally in the air."

"Sorry, kid. You lost me, 'cause I was using a figure of speech."

"Yeah, I know. The new portal ridge I closed up out on the quad. That's the issue."

"It's closed, Cheyenne. And inactive. I don't see the connection."

Cheyenne tapped the activator behind her ear. "But I did. Now we have more blight leaking out of the portals into the air, and it's making the closest thing we can get to human zombies."

The general's green eyes narrowed. "You saw it?"

"Activator. Yep. I don't know why I can see it on this side and not over there, but it's like a giant gas leak with some random in-between smoke mixed up with it. That's why everyone's acting like they've lost their minds."

"Huh." Maleshi tapped her lip as she peered through the rectangular window again, then shrugged. "Well, they'll have to deal with it."

"What?" Cheyenne stayed where she was as the general turned around and stalked back to the desk and her rolling briefcase. "What do you mean, deal with it?"

"It's pretty self-explanatory, kid." Maleshi grabbed a stack of paper off the desk and shoved it into her open bag. "Look, there's not a whole lot we can do until Venga's work can wipe out the blight on the other side. Then the leaks will stop over here. Humans are used to brain fog, right? It happens all the time."

"Not from a magical airborne poison."

Maleshi scoffed, zipped up her briefcase, and grabbed the perpetually extended handle before rolling the thing after her. "Okay, fine. It's a little different. And maybe it hasn't happened like this on a mass scale, but they'll be fine, kid. If this is the only way they're affected by this leak, or whatever it is, it's not the end of the world." She leaned sideways to knock twice on the closest desk. "Huh. Not even sure that's real wood."

"So you're not concerned."

"Of course I'm a little concerned, but seriously, a little bit of disorientation never hurt anyone. Besides, fall break is coming up in two weeks. Everyone's gonna write this whole thing off as autumn jitters. No big deal."

"Except for when it gets worse."

Maleshi stopped beside Cheyenne and turned to look at her head-on. "But it's not worse. Not yet. If it gets to the point where it needs to be dealt with, then we'll deal with it. Until then, you and I both know there are a few things currently inhabiting top-priority space. Right?"

Cheyenne frowned.

"Hey, if you took care of all the other more important issues on your own without me even knowing about it, congratulations."

"No. I haven't."

"Oh. Well, there you go. First things first in order of importance, kid." Maleshi nudged Cheyenne's shoulder with the back of her hand. "Just gotta work your way down the list."

"Yeah, okay." Rolling her eyes, Cheyenne turned to follow the general dressed as Maddie Bergmann back out of the classroom. "Oh, hey. By the way, thanks for the 'getting out of teaching undergrad classes free' card."

"You're welcome. I'd ask what your students had to say, but I have a feeling the answer's 'not much' today."

"Yeah. They brought it up, though. Enough for me to figure out I apparently sent my entire class an email saying class was canceled on Friday."

Maddie turned the doorknob. "That is convenient."

"How'd you pull that off?"

"Please, Cheyenne." When they stepped into the slowly emptying hall, the door pulled shut behind them with a click. "I found my way into your university email and sent a convincing Cheyenne Summerlin email. I'm sure you already know how easy that is to do."

"Yep. But you didn't send the same email to your class."

"Of course not. That would be weird." Maleshi took off down the hall to wherever she was headed next. "I took a sick day. But I did let the other graduate instructors and professors know that you were working through some personal family issues and that, as your mentor and the one who suggested you teach for your master's, I approved your long weekend. No questions asked."

"And this doesn't count against me as a strike or whatever."

"Nope. You're in the clear, kid."

"Cool. Thanks."

"I have to get a move on, so if there's nothing else?"

Cheyenne shrugged. "No, that's it. Oh, and that meeting with the colonel and the Bull's Head is tonight. Just a reminder."

"Oh, sure." Maleshi shrugged. "Yeah, I might show up. It depends on a few other things I have in the works."

"Like what?"

"Hmm." Maleshi kept moving down the hall and didn't turn to look back at the halfling when she added, "Like private things that don't have anything to do with you. I'll text you the terror twins' numbers. At the very least, they should be there if it comes down to a fight."

"Yeah, okay. See you tonight." Cheyenne sighed when the general disappeared around the corner without another word. "Maybe."

Her cell phone vibrated in her pocket, and she pulled it out to find the goblins' numbers already shared with her from Maleshi's phone. She snorted. *Noose Girl and Firebird. Only Maleshi would come up with names like that.*

CHAPTER THIRTY-NINE

It took Cheyenne under ten minutes to run in enhanced speed all the way back to her apartment from the VCU campus. Ember was still sitting on the couch, a bowl of popcorn in her lap now as she stared at the TV. Her eyes widened when Cheyenne burst through the door, dropped her backpack on the floor against the wall, and headed straight to the kitchen.

"Whoa. You're back early."

"Yeah." Cheyenne flung open the cabinet above the sink to get a glass for some water. "Class got out early."

"Okay. That statement's lacking the usual excitement that comes with it."

Cheyenne chugged the entire glass of water in one go, then took a huge breath and filled it again. "Maybe that's because it wasn't for any of the usual reasons."

"Uh-huh." Ember shifted on the couch and folded her arms over the back of it, resting her chin on her forearms as she watched her friend down another glass. "Whenever you're ready. I'm listening."

"Damn." Cheyenne stared at the empty glass, briefly considered drinking another, then stuck it in the dishwasher instead. "Didn't know I could get that thirsty."

"I meant, whenever you're ready to tell me about why you're back now instead of in half an hour like you normally are."

The halfling wiped her mouth. "Sorry. Did I interrupt something?"

"Very funny."

"That new portal ridge I closed on campus? It's leaking."

Ember frowned. "I'm having a hard time picturing that."

Cheyenne stepped into the living room and shrugged. "Leaking the blight and some in-between shit. Which is now airborne, apparently."

Ember wrinkled her nose. "Not good."

"Nope. I mean, it's better than the blight the way we've seen it before popping on out through an active portal. That would be a serious issue, but this makes people confused and slow and fuzzy. In the head."

"By people, I'm guessing you mean humans."

"Well, yeah."

"Also not good."

Cheyenne nodded and walked slowly to the leather recliner. "True. Also not high on the priority list. And before you ask how I can possibly think that, I already talked to Maleshi. She doesn't think it's that big of a deal for now."

"So you're focusing on the more important things. I get it."

Tilting her head, Cheyenne stared at her friend. *I didn't expect that, but okay.* "Right. Hopefully, the airborne leak will clear up once we take care of everything else. It's gonna be a weird scene on the quad out there until then."

"Assuming it doesn't get any worse before it gets better."

"Yeah, Em." Cheyenne lowered herself into the recliner and closed her eyes. "That can be said about pretty much everything we've got going on right now."

The living room fell silent but for the high-intensity action scene playing out on the TV at a barely-above-a-whisper volume. Ember paused the show she was streaming and tossed the remote on the coffee table. "You okay?"

"Yep. Just trying to switch mental gears here." Cheyenne kept her eyes closed and focused on her breathing. "And wondering why you're asking."

"You look tired."

"Ha. Well, I didn't sleep as well as I wanted."

"Yeah, I don't mean the dreams. You're pale. I mean, paler than normal. You just chugged two glasses of water in under a minute, and you have leaves in your hair."

Cheyenne opened her eyes and glanced at the tangles of her black wavy hair falling over her shoulder. "Drow speed to the school and back."

She picked the leaves she could see out of her hair and leaned forward to set them on the coffee table.

Ember stared at the dried, crumbling mess with a frown. "You've got three blight-poisoned holes in your body, and you thought it would be a good idea to run all the way to VCU?"

"It worked, and I didn't even have to stop. Not once. Leveling up with drow speed, right?"

"Leveling up with recklessness, maybe."

"I'm fine, Em."

Ember floated off the couch and approached her friend. "You don't look fine. Honestly, you kinda look like when you woke up from your twelve-hour nap after the fight with Ba'rael you didn't technically win."

Cheyenne looked at the fae with a raised eyebrow. "Seriously. I'm good."

"Cheyenne, this is your healer speaking. Quit playing tough drow and let me do my job."

"It's not your job to be my healer, Healer."

Ember folded her arms. "No, but it's my job to help you, make sure you have everything you need, and in this scenario, it's also to look out for you and make sure you don't run yourself into the ground. 'Cause I have a feeling you will if nobody says anything."

"Okay, fine," Cheyenne said, "What do you want me to do?"

"Chill out for a sec, for starters. Have you checked the black streaks since last night?"

"Nope."

Ember gave her friend a pointed stare and waited for the halfling to pull down the collar of her shirt with an exaggerated sigh. Then the fae bent over for a closer look. "All right. Looks like the darktongue's still doing its job, so that's the good news."

"Sounds like there's bad news too."

"The bad news is," Ember said, turning slightly to glance at

Cheyenne's backpack beside the door, "that the canister only has a few doses left."

Cheyenne pressed her lips together. "A few could be anything, Em."

"Yeah. In this case, it's three. I think."

"Oh, good. So that's, like, a conservative guess."

Ember wrinkled her nose. "No, I'd say that's pretty generous. It might even be two."

"Right. And we didn't bring any refills."

"It's not like we had time to think about that. You puked all over Venga's lab, then the Sorren Gán did its weird puppet trick or whatever that was."

"Yeah, I know. I'm not blaming you." Cheyenne sat back in the recliner and swallowed. "But I'm glad you told me. Whatever's left in there, I'll use it sparingly. Like at least once before we head into this Bull's Head meeting tonight."

Ember floated away from her friend to quit hovering and shook her head. "You're going for darktongue courage, huh?"

"Trust me, the last thing I want to do is go into that meeting all hopped up on serum. Okay? It's to keep me from going down if somebody hits me in my three weakest points. Which someone's bound to do, 'cause that's what happens."

"You could try wearing some kinda armor."

Cheyenne frowned at her friend, and Ember couldn't hold back her laughter anymore. "Funny."

"I had this vision of you storming in and clinking around like the guards in Hangivol. You in orc-sized armor plates!"

"Okay. I get it. And armor's off the table, 'cause we have to go into this thing quietly. That's the whole point of a sting, you know."

"Oh, it's a sting now." Ember settled on the couch, leaning back as her magic lifted her legs up to stretch out in front of her. "I had no idea the ex-FRoE agent and the halfling who never officially worked for the FRoE were running their own operations now."

"You know what I mean." Cheyenne leaned forward and grabbed her buzzing phone out of her pocket. "Speaking of the ex-agent..." She accepted the call. "Rhynehart."

"I sent you an email. See? This is how you send someone an email with absolutely no explanation and fill them in on what it means at the same time."

"Hey, you have your way of communicating, and I have mine."

"Yeah, well, check it out so we can go over a few things."

"Right now?"

There was a slight pause. "Yeah, right now. Come on. I'm trying to keep all the information from being in one place, okay? Let's go."

Cheyenne stood from the recliner and rolled her eyes at Ember before turning to head up the stairs to the mini loft. "Okay, give me a second to get to my computer."

"Uh-huh."

The long silence after that made her wonder if he'd tell her never mind, call him when she was ready. As Glen powered up, Cheyenne sat in the desk chair and turned slowly back and forth. "So."

"You have the email yet?"

"Still waiting."

Rhynehart smacked his lips. "This isn't how I planned this conversation to go."

"Well, maybe it's 'cause the best way to send someone an email with absolutely no information and fill them in on it after the fact is to let them call you. Wait, didn't I already do that?"

"Whatever. Just tell me when you're ready."

Cheyenne set her phone down on the desk and logged into her system. It only took her five seconds to pull up her email, but she gave it another twenty before she picked up the phone and pressed it against her ear again. "Okay. I'm looking at names. This is who's coming with us, right?"

Rhynehart grunted. "I guess that part wasn't as hard to figure out."

"Not really."

"Yeah, Cheyenne. This is who's coming."

She read quickly through the names one more time, Bhandi, Tate, Yurik, Jamal, and someone named Michael Todd. *Guess he's replacing Payton with a new guy.* "Okay. What about our friend with the eyepatch?"

"Yeah, she opted out. Didn't wanna be a part of it, and that's fine."

"You trust her to keep this whole thing to herself even after the fact?"

Rhynehart cleared his throat. "Yeah, I do. She's kept her mouth shut about the lizard escapee, so I don't see a problem."

"And what about this new guy? You trust him?"

"Yeah. He's an old buddy of mine. More like me than like you if you know what I mean."

So, he's a human agent. Cheyenne sat back in her chair and kept spinning back and forth. "Uh-huh."

"Honestly, I wasn't even gonna ask him, seeing as you two don't know each other. But one of the assholes on this list you're looking at opened her big mouth and spilled all the secret beans."

Cheyenne snorted. *Bhandi. That was easy.* "And he wanted in."

"Yeah, he wanted in. I'm not on the payroll anymore, so it doesn't feel like a conflict of interest at this point if I bring a friend along for the ride. You got a problem with that?"

"Nope. As long as he can handle himself, it's all good."

"Great." The soft gurgle of Rhynehart chugging something filled her ear. Then he sighed and continued, "Last thing. We're scrapping the meetup in Alexandria."

"Something wrong with it?"

"Not other than the fact that it's public, and I'm not interested in going over all this in a public setting."

Cheyenne tilted her head. "Well, we sure as shit aren't meeting at my place."

Below her in the living room, Ember pumped a fist in the air as she stared at the TV again. "I second that refusal."

"Who's that?" Rhynehart asked. "Am I on speaker?"

"It's Ember. Because we share an apartment. And no. She wants a planning party over here as much as I do."

"That would be stupid anyway. You're two hours out from where we're headed tonight."

"Yeah, I know."

"So we're meeting at my place."

She almost burst out laughing at that one and centered her focus on the address at the bottom of his email. "Congratulations, Rhynehart. I did not see that coming."

"I'm off the map. I got sacked after thirteen years of perfect service under that asshole, and seeing as my old superiors haven't said shit to me about any of it after the fact, I figure I'm off their radar. No one's gonna be checking us out at my place. As far as they're concerned, it's like I never existed."

"And you don't think they'll draw a connection between you and me?"

"Why would they?"

Cheyenne rolled her eyes. "Oh, I don't know. Maybe because you're the one who took me out on every major op where my skills were specifically required."

"Yeah, but we're not friends."

She laughed. "Okay. You have a point."

"Great. Now we're on the same page. So, you have the address. If we're still looking at a two o'clock meetup, I say we use that extra time to go survey the site beforehand."

"Bad idea."

Rhynehart sighed heavily through the phone. "I fail to see why reconnaissance is a bad idea."

"The guys who are gonna be there tonight probably have all kinds of gear already set up to keep an eye on the place. Surveillance and security. Not the kind that records and sounds off alarms, either. I mean the kind that explodes and fires rounds."

"Yeah, yeah, okay. I get it."

"I don't wanna blow our chances with this, Rhynehart."

"Fine. But I don't wanna go into the place like a complete idiot without knowing exit and entry points, blind spots, or where the hell I'm supposed to take a left turn or a right turn. You get that, right?"

"Sure." Cheyenne tilted her head and lifted her shoulder to hold her cell phone in place so she could pull up her VPN and get started. "I can get the layout for you."

"You're shitting me."

"Nope. Give me, like, ten minutes, and you'll have another email. I won't make it all complicated this time, so don't worry."

Rhynehart scoffed and chugged more of whatever he was drinking. "You know, when you say, 'Don't worry,' that's when I start to worry."

"That's on you. You'll feel better when you have a visual in front of you."

"You're talking about actual schematics, right?"

"Yeah, whatever exists, I'll find it. We can go over it with everyone in person before we head out."

"Fine. I'll wait for that email."

"Cool." Cheyenne grabbed the phone again and hung up without taking her eyes off the screen as she logged back into the dark web. *Not like an old factory-turned-showroom is a super-secret place, but it'll be a lot easier to find this way. Then maybe Mr. Ex-Agent will finally stop whining.*

CHAPTER FORTY

After she found everything she needed and sent it to Rhynehart, Cheyenne pulled up Byrd's number she only had in her phone as belonging to "Firebird" and made the call.

"Who the fuck is this?"

She laughed in surprise. "Cheyenne."

"Oh, hey. What's up, kid?"

Shaking her head, Cheyenne spun around in her desk chair again. "Meeting with the Bull's Head tonight."

"Tonight? Fuck, yeah! Hey, you hear that?"

Lumil shouted across the warehouse, "Somebody's getting fucked tonight?"

"Yeah, by us!"

Oh, jeez. Maybe I should've reconsidered.

"Okay, kid. So, where are we going? What's the deal? You know us. We're ready to get this shit done any time, any day. You tell us what's up."

"Hammer's comin' down, Cheyenne!" Lumil shouted again. "You hear me? Coming down!"

Cheyenne cleared her throat. "Cool, guys. Maybe chill a little. We're all meeting up at Rhynehart's place at two. I'll text you the address, okay?"

"Rhynehart? You mean that pissed-off human who almost pissed his pants before agreeing to help us break Ve—"

"Yeah, him. And we're not going through all that over the phone, okay?"

"Oh, shit. Yeah. Sorry." Byrd chuckled and took a huge, crunching bite of something. "We'll be there. Let us know where."

"Yep. That's incoming. See you guys in a bit."

"We're gonna rip those assholes a new one!" Lumil shouted.

Byrd roared his approval over the phone, and Cheyenne jerked her cell away from her ear before ending the call. "Fuck."

How did anyone put up with them camping out in the warehouse for so long?

"You good?" Ember called.

"As good as I'll ever be, talking to the goblin destroyers over the phone."

Ember chuckled. "Have they heard you call them that yet? 'Cause I have a feeling they'd take it as a compliment."

"They take everything as a compliment as long as it's not coming from one of them." With a snort, Cheyenne stood from her chair, ran Glen through the shutdown cycle, and grabbed her phone. "I guess it's time to think about heading out soon."

"Where are we going first?"

"Rhynehart's place. It's like an hour and a half out."

"Cool. We have an extra hour."

Cheyenne's black Vans clanged on the metal mesh of the stairs as she jogged down them. "Yeah, and that hour's pretty much spoken for. I gotta get my car."

"Oh, yeah."

"Lee told me twenty-four hours. That's almost up."

"Hey, now that you mention bringing the goblins with us," Ember asked as she watched Cheyenne walk slowly across the living room as she searched for Lee's number, "do they know that this isn't a 'run in screaming and blasting magic' kinda deal?"

"Not yet, but they will when they meet us closer to DC."

"I mean, yeah, it's great to have them there against the Bull's Head 'cause they know what those guys are capable of. We're not trying to be gentle with the loyalists, right?"

Cheyenne paused and looked up from her phone. "No way. The Bull's Head can suck it. I'll make sure the goblins know not to mess with anyone else. We can't roll in and blast a top FRoE official who's also a US colonel completely off the map. Guess this is one of those delicate situations."

"Ha. You and delicate don't go together in any kind of fight."

Cheyenne looked back down at her phone and found Lee's number. "Maybe not the fighting, Em. But I've got the only working activator on this side of the Border, and it's a GoPro on its own secure server. We're good."

"Blackmail." Ember pointed at her. "That's the angle you're taking."

"Hey, if it gets the job done without us having to make things messy, then I'm gonna blackmail the fucker." Before she could send a call to Lee's number, her phone buzzed in her hand with an incoming call from the car enthusiast. *Perfect timing.* "Hey, Lee."

"Cheyenne. Hey. Glad I caught you."

"I mean, I was about to call you anyway, so this works."

"Oh. Yeah, listen. I took a look under the hood for fun. Kinda couldn't help myself. I found something I can't in good conscience let slide."

"What?"

"Sorry, Cheyenne. You can't keep driving this thing around until it's taken care of."

"Oh? What's the issue?"

"Like a big, complicated mess. I won't bore you with the details. I'm gonna need one more day to get this all taken care of for you. I know I said twenty-four hours."

"Yeah, but if you found something that makes the car undrivable, that's not a problem." *Except that I don't have a ride.* "You sure it'll be finished tomorrow?"

"Absolutely. One hundred percent." Lee cleared his throat. "I tell you what. I'll chop off a good thirty percent of the cost for the inconvenience. I like to think I'm a man of my word, at least these days, and I want to make sure I do right by you and this Porsche, yeah?"

"I should pay you thirty percent more for catching the issue. You know, I understand enough about cars that you can tell me what happened."

"I'll show you everything when you come to pick it up tomorrow. Now, I know we just met, and you don't have any reason to trust that I'll take care of this thing the way it needs to be done."

"Lee, it's fine. Seriously." Cheyenne took a deep breath and nodded. "Whatever you have to do, it's all good. I'll wait for your call tomorrow, then."

"Excellent. Talk to you then." He hung up first, and she blinked at her phone as the call screen returned to her home screen. "Shit."

"No car."

"No car." Cheyenne wrinkled her nose. "I'm not in the mood to run all the way to DC, not to mention that I'd have to carry you if we wanted to get there at the same time."

"Yeah, I wouldn't let you do that anyway."

"Well, thanks, Em. So now what?" Cheyenne grabbed her backpack and pulled out the injection canister before sticking it in her coat pocket. "We call an Uber to drive us almost two hours?"

"Hold on." A slow, mischievous smile spread across Ember's lips. "Give me, like, two minutes. I got this."

The fae spun and zipped across the living room, through the front door, and out into the hall before Cheyenne had a chance to say anything.

"Okay."

Through the open front door, she heard her friend's loud, swift knock on Matthew Thomas' door across the hall. Then that door opened.

"Ember." He sounded surprised and hopeful and terrified all at the same time.

Oh, for real?

"All I need from you right now is to move out of the way so I can come inside," Ember said sternly. "This won't take long."

Cheyenne grinned. *I gotta see this.*

She stepped into the hall as Matthew's front door closed with Ember and their neighbor on the other side of it. Even though the conversation was most likely supposed to be private, given the closed door, Cheyenne's drow hearing picked up every last word.

"I'm serious," Ember said. "If you ever want to talk to me again like we used to, you'll do this. You won't ask why or for how long or anything else. I think we both know this is the least you can do after the massive shitstorm you helped create."

"Ember, I didn't know."

"Doesn't matter. Cheyenne could've done a lot worse than show you a video of her fighting those things your program's powering. She still might, honestly, but that depends on the choices you make from here on out."

Matthew scoffed. "I don't see how this makes up for whatever's happened because of a program I built."

"Don't even try to pretend you're still useless. You saw it in action. You know what your part was, and I'm not here to argue the details with you. Are you gonna man up and do this or not?"

"This is ridiculous."

"This is your last option."

Cheyenne cocked her head when their voices fell silent. *Uh-oh.*

Then the front door flew open, and Ember floated swiftly into the hall. The door slammed shut behind her, and she stopped when she saw the halfling standing in the hall with a sheepish grin. "You heard all that?"

"Couldn't help myself."

"Whatever." Ember shot a scathing glare at Matthew's closed front door, then floated down the hall.

"I didn't hear a definitive ending, though. How did it go."

Ember shrugged. "Hard to say. Come on."

"Right. So we're calling an Uber, then?" The jingle of keys being tossed in the air made Cheyenne look up in time to see a set of keys flying toward her. She snatched them before they could hit her in the face, and Ember brushed past her to the elevator.

"Nope," the fae said. "We have a ride."

"Well, look at you."

"I can be persuasive too, you know."

Cheyenne stopped behind her friend as Ember punched the elevator's call button. "You sure it's not because you've got the cyber-security guru next door falling head-over-heels in love with you?"

"Yeah, I'm sure. Unless you're ready to admit that you only let someone into your personal space when it's a bone drow in a darkseller bazaar you drooled over for hours."

The elevator dinged, and the doors opened. "Touché, Em. I give you full credit for the persuasion."

Ember floated into the elevator and turned around to shoot her friend a pert look. "Great."

When they reached the apartment's parking lot, Cheyenne lifted Matthew's keys and clicked the remote lock button, listening for the sound of locks or a little chirp or a beep. "Okay, we're looking for a Mercedes."

"That doesn't narrow it down."

"Well, it's not like the model and year are on the key fob." Cheyenne clicked again as she turned right down the sidewalk before stepping down onto the asphalt. "Guess we can't call him and ask what kinda car he drives, huh?"

"You can. I'm not talking to him again until we finish this whole 'Bull's Head with Combined Reality's programming software' crap."

"Yeah, I'm not going back up there." The next time Cheyenne clicked the lock button, a short beep and flashing headlights came from two rows down.

"No way." Ember laughed and floated faster through the rows of cars, unconcerned about being seen racing that quickly without bobbing up and down like someone whose feet actually touched the ground. "Hit it again."

Cheyenne did, and the Mercedes-Benz S-Class beeped again with another flash of its headlights. "You know what? I have no problem giving the guy credit for his taste in cars."

"Yeah, no shit." Grinning, Ember stared at the steering wheel through the windshield. "Man, when I feel good about getting behind the wheel again, I'm taking this out again all by myself. And yeah, I do think he'll let me."

"He better." With a chuckle, Cheyenne unlocked the Mercedes and opened the driver's side door. "Never thought I'd say I'm looking forward to the drive up to Rhynehart's house."

"Ha. First time for everything, right?"

"Yeah, and a last time, too."

CHAPTER FORTY-ONE

They pulled onto Rhynehart's street in Bennsville, Maryland an hour and forty minutes later. Cheyenne drove slowly, scanning the address numbers on the mailboxes and the front porches as they passed.

"Oh. Yep." Ember pointed at a house up ahead on the right. "How much you wanna bet the house with two shiny black SUVs is the one we're looking for?"

"Yeah, that's definitely it. His Jeep's in the driveway."

When they got out of the car, Cheyenne tossed the keys over the roof and nodded when Ember caught them. The fae raised an eyebrow and pressed the lock button on the fob. The beep made her grin. "I don't think this is anything like how much you like locking your car."

"Nowhere close." Cheyenne headed around the Mercedes to Rhynehart's driveway and shrugged. "Still sounds nice, though."

"Sure." Ember looked up and down the street, then turned to follow her friend to the ex-FRoE agent's front door.

Cheyenne got one knock in before the front door jerked open and a woman's shimmering face morphed from purple to light-human-tan and back to purple again.

"Hey, Goth drow." Bhandi grinned. "Get the hell inside, huh?"

"Good to see you too." Cheyenne stepped into the entryway of

Rhynehart's ranch-style house and took a slow look around. "Everyone's already here, aren't they?"

The troll woman scoffed. "Shit, Cheyenne. You know that's rule number one."

"Don't be late. Yeah, I know."

Ember leaned toward her and whispered, "They have rules?"

"Not really. Pretty sure it's more of a running joke."

They followed Bhandi through the front hall into Rhynehart's living room and dining room all in one.

The troll woman clapped her hands and spread her arms. "And now it's a party!"

Rhynehart, Yurik, Tate, Jamal, and the human new guy looked up from where they all stood over spread out sheets of paper on the dining table. On the other side of the table were two black composite crates and two duffel bags of gear.

Tate jerked his chin at Cheyenne and Ember. "You made it."

"Had to talk our neighbor out of his car first." Ember shrugged. "That's why we're a little late."

Rhynehart's gaze flickered to Cheyenne. "You're the one who set the time."

"Yeah, I know. Sorry. Good thing we still have over four hours as a buffer, right?"

He didn't say a word, just returned his attention to the papers she now saw were the printed schematics of the building they'd be storming through in about four hours.

The only other human in the room besides Rhynehart grinned and stepped around the table. His short brown hair was gelled up in spikes, and he stuck out his hand with a nod. "So you're the drow halfling, huh?"

Cheyenne's fingers moved quickly at her side when her activator prompted her to drop her illusion charm. The man's eyes widened a little, but he didn't step back or lower his hand as he found himself standing in front of the same Cheyenne with a totally different look.

"Cheyenne." She grabbed his hand and shook it.

"Todd."

"That's your last name, isn't it?"

"Yeah. Michael Todd. Most people get confused by two first names, and Todd's shorter."

Cheyenne nodded and stepped back. *I have nothing to say to that.*

"I'm Ember." The fae reached out to shake Todd's hand too, and his grin widened even more. "You're the fae."

"Good guess."

"It's the hovering." The man glanced at her shoes, which were floating an inch off the floor. "And I heard you're always with the halfling these days."

Ember snorted, and Cheyenne shot another pointed glance at Rhynehart. He didn't look up from studying the schematics laid out on the table.

"Sounds like you know all about us, then." Ember rubbed her hands down the sides of her pants and nodded. "So, this is everybody who's coming with us, huh?"

"Seems like it," Rhynehart muttered. He looked up when a plastic click came from the back of the house, followed by the quick clatter of nails scrabbling across the hardwood floor. A small white Maltese trotted into the room from the kitchen, eyeing Rhynehart's odd collection of guests with wide brown eyes, tail wagging furiously. "That's Tammy."

Cheyenne swallowed a laugh. "Tammy."

"She already had the name when I got her." The agent met her gaze and stared. "Is that a problem?"

She ignored his bad mood and watched the dog happily approach the table and everyone gathered around it.

"Aw, look at this little thing." Yurik bent down and stretched his hand out to the dog. Tammy skittered backward and gave that grating, yapping bark intrinsic in canines of her size, and jumped back and forth in front of him until he straightened and pulled back his hand. "Well, shit. You get her as a guard dog, Rhynehart?"

Tate and Todd burst out laughing.

"Guess she's not into goblins."

"Yeah, especially weirdly beefy ones," Tate added.

Yurik sniffed and rubbed his nose with the back of a hand, smooshing it against the giant iron bullring through his septum. "Whatever, man. Most dogs love me."

"Well, keep that thing away from me." Bhandi shot Tammy a sideways glance and grimaced in disgust. "I'm not into animals."

Yurik snorted. "Could've fooled me."

The troll woman clicked her tongue and waved him off. "Man, you're butt-hurt 'cause an oversized rat didn't wanna be your best friend."

"She's not a rat," Rhynehart countered without looking up from his printed plans.

"You need to get your eyes checked, man."

Tammy stopped on her curious path around the table to sniff Cheyenne's black Vans, but that was as much attention as the dog gave her. Then she trotted around the table, ignoring Bhandi and giving Yurik a wide berth before stopping in front of Jamal. The dog sat back, let out a small whine, and pawed the massive ogre's shin.

"Oh, shit. Look at that." Tate folded his arms and grinned at the ogre. "She likes the big guy."

Jamal grunted and dipped his head to watch the tiny Maltese paw his pant leg.

Rhynehart glanced quickly at his pet, then up at Jamal and shrugged. "You can pick her up if you want. She won't stop until you do. Your call."

The ogre's yellow eyes moved slowly around the circle of magicals and human agents, who were all watching his response with amusement. Grunting again, he bent over to scoop Tammy up and cradled her against his massive chest. The dog fit in one meaty gray hand, and Jamal's only reaction when she lapped his neck and chin without stopping was to blink quickly and stare at the table.

Bhandi wrinkled her nose at the display. Yurik and Tate sniggered.

Cheyenne widened her eyes and folded her arms. "As cute as that is, we didn't come here to play with your dog, Rhynehart."

The man looked at her with a blank expression. "Then do what you came here to do."

"Yeah." Bhandi folded her arms too and stepped away from the table as Tammy tirelessly licked Jamal's neck. "I wanna know how the hell you found out about this thing in the first place."

Cheyenne shrugged. "Got it off the colonel's computer."

Tate narrowed his eyes. "How the fuck did you do that?"

Ember said, "You're surprised?"

The troll man with tattoos covering every inch of his purple flesh cocked his bald head and shrugged. "Maybe if it was anyone else."

"Okay, here's the deal." Cheyenne glanced at Ember, who gave her the silent go-ahead to tell the whole story. *Not that I need her permission, but it's nice to have some non-FRoE backup this time around.* "Full transparency, 'cause you guys stuck around through a lot of bullshit. With me. With L'zar. With what Rhynehart's apparently calling Operation Free Lizard."

Bhandi grinned and shook her head.

When Cheyenne's questioning gaze settled on Todd, the man jerked his chin at her. "Yeah, I know you guys broke the scaleback out of the Dunk Tank. You don't have to skirt around it."

Guess Rhynehart really does trust the guy. Or he's puttin' it all out there 'cause he doesn't have anything else to lose.

"Fine. So, here's what we're up against. Colonel Thomas has been feeding classified FRoE information, if that's a real thing, to a group of O'gúleesh called the Bull's Head. They're Crown loyalists."

"Wait, what loyalists?" Bhandi shook her head.

"The Crown," Ember put in.

"What the fuck is that?"

"Seriously? Ba'rael Verdys. The Spider. Drow ruler of Ambar'ogúl for the last few thousand years."

Todd let out a low whistle. "That's a long time."

Ember spread her arms. "None of that rings a bell?"

"Wait." Tate ran a hand over his bald head. "You mean there's an actual leader over on the other side?"

"Shit." Bhandi chuckled. "I thought it was a bunch of backwoods magicals who've never seen a car or a cell phone before. They're organized over there?"

The fae cocked her head. "Given that you guys are supposed to be helping Earthside magicals, your level of cluelessness is concerning."

Cheyenne raised an eyebrow and shot her friend a sidelong glance. "Told you."

"But you guys were at Bianca's house the other day when we brought all this up."

Yurik's eyes widened. "No fucking way. You were serious about that whole drow royalty shit?"

Cheyenne tilted her head. "I didn't think I made it sound like a joke."

"Damn." Tate folded his arms, his tattooed biceps bulging against his hands as he glanced at Rhynehart. "And you didn't think it was important to confirm that kinda thing with us, huh?"

Rhynehart sighed. "She didn't make it sound like a joke."

"Well, shit."

"That's not important right now." Cheyenne nodded at the printed building plans on the table. "So let's stick to what is. Colonel Thomas is feeding intel to the Bull's Head, none of whom realize at this point that things have changed on the other side of the Border, and they're carrying out nonexistent orders. The colonel's nephew built a program for the Bull's Head five years ago that makes O'gúl tech work Earthside."

"They have tech too?" Yurik's eyes widened.

"Remember that tunneling machine that came down on us in Peridosh?"

"Fuck me sideways," Bhandi muttered.

Cheyenne frowned at the troll woman and shook off the odd remark. "That came from the Bull's Head, who's been smuggling machine parts across the Border and powering them with the colonel's nephew's program while he feeds them information. I'm guessing a lot of that is about me, based on personal experience. And there's probably a lot of stuff he's been feeding them directly from the FRoE systems."

"Which ones?" Todd asked.

"All of them, if I had to guess. The A.S.S. and the B.I.T.Ch. Are there any others with awesome acronyms I don't know about?"

Rhynehart stared at the table. "That's pretty much it."

"There you go. So, beyond it being way too shitty that you guys have all your secrets handed over to a group of O'gúleesh who don't give a fuck what happens to any of us on this side, I'm, like, ninety-nine-percent sure that what we went up against last month—the black-market shit Q'orr was hawking, the kidnapped kids, the bomb that put you in the med ward—was all the Bull's Head." Cheyenne nodded at Jamal.

The ogre finally lowered Tammy away from his chin where she couldn't reach him anymore and let out a low growl.

"Yeah. This isn't the normal crap you're used to dealing with. Not refugees turned thugs right off the reservations, trying to get a leg up on life Earthside." Cheyenne shrugged. "These are magicals straight from the capital of Ambar'ogúl who want to wipe out any resistance over here before the war they still think is coming shows up."

"But it's not, right?" Yurik asked.

"No." Ember shook her head. "Because Cheyenne fought the O'gúl Crown, and now the Spider's out of the picture."

"Wait, so who's leading shit over there?" Bhandi pointed at the halfling. "Is it the Goth drow?"

Cheyenne glared at her. "Does it matter?"

"Yeah, kinda. I mean, that's a big deal if we're standin' around planning a private sting op with a goddamn queen or something."

"Well, you're not."

Ember grinned. "But she does get certain perks over there."

Cheyenne scowled at her friend, and Ember shrugged. "But hey, at least two of you will be happy to know there's a troll on the throne now."

"Why would that make us happy?" Tate looked at Ember and Cheyenne.

"I mean, because you and Bhandi are trolls." Ember shook her head. "Okay, maybe I was wrong."

Rhynehart cleared his throat. "So, the plan."

"Yeah." Cheyenne pointed at the schematics on the table. "I pulled the date and time right off the colonel's computer. It was on a private server hidden in a whole bunch of different files, but I found it. He's meeting with the Bull's Head again tonight, seven o'clock at the showroom in Westphalia. I wouldn't be surprised if the hefty withdrawal he made from an account I don't think anyone's supposed to know about was for this meeting."

"You think he's paying them too?"

"Probably."

"Wait, the colonel's paying these assholes and feeding them intel?" Yurik shook his head. "That doesn't add up. What's he getting out of it?"

Cheyenne took a deep breath. "I don't know."

"You think they're bringing him black-magic shit or stolen kids or something?" Todd asked.

"You know, at this point, I wouldn't be surprised by anything."

Tate chewed the inside of his lower lip. "But the colonel's a human. He won't be able to use any of it."

"Not without the program his nephew built, at least." Cheyenne glanced at the agents standing around the table. "Honestly, I don't care what he's trying to get out of it. He's been funding and supporting the bastards who stole those kids, he blew up that construction site, fought us every step of the way, and kept coming for me. They'll probably piss themselves at the chance to get at me when we show up, but we have a few advantages."

Ember laughed. "Yeah, mainly you showing up."

"And that we know what they're doing," Rhynehart added.

"Yeah. Plus, they won't have any backup coming in from the other side."

"Don't you have to cross the Border through a portal to get here?" Todd asked.

"For the most part, yeah."

Yurik blinked. "What the fuck?"

"Doesn't matter. What we need to do has two parts. I wanna nail the colonel in the act of dealing with the Bull's Head, so we can't let them know we're there until either the money's changed hands, or the guy incriminates himself enough to get him locked up, no questions asked."

"That's not exactly a foolproof plan." Todd met Rhynehart's gaze. "It's the word of a US colonel against a bunch of magical agents, a halfling nobody's heard of other than being L'zar's kid, and an ex-agent who got canned for breaking out a high-security inmate."

Rhynehart cleared his throat. "Allegedly."

"Whatever. No one's gonna take us seriously. Especially not you, man. No offense."

"Let me take care of that."

"Yeah? You have more neat tricks up your sleeve, halfling?"

Cheyenne glanced around the table. "The Bull's Head aren't the only ones with working tech on this side. I'll just say mine's better."

"No shit?" Bhandi snorted. "You got some James Bond shit goin' on, Goth drow?"

"Please." Cheyenne's smile grew a little. "You guys can take down whoever the hell you want when we're there, just not the colonel, and only after they make a deal, or he runs his mouth about what they're doing."

The agents nodded and shrugged in agreement.

"You said they'll have machines there. Surveillance." Rhynehart finally looked at her again. "What do we do about those?"

"If it's active when we get there, I'll be able to shut everything down long enough for us to get in without setting off alarms, at the very least. Probably longer. I can't get them all, so we'll probably be fighting magicals and machines. So there's that."

"Any tips for blasting those things to pieces?" Yurik asked. "You know, for those of us who can't make the ground swallow up a giant machine."

"Yeah. They all have something like a head, I guess. The control center." Cheyenne pointed at her own. "Focus on that, and eventually you'll take it down. Unless they're super tiny. Then you blow 'em up."

"Huh."

The dining room fell silent, then Rhynehart drummed his fingers on the tabletop. "So after that highly educational briefing, let's talk ops. The best points of entry are here, here, and here. I don't think these guys are gonna be walking in all together and holding the colonel's hand, so we know at least two of these entrances are already…"

As Rhynehart explained whatever plan he'd come up with on his own, Cheyenne's activator flashed in her vision with yellow light. She frowned and followed the prompts, turning to scan his living room. The yellow light flashed faster, switched to orange, and then that stupidly loud alarm blared in her head. The displayed warning was an extra precaution, apparently.

Incoming threat detected, source location unknown.

CHAPTER FORTY-TWO

S hit. Cheyenne turned the alarm's brain-splitting volume down to a background drone and kept searching.

Ember leaned toward her and quietly asked, "What's going on?"

"Something's wrong." Cheyenne turned around and scanned the hallway into the kitchen, then the hallway to the front door. The orange light flashed brighter and lit an arrow in her vision that steadily grew larger and blinked furiously.

"What is it?"

"I don't know."

Rhynehart stopped talking and looked up at them. "Am I boring you?"

Incoming threat detected. Arrival in 00:24.

The seconds counted down in Cheyenne's vision, and the blinking orange arrow came into clearer focus as it moved up the far wall of the living room, turned into the ceiling, and moved slowly to the center of the living room and their little gathering at the table.

"Something's coming."

Rhynehart glared at her. "Just a feeling you have?"

"It's in the fucking wall, Rhynehart. I can see it." She pointed at the orange arrow in her vision, then summoned a crackling sphere of black drow energy. "If anyone brought anything useful in those crates, I'd get it out."

Tate, Yurik, and Bhandi darted to the crates on the other side of the table without a word. Todd frowned at them as Jamal slowly lowered a panting, whining Tammy to the floor. "You guys jump to it 'cause she says she sees shit in the walls?"

The crate's locks clicked, and Bhandi flung open one of the lids. "Makes no sense if you haven't been in the field with her, man."

Yurik hauled one of the large black duffel bags onto the table and nodded at Todd. "This is yours, right?"

"Yeah."

Tammy started barking wildly, growling and yapping and darting all over the place with nowhere to aim her warning.

Rhynehart spun and leaped to the table beside the couch on the other side of the room. A drawer slammed open, and he turned around again with pistols in both hands. "What the hell is it?"

"If I knew," Cheyenne muttered, "I wouldn't be standing here waiting for it to—"

The ceiling two feet away from the center of Rhynehart's dining table erupted in a shower of drywall, dust, and chunks of plaster, and a violent spray of reeking sewage cut through the air between Bhandi and Jamal.

"What the fuck!" Bhandi leaped away from the spray. She swung her fell pistol up to the ceiling as a dull silver head burst from the hole. The troll squeezed off one shot before the war machine's plated head darted toward her like a striking snake and knocked her backward. She slipped on the growing puddle of sewage and went down hard.

Rhynehart fired, but the bullet pinged off the machine's metallic head and buried itself in the far wall of the living room in another spray of plaster.

"No bullets!" Cheyenne launched her energy sphere at the war machine and knocked the head sideways against the ceiling. "Seriously, you're gonna kill one of us instead."

"Then what the hell do you suggest?"

More water and sewage burst farther down the pipe in the ceiling, then an eight-foot section of drywall collapsed in the center of the room. The long, segmented metal body of the war machine hit the dining table and knocked it to the ground. Whirs and clicks emanated from the thing as it lifted itself out of the plaster chunks and sewage, coiling and lifting its elongated head to scan the magicals and the two humans in the room.

"Jesus Christ, it's a fucking shit snake!" Yurik lifted a fell rifle from one of the crates and powered it up. The low whine rose quickly in pitch as the fell energy's green glow came to life within the rifle's moving parts.

"Wait!" Cheyenne reached out to him, but he fired his first shot anyway and struck the machine snake below the head.

The thing let out a low, metallic hiss as red and orange lights flashed on its featureless head. The end of its tail, which was eight inches in diameter, swung back to knock Yurik aside, and the goblin's rifle fired again but went wild into the ceiling and the reeking mess still spewing from the pipes.

Cheyenne launched two more energy spheres at the snake, but they barely made a difference. The machine headed swiftly toward Rhynehart, rearing up again and preparing to strike.

Tammy yapped incessantly, scrabbling around on the slippery floors and falling all over herself. Jamal almost knocked into her when he stomped to the war machine's segmented body and reached down to pick it up. The thing squirmed in his grasp and whipped away from Rhynehart. Jamal roared and hauled the machine across the room.

"Wait, wait!" Cheyenne shouted. "Don't try to—"

The ogre slammed the snake machine on the floor, and a series of segmented panels on the thing's back lifted. A swarm of tiny insect-shaped machines lifted from the panels and buzzed around the room, firing green and red and yellow bursts of magic in every direction.

"Oh, hell, no. I hate those things!" Ember fired brilliant flashes of violet light from both hands.

Bhandi, Tate, and Yurik lifted their fell weapons, and they all took aim at the segmented body writhing on the floor as Jamal tried to wrestle it. Sewer water splashed all over the place, splattering the walls and the magical agents as they fired round after fell round.

Cheyenne's activator highlighted the tiny whirring bodies of the flying insect-machines, and she selected the prompts to take them out one by one. Silver light flashed at her fingertips as she flung the machine-bugs against the walls and ducked others coming at her.

Tammy kept barking and darting back and forth, trying to avoid the snake machine's lashing tail.

"Fuck this." Todd jerked open the duffel bag and pulled out a massive weapon that looked like a crossbow with the head of a medieval battle ax attached. He slammed aside the heavy safety bar, and the fell weapon powered up with a shrill whine ten times louder than any fell rifle.

"What the hell is that?" Cheyenne raised a shield in front of Ember as five tiny metal bugs darted toward the fae. They smashed into the shield of dark light and sparked madly as they fell into the rank puddle on the floor.

Todd hefted the huge weapon in his arms and leered at the war machine. "Say hello to my little friend."

Cheyenne rolled her eyes and summoned two more energy spheres in her hands. "Fucking moron."

"Dude!" Tate glanced quickly at the human agent, then fired another fell shot as the snake bucked and sent Jamal staggering backward. "Watch where you aim that thing!"

The wide, flat head of Todd's weapon let out a high-powered whine and flashed green light. The burst of fell energy sent the agent slipping back across the wet floor, and the shot went wild after the recoil. Rhynehart's coffee table splintered, and Todd slapped a lever on the side of the weapon before his next shot.

Cheyenne fired energy spheres at the base of the metal snake's "head" before she heard the man scream, "Fire in the hole!"

The fell blast from his weird-ass crossbow filled the room with a deafening crack and blazing green light, but it didn't stop at one shot. A stream of fell energy arced from the end of the weapon and sprayed across the room in a continuous line, smashing through walls and cutting through furniture as Todd struggled to aim the powerful thing vibrating in his arms.

Sparks flew off the snake machine when the green light hit it, and the fell-powered laser shredded the metal segments with squeals and the cracks of exploding parts.

"Not the head, *not the head!*" Cheyenne shouted, slipping on the wet floor as she tried to race to Todd and his uncontrollable weapon.

Bhandi stared at her and shouted, "You said to take out the head!"

"Not this one. Todd!"

The agent laughed madly as he held onto the weapon spewing concentrated fell energy, his face reflecting the eerie green light. "Holy shit, look at this!"

Jamal's huge fists whaled on the snake machine's head as it bucked and jerked beneath the fell-powered weapons fire.

"Cut it off!" Cheyenne shouted, but Todd was too busy playing lunatic with a fell laser to listen. She slipped again and almost fell on her ass in the growing puddle of sewage still spraying from the broken pipes in the ceiling and reached out with her black lashing tendrils instead.

"Hey!" Todd stared at the tendrils curling around his arms and the fell weapon, which Cheyenne jerked down and away.

The fell laser cut through the snake machine's segmented back with another squeal of shredded metal, and Jamal's next punch sent the thing's head flying across the room. It clanged against the far wall as the rest of the war machine's body erupted under the fellfire, then the weapon shut off with a whirring click.

Rhynehart's house was silent but for Tammy's continued yapping, the hisses and sparks of the destroyed war machine, and the dwindling spatters of sewage on the floor as the pipes ran dry. A plume of green-gray smoke rose from the end of Todd's weapon. He jammed the butt of it against his hip and leaned forward to blow the smoke away. "That fucking did it."

"Fuck, Todd." Rhynehart stared with wide eyes at the destruction in his living room, then glared at his friend. "Did you get clearance for that thing?"

"Not exactly."

Jamal splashed across the floor and hauled the dining table back onto its legs.

"Thanks, bud." Todd nodded at the ogre and dropped the weapon on the table with a thud.

Ember pointed at the empty weapon. "Is that a laser?"

"Kinda, yeah." The man slapped a hand on the weapon. "Does a bunch of other cool shit too. Just passed the initial testing stages, so it's not standard yet."

"I wonder why."

Bhandi wiped a smear of sewer water and shit off the front of her shirt and flung it into the puddle on the floor. "This is a new low."

"My fucking house." Rhynehart leaned against the back of the couch, the half that hadn't been shredded by the fell laser, and blinked. "How the fuck did this happen?"

"You mean, you didn't see the giant shit snake fall out of your ceiling and attack us?" Yurik glanced between the destroyed husk of the war machine and Rhynehart's dazed expression.

"And I don't think there's supposed to be this much shit in your ceiling on a regular basis, man." Tate stepped out of the puddle on the floor that had finally stopped growing and stared at the gaping hole in the ceiling. "Like, that doesn't even make sense."

Rhynehart smiled thickly. "It's an old house."

"You have insurance, right?" When Rhynehart glared at him, the tattooed troll lifted both hands in surrender and shrugged. "Just thought I'd ask."

"Is that how these things move around all the time?" Todd asked as Cheyenne sloshed across the floor to the immobilized snake machine. "In the fucking sewer pipes?"

His boot kicked it with a clang, and the broken machine threw up another flare of sparks as it rolled.

"Dude, lay off." Tate shook his head. "You don't know what kinda shit you're gonna set off doing that."

"What, like a bomb? Please." Todd sneered.

"No!" Jamal whirled on the man, grabbed a fistful of Todd's shirt, and hauled him away from the motionless machine. "No fucking bombs."

"Whoa, Jesus. Okay."

Cheyenne's activator located the snake machine's severed head, which had rolled under the relatively unaffected TV stand at the back of the room off the kitchen. She headed to it, creating dark, smelly footprints behind her.

"It's the first time I've seen one move through the walls like that. First one shaped like a snake, too." She crouched by the entertainment system and tipped the whole thing sideways to reach underneath for the metallic head. The furniture piece, which had a large TV, the cable box, and an Xbox console with at least twenty different games on it, crashed back down to the floor, and she stood with the snake's head in her hand. When she turned around, all the agents were staring at her. "What?"

Todd cleared his throat. "You lift cars like that too, or what?"

Cheyenne ignored him and returned to the sopping-wet dining room. "Just for future reference, when there's an ambush by one of these things, go for the head but keep it intact, okay?"

"Why?" Jamal grunted.

"Because I can trace this thing to where it came from, or at least get a good look at why it was here, what it heard, and if it relayed anything back to its operator." The blank looks aimed her way made her roll her eyes. "If it was spying on us and told the Bull's Head what we're up to."

"Oh."

"Yeah, good thinking."

"Fucking shit snake."

Bhandi smacked Yurik's shoulder with the back of a hand and glared at him. "Man, you've said that three times now. Cut it out."

"You were counting?"

Ember started when one of the fallen bug-machines leaped two inches and threw up sparks. A blast of purple light erupted from her fingers and blasted the tiny war machine into specks of ground metal that slowly drifted into the puddle of muddy brown water beneath her.

"You okay, Em?"

"I'd be better if I could've stomped on it."

"Yeah, what's with that anyway?" Todd asked.

"None of your business."

CHAPTER FORTY-THREE

Cheyenne focused her attention on the metal snake head in her hands, which pulsed muted red light in three different locations but didn't move or make any noise. Her activator pulled up the coded commands scrolling through the head's mechanisms. *Matthew's code. This isn't O'gúleesh.*

She pulled out the war machine's last accepted command and the images it had stored, presumably to return to whatever Bull's Head member had sent it here. With a grimace, she chucked the head onto the table beside Todd's not-quite-approved fell weapon. "Well, at least we know it didn't hear our conversation."

"You can tell all that by looking at its head?" Yurik asked.

"It's a little more complicated than that, but yeah." *It's gonna take a hell of a lot more work than I thought to introduce activators to these guys. But they'll be better for it. If I don't strangle them first.* Cheyenne turned to Rhynehart and shrugged. "It got here just before I realized it was here, so the good news is, it hasn't been hanging out in your walls, waiting for a reason to attack."

Rhynehart looked up to meet her gaze. "Then the bad news is that it was sent here without knowing it would find a group of magicals and FRoE agents with fell weapons hanging out in my living room."

She gave him a sympathetic frown that felt more like a grimace. "Yeah."

"Wait, isn't that a good thing?" Todd asked. "I mean, 'cause they don't know we were here or that we're planning to run this op on their doorstep tonight."

"Yeah, if you're not me, I guess that's a fucking good thing." Rhynehart peeled himself away from the back of the couch and kicked the severed end of the side table lying in the muck in front of him. The wooden piece sailed under the dining table, and the splash of kicked-up sewage made Tate and Yurik jump away from him.

"Whoa, hey."

"Come on, man. That's disgusting."

"You're damn right it's fucking disgusting," Rhynehart shouted. "Those motherfuckers sent a goddamn weapon into my house to take me out!"

"Wait, to kill you?" Yurik cocked his head and frowned. "Man, you're pissed."

"Oh, you have no idea."

"He's right, though," Cheyenne said. "If no one knew we were meeting here, then they sent the machine for Rhynehart. They know he's not active FRoE anymore and assumed he'd be alone and unarmed, without any way to see it coming."

"Damn." Bhandi rubbed the back of her neck. "We could use that against them too if he had a way to prove it."

"We don't have to prove shit." Rhynehart kicked another spray of sewage across the room, then stomped to the side table again with his firearm in hand. Instead of returning it to the drawer, he slammed it down beside the untouched laptop. "I'm done with that asshole. He only fired me to make it legal and by-the-book. Then he tried to take me out for real and make it look like…what? Some kinda fucked-up accident? A break-in?"

Yurik snorted and stared at the hole in the ceiling. "Dude, nobody breaks into houses through the shit pipes."

"Unless they have these machines and don't have to do it in person."

"I wanna know how these magical shitbags found you." Todd folded his arms and jerked his chin at Rhynehart. "You're not in the system anymore."

"Todd." Tate hissed out a sigh and shook his head. "Totally went over your head, didn't it?"

"What? You think Colonel Thomas handed over your address and told those assholes to take you out?"

"Most fucking likely." Rhynehart glared at his destroyed living and dining room, his nostrils flaring. "I need some air."

He spun with a smaller splash and stormed through the kitchen to the back door.

"For real? After everything you've done, you think he'd turn on you like that? A fucking colonel?" Todd raced after his friend, shouting in surprise and disgust when an extra slosh of sewer water sprayed on his pants and into his boots. "Fuck, man."

Rhynehart didn't bother to close the door behind him when he shoved it open and stomped out into the backyard. Their conversation drifted inside, louder than either man intended.

"Do you hear how crazy you sound, man?"

"I'm not crazy, Mike. This hole just keeps getting bigger."

"And you're gonna take her word for it? L'zar's daughter? The halfling, Brian? Come on!"

"Don't fucking say my name," Rhynehart hissed. He shot a wide-eyed glance through the door, with a straight line of sight into the destroyed living room and the six magicals standing there staring back at him, then slammed the back door shut and stalked down the side of the house.

Yurik raised his eyebrows at Cheyenne. "Ouch."

Bhandi shrugged. "He's human. They don't know shit. Don't worry, Cheyenne, he'll figure it out."

Cheyenne tilted her head to give the troll woman an expressionless stare. "I don't give a shit what he thinks as long as he doesn't screw this up for the rest of us."

"Nah. He probably won't."

A fast, steady lapping sound rose from beneath the table as Tammy's canine curiosity got the better of her.

"Oh, fucking gross." Bhandi sloshed backward and peered under the table. "I bet he lets that thing drink outta the toilet too."

"So." Jamal clasped his hands together and looked around at each of them. "We gonna eat before we do this or what?"

"Dude." Yurik shook his head at the ogre, his eyes wide. "Worst timing."

Jamal grunted. "I don't like going in on an empty stomach. Gotta eat somethin'."

Bhandi gestured at the floor. "Well, if it's good enough for the rat-dog…"

"I'll order takeout." Jamal pulled a cell phone from the pocket of his black fatigues and took off to the back of the house, his thick finger stabbing delicately at the screen. When his boots clomped across the kitchen, Tammy whined and sloshed through the muck after him, the tags on her collar jingling.

"Man, it fucking stinks in here." Bhandi shook her head and slogged after the ogre and Rhynehart's dog.

"Sucks to be Rhynehart, right?" Tate took a quick look around and nodded at the back door. "If the big guy gets food on the way, we're eatin' outside."

"You comin'?" Yurik asked as he followed Tate to the kitchen, turning around to look at Cheyenne and Ember.

"Yeah, in a minute." Cheyenne wrinkled her nose, trying to ignore the smell, which hit her at least ten times harder than anyone else. When the back door shut again behind Yurik and Tate, she turned to Ember and sighed.

"You feel responsible for this, don't you?"

"Can you blame me?"

Ember shook her head. "Not really."

Cheyenne gazed around the destroyed room, and at the same time, inspected the command prompts the activator pulled up in her vision. "I can't believe I'm about to do the guy a favor just because I can."

"See? You can be nice." Ember raised her hand, and a halo of violet light flared around it. "And if nothing else, it proves you're not like L'zar, this does."

With a snort, Cheyenne stepped out of the rippling puddle of muck on the floor and pointed at the mess before selecting the spell she wanted from the activator's options. "Sure. But if Rhynehart thinks he owes me big-time again after this, I won't argue."

Twenty minutes later, Rhynehart jerked open the back door and poked his head inside.

"There must be something seriously wrong with you." He blinked, opened the door wider, and stepped into the kitchen. "What the fuck?"

"Oh, hey. Yeah." Cheyenne dropped the last piece of shredded metal on the pile of segmented war-machine fragments in the corner with a flick of her fingers. "You're welcome."

"How did you…" The man walked slowly into the living room and couldn't stop staring. "Help me out here, halfling."

"Well, you might wanna put a new seal up there. Maybe a fresh panel. I don't know how long that'll hold." Cheyenne pointed at the ceiling, which was mostly restored but didn't look very stable. "And I don't know shit about plumbing."

Ember floated back through the front door and closed it behind her, then dusted off her hands and grinned at the stunned ex-agent. "What do you think?"

"I have no fucking clue." Rhynehart peered under the table, then pointed at the still-severed couch. "Couldn't fix the furniture?"

"Meh." Cheyenne shrugged. "That's an ugly couch, man. Good excuse to get a new one."

Bhandi came in through the back and barked a laugh. "You finally picked up cleaning-crew duty, huh?"

The other agents filtered in behind her, looking as dumbstruck as Rhynehart.

"How the hell did you do this?" Yurik asked.

Ember laughed. "Seriously? I mean, I know none of you are fae, but magic is a thing. So are spells."

"Huh?"

Cheyenne and Ember shared an exasperated glance. "And you wanna give them activators."

"There's gonna be a serious learning curve with these guys, yeah."

"Wait, Cheyenne's not fae, either. Don't tell me you know spells too." Tate squinted at the halfling. "But if you do, you should say that."

"Kinda." Cheyenne almost tapped the activator behind her ear but realized none of them would understand what that meant. "It's all part of the O'gúl tech I have on me. Helps with a lot of things."

"Yeah, no shit."

"So when do we get our own? Whatever they are?" Bhandi asked.

"It's on my list. But let's stay focused on one thing at a time, huh?"

"After we wipe out these machine-controlling assholes, then?"

"It's gonna take a little more time than that." Cheyenne shrugged. "They don't exist on this side. Yet."

"No kidding. So you're gonna bring us our own secret stash of whatever lets you do all this?" Yurik frowned at the clean floors, then glanced at the pile of destroyed snake-machine parts. "Where'd you put the mess?"

"Oh, yeah." Ember stuck a thumb over her shoulder at the front door. "Your front garden got some extra fertilizer. Hope you don't mind."

Rhynehart gave her a blank look and shook his head.

"Great."

A knock came at the front door, and everybody turned to stare at it.

"Food's here," Jamal grumbled and stuck a hand in his pocket to pull out an illusion-charm ring and stick it on his finger.

"Masks on," Bhandi muttered.

The room of two humans and six magicals transformed into six almost-regular-looking people seconds before Jamal opened the front door.

"Order for Jamal." The kid in the Jimmy John's shirt gave the huge, ridiculously muscular man with brown hair flopping into his beady eyes a nervous smile and lifted the bulging plastic bags in each of his hands.

"Yep." Jamal reached through the door to take the bags. "I tipped on the website."

"Oh. Yeah, okay. That's cool."

Tammy came racing through the house, yapping as her nails clicked across the floor.

"Hey, by the way." The kid wrinkled his nose and glanced at the front garden. "Not trying to get in anyone's business, but it smells out here. You might wanna check for a backup in the pipes or something, you know?"

"Sure." Jamal jerked his chin at the delivery driver and turned, pulling the door closed with a huge elbow.

Rhynehart's dog stopped in the doorway and barked furiously at the kid as he turned to head down the drive. The kid's smile faded when he saw the white Maltese covered in brown sludge. "Uh, cute dog."

"Uh-huh." Jamal elbowed the door, and the Jimmy John's kid turned around two more times to stare at Tammy before the door shut and muffled her barking. "Food."

Everyone gathered around the table as he brought in the plastic bags.

"Tammy. Hey." Rhynehart headed to the front door and stopped. "You cleaned my whole house, halfling. Would it've killed you to do the same for my dog?"

Cheyenne snorted. "She was outside with you, and I'm not a groomer."

Bhandi and Yurik burst out laughing as they sifted through the plastic bags on the table. Jamal bit off a quarter of his sandwich at once and grunted again.

Grimacing, Rhynehart bent to pick up his soiled Maltese and shook his head. "Leave me a sandwich, huh?"

"Where you goin', man?" Tate called through a mouthful.

"To give Tammy a bath and change my clothes. If you didn't bring any, don't expect me to loan you extras."

As the agents dug into their late lunches or early dinners, Cheyenne grinned and pulled out her cell phone. *He can act pissed off all he wants. Anyone would be grateful for not having to clean sprayed sewage off their walls.*

Bhandi slid a wrapped sandwich to her across the table. "Unless you don't wanna eat. Then I'll take care of it for you."

"Hey. You can't call dibs on someone else's sandwich."

"I can if she's not gonna eat it, Greenskin."

"Yeah, I'll eat it. Give me a sec." Cheyenne turned away from the table to send Byrd a text.

Where are you guys? We said 2:00.

She didn't get an immediate reply, so she stuck her phone back in her pocket and grabbed the sandwich.

"Hey, you know what?" Todd swallowed his food and jerked his chin at the other agents. "This gives a whole new meaning to shittin' where you eat, right?"

The magical agents stared at him, and Bhandi scoffed. "You should stick to lasers, man. Comedy's not your thing."

"I thought it was funny." He bit into his sandwich again and chuckled.

Cheyenne and Ember glanced at each other, and the fae lifted her sandwich in a silent toast.

Yeah, another day hanging out with FRoE agents. As long as they have their heads in the game when we roll into that meeting.

CHAPTER FORTY-FOUR

Rhynehart emptied a scoop of dog food into Tammy's bowl and scratched behind her ears as she sniffed her dinner. "Good girl." He stood, glanced at his tactical watch, and turned around to look at his lounging guests in the other room. "6:15, people. Time to move out."

Yurik grinned at him as the man rejoined everyone else. "Hey, they didn't take your watch."

Tate snorted and shook his head.

"Nope, they didn't take my watch." Rhynehart stuck his hands in his pockets and frowned as he headed to the front door. "Tried to take my life. No big deal."

"That's not what I meant." Yurik sighed and gave up when the human agent disappeared through his front door. "Damn."

"What're you tryin' to do, sayin' shit like that?" Todd shook his head as he zipped up the duffel bag with the fell laser inside.

"What? I'm staying positive."

Cheyenne clapped a hand on the goblin's muscular shoulder. "Maybe stay on task with this one. I bet he'll find a silver lining once the man who used to be his boss and ordered his murder falls off his high horse."

"Yeah, but what about before then?" When nobody answered, Yurik turned around with a scowl and picked up the second duffel bag. "Can't be gloomy and shitty all the time."

"Have you ever seen Rhynehart laugh?" Bhandi asked.

"No."

"Then, there's the hole in your logic."

Jamal grunted and stooped to pat the top of Tammy's head when she padded up to him with a whine. "Bye, dog." After slipping on his mask on again, he put one crate on top of the other and picked them both up before turning to the door.

"Time to roll." Tate slipped on his mask too and grinned at Ember as he passed her on the way to the door. "Don't be nervous, fae. We've got your back."

"I'm not nervous." She shot Cheyenne a confused smile and floated along beside the bald, tattooed troll. "Why would you think that?"

The others followed them through the front hall. Jamal grunted when the corner of the top crate bumped the wall.

"Watch it, big guy. This way." Bhandi tapped his huge arm and directed him around the corner out the door.

Tate held the door open for everyone and chuckled when Ember stared him down. "No, seriously. Do I look nervous?"

"I mean, not now. But you did." He puckered his lips and blew Tammy a quick kiss before closing the door in the dog's face. "It's nothing to be ashamed of, Ember. Everyone's a little nervous their first time."

"Ha!" She turned around and grinned at him as he caught up to her on the driveway. "That's what you're trying to do. I'm the fae who used to ride through Peridosh in a wheelchair, which means I've never been in a fight before."

"I mean, kinda. Yeah."

The cobbled-together team stopped at the two black SUVs parked in front of Rhynehart's house, and Ember met Cheyenne's gaze. "Tate thinks this is my first fight."

"Huh."

"Okay, maybe it's not." With a nervous laugh, the troll man rubbed the back of his bald head. "But you haven't gone on an op with us before. Not like Cheyenne, anyway. So that's a first, at least."

"You know what I think?"

"Huh?"

Ember folded her arms. "I think this is your first time doing anything with a fae."

"Pshh. So?"

"So don't be nervous, Tate." She patted his shoulder. "I've got your back."

Ember climbed into the back seat of one SUV after Bhandi as Yurik went around the front to the driver's side. Tate frowned at Cheyenne and spread his arms. "But she hasn't done anything like this, right?"

Cheyenne slipped into the back seat and grabbed the door handle. "Ember's been in more high-level raids than you have, man. I promise." Then she shut the door and fought back a laugh as the troll man stood beside the car in disbelief.

"This isn't a damn videogame," Tate muttered. "Raids?"

Yurik gently honked the horn, and the tattooed troll jumped and yanked open the passenger door.

Todd, Rhynehart, and Jamal got into the second SUV, then the drivers started the engines and both vehicles pulled away from the house, leaving Rhynehart's black Jeep and Matthew Thomas' Mercedes behind.

Cheyenne pulled out her cell phone again and sent Lumil a text this time since Byrd still hadn't replied.

We're heading out now. Couldn't wait for you. Meet us there.

She added the address of the meeting location and sent it before slipping her phone back into her pocket. *They're more likely to get themselves into trouble than out of it. Whatever's holding them up, I hope they figure their shit out.*

Ember looked at her with raised eyebrows. "Still nothing?"

"Nope. They'll be there or they won't. I'm not gonna worry about trying to figure it out."

"Right." The fae's gaze dropped to the neckline of Cheyenne's shirt. "What about your shoulders?"

Cheyenne glanced down at where one of the dart wounds was still open beneath her shirt. "Well, they're not breaking any records at least, for the worst or the best."

Bhandi snorted. "What are you talking about?"

"Nothing." Reaching into her pocket, Cheyenne pulled out the injection canister and handed it to Ember. "You mind?"

"Sure."

"Whoa. Shit. What the hell is that?" Bhandi laughed and stared at the canister as Ember turned it over in her hand. "You bring your own weapons, Goth drow?"

Cheyenne moved her trenchcoat out of the way and lifted her shirt to give Ember a clear shot. "Have you ever seen me bring weapons?"

"I mean, not yet." The injection canister hissed when Ember pressed it against Cheyenne's side. Bhandi threw her head back and cackled. "No fucking way!"

"What?" Tate turned around in the passenger seat as Cheyenne closed her eyes and leaned her head back against the headrest. "I missed something."

Bhandi pointed at the canister in Ember's hand. "The Goth drow brought herself an extra boost, man."

Yurik snorted and looked into the rearview mirror. "Bullshit."

"Yeah, that's what you'd think." The troll woman slapped her hand on the door's armrest. "She's fucking juicin' over here!"

"Damn, Cheyenne." Tate raised an eyebrow and glanced at the halfling before turning around again in his seat. "Never would've pinned you for the type."

Cheyenne hissed, her head rocking to the window as she let the wave of darktongue euphoria wash over her. "You guys are idiots."

"Hey, I know what I saw." Bhandi snorted and gestured at Ember and the canister. "And you had your friend do it for you."

"Wait." Ember flipped the canister to the troll woman. "What do you think this is?"

"Juice."

The fae shook her head.

"Steroids," Yurik clarified, shaking his head as he glanced one more time in the rearview mirror and kept a safe distance behind the other SUV. "Obviously, magical steroids. Did she even tell you what's in that thing before gettin' you to pump her up like that?"

"Oh, my God. Here." Rolling her eyes, Ember handed the canister back to Cheyenne.

"Thanks." The halfling took the long cylinder of metal. It felt like she was moving through syrup when she tried to find her coat pocket again.

"See, this is the way to be about everything." Bhandi grinned and bobbed her head. "No shame. No fucking shame. She pulls it out in front of everyone like, 'Bam. We're goin' in, and I'm gonna take advantage of drow magic and 'roid rage. I don't give a fuck who knows about it.'"

"Stop talking." Cheyenne's eyes fluttered open and she swallowed. "You have no idea what you're talking about."

"Sure I do. We've seen that shit before. Little goblin punk named Rugen. Man, that guy lasted, what? Two months in our unit?"

"Three." Tate chuckled. "He was decent, I guess. When he didn't forget to bring his pumpers with him."

"Totally useless otherwise." Bhandi leaned forward to look past Ember at Cheyenne. "What the hell are you doing? You don't need that shit."

"Yeah, I know." Taking a deep breath, Cheyenne blinked heavily as the rest of the buzz faded from her system. *Feels so much better.* Then she met Bhandi's gaze and raised an eyebrow. "It's medicine."

"Ha. You know how many times we've heard that excuse? And everybody thinks they're so goddamn smart, nobody's gonna notice."

Cheyenne looked at Ember, and her friend shook her head. "Guess they need proof."

Yurik frowned at her in the rearview mirror. "Proof of what?"

Cheyenne hooked a finger through the collar of her shirt and pulled down to give the magical agents a nice view of the dart wound there and the black streaks snaking farther and farther away from it.

Bhandi sucked in a sharp breath and brought a fist to her mouth. "Oh, shit."

Tate spun in the passenger seat and gripped the seatback to turn even farther.

"What the hell happened to you?" Bhandi tried to lean closer until Ember nudged her away with a shoulder.

"I'm sitting here, remember?"

"Yeah, sorry. Seriously, Cheyenne? That looks fucked up."

"I'm not gonna lie. It feels the same way." Cheyenne dropped her head back against the headrest again. "And I have two more like it."

"So, that really was medicine?"

"Pretty much. And yeah, I'm fine. I'll be fine. It's not gonna jeopardize this thing. That's what that fun dose of meds is for. We all on the same page now?"

"Yep." Bhandi sat back in her seat and stared at Yurik's headrest.

"You keep rollin' out one surprise after another, halfling. I'll give you that." Yurik chuckled. "I knew you wouldn't take steroids."

"I'm pretty sure they wouldn't work on me anyway."

"How come?"

"Because nothing else does." Cheyenne glanced out the window at the street signs streaking past them on the highway. "Only alcohol and really strong magical meds from the other side. This stuff would probably take out a horse, honestly."

Ember laughed and clapped her hands over her mouth before muttering, "Yeah. It probably would."

"As long as you're good to go when we move on those assholes," Tate said, giving her a final once-over before facing forward again, "I don't care what you have to do."

"Then we're on the same page."

CHAPTER FORTY-FIVE

At 7:01, Cheyenne moved quickly and silently with the FRoE agents through the showroom building. All the lights were off from the east wing where they'd decided to enter to the larger reception hall at the north end. *At least these guys have enough experience to guess the best door to break down.*

The doors had been unlocked, which made her warier, but this time, she knew she was part of an operation from the very beginning. *I won't screw it up for everyone else who's on the same team.*

Cheyenne scanned the walls and the dark corners as Rhynehart directed his agents with silent signals behind her. They moved down the hall, pausing to clear the next section of it before making their way closer to the north end. Cheyenne only found two security cameras in the east wing and shut them off with the activator's help. *These don't belong to the Bull's Head, but at least we're covered. Now I gotta find the war-machine cameras.*

As they closed in on the north end of the building and the corridor that led into the open reception hall with enough room for a whole gathering of O'gúl loyalists and FRoE traitors, her activator didn't find a single piece of working O'gúl tech. Rhynehart kept shooting her questioning glances, and her only reply was to shake her head and keep moving.

Then she heard the voices. It didn't matter if the rest of her team heard them too. Cheyenne squinted at the closed doors into the reception hall, and without having to place her hand against them, without even closing her eyes or accepting the activator's help, the image of the door changed. *Holy shit. Drow vision's gotten superpowered, apparently.*

The shimmering outlines of Bull's Head magicals on the other side of the doors came into view, surrounded by different glowing colors according to race. *No humans. Not yet, anyway.*

Turning silently back to Rhynehart, she opened and closed both hands three times, then pointed at the doors. *Yeah, I'd say thirty's a pretty good count.*

When the agent pointed at himself to ask if there were any humans, she shook her head. Whatever other signals he gave to the rest of his team were quick and efficient and sent the other agents out in different directions along the corridors. *Guess they planned this part too, and I missed it. If we all had activators, it'd be almost as good as telepathy.*

The thought almost made her snort, but she kept quiet and focused instead on the conversations inside the reception hall.

"I said not yet, Pendra."

"So, you're telling me you want that human to come barging in here without any defenses set up?"

"Why the hell do we need defenses, huh? We got the bastard working for us. Eating right out of our fell-damn hands."

The creak of metal hinges opening on the other side of the doors momentarily drowned out the low background noise of at least two dozen Bull's Head loyalists inside getting ready for this meeting. Then came the rustling clinks of small metal parts shifting around.

"You trust these humans too much, brother."

"Nah. I only trust 'em as far as I can spray their blood across the wall." Both magicals chuckled. "Look, he's the one who set this up. We have what he wants, and if this turns into anything other than a demonstration, we'll give him way more than he can handle."

Metal war-machine parts clanked together, and Cheyenne's enhanced drow vision brought up the shapes of multiple stacked crates and large, amorphous shapes that didn't belong to magicals and didn't move or glow.

War machines. If this is supposed to be a demonstration, it explains why we didn't have to fight off any spy bugs on the way in.

A gentle tap on her shoulder made her whirl. Rhynehart stepped back, pointed at his eyes, then gestured around the corner at the other side of the reception hall. He headed that way, moving silently and looking back only once to make sure she was following.

This is worse than Charades.

They turned down a narrow hall at the end of the corridor, and Rhynehart led her up a dark flight of stairs at the west end of the reception hall. When they reached the top, Tate briefly glanced their way. He knelt in front of a low ledge supporting a huge pane of glass running down the length of the reception room below. His fell rifle was propped on his thigh, held in both hands, and he lowered his head again to watch the movements below them through the scope.

Look at that. We get our own private show with a bird's-eye view.

Farther along the upstairs hall, she saw Yurik standing in front of the window with his weapon trained on the meeting room. Ember hovered next to him and nodded at Cheyenne when they looked at each other. Cheyenne nodded back, then searched for the other magicals on their team. When Rhynehart caught her attention again and pointed down through the window to the opposite side of the reception hall. The lights inside the room below were too bright to make out much at first, but she pulled up a magnified view through her activator and found the darkened outlines of Bhandi, Jamal, and Todd through the set of smaller windows. *Everyone's in their places. They're a hell of a lot better at this than when we broke the necromancer out of Chateau D'rahl, that's for damn sure. Probably 'cause there's no nightstalker or drow-thief convict breathing down their necks.*

Nodding at Rhynehart to show she understood, Cheyenne stepped slowly to the window and peered down into the reception hall. Sure enough, the odd shapes she'd seen through the doors were fully built but not-yet-activated war machines. One tunneler, two heavy tank-looking things, a machine that looked like a grenade launcher on legs, and a narrow flattened contraption with two metal sheets that looked like wings extending from a central base. *Well, if people didn't freak out about war machines digging up out of the ground, they'll definitely have an issue with giant flying weapons. Freaked-out humans are a no-go.*

The dozens of Bull's Head loyalists down below moved quickly back and forth, calibrating the assembled machines, checking whatever other inventory they'd brought with them, and patrolling lazily with automatic weapons at the ready. None of them that she could see carried fell weapons, so her team had an advantage that way.

We'll keep it as long as those war machines stay dead. I doubt they will.

The doors on the north end of the reception hall opened with a bang, and in walked Colonel Les Thomas. Despite the thick window separating the second story from the room below, Cheyenne could hear the man's shiny black shoes clicking on the floor as he entered. The man paused, looked around at the assembled machines and the supply crates and the loyalists who'd stopped moving to stare at him, and clasped his hands behind his back. "Where's Welyk?"

"You're late." A tall, gangly magical with what looked like spikes where his shoulders should have been beneath the oversized hoodie stepped casually forward from behind a stack of crates.

Bingo. They already know each other. This is almost too easy. Cheyenne selected the prompted command on her activator to zero in on the scene below and marked the place where whatever her O'gúl tech recorded would start when she turned this into evidence later. *And leverage.*

For good measure, she had her activator turn up the volume, then it was almost like she stood down there with the Bull's Head people, every word coming in crisp and clear.

Colonel Thomas jerked his chin at Welyk and met the guy in the center of the reception hall. "I had a few of my guys surveil the premises. Just a standard precaution. You know."

Welyk wrinkled his squashed, mottled brown nose and revealed sharp upper fangs on either side of short, stubby yellow teeth. "Everything we've got is right here in this room. Colonel."

"I believe you. I just don't think either of us would be pleased to find ourselves joined by a third party."

"No. We wouldn't be." The loyalist stuck out his hand to the colonel, a dry, spindly brown appendage with knobby knuckles and skin that looked more like tree bark than flesh. Colonel Thomas shook Welyk's hand, then clasped his hands behind his back again and turned to look at one of the tanks. "That's impressive."

Welyk's grin looked more like a snarl, and he gestured at the machine. "That one'll do about everything but take prisoners."

The loyalists around him laughed.

"An acceptable lack for something that size." Colonel Thomas tilted his head. "But does it work?"

The laughter died abruptly, and a pale-yellow tongue flickered out between Welyk's sharpened front fangs. "It works. They all work."

"I'm very much looking forward to seeing them in action, then. One moment." The colonel turned halfway around to look back through the open door he'd entered. "Well?"

"All clear, Colonel."

Cheyenne recognized the voice before its owner stepped through the open doors on the north end. Seeing him in the flesh two seconds later made her rage flare up that much more intensely. *What the actual fuck?*

"Excellent. Thank you, Major." Colonel Thomas nodded and gestured with an open arm. "Welyk, this is Major Carson. When you and I approve all the finer details, he'll be taking over the transfer from here."

Yurik jerked his head away from his rifle scope to look up at Rhynehart with wide eyes. Rhynehart grimaced, his fists clenching at his sides. Cheyenne clearly heard the man's teeth grinding together, but no one made a sound behind the second-story window.

Sir's been in on this from the beginning. The whole fucking time. Or maybe the colonel asked him last-second to tag along, but it doesn't fucking matter either way. They're both going down. She made sure to spend plenty of time recording Major Guy Carson so no one could argue later that it hadn't been him standing right next to Colonel Les Thomas. Fuckers.

The gangly magical sneered at the human FRoE officials. "Whatever you say."

Sir grunted and gave Welyk a stiff nod, his hand resting on the butt of his pistol holstered at his hip.

Even without the activator's help, Cheyenne could see the man's mustache twitching as he slowly scanned the room, where almost three dozen magical assholes were staring him down.

"Now." Colonel Thomas lifted his chin at the tank machine again. "Let's talk about our next steps."

"We've got command cases behind me with Haltigar." A hulking orc with both tusks tilted to the left side of his face folded his arms and sneered at the colonel. "Those take a little trial and error at the beginning. More error recently, now that I think about it."

Thomas glanced quickly at the orc and shook his head. "What do you mean?"

"The system your nephew got up and running for us isn't sailing along the way we'd hoped at this point."

"Really? The last time you and I spoke, you said the program did everything you wanted without a hitch."

"Yeah, and now it's not." Welyk hocked up a huge ball of phlegm and spat it across the room. "Something happened. I'm not a fan of someone promising me one thing and falling short. You get what I'm saying."

"Of course. I'll have a chat with my nephew about it. If you can tell me what specifically isn't working out the way you'd hoped, I will ensure he addresses the issue as quickly as possible."

"Systems aren't updating. Syncing with the new data used to be automatic, and that dropped first." Welyk drew his forearm under his squashed nose and sniffed. "Now it won't even make the connection when we go in manually, and that's a real pain in the ass."

Cheyenne thought, *Sounds like Matthew took our strong advice and shut down the account updates after all. Points for our neighbor.*

"No doubt." The colonel nodded. "I'm sure you already know there are always bugs and new patches rolling out that take a little more time than others to filter through. Don't worry about it."

"Oh, I'm not worried, Colonel. I'm annoyed."

"Well, if you don't get a visit from my nephew or by someone on his team by the end of the day tomorrow, you won't be the only one. I'll take care of it."

Welyk shook a spindly finger at the man. "Yeah, make sure you do. I guess that gives you a day to play with your new machines, doesn't it?"

"At the very least." Colonel Thomas headed after the slow-moving, stooped Welyk as they made their way through the stacks of crates and the deactivated war machines.

Cheyenne felt Rhynehart studying her, but she didn't want to look away from the scene playing out below them. *That's what the asshole's getting out of all this. Thomas brought them his top programmer, fed the Bull's*

Head intel to keep them happy, and waited for the perfect moment to buy his own fucking war machines. What the hell for?

362

CHAPTER FORTY-SIX

Beside Cheyenne, Tate shifted his rifle's position on his thigh and let out a slow breath.

Right there with you, man. This is fucked up.

"I was hoping for a demonstration," Colonel Thomas said casually as he stopped to appreciate the grenade launcher on legs.

"Yeah, we deliver, Colonel. You're getting exactly what you asked for today, as long as you hold up your end of things."

"Five years, Welyk. I'm not going to start disappointing you now."

At the other end of the reception hall, Sir stood rigidly with his hand resting on his weapon. Five more FRoE agents had trickled in behind him while the colonel and today's Bull's Head leader took their tour around the merchandise. Cheyenne quickly scanned each of their faces. *Of course, they're not anyone I'd recognize. And they're human. This whole thing's been covered up from the start.*

"What's this one?" Colonel Thomas gestured at the launcher.

"Oh, yeah. This one's fun." Welyk nodded brusquely at a sniggering skaxen, who turned around and rifled through an open crate behind him. "These are blood-trackers."

"Hmm." The colonel's eyebrows lifted.

"We've got a specific one for every known race of magical this side of the Border. That's how they find their targets, Colonel. They lock onto the blood." Welyk stepped aside to let the skaxen load a large metal canister into the launcher at the top of the war machine. "Back home, we can customize these things to a specific individual, but the technology's a little delayed Earthside. Nothing against your nephew; it's not possible over here, but that doesn't make it any less effective."

"Interesting."

The skaxen slammed the canister into place, then hopped away from the machine to grab a black metal box from inside the open crate. "You wanna see how it works?"

"That's why I'm here."

With a shriek of glee, the skaxen smacked the side of the box, and a panel opened to reveal a small lever and multiple crude dials on the surface. His tongue flickering in and out between sharpened teeth, the rat-faced magical scanned the room and called, "Hey, Thel! Just so you know, I heard what you said about my face!"

A scarred gremlin spun around with wide eyes as the skaxen jerked down the box's lever. "What are you doing, *dae'bruj?*"

The skaxen cackled as the launcher flared to life, whirring and clicking and flashing ribbons of yellow and orange light. The four legs beneath the launcher's base stretched out and pinged on the floor before rising to their full height.

"Turn that shit off," the gremlin screamed.

Faster than the bulky parts looked capable of moving, the launcher swiveled toward the gremlin, took two steps forward, and fired a burst of yellow-brown light. The gremlin screamed and dodged out of the way, shoving other loyalists aside as he darted across the reception hall to the open doors at the far end. The launcher whined and followed him with its swiveling head, but the blood-tracker bolt it had fired was enough to get the job done. The yellow shot of magic zipped around the room, changing its course to head after the gremlin no matter which way he ran. He screamed when the yellow magic crashed into his back and sent him flying face-first across the floor. Yellow sparks darted across his body like an electrical current, and the gremlin jerked and bucked on the ground beneath the jolting attack until he finally fell still. He didn't get up again.

Some of the loyalists burst out laughing. A troll roared and pumped his fist in the air.

"Incredible." Colonel Thomas' slow clap barely rose above the loyalists' amusement as he grinned at the launcher. "Can it only be fired manually?"

"Not if your nephew's system works the way you promised us it would."

"Oh, it will."

Welyk sneered at the man. "Then, sure. Every hunk of metal parts in this room can be automated for pretty much whatever you want."

"Good. I like this one in particular." The colonel shook a finger at the blood-tracker machine. "That'll come in very useful."

The gangly loyalist sniggered. "New training or something?"

"Training? No. This is quality control, Welyk." Colonel Thomas stroked his chin, his smile growing. "The refugees taking up our resources at the Border reservations step out of line far more often than any of us expected in the beginning."

Welyk gave a low chuckle. "Not as easy to control as humans, huh?"

"Not with human methods, no, but you're helping me change that."

"Sure. Easy to intimidate with something like this."

"Indeed. I'm not above using force when it's called for, even on my own. Much like yourself."

They both turned to look at the dead gremlin lying face-down in front of the double doors. Welyk's fanged grin returned. "That one was a pain in my ass anyway. So, does it hold up to your expectations, Colonel?"

"I think it does." Thomas turned to Sir and the other FRoE agents watching the room with masks of indifference and snapped his fingers. "Get it."

One agent moved swiftly through the open doors and returned with a large briefcase.

"I'm sure you understand the need for discretion with this," the colonel said as he accepted the case and turned to Welyk. "And cash."

"Well, I wasn't expecting a stack of *veréle*," the lanky magical muttered. The loyalists around him sniggered.

"What was that?"

"Nothing important, Colonel." Welyk grinned, his tongue flicking between his fangs again. "These crates behind me have all the control cases you'll need for each of these machines. If you find yourself wanting anything a little more specific after this, we'll see what we can come up with for you."

"Good to know."

The skaxen came forward with the black control box clamped between his black-clawed orange hands. Welyk took it from him, then extended the box to the colonel and paused. "Before we finish this transaction, there's one more thing I need from you."

Colonel Thomas lifted his chin and faced the loyalist square-on, clasping the handle of the briefcase in front of him with both hands. "You gave me a price for these. I came here trusting you wouldn't change the terms."

"No, I'll take the money. But all this talk about what's been happening in your magical prison and outside of it got me thinking. I want everything you have on the halfling."

The colonel briefly shook his head. "What halfling?"

Cheyenne held her breath. *What a piece of shit.* She wasn't sure if she meant Welyk or the colonel or both.

Welyk sneered at the FRoE official and spread his arms. "The drow *mór úcare*, Colonel. Cheyenne Summerlin."

"Oh." Thomas turned to his gathered agents and gestured at Sir. "Major Carson has spent far more time with her than I have. Major?"

Sir swallowed thickly, one eye twitching. "Colonel?"

"Give this magical what he wants. Everything you have on the halfling."

Mustache writhing, Sir stood rigidly and stared at his superior and the Bull's Head scum leering at him.

Jesus, he looks like a fucking deer in the headlights. Cheyenne bit her bottom lip and glared down at Sir. *If you start talking, I swear I'll take you down.*

"Major, this is hardly classified information," Colonel Thomas said sharply. "And I don't appreciate you hesitating on this. We're closing on this deal, so start talking. Now."

Sir cleared his throat and glanced at the ground. "Sir."

"That's an order, Major."

Fuck this.

"The halfling—"

Cheyenne summoned two crackling spheres of black energy in her palms and slammed them against the window before Sir could get out another word. The entire pane of thick glass shattered, raining down on the gathered magicals and FRoE agents. Those directly beneath it darted out of the way, and Cheyenne leaped from the second-story balcony she'd created to land on a pile of glass.

Welyk snarled and raised his hand over the black control box in his palm. She swept it out of his grasp with a burst of telekinetic force and sent the box into the far wall.

"Guy Carson's a fucking idiot." Cheyenne shrugged and summoned two more energy spheres in her open palms. "And a traitor. You can't trust anything that sprays out of his mouth. Why don't you ask the halfling to her face?"

Colonel Thomas pressed his lips together and looked at her. "I think we're done here." He glanced at Sir and the other agents and nodded. "Take care of her, will you?"

"Don't fucking move," Rhynehart shouted from above. The Bull's Head loyalists and Colonel Thomas' band of trusted human agents looked up to find Rhynehart, Yurik, and Tate training their fell weapons on the gathered party. Then Jamal stomped through the open double doors on the north end of the reception hall, a rifle tucked under each arm. Todd moved quickly behind the ogre, holding the newly tested fell laser cannon with both hands. Bhandi filtered in behind him, decked out in full dampening gear, vest, helmet, and gloves. She passed Todd and slapped at his helmet to lower his visor for him before gripping her rifle again with both hands.

Colonel Thomas looked at Rhynehart with wide eyes. "I'm surprised to see you here, Captain."

"Yeah, I bet you are." Rhynehart didn't move a muscle, his fell weapon trained on the center of the colonel's chest.

Welyk snarled and darted for the control box on the ground. Cheyenne fired one of her energy spheres at the ground in front of the gangly loyalist's feet, and he stopped short. "I don't usually give warnings, but I'm trying to do things a little differently these days. Don't fucking move again."

His yellow eyes narrowed, and he slowly moved a hand to his hip for whatever he'd stashed in his pocket. But he didn't try to slip past her again or attack, even when the other loyalists summoned their own attack spells in blue and orange sparks and jolts of yellow and red light. The air practically vibrated with so much magic drawn up and held in stasis, and everyone waited for someone else to make the first move.

"So here's the thing, Colonel." Cheyenne waited for the man to look at her again. "You get one chance to back away from this deal you almost made. Take your money and your idiot backup with you. Call this whole thing off, and I won't have to take you down."

Colonel Thomas chuckled. "I don't think you're in any position to make demands like that, Miss Summerlin. If this is all the backup you brought with you, you're outnumbered at least five times over. And as I'm sure you overheard, these O'gúleesh have been looking for you."

"Yeah, these guys have been looking for me for months. It's nothing new."

"I see." The colonel's gaze swept around the static-filled reception hall one more time, and he glanced briefly up at Rhynehart, Yurik, and Tate on the second floor. "I'm not in the habit of submitting to anyone else's demands. This little display of yours doesn't make you that much more intimidating."

Cheyenne blinked slowly. *Jesus, it's like this guy wants to fight.* "I'm not trying to be intimidating, Colonel. I'm trying to give you an out. How hard is that to understand?"

"Well, thank you for clarifying. I don't need an out." Colonel Thomas turned to Sir again and nodded. "Major. Remove her."

Major "Sir" Carson bristled, his eyes bulging and his face turning its usual deep crimson that meant he was either very drunk or very pissed or both.

"This isn't a discussion, Major Carson." The colonel widened his eyes. "I didn't realize you'd forgotten how to follow the chain of command."

With a low growl, Sir turned to Cheyenne and started to draw his firearm. His mistake was looking up to meet the drow halfling's glowing golden eyes as he did so. Cheyenne tilted her head and stared him down. *Don't you fucking do it, Guy. You know what I'll do to you.*

Sir swallowed and went perfectly still.

"What the hell is going on?" Colonel Thomas shouted. "Carson! I said—"

"He heard what you said." Cheyenne turned her attention to the colonel again. "He's not gonna do what you want. Which is surprising, seeing as he's been doing what you want for a long time, apparently."

"I don't know who you think you are."

"Well, lucky for both of us, I know exactly who I am." Her energy spheres crackled with intensifying black and purple light and grew to twice their usual size in her hands. "If you wanna find out the hard way, keep being a dick. I'm giving you an option."

"You said that, and I said I don't—"

"Yeah, you don't submit to demands. I get it. How are you with blackmail?"

"What?"

The reception hall fell eerily silent except for Sir's heavy breathing and the crackle and hiss of so many attack spells held at the ready in so many hands, just waiting to be let loose.

"Step down from your position, Colonel." Cheyenne raised her eyebrows. "Leave the FRoE. You're basically at the top, right? So there won't be a bunch of hoops to jump through. Walk away, and I won't send this video to anyone who will make you step down. Trust me, I'll use it to end you if you don't take my offer. I'm sure Major Carson can back me up when I say I don't bluff."

Colonel Thomas' nostrils flared as he glared at her. "Except for now."

"Nope. I have this whole meeting tonight recorded."

"Bullshit."

In a fraction of a second, Cheyenne selected her activator's command to share everything up to this point with one specific private number. The jingle of an annoying piano-keys ringtone cut through the silence in the reception hall. She glanced at the colonel's jacket pocket. "Sounds like you got a message. You should probably check that."

Colonel Thomas jammed his hand into his pocket and whipped out his cell phone. His eyes widened, then he pressed the play button and the video came up on his screen.

"I had a few of my guys surveil the premises. Just a standard precaution. You know." Les Thomas' recorded voice came through loud and clear as the video played.

"Everything we've got is right here in this room. Colonel."

"I believe you. I just don't think either of us would be pleased to find ourselves joined by a third party."

"No. We wouldn't be."

With a snarl, the colonel stopped the video and shoved his phone back into his pocket. "Whatever you think you're going to do with that, you've overestimated yourself."

Cheyenne snorted. "I don't think so."

"You won't leave this building tonight, Miss Summerlin, and your little home movie dies with you."

"That's a no, then, right? You're not gonna step down and take the easy way out?"

"Major Carson!" the colonel barked. "If you don't pull your head out of whatever hole you've buried it in, I will ruin you. Take her out!"

Sir cleared his throat, blinking rapidly, and finally found at least part of his voice. "With all due respect, Colonel, I don't think this—"

"I'm the one who does the thinking." Les Thomas stormed toward Guy Carson until they stood toe to toe. "Respect or no, Carson, I've had enough of your insubordination. Don't forget how much you have at stake in this."

Sir stared straight ahead as his ranking officer fumed in his face. "Sir, I don't—"

"You do because I say you do. How do you think Alice will feel when she finds out about everything you've been doing over the last thirty years? That you've been lying to her all this time? It would kill her, wouldn't it?"

Sir's eyes flicked to the colonel's, twitching almost uncontrollably now, but he didn't say a word.

"This transaction tonight will be completed, Carson, whether you like it or not. These magicals, all of them, don't belong in our world. You know that as well as I do. I'm not backing down until I have them either under my thumb exactly the way I want, or we toss their asses back where they came from. If I can't keep them out, I *will* keep them in line, you understand? So, Major, do your job and keep this halfling bitch in line."

"Sir."

"And these agents under your command! We are the ones who own this world, Carson. Not them."

"It's all bullshit, Major," Rhynehart called from the second story, stepping forward with his fell rifle aimed at Colonel Thomas' chest. "He's not gonna use all this for magicals. Not even for current agents. He sent a fucking machine to my house to take me out, and I'll do whatever I have to."

Sir moved faster than any of them expected. He released his firearm from its holster and swung up to the second story. A second later, the report of a single shot cracked through the room, and Rhynehart staggered backward with a shout. The rifle hung by his side from one hand, the other rendered useless by the bullet that had lodged in his shoulder outside the safety of his bulletproof dampening vest.

Guess we'll have matching scars.

"What the fuck?" Yurik shouted, though he didn't remove his eye from the scope of his own rifle. "Rhynehart?"

"Fuck." The human agent staggered against the wall of the corridor on the second story. "Shoulder. I'm fine."

"You're a piece of shit, you know that?" Bhandi screamed, stepping forward to stand squarely beside Jamal, her rifle centered on Sir.

Sir gritted his teeth, breathing heavily and seething as he aimed his weapon at Todd. "That's not up for debate."

"Now that you've gotten that out of your system," Colonel Thomas muttered, "I suggest you continue with the rest of it."

"Move, and I'll blow your fucking brains out!" Tate shouted from above.

Cheyenne scanned the room: the tense FRoE agents and their commanding officers, Welyk and his sneering Bull's Head loyalists, their faces shimmering the colored light from their spells, and the deactivated war machines waiting to be purchased and used against the O'gúleesh who made the crossing as refugees, not prisoners. *We can call this an O'gúleesh standoff, right?*

Then her activator pulled up movement in the top right corner of her vision. And the left. One after another, multiple blinking yellow arrows appeared in her vision, moving closer to the reception hall and picking up speed. *Somebody finally activated the spy machines. And here I thought we had a chance of walking away without a fight.*

"Major Carson," Colonel Thomas muttered.

Cheyenne's activator blared an alarm when a scuttling war machine like a two-foot-long spider crawled silently along the wall to her left and climbed up to the second floor. Her hand lashed out and sent a double-sized black energy sphere into the machine. The metal spider squealed when she knocked it to the ground, sparking and hissing mechanically as its legs scrambled to find purchase upside down.

The next two seconds of stunned silence seemed to last forever. *Yeah, now we're in for it.*

Then the walls and the floor and all the dark corners of the reception hall moved as the dozens of other small war machines abandoned their stealth sequences and streamed toward Cheyenne and her rebel team of FRoE agents instead of O'gúleesh magicals.

Welyk snarled, spit flying from his sharpened fangs as he launched a bolt of flashing light across the room. Then all hell broke loose.

CHAPTER FORTY-SEVEN

"Remember the heads!" Cheyenne shouted as she ducked a flung green fireball and launched an energy sphere at an oversized metal wasp.

"As in, aim for them this time or what?" Bhandi shouted, squeezing off fell shots left and right.

"As in, take them off!" She lifted a shield in front of her before a swarm of glinting metal beetles with needle-sharp spikes where their faces would be flew toward her.

Spells blasted in all directions from the Bull's Head loyalists, who roared and snarled and leaped atop stacked crates to get better shots at their targets.

Colonel Thomas pulled his own firearm and squeezed off a few rounds at Jamal before the FRoE agents he'd brought with him formed a protective line around their commanding officer. Jamal staggered back against the force, but his bulletproof dampening vest caught the bullets instead of his chest. With a roar, he slammed the sides of both fell rifles against his chest and powered them up with high-pitched whines, then unleashed blast after green blast.

A loyalist goblin screeched with laughter and punched another metal box she'd pulled from one of the crates. "You're finished now, *mór úcare!*"

One of the two tank machines rumbled to life, blinking red and yellow lights before the heavy metal tracks started turning and it growled across the floor. Cheyenne lifted another shield to block the burst of crimson light spewing from the war machine's rotating head. She ducked, turned to reach out with her black lashing tendrils, and pulled a leaping skaxen out of the air with a sharp tug. The rat-faced magical yelped and hit the floor, and the spray of yellow darts the guy had meant to aim at Todd and Bhandi went wild and crashed into the high wall opposite the second-story windows.

Todd jammed down the lever on the fell laser and screamed in excitement and effort as the column of fell energy flared across the reception hall. It seared through metal crates and the floor and the tip of the flying war machine's wing, spraying like an out-of-control water hose. He tried to aim it at the rumbling tank coming for Cheyenne, the floor now trembling beneath the heavy machine's movement. The fell laser nicked the edge of the tank with a squeal of shredding metal and a thick shower of sparks, then a troll loyalist darted past Jamal's double-firing rifles and crashed into Todd.

The human agent roared as he staggered back. The fell laser changed trajectory and moved up the back wall of the reception hall, cutting through the plaster and metal and brick and dropping huge chunks of the wall on the loyalists on the other side.

"Get that tank!" Cheyenne shouted.

Bhandi squeezed off fell rounds left and right, taking out two snarling goblins leaping at her before she turned and blasted both a dart of crimson light and another fell shot at the goblin grappling with Todd. The goblin shrieked and dropped.

"I'm on it!" Todd roared and aimed the crossbow-axehead-laser back toward the ground floor. The loyalists in his constantly spewing line of fire leaped into toppling stacks of crates and over each other. An ogre who didn't move fast enough got his left arm and most of his left leg shaved off as the laser moved toward the growling tank.

Yurik and Tate picked off loyalists one by one from the second story, occasionally having to aim their barrels up to shoot flying, whirring war machines out of the air.

Cheyenne lifted a second shield when the tank unloaded another spray of red light in her direction, then raised a hand to knock another oversized metal wasp from the air with telekinetic force. The thing let off a burst of metal shards, and she darted away from most of it before the tail end of the attack sent two steel barbs, each an inch long, into her thigh.

With a roar, she spun again and slammed into an orc's chest. Staggering back, she looked at the sneering loyalist, his tusks covered with deep engravings shaped like flames. The orc chuckled darkly, his yellow eyes glowing, and grabbed two thick black disks of metal off his belt. They were already beeping and flashing orange.

Shit. Cheyenne summoned a black energy sphere, but before she could throw it at him, a stream of opalescent violet light hit the orc's side and sent him flying across the room. The disks in his meaty green hands exploded into two swarms of tiny black machines that peppered the closest living thing, which happened to be the orc and the two gremlin loyalists he'd bowled over.

Their screams cut through the air over the explosions of fellfire, the crackling hiss of unleashed magic, and the roar of the activated tank that wobbled dangerously across the ground as Todd seared through one side of the tracks. Cheyenne looked quickly up at the second story to find Ember staring down at her with both arms outstretched, her eyes wide. Then a Bull's Head troll launched a streak of zigzagging blue energy at the fae, and Ember returned her attention to the battle.

Definitely not her first time. She can handle this.

Cheyenne spun again and found Sir standing against the side wall of the reception hall, his pistol raised in both hands but not discharging as his eyes flicked back and forth across the chaos. *Coward.*

The FRoE agents who'd come in with him and Colonel Thomas had formed their own tight knot a few yards from him, looking confused as they fired at any Bull's Head magicals who headed toward them in battle rage, forgetting they were supposed to be on the same side as Colonel Thomas and his men. So far, none of the colonel's agents had made a move on Rhynehart and his rebel team. *We'll see what happens when all these screaming loyalist idiots are on the ground.*

One of those screaming loyalist idiots barreled toward her. The goblin was skinny and haggard-looking, his turquoise skin covered in boils as he ran at Cheyenne and swung back a fist sparking green light.

Cheyenne slipped into drow speed and met him halfway, catching his fist in her own before he knew what hit him. She summoned a black energy sphere and felt the goblin's bones crack in her grip before she threw him across the reception hall.

She didn't have time to see where he landed. The steel barbs embedded in her thigh zapped her with an electric charge, and she bellowed in rage when her leg went numb from thigh to toe. It forced her out of enhanced speed, and her activator prompted her to jerk them out of her flesh without touching the barbs before disassembling them into sparking segments she tossed at the orc leveling some kind of black metal grenade launcher at Jamal. The orc screamed and dropped the weapon to clamp his thick hands over his face, now peppered with barb segments, blood, and sparking green light.

Everyone ducked when the tank finally exploded under Todd's fell laser. Shards of metal, sprays of small gears and whirring levers, and an eruption of dark blue flames filled the reception hall. Cheyenne raised a shield in front of herself, which gave her enough time to try to stomp some feeling back into her leg. Before the rest of the debris hit the ground, the fighting picked up again.

"Cheyenne!" Bhandi called and cracked the butt of her fell pistol into the skull of a Bull's Head skaxen who'd caught fire from the explosion.

Cheyenne turned to the troll woman and caught a glimpse of Colonel Thomas running away from the melee before he disappeared through the open doors and left the hall. *Wow. At least Sir has the balls to stay here.*

She slipped into drow speed and let out a sharp growl when her half-numb leg wobbled under her. But she ran across the debris-strewn floor as flashing spells and blue flames and fell shots hung suspended all around her. By the time she reached the doors, she was moving almost at full speed despite the cramp threatening to take over her thigh.

Then she was out in the darkened hall, but Colonel Thomas was gone. *I won't find him like this.*

Falling out of enhanced speed, she stopped in the dark corridor and cocked her head. The echoing sounds of battle behind her overwhelmed everything else, but she dampened it with the activator and let her drow hearing pick up the rest.

Hurried footsteps came toward her from the branching corridor on her right. *There you are.*

Cheyenne took off running, following the sounds of the colonel's footsteps and his slightly labored breathing. Her steps hardly made a noise on the slick floor, then she skidded around the corner and saw the heel of the man's boot disappearing into a dark room at the end of the hall. *Gotcha.*

She ran after him and darted through the doorway. "Pretty sure this is a dead-end, Colonel."

Thomas fired two shots that cracked against the wall behind her head. The third hit the shield of dark light Cheyenne threw up in front of her and ricocheted. The bulb in the overhead light shattered and rained glass on the empty room.

The colonel squeezed off another shot like an idiot and almost took himself out of the game when the bullet bounced off her shield and struck the wall behind him two inches from his head.

Cheyenne grinned behind her shield. "You should probably stop."

Thomas fired again, but the only sound was the click of an empty chamber. The man snarled at his weapon and tossed it across the room with a clatter. Then he spread his arms and glared at her. "If you're gonna kill me, now's your chance."

"Tempting." Cheyenne waved the shield down and cocked her head. "But not why I'm here."

"Well, I'm not stepping down from anything." Colonel Thomas lifted his chin and took a deep breath. "So you either fight me and kill me, or you're wasting both our time."

She gave him a mocking grimace. "I mean, if you fight anything like you aim your weapon, you don't have a chance."

What came next happened all at once. Colonel Thomas' eyes darted to the dark corner behind Cheyenne on the right. Her activator blared to life with a warning alarm and flashing lights. She felt a shift in the air behind her, the hair on the back of her neck rising and tingling even as she spun toward the corner.

The massive war machine that had waited silently in half-activated stealth mode moved faster than any other machine she'd seen. Two segmented, whirring tentacles that looked way too much like an in-between monster swept across the room toward her. Cheyenne got off two crackling black energy spheres before the tentacles connected with her chest and knocked her against the wall.

She roared in surprise and pain, pinned against the wall with her feet four inches off the floor. Slapping both hands on the whirring tentacle arms, Cheyenne summoned the blazing black fire across every inch of her skin before she formed the coherent thought to do so. The tentacle jerked beneath her hand, crushing her harder against the wall even as her black fire raced up the metallic appendage to the war machine's body, which was coming to life with blinking lights and an animalistic groan.

Before the thing fell away from her under her attack, it activated a line of opening panels against Cheyenne's chest. A pain worse than anything she'd known, worse than Venga's surprise potion dose, worse than the blight poison spreading through her, worse than being crushed nearly to death by an in-between monster, shot into her chest and coursed through her entire body.

Her scream was the only thing in her awareness.

The next thing she knew, she was lying in a crumpled heap on the floor against the wall, the war machine's tentacle spasming and sparking beside her before falling still. The black flames racing up and down her body snuffed out. Cheyenne lay panting heavily under the spasming agony racing through her limbs and throbbing through her head. When the dart wounds in her shoulders and hip erupted in agonizing bursts under whatever the war machine had injected into her, her first reaction was to scream.

But no sound came out.

I can't move. Why the fuck can't I move?

Her racing pulse pounded in her ears, and no matter how hard she tried to roll over, open her mouth, or lift a finger, she was useless.

A low chuckle echoed around the dark, empty room, followed by slow footsteps drawing closer. Then two black boots streaked with the ghost of a reflection from the soft light in the hallway stopped three feet from Cheyenne's face.

With an overwhelming amount of effort, she managed to lift her gaze up the length of Colonel Thomas' legs until they settled somewhere close to his face.

Fuck you.

She could only think it at this point. The rest of her didn't work.

The colonel reached back beneath the hem of his jacket and drew a second service pistol from the cross-body harness hidden there. The weapon hung at his side as he cocked his head and studied the immobilized drow halfling lying in front of him. "They told me it would be agonizing."

Cheyenne glared at him, refusing to blink. Her panting breath quickened only a little beneath the blazing pain coursing through her, not nearly as strong as her fury.

"I'm sure it won't surprise you to hear I've been watching you for some time now, Cheyenne. Of course, I had no idea who you were in the beginning, and I didn't really give a shit. Major Carson handles the underlings fine, or at least he did. You made a splash when you helped the agents technically under my command unravel the work my associates were so driven to complete. You caught my attention."

A choking sound burst from her throat as she struggled to move. *As soon as this shit runs its course, I'm gonna rip his head off.*

"You won't be able to fight this." Colonel Thomas lifted his pistol to wave it back and forth over her body, pointing at her with the barrel of his firearm like it was a baton. "I know you probably still believe you can fight this, but the Bull's Head made it specifically for you. Obviously, I didn't know they worked with race-tracking explosives before this, but Welyk assured me the injection you received would take you out of the game. It's very impressive what you can do. Even more impressive, I think, is the fact that those magicals managed to lock onto your magical signature, as they call it, to manufacture what's most likely the only thing that can take you down."

The man squatted in front of her and leaned forward with a sneer.

"You're too rash. Quick to fight off one of these machines in that disgusting marketplace they built underground. You sealed your fate by trying to be a hero. Your kind doesn't deserve what you've taken from us. I plan to take it back." He cocked his head and gave her a mocking frown. "What's wrong? Can't think of anything to say?"

I'll fucking kill you. What came out instead was a wheezing moan, but her lips did finally move.

Colonel Thomas widened his eyes and nodded. "You must be fighting hard in there to even get that much out."

Cheyenne's foot twitched against the floor.

The man glanced at her foot, then shrugged. "Major Carson said you healed quickly."

"You…" Cheyenne swallowed, which encouraged her. *Here we go.* "You have…no idea…" Forcing all her willpower into it, she managed to shake her head a quarter of an inch.

"Oh, you're here to prove us all wrong, aren't you?"

Jesus. And I thought fighting Ba'rael was bad.

Clicking his tongue, the man shook his head and let out a humorless chuckle. "I don't think you'll heal very quickly from a bullet to the head."

Fuck. Cheyenne struggled to move, but all she managed was a quick jerk of her entire body.

Colonel Les Thomas stepped back and raised his pistol to level it at Cheyenne's head. "You did your best, Miss Summerlin. It wasn't enough."

"Fuck you."

The gunshot cracked through the room and brought a new level of searing pain through her head. *I'm not supposed to feel this.*

Cheyenne groaned, clenching her eyes tightly against the high-pitched ringing in her ears and the pain and the fact that she still couldn't fucking move. Through the muted echo of her ringing ears, she heard a sharp crack, and something heavy thumped to the ground. Then she opened her eyes and found herself staring at Colonel Thomas' face on the floor next to hers.

"What?" She looked up as Sir stepped the rest of the way into the room. "You."

Sir holstered his pistol and dropped into a squat beside the colonel to check the man's pulse. His upper lip twitched when he found it, then he stood again and stepped away from both bodies on the ground. "Yeah. Me."

Cheyenne swallowed thickly, growling a little before she managed to say more than two words at once. "Change of heart?"

"You could say that. And now I guess we're on the same goddamn side, halfling. Wasn't sure I wanted to be, but I'm pretty sure Alice would stop talking to me forever if she found out I didn't do everything I could to grow a fucking conscience."

"Or a pair of balls." Cheyenne let out a croaking laugh.

"Fair enough." Sir sniffed and folded his arms. "I'm trying to do what's right, Cheyenne. Hard to figure that shit out when everyone's got as many goddamn secrets as a fat-ass catfish has whiskers. You were right, though. Les wasn't who I thought he was."

"I know I was right." Cheyenne finally managed to move, which was only a slight roll off her side until her upper back and her head thumped into the wall. "You should listen to me more."

"Yeah, I said you were right, okay? You win." Sir's mustache bristled beneath his deepening frown. "So why the fuck are you just lying there?"

A raw chuckle escaped her. "I know, right? 'Cause I can't fucking move."

CHAPTER FORTY-EIGHT

In the middle of the chaotic fight still raging through the reception hall, the doors at the back behind the Bull's Head's stash of war-machine parts and control panels and crates burst open.

"The deathflame's coming for you, fuckers!" Lumil let out a shrieking battle cry and sprinted into the room, red runes already spinning wildly around her fists. She dropped to her knees and slid beneath an orc's launched attack of blazing darts of orange light and brought her fist up into his groin. The orc howled and dropped halfway to his knees before Lumil's other fist cracked into the underside of his jaw. "Ha!"

Byrd cackled, spit flying out of his mouth as he launched heavy columns of green flames at the unsuspecting magicals turning around in surprise. "Assholes don't know what hit 'em!"

Up on the second-story balcony, Ember laughed in surprise and shot a stream of violet light at one of the last flying war machines trying to get close enough to attack her. "It's about fucking time."

Beside her, Tate finished tying a makeshift tourniquet around his thigh, which two flying machines had mashed up pretty badly. He cocked his head when he heard Lumil's and Byrd's roaring shouts and the screams of Bull's Head loyalists meeting their red fists and his green fire. "Did you know they were coming?"

"Kinda gave up hope on that one." Ember darted back from the edge of the glassless window when a snaking metallic arm shot up over the ledge to pull itself up. She blasted it away with more violet light and shrugged. "Guess they came through."

Yurik squeezed off more shots with his fell rifle, then stopped. He jerked his head away from the scope with wide eyes. "Holy shit."

"What?"

Ember peered over the edge of the balcony to see a zigzagging streak of silver light blazing across the reception hall. Maleshi's snarling face appeared in brief bursts as every loyalist she met screamed and choked and dropped to the ground. Sprays of blood erupted left and right as the Bull's Head magicals met General Hi'et's fury and the sharpened edges of her silver claws.

Jamal, Bhandi, and Todd paused in picking off the loyalists coming after them. Bhandi ripped off her helmet when Maleshi's silver lightning streaks darted to their side of the reception hall. "What the actual fuck?"

The general stopped beside her with a snarl. "You're welcome."

"Watch it!" Todd lifted his fell laser cannon in both hands again as the war machine with a lasered-off wingtip groaned to life.

Maleshi darted away from them in a burst of light, and a second later, she was on top of the flying machine, slashing it to ribbons with her claws. Bhandi slapped a gloved hand on Todd's laser weapon and lowered it back down in front of him, shooting him a warning look.

"Yeah, okay." The human agent shrugged and let Maleshi do her thing.

In under a minute, the general had slashed through all the remaining working war machines and Bull's Head loyalists, except for one. Welyk struggled against the pulsing silver ties of the nightstalker's magic that had secured his arms behind his back and cinched his ankles. "What the fuck do you want, Hi'et?" he snarled.

Maleshi looked down at him with a raised eyebrow. "A chat. Things are changing, *dae'bruj*."

"You don't know what you're talking about. When the Crown gets—"

"The Crown doesn't want anything to do with you, shriveled-up shit. He has plenty of more important things on his plate than listening to your pathetic excuses."

Welyk stopped struggling, his yellow eyes wide as he craned his neck at the nightstalker. "He?"

"The Ironbreak. Didn't you hear? Now shut up before I change my mind." Maleshi stalked away from him and looked around the destroyed room littered with war-machine parts, body parts, and blood. "Where's Cheyenne?"

Ember pointed at the open doors behind Jamal, Bhandi, and Todd. "She went after the colonel that way."

The remaining FRoE agents who'd shown up with Colonel Thomas tried to sneak away. Bhandi smacked the side of her weapon and lifted it as it powered up again with a whine. "Don't move, assholes. You're not walking away from this clean."

The human agents stopped and glared at her. Jamal raised one of his fell rifles and grunted. "Weapons down, dipshits."

One by one, the other agents' firearms hit the floor, and they backed up against the wall under the direction of Bhandi's fell pistol.

"Hmm." Maleshi watched the scene with indifference, then her silver eyes narrowed. "You'll probably wanna join me, Ember."

"Yep." The fae turned to Tate, then glanced at Rhynehart. "As soon as I know she's okay, I'll come back to help you guys."

Sitting with his back against the wall and looking paler than usual, Rhynehart snorted. "What are you gonna do about a bullet in my shoulder?"

"You'll see. Just two minutes." Ember turned and floated down the hall to the dark stairwell in the back. She emerged again on the ground floor as Maleshi marched past her.

"Did you see where she went?"

"Not after she left the massacre back there." Ember looked over her shoulder at the open doors.

"I'm in here!" Cheyenne's croaking shout was loud enough for them to hear. Maleshi pointed at the branching hallway on their right, and they hurried that way.

Sir stepped out of the room at the end of the hall and froze when he saw the nightstalker woman and the fae floating beside her. He lifted both hands in surrender and slowly shook his head. "Whatever you're thinking, I didn't do shit to her."

"Oh, yeah? That's very reassuring." Ember glared at him and floated past Maleshi. "Cheyenne?"

"Come on in, Em."

Ember reached the open door and stopped in front of Colonel Thomas' body. Then she saw Cheyenne sprawled against the wall and the deactivated, tentacled war machine lying in a broken heap in the corner. "What the fuck?"

"I know."

"Jesus, Cheyenne! I thought you were smart enough not to go running into a trap by yourself!"

"Yep. Me too. There's a first time for everything, right?" A weak chuckle escaped the halfling, and she grimaced. "But now you're here, and I could use a little help."

"Okay. With what?" Ember floated cautiously around the colonel's body to approach her friend.

"As far as I know, that machine pumped me full of something that pretty much wiped out all my magic. And motor function. Couldn't talk there for a while, but that's obviously improved."

"Oh, my God." Ember let out a heavy sigh and sank down to sit beside Cheyenne in a flash of violet light. "If you can't move, how'd he get on the floor?"

"That was me." Sir leaned against the doorframe and shrugged. "Surprises all around, huh?"

Ember frowned at him, then glanced at Les Thomas. "Is he dead?"

"Ha. I fucking wish." Sir's mustache bristled as he glared at his superior. "Wasn't a fatal shot, but he's gonna have a hard time figuring out which one hurts worse, the bullet hole in his side or the massive concussion."

"Congratulations," Cheyenne muttered. "Can we focus on the person who needs healing?"

"Sorry." Ember turned back to her friend and looked her over. "So, I'm drawing out poison or something?"

"Whatever you can, Em. I'd like to move and use my magic at the very least, but I'll take whatever."

"Right." Placing one hand on Cheyenne's shoulder and the other on the halfling's waist, Ember took a deep breath and closed her eyes. Warm golden light bloomed beneath her palms, and she breathed slowly. "Oh."

"Oh, what?"

"Oh, I can feel it." Ember tilted her head. "Like a giant off-switch."

"Yep, that's about right. Please tell me you can turn it back on."

"That's what I'm trying to do, so shut up and let me."

Maleshi snorted and folded her arms. Sir quickly stepped away from the doorframe and backed up into the hall, staring at the nightstalker he hadn't known was right beside him. The general jerked her chin at him and wiggled her eyebrows. "How's it goin'?"

He glared at her, then looked at the ceiling. "This whole fucking day is nuts."

Ember's hands trembled slightly as her healing magic did its work in Cheyenne's body. A smoky gray film rose from her prone form and dissolved quickly in the air. She coughed a few times, groaned, and pushed herself up off the floor to sit against the wall. "Thanks, Em."

The fae let out a slow breath and opened her eyes. "That was a lot."

"And you're good at what you do." Cheyenne sucked in a sharp breath and clenched her eyes shut.

"What's wrong?"

"Pain." A wry chuckle escaped Cheyenne, but it cut off abruptly under the growing pain of her first attempt to stand. "Lots of it still."

Ember frowned. "But I got it all out."

"I think this was a preexisting condition." Pulling down on the collar of her shirt, Cheyenne exposed one of her shoulder wounds and the black streaking lines of blight spreading away from it. "Fuck."

"Oh, my God." Ember leaned toward her friend's shoulder. "That looks really bad."

"Keeps getting worse, doesn't it." Cheyenne lifted her shirt back into place and gritted her teeth. "At least we can check one of the things off the to-do list now."

"I'm so sorry." Ember floated back up and offered her friend a hand. "I didn't know I'd make it worse."

"How could you?" Cheyenne grimaced again when Ember helped her to her feet. "It's not your fault."

"I'm not helping, either."

"Ember." Cheyenne dipped her head and held her friend's gaze. "I'd rather have longer black streaks in my skin than be paralyzed, okay? Being paralyzed is how I almost got shot in the head. I'll be fine."

She gave Ember's shoulder a light, reassuring squeeze, then stepped past Colonel Thomas' body without looking at him. "So, what's the plan for taking out the trash?"

Sir looked at her sharply, then glanced at the colonel's body. "One that makes me wanna tear what's left of my hair out. I'd love to kill the fucker, but we need to do this by the book if we're gonna keep this from happening again."

"You mean, you're not into turning on your boss just for fun?"

"I think your humor's been paralyzed too, halfling."

"Whatever. For the record, I agree with you. By the book." Cheyenne reached into her coat pocket and pulled out the darktongue injection canister.

"What the fuck is that?"

"Medicine. Why does everyone suddenly give a shit?"

Ember floated out of the room and frowned. "That might be the last one."

"Yeah, I know, Em." Cheyenne lifted the bottom of her shirt and pressed the canister against the side of her stomach. It clicked and hissed, and she closed her eyes. "I need a minute."

"I swear on the body lying in that room, halfling, if you're fucking juicing—"

"It's not steroids!" Ember shouted at the same time that Cheyenne growled it out.

Sir grimaced so hard that his upper lip lifted to reveal his top teeth. "Calm the fuck down, will ya? Christ. You magicals have anybody who can carry Colonel Fucktard outta here, or do I need to go hunt down a stretcher?"

Maleshi chuckled, making the man jump and stumble away from her in surprise. "I can remove him for you, but you might not see him again."

"Then forget it." Waving her off and trying to look casual about it, Sir pressed his back against the wall and pulled out his cell phone. "I'll make some calls."

Cheyenne reached out to steady herself against the doorframe as the hallway spun all around her. *I would've thought I'd built up a tolerance to this stuff by now.* "How's everybody out there?"

"Well, I'm here." Maleshi spread her arms. "How do you think everyone's doing?"

"So, all the loyalists are dead."

"All but one, kid. I've got some pretty special plans for Welyk if I do say so myself."

With a deep breath, Cheyenne opened her eyes and blinked off the spinning warm and fuzzy daze from the darktongue serum. "What about everyone on our side? I mean, besides Rhynehart."

Ember flicked her gaze to Sir and slowly shook her head. "That was fucked up, man."

"It was me trying to buy some goddamn time." Sir grunted. "He's not dead, and it fucking worked."

"Tate had his leg ripped up by some machine bugs," Ember said, turning back to Cheyenne. "He's trying to laugh it off, but I don't think he's going anywhere on his own."

"Okay." Cheyenne ran a hand through her bone-white hair and took another deep breath. *Starting to feel like me again. Let's get going on this.* "I guess you better go take a look at them both."

"Wow." Ember laughed and playfully rolled her eyes. She floated past Cheyenne and gave her friend an exasperated look as she headed down the hall. "I pulled poison out of you that was tailored to your magic. I'm quite sure I can heal a bullet hole and a mangled thigh, thanks."

The fae took off and disappeared around the corner to the reception hall, and Cheyenne looked at Maleshi. "Glad you showed up to the party, by the way."

"Well, you know me, kid. I can't let everyone else have all the fun." The general glanced at Sir and shot him a wink.

The man vigorously shook his head and got busy making whatever calls he'd said he'd make.

Cheyenne pushed herself off the doorframe and headed slowly down the hall, finding her legs again after the darktongue serum's initial hit wore off most of the way. Maleshi fell in line beside her with her hands clasped behind her back. "I also showed up because the idiot twins begged me to help them out."

"What?"

"Apparently, they spent an unconscionable amount of time arguing over whose GPS worked better and whether the address you gave them was the right one in the right city."

Cheyenne snorted.

"I know. They're useless for pretty much everything that doesn't have to do with bashing in skulls and tossing magic around."

"So you ported them here last-minute and figured you'd join in just because."

"I ported them in last-minute and let General Hi'et unleash what she'd been waiting a very long time to unleash on the Earthside Bull's Head." Maleshi glanced down at the cuffs of her jacket sleeves, which were covered in sprays of drying loyalist blood. A brief flash of silver light illuminated at her fingertips and the bloodstains disappeared. "If I had to guess, I'd say we've now collectively taken out at least eighty percent of the bastards who still think they're answering to the Spider on the O'gúl throne. Maybe eight-five, but that might be stretching it."

"Well, it's a start." Cheyenne stuck her hands in her coat pockets as the doors to the reception hall came into view. "We still have a lot of cleanup to do after this."

Maleshi chuckled and passed the halfling on their way through the doors. "Piece of cake, kid. I can clear away my messes almost as quickly as I make them."

Yeah, wish I could say the same.

CHAPTER FORTY-NINE

After Ember's successful healing on Rhynehart and Tate, they all came back downstairs to the main level of the building to join the rest of their team, the goblins, and Maleshi. Bhandi jerked her chin at Tate and Yurik when they stepped through the double doors. "Looks like you get another battle scar to show off on poker night, huh?"

Tate slapped his newly healed thigh and grinned. "No scar. That fae knows her shit."

Ember shook her head, though she couldn't keep a small smile off her face. "She also knows how not to get shredded by giant flying beetles, but I guess that's beside the point, huh?"

"Ha!" Bhandi pointed at the fae and grinned. "You're funny." The next second, both hands were on the grip of her pistol as she swung it toward the FRoE agents she'd kept pressed up against the wall. Her grin vanished. "Just because I'm laughing, it doesn't mean I've forgotten about you. Don't even think about it."

One of the human agents with a shaved head glanced around and frowned. "About what?"

"Whatever the fuck you're thinking about. It's that simple."

Rhynehart stepped up beside Cheyenne and let out a low whistle as he gazed at the loyalist bodies and the shredded machine parts all over the reception hall. "Hell of a sting."

"Right." She shot him a sidelong glance. "Little bit of an improvement over the first one, huh?"

"For you, maybe. I'm the one who got shot this time." He nudged her arm with his elbow and glanced down at his open hand and the blood-smeared bullet resting there. "But I did get a souvenir."

"Nice. I didn't have that luxury, or a fae to pull it out of me half an hour later. I think you drew the lucky straw here."

"Whatever." Rhynehart shoved his hand and the bullet into his pocket and stepped aside at the sound of a dozen pairs of footsteps marching down the hall toward them.

Sir appeared outside the doors first and pointed down the hall on the other side. "First right. Room at the end of the hall. He's out cold, but if he wakes up and starts making threats, he's already got a soft spot on his skull. I won't ask if you had to use it."

Two of the men in dark-gray fatigues nodded and took off down the hall to grab Colonel Thomas.

"Who are those guys?" Cheyenne muttered.

Rhynehart shrugged. "FRoE MPs, more or less."

"You guys have your own police?"

"Hey, I'm not included in that group anymore, but yeah. Usually, they show up when somebody gets a little rowdy on base. Haven't seen them in the field for a long time."

Cheyenne shrugged. "First time for everything, I guess. Hopefully, it's the last time too."

She looked and caught Sir's gaze as he stepped through the doors, with the rest of the MPs in dark-gray fatigues behind him.

"This is what I mean by cleanup, halfling." Sir glanced at the MPs and gestured at the agents guarded by a snarling Bhandi and one of Jamal's casually aimed rifles. "When you get back to base, hold 'em on the north end. I don't want anybody talking about this until we have a few things sorted out."

"Major." The closest MP nodded and pulled a pair of handcuffs off his belt as he approached Bhandi and Jamal. "We'll take it from here."

"Great." Bhandi wiggled her eyebrows at the guy. "You're welcome."

"Wait a minute." The bald human agent leaned forward as his hand was jerked behind his back and cuffed by another FRoE member who could've been his drinking buddy on any other day. "Sir, we were following orders. *You* were following orders! Hey!"

He struggled against the MP's grip on his arm as the other man dragged him to the doors. "Where's Colonel Thomas? This is ridiculous. He said no one would touch us. You can't do this!"

Sir eyed the man. "Colonel Thomas took a bullet and is gonna wake up in the north end, probably in a holding cell next to yours, until the board decides what to do with all of you."

"We were following orders!"

"Orders don't mean shit from someone who's endangering the entire planet, fuckwad," Sir spat, leaning into the agent's face as the MP jerked him to the doors.

The other agents were cuffed and led out also, though they put up a little more of a struggle. One of them got the butt of a service pistol to the head and dropped like a sack of potatoes. That shut the rest of them up.

Rhynehart folded his arms and looked at Sir. "First time I've seen someone defy a colonel's orders and end up at the top of the food chain."

"Yeah. I'm a lucky fucker like that." Sir glared at him. "What are you staring at?"

"The man who shot me." Rhynehart slapped his healed shoulder. "And someone whose bullshit I don't have to put up with anymore."

Sir scoffed and spread his arms. "You wanna shoot me back, is that it? Think we'll be even after that? I'm so goddamn tired of listening to you whine like a fucking wounded puppy, Rhynehart."

"Fuck you."

Sir jerked his head back in surprise. "You think I'm gonna let that fly? You should be thanking me."

"Okay, both of you need to stop." Cheyenne stepped between them and shook her head. "You can kiss and make up later, okay? Or not. Whatever. Right now, we need to clean the rest of this shit up."

The reception hall filled with blazing flashes of silver light as Maleshi darted back and forth across the room. One by one, the Bull's Head bodies she'd shredded disappeared from the blood-streaked floor. Then the clink of metal parts echoed around the walls.

"Goddamn!" Todd slapped a hand to his head as he tried to keep his eyes on the general, who was working at enhanced speed. "How the hell does she do that?"

"Nightstalkers." Bhandi punched the human agent in the shoulder and snorted. "I'm guessing you've never seen one before, huh?"

Yurik burst out laughing. "She hadn't either until a few days ago, man. Don't let her say it like she's an expert."

Bhandi scowled at the muscular goblin and shook her head. "Dick."

"She can't do that!" Sir stepped forward, tried to point at Maleshi's darting form, then gave up and pointed at Cheyenne instead. "This is evidence. Make her stop."

"Yeah, I'm smarter than that. But if you wanna give it a shot, go ahead."

He clenched his fists and roared, his face trembling. "We need this shit, halfling. I swear if you don't get your creepy fuck of a furry-ass friend to cut it out, I'll—"

Maleshi stopped in front of him in a burst of silver light and grinned. "You'll what?"

"Fuck!" Sir staggered away from her.

"Really, though. I'd love to hear what you come up with."

Sir blinked quickly and stared at the now-empty reception hall behind the general. "This whole goddamn shitshow isn't worth a flying fuck if we don't have those machines!"

Maleshi tilted her head and nodded slowly. "You're the one who's always screaming over the phone, aren't you?"

Sir's eyes widened as he glared at the nightstalker, his entire body trembling.

"Jesus. Relax." Cheyenne shooed Maleshi off, and the general chuckled as she walked casually past the livid major. "I got the whole meeting on camera, remember?"

Sir let out a long, low growl, and his rage seemed to seep out of him with it. "The fucking video."

"Yeah. If there's anything else we need to clean up this mess beyond this right here, I'll let you know."

Glaring blankly across the room, Sir let out a heavy sigh. "The cleanup crew's already on their way."

"See? Taken care of." Cheyenne scanned the options brought up by her activator and selected two simple, clear-cut commands. "And you know what? I'll go ahead and send that fun little homemade video out to the rest of your superior officers right now. Then we're done with it, and it's out of the way."

"Wait a minute." The major spun toward her. "Hold off on that, at least until we're off the premises."

She shrugged. "Already done."

For a moment, he glared at her with unblinking beady brown eyes. Then his lip twitched, and he grunted. "How the fuck did you do that?"

"Grabbed their secure emails with everything else off the colonel's computer. The rest is O'gúl tech you wouldn't understand even if I took the time to explain it to you. Nothing personal, Major. You're a human."

"Uh-huh." Sir bit his lower lip to keep from bursting out with whatever crude, senseless diatribe he so obviously wanted to spray at her.

Cheyenne fought back a laugh. "Aren't you gonna call me a weird-ass name and make ridiculous threats you can't follow through on?"

"Aw, does the halfling want a goddamn cookie?" He sneered and flipped her the bird.

"Close, I guess." With a nod, she turned away from him and headed to Rhynehart and the rest of their team. "Oh, and thanks for the backup, by the way."

"Don't let it go to your head, halfling." Sir still clenched his fists at his sides, but at least his head didn't look like it was going to explode. "You can pay me back later."

"Nope." Cheyenne turned back to him with a grin and spread her arms. "That was the start of you and me being even. Sir."

Bhandi and Yurik sniggered at the major's dumbfounded expression and the fact that he had absolutely nothing to say. Fortunately for Major Carson, his phone rang, and he had an excuse to turn away from the agents more or less under his command so he could answer the call.

"So, what now?" Tate asked, slipping his head and shoulder through the strap on his rifle.

"Well, the cleanup crew's on the way, apparently. The FRoE board members are probably pulling out the bowls of popcorn to watch that video of Colonel Thomas fucking himself over, and no one has access to those war machines anymore."

"Come on, kid." Lumil marched toward them, spreading her arms. "Not no one. Where do you think Maleshi chucked all that shit, huh?"

Byrd snorted. "I don't know why you're so happy about it."

"That's because you're a moron. We won, moron."

The goblin man leaned toward her with wide eyes and tapped his forehead. "If you're so smart, you think about where Maleshi dumped it all."

"In the fucking warehouse."

Byrd blinked. "Yeah. And where do we live right now?"

"Damnit, Maleshi!" Lumil whirled to the doors through which the general had disappeared. Then she stopped to point at Cheyenne. "Next time, we'll be on time. Or something."

"Not if you keep putting in the wrong address," Byrd shouted as he stormed out after her. "It's called a zip code, not an actual code you need to fucking unscramble. I don't get it."

Cheyenne and Ember exchanged quick glances as the goblins' bickering faded down the hall. Jamal chuckled. "I like them."

"Wow." Cheyenne blinked at him in surprise and couldn't hold back a laugh. "I think you're the first."

"They're always like that, aren't they?" Yurik asked. "That seems like a regular thing."

"Unfortunately, yeah." Cheyenne shrugged. "They can fight, at least."

No one else had anything to say, and the reception hall fell silent. Sir turned to face them and pulled his cell phone away from his ear. "What the fuck are you shit-for-brains staring at? Get outta here."

"Guess we have our orders." Todd hefted the laser cannon to his shoulder, jamming the lever in the process and powering the thing up with a loud, squealing whine.

"Fuck, Todd!"

"Whoa, whoa. Watch it!"

The magical agents ducked away from the weapon and scowled at him. Jamal grunted and plucked the laser cannon out of Todd's grip before slamming the activating lever back down. The green glow at the weapon's head faded quickly, and the ogre tucked the fell cannon under his arm. "You're done."

Todd scoffed. "Fine, but that thing was fucking awesome. Later." He jerked his chin at Cheyenne and Ember, then shot the rest of the agents a wide-eyed look. "You need an invitation or what?"

Shaking their heads and grabbing the rest of their gear, Bhandi,

Tate, Yurik, and Jamal followed their human fifth out the open doors. "Next time you need a bunch of weird shit blown up, Cheyenne, you know who to call."

"Yep. Thanks."

"Oh, hey." Bhandi spun around and spread her arms. "Victory drinks?"

"Not tonight."

"Yeah, whatever." Laughing, the troll woman hurried after the rest of them.

Ember smiled. "No victory drinks, huh?"

"I think I need to lay off everything for a while, Em." Cheyenne ran a hand through her hair and turned around to glance at Rhynehart. The man stood with his arms folded, staring at Sir as the major finished his phone call. "I feel like I've had too much shit pumped into me over the last few days. Until I get the worst of it out, I think I'm gonna take it easy."

They both glanced down at Cheyenne's shoulder wounds. Ember nodded. "I think that's a pretty good call."

"Rhynehart."

"Yeah."

"Keep me updated."

He raised his eyebrows at her, the only expression he could manage. "You too."

Cheyenne nodded, then she and Ember stepped into the hall and turned in the direction of Lumil and Byrd bickering at each other.

"Okay, this might sound a little weird," Ember said, "'cause I know it's totally different. But this felt like an anticlimactic victory."

"Maybe because you got to fight this time." Cheyenne shook her head. "One-on-one battles *are* different."

"Yeah, maybe." They turned the corner, the goblins' voices growing louder ahead of them. "What's gonna happen with Rhynehart?"

"I have no idea, and I don't care."

Ember stared at her friend as they moved down the hall. "Bullshit."

Cheyenne snorted. "What? How is that bullshit?"

"You care. I bet you could get him his job back."

"Oh, sure. 'Cause I'll have a lot of say in how things are run, huh?"

Ember grinned. "Yep. You will have a lot of say. That was the plan, right?"

"To say who gets their old job back? Maybe." Cheyenne shrugged. "I was thinking more along the lines of revamping the whole reservation experience for the refugees. You know, bringing them activators, teaching Earthside magicals how to use them."

With a burst of laughter, Ember shook her head. "Seriously? You wanna keep teaching?"

"You know, I think I might be a better teacher with O'gúl tech than undergrad."

"I don't doubt it. Before you become Professor Royal Drow, though, you should get Rhynehart his job back."

Cheyenne snorted. "I'll think about it. If he even wants it after all this."

The metal door at the end of the hall jerked open, and Lumil poked her head inside. "You guys comin', or what? It's not like we have all night."

"What the hell are you talking about?" Byrd called from somewhere outside. "We don't have shit else to do."

"They don't know that." Lumil whirled on him and let go of the door, forgetting about it altogether. "You know what? I'm sick of your constant whining."

The door clicked shut, and only muffled voices made it through. Ember stared down the rest of the hall and shook her head. "I'm so glad we don't have to drive back to Richmond with them."

"Trust me, one car ride with those two is more than anyone deserves in a lifetime."

"And Persh'al was stuck with them for how long?"

"Centuries."

CHAPTER FIFTY

They had Maleshi port them back to Rhynehart's house to pick up Matthew's car before they headed home.

"Thanks, General." Cheyenne turned to her and spread her arms in a mocking bow. "Always a pleasure."

"Uh-huh." The nightstalker stood in the middle of the residential street in her human illusion, arms folded, and watched Cheyenne walk quickly to the driver's side door. "Cheyenne."

"Yeah." Cheyenne caught the keys Ember tossed over the roof of the car and pressed the unlock button on the key fob. "What's up?"

"How you feelin'?"

"Definitely not like I got pumped with magically tailored poison, almost got shot in the head, and had to spend five minutes in a room with Sir while paralyzed, so I'm fine."

Maleshi shot Ember a questioning glance. The fae looked between them, then decided opening the car door and slipping into the passenger seat was the best option. "Good to see ya."

The door shut behind her, and she pretended to be seriously involved in her cell phone.

Cheyenne blinked. "Someone's ready to call it a night."

"Or maybe someone doesn't want to say something she knows she should, but that will make her friend a little pissed because it's not good news. And that friend doesn't like anybody worrying about her."

"Hmm." Cheyenne shrugged. "I don't know. You'd have to ask her."

With a quick glance at the mostly dark houses lining the street, Maleshi stepped over to Cheyenne and stopped at the hood of the Mercedes. "I heard you both say things were looking a lot worse."

"Come on, Maleshi."

"How much worse?"

Cheyenne scoffed and looked at the street instead of at the general's concerned frown. "Just a little."

"I wanna see."

"No, it's okay."

Maleshi crossed the space between them in a flash of silver light and tugged down the collar of Cheyenne's shirt.

"What the hell?" Cheyenne smacked the general's hand away. "Not cool."

"Neither is that." When the general shook her head, it was barely perceptible. "If that gets any worse, I want you to call me."

"I'm fine."

"For now. None of us know how long that's gonna last, kid. If it gets worse, we're making the crossing again. If Venga can't figure out how to heal that, I will."

Cheyenne sighed. "I still have to figure out how to clear the rest of that curse off my mom. I'm not crossing over until I know she's in the clear."

"I'm sure it's occurred to you that you might not make it that long."

They stared at each other, then Cheyenne laughed bitterly and nodded once. "I'm not gonna thank you for the pep talk, 'cause that was shit. But thanks for showing up to help with the Bull's Head."

"Cheyenne."

"Yeah, I heard everything you said, and I'll make sure you know if I'm dying." Cheyenne jerked open the car door and slumped behind the wheel. She started the engine and waited for the general to quickly cast another portal, glance up and down the street, and disappear through it.

"Sorry," Ember muttered.

"I mean, you didn't throw me under the bus."

"I didn't make that any less awkward, either."

"True."

Ember glanced at her friend as Cheyenne pulled away from the curb to take them home to Richmond. "You'll be okay."

"I know."

"We'll figure out how to get that shit out of you. I promise."

"I know, Em."

"And whatever we have to do to take care of your mom, I'm right there with you. Then we'll make the crossing and fuck shit up over there too if that's what it takes."

Cheyenne shot her friend a sidelong glance. "Thanks, Em."

"You're welcome."

They got back to their apartment building a little after 10:00. Cheyenne's barb-electrocuted thigh twitched every few steps when they left the elevator on the top floor and headed down the hall. *I'm out of darktongue, so it's either power through with nothing or power through with salve after this. Awesome options.*

She handed Ember their neighbor's car keys and shrugged. "You took 'em. Makes sense you get to give 'em back."

"I'm not expecting a thank you either way." They stopped in front of Matthew's front door, and Ember knocked firmly.

The door opened almost immediately, and Matthew Thomas stared at them with wide eyes. "What happened?"

Cheyenne and Ember exchanged glances. *We definitely look like we were in an explosive fight.* "Just a normal Monday night, Matt."

His nostrils flared, and he stared at Ember. "Please tell me my car wasn't involved."

She gave him a tight smile and tossed his keys in a high arc so he'd have enough time to catch them. He did, then frowned at her. "Thanks for the car."

The fae spun without another word and floated quickly across the hall.

"Ember. Hold on."

"I wouldn't try anything right now." Cheyenne propped her hand on the doorframe to block him from running after her friend. "It's been a weird day."

Matthew sighed heavily and looked at her. "Obviously. Is she okay?"

"Yeah, don't worry. I'm the one who got her ass kicked. So, let me ask you something."

The front door to her apartment closed behind Ember, and Matthew chewed the inside of his cheek. "Okay."

"How close were you to your uncle before you found all the stuff that made you freak out about him?"

Her neighbor blinked quickly and stepped back. "I mean, fairly close. I thought. Why?"

Cheyenne shrugged. "You might be getting a phone call in the next few days. If the FRoE even allows the one phone call. Just a friendly heads-up, 'kay?" She tapped the doorframe twice, then turned around to head for her own front door.

It took until she got to the door for Matthew to mentally piece together what she'd said. "What do you mean, one phone call? What happened?"

"We made a deal, Matthew. Ask me tomorrow." She stepped inside and closed the door behind her without looking back. Then she pressed her back against the wall and let out a massive sigh. Matthew's door closed, and she turned the deadbolt. "That was rough."

"You mean giving him a heads-up that his uncle might be calling him from military prison or FRoE prison or wherever? Or the whole day?"

"I'm gonna blanket this over and say the whole day, Em. And I'm fucking glad it's over." Cheyenne had to fight extra hard not to stumble over her own feet on her way to the closest black leather recliner. She slumped into it with a groan and closed her eyes. "I can't even imagine what it would be like to go to sleep right now."

"Is it 'cause you feel a little bad about leaving him hanging like that?"

"Who, Matthew?"

"Yeah." Ember thumped her head against the couch cushion. "Because I do. Not saying it'll keep me up all night, but I mean, he's gotta be really confused."

"Yeah, I know." Cheyenne ran a hand through her hair, pulling out stray flecks of exploded metal, and something that like looked like a chip off some magical's claw. She grimaced and dusted it off her hand onto the floor. "We can't drop everything we're doing to comfort our confused neighbor, though. Not tonight. I gave him as much of a break as I could handle, and he'll have to wait for the rest."

"You did tell him to ask again tomorrow."

"I did. And we still have a lot of work ahead of us. Bianca and the curse. Dealing with whatever fallout comes after us when the FRoE board realizes that video is one-hundred-percent real. And whatever the hell's wrong with me." Cheyenne rubbed the back of her neck and closed her eyes. "It's never-ending."

"I mean, there *is* a bright side."

"Oh, really?"

"Yeah. You don't have to fight anyone to the death the next time you roll into Hangivol."

Cheyenne snorted. "There is that."

"And technically, no one's trying to kill you anymore on either side of the Border. You're in a safe zone."

"Safe zone."

"Yeah. I mean, I don't wanna jinx it or anything."

"Then don't jinx it, Em." Cheyenne grinned at her friend, and Ember pressed herself back against the couch with a frown. "What?"

"That was the smile of a lunatic." Ember raised an eyebrow. "I feel like I should ask if you're okay."

"Nothing I can't handle." Cheyenne clenched her jaw and swallowed. *So far.*

"But?"

"But everything fucking hurts." She reached into her coat pocket and pulled out the injection canister.

"Hey, maybe you should hold off on that."

Cheyenne lifted her shirt and jammed the end of the canister into her stomach below her ribs. Nothing happened.

"Well, at least we know that was the last one." She tossed the canister over the arm of the chair and raised her eyebrows. "I'm gonna go with the next best option, which is still pretty shitty."

"Okay, I'm a little worried about what that might be."

With a grunt, Cheyenne pushed up out of the chair, grabbed her backpack from off the floor beside the couch, and took it with her to her room. "Sticking with darktongue, Em. It's down to the salve now. If you hear me screaming, you'll know why."

"Do you want any help?"

"Nope."

"Seriously, Cheyenne. It might be better if you have—"

"Space and a room to myself. Good night, Em."

Ember bit her lower lip and stared after the halfling shuffling toward the other end of their apartment. "Night. Let me know if you need anything."

Cheyenne's bedroom door slammed shut. Ember nodded and turned on the couch, lifting her legs with a flash of purple light to stretch them out in front of her. Then she snatched the remote off the coffee table and pulled up the new show she'd started streaming.

"Yep. I'll be here doing my thing. Watching TV. Definitely not trying to listen to my best friend."

Cheyenne's erupting roar came through her bedroom door with perfect clarity before it died in a hiss and a low growl. Then came the clatter of a glass jar toppling onto the floor and rolling across the room.

Ember turned up the volume on the TV.

<hr>

When Cheyenne finished smearing the sticky white goo on the barb holes in her thigh and the black-streaked dart holes on her shoulders and hip, she let herself lie on the floor with her arms spread out at her sides. *Let it do its thing. Don't move.*

Her eyelids fluttered closed, and she had no idea how long she lay sprawled out like that in the semi-darkness of her room, lit only by the standing lamp shaped like an upside-down chandelier. When she felt like she could move again, she pulled her phone out of her back pocket and checked for new notifications.

No missed calls. No Eleanor or Bianca or L'zar trying to reach me for one more thing that went wrong. That's a plus.

Gritting her teeth, she rolled slowly onto her side and fought through the pain practically everywhere before staggering to her bed.

She kicked her shoes off, didn't bother undressing, and settled down on her bed in the least painful position she could manage. It wasn't remotely close to comfortable.

Here's to another night of awful fucking sleep. Still, I'll take endless pain over dreaming about my parents like that again.

CHAPTER FIFTY-ONE

Everything still hurt when Cheyenne woke the next morning, but it wasn't nearly as bad. With a groan, she slapped the bedside table until she found her phone. The light of the screen was way too bright.

Nine thirty? Holy shit.

She pushed up off the comforter and sat there for who knew how long, staring at the floor. Then her phone buzzed in her hand with an incoming text from Ember.

If you're not dead, I made quiche.

Cheyenne snorted and grimaced at the pain even that sent through her head. *This is gonna be a long day.* She pushed off the bed and moved painfully toward her bedroom door. It opened silently, and she blinked against the morning light spilling through the north-facing wall of windows on the right. "We need to get some curtains or something."

"Oh, good. You're still breathing. And walking and talking." Ember looked up from the quiche fresh out of the oven on the center island and shot Cheyenne two thumbs-up, grinning. "You still eat, right?"

"Only one way to find out, but I'm gonna take a shower first. Maybe that'll help."

"Sure. If you pass out in there again, do you want me to come in before or after you burn yourself to Goth-lobster status?"

"Very funny. I'm not gonna pass out."

Ember set a slice of quiche on a plate and licked steaming egg off her finger. "So, after. Got it."

Cheyenne rolled her eyes and went into the bathroom to start the water and let it heat up. She got a quick glimpse of her wounded shoulders in the mirror when she peeled off her shirt and forced herself not to look any closer. *It's not gonna make you feel better, and it's not gonna heal the stupid things. One issue at a time.*

Stepping under the steaming water was only hard until she was all the way under it. Compared to the agony of being poisoned by the tentacled war machine or even to all the darktongue salve the night before, near-boiling water streaming over her was nothing, and it helped the worst of the pain in her hip and shoulders smooth out into something that felt more manageable.

By the time she toweled off, got dressed, and stepped out of her bedroom with wet hair, Ember was on the couch with the stack of loose spellbook pages in her lap. "Well, at least you're walking around like you feel better."

"A little, yeah. You didn't eat all the quiche, did you?"

"I wasn't that hungry. I put the rest of it back in the oven."

"Thanks." Moving slower than she wanted to, Cheyenne banged around in the kitchen, getting a plate and silverware and scooping a giant slice of quiche out of the pan. She opted for standing over the kitchen island to eat as much as she could quickly before having to move much again. "This is really good."

"Right?" Ember looked up from the spellbook and nodded. "Figured I'd try it. And no, I did not cook that shit from scratch."

Putting the dishes in the sink was as much as she could handle for cleanup, then she ran a hand through her still-damp hair and headed back into the living room to take her usual seat in the recliner. "Okay. So, for the record, I'm glad that that serum lasted as long as it did."

"It sucks without it, huh?"

"Yeah, Em. I know I have to hurry up and figure out how to keep my mom safe and out of this craziness, and at the same time, I wanna sit here all day and do absolutely nothing. So. That's my biggest issue today."

Ember finally put down the loose page she'd been studying and gave her friend a sympathetic smile. "I wish I could help."

"Yeah, I know. But I heal quickly, right? I'm waiting for that to happen."

They fell into a slightly awkward silence, and Cheyenne closed her eyes. She thought she was about to drift off to sleep before her phone buzzed in her back pocket. This time, the text was from Lee.

She's ready as promised. Stop by whenever you want.

"I guess there's one good thing about today."

Ember looked at her with a cheesy grin. "Somebody else found the solution to all your problems, and now you get to enjoy what would otherwise be a pretty sweet life?"

"Huh. Was that supposed to make me feel better?"

"I don't know. Figured it was worth a shot."

Cheyenne snorted. "My car's ready."

"Oh. Yeah, that's a good thing."

"Except I don't have any way to get there, and I am not superspeed-running to Lee's property. Not now."

Ember pursed her lips. "Want me to borrow Matthew's car again?"

"Nice try." With a sigh, Cheyenne returned Lee's text to let him know she'd be there at some point today. Then she pulled up Maleshi's number to start a new text. *Worth a shot, I guess.*

I need a portal.

The reply she got was almost instant and would have made her laugh if laughing didn't hurt so much.

Congratulations.

Okay, I'll try again.

Pretty please, General. Will you please get over here and open a portal for me so I can get my car that you destroyed?

Cheyenne closed her eyes and dropped her head back against the headrest. "Em, I might ask you to grab the neighbor's keys again. Depending on what kinda mood Maleshi's in."

"Uh-oh. What happened?"

Before Cheyenne could reply, a dark circle of light bloomed in the air beside the coffee table, and the general stepped through into their apartment. "I'll tell you one thing, kid. You know how to take a grudge and wrap it up in a polite little package. That's for sure."

Opening her eyes, Cheyenne looked at the nightstalker and shrugged. "I do what I can."

"And you still look like shit."

Ember blinked. "Whoa."

"I'm not wrong." Maleshi stepped over to Cheyenne's chair and leaned down to look the halfling dead in the eye. "At least you haven't thrown in the towel."

"I haven't thrown in the towel even a little, okay? But I can't drive a towel to do all the other stuff I have to do. I need my car, and you're faster than an Uber."

"Cheaper too, apparently." Maleshi straightened, staring at the halfling until Cheyenne ran out of patience.

"Seriously. Please?"

"Can you walk?"

"What?" Cheyenne snorted. "Of course I can walk."

"I wanna see you get up out of that chair and walk to the portal I'm gonna cast right here." Maleshi backed up until she was almost at the front door and pointed at the floor in front of her. "Then you can go through it and get your car."

"You don't think I can walk. I took a shower."

"Good for you. Come on." The general waved her forward, and Cheyenne rolled her eyes as she pushed up out of the chair.

"See? I'm good."

"Walk, kid. I said, walk."

Cheyenne moved slowly toward the nightstalker with a deadpan stare. Then she stopped and spread her arms. "There. Portal."

"Hmm." Maleshi looked at her. "Based on how you look right now, I honestly didn't expect you to manage that."

"Thanks."

"Sure. Where do you wanna go?" Cheyenne pulled Lee's address up on her phone and waited for Maleshi to read it. The general opened up the portal between them and shrugged. "There you go. Super easy."

"Thank you. I really do appreciate it."

Maleshi gave her a thin smile. "I know."

"Wait, wait." Ember shook her head and pointed at Cheyenne's bedroom door. "You can't go yet."

"Ember, I don't have anything else to do."

The fae's fingers flashed with violet light. Two more purple streaks burst out of Cheyenne's open bedroom door and hurtled across the living room before her black Vans thumped on the floor in front of her.

Cheyenne looked down at them and grimaced. "Shit."

"Yep." Maleshi rubbed her lips. "You'll definitely need those."

"Okay. Nobody says anything else. I'll be fine." Cheyenne stepped into her shoes, then grabbed her trenchcoat off the armrest of the couch. "I'm going to get my car, then I'll come back here and take a nap or something."

"Good plan."

Ember nodded. "I don't have a problem with it."

"Right. You're both looking at me funny."

A loud knock startled her out of her thoughts, and everyone looked at the front door.

Great.

"Ember? Cheyenne?" Matthew paused his knocking only long enough to call their names before he was at it again. "It's Tuesday. I have a lot of questions, and you promised me answers. So open up. Please."

Cheyenne let out a long sigh and looked at her friend. "I can't deal with this right now."

"Totally fine. Go get your car."

"Ember? Come on. Please open the door." The knocking continued.

Maleshi clicked her tongue. "Poor thing."

"Not really, but okay."

The general flicked her fingers at the front door, which opened with a flash of silver light, and Matthew Thomas stumbled into their apartment. His eyes widened when he saw Maleshi, Cheyenne, and a portal between them; he couldn't decide which part of it troubled him more. "You!"

Maleshi gestured at herself. "If you're talking to me, then yeah. I guess that would be pretty accurate."

"I saw you." Matthew looked at Cheyenne. "She was in that footage."

"Yep. Maleshi, Matthew, you've been introduced. I gotta go."

"Wait, wait. Cheyenne, you said you'd tell me what's going on with my uncle!"

"Feel free to hang out with Ember and the general." Waving him off, Cheyenne hurried through the portal and disappeared.

The dark window of light closed behind her with a soft pop, and Matthew staggered forward in surprise. "What? Where did she go?"

Maleshi folded her arms and grinned at the baffled human. "I'd almost forgotten you're the one who made so much trouble for us. And by us, I'm only referring to my own involvement over the last few months. But you've been at it for a few years, right?"

Matthew swallowed thickly. "What?"

Ember nodded. "Five years."

"Oh. That's a fairly long time for humans, isn't it?"

"Long enough to make a lot of bad choices and still have no idea what's going on." With a shrug, Ember let out a humorless chuckle. "Hopefully, turning over a new leaf doesn't take nearly as long."

Matthew couldn't decide who to look at, but he eventually staggered over to Ember on the couch as he stared at the general. "Ember, seriously, you guys told me you'd explain everything after you did whatever you had to do last night."

"Really?" Maleshi's grin widened. "He's expecting a full debriefing, is that it?"

"I guess we can call it that."

Chuckling, the general lowered herself into Cheyenne's usual recliner, then gestured at the second one beside her. "Come sit down and get comfortable, Matthew. If Ember's okay with it, I'd love to sit in on this and fill in the missing pieces."

"I'm totally fine with it." Ember looked at Matthew, folded her arms, and nodded at the empty chair. "Take a seat."

"I don't even know this…whatever she is." Matthew steadied himself with a hand on the back of the couch. When neither the fae nor the grinning nightstalker said anything else, he cleared his throat. "She's not gonna leave, is she?"

Maleshi slowly shook her head and crossed one leg over the other. "Not until we've been over everything in detail. It'll be fun."

"Uh-huh." Slowly, the nervous Matthew Thomas inched his way

past the couch and stiffly sat in the leather recliner, staring at General Hi'et the whole time.

"There you go. Not so bad. Ember, would you like to kick off this little powwow, or should I?"

"I'll go first." With a flash of purple light, Ember swung her legs off the couch cushions so they dangled over the edge toward the floor as she faced Matthew head-on. "I have a lot to say."

CHAPTER FIFTY-TWO

Cheyenne sighed when she stepped through the portal and found herself on the gravel drive inside the front gate of Lee McDurn's estate. She turned around, scanning the empty gate tower she couldn't imagine Lee hired anyone to man and trudged up the road toward the circular drive at the end and the main house behind it. *She got me close enough, I guess.*

Her black Vans kicked up sprays of dusty pebbles as she headed up the road. A light autumn breeze whipped through her hair and sent dried leaves skittering across the drive in front of her. Lee didn't see her turn around the corner of the garage until she stopped and cleared her throat.

"Oh. Cheyenne!" The man looked up from the paperwork on his desk and grinned. "That was fast."

"Yeah, I had a friend drop me off."

"Huh. Funny. I didn't hear anyone drive up past the gate."

She gave him a small smile. "The kind of friend who doesn't need a car."

"Ah. I see. You're not the only one, then." He dropped his pen on the stack of papers on his desk and walked around it heading toward her.

"Well, I don't always need a car, but I can't always get around without one, either."

"Good thing you brought your car to me and she's all fixed up and ready for you, huh?" Lee extended his hand for a quick shake, then spun again and waved her after him into the garage. "Come on. She's a little farther down the line today. Closer to some of my tools and whatnot."

"Sure." Cheyenne stuck her hands in her pockets and quickly glanced at the framed photograph of Lee and his daughter that hadn't moved since she'd brought it up two days ago. *Yeah, we don't have to go there again.*

"All right. Here we are." The man chuckled and readjusted the huge cream-colored Stetson on his head. "Now, if anything stands out to you as unacceptable, you let me know."

"Holy shit."

He grinned at her and nodded slowly. "I'll take that as a good sign, sure."

With a laugh of disbelief, Cheyenne peered through the driver's side window and shook her head. "You did all this in two days?"

"Mm-hmm."

"Lee, you made me a Gothmobile."

He laughed sharply. "Is that what they're calling it these days?"

"Well, that's what *I'm* calling it."

"Go ahead and get in. Take a look."

Cheyenne didn't hesitate to open the door and slip behind the wheel, the center of which was now covered with small silver studs that matched nearly half her clothes. Her smile widened as she scanned the changes to the inside of her car: the silver skull at the top of the gearshift, the swirling flame designs in black and silver that covered the dashboard and the glovebox, the tiny black skulls decorating the seatbelts that were barely visible from more than a few inches away. "This is awesome."

"Wait 'til you turn her on." Lee ducked to watch her in the driver's seat and nodded at the fob lying in the center console with a new silver rim around the black. "Go ahead."

When she pressed the keyless start button, the Panamera's engine turned over with a purr. The entire dashboard lit up in various shades of purple light instead of the usual blue, green, and white. "Oh, man!"

"Overhead lights, too."

Cheyenne looked at the roof of the car to find the dome light had been replaced with a rounded silver-and-black skeleton hand. When she switched on the light, it was the same dark-purple as the lights on the dashboard, and she laughed. "This is insane."

Lee chuckled and rubbed his upper lip. "In a good way, right?"

"Absolutely." She got out of the car and laughed again at the purple light in the wheel well. The license plate holders on the front and back were both made of tiny silver skulls stacked on top of each other, and looking in through the front windshield, the mount for the rearview mirror looked like it was made out of silver chains. She couldn't find a single dent or scratch on the body as proof that she'd been stupid enough to let Maleshi drive her car. "Yeah. Definitely a good insane. What about the engine problems?"

Wrinkling his nose, Lee folded his arms and stepped back. "Yeah. There weren't any. I had this feeling, you know? Wanted to see if I was right."

Cheyenne looked at him and couldn't stop grinning. "What if you hadn't been?"

"Well, you know. I would've reversed the whole thing free of charge and reminded myself not to stick my nose too far into other people's business."

"This is definitely the best experience I've ever had with bringing my car into the shop."

He laughed, nodding slowly, and took her hand when she extended it.

"Seriously. Thank you. I kinda needed something like this today."

"I'm glad to hear it. Listen, if you have any other issues with this car or anything else, give me a call. Or if you want some updates to the Gothmobile. Whatever."

She snorted. "Yeah. You will be my guy for a while."

Lee hit a switch on the far wall of the garage, and the door lifted and slowly swung out, letting daylight in. "You'll be able to drive her right outta here. I'll draw up a final receipt."

"Yeah. Sounds good. Do you take credit cards?"

"If I told you not to pay me and that the fun I got out of this project was more than enough, would you let it go at that?"

"Nope."

"I didn't think so. Yeah, I take credit cards." He nodded at the other end of the garage and took off that way.

Cheyenne gave herself a moment longer to look over the Panamera from the outside and shook her head. He'd just done it. What kinda crazy person remodeled the inside of someone's car without asking? This was the best thing she'd seen in months.

Laughing, she found her severely improved mood making it a lot easier to move around and at least ignore most of the pain in her body as she joined Lee at his desk. They worked out the final price, she handed him her card, and they waited for his machine to print a receipt.

"That's what I call a good deal, Cheyenne." He tapped the desk. "We're both happy with the final outcome but not satisfied with the price."

"Because what you did is worth way more than you'll let me pay you."

"We'll be arguing about this all day if I don't change the subject." With a quick rip of the serrated paper, Lee handed over her receipt and raised his eyebrows. "So, this is me changing the subject. You give that friend of mine a call yet?"

Stuffing the receipt into her pocket, she shook her head. "No, not yet. I thought I was gonna have to put it off today, but I'm feelin' like things are lookin' up now."

"Ha. Yeah, custom work tends to have that effect." He held her gaze, his lips twitching in and out of a smile as he held back a laugh. "I'm interested to know how things work out for you once you make that call. If you feel like tellin' me."

"Do you know a lot about the magical world?"

"Enough to hold my own in a conversation about it, sure. That's neither here nor there today, is it?" He gave her a curt nod and pointed at the Panamera three cars down. "Now get outta here."

Cheyenne laughed and headed to her car. "Thank you. I'll keep you updated."

"Sounds good."

"And if you end up with a bunch of new customers knocking down your door after seeing what you did to my Porsche, you have only yourself to blame."

Lee threw his head back and laughed, slapping a hand on his belly. "I've learned to deal with it. Drive safely."

"Yeah, I will." Safe and fast weren't mutually exclusive. She slipped into the driver's seat again, strapped herself in, and closed the door. *This is exactly what I needed today. If Maleshi even looks at this thing the wrong way, I'll... Shit, I don't know.*

Cheyenne backed the Panamera smoothly out of the garage and raised her hand for a final wave at Lee through the window. She laughed when her hand came down on the silver skull as she shifted into drive. "Fuck, yeah."

Then she was heading down the gravel drive and out through the open gate, the ride feeling smoother than she remembered. *I don't care if he did that or if I'm too stoked about this to feel any bumps.*

Once she reached the end of the gravel drive and turned onto the frontage road leading back toward downtown Richmond, she pulled out her cellphone and found the number she'd saved for Inolu. *Might as well take advantage of the good mood. Let's see what's up.*

She connected her phone to the car's Bluetooth and sent the call. Her foot pressed down bit by bit on the gas as she stared down the straight shot of asphalt in front of her. The call rang and rang, and as she was about to hang up and try again, the ringing stopped with a click, and the strangest voicemail greeting filled the inside of her car.

"Yes, you called the right number." The female voice was flat and droned like the speaker couldn't possibly have been more bored than she was at the time of recording it. "And yes, this is Inolu. If you haven't already been made aware by whatever idiot gave you my number and didn't mention these things beforehand, I don't do consultations after nine o'clock at night or on the weekends. No exceptions."

Cheyenne snorted. For real? It sounds like she's reading an instruction manual.

"The following is a list of services you will not find under my current offerings. No love potions. No reincarnations or bringing any living creature back from the dead. I don't do temporary IQ increases or permanent physical restructuring. No reanimation. And yes, that includes first-time animation. Inanimate shit doesn't need to move."

The halfling barked out a laugh. "Oh, my God."

"I also don't provide my services to minors, human or magical, without the written permission of an accompanying adult and a signed waiver. I will not be held accountable for your stupidity. And no, I still do not accept online payments. The internet can suck it. Now that you've listened to all this incredibly interesting bullshit, we can move on. If you don't leave a message after the beep, you'll never hear back from me. I don't answer calls as a general rule, but I do call back within twenty-four hours. Lay down your issue, ailment, unfulfilled desire, or specific request for vengeance, and I'll return your call as soon as possible. So, yeah, I guess that's it."

The line clicked again, followed by a two-second beep, and Cheyenne cleared her throat to make sure she wouldn't laugh when she started talking.

"Yeah. Hi." *Guess I might as well start with the thing that gets every other magical's damn attention. Can't hurt with this one.* "I got your number from Lee McDurn. He said you might be able to help me, so I thought I'd give this a shot. My name's Cheyenne Summerlin. That might not mean anything to you, but if it does, maybe it makes a difference. I don't know anymore. I'm L'zar Verdys' daughter, and I need help with a personal problem. A curse. Not on me, on someone close to me."

Wrinkling her nose, she shook her head and glanced briefly at the dashboard as if she could see Inolu in the touchscreen window. *Cut it out with the verbal diarrhea and leave the damn message.*

"Anyway, I'd like to know what you can do for me. So, call me back." She left her phone number just in case, then snatched up her phone and ended the call. "Jesus. That was a mess." *There's no way my voicemail was the weirdest one she's gotten. Didn't expect Inolu to be a woman, either. Or female magical. Whatever.*

Cheyenne forced herself to focus on the drive home.

About ten minutes out of the Pellerville Gables Apartments, her phone rang. Cheyenne connected it to the Bluetooth one more time and accepted the call. *That was fast.*

"Hello?"

"This is Inolu."

Cheyenne smiled at the highway stretching out in front of her. "Hi. Thanks for calling me back."

"I haven't heard the Weaver's name in a long time, Ms. Summerlin, and certainly not invoked. You've definitely caught my attention."

"Ah." Cheyenne wrinkled her nose but managed to keep the distaste out of her voice. "I thought that would do it."

"I'm assuming your request is fairly urgent."

"Yeah. Fairly." Cheyenne readjusted her grip on the steering wheel and cocked her head. *I wonder what gave it away.*

"Then I'd like to see you as soon as possible. I'm free now. Be at this address in the next thirty minutes, and I'll take fifteen percent off my regular consultation price." Inolu's bored, monotonous voice rattled off an address. "And make sure you're alone. I'm not a fan of moochers or stowaways."

"What? Yeah. I'm alone. Can you repeat that address?"

Inolu scoffed. "No, but I'll text it to you. This is a cell phone, right?"

"Yeah."

The line went dead, and the Bluetooth call ended. Cheyenne frowned at her dashboard and took a deep breath. "Okay, guess I'm going to hang out with a bane-breaker who doesn't sound like she enjoys her job but won't give me a chance to say no. This is gonna be weird."

CHAPTER FIFTY-THREE

After plugging Inolu's address into her GPS, Cheyenne ended up in South Richmond fifteen minutes later. After sticking her activator behind her ear, she slipped into drow mode long enough to select the command for her illusion charm and went to her human-Goth self. There was no one around before noon on a Tuesday to see it.

She had to pay for parking in the public lot before she stalked across the street toward the line of row houses and Inolu's alleged home. Every few steps, she looked over her shoulder to take another glance of her newly Gothed-out Panamera, and when she pressed the lock button on the key fob, the ensuing chirp and flash of purple at the top of the headlights brought another small smile to her lips.

Okay, that made it worth it.

She walked down the row of two-story homes and stopped at the address she'd been given. The brick exterior was a faded green-yellow, and the front door was navy-blue with black trim. The shutters and trim around the rest of the unit were black too, and Cheyenne narrowed her eyes. *Right. Bored-sounding bane-breaker. Obnoxious paint job. I have no idea what to expect.*

She knocked swiftly on the door and waited.

A buzzing whir came from a panel mounted on the narrow side wall of what was supposed to be the front stoop. Cheyenne looked up and found a relatively sophisticated swiveling camera lens spinning, readjusting, and zooming in to get a clear image of her face. *Normal Earthside tech, at least. Not off to a terrible start.*

"State your name." Inolu's droning voice had a metallic, robotic tinge to it as the camera lens kept twisting and zooming in and out, with Cheyenne as its central focus.

The halfling cleared her throat. "Cheyenne Summerlin." *First time I've come out and said it in public. Maybe the first time it hasn't meant anything during an appointment.*

"State your business."

Cheyenne narrowed her eyes at the camera. "We spoke on the phone."

"Consultation or repeat visit?"

"What?"

"It's a standard series of questions, Miss Summerlin. I record and collect this data for all clients, visitors, mail carriers, delivery personnel, salespersons, survey providers, and the unsuspecting morons who somehow find themselves on my doorstep instead of any of my neighbors' where they belong. Consultation or repeat visit?"

Cheyenne widened her eyes at the camera, then finally looked away and stared at the door instead. "Consultation. First one ever."

"Please refrain from providing extraneous information or smart-ass comments, Miss Summerlin. It junks up my data categorization, and I don't enjoy having to start the process all over again."

The camera lens spun repeatedly and stretched out on a long lever toward the halfling with a constant whir that didn't let up. Cheyenne glanced up at the thing's opening shutter and shrugged. "Sorry."

"Are you alone?"

"Yeah."

"Do you currently have on your person anything fragile, liquid, perishable, or potentially hazardous, including lithium batteries and perfume?"

Cheyenne couldn't help an exasperated laugh. "Define potentially hazardous."

"Answer the question, Miss Summerlin."

"I mean, if we're going by the regular post-office rules, then no. I don't have anything like that on me." *There's one good thing about being fresh out of darktongue serum. I'd have to hand over my injection canister for inspection. Jesus.*

The camera stopped whirring and retracted back into place behind the panel on the narrow side wall. Something heavy and metallic clicked into place behind the door, followed by a loud buzz.

"You may enter," Inolu droned. "When the door opens, please stand inside the red circle and try not to move. The standard security scan lasts twenty-two point three seconds. Unless, of course, you don't consent to said security scan. In that case, you can turn around right now and get the fuck off my property."

"Whoa." Cocking her head, Cheyenne held up both hands as if Inolu stood right in front of her with a loaded shotgun instead and fought back a laugh. "I consent."

"Very good." The navy-blue front door opened swiftly to reveal a short, dark entryway.

The only thing Cheyenne could see at first was the bright-red circle painted on the wooden floor two feet inside. *Stand inside the red circle. This better be worth all the bullshit.*

She stepped forward and centered both feet in the designated area. The front door shut on its own with a bang, and the entryway fell into complete darkness. The next second, there was another buzz, and a dark orange light flared to life in a rectangular doorway around Cheyenne like a metal detector. *Security scan. Right. The kind I can apparently feel on my skin.*

A loud, rhythmic click sounded around her, and while the one and only time Cheyenne had had an MRI was when she was ten, the memory of it came back to her with surprising intensity. But she did as she'd been told and tried not to move. The clicking continued, and she thought she felt an unwelcome heat stretching toward her from the orange light.

"Hello?"

No one answered, and she couldn't see anything but the orange light and the complete darkness everywhere else. *Twenty-two point three seconds. I'll be fine.*

The warmth intensified into a slightly concerning heat on her skin.

"This isn't something I should be concerned about, is it?" She blew out a quick breath. "Listen, you didn't say anything about a heater, okay? This doesn't feel…"

The clicking sped up into a startling crackle, then the orange light burst with blinding intensity and a flash of blood-red. The dart wounds in Cheyenne's shoulders and hip felt like they were ripping open all over again. She thought she shouted for Inolu to stop the fucking scan, and then she wasn't thinking anything. Fortunately, that happened before she hit the floor in the bane-breaker's front entryway and lost consciousness.

The next thing she was aware of after that was the gentle crackle of a fire somewhere close by and a complete lack of heat from it. Cheyenne's eyelids fluttered open, and it took her a few times of rolling her gaze around the room before she remembered where she was and how she'd gotten there. *But I didn't walk into a living room.*

With a sharp breath, she pushed up onto her elbows and groaned at the ache splitting her skull. *This has to stop.*

The room spun around her until she held still long enough for it to settle again. Swallowing thickly, Cheyenne sat up a lot more cautiously and found herself on a raised pallet covered in thick quilts. On her right, the fire she'd heard crackled in a real hearth—a regular fire, small, with nothing ominous or magical about it. The rest of the room, however, was incredibly dark, even with the smoke going up through the chimney like it was supposed to.

She turned as much as she could to look behind her, searching for the entrance to the room or at least a sign of the entryway where she'd been scanned and knocked unconscious. But the room didn't have any windows or doors or exits to other parts of the house. *If I'm even still in the same house. What the fuck?*

When she opened her mouth and took a breath to ask the same question out loud, Inolu's droning, bored voice beat her to it. "You're full of surprises, aren't you?"

"You know, you don't sound very surprised." Cheyenne turned to the wingback armchair in front of the fire. A narrow hand with long, slender fingers reached out and tossed something into the fire, resulting in a loud crack and an instant puff of smoke that quickly disappeared up through the chimney. She blinked and waited for the hand to reappear. *It looked like her veins were glowing green. Assuming that's her.*

"I prefer not to show all my cards at once, Miss Summerlin." The armchair let out a soft creak when the owner of the hand and voice shifted her position.

"Call me Cheyenne. Please." She closed her eyes and let out a slow breath. "And then you might tell me why your standard security scan knocked me on my ass."

"You landed on your face, believe it or not," Inolu drawled. "And the sarcasm I detected in your delivery of the word 'standard' leads me to the conclusion that you find it an inaccurate description."

This lady's nuts. "Personally, yeah. I think 'standard' is defined as harmless and the same for everyone and nothing to worry about. If passing out is the standard for all your clients or whoever, I guess one of us is wrong."

"In that hypothetical case, Miss Cheyenne, you would be incorrect. But you are not."

"So that wasn't standard."

"No, my security measures are perfectly standard under your definition and mine. You are the abnormality in this scenario."

Cheyenne snorted. "Excuse me?"

"You're excused. If you'd like me to break it down even further for you, I will. You misrepresented yourself and your magical state. You failed to make me aware of certain discrepancies on your physical person, and because of that, you went against fucking standard protocol."

"Are you saying me passing out inside your front door is my fault?" Cheyenne pressed her hands down on the quilt-covered pallet and scooted over to the edge. "Because I didn't ask to be shocked unconscious by a weird-ass light that was only supposed to last twenty-two point three seconds."

"Yes. It's your fault." Inolu's long inhale seemed abnormally loud even for both of them being in the same room. "But I'm impressed that you remembered the length of the scan, which would have completed its sequence if it hadn't found some serious issues in the process."

Cheyenne stared at the back of the wingback armchair facing the small fire. *This was a bad idea.* "Yeah, I'm good with numbers and remembering details."

"Yes. So am I."

"Great. I think that's about the only thing we have in common. So I'm gonna go." Cheyenne pushed herself to her feet and almost fell onto the pallet again when her hip and knee wobbled beneath her. She steadied herself, made sure she wasn't about to fall over again, and headed to the other side of the dark room opposite the fireplace.

"Don't be an idiot," Inolu muttered.

The halfling paused and gritted her teeth. "Great advice. Where's the door?"

"You won't find it because it isn't here. Not now, anyway."

"Well, bring it back." Cheyenne turned around to face the armchair and forced her anger back down where she could keep a handle on it. "Right now."

"No." The bane-breaker's hand appeared again and stretched out beside the armchair to hover over a well-polished round side table. A silver coil glinted within those slender fingers, which were streaked with glowing green lines that looked exactly like veins. "First, I'd love to hear your explanation for how you managed to bring an O'gúl activator into this fucking backward world. That's not a part of our original agreement, of course, but I won't charge you for it."

"You took my activator?" Cheyenne stormed toward the outstretched hand over the side table. "You can't take shit off someone when they're passed out in your house."

"But I did." The silver coil clinked down onto the side table, and Inolu flipped her hand over, spreading her fingers as if they were having a much more casual conversation face to face. "And you scheduled this consultation to talk to me about your little curse problem. As agreed, that's what we'll do. You're not leaving until your consultation is completed, so sit your lying ass back down and let's begin. Shall we?"

"I didn't have a chance to lie to you. Your fancy scanner knocked me unconscious first."

"Lies of omission, Cheyenne. I shouldn't have to explain to you how that works."

"What's that supposed to mean?"

"Lots of things. Probably. And the only reason you didn't walk away from that scan is that my system detected a threat and dealt with it in the most appropriate way."

Keep it together, Cheyenne. Her hands clenched into fists at her sides. *If she does anything outright stupid, you can tear her apart then. Just don't lose it. You came here for Mom.* "I think you misinterpreted me as a threat."

"I did no such thing. It was my algorithm, which admittedly has its own faults. Fewer than either of us, though."

With a heavy sigh, Cheyenne took two long, swift strides to the round side table and snatched the activator. "Don't take my shit again, got it?"

She leaned forward to sneak a look at the magical sitting in the chair, but there was no one there.

"Don't lie to me by leaving out the most relevant information," Inolu said from the other side of the room, "and then yeah, you have a deal."

Cheyenne spun and found the bane-breaker draped in an oversized sweater over vertically striped leggings standing on the opposite side of the raised pallet. Her eyes widened as she looked the magical woman over. *What is she?*

Inolu gave Cheyenne the same deadpan stare the halfling used on everyone else. "Go ahead. Make your useless comments, and then we can get down to business."

"Nice leggings."

The other woman cocked her head. "Really? That's all you have to say?"

"Anything else is none of my business." *Maybe I misjudged her. Easy to do when she apparently doesn't let anyone look at her. I might not either if all the veins in my body glowed green like that.*

Inolu's short brown bob fluttered around her cheeks when she lightly tossed her head. Round, luminous eyes the same shade of green as the veins racing across every visible inch of her amber-colored skin swept over Cheyenne in return. "Fair enough."

"Okay." Cheyenne stuck the activator behind her ear, her eyelids barely fluttering anymore at the pinch of the tech syncing with her magic. Unfortunately, the activator didn't have anything unusual to show her about this new magical associate. "Let's have this consultation, then, huh?"

"Yes." Inolu gestured at a low bench in the center of the room. "You can sit wherever you like. I prefer to keep my distance from everyone, so if you're offended by my four-foot radius of personal space, that's your problem."

Cheyenne slowly stepped over to the bench, glancing at it briefly before she sat. "I totally get it. So if we're on the same page, what's the 'most relevant' information I left out? You didn't give me a chance to tell you why I'm here. In detail, I mean."

"It's not like you insisted on telling me, either." They stared at each other, then Inolu lowered herself gingerly onto the pallet and folded her hands in her lap. "I want to know if the curse you need help with is the one you carried into my house or something else entirely."

CHAPTER FIFTY-FOUR

"What?" Cheyenne snorted. "No. I'm not cursed."

"Huh. That's amusing." Inolu's green eyes narrowed but shone brightly in the dark room. "The clueless halfling came to the bane-breaker for assistance, but she's sure she's not cursed. Should I be paying you for this consultation instead?"

Cheyenne swallowed. "No."

"That's what I thought. So spill it."

She's gotta have multiple personalities in there or something. Not that there's anything wrong with that. She talks like at least three different people all wrapped up together. "You know, maybe if you gave me a hint, I'd have a better answer."

Inolu blinked rapidly. "How would I give you a hint when I'm the one asking the question?"

With a confused frown, Cheyenne shook her head. "I mean, I don't know what makes you think there is a curse. On me."

"You really are special, aren't you?" Inolu held up one open palm, then the other. "Epically brilliant over here, and mind-blowingly stupid over here."

"Okay, watch it."

"The fucking holes in your flesh and the poison practically eating you alive." Inolu flicked her wrist and pointed in quick succession at all three of Cheyenne's blight-poisoned wounds, one after the other. "Don't tell me you had no idea they were there."

"I wasn't gonna say that." The halfling turned her head to eye the bane-breaker. "How the hell did *you* know they're there?"

Inolu narrowed her eyes and said in a flat, inflectionless voice, "Standard security scan."

"Right." Cheyenne gave her a bitter smile. "And your scan thought this poison inside me was a threat to you?"

"No. A threat in general, so it wasn't wrong."

Blinking slowly, Cheyenne opened her mouth for one of her usual quips in reply and found she had nothing to say to that. She shrugged instead and waited for the other woman to continue the consultation.

"I guess my question's already been answered, no thanks to you."

"Oh. Sure."

"So now we'll move on. What is the actual curse for which you chose to seek out my services?"

Cheyenne rubbed her hands down her thighs and leaned forward with a small grimace. *Do I have to think about wording this delicately, or is it 'throw it at the wall and see what sticks?'* "It's my mom."

Inolu's green eyes widened, and the first brief flicker of a smile passed across her lips. "The mom who made L'zar Verdys your father?"

Cheyenne scrunched her nose. "Yeah. That's kinda how it works." *And if she goes any farther down that rabbit hole, I'm outta here.*

"I see." Inolu lightly bit her lower lip, her gaze flickering around the dark room. Then she barked a laugh and wiped away all traces of amusement two seconds later. "Well, what the hell's wrong with her?"

"Jesus." Cheyenne snorted. "I think you have less of a filter than I do."

"So?"

"So it's surprising. And refreshing, maybe."

"Whatever. You're paying me to help you with this problem, not to be your friend. So answer my question."

Fighting back a laugh, Cheyenne shook her head and studied the floor. *Where do I even fucking start?* "Okay, so in the interest of not leaving anything out and getting knocked unconscious by whatever else you might have stashed away in here—"

"Oh, many things, I assure you."

"Right. I'm gonna tell you everything."

"That's the first intelligent thing you've said since you left that excruciatingly awkward voicemail on my incoming messages."

Cheyenne stared at the tactless magical with glowing green veins and raised her eyebrows. "Wow."

"You're welcome."

"Okay. Is it possible for me to try explaining this to you without you interrupting me?"

Inolu shrugged. "Probably not, but I'm always willing to be proven wrong. It so rarely happens these days."

"Uh-huh. Well, do your best." Cheyenne cleared her throat and figured she'd start the story with the new portal ridge that had popped up in her mom's backyard and had since been destroyed.

By the time she finished laying out the details she thought were remotely relevant, Inolu had drawn her striped-legginged legs up under her on the pallet and crossed them. She grabbed her ankles and leaned forward, hanging on the halfling's every word with an expression somewhere between bubbling glee and wary caution.

"So I need to figure out how to break the rest of this curse on my mom," Cheyenne finished. "You know, get her to stop breaking out with new runes burning into her skin. I mean, I know for a fact it's ridiculously painful, though she won't say it."

"Oh, naturally." Inolu nodded. "Yes, that sounds excruciating."

"Uh-huh." Cheyenne raised her eyebrows and forced herself to continue. "And I need to separate her from everything else that's going on, so she doesn't get sucked into it like this again. Ambar'ogúl's not her world. Its problems shouldn't be hers, either, so whatever I have to do to clear the slate for her, I'm ready to do it."

Inolu cocked her head. "Clear the slate."

"Yeah. Keep her safe."

"Ha! Keep her safe!" The bane-breaker threw her head back and cackled, rocking back on the pallet with a firm grip on her ankles. "You think you need to separate her? Pull her out of the very center of every-thing." Her laughter echoed around the room and pierced Cheyenne's ears at the right frequency of annoying so one of her eyes started twitching. "You're a fucking idiot!"

"Seriously, I've put up with you insulting me since our first conversation. I don't mind eccentric. I get that. Different strokes for different whatever. But if you call me an idiot one more time, I'm gonna lose it on you, and I don't want to."

Inolu's laughter died into a light chuckle, then she leaned forward and widened her eyes. "Then give me a reason not to."

Just breathe, Cheyenne. If she knows breaking curses like she knows writing algorithms, this is exactly who you want to help you.

The other woman's smile faded slowly, and she tilted her head, studying Cheyenne as if she were a strange new species of macabre insect instead of a halfling coming to her as an alleged new client. "I think you already know what the missing piece is, Cheyenne."

"I really don't." Cheyenne shook her head and forced herself to keep breathing evenly. "If I did, I wouldn't be here."

"Hmm. You know, I used to be scared of what I knew I understood and thought I didn't want to."

"Right." Cheyenne swept her gaze around the dark, windowless room with no doors. "You've obviously made a huge improvement."

"How about this?" Inolu propped her elbows on her thighs, steepled her fingers, and tapped them against each other over and over. "We're coming up on what I tend to think of as my private time."

Cheyenne raised her eyebrows and paused. "Then I will definitely take that reappearing door right now."

The other woman scoffed. "Don't be such a prude. I want you to stay. You don't have a choice, but it feels better to tell you that's what I want. We'll ask the Underman together." Inolu moved her green-glowing hand in an undulating wave in front of her face, staring at the internal light seeping from her veins through her amber skin. "What do you think about that?"

"I have absolutely no idea, but I do think I should probably go home and come back at a better time."

Inolu chuckled and shook her head. "You won't be going home tonight, Cheyenne. That's impossible."

"Tonight?"

Inolu grinned and wiggled her eyebrows.

"Okay, whatever you're trying to pull, it's not gonna work on me." Cheyenne pulled her cell phone from her back pocket and snorted in disbelief. "I can come back later today, or maybe tomorrow." She stopped when she looked down at her phone's illuminated screen and saw the time. *Eight fifty-eight? What the fuck?*

Beneath the clock were three unread texts from Ember, all of them asking the same thing. Where was Cheyenne, was she okay, and did Ember need to call in the nightstalker rescue team or not?

Cheyenne cleared her throat. "You could've told me I was unconscious for eight hours, Inolu."

"Ah." The bane-breaker closed one eye in thought. "Eight hours and fifty-one minutes. Almost fifty-two now."

"Even better." Cheyenne unlocked her phone and pulled up her text history with Ember to finally get back to her friend. The minutes changed to 8:59, and her phone that still had over half its battery life blinked off. Nothing but a black screen. She looked at Inolu and pressed her lips tightly together. "I thought you said you don't take clients or calls after nine or on weekends."

"Well, you're already here, aren't you?" Inolu shrugged, rocking back and forth with her legs crossed and her hands gripped tightly around her ankles. "You'd never make it out before he got here anyway."

A high-pitched, squeaking giggle erupted from the bane-breaker's mouth. "The Underman is coming, and he really wants to meet you."

"Yeah, I'm not sure I wanna meet him." Cheyenne stood from the bench and slipped her phone back into her pocket.

"Sit down and show some respect!" Inolu spat. Her green eyes widened and started pulsing with brightening light. Her glowing veins echoed the undulating rhythm.

"Shit. Okay." Not daring to take her eyes off the woman, Cheyenne slowly lowered herself back down on the bench and waited. "Anything I need to know?"

"You will speak to him, Cheyenne." Inolu hunched her shoulders in eager anticipation as she rocked back and forth. "You will hear his voice, and he will hear yours, and then you'll have your answers. If you don't already. Ha."

"Okay." The halfling gazed around the room again, searching for any sign of a door or a materializing window or anything out of the ordinary her activator might pick up on for her. *Not that this Underman guy would necessarily* need *a door. This is magic.*

A burst of bitingly cold air whipped through the room and snuffed out the fire—sparks, embers, glowing coals, and everything—in a split second. If there had been any lights on, they were off now. Even the green glow of Inolu's eyes and veins was gone.

Fuck.

Cheyenne forced herself to breathe slowly and wondered if the activator had any way to pull up something like night vision. *But I'm already thinking about it, and it's not pulling up a command prompt. Yeah, this thing's as dead as my phone.*

A long, slow, rattling breath filled the darkness.

Cheyenne tilted her head, trying to pinpoint the source of the sound, which came from everywhere and nowhere at the same time. "Inolu?"

A single orb of bright green light illuminated in front of her and was quickly joined by a second. Then both orbs narrowed, squishing in on themselves before the green light spread and grew to reveal an unnaturally wide grin that revealed shining black teeth. A low chuckle followed, and it wasn't Inolu's, nor was it her voice when the deep, growling tone reverberated through the room like a thunderstorm. "Not quite."

"Right." Cheyenne took a deep breath. "Am I talking to the Underman now?"

The glowing green grin spread unnaturally wider in the darkness. "You are. And I get to look upon Ambar'ogúl's Black Flame with my very own eyes." That dark, wheezing chuckle came again. "Well, they're not technically mine. But no one ever said Inolu didn't take care of herself. She really does. That might be the only reason we've been able to do this as long as we have."

"How long is that, exactly?" *What the hell else am I supposed to say to this thing? I don't even know what's happening.*

The green eyes floating suspended in the darkness slowly blinked. "Longer than you can imagine. But you didn't come here to talk about me and Inolu, did you?"

"No. I came here for help with my—"

"Bianca." The name purred from the Underman's disembodied throat. "Yes, we know."

I haven't said her name since I've been here, but this is already way past the point of making sense.

"That's right. I need to know how to the break the rest of Ba'rael's curse on her and get her as far away from all this messed-up shit as I possibly can. Preferably forever."

The glowing green grin opened wide as the Underman let out a rumbling laugh that made Cheyenne's brain feel like it was rattling around in her head. "Oh, no, no, no, you delightfully stubborn drow. You've got it all wrong."

I don't think I've been called that before.

"I'm sure I know what I need to do with my mom, okay? I need help with the how part."

"How to remove Bianca from the equation and spirit her away to some fabled safe place?" The Underman laughed again and sucked in a long, noisy breath. "Trust me, Cheyenne. That's the last thing you want to do."

CHAPTER FIFTY-FIVE

I don't care how much this demon-thing thinks it knows. I'm not buying it.

Cheyenne Summerlin narrowed her eyes at the Underman's bright green grin illuminating the pitch-black darkness of Inolu the bane-breaker's doorless living room. "What are you trying to say?"

A whispering laugh like dry leaves blowing down a sidewalk spilled from the Underman's open mouth, or Inolu's mouth, or however this kind of magical possession worked. "You already know."

"See, I'm done with people telling me that." Cheyenne clenched her fists in her lap. "So lay it out for me. 'Cause it sounded a lot like you said I can't keep my mom safe."

"Oh, not in the way you're trying so hard to convince yourself is the only option."

"Careful."

"Of what, Cheyenne?" The glowing green Cheshire Cat grin of the magical being taking over Inolu Frosh's body for this little chat widened. "Whatever you think you could do to me has already been done. Inolu and I have been bound together for quite some time. I will place my bets on her strength over yours." The luminous eyes flickered over Cheyenne's body. "Especially in your condition."

My condition. Bullshit. I'm fine.

"So then tell me how to break this curse on my mom." Cheyenne almost lurched off the bench, fighting back the urge to wrap her hands around the Underman's neck she couldn't see and squeeze. *Inolu's neck. This guy doesn't have a body.*

"Bianca Summerlin must fulfill her purpose in this grander design, drow." The Underman cocked his head and studied her. The mad grin never wavered. "Like I said, you already know what that is."

"Uh, no." Cheyenne briskly shook her head, her jaw clenching as she forced out the rest of her words. "My mom has nothing to do with this 'grand design' or any of the crap I'm trying to clean up on both worlds. Tell me how to save her, or this consultation is over."

The Underman let out a high, shrieking cackle. Inolu's green-illuminated head rocked back with the force of the being's amusement. Cheyenne could've sworn she felt the ground rumble beneath her. "You're such a refreshing change, Cheyenne. We've been here for so long, watching these cowering, trembling magicals lose their way and come here begging for our help. And you? You walk right into our midst with anger and denial and a firm belief in your ability to rip open the threads of the Weave to suit whatever you think is best. You know who you remind us of, don't you?"

Cheyenne turned her head away from the glowing face in the darkness but couldn't stop staring at it. "Don't."

"You are very much L'zar's daughter, aren't you?"

She sighed bitterly. "I told you not to say it."

"You can tell me whatever you want, Cheyenne. I see you. I've been observing you for quite some time, along with other select souls under my watchful gaze. Many of us have been watching you and your grinning Weaver of a father." The Underman let out a small hum of consideration and cocked his head. "But of course, that doesn't make a difference to you one way or the other, does it? It should."

Cheyenne scoffed. "I didn't come here to talk about a bunch of disembodied demons stalking me." *At least, I think they're demons. Who the fuck knows?* "And I'm so done with prophecies and vague riddles and beating around the fucking magical bush. Do you have a straight answer for me or not?"

"Of course I do."

"Then tell me what I have to do."

Faster than she expected, the Underman's glowing face shot across the pitch-black living room until it hovered mere inches from hers. She sucked in a sharp breath and leaned backward, hoping the bench was as wide as she remembered so she wouldn't fall off the back onto her ass.

A slow creaking sound emanated from the Underman's open mouth as he studied her through the bane-breaker's eyes. "It's about time someone offered you the carrot and not just the stick."

She frowned. "I'm gonna assume you're talking figuratively here. Then I'm gonna tell you to back up out of my personal space."

He let out another deep chuckle. "Here's your straight answer, Cheyenne. The fate of Bianca Summerlin, her half-drow daughter, and both worlds is the same."

The base of Cheyenne's spine burned with a renewed flare of anger. "Nope. Try again, demon."

"You're so cute." A green-glowing hand materialized out of the darkness and reached toward the halfling's face. Cheyenne jerked her head away, squinting against the sudden drop in temperature when Inolu's possessed fingers came close to her cheek. "There is no trying again. If she is to live and if you want to live, take the vessel with you across the Border."

"No." She swallowed thickly. "No, that's not how this works."

"Oh, really?" The Underman drew away from her, still grinning. "Didn't you say you needed help with the how?"

Cheyenne couldn't look at the grotesquely wide smile stretching across Inolu's face. A knot in her gut clenched tighter with each second, and she shut her eyes. *This isn't happening. Ember brought it up, and I shut that idea down as fast I could because it's not true. Mom can't be a part of this, not like I am. She didn't do anything. This asshole's fucking with my head.*

Taking a long, slow breath through her nose, Cheyenne forced herself to look at the Underman's glowing face again. "What's the vessel?"

"Not what, Cheyenne. Who."

No, no, no. This is wrong.

Another low chuckle rose from his grinning mouth. "L'zar Verdys has done his part in this world, but he has yet to finish what he started Earthside. Now that you've reached this pivotal moment, it falls to you to mend the break in the Weave."

"I told you I was done with riddles," Cheyenne growled. "Just tell me!"

The Underman retreated again to the pallet where Inolu had been sitting before her possession began. "Bianca Summerlin must present herself in Ambar'ogúl as the vessel. The final part of the whole. The final part of *your* whole."

"You're insane." She stood, wanting more than anything to storm out of the room and take her questions somewhere else. *I can't see shit in here.* Gritting her teeth, she forced herself to breathe evenly and do the only thing she could—stand there and try to weasel something out of this demonic douchebag that made sense. "There's no way she's the vessel. I'm not buying it."

"You would not exist to break the Spider's chains around both worlds without your dear human mother." The Underman swayed from side to side, leaving a trailing glow of green behind. "And neither world will exist the way we've always known them if you do not finish what L'zar started when he sought not to reap what the drow have sown but to burn it. And it will burn, Cheyenne, either beneath the lifeforce of the deathflame purging Ambar'ogúl with the vessel's strength or beneath the fires of the Undoing created to consume us. One way or the other, nothing as you know it will remain the same. The choice you must make is whether you are willing to do whatever it takes to guide the rewriting of your worlds. If not, that rewriting will end you and everything you hold dear—and everyone. Including Bianca Summerlin."

A cold shiver raced up Cheyenne's spine. *No. Just no.* "Are you fucking serious?"

"It's very simple, drow."

"It's not simple. It's a fucking joke."

"Yes." A rumbling laugh filled the black room. "Right now, maybe it is a joke. Very soon, there will be no laughter if you do not fulfill your purpose."

Goddammit! Cheyenne's nails bit into her palms as her mind raced with everything this meant. *This demon's full of shit. He has to be.*

"I'm not taking her across the Border, asshole," she snarled as the heat of her fury egging on her drow magic pulsed from the base of her spine. She could even feel it in her head this time, like a constant ache throbbing behind her eyes with each heartbeat. "There has to be another way."

"Oh, of course there is. Two choices." The eerie glow lighting up nothing but Inolu's face and the Underman's unfailing smile flickered. "You can take the vessel to Ambar'ogúl and do what must be done. Or you can refuse. That way lies death and destruction and agony, blah, blah, blah."

"You're lying."

The demon cackled again.

Cheyenne lost it.

Her skin rippled to life with black flames, which only gave off a miniscule amount of light. Without thinking, she lashed out at the Underman using the bane-breaker as a conduit and shot a stream of black fire at the center of that insufferably grinning face.

Still laughing, the Underman lifted two glowing hands and stopped Cheyenne's drow fire without any effort. The flames crackled and churned between those outstretched hands. "This has been an entertaining encounter, I will give you that. I already told you how cute you are, didn't I?"

"Fuck you!" Cheyenne lunged at the face in the darkness with a snarl.

The Underman flicked his wrists, and her captured black fire snuffed out. A howling gale whipped through the dark room, and an unbearable weight settled on Cheyenne's chest.

She choked, gasping for breath, but there was no air left in the room. Lurching toward that goddamn grin, she forced herself to keep moving through the agonizing burning in her lungs. One leg gave out, then the other, and she dropped to her knees halfway to Inolu's pallet.

I'll fucking kill him. I don't care what that thing is. Dead or alive...or... I'll rip his...

The green grin and glowing eyes squinted in amusement blurred in her vision. The rest of the Underman's rolling laughter faded from her ears as if retreating down a long tunnel. Then Cheyenne had nothing left inside her to keep fighting.

CHAPTER FIFTY-SIX

Cheyenne gasped and jolted awake. Immediately, she pushed off the cold, hard stone floor until she was sitting up and looked around, blinking furiously. *Too bright.*

When her eyes finally adjusted, she realized she was in an entirely different room. Sunlight streamed through the sliding glass doors in front of her. Outside, a crow swooped down to land on the nearly bare branch of a tree in the back courtyard. Cheyenne glared at the bird, then looked quickly over her shoulder.

I'm in a kitchen. What the hell?

A soft pop and thump came from behind her on the left, and she looked over the other shoulder.

Inolu sat in one of the two chairs at her round kitchen table, popping hard, deep-purple berries off a sprig of some plant before chucking them into the lime-green ceramic bowl on the table in front of her. The whole time, she stared at Cheyenne, looking as bored as she had the first time they'd met.

Cheyenne cleared her throat. "Are you serious? You can't just knock me out and move me into a different room again while I'm unconscious."

The bane-breaker shrugged. "I didn't. Your consultation is concluded, though."

"Yeah, no shit." Grimacing, Cheyenne pushed to her feet, dusting off her hands on her black pants as she looked around the normal, clean, brightly lit kitchen. *I'm missing something here.*

"These are for you." Inolu produced two large, corked vials, one of a dark-purple glass, the other light brown, and slid them across the table to her client.

"I don't want anything from you." Cheyenne swallowed and glanced around the kitchen, trying to find the best way out of there.

"The Underman says the purple one will help with the poison eating you from the inside out," Inolu continued, unfazed by the halfling's rejection.

"Oh, yeah?" Cheyenne looked sharply at the bane-breaker, who'd gone back to plucking berries and dropping them into the bowl as she stared at the halfling. "Your demon buddy told you to hand it over, huh? Nice try. I'm not falling for it."

"Whatever. The brown one is for the human vessel. To make her strong before the crossing. You know, so she doesn't spontaneously combust or something."

Cheyenne narrowed her eyes at the bane-breaker, who no longer tried to hide her green-glowing veins or the constant light behind her eyes. "Do you want me to hurt you?"

Inolu snorted. "Right. Because you were so successful with that the last time you tried."

"I don't care what just happened. I'm not taking my human mom across the Border because the demon living inside you told me to."

The bane-breaker's rhythmic plucking paused as she studied the drow looming over her in the center of her kitchen. With a click of her tongue, Inolu shrugged and lowered her gaze to the small branch in her hand. "Then we'll all burn. Now get the fuck out of my house."

"I thought you'd never ask."

"I didn't."

With flaring nostrils, Cheyenne stormed past the table to the other side of the kitchen. She stopped, spun around, and leaned over the bane-breaker to snatch the two vials off the table. *Just because this isn't happening, it doesn't mean these won't be useful.*

The second the glass vials clinked together in her hand, Inolu spun around in her chair and shoved Cheyenne squarely in the chest. "That wasn't an invitation to loiter!"

The force of the magic behind the shove propelled Cheyenne across the kitchen. The soles of her black Vans squeaked on the stone floors. "What the hell are you doing? Hey!"

Before the spell zapped her sideways down the hall, she caught a final glimpse of the bane-breaker returning her attention to the berries.

Cheyenne bashed into the corner of the hallway, sending a flare of searing pain through her poisoned shoulder. She snarled and reached out, trying to grab a passing doorframe or bookshelf, but she was moving too fast. "Make this thing stop!"

The spell bashed her against another corner before sweeping her into the narrow entrance hall inside the front door. Cheyenne tried to brace herself against the floor scraping by beneath her, but she couldn't get traction. The red circle painted on the floor rushed by her, then the front door flew open. Sunlight spilled into the entryway, Cheyenne was tossed onto the front stoop, and the door slammed shut in her face.

Staggering under her full weight, she snarled at the door and lunged at it. "Inolu! Hey! Open this fucking door!"

Cheyenne pounded on the navy-blue wood with her fist, the potion vials clinking together in her other hand. Her drow magic threatened to flare out of her control for the first time in months. *Get it together, Cheyenne. You can't go full-drow apeshit out here in the middle of the street. Get back in there first.*

"Inolu!" The next time her fist came down on the door, an orange jolt of energy zapped through her hand and up her arm. The magical burst knocked her sideways as if someone had punched her in the shoulder, and Cheyenne snarled. "What the hell's wrong with you?"

The whir of the swiveling camera lens made her stop. She looked at the opening and closing shutter and hissed.

Inolu's voice came from an intercom hidden somewhere on the front stoop, tinny and robotic-sounding. "Do what you have to do, Cheyenne, but if you're too much of an imbecile to take the Underman's advice, don't even think about showing up at my door again."

The camera lens jerked quickly away from Cheyenne to center on the street, then whirred closed again and retracted into the small black box on the side wall.

Fuck.

Cheyenne glared at the door, fuming, and shoved the glass vials into her coat pocket. "Bitch."

Clenching her jaw, she spun away from the landing and headed down the few steps to the sidewalk. Then she realized what she'd been missing before she was tossed out onto the street like a sack of drow garbage. *It's light outside. Either they're both liars, or I was in there way longer than I thought.*

Snatching her phone out of her back pocket, Cheyenne stalked across the street to the parking garage. She had to turn her phone back on after whatever interference from the demon-possessed bane-breaker had turned it off. The lock screen lit up under the crisp early-November morning light.

Ten o'clock in the morning? Are you shitting me?

The notifications banner on her lock screen had filled up so much, they'd all smooshed into a single line. She had seven missed calls, three new voicemails, and four unread text messages.

Cheyenne stomped back to her car, unlocked her phone, and went for the texts first. They were all from Ember.

So I guess you're not gonna make it home for dinner, right?

Okay, not that I care, but it's weird that you're not back. All good?

I called you. It's almost midnight. Maybe toss a fae something, huh?

Where the fuck are you?

Cheyenne closed the text app and pulled up the missed calls. Only two of them were Ember; the other four were from numbers she didn't recognize. The fae had left a voicemail both times she'd called, and the third message was from an unknown number too.

Normally, she wouldn't have bothered to listen. But she'd told L'zar to figure out how to use cell phones if he insisted on being Bianca's fucked-up drow keeper. *Please don't let this be a call from him.*

She played the voicemail and stuck the phone to her ear as she reached into her coat pocket and thumbed the automatic unlock on her key fob by feel. The Panamera chirped at her from two rows up and one to the left.

"This is a confidential voicemail for Miss Cheyenne Summerlin," a woman's voice droned in the recording. "My name is Helen Holder, personal secretary for Major General Van Lurig with the organization you've had unofficial dealings with for the last few months. Your presence is requested on base tomorrow afternoon at one-thirty for a debriefing on the events of last night at the showroom in Westphalia, specifically regarding further punitive action to be taken against Colonel Les Thomas, Major Guy Carson, and Captain Brian Rhynehart. Major General Van Lurig and the remaining members of the board believe you can shed further light on the situation and will not be moving forward with future injunctions until this debriefing takes place." The woman cleared her throat. "I was told to include in this summons that although your presence is requested, Miss Summerlin, do be aware that failing to appear at one-thirty tomorrow afternoon will result in our organization enacting certain disciplinary protocols to ensure you present yourself on base. And we both know you don't want that."

The message ended with a click.

Cheyenne rolled her eyes and lowered the phone from her ear as she approached her newly Gothed-out Porsche. Even the sight of the purple lights on the dashboard and interior doors when she opened the driver's side door wasn't enough to pull her out of her funk.

First this bane-breaker and her psychotic demon puppeteer, and now the fucking FRoE. I didn't know it was today until ten minutes ago, and it's already started off like shit.

Slumping into the driver's seat, she pulled the door closed and took a steadying breath. Another glance at her phone showed her Helen Holder's voicemail had been left yesterday at 5:23 p.m.

"Great. Three hours 'til I have to show up for 'save Sir's ass' duty. I need to hit something." She strapped herself in, turned on the car, and called Ember before putting the call on speaker.

The line rang once.

"What the hell, Cheyenne?"

"I know."

"Seriously. This is, like, the one time I ever call or text you, and absolutely nothing."

The Panamera peeled out of the parking garage with a squeal of tires. "I know, Em."

"I don't get it. You get sucked into some kinda time warp or something? 'Cause that's the only thing I can think of that would make sense."

Gripping the steering wheel so tightly her hands squeaked on the leather, Cheyenne pulled to a jerky stop at the next stop sign before taking the left turn way too fast. "I mean, I guess it was kinda like that, yeah."

Ember paused. "What?"

"Look, I'm on the way home right now. I'll tell you then."

"Yeah. Fine." The fae cleared her throat. "And just to be clear, I don't need you to always tell me where you are or what you're doing. Honestly, I'd probably rather not know half the time, except for when you have poisoned blight holes in your body and no more darktongue serum."

Gritting her teeth, Cheyenne tried not to let herself drive angry all the way back to their apartment on the north end of Richmond. "I'm sorry, Em."

"Yeah, I know."

"For the record, the last twenty or whatever hours for you have only felt like maybe three hours for me."

Ember sniffed on the other end. "Yeah, you can tell me how the hell that's even possible when you get here."

"Uh-huh."

The line went dead, and Cheyenne glanced quickly at her phone in the center console to be sure the call was over. "Shit."

So that's what Ember Gaderow sounds like when she's pissed off. Maybe she'll buck up when she hears she was right. I can't believe I'm thinking that.

CHAPTER FIFTY-SEVEN

The second she stepped out of the elevators on the top floor of their building at Pellerville Gables, Cheyenne heard voices. Both of them came from behind the door to the apartment she shared with her best friend—Ember's voice and Matthew Thomas'.

Fuck this.

Rolling her eyes, she jerked on the doorknob, knowing it wouldn't be locked with their who-knew-how-friendly neighbor walking in and out of their place again, apparently whenever he wanted. As soon as the door opened, Ember and Matthew stopped talking.

Cheyenne folded her arms and didn't bother to close the door behind her when she stepped inside. "So I disappear for a night, and you make yourself right at home again, huh?"

"Hey, Cheyenne." He sat on the couch with Ember, though they each took up opposite sides with the whole center cushion between them.

At least I didn't walk in on them cuddling. Ugh.

She stared him down without a word.

Ember cleared her throat. "Hungry?"

"No."

Matthew nodded and leaned over his lap, running his hands down his long thighs. "I had some more questions this morning, okay? I had the chance to sleep on everything Ember told me yesterday before you popped out of here with the cat lady."

"Nightstalker." Ember and Cheyenne said it at the same time.

"Right." Their neighbor frowned. "I guess I owe you one, huh?"

"I didn't do anything, Matthew. To you or for you." The halfling shrugged out of her trenchcoat with a grimace and didn't sling it over the armrest of the couch like usual because he was sitting there. She headed for her regular seat in the closest black leather recliner, draped her coat over the armrest of the other recliner, and lowered herself to the cushion, trying to keep her face from showing the pain. *Looks like passing out twice and sleeping through most of the last day doesn't have any effect on blight wounds. Whoever said the body heals most during sleep can go fuck themselves.*

She settled both arms gingerly on the armrests and cocked her head at their neighbor. "So, what do you owe me?"

"An apology, for one." Matthew ran a hand through his hair. "A real one where I say I know I was a dick, I should've believed you from the beginning, and I'm sorry I didn't take you seriously."

"I guess that's a good start." Cheyenne shifted to the left to remove some of the weight from her screaming right hip, which was full of poison that was spreading farther through her body by the hour. "Anything else?"

"Yeah." Matthew glanced at Ember, then braced his forearms against his thighs and dipped his head between his shoulders as he studied the halfling warily. "A thank you."

She snorted. "You know, if I wasn't this close to chopping my own arms off just to feel better, I might know what the hell you're talking about."

"For going in last night to stop him. Les." Their neighbor frowned at her, chewing the inside of his cheek. "What Ember told me and what I know about him match up enough that I can say I don't think he would've stopped. Not on his own, at least."

"Yeah, probably not." Cheyenne grunted out the rest of her words. "Asshole bigots in positions of power usually don't step away from their genocidal tendencies out of the blue and start reevaluating their life choices."

Matthew's gaze fell to the floor, and he seemed to have an awfully hard time looking up at her again to meet her gaze. "I meant, you know, if anyone was gonna stop him, I guess I'm glad it was you. Both of you."

"Cool." Cheyenne thumped her head back against the cushion and closed her eyes. "We'll let you throw us a party later."

Matthew and Ember exchanged quick glances, then their cyber-security millionaire neighbor slapped his thighs and pushed himself to his feet. "Pretty sure this is my cue to go home. Thanks for explaining things, Ember."

She gave him a tight smile but didn't bother standing. "Well, we told you we would."

"Yeah, and I appreciate that. Sticking to your word and everything." He stuck his hands in his pockets and frowned at the long wall of windows on the north side of their apartment. "Not a lot of that goin' around right now."

With a brief nod to no one and nothing in particular, Matthew hurried to the open front door. His hand came out of his pocket to pull the shut door behind him, and thirty seconds later, the sound of his apartment door opening and shutting came from across the hall.

Ember stared at her friend, waiting for Cheyenne to start the conversation they both knew they needed to have. The drow sat motionlessly in the recliner, her legs splayed out in front of her and her hands dangling limply over the ends of the armrests. *Like she sat down in her Goth-girl throne just to kick the bucket. Jesus, Ember. You're full of morbid shit today.*

"So." With a flash of purple light, the fae lifted both legs onto the couch and leaned back against the armrest in her favorite position. "You gonna tell me what happened?"

"Yep." The word whispered out of Cheyenne, and she swallowed thickly before clearing her throat. "I'm thinking about the good old days, Em. Back when I could stick myself with a metal canister and not feel anything for hours."

"The good old days as in less than forty-eight hours ago?"

"Yeah. I miss 'em."

"Want some water or something?"

"Nope."

Ember folded her arms. "How bad is it?"

"Bad enough. Not as bad as it could be. And please don't ask to see right now. I just need to sit here and not be touched by anyone or moved around by magic or whatever."

"Just by looking at you, Cheyenne, I know I don't wanna see. My imagination's in a lot better shape than you are right now."

With a snort, Cheyenne finally opened her eyes and looked at her friend. "That might be taking it a little too far."

"I don't think so." Ember didn't look like she was joking. "Was that why you pulled a disappearing act?"

"Because of the blight-poisoned dart holes in my body? Not really."

The fae blinked. "You gotta give me something here."

"Yeah, I know. Okay." Cheyenne took a deep breath and nodded. "I went to pick up my car yesterday."

"Uh-huh."

"Which, by the way, didn't have anything wrong with it. Lee tricked it out as a surprise. It's insane, Em. Not huge changes, but he did this thing with—"

"You're stalling."

"I mean, it's all true."

When Ember raised an unamused eyebrow, Cheyenne cleared her throat.

"Okay, fine. I was on my way home. Finally decided to call the banebreaker, Inolu Roth, and she told me to come by for a consultation. Like she's some kind of doctor."

"The kind that deals in curses."

"Yeah, Em. And not just her. She's sharing her body with this thing— a demon-spirit-magical something. I don't know. I guess I wasn't supposed to be there as late as I was."

"What time did you get there?" Ember's eyebrows furrowed.

"I don't know. Mid-afternoon. That chick's crazy, Em. She's got this whole security system. Knocked me flat on my ass, and the next thing I know, I wake up, like, in this study pulled right out of the eighteen hundreds. Then she—"

"Whoa, whoa. Hold on a second." Ember held up a hand to stop her friend and blinked quickly. "Her security system knocked you out?"

"Kinda. Apparently, her algorithm didn't pick up that the poison I'm carrying around isn't a bomb or something."

"Seriously?"

"What?"

Ember's eyes widened, and she took a deep breath. "I've heard a lot of crazy stories from you, but I could at least follow those ones through from beginning to end. I have no idea what the hell you said."

"Oh." Cheyenne cleared her throat and tried to push herself up a little straighter in the recliner. Her shoulders burned with even the smallest movement of her arms, and the pain in her hip might only have been lessening because that side of her seemed to be going numb. *Pull it together. Doesn't matter how much this shit hurts right now. The last thing I need is to go all raving-drow lunatic because of it. Yeah, that sounds like someone I know too.*

She shook her head. "Okay, let's forget about the details right now."

"With everything we're still trying to do, don't you think the details are kind of important?"

"Not all of them." Cheyenne had to look away from her friend's confused frown and settled for staring at the ceiling instead. "I had a little chat with this demon-thing, I guess, and he told me… Jesus, I can't believe I'm about to say this right now, Em, but maybe you were right."

Ember shifted toward her and slung her elbow over the armrest behind her. "About what?"

Cheyenne grimaced and slowly looked down to meet the fae's gaze. "That Bianca has more to do with all this than any of us thought."

Her friend's eyebrows rose. "What did the demon-thing tell you?"

"It doesn't even make sense." Shaking her head, Cheyenne tried to steady her breathing as the heat of her anger made a surprisingly strong comeback. "It can't make sense. I mean, she's human. And none of this was supposed to happen. The curse was a side effect. An accident."

"Cheyenne." Ember leaned forward, getting ready to push herself off the couch if she had to. *This is what people with fevers and head injuries sound like.* "Just say it."

The drow gritted her teeth and clenched her eyes shut. "The bane-breaker and the thing inside her both said that Bianca's the vessel, Em. That if I don't take my human mom across the Border to do whatever the vessel's supposed to do, everything will burn. Whatever the hell that's supposed to mean."

"To Ambar'ogúl?"

Swallowing thickly, Cheyenne opened her eyes again and slowly nodded.

"Okay, well, how much can we trust a demon?" Ember ran a hand through her violet-streaked hair she hadn't bothered to cover with an illusion charm now that Matthew knew who and what she was. "I mean, did the thing sound like it knew what it was talking about?"

"Does anyone these days?" Cheyenne stared at the coffee table. "I have no idea, but I can't let myself believe that this is a thing, Em. That she's involved in this and has to be there to do whatever. I mean, humans don't make the crossing. That's a pretty known fucking fact."

"So was O'gúl tech malfunctioning when anyone tried to bring it across Earthside. Until you did it."

Cheyenne grunted. "That's not the same thing."

"I mean, if you're talking about known facts," Ember spread her arms, "it's looking more and more like those don't even exist."

"That doesn't mean a glowing asshole using the bane-breaker as a puppet is right." When she lifted a hand to her head, meaning to run it through her hair, the pain in Cheyenne's shoulder flared, and she gingerly lowered her arm to the armrest again. "There has to be another way. Some other loophole out of this. 'Cause I am not ferrying Bianca Summerlin through the in-between so she can be poked and prodded by a bunch of magicals who think humans are dull, slow, powerless idiots."

A tiny smirk flickered along Ember's lips. "Pretty accurate, though, right? In comparison, I mean."

Cheyenne flicked her gaze up and slowly shook her head. "Not funny right now."

"Okay, fine. I get it. You don't want to stretch your mind as far as it has to stretch to wrap around something like this. If I felt as bad as you look right now, I wouldn't wanna think about anything either. Especially not Bianca in Ambar'ogúl."

"Jesus."

"But hear me out. Just for a second, okay?" Ember swung her legs off the couch and leaned over them, trying to hold her friend's unsteady gaze. "You aren't the vessel. I'm willing to put stock in that based on what happened to you when Venga thought you were. And I don't care what you say, that's not happening again."

"Em!"

"I'm not done. Your cousin's been coming to you in dreams, talking about the vessel. About putting two parts of a whole back together. I wouldn't normally say the arrow points immediately to your mom, but she's already neck-deep in this. Ba'rael's curse is on her skin, Cheyenne, and she's your *mom*. The only woman who managed to raise one of L'zar's kids to 'kick ass and overthrow the Crown' status."

Both girls grimaced at the unwelcome visual of L'zar doing anything intimate with anyone.

"You get the picture."

Cheyenne's nostrils flared. "I wish I didn't."

"And we can't ignore the blazing sign that literally burned itself into your mom's body. *Vessel.* You have a good explanation for how that's just another random O'gúleesh rune like all the others?"

"Em, I could write 'troll hooker' on my forehead, and that wouldn't make me one."

The fae snorted. "Thank God."

When Cheyenne clenched her eyes shut and didn't look even slightly amused, Ember straightened, her small smile disappearing. *She really is in bad shape.*

"I think we should at least talk to someone else about this. Maybe even give it a try."

"No." Cheyenne shook her head. "I'm not doing that to Bianca. She's already been through way more than she should have because L'zar decided to fuck around with prophecies and his sister's shitty pride or jealousy or whatever the hell it was. I'll figure it out. I just need more time."

Ember cocked her head, wanting to scream at her friend to stop being so fucking stubborn. That might be more than she could handle right now, though. "It doesn't look like you have a lot of time left, Cheyenne."

"You don't know that."

"Sure, but I know I've never seen you look like that before."

"I'm fine." Gritting her teeth against the pain, Cheyenne pushed out of the chair.

"You're very obviously not," Ember countered.

"I probably just need some food or something." Her right leg wobbled beneath her weight and the dizzying jolt of pain bursting through her hip. She stumbled sideways to the other recliner and slapped her hands down on the leather to keep from falling. Her other leg bumped the armrest and her trenchcoat, and the two vials in the pocket clinked against each other.

Cheyenne froze and glared down at her jacket.

Ember was on her feet now, with an inch between them and the floor. "What is that?"

"Nothing."

"Don't do that." The fae floated around the coffee table, eyeing the trenchcoat. "You tell me all the things, remember? 'Nothing' is the excuse you use for everyone else."

"It doesn't matter, Em." Cheyenne straightened and reached down for her coat.

The trenchcoat flashed with violet light, whisked away from the recliner, and settled into Ember's outstretched hand. They stared at each other for a moment, then Ember raised her eyebrows. "Guess you should go eat something. Might make you a little faster."

Cheyenne rolled her eyes as Ember shoved her hand into the correct pocket on the first try. The two potion vials glinted under the overhead lights, and the fae studied them before using them to point at her friend. "Party favors from a demon?"

"Yeah, I don't know."

Ember tossed the trenchcoat back on the recliner and studied the vials. "Somehow, I'm not feelin' this whole 'bane-breaker gave me potions but didn't say shit about what they're for' vibe."

"And I'm not feeling this whole 'let's interrogate Cheyenne and go through her stuff because we can cast spells' vibe, either."

"You know what?" Ember eyed her friend. "If we don't figure out how to heal you, I'm sure you'll be feeling a dead vibe. Probably soon. In case you haven't noticed, that's why I'm interrogating you and going through your stuff. No dead vibes. Got it?"

Cheyenne had to look away as she muttered, "I'm fine."

"What are these for?"

"I have no idea. Inolu told me, but I'm not into trusting magical shut-ins who might have OCD and definitely don't have a social filter."

Ember snorted. "So, you're second-guessing yourself then too, huh?"

"No." Cheyenne dipped her head. "Okay, that does kinda sound like me sometimes, but I'm talking about the bane-breaker."

"Just tell me what they're for, Cheyenne. Or what she said they're for."

"Fine. The brown one's for Bianca. To make her strong for the crossing, or whatever."

Ember looked down at the vials and raised her eyebrows. "Huh. That's kinda cool. And the purple one?"

"It's a healing potion." The words came out in a rushed mumble as Cheyenne brushed past the recliner and half-stumbled, half-limped to the bathroom.

"She gave you a healing potion, and you haven't taken it yet?" Ember floated after her. "What are you doing?"

"I'm gonna take a shower."

"Not before you take this." Ember moved faster, trying to get to the bathroom before Cheyenne did. "Seriously, Cheyenne. You don't think a healing potion from a magical who deals strictly in curses and spends at least half her time getting rid of them won't help you?"

"Nope." Cheyenne grabbed the bathroom doorknob, opened the door, and froze when violet light flared in front of her and slammed the door shut again. "Not cool."

"Take the potion."

"No way." Opening the door again, Cheyenne shot Ember a disgusted frown over her shoulder. "I'm not putting anything in my body that that crazy chick handed over for fun. She's possessed. And she didn't charge me for it, so it can't be that helpful."

"Or maybe she knows what'll happen if you don't take it and doesn't give a shit about the money." The bathroom door slammed shut again, followed quickly by the rush of the showerhead.

Ember turned halfway to the kitchen, then stopped to glare at the bathroom door. *Maybe she cared about you not being poisoned by the blight and that stupid, hard-ass drow head that apparently runs in the family. It's like you don't even want to get better.*

With a frustrated snort, she floated back to the couch and slumped down on it. Ember's legs lifted up onto the cushions again with a flash of violet light, and she stared at the two five-inch vials in her hands. *She wouldn't let that shit kill her just to keep her mom out of this. Right?*

CHAPTER FIFTY-EIGHT

A shower was supposed to be quick, simple, and practical. Cheyenne's wasn't any of those things. She couldn't stop thinking about the Underman's glowing grin as she tried to scrub away the dirt of the last few days and the creepiness of the last twenty-four hours, all while trying not to make any sudden movements that would make the pain in her shoulders and hips even worse. That was hard to do with a full head of hair needing to be shampooed, no matter what color it was.

What the fuck was that thing, anyway? Said he'd been with Inolu for a long time. They had an arrangement. What kind of messed-up ritual does someone have to do to literally share their body with a thing like that?

She shuddered when she remembered the cold sharpness emanating from the Underman-Inolu's hand when they'd reached for her face, even under the steaming-hot water. *Yeah, I don't think I wanna know.*

Toweling off wasn't all that bad as long as she didn't try to dry the hard-to-reach places, which was pretty much everywhere at this point. Cheyenne pulled her blow-dryer out of the drawer, plugged it in, then tried to lift the thing to her head. The blow-dryer clattered on the countertop five seconds later. *Fuck this.*

With a towel wrapped loosely around her, she moved slowly out of the bathroom to her trenchcoat on the recliner and managed to pull her activator out of the pocket without the towel dropping to her feet.

Ember looked up at her from the couch, hardly paying attention to her show on the TV with the volume turned way too low. "Feel better?"

"I don't know yet."

"Huh. Maybe you should take a healing potion."

"I'm not taking anything right now, Em." The drow shuffled toward her bedroom. "Not until I know for sure what's in that vial."

"Yeah. I wonder what it could possibly be."

Cheyenne ignored her and closed the bedroom door. The towel dropped to the floor, and she stuck the activator behind her ear. The sharp pinch in her neck felt stronger this time, and her eyelids fluttered for seconds longer than they usually did when the tech synced up with her magic. *But I can still use the damn thing. That's all I need.*

She selected the command prompts for what she wanted, flicking her fingers around the room without having to move her arms. Dresser drawers opened to launch a shirt, pants, and underwear onto her bed. Her backpack unzipped itself, and the brown glass jar of darktongue salve spun end over end in the air before joining her outfit.

At least that still worked.

When the activator didn't pull up any prompts for self-healing or instructions for poison-canceling spells, Cheyenne shook her head. *Of course not. That would be way too easy.*

It did pull up spells for magicking her clothes onto her body in under twenty seconds. She brushed down the front of her long-sleeved black shirt with red lace around the collar and in a thick line down each arm. *Shouldn't get too used to that, but I'm sure this counts as a necessary exception.*

She sat down on the bed, reached for the jar of darktongue salve to unscrew the lid, and dipped her fingers into the glistening, sticky white salve. "Just sticking to what I know works. Mostly."

Then she steeled herself for what she knew hurt like a bitch every time.

After twenty minutes of trying to drown out the sounds of Cheyenne enduring another application of darktongue salve, Ember didn't even bother to open her eyes when her friend's bedroom door opened. "Oh, good. You survived."

"Yeah." Cheyenne stretched her neck as far as she could toward each shoulder and sniffed. "It works for now."

"And when it stops working?" Ember opened her eyes and watched the drow lumber across their apartment to the kitchen. "What are you gonna do then?"

"I'll figure it out, Em. Just like I always have."

Ember sat up on the couch and looked over the back of it with a frown. "You're gonna have to make a choice sooner or later. You know, I have a feeling you'll change your tune when you can't get up and move around. When your magic stops working because the blight's shut everything down. I'd like to avoid seeing you get to that place, though."

Cheyenne grimaced as she opened the fridge, her shoulder protesting even that much movement. She peeled down the collar of her shirt to take a quick look at the dart-hole. *Shit. Being knocked around by a bane breaker and getting pissed off and running out of serum make for one killer combination. And that was the worst choice of words.*

"I won't get there." She reached into the fridge for a takeout container. "What's this?"

"Italian." Ember shrugged. "Felt kinda weird to cook something when I couldn't decide if you'd been blown up, strangled by that poison, or just wanted everyone to leave you alone."

The drow snorted. "I wouldn't ignore that many phone calls and texts on purpose."

"Yeah, I know. That's why it was weird." Ember nodded when her friend raised the container with a questioning glance. "Yeah, go ahead. I already ate breakfast."

"With Matthew?"

Ember stared at her as Cheyenne popped the container into the microwave and tried to hide that the darktongue salve hadn't worked to take down the pain. "Only because he brought it to me."

"So you could answer his other questions over coffee and a scone, huh?"

"Actually, it was a breakfast sandwich from the deli across the street. Really freakin' good, too."

Cheyenne glanced at her friend with a small smile. "How'd he take it?"

"Despite how surprised I am that you even care, he took it pretty well." Ember slung her arms over the back of the couch to hold herself up and peer over it into the kitchen. "I mean, yesterday was pretty much me just giving him the facts about the colonel, the war machines, and what we found out before and after we stormed into that showroom to stop him. I don't think he was expecting anything close to what I told him."

"Who would?"

"True."

The microwave beeped, and Cheyenne took out the steaming container of leftover chicken cacciatore before rummaging loudly through the silverware drawer for a fork. "And he came back this morning?"

"To ask questions. I guess he needed a few hours to let it all settle before he could wrap his mind around what he still wanted to know."

Blowing on a hot forkful, Cheyenne leaned far over the kitchen island and her leftovers so she wouldn't have to lift the fork farther than her aching shoulder could handle. "What did you tell him about me?"

Ember let out a surprised laugh. "What?"

"Not to say you guys don't have anything better to talk about. There are some things I don't necessarily want him to know about that night."

"You mean like the fact that you have a magical poison spreading through your body, the Bull's Head made a drow-paralyzing agent specific to your DNA, and the combination almost got you shot in the head by Les Thomas?"

Cheyenne almost choked on her mouthful and leaned farther over the container. "Yeah, Em. Like that."

"No." The fae pursed her lips, trying to hide a smile, and shook her head. "I didn't tell our neighbor about all your personal issues."

"Okay. And I appreciate it." Their apartment fell silent for the next three minutes while Cheyenne shoveled warm chicken and tomato sauce and noodles into her mouth. She finally had to stop to get herself a glass of water, and when she returned to the island, Ember was still watching her intently. "I'm not gonna keel over while eating your leftovers, Em."

"Hey, neither of us knows that for sure, do we?"

The drow chugged half her water and gave the weakest, lamest shrug possible. *I can't even use body language with this crap inside me. This sucks.* "So, what are you gonna do with the neighbor guy?"

"What do you mean?"

"I mean, you invited him over for breakfast."

"I didn't invite him. He texted me and asked if we could go over some more things. Then he offered to bring food." When Cheyenne went back to eating the rest of her re-heated meal, Ember sighed. "I'm kind of giving him a second chance."

"Huh. How does that work, exactly?"

"I don't know, okay? I mean, his brain practically exploded yesterday when I spilled the beans about his uncle. And he kept apologizing the whole time." Ember snorted. "Both cute and annoying. I had to tell him to shut up so I could finish talking."

"Good call."

"I don't know how to read him." Ember slid back down on the couch and leaned against the armrest again. "He took way too long to give up any information we could use when we needed it. And he seems like he wants to help, like he wants to make sure something like a FRoE official commissioning war machines from Ba'rael's Earthside thugs never happens again. But he's not the guy I thought he was when we met."

"Well, don't beat yourself up too much." Cheyenne licked the fork clean, tossed the empty container in the trash, and dropped the fork into the dishwasher with a clink. "You've only known the guy a few weeks."

"I know that. And I'm not beating myself up." Ember rolled her eyes. "I liked having a cool neighbor who was fun to hang out with while you ran all over Virginia doing your 'secret double life as an unofficial FRoE agent' thing."

Cheyenne walked slowly to the second recliner and reached for her jacket. "You're not gonna mention the part about you being head-over-heels for our billionaire tech mogul right across the hall?"

Ember scoffed. "Yeah, okay. And he's nice to look at. Trust me, though. I'm not heartbroken or pining for the guy. I'd be able to forget about the whole thing a lot easier if he didn't live right across the hall."

"True." When trying to slip into her trenchcoat didn't pan out, Cheyenne grunted and selected the activator's prompted spell to magic the thing onto her instead. "He might be useful for other things, once we fix this whole 'two dying worlds' thing."

The fae's eyes widened. "That's one awesome spell."

"Oh. Yeah." Cheyenne stuck her hands in her pockets and felt around to make sure she had everything. "I'd offer to show you how, but…"

"Activator. I get it." Ember gave her a once-over. "Going somewhere?"

"Yeah." With a grimace, the drow pointed at the door with her thumb. "Got a call from Major General Van Lurig's hotshot personal secretary. Same FRoE official who interrogated me when L'zar got out. One of them, at least. They want a debriefing about the other night."

Ember sucked in a breath through her teeth and wrinkled her nose. "That sounds like a real mood-killer."

"Tell me about it." Despite how much she didn't want to do this today, or at all, Cheyenne couldn't hold back a wry laugh. "The lady threatened me in a voicemail. They'll enact disciplinary protocols if I don't show up."

"Those people are insane."

"I know. Hopefully not too insane to listen to me this time. I gotta go."

"Yeah. Good luck."

"Thanks. Feel free to tell Matthew all about it when I get back."

Ember rolled her eyes. "Very funny."

CHAPTER FIFTY-NINE

*I*f *there was ever a good time to sit down with those idiots and start telling them what needs to change, I guess now is it.*

Cheyenne stepped out of her car in the parking lot of the FRoE compound at 1:15 and locked the doors. The Panamera chirped and flashed a dim violet glow from the tops of the headlights. She headed for the front door, slipping into drow mode on the way. *Yeah, Lee outdid himself.*

She walked slowly past the line of glistening black FRoE vehicles, three of which were black Jeeps like Rhynehart's. *But not his. Rhynehart's unemployed now.*

The compound's front lobby was just as empty as that weird row of cubicles lining the back wall, but that didn't last very long.

"I swear to the brilliant asshole who invented fellwine, Grot. If I even smell your fat ogre fingers on my cards, that ugly mug of yours is gonna pay for it." Bhandi emerged from the short, narrow hallway leading to the common room and snorted. "Cheating asshole! 'Sup, Goth drow?"

Cheyenne jerked her chin at the troll woman in black fatigue pants and the standard-issue black t-shirt. "How's it goin'?"

"Can't complain." Bhandi shrugged and ducked into the closest cubicle to rummage around in one of the drawers. "Some of the others might not be able to say the same, though."

"They get in trouble after the other night?"

"Ah-ha!" Bhandi lifted a pen in the air, then slammed the drawer shut. "'Get in trouble.' What is this, first grade?"

Cheyenne cocked her head. "I'm having a hard time figuring out what first grade and this whole thing with Colonel Thomas have in common."

"For real? First grade sucked. Probably because I went to a shitty school, though. Shitty neighborhood too, growin' up." Bhandi flashed the drow a mischievous grin. "I got sent to the principal's office more times than I could even count back then. Not as much as you, though, huh?"

"No principal's office for me."

"No way." The troll woman raised her hand to bring it down to Cheyenne's shoulder, but the drow lurched away from her. "Right. No touching. I knew that. So, what? Were you like one of those goody-two-shoes kids who did everything right and never got in trouble and cried when you got an A-minus on your report card?"

Cheyenne snorted. "Not exactly."

"I mean, it's cool if you were. You turned out pretty fucking badass."

If Mom had had a principal's office to send me to, she would've used it every single day. "Well, thanks."

"Yeah, for sure. Hey, why are you even here?"

"Debriefing."

"What, you mean about the other night?"

Cheyenne nodded.

"Well, shit. No one called any of us in for a debriefing. Just kept it all hush-hush." Bhandi scratched beneath her scarlet braids with the end of the pen. "I mean, it's not like word doesn't get around on its own in this place anyway, but I'm surprised they called you in. You're not even on the payroll."

"Tell me about it." Cheyenne stuck her hands in her pockets and forced herself to relax her throbbing shoulders. "So, everyone else on our temporary team or whatever, they're all good?"

"Hell, yeah." Bhandi nodded at the short hallway leading to the common room. "Tate's still walkin' around with a limp, but I call bullshit. That fae friend of yours healed him up better than any of the idiots calling themselves healthcare providers in the med bay. He's milkin' it at this point."

"Good. I'm glad you guys didn't get any blowback from that whole thing."

"Are you kiddin'? We might as well be fucking heroes!" Bhandi threw her head back and laughed. "Except for Todd. He basically got a slap on the wrist for pulling out that fucking fell laser before it got the official stamp of approval. A hard slap, but whatever. Saved all our asses, right?"

Cheyenne gave the troll woman as genuine a smile as she could manage. "Yeah. Right after he almost took our asses out, but whatever."

"Yeah. Whatever."

"Bhandi!" The gruff bark echoed toward them from the other side of the hall. "How long does it take to find a fucking pen?"

"No, I think the question is, 'How many ogres does it take to find a pen?'" she shouted back. "Answer's zero, by the way. 'Cause they're all too fucking stupid."

"You're holdin' up the game!"

"I'm busy! Gimme a minute." Bhandi shook her head and pointed at the hallway with the pen. "That fuckin' guy. Laughs his head off in the field, but Texas Hold 'em is apparently life-or-death."

"Man, who the hell are you talkin' to?" Heavy footsteps thumped down the hall, then a massive ogre with warty brown boils over every inch of his skin like a toad's entered the lobby. He was even bigger than Jamal, his blunt, crooked teeth jutting out from between his lips in every direction. He caught sight of Cheyenne and sneered. "That fucking bitch, huh?"

"Hey!" Bhandi thrust the pen at him. "We've been over this, wartface. This drow's a goddamn hero."

Cheyenne looked the ogre up and down with a raised eyebrow. *Not the first moron to call me a bitch. If he wants to go, I'll let him throw the first punch.*

"Hero?" Grot's upper lip caught on his snaggled teeth when he stretched his huge head out on his thick neck and growled at her. "All I see is a fucking traitor. That's what all you drow are, ain't it? Sneaking your way into every dark little corner to chew things up from the inside out."

"Watch it, bud." This time, the tip of the pen in Bhandi's hand flickered with a deep maroon light. "It'll be pretty hard to say you can't find a pen when you've got one stuck in your fuckin' eyeball."

The ogre grunted. "Should've taken you out the first time you stepped in over your head, drow."

"Oh, yeah?" Cheyenne cocked her head. "When was that, exactly? I've done that a lot."

Bhandi choked back a laugh. Grot snarled. "Showin' your face round here. Better watch your back."

"Better watch your fucking mouth!" Bhandi shouted. "I don't care what the pot's up to, asshat. Keep it up with this conspiracy shit, and I'll take your stuff anyway."

Grot's yellow eyes darted to the troll woman. He hunched his shoulders and spread his arms in a challenge. "Try it. I dare you."

Bhandi shot Cheyenne a sidelong glance. "Never back down from a dare, right?"

"I mean, maybe, when it's stupid."

"What the hell happened now?" Yurik barreled down the short hall and ducked under Grot's arm when the enormous ogre turned to see who was coming. "Come on, guys. We've made it this far without tearing each other apart over stupid shit, so how abou…Cheyenne."

She raised her eyebrows at him.

"Shit. I get it." The muscular goblin with the thick bullring through his septum glanced between Bhandi and Grot, then smacked the back of his hand against the ogre's beefy forearm. "Get back to the table, huh? I saw Zolu tryin' to sneak a peek at your hand."

"I'm gonna kill that fucking troll." Grot pointed a thick, grimy-nailed finger at Cheyenne with another snarl. "And you too if you don't watch it. Ain't no room for drow in here."

With a grunt, the ogre whirled and stomped back down the hallway, ducking to squeeze his massive frame between the walls.

"Just ignore him." Yurik shook his head. "He's always that pissed off."

Cheyenne frowned at Bhandi. "That's the ogre who laughs in the field?"

"Pretty hard to imagine, huh?"

"What're you doing here?" Yurik asked.

"Debriefing." Bhandi and Cheyenne said it at the same time.

"Shit." The goblin folded his arms, then lifted a hand to rub his chin. "Nobody said anything about a debriefing."

"Yeah, well, I guess I'm special." Cheyenne wasn't trying to be funny, but both agents sniggered anyway.

In the common room, Grot roared in anger, followed by the crash of a table being overturned and the poker pot spilling onto the floor.

"Hey, what the hell's your problem, man?"

"You, fuckface. You look at my hand?"

As the magical agents scuffled in the common room, Cheyenne pointed down the hall. "Not that I give a shit, but is that something I should pay attention to?"

"Nah." Yurik waved her off. "He's always breaking shit."

"Yeah, I was talking about the whole 'watch your back' thing. What's that about?"

Bhandi and Yurik exchanged glances, and the goblin rubbed the back of his neck. "You won't hear about it at your debriefing, so I guess it's technically not a thing."

"For fuck's sake, man." Bhandi hissed and turned to Cheyenne. "This whole thing with the colonel started some real shit with the rest of the operatives."

"Don't say it like that." Yurik scowled. "Just a little friction."

"Friction? Man, it's like a damn civil war in there!" When Cheyenne and Yurik stared at Bhandi, she shrugged and rolled her eyes. "Okay, maybe that's a small exaggeration."

"It'll blow over, Cheyenne." Yurik folded his arms again. "Just needs a little more than two days, you know?"

"Yeah, I get the whole time thing." Cheyenne stuck her hands in her pockets and studied two of the only FRoE agents she might as well call her friends. "But I'm still not getting why there's an issue. We figured out what the colonel was up to, exposed him, and stopped his lunatic plan from going any farther. What's there to be pissed about?"

Bhandi slipped the writing tip of the pen under one purple-tinted fingernail to scrape out whatever was beneath it. "Some of these bastards are way too serious about the chain of command if you ask me."

"Like live-and-die-by-it serious," Yurik added.

"And we just put a high-ranking official behind bars." Cheyenne took a deep breath. "Do they know what he was trying to do?"

"Fuck yeah, they do." Bhandi pointed the pen at Yurik. "We've been telling everyone, and it's not like we don't have our story straight. Kinda hard to mix things up when you know the damn truth."

Yurik sniffed, and the bullring through his septum bounced against his upper lip. "Yeah, but they're not ready to hear it."

"So, everyone who wasn't there the other night thinks this is some kind of huge conspiracy to take out commanding officers?"

"Not everyone." Bhandi glanced over her shoulder at the hallway and shrugged. "It's about half and half. Hell, Cheyenne, anyone who's been in the field with you knows what's up. We're not all brainless idiots, just the dumb ones."

Cheyenne shook her head. "That's still a stretch. Even for FRoE agents."

"It probably doesn't help that you were involved," Yurik added hesitantly.

"Me specifically?"

"Yep."

Bhandi glared at the empty hall. "The other half is pretty much convinced you're here to dismantle this place and take control of the whole damn organization. I don't know. It sure as shit isn't to force your fashion sense on us or anything. Standard issue's already black on black."

The troll woman snorted at her own joke and didn't seem to care that no one else thought it was funny.

"So, me refusing to go on ops, saving that team from a collapsing building, finding the stolen kids, and standing up to Sir means I wanna take all this for myself, huh? Is it because I had Rhynehart bring a team up to my mom's place, or what?"

"Nobody knows about that," Yurik muttered. "Off the A.S.S. and everything. And it's not something you did, per se."

Bhandi gave an exasperated sigh and delivered the punchline for him. "It's 'cause you're a drow."

"Seriously?"

Yurik winced. "There's gotta be a better way to say that."

"No, I'll take the bare-ass truth every time." When Bhandi's head whipped sharply to Cheyenne, the drow smirked. "And no. I wasn't referring to you specifically."

"Good." The troll woman's scarlet eyes flickered to the hallway. "What happens in Peridosh and all that. Don't forget."

"Sorry, Cheyenne." Yurik gave her a sympathetic frown. "We know you being a drow doesn't have anything to do with the way you operate."

"Other than making you seriously badass when we're goin' after targets," Bhandi added. "And you're only half-drow."

"They all know that too, don't they?"

"Yep. Doesn't make a difference, though." The goblin man rolled his shoulders back. "Dumbasses are gonna think what they wanna think, no matter how many times we lay out all the facts."

"Trust me, Goth drow. The facts make you look really good." Bhandi winked.

"Well, don't talk me up into something I'm not, okay?" Cheyenne pulled her phone out of her pocket to check the time. Three minutes 'til showtime. Guess being early paid off. "And it's not like I put a lot of stock in what anyone around here thinks."

"Not even your friends?" The troll woman exaggerated a grimace. "Ouch."

"I already know what you guys think." Turning to the opposite end of the lobby, Cheyenne nodded at the agents. "I gotta get to this thing. Tell Tate I said hi, and that most people quit faking injuries after grade school."

Bhandi barked a laugh. Chuckling, Yurik followed her down the hall into the common room. "That's what I said. Good luck in there, or whatever."

"Yeah. Thanks." Cheyenne headed across the lobby, shaking her head when Bhandi's shout echoed after her.

"What the fuck's wrong with you, Grot? You can't be a civilized biped for two minutes while the grownups have a conversation? No. No, put that fucking table down. Goddamn, you're a sore loser."

CHAPTER SIXTY

Cheyenne hadn't made it six feet down the wider corridor on the opposite side of the lobby before a woman in a chocolate-brown pantsuit at least one size too small power-walked over to her. "I see you got my voicemail."

"You must be Helen."

The woman nodded curtly and readjusted her tiny glasses by their thin silver rims. "Ms. Holder, if you don't mind."

Cheyenne fought not to roll her eyes. Then don't leave your full name on a voicemail. "Sure."

Helen looked her up and down and lifted her chin. "I honestly didn't expect you to be this punctual, Miss Summerlin, or I would have come down to fetch you earlier. This way, please."

Fetch? What the hell did they tell her about me?

Sighing, Cheyenne bit the bullet on anything she might have said in response and followed Major General Van Lurig's personal secretary through the base.

Even their elevator ride up to the third floor on the north end of the compound was silent. Helen stared at the closed doors in front of her, her hands folded together, and didn't make any attempt at conversation.

I'm not going to, either. Not if she had to fetch me like a dog.

When they reached the top floor, the woman walked briskly out, turned immediately down another hallway on the left, and didn't bother slowing down to make sure Cheyenne followed. The drow gritted her teeth and hurried after her, putting most of her attention into not limping on her right leg no matter how unstable her hip felt.

I better be able to sit down for this.

After three more sharp turns down different corridors, they reached a much wider hallway with five waiting-room chairs with metal legs and cheap, fraying upholstery lined up against the right-hand wall. Directly across from them was an unmarked door, and that was it.

"Take a seat, Miss Summerlin." Helen gestured at the chairs. "They'll call you in when they're ready."

"I guess being punctual wasn't that big of a deal, then, huh?"

The woman gave her a blank stare, and Cheyenne shrugged as she headed for the closest chair on the end.

"Do try not to go sniffing around in the meantime."

Cheyenne sat and slowly looked the woman up and down. "Do I get a treat for good behavior, too?"

Helen blinked quickly, glanced at the closed door, then turned swiftly on her heels and headed down the hallway again. Her thick wedges thumped across the flattened, colorless gray carpet before she disappeared around the corner.

If dogs could talk back. Cheyenne hissed and shook her head.

After waiting what felt like way longer than what could acceptably be called 1:30 sharp, she pulled her phone out of her pocket to check the time. *Five minutes. Jesus. That's it?*

Cheyenne propped her forearms on her thighs and leaned forward. One foot started bouncing all on its own, and she had to force herself to stop when even that small movement jolted her unhealing wounds. She leaned gingerly against the seat's nonexistent back cushion and stared at the door.

What the hell's taking them so long?

She poured her focus into listening, but her drow hearing didn't pick up a single voice. *Either everyone's just staring at each other in* there and wasting my time, or they soundproofed another conference room. Great.

Her activator didn't pull up any wards or spells on the door or the room beyond, and there definitely wasn't any tech between these awful waiting-room chairs and the board members on the other side. As she stared at the door, her drow vision took over, and the opaqueness of the wood and the surrounding walls faded. The blurry outlines of seven figures illuminated. Only one of them glowed a bright yellow-orange color.

One magical and six humans. Can't make it an objective meeting with those numbers.

Squinting, Cheyenne tried to improve the clarity of the outlines and at least get an idea of who was waiting for her besides Major General Van Lurig. But the closest human form stood and moved across the room.

The door opened, and Cheyenne lost all her focus when the outline of the human's head was suddenly Rhynehart's face. He froze when he saw her, then quickly collected himself and stepped into the hall, closing the door behind him.

She blinked. "What are you doing here?"

"I could ask you the same thing." Frowning, Rhynehart stepped past her down the line of chairs and took the one at the opposite end. "They called you in for a debriefing?"

"Yeah." She swallowed and looked him over. "You too?"

His jaw muscles worked over and over as he slumped back in the chair and folded his arms. "Not gonna lie. It's one of the last things I expected."

"Yeah, no kidding. But you're done now, right?"

He gestured at the door. "They asked me to stick around. Didn't make any sense until thirty seconds ago. Now it looks like they're pulling us in one by one to corroborate our stories. Feels like being called to the fucking principal's office."

I still wouldn't know.

"What did you tell them?"

Rhynehart slowly turned his head to look at her. "The truth, Cheyenne. That's what they want."

"As long as it's the truth they wanna hear, right?"

He closed his eyes. "Just the truth. For fuck's sake, don't try to give them anything else."

"I'm well aware of what's riding on whether or not they believe us, but thanks for the warning."

The door opened, and the large ogre woman Sheila poked her head out. She didn't give Rhynehart a glance, instead staring at Cheyenne as she muttered, "You're up."

"Right." The drow pushed to her feet, gritting her teeth against the throbbing pain spreading pretty much through her whole body at this point.

"And maybe don't hold anything back this time," Rhynehart murmured.

"Yeah, I know what the truth means."

He watched her hobble to the slowly opening door as Sheila released her hold on the doorknob and returned to her place inside the conference room. "You okay?"

"Peachy." Cheyenne stepped through the door, pulled it shut behind her, and turned to face the FRoE board for the second time in less than a month.

"Have a seat, Miss Summerlin." Major General Van Lurig gestured at the open seat at the head of the table. The woman's short, slightly graying hair made her look distinguished instead of old, especially when she was surrounded by three other high-ranking male officials with fully gray or white beards and a lot less hair. And then, of course, anyone looked distinguished sitting two chairs down from Major Guy Carson.

The man sat back in the rolling conference chair, both arms draped over the armrests, and glanced at her briefly before settling his gaze on the much smaller conference table than the last time they'd all met like this.

Great. Now it feels like I'm on trial.

Cheyenne pulled the chair away from the table and lowered slowly into it. Every board member and Sir watched her intently. The major's eyebrows flickered together when Cheyenne grimaced and wiped the expression off her face again in a second.

"First, Miss Summerlin, I want to thank you for agreeing to meet us here on such short notice." Van Lurig folded her hands on the table at the opposite end and nodded. "We very much appreciate your cooperation, especially when you're under no obligation to join us for these proceedings."

"Huh. Helen seems to think differently."

The man sitting on Van Lurig's right bowed his head so he could pinch the bridge of his nose without having to lift his elbow from the armrest.

Van Lurig glanced at him, then cocked her head. "Yes, she takes her job very seriously. As do we."

"I hope so."

The major general held Cheyenne's glowing golden gaze for a moment longer, expressionless, then cleared her throat. "Before we go any farther, I want to ensure there aren't any oversights in this. So I'll make the introductions I neglected the last time we met. My name is Catherine Van Lurig."

"Major General, right?"

The woman dipped her head in agreement. "This is Lieutenant Colonel Lance Oppenhaur."

Van Lurig gestured at the man rubbing his temples, and he slowly lifted his head.

"Colonel McMillen."

The man with no beard and no hair nodded grimly at Cheyenne.

"Mr. Anderson Weber."

The man with a closely trimmed goatee and large round glasses tinted yellow raised his eyebrows and stared unblinkingly at Cheyenne.

So not everyone's military. I have no idea if that's better or worse.

"And, of course, you're already acquainted with Major Guy Carson."

Cheyenne leaned back in her chair and stared at Sir. "Yep."

He swiveled toward her but didn't bristle, flush, scowl, or cuss her out. The guy could have been another board member sitting here with the others, objectively listening to an unaffiliated drow halfling describe the process of bringing down one of their own who had betrayed them and their entire organization.

Probably 'cause he's the one with his ass on the line this time.

"Now, Miss Summerlin."

"Please stop calling me that." Cheyenne looked quickly at the major general and lifted her hands from where they'd been dangling over the ends of the armrests. "We don't all have to be on a first-name basis, but I don't answer to Miss Summerlin. It's a personal thing."

"That's fine." With a raised eyebrow, Major General Van Lurig glanced down at the three pieces of paper spread out on the table in front of her and nodded. "Cheyenne, we'd like to ask you to describe for us in your own words how you first became aware of Colonel Les Thomas' personal and financial dealings with the magicals in possession of what are currently being referred to as war machines."

Cheyenne fought back a snort. *I wonder who suggested that name.*

"My neighbor."

Van Lurig studied her. "Please elaborate."

"I live across the hall from the colonel's nephew Matthew. Ever heard of him?"

"No. Despite what you may have heard, we don't generally make it a point to delve into our colleagues' private lives."

When Cheyenne looked at Sir, the man glanced quickly away to stare at the table again. The only sign of his frustration was one hand balling into a fist on top of the armrest.

Relax, Major. I'm not here to talk about Alice and your secret home life.

She looked away from him and found the board members staring at her expectantly. "That's how I found out."

"So Colonel Thomas' nephew told you what his uncle was planning?"

"Oh. No." Cheyenne dropped her head back against the cushion of the office chair. "I hacked into the control center of one of those machines and followed the data stream back to Combined Reality's servers. Wasn't that hard. After I found the program was being run from those servers, all I had to do was walk across the hall."

I mean, that's an oversimplification, but whatever.

Oppenhaur cleared his throat. "Combined Reality?"

"Yep."

The man glanced at Van Lurig, who looked back down at her notes. "I'm not familiar with the name."

"It's one of his smaller nested companies," Cheyenne said.

"Colonel Thomas' company?"

"No, his nephew's." She frowned at the board members and waited while the major general made a notation on one of her loose papers.

This is gonna take forever. I should've stuck with giving them only the important parts so they don't hurt themselves trying to keep up.

"And you obtained this information illegally?" the woman asked.

"Nope. Just from the privacy of my home. I mean, you can't blame me for getting to know my neighbors, right?"

The board members looked at her again, but no one said a word. Sir didn't take a break from staring at the table.

"Describe what happened when you 'walked across the hall,' as you put it."

Cheyenne blinked slowly. "I talked to Matthew about it. It took a while, but he finally told me his uncle had connected him with the magicals running these war machines and letting them loose all over the place. Which I know you know about already."

"We do, yes. Cheyenne, do you have any verifiable proof that Colonel Thomas was involved in this alleged weapons deal with the aforementioned group of magicals?"

"Well, yeah." Cheyenne frowned. "And I emailed it to all of you. Didn't you get it?"

Colonel McMillen drummed his fingers on the table. "We did. Just wanted to confirm it was you who sent it."

"Who else would it be from?"

"At this juncture," Van Lurig added, "we have to turn every stone and explore every avenue, Cheyenne. The severity of the charges against Colonel Thomas warrants a particularly thorough approach. You understand."

"Sure." *Should've been more thorough when you brought the asshole onto the board.*

"Is there any other evidence you would like us to be aware of at this time?"

Cheyenne's first reaction was to say no and keep skirting along through this meeting, hopefully, a lot more easily now that they'd gotten over the apparently confusing parts about Matthew Thomas and Combined Reality. But then she remembered Rhynehart still sitting out in the hall. *He definitely told them. I'm screwing us both over if I don't.*

"Yeah. I also uploaded personal files from the colonel's computer in his office on base and sent them to Rhynehart."

"Captain Brian Rhynehart?"

Cheyenne cocked her head. "That's the one."

Her sarcasm was lost on all five officials sitting at the table.

"Why him?"

"Because I needed his help. And I guess you could say we trust each other to a certain extent."

"Even though he was no longer on active duty or an employed operative of this organization at the time. Is that correct?"

Cheyenne nodded. "Because Colonel Thomas fired him on a hunch."

"What type of hunch, Cheyenne?"

Jesus Christ. I'm gonna end up ripping my eyeballs out before this is over.

"The kind traitorous assholes have when they're dirty and they don't want anyone to dig up all their shit, okay?"

The board members blinked at her. Van Lurig made another notation. "So you believe Colonel Thomas anticipated an investigation into his dealings, specifically instigated by Captain Rhynehart, and relieved the man from duty in order to prevent said investigation."

"Yeah. And he didn't just fire the guy. He had one of those machines sent to Rhynehart's house to kill him. Which it would have if Rhynehart had been alone in his house."

"So, you were there too?"

"Yes!" Cheyenne gave a long, heavy sigh. "Look, Thomas knew we were onto him, okay? He fired Rhynehart without a justifiable reason, then he invited me to his office here for a private chat. That's where I got the files from his computer that told me exactly when and where he was meeting with the Bull's Head."

"What's that?"

The drow's eyes widened. "The magicals with the machines. And I shared it with Rhynehart because he had nothing left to lose, and I wanted to take Thomas out the right way, without leaving room for any mistakes. Because in case you haven't noticed, he's been fucking around with those machines, funding their operating systems and whatever else the Bull's Head needed, and making things damn hard for everyone. I'm sure you can agree with me on that one."

"Yes, we can."

"So we pulled a team together, made a plan, and went with it. The colonel tried to kill me too, by the way. Held a gun to my head and would've pulled the trigger if Major Carson hadn't shown up on time."

All board members turned to look at Sir next. The man glanced up from the table with wide eyes and glanced around at his superiors. "You don't have to look at me like that. You've already heard this part."

"And we appreciate hearing it again from Cheyenne's perspective." Van Lurig made another note. "To the best of your ability and in as much detail as you can, describe the confrontation at the showroom in Westphalia two nights ago, where Colonel Thomas was subsequently detained."

Cheyenne looked at Sir, and he jerked his head at the major general.

No wonder Rhynehart went into my scheduled time. I should've just written a fucking report.

CHAPTER SIXTY-ONE

When Cheyenne finished recounting the entire night from her memory, which was still sharp enough not to leave anything out despite how uncomfortable she'd become in the office chair, she rolled backward away from the head of the table and stretched out her legs. "And that's it."

"Thank you, Cheyenne."

Mr. Weber leaned forward and tapped his pen on the table, despite not having anything on which to write with it. "I have one more question if you don't mind."

Cheyenne couldn't help from rolling her eyes this time. "I kinda do mind, but go ahead."

"We've heard multiple accounts of these war machines being on the premises on the night in question. Most notably, before you made an appearance and confronted Colonel Thomas. We also have visual confirmation of the machines in the footage you so graciously sent out via private email." The man cocked his head, his pen still tapping. "Which, I might add, should with good reason be in the custody of this organization as we speak. So what happened to the machines?"

For a moment, the conference room fell tensely silent. *They want to hear the truth. Sir and Rhynehart have already told them everything, and it's not like they know more about Maleshi than I do.*

Crossing one ankle over the other, Cheyenne waved off the question. "Some nightstalker rolled in, opened a portal, and took 'em all."

The board members shared confused glances.

Van Lurig looked down at her notes again. "Was this the same nightstalker who singlehandedly incapacitated every single member of the magical group selling this weaponized technology while you and Major Carson were otherwise indisposed?"

"Yep." Cheyenne watched the woman slowly write another note to herself. "Not all of them, though. She saved one for later."

"I'm sorry?"

Sir grunted, and Cheyenne couldn't tell if he was pissed off at her lame joke or trying not to laugh.

"The nightstalker took the one survivor as her prisoner. Does that clear it up?"

"Yes, thank you. Do you know what happened?"

"No." Cheyenne shook her head. "I have absolutely no idea where she took the poor bastard or what she did or will do to him."

Colonel McMillen shifted in his chair. Across from him, Lieutenant Colonel Oppenhaur dipped his head again, this time to massage his temple with one hand. The silent seconds stretched on.

Yeah, this 'make the halfling wait just for fun' bit isn't gonna fly.

Cheyenne slapped her hands on the armrests and swiveled back and forth in the chair. "Now you have all the details. Should be pretty helpful in making a decision. I'd recommend kicking Les Thomas out on his greedy, magical-hating ass, but you guys are paying yourselves the big bucks, so I'll leave it up to you. If there's nothing else?"

"Actually, Cheyenne." The major general slowly set down her pen, removed her narrow reading glasses to place them on the table too, and sat back in her chair to fold her hands in her lap. "There is something else we'd like to discuss with you, and it has much more to do with your unique perspective and opinion than anything else."

Cheyenne relaxed back into the chair again and glanced at Sir. "No more questions?"

"No more questions." Van Lurig offered a thin smile. "We've concluded the debriefing, so think of this as more of a consultation, if you like."

"Huh." *I might get up and dance if they ask me what they should do with Sir.* "Okay. What can I help you with?"

Sir's bushy eyebrows twitched over his beady eyes when he scowled at the table. But still, he was playing the good underling who'd barely managed to redeem himself and kept his mouth shut.

"For some time now," Van Lurig continued, "we've been acutely aware of a need to make certain changes within this organization. No, we haven't been around long, but we've accomplished quite a bit in the last two decades. Be that as it may, this organization was founded as a defense protocol first and was never quite restructured in ways I personally feel would have prevented this whole incident in the first place. Now that we're aware of what Colonel Thomas felt was possible and necessary to accomplish within his role both on this board and as a commanding officer, the subject of an organization-wide restructuring has become something of a top priority. A necessity, if you will."

"Uh-huh." Cheyenne narrowed her eyes at the major general. "Probably a good choice."

Van Lurig spread her arms. "Well, do you have any ideas?"

Too surprised to think about the pain radiating from her shoulders down her arms, Cheyenne leaned quickly forward in her chair and gaped at the woman. "You're asking me?"

"Yes."

"For ideas on how to restructure the FRoE so Les Thomas wannabes don't kick up another shitshow like this one."

Van Lurig cleared her throat. "I didn't use those exact words, but yes, Cheyenne. That is the gist of it."

"Yeah." A small smile crept across the drow's lips, and she nodded slowly, gazing at each of the board members in turn. *They made this too fucking easy.* "Yeah, I have some ideas."

"We'd love to hear them."

Cheyenne rolled her chair back to the end of the table and pointed at the woman's papers on the opposite end. "You're gonna want to get that pen ready."

The major general didn't move to pick up her pen, but Cheyenne was too engulfed in the ideas she'd been mulling over for weeks to care.

"Okay, first of all, whoever had the dumbass idea to only bring on

Earthborn magicals as agents should be fired. Unless it was Les Thomas. Then you've already covered that."

"So, you see an issue with employing magicals as operatives and reservation guards."

"And you don't?" Cheyenne let out a bitter laugh. "Seriously, I bet it was Thomas' idea. How the hell are Earthborn magicals who've never made the crossing and never stepped foot in Ambar'ogúl supposed to know how to deal with refugees when they show up on the reservations? They're not. The only thing they can do that human agents can't is throw spells in between fellfire shots and trick the O'gúleesh into thinking they have support and someone who understands what they're going through when they end up Earthside."

Colonel McMillen cocked his head. "And you're suggesting what? That we offer these refugee magicals some sort of counseling?"

"What? That's not even remotely related to what I said." The drow set her hands on the table and leaned forward. "But now that you mention, that wouldn't be a bad idea. What I'm saying is that you need magical agents who've been Earthside long enough to know how things work here but who haven't been human-washed."

"Human-washed?"

Lieutenant Colonel Oppenhaur leaned across the table toward his colleagues and muttered, "Like brainwashed, right?"

"Or whitewashed." Mr. Weber stroked his chin. "Perhaps greenwashed."

Van Lurig frowned and shook her head. "Well, we don't do that."

"Hey, it doesn't matter what you call it," Cheyenne cut in, startling the board members out of their little huddle. "The point is, your Earthborn magicals are seriously underequipped when it comes to handling any refugees who might make trouble when they come across, or connecting with them in any way other than also being magicals. They especially don't have what it takes to handle what was happening with Les Thomas. You didn't even know what the Bull's Head is. Your agents sure as shit didn't. And unless you're ready to start handing out those fell lasers Todd was spewing around the place—"

"No!" Mr. Weber shouted. Then he cleared his throat, sat back in his chair, and tugged the lapel of his sports jacket. "No, that model hasn't been cleared for field use yet."

"Then you're gonna need to up the game with something else," Cheyenne growled, "Because the way things are now, your agents can't take down those machines if they get into the wrong hands. They were clueless when a rogue magical snuck onto Rez 38 pretending to be one of them and opened the gates to smuggle all that black-magic shit into Virginia. You know, the stuff they were selling to kids. They have no idea what to do when it comes to O'gúl magic and all the crazy shit those refugees bring with them across the Border. Trust me, it's a lot. And they're useless when it comes to connecting with the refugees. You know, like explaining the differences between what was normal in Ambar'ogúl but will get them into trouble if they try it Earthside. Which is also a serious problem."

She took a deep breath and glanced at each of the board member's frowning faces. "Stupid stuff too. Like a family of trolls making an entire basket of underwear that looks more like leftover scraps from a boho-chic store and handing it off as a thank you gift."

Sir grunted and looked slowly up at her.

"Just as an example." Cheyenne shook her head. "But your whole system is fucked. You're paying attention to the wrong things. Detaining and threatening when you should be teaching. The refugees come here for good reasons, and no one's bothering to help them learn what living Earthside really means. You give them a cookie-cutter box as a house, feed them sometimes, stick them in your system, then throw them out and let them fend for themselves. Trust me, if you spent some time listening to these magicals and then working with them to show them what's up on this side, you wouldn't have to fund nearly as many agents or secret ops to pick up the messes they make over here. And yeah, I'm saying that is your fault.

"And for fuck's sake, your agents need to know what they're dealing with. I mean, yeah. They can fire fell weapons and beat the shit out of angry magicals breaking any number of laws because that's the only way they've figured out on their own how to get what they want. But what happens when hardcore magical shit hits the fan, huh? Your teams are useless. They can't cast spells, they don't know anything about dangerous magic other than how to clean up after it, and they have absolutely no idea what's happening on the other side to cause these problems in the first place. So yeah, if you wanna keep your high-ranking human officials from hating magicals and buying O'gúl tech from even worse magical assholes because it seems like the only way to keep everybody in line, you need a complete overhaul. From the bottom up."

Breathing heavily, Cheyenne thumped back in her chair and folded her arms. The movement shot sharp pain through her shoulders, and she gritted her teeth.

The conference room fell deathly silent as the board members and Sir stared at the drow halfling who'd said more in the last five minutes than she'd said to all of them combined over the last two months.

Standing against the left-hand wall with her hands clasped behind her back, Sheila snorted and dipped her head.

Van Lurig looked at the ogre and raised an eyebrow. "You're obviously amused by this summary."

Sheila glanced briefly at the major general and didn't wipe the small smile off her dark-gray lips. "Permission to speak freely, sir?"

"Go ahead."

Nodding at Cheyenne, Sheila stared at the table as her smile widened. "I don't think anyone's had the balls to say all that out loud."

"I see." The major general looked slowly at Cheyenne again and reached for her pen. "Is there anything else you would like to get off your chest, Cheyenne?"

The drow unfolded her arms, gritting her teeth against her aching shoulders, and gripped the armrests instead. "Not at the moment. Should I call your secretary if anything else comes to mind?"

Sheila barked a laugh, immediately cut it off, and cleared her throat.

"That won't be necessary. You already have my email address." Van Lurig glanced at the three other board members, who returned her gaze with varying degrees of shock. The woman nodded and glanced down at her notes to scribble something else in the margins. "Thank you for your time, Cheyenne. That will be all for now. Please wait outside for a moment longer while we discuss your suggestions."

"Sure." With a final warning glance at Sir, Cheyenne pushed out of the chair and headed for the door. She was not sure that had been the best way to lay it all out there, but they'd asked.

Rhynehart was still sitting in the chair on the end when she stepped into the wide hallway and closed the door behind her. He looked at her with a raised eyebrow. "How did it go?"

Cheyenne cocked her head. "Let's say it was more than any of us expected."

The uncomfortably hard chair creaked when she sat. Rhynehart folded his arms and leaned his head back against the wall. "I guess it could be worse."

"If they don't pull their heads out of their asses and start taking all this seriously, it will be." They sat in silence for a moment longer, and Cheyenne's breathing finally settled down into something resembling normal. "You hear about half the agents downstairs who think the drow halfling's trying to stage a coup and take over the FRoE from the inside?"

"Tate mentioned something about that, yeah."

"It's not true." *Though if anyone heard me running my mouth in there, they'd say I proved their point.*

"Trust me, Cheyenne. I may be unemployed, but I can still tell the difference between someone who wants nothing to do with this organization and someone who's trying to weasel their way in to take control." Rhynehart shot her a sidelong glance. "Earthside, at least."

"Yeah, one coup was enough." She closed her eyes and took another slow, steady breath. "If I wanted to be drow Leader of the FRoE, I would've done it already. This is nothing compared to the Heart."

"The what?"

"Never mind." *Not like he'd understand a single thing I could say about dethroning Ba'rael the Spider.* "So, what happens next?"

"No clue." Rhynehart shifted in his equally uncomfortable chair. "At the very least, though, it's nice to know we have a team of agents who were there with us the other night. They have our backs. And now the board's heard the same story at least three times. They'll come around."

Cheyenne squinted at him. "You're trying to get your job back, aren't you?"

He shrugged. "Well, it's either that or take up watercolor painting. Only one of those has a stable future."

She snorted. "Of getting paid or of not getting killed?"

"Very funny."

CHAPTER SIXTY-TWO

They waited in that hallway for another thirty minutes before the door opened again. Major General Van Lurig, the other board members, and Sir filtered out of the conference room in quick succession. Van Lurig had ditched her notes and stopped along the wall, nodding at Sir. "Now would be the appropriate time, Major."

Sir scowled and cleared his throat. "Yeah, all right."

"Excuse me?"

"Yes, sir." The major ran his fingers over his mustache and sniffed. When he turned to Cheyenne, he could only look at the wall behind her head instead of her face. "Cheyenne. I want to apologize for putting my insecurities above the best interests of this organization and its operatives. You handed over all the information I needed to make an informed decision, and I made the wrong one. I stood behind Colonel Thomas and failed to act until the last minute. Almost cost you your life. So please accept my apology."

Is he for real right now? Cheyenne's eyes had grown so wide, they started burning before she realized she should probably blink. "Yeah, but then you saved my life. So, apology accepted, I guess."

"Anyway." Sir's eye twitched, then he cleared his throat and pivoted one step to the former agent. "Captain Rhynehart, I apologize for not saying anything when you were removed from duty with no actionable evidence to support it. I know you've put this organization before everything else for the last thirteen years, and as your commanding officer, I failed to speak up on your behalf. So please accept my apology."

Rhynehart shook his head. "Not yet."

"What?" The crimson flush finally made a comeback on the major's cheeks and up the sides of his neck. "Why the hell not?"

Van Lurig lifted her chin. "Major."

Sir looked like he was ready to explode, and he forced his clenched fists open at his sides. "Why?"

Rhynehart shrugged. "You left something out."

Sir's jaw muscles worked as he took a slow, heavy breath. "Fine. Sorry I shot you." He pointed sharply at the agent. "But you know why I did it."

"Major Carson," Van Lurig said calmly. "We discussed this. An apology does not include a rebuttal."

A slow, tense hiss escaped the major's clenched teeth.

Rhynehart shrugged. "Apology accepted."

"Fucking great." Sir spun around and stormed past the board members down the hall. They followed him swiftly without another word before disappearing around the corner.

Cheyenne stared after Sir, expecting him to turn around and offer some kind of quick jab or at least a scowl. He didn't. "What the hell just happened?"

Rhynehart rubbed his mouth and stared at the end of the now-empty hall with her. "Pigs'll start flying now, I bet."

Sheila stepped into the hall with a small smile and jerked her chin up at the drow and the ex-operative. "You're gonna want to head after them."

Rhynehart frowned. "Any specific reason?"

"You think they tell me shit?" The ogre woman shook her head. "All I know is they want you both downstairs in the common room with everyone else. Kinda my job to get you down there."

When she gestured down the hall, Cheyenne and Rhynehart both stood and headed after the board members. The drow looked over her shoulder at the ogre woman lumbering slowly behind her. "Did you know he was gonna do that?"

"Make an apology?" Sheila shrugged. "They pay me to follow orders, not listen in on private conversations."

She said it blandly, but Cheyenne didn't miss the small smile flickering on the corners of the agent's lips. "Yeah, you knew."

"So, you do know why we're being ushered down to the common room," Rhynehart added.

"That's beyond both our paygrades."

"Shit."

They had to wait for the elevator to come back up to the top floor before they stepped inside for the awkwardly silent ride down to the ground floor. By the time they made it to the east wing, across the empty lobby, and down the short hall, the common room was packed to the brim with agents. All the seats around the row of tables were taken, as well as the armchairs scattered around and the couch in front of the fireplace. The rest of them had to stand, talking to their neighbors in low voices about what the hell was going on.

"Hey, Cheyenne." Tate nodded at her and squeezed his way through the gathered agents to head her off while Rhynehart and Sheila made their way to the far side of the common room to join the board members and Sir. "What's going on?"

"No clue." She glanced at his leg. "How're the wounds?"

"Oh. You know." The troll man rubbed his bald, tattooed purple head and shrugged. "Doin' all right."

"Good. Ember knows what she's doing."

He cleared his throat. "Yep. You should keep her around. But for real, though. Yurik said they called you in for a debriefing. Is that true?"

"Yeah." She stuck her hands into the pockets of her trenchcoat and stared at the board members muttering to each other. Helen the secretary appeared seemingly from nowhere and hurried to Major General Van Lurig to hand over a large tablet in a heavy-duty protective case. "Debriefing that turned into a consulting session, apparently."

Tate wrinkled his nose. "What'd you wanna consult the board about?"

"I didn't. They asked for my opinion."

"What the fuck about?"

A crackle of static rose through the speakers dotting the common room's ceiling as Van Lurig placed a Bluetooth headset on her ear. She tapped it once. "How's the sound?"

Her secretary glanced at the ceiling and nodded curtly before muttering something in reply.

"And the live broadcast is all set up? And we're recording from where? Oh, I see it there in the back. Thank you, Helen."

The woman stepped aside in her smart, slightly too-small pantsuit and smoothed the sides of her blazer. Her gaze swept across the crowded common room, stopped for a second on Cheyenne, then kept moving.

Cheyenne leaned toward Tate without taking her eyes off the board members. "Maybe I'm wrong, but I get the feeling this doesn't happen very often."

"Try never." The troll man folded his arms. "This is fucking weird."

A few agents grumbled and stumbled aside as Bhandi pushed her way through, followed by Yurik. The troll woman glared across the room and cracked her knuckles. "What the fuck is this?"

"How should I know?"

Yurik nodded at Cheyenne. "You know anything?"

She shot him a sidelong glance and shook her head. "I don't even work here."

"Shit." The muscular goblin shoved his hands into his pockets and frowned. "Already doesn't look good."

Van Lurig cleared her throat, and the sound was amplified at high volume through the speakers. "Start the broadcast."

A soft beep came from the wall behind Cheyenne. She turned slightly to see two small round cameras mounted on the wall, capturing the meeting and Major General Van Lurig's speech from different angles. *Broadcast to where?*

"This is Major General Van Lurig with an urgent announcement for every agent, officer, reservation guard, and the Chateau D'rahl personnel. By now, I'm sure most of you have caught wind of no doubt disturbing news regarding certain events two nights ago in Westphalia. Now you'll hear it straight from me, with my fellow commanding officers and board members at my side in full support of delivering this message.

"Colonel Les Thomas was apprehended at approximately oh-one-hundred hours Tuesday morning after a confrontation with a rogue band of magicals who circumvented the Border reservations, the intake into our registered migrant system, and detection by our top teams for quite some time. It has come to our attention that Colonel Thomas had been in contact with this group for the last five years at least, funding a private operation through a combination of FRoE resources and his own to aid these rebels in smuggling illicit supplies across the Border. These supplies were intended to be weaponized as a safeguard against magicals, both refugees and Earthborn, at an undisclosed time in the immediate future. We can only assume Colonel Thomas believed this would aid the organization's founding purpose, but I want to make it perfectly clear that he was mistaken."

The woman paused for added effect, sweeping her gaze across the crowded room and making a point of staring straight at each of the cameras in turn.

Cheyenne raised her eyebrows. Points for public speaking, at least. She's good.

"She's putting it all out there?" Tate whispered. "Not a good look for the board."

"Man, who gives a fuck about the board?" Bhandi spat. "They couldn't see the traitor sitting at the same fucking table with them."

"Just saying."

Clasping her hands behind her back, Van Lurig glanced down at her feet for a moment, then lifted her chin even higher than before. "The FRoE was founded on the principles of protection and security, first and foremost. For this country, this world, and yes, for magicals seeking a new life Earthside as well. I'd be bullshitting all of you if I said we have executed these principles with flawless adherence to the safety and wellbeing of everyone who crosses through Earth's Border portals, the Earthborn magicals such as yourselves, and the human civilians who come in contact with them. This incident with Colonel Thomas has brought to light a number of this organization's shortcomings, and we intend to change that.

"Colonel Les Thomas will receive a fair, private trial, and we will take disciplinary action proportionate to his crimes. Any and all questions or concerns you may have regarding these events may be directed to Ms. Helen Holder in writing, and we will provide whatever further information possible as time allows. Now." Van Lurig gestured with a sweeping arm at Sir. "Major Carson has additional items to address."

Sir had barely managed to fumble around with the Bluetooth headset Helen had given him, but he froze when the major general mentioned his name. Helen leaned toward the man, and the awestruck silence in the common room made it only too easy to hear her low mutter. "You have to turn it on, Major."

"How the hell do I do that?" Sir grumbled, ripping the headset off his ear to turn the thing over.

Helen pressed the headset's power button, shot him a judgmental look, then nodded. "You're live."

"Still? Shit." The amplified rustle and thump of him trying to jerk the headset back onto his ear crackled across the sound system, then he stepped forward to where Van Lurig had been standing and cleared his throat.

"Major General Van Lurig is a lot better at these damn things than I am. I'll be quick about it. We're making some changes around here, in case you didn't figure that out on your own already, which you should have if you've been paying attention. Protocol updates will roll out on an ongoing basis, but two things are happening right now." He glanced quickly at Van Lurig, who nodded curtly. Then he pulled a crumpled index card out of his pocket and scowled at it. "I guess I'm the one to bring 'em up. First, effective immediately, Captain Rhynehart is reinstated and will report for active duty in his previous role as a field operative and team leader, with recognition for his service to this organization despite having been relieved by Colonel Thomas."

Sir turned to look at Rhynehart this time, who stood with his arms folded and stared blankly at the major. "Yeah, we'll talk about what that means for you when the whole goddamn world isn't watching."

A few subdued sniggers rose from the agents gathered in the common room. Van Lurig closed her eyes and slowly shook her head.

"What are you laughing at? None of you has the *cajones* to fight off a robot snake and take a bullet in the shoulder, okay? Take a lesson from this guy and shut the hell up." Clearing his throat again, Sir glanced one more time at the index card. One eye twitched, and his mustache bristled before a low, disapproving growl escaped him. "And finally, Cheyenne Summerlin will officially join the FRoE as a consultant to the Board of Directors, also effective immediately. You're dismissed."

"What the fuck?" Cheyenne's mouth slowly dropped open.

"Well, look at that." Yurik looked her up and down and chuckled. "Now you *do* work here."

"No, I don't." Gritting her teeth, she glared at the line of board members, Sir, and Rhynehart all standing up there in front of the entire organization. Not a single one of them looked at her. *These assholes just assumed I'd be down with this?*

Sir jerked the headset off his ear and turned to face the board members. "I don't know what the fuck to do with this thing. Here. Just take it."

The sound system crackled noisily again when he slapped the headset into Helen's open palm. Then he stalked to the hallway leading into the lobby and disappeared. Helen turned off his headset, and Van Lurig stepped forward again. "That concludes this announcement. Thank you all for your time."

The speakers clicked one final time when she turned off her headset and removed it, then Helen deactivated the broadcast with quick, efficient taps on the tablet. The board members filed out of the room, their footsteps echoing in the tensely silent common room. The second they disappeared down the short hallway, the room exploded in dozens of heated conversations.

"Check you out, Goth drow." Bhandi folded her arms and grinned at Cheyenne. "Consultant to the Board of Directors. No fucking shit. How much they payin' you for that?"

"They're not." Cheyenne tried to slip past the troll woman, but Yurik leaned in front of her with a confused smile.

"Come on, Cheyenne. You can't expect us to believe you're gonna keep doing this for free. You got a major promotion."

"They can't promote me if I never agreed to it." She cocked her head at him with a warning look. "I need to go set some things straight now. Again. Do you mind?"

"Whoa, yeah. Sure." Yurik raised his hands and straightened out of her way. Chuckling, he turned to face her as she headed toward the hallway. "Congratulations, by the way."

Tate rolled his eyes. "You don't congratulate someone for something they don't want, man."

"Nah. She wants it. You just can't tell."

"Man." Bhandi barked a laugh. "We took her drinkin' for the first time in Peridosh, and now she outranks all you fuckers."

"Yeah, and you."

"You think I don't know that? Come on. I put two hundred bucks down on this whole assembly being about Colonel Assface and his fuckup. I need to collect my winnings."

"Hold on." Tate set a hand on the troll woman's shoulder and nodded at the hallway into the lobby. "We might have a problem."

CHAPTER SIXTY-THREE

Cheyenne was so busy fuming about the board's curveball, she didn't see the massive ogre Grot and the half dozen other agents shoving their way over to her until the guy's gigantic shadow passed over her. Grot stepped in front of her and growled. "I told you to watch yourself, drow."

She glared up at him. "Yeah, I get told a lot of things. Doesn't mean I have to listen."

When she tried to step around him, Grot nudged her shoulder with the tips of his meaty fingers. Cheyenne shouted in pain, her wounded shoulder flaring with agony as she stumbled backward. One of Grot's disgruntled fellow agents sniggered behind her and shoved her forward again with both hands. "You're not going anywhere, you fucking—"

Cheyenne spun and threw a vicious right hook into the squat goblin's jaw. His head whipped sideways. "Fuck you!"

"That's how you like to play, huh?" Grot folded his arms. "Looks like someone's a little touchy."

Seething, Cheyenne gritted her teeth against the dizzying pain in both her shoulders and summoned a crackling orb of black-and-purple energy in her hand. The pissed-off agents backed away, and she glared at the ogre. "I don't like being touched. Period. Now get out of my way."

"I heard you like magicals getting in your way." The goblin woman beside Grot with a small burn scar on her cheek sneered and tilted her head from side to side to stretch out her neck and shoulders. Her spine popped with each movement. "That's why you're here, right? Fucking drow halfling can't get in with her own kind on the other side, so you're gonna try playing badass ruler in our house."

So much for drow royalty on Earth. Cheyenne shook her head. "You have no idea how long I've been trying to get away from this. I don't give a shit about ruling anything."

"Major General says otherwise." Grot slammed a fist into his other palm. "But what does a human know, huh? Why don't we show her who you really are?"

"Good fucking luck." Cheyenne tried to muscle past the huge magical again, and when he reached for her arm, she launched her crackling black orb into his foot.

Grot roared. "Drow bitch."

"What the fuck are you doin', huh?" Bhandi pushed her way through the spectating agents, shaking her head. "You wanna get picked up by the MPs too?"

"I wanna bury this little snake is what I want." Grot glared at Cheyenne.

"You're not thinking this through, man," Yurik added as he and Tate joined the paused brawl. "And you're an idiot if you think Cheyenne wants to turn our shit inside-out. You touch her, you're breaking rank."

"She doesn't have any rank," the goblin woman snarled.

Bhandi rolled her eyes. "Jesus Christ, Malfi. This giant shit-for-brains has an excuse. He's an ogre. But you're even dumber than him."

"You can't touch her, man," Tate added. "You think they'll let that slide? She's basically on the fucking board."

Cheyenne glared at the tattooed troll, who gave her a discrete wink and nodded.

"Bullshit." Grot glared at the three other agents coming to the drow's defense, his eyes narrowing to glowing yellow slits. "Show me a contract, and maybe I'll listen."

Yeah, that would be the place to start, wouldn't it?

"Fine." Yurik raised his hands and shrugged. "You wanna give it a try? That's your call. But you'll have to go through us first. Might not play out the way you want, right?"

"Oh, yeah. 'Cause of all that nerve damage, right?" Bhandi exaggerated a thoughtful frown. "Hurts real bad still, doesn't it? Huh. Now, where was it exactly you got that electrical spear tip shoved through your nasty-ass skin?"

Malfi shouted in surprise when she was shoved aside, then Jamal stomped to Grot, expressionless. "Right here."

He slapped a hand down on Grot's pectoral muscle and grabbed a handful of the other ogre's boil-covered flesh beneath the standard-issue black t-shirt. Grot bellowed and tried to jerk away, but Jamal's other fist crashed into the side of the huge ogre's head. The agents who'd gathered to watch stepped back, some shouting encouragement but most of them watching quietly. Cheyenne caught half of them grinning at the display, and the other half shot her hateful grimaces without bothering to hide it.

Grot dropped to his knees with Jamal's hand still gripping his chest. "Stop."

Bhandi threw her head back for an exaggerated laugh and slapped Yurik's back. "Puts a whole new spin on titty-twister, doesn't it?"

Yurik rolled his eyes but chuckled anyway.

"Jamal, you fuck!" Grot roared again, breathing so heavily under the pain that thick wads of spit flew from between his lips. Half of them dangled beneath his chin.

Jamal wrenched his hand away, then smacked the back of the other ogre's bald head for good measure. "Quit fuckin' around."

Then he stepped aside, looked at Cheyenne, and gestured at the now-clear path into the hall.

"Thanks." She nodded at him and stormed toward the hall, ignoring the heaving ogre on his knees and all the FRoE agents' gazes burning holes into the back of her head. *I didn't ask for this, and I sure as shit don't need it right now.*

"See ya, Cheyenne," Tate called after her.

"Yeah, a lot more now, huh?" Bhandi added. "Goth drow's here to fucking stay!"

"Dial it down, huh?"

"Why? It's true. Hey!" Bhandi's voice followed Cheyenne down the short hallway. "You keep your hands to yourself, ogre. Got it? Now everyone on base knows how to bring down your giant fuckin' ass."

Cheyenne blocked out the other conversations rising behind her and hurried into the lobby. *Maybe I can catch them at the elevator.*

She slowed when she found the general major and Helen standing on the opposite side of the lobby, their heads dipped to each other as they stared at the tablet in Helen's hands and discussed whatever the hell was on that screen.

"Major General." Cheyenne cleared her throat and unconsciously gripped her bicep below her screaming shoulder. "We need to talk."

Van Lurig turned and glared at the grimacing drow stalking toward her. "I didn't take you as the type to file complaints against our operatives, Cheyenne, but is that something you need to do?"

"File a complaint? No." Cheyenne shook her head. "I couldn't care less about that."

"Then what's the problem?"

The drow stopped four feet away from the major general and tried to catch her breath. The room spun a little around her, and she swallowed. *I need to sit down.* "The problem is your little announcement back there."

"Really? I think it went rather well." Van Lurig nodded at her secretary. "Take that up to my office, Helen. Thank you."

"Sure. It went well. Until that last part, when you said I'm your new consultant."

"We discussed this during our meeting, Cheyenne."

"No, we definitely didn't. You asked for my opinion, and I told you. I didn't agree to work for you."

"I like to think of it as more of a partnership."

"Which you've obviously never done before. A partner would ask the other partner if they even wanted the gig."

Van Lurig blinked slowly. "You brought up some crucial points in our meeting. Am I to believe now that your passion for the changes we fully intend to make in this organization was not genuine?"

"No." Cheyenne clenched her eyes shut. "No, those are all things you need to do."

"And we need your insight to help us accomplish that." The woman clasped her hands behind her back and eyed the drow. "You're in a unique position, Cheyenne. You understand both worlds, maybe even more than the rest of us understand."

"Well, yeah."

"And from what I've heard, you're more than capable of leading a new phase within this organization. I don't see any reason why you wouldn't take full advantage of this offer."

"I can take advantage of it, sure. As long as you don't keep roping me into something without talking to me about it first." Cheyenne tried to shake the dizziness out of her head, but that only made it worse. "And it'll have to wait. I have other things that are a lot more important than this FRoE overhaul right now."

"Really?" Van Lurig raised her eyebrows. "Like what?"

Cheyenne grimaced. "I can't tell you."

"Hmm. Well then, I suggest you get your priorities in order over the next few days. We want you back here at seventeen-hundred hours this Monday to work on implementing these changes. And try to get some rest." The general major looked her over. "You don't look well."

Cheyenne blinked at her, and the woman spun smartly on her heel to march to the opposite hallway. Van Lurig glanced at her watch and disappeared around the corner.

Get my priorities in order. Shit. She knows I can't walk away from this. And now I have less than a week to suck the blight out of Ambar'ogúl and save Bianca before I have to play FRoE consultant.

Turning quickly, she staggered to the front doors and had to stop to collect herself. *Just pull it together and get home, Cheyenne. You'll figure out the rest of it.*

CHAPTER SIXTY-FOUR

Ember jolted when a hard thump came from the front door. A second later, the door burst open, and Cheyenne stumbled into their apartment. "Oh, shit."

"I'm fine." The door slammed shut, and Cheyenne made her way in a hunched-over crouch to the kitchen.

"No, you're not." The fae floated off the couch in a flash of purple light and headed after her friend. "Cheyenne, seriously. You can't keep ignoring this. Look at you."

Without stopping to argue, Cheyenne nearly fell over against the kitchen counter before she jerked open the cabinet above the sink and pulled down a glass. Water sprayed crazily from the faucet when she turned it on too hard, but she didn't care. *Why the fuck am I so thirsty?*

"You need to take that potion."

"Nope." Cheyenne lifted the overflowing glass to her lips and guzzled the whole thing. Then she stuck it under the faucet again.

"Yes." Ember stopped on the other side of the kitchen island and stared at her friend with wide eyes. "You need to take that potion and start using your brain again. Seriously, it's okay to put the whole stubborn-drow thing on hold for all of five seconds. 'Cause that's how long it takes to down a potion. Just take the help where you can get it."

Cheyenne finished chugging down the second glass of water, then set the glass on the counter with a sharp clink. "Not when I don't trust the magical trying to help me."

"So, it's because you don't trust the bane-breaker? Fine. Then we'll get a second opinion."

"I need some rest, Em." When Cheyenne took her first step away from the counter, her bad hip gave out, and she nearly dropped.

"You know, something tells me you lying down right now like this is just as bad as going to sleep with a concussion. Or worse."

"Nothing happened to my head." Cheyenne staggered to the kitchen island and propped herself up there instead.

Shaking her head, Ember pulled out her phone, swiped angrily at the screen, then lifted it to her ear. "Hey. We need you over here. Not good."

"Who are you calling?" Cheyenne blinked heavily at the countertop, which now floated in and out of four different versions of itself.

"Help. From a magical you do trust." Ember shoved her phone back into her pocket and reached for her friend's arms. "Then maybe you'll listen to someone who isn't pumped full of magical poison and can think clearly."

A soft pop came from the living room, then Maleshi stepped through her portal's dark circle of light, facing the other end of the apartment.

"What happened this time, huh? You stick your fingers in the wrong —" The general turned. When she saw Cheyenne, her eyes widened and her playful smile disappeared. "Holy shit. We need to move now."

She bolted across the living room in a flash of silver light. "Let's go, kid."

Cheyenne shook her head, slumped on the island now. "I'm fine."

"You're dying, Cheyenne, and I'm not gonna let that happen." The general grabbed one of Cheyenne's arms to drape over her shoulders, and the drow almost dropped in the split second without the extra support.

Ember reached toward the living room, and a burst of violet light streaked from the coffee table into her outstretched hand. The potions vials clinked together, and she handed the purple one to Maleshi. "Here. Tell her she has to take it."

The general squinted at the dark glass. "What is it?"

"A healing potion."

"Why the hell won't you take it, kid?"

Cheyenne grunted. "We don't know that's what it is."

"She got it from a bane-breaker," Ember added.

Maleshi froze. "There's a bane-breaker Earthside?"

Ember stared at Cheyenne, and when her friend didn't willingly offer the information, she dove in for her. "Yeah, she went to her last night. Inolu Frosh. She gave Cheyenne these potions. One to heal her, and the other one's for Bianca before she makes the crossing."

The general choked in surprise. "Oh, so she's an insane bane-breaker?"

"No. Inolu and the Underman said Bianca's the vessel. You know, the one Venga said he needs."

"Yeah, Ember. Thanks. I know which vessel you're talking about." Maleshi glanced at Cheyenne. "Is she serious?"

"Jesus Christ, Em. You couldn't wait five minutes?"

"Hey, if you're not gonna spit it out, I sure as fuck will." Ember thrust the potion under her friend's nose. "Take it."

"No."

Maleshi glared at the potion and nodded. "I have no idea what to think about a healing potion from a bane-breaker, kid. If Corian were here, I'd ask him. There aren't a bunch of other magical brains for me to pick at the moment, not Earthside. So we need to talk to L'zar."

"No fucking way." Cheyenne struggled to pull her arm off Maleshi's shoulder. "I don't need to go to L'zar for help. He's done enough."

"You don't have a choice!" Maleshi snarled. "And you're obviously not in a state to make this kind of decision for yourself. We're going to L'zar."

The general cast a new portal, working around her arms full of poisoned drow. Another window of dark light opened in the space between the kitchen island and the back of the couch, then Cheyenne wrenched away from Maleshi and staggered to the couch. "I just need to lie down."

"You need to shut the fuck up and come with me!" The general lurched after Cheyenne and grabbed her wrist.

Cheyenne's entire body was on fire, and she barely felt Maleshi's grip, but her shoulder exploded with agony when the nightstalker tugged lightly on her wrist, and she spun with a snarl, wrenching her wrist away. "Just give me a fucking minute!"

The apartment spun around her, and she couldn't tell which of the three Maleshi Hi'ets in her vision was the right one to focus on. *What am I doing? This isn't supposed to happen.*

"I don't think you have that long." Maleshi rolled her shoulders back and pointed at the open portal. "You're going through that thing one way or another, kid. Even if I have to drag you through it."

"You can try." Cheyenne's breath came in shuddering gasps as she tried to focus her gaze on the nightstalker's glowing silver eyes. "I'm done with everyone making decisions for me."

"Well, it's happening one more time. Come on." Maleshi headed toward her, and Cheyenne summoned a sparking black energy orb in one hand. "All right, cut the bullshit."

Cheyenne tried to walk away, but her legs gave out, and it wasn't just her hip this time. Black dots danced in the corners of her vision, and a rhythmic rushing pulse filled her ears. "L'zar can—"

"Tell us whether or not that potion's a good bet? Yep. Now get through this portal."

"Stop!" Cheyenne hurled her energy sphere at the nightstalker and crashed to her knees at the same time. Her drow magic jumped from her hand and snuffed out mid-air. Two purple sparks leaped from where the rest of it had disappeared, and that was it.

Ember's jaw dropped. "Fuck."

"What?" Cheyenne gazed down at her hand and summoned another black energy orb, more like a crackle of black sparks and a second-long hiss.

"That is what I call a big fucking uh-oh." Maleshi stalked over to Cheyenne and helped her stand again. "Come on. Get on your feet and walk through this portal. Then we'll have our answers. Ember, don't forget those potions."

"Trust me, I won't." Ember stared at them as they made their way to the portal. Swallowing thickly, she floated through behind them.

The foyer of Bianca Summerlin's estate house was empty and quiet. Maleshi guided Cheyenne to the stairs and lowered the drow to the bottom steps. "Just stay right here, okay? Don't worry, kid. I'll make this as delicate as it can be."

The general's fingers moved quickly as she cast her human illusion in a flash of silver light. Ember did the same, though her feet still hovered an inch above the floor. "Do we need to make sure she doesn't fall asleep or something?"

Maleshi shrugged. "Nah. What we just saw, or didn't see, is enough to keep her up for a while."

As the general headed around the wide staircase toward the back of the house, Ember eyed Cheyenne. "We'll figure this out. And that's not permanent. Trust me."

Cheyenne blinked heavily and stared at her open palms, her forearms propped on her thighs. "If anyone would know, it's you."

"Yeah."

The drow kept staring at her hands even after Ember and Maleshi disappeared. She tried to summon another energy sphere, one in each hand, but the results weren't any better than the last time. Probably worse. Even the spray of purple sparks petered out into nothing, and then she had to give up. *Okay. Now it's pretty bad.*

Ember and Maleshi reached the back of the house and stopped beneath the staircase. The back wall of windows gave them a perfect view onto the veranda, complete with a strangely domestic image of Bianca, Eleanor, and L'zar sitting around the wrought-iron patio table. L'zar grinned as he spoke casually, gesturing lightly with his long, slender fingers. Eleanor scowled at him with a raised eyebrow, but Bianca wore a calculating look even as she sat rigidly on a cushion brought out from inside, careful not to let any other part of her body press against the chair.

"Well, that's certainly not what I expected to see," Maleshi muttered.

"Super weird." Ember nodded at her. "I'll go talk to them."

"And I can't, because why?"

"I've been here more than you. I know they like me." Ember floated toward the French doors without waiting for the general's consent.

With a wry chuckle, Maleshi folded her arms and watched.

Eleanor was the first to notice the movement inside. When she looked at the French doors and saw Ember slowly opening them, her disapproving scowl vanished beneath a wide grin. "Ember! What a wonderful surprise."

Bianca and L'zar both turned to see the fae hovering in the open doorway. Bianca offered a small smile. "While I agree it's wonderful to see you, Ember, I have to say I'm not a fan of surprises."

"I know. And I'm sorry. There wasn't enough time to call first, and I honestly don't think there's enough time to explain, either."

Bianca's smile faded. "Where's Cheyenne?"

"In the foyer."

"Why didn't she come out with you?"

Ember looked at L'zar. "That's what we need to talk about. Just L'zar first, though. Sorry."

The drow chuckled and pushed languidly out of the patio chair. "It seems our daughter's taken after me in the drama department. Excuse me, ladies. I won't be long."

Eleanor scoffed. "You could never come back, and it wouldn't be long enough."

L'zar pointed at her as he headed toward the doors and winked. "Not the first time I've heard that one either."

Bianca swallowed thickly and stared after the human-looking fae leading the drow thief back inside. She caught a glimpse of Maleshi, all wavy black hair, green eyes, and sternly straight lips, standing in front of the dining table beneath the stairs. The general met her gaze and dipped her head in acknowledgment before turning to follow Ember and L'zar around the staircase.

"Something's wrong."

Eleanor rolled her eyes and took a long drink of her iced tea. "Of course something's wrong. He's here."

"I mean with Cheyenne."

"Oh, whatever it is, we both know she can handle it." The housekeeper brushed a small droplet of condensation off her cardigan. "Are you sure you don't want me to get you a drink? I'm happy to."

"Thank you, Eleanor, but no. I'd like to sit out here for a moment longer if you don't mind keeping me company."

Eleanor studied the other woman's intense gaze aimed directly inside and nodded. "Sure, we'll stay. I don't mind."

CHAPTER SIXTY-FIVE

"General, if you wanted my attention, you didn't have to send the fae outside to fetch me." L'zar's long, slow strides made him look like he was floating down the wide corridor between the central staircase and the kitchen. He turned halfway around to raise eyebrows at Maleshi, still all jokes and smiles. "I don't see why you're in such a mood, either."

Maleshi nodded at the front of the house. "You will."

"Well. Now I'm intrigued."

Ember rolled her eyes as she floated ahead of him and rounded the base of the staircase first. Cheyenne looked slowly up at her with a pained frown but didn't say a word.

"I have to say, Bianca and I share the same sentiment, which has been happening quite a lot over the last few days if you can believe that." L'zar turned and walked backward to watch Maleshi as he spoke, spreading his arms. "Cheyenne's a grown woman. She should speak to us herself if it's so important."

"If I knew I could walk across this house without eating shit, L'zar, I would have."

The drow thief froze at the sound of his daughter's voice and slowly turned. His gaze dropped to the foot of the stairs, and his careless, crooked Weaver's smile disappeared. "What happened?"

"Same thing, different day."

Ember folded her arms. "The poison's getting worse."

"Thanks, Em. I got it." Cheyenne looked at her dad, using all the strength she had left not to lean back against the stairs and drift off to sleep. *I'd have a better chance of not feeling anything if I'm unconscious.* "I'll tell you what's going on now as soon as you tell me how she is."

"Bianca?"

She gave him a deadpan stare. "No. The Queen of England."

For once, he ignored her sarcasm and maintained a surprising level of seriousness as he glanced at the back of the house. "Well, she hasn't gotten worse, at least. Can't say the same for you, can I?"

"Just tell me."

He took a deep breath. "The pain's obviously getting to her. It was an interesting experience listening to her dress herself this morning."

"Better or worse than hearing someone slather darktongue salve all over their wounds that won't heal?" Ember muttered.

L'zar narrowed his eyes at the fae. "Hmm. I can't say I've come across that one."

"L'zar." Cheyenne closed her eyes. "How bad is it?"

"Bad enough that she doesn't want to touch anything, and I do mean anything. I was surprised to see her sitting outside on that cushion."

"Any new runes?"

L'zar dipped his head and shook it briefly. "Not that I've seen, and she hasn't mentioned anything. Not that I'm convinced she would tell me."

"She'd tell you." Swallowing through another grimace, Cheyenne looked at him and nodded. "So, at least we're good there."

"Quite. And now I believe you have some information to add to this exchange." L'zar cocked his head. "Specifically, why you look like someone who refused the deathflame in a fighting pit but wasn't hit badly enough to die."

"I'm—" *Not fine. I have to quit saying that.* "The poison's getting worse."

"Yes, that's quite obvious." L'zar frowned at Ember and Maleshi. "Don't tell me you needed my opinion on that."

Ember nodded as Cheyenne slumped over her bent legs. "She found out important things for healing herself and about the blight."

L'zar's eyes widened, and he flashed his daughter a feral, gleaming grin that was entirely wasted on her. She couldn't stop staring at the floor. "Is that right?"

"Alleged healing," Cheyenne muttered.

"You need to tell him, kid." Maleshi folded her arms, clearly unhappy about letting Cheyenne just sit there as the seconds ticked by. "We need his help."

"No, we don't. We want his opinion. Those are two totally different things." Cheyenne swayed where she sat and started to tilt sideways. Ember floated toward her, but the drow steadied herself against the banister and shook her head. "I don't need help sitting."

"But you obviously need help explaining what Inolu told you." Ember gestured to L'zar. "Unless you're ready to start talking."

L'zar blinked quickly and tapped a finger against his lips. "I rather like that name. Inolu. Do go on."

"She's a bane-breaker."

He shot Maleshi a sharp glance, but the general's only reply was to shrug and shake her head. "Earthside?"

"Yeah."

"Interesting."

Ember sighed. "And what did she tell you?"

"I got it, Em. I need a minute to put it all together." Clenching her eyes shut, Cheyenne bowed her head and weakly rubbed her eyebrow. *This is the worst combination. He's gotta be loving this, his daughter running to him like a scared little kid because she can't make up her fucking mind. I don't want his help, but I don't have any other options.*

Taking a deep breath, she lifted a head that felt like it weighed a hundred pounds and met L'zar's gaze. "I went to Inolu to see if she could do anything about the curse on Bianca. You know, like remove it."

"Yes, I'm aware of a bane-breaker's purpose."

"Right. She told me there wasn't any way to remove the curse with a spell or a potion or whatever. Then I guess I stuck around too long, 'cause the Underman showed up and told me the rest of it." *I hate this.*

"The Underman. Sounds like a bad spinoff of *The Mortician*." L'zar chuckled, even when no one else found any humor. "Who is he?"

"I don't know. Some disembodied magical thing. A demon. She channeled him, and he told me…"

Maleshi nodded. "Keep going. This is taking too long."

L'zar looked quickly at Ember and Maleshi, and his grin widened again. "Don't you love the suspense? I find it so rare these days."

"Shut up and listen to her," Ember snapped.

"Well, now." He pointed at her. "Somebody's getting awfully pushy."

"He said Bianca's the vessel," Cheyenne blurted. "That her fate's intertwined with Ambar'ogúl. And me."

All traces of amusement vanished from L'zar's features. His golden eyes burned fiercely when he lowered his gaze to look his daughter in the eye. "No."

"That's what I said."

"Bianca is not the vessel."

Cheyenne laughed weakly. "We're on the same page about something. Good. Now we can drop this shitty idea."

"I'm gonna stop you right there." Maleshi stepped over to L'zar and leaned toward him. "I know this isn't what you want to hear, but we don't know enough to be able to say it's not true."

L'zar stared blankly at nothing, though his gaze was aimed hazily at the top of Cheyenne's head. "That's impossible."

"Is it really?" Maleshi gestured at Ember. "Because I can't think of a reason why a bane-breaker would offer a shielding potion and tell Cheyenne it's for her mother."

"There are always other threads, General."

"And it's our responsibility to look at all of them. You know that better than anyone."

L'zar looked at the nightstalker with more fear in his eyes than she knew he was capable of feeling. Even more than when he'd approached the Sorren Gán for a second time. "Maleshi."

"Your daughter is running out of time, L'zar." The general frowned, unable to look away from the horror flaring behind his eyes. "Faster even than Bianca."

"But we might be able to reverse that," Ember added. "At least long enough to get Bianca across the Border."

Cheyenne groaned. "Ember, come on."

"What is it?" L'zar hissed.

The fae pulled the two vials out of her pocket and extended the purple one to him. "A healing potion, also from the bane-breaker."

"Cheyenne, why haven't you taken this?"

"Really? If a bane-breaker handed you a potion for free and said, 'Hey, you're fine. This'll heal the blight inside you, no problem. Now take your human mom across the Border because the demon living inside me said it'll work,' you'd just gulp the whole thing down and call it a day?"

"No, but I would seriously consider why I had an issue taking a bane-breaker's word for what it's worth."

"I don't know what it's worth, L'zar. Neither do you, or you wouldn't be talking circles around this." Cheyenne swayed again and shook her head. "I don't see why this is such a big deal. Everyone's been telling me I need to be more discerning, right?"

"Not with your life." L'zar's nostrils flared as he stared at his weakening daughter. Then his hand whipped out to Ember. "Give it to me."

"Yep." Ember gingerly set the vial in the drow's palm, then stuck the potion for Bianca back in her pocket.

"General." Breathing heavily, L'zar gave Cheyenne one more scathing glance, then spun quickly to the door. Maleshi followed him, and they stood in the foyer, their heads bent toward each other as he turned the vial over and over in his hands. "Did you know about an Earthside bane-breaker?"

"I'm as surprised as you are."

L'zar lifted the vial and wafted it back and forth under his nose. "That's tillhorn powder."

Her eyes widened. "Are you sure?"

The potion waved back and forth under her face, and Maleshi hissed. "And rattlebrim."

"Ah. Yes, that's the undertone that threw me off."

"Whoever this Inolu is, she couldn't have brought these ingredients across the Border with her."

L'zar scowled at the vial as he lifted it to the overhead lights and studied the liquid inside through the purple glass. "Indeed. The half-life for both of those is what, three days?"

"That's a generous estimate." Maleshi folded her arms. "So how the hell did she get her hands on something like that Earthside?"

"If I knew the answer to that, General, I would have cooked this up myself." L'zar tapped the vial's cork, which lit up with a white glow before removing itself from the vial and hovering two inches above it in the air. Then he dipped his pinky into the glass and dabbed a drop of deep-blue liquid on his tongue. "Fuck it. This is as good as it's gonna get."

"Okay." They headed back to the foot of the grand central staircase. "And we have our answer, kid. Take the potion."

Cheyenne's drooping head wove from side to side between her shoulders. "Will it get this shit out of me?"

"We can't promise that, no. But it'll keep the poison at bay long enough to buy us the time we need."

"You mean, the time we need to make the crossing with Bianca, right?" Cheyenne's voice was weak now, her entire body drooping like she was talking in her sleep instead of having the life drained out of her by Ba'rael's blighted poison.

"Maybe," L'zar said. "Maybe not. But you need to."

"If you don't know, I'm not taking it."

L'zar glared at her, and the floating cork dropped to the floor and bounced across the polished hardwood. He slowly walked to the foot of the stairs and lowered into a crouch in front of his daughter. "I know why you don't want to take it. Because if the bane-breaker was telling the truth about this, it makes everything else she told you true as well. I can assure you, I don't want Bianca to be a part of this any more than you do."

"You made her a part of this." Cheyenne's breath came in slow, shallow bursts. "You made all of this. Just because you couldn't keep your hands out of the fucking Weave, right?"

He blinked and dipped his head to get her to look at him. "I might have manipulated the Threads in the past to get what I thought I wanted, Cheyenne, but I have no reason to lie to you about this. Not when you're fading right in front of my eyes."

"Like you give a shit." Cheyenne's lips felt swollen now, her words stumbling awkwardly through them as if they were numb. She couldn't get her gaze to settle on anything, and nothing made any sense. *I don't even know what he's talking about.*

"Don't say that," L'zar whispered.

What am I talking about?

"Suck it up, kid," Maleshi said sharply. "Now isn't the time to push that grudge."

"I'm not fucking drinking that."

Ember took a sharp breath. "Something's wrong."

"I think everyone's aware of that, Ember."

"No, I mean she's not hearing us." The fae floated over to the stairs. When L'zar saw her, he stood and held the potion vial out to her. "She'll listen to her *Nós Ani.*"

"I'm not so sure." Ember bent down in front of her friend. "Cheyenne, can you hear me? I don't know what's happening right now, but I can see it. You need to fight it."

L'zar rolled his eyes at Maleshi. "What is she talking about?"

The general ignored him and stared at Cheyenne, who still swayed where she sat on the stairs but now snarled with every exhale.

Ember lowered herself to her knees, held up by her magic, and dipped her head even lower. "Cheyenne?"

"Fuck off."

"You need to snap out of it!"

"Get the fuck out of my face!" Without warning, Cheyenne's hands lashed out with incredible speed to shove Ember forcefully away.

Ember flew toward the front door but stopped herself with a flash of violet light and slowly lowered herself to the floor.

"Cheyenne!" L'zar snapped.

Her head whipped up to fix him with a burning glare, and she hissed. For a fraction of a second, L'zar couldn't think or move. The sight of his daughter's eyes glistening pure black above the snaking lines of black poison trailing up her neck from beneath the collar of her shirt made everything else cease to exist.

"Fuck, we took too long," Maleshi whispered. "She's already gone."

"No, she's not." Ember reached out to her friend with both hands. "Sorry in advance."

Cheyenne roared and leaped from the stairs toward the fae. A stream of blinding yellow light shot from Ember's palms and struck the blighted drow in the chest. Tendrils of thick golden light wrapped around Cheyenne's body a second before her back and head hit the staircase, pinning her arms at her sides. The drow screamed, unable to move beneath her *Nós Ani's* spell. "You fucking bitch!"

"Jesus." Maleshi's mouth popped open.

"We need to do something." L'zar eyelids fluttered as his panic overtook his ability to think.

"I got it." Ember floated swiftly to him and held out her hand. "Give me that."

"What?"

"L'zar! The potion!"

"Yes." He handed it over, his mouth working soundlessly as Cheyenne hissed and spat on the staircase.

Ember raced to the stairs and hovered beside Cheyenne, kneeling on the step by her friend's head in another flash of violet light. "One way or another, right?"

The golden light flashed behind Cheyenne's eyes again, warring with the blackness that hadn't completely taken over. "Ember, don't."

"We're out of options."

"I'm not gonna!"

Ember pointed at Cheyenne's mouth, and violet light forced the drow's jaws open and held them there. "You don't have to thank me as long as you don't die."

She brought the potion over Cheyenne's open mouth and poured a thin, trickling stream of it down her throat.

Cheyenne choked and coughed, held down by the fae's spell, but almost immediately, the blackness filtered out of her eyes. The fury behind them was almost worse.

Ember floated upright again and backed away, waving her hand to release her spell. Cheyenne sat up with a gasp, coughed again, then stared at the fae in disbelief. "What the fuck, Em?"

"Someone had to get you to take this, and you were too much of a stubborn asshole to get that through your drow head before we ran out of time."

Cheyenne tried to stand, but her feet slipped out from under her, and she crashed to the stairs, sliding down until her shoes squeaked against the hardwood floor. "You held me down and drugged me. How is that…"

Maleshi pressed her knuckles to her mouth. "Is it gonna work?"

"It looks like it already is." Ember stared at her friend. "At least she sounds like herself."

Cheyenne's eyelids fluttered as she struggled to push off the stairs. *What the hell's wrong with my body?* "This is how we do things now? We're forcing who the fuck knows what down each other's throats to see what...what is..."

Her eyes rolled back in her head, and she dropped against the stairs again. This time, she didn't move.

L'zar inhaled sharply through his nose and pushed his long white hair away from his face with both hands. "Ember."

"I didn't do it for you, but I guess you're welcome."

Maleshi folded and unfolded her arms, too shocked to know what to do with them. "She's not gonna be happy with you when she wakes up."

Ember turned slowly to look at the general, her eyes shimmering with tears. "I can live with that. So can she."

CHAPTER SIXTY-SIX

When Cheyenne woke up again, her first thought was to wonder who the hell had poured sand down her throat.

No, not sand. Just that damn potion.

With a groan, she rolled over and blinked heavily. Her vision still swam with multiple versions of everything, but she managed to pull her focus together and found herself staring at the rug on the floor of her old bedroom in Bianca's house. *They couldn't have put me in the guest bed?*

Cheyenne tried to push up and managed a half-hearted jerk before she flopped back onto the mattress. She heard movement in the room and looked at Eleanor sitting in an armchair she'd brought in. "Eleanor."

"Hey, sweetheart." The housekeeper slowly stood. "How are you feeling?"

"Thirsty."

"Of course. Here." Eleanor hurried to the desk below the window and poured a large glass of water. By the time she reached the bed, Cheyenne had succeeded in pushing herself all the way up to sit back against the headboard.

"Thanks."

Eleanor stared with wide eyes as the drow downed the whole glass in ten seconds.

"Do you mind refilling it?" Cheyenne had to force herself to meet the woman's gaze as she held out the glass. *If they told her and Mom what happened, that would explain the awkwardness.*

The housekeeper grabbed the pitcher and filled the glass again without taking it out of Cheyenne's hand. Once the drow had downed that too, she leaned her head against the headrest and closed her eyes.

"Anything else I can get you?"

"Not right now." Cheyenne grimaced. "Are Ember and Maleshi still here?"

"Maleshi. What a name." Eleanor took the empty glass with a weak, humorless chuckle. "They're still here, sweetheart. I'm a little surprised Ember didn't want to sit with you, but she told me she had a feeling you wouldn't want to see her first thing when you woke up." The pitcher and glass clinked down on the desk, and the housekeeper stuck both hands on her hips. "Want to tell me what happened?"

"Not really."

"Fair enough. I just pulled a rack of lamb out of the oven, and I'm going to fix you a plate."

"Eleanor, I don't want anything."

"Don't even try to talk me out of it, Cheyenne. I wasn't asking if you wanted to eat. I'm telling you you need to. You look a lot better than the last time I saw you, but you're still alarmingly pale. Even for you."

Cheyenne laughed.

"I'll be right back." Gently patting the drow's thigh, Eleanor nodded with a sympathetic smile, then left the room and softly shut the door behind her.

Cheyenne swallowed. *I look better, huh? So the potion worked?*

She pulled her shirt collar down and glanced at the poisoned wound in her left shoulder first. "Holy shit."

The dark, snaking lines of the blight had almost entirely retreated, though the wound was still dark and open, surrounded by angry red flesh. Moving quicker, she checked the other shoulder, then slumped against the pillows to pull down the waistband of her pants and check her hip.

"Jesus. It worked."

Running a hand through her hair, Cheyenne stared at the opposite wall of her childhood bedroom, then took a deep breath. *Better test it out.*

She moved slowly at first, anticipating pain flareups, but in comparison with how she'd felt when Maleshi ported them into this house, she was practically pain-free. "No way."

A small laugh escaped her when an experimental lift of her arm told her the same thing. The potion had worked, at least when it came to reversing the damage. The wounds still weren't healing, but that felt pretty irrelevant at this point.

They were right. Shit. Cheyenne sank back down onto the edge of the bed and closed her eyes. *They were right.*

A brief knock came on the bedroom door, then Eleanor stepped back inside, looking pale and worried.

"What's wrong?"

The housekeeper wrung her hands and couldn't look the drow in the eye. "Well, I know I said I'd bring you food, but I'm confused."

"Something wrong with the food?"

"Not at all. Only that it might be on its way to getting cold." Eleanor cleared her throat. "Everyone's downstairs at the dining table, Cheyenne, and they all refuse to eat anything until you come down to join them."

"What?" Cheyenne squinted. "They're staging a dinner strike."

"It would seem that way, yes." Eleanor patted the back of her head and the graying bun there. "It's highly unusual, and I hardly think insulting me and my cooking is going to be of much use to anyone."

"Jesus." Rolling her eyes, Cheyenne pushed up off the bed and approached the housekeeper to set a gentle hand on the woman's shoulder. "It was Mom's idea."

"Oh, most definitely."

"She knows how to push both our buttons. You can go tell them I'm coming if you want."

"Absolutely not." Eleanor scowled at the open bedroom door and the staircase's banister beyond. "I'm not stepping foot in that room again until everyone's eating what I cooked. Do you know how often we have six people sitting down for a meal in this house?"

"Hardly ever, I know."

"That's right. Way too much work to let it all go to waste." Eleanor snorted and folded her arms. "I'll come down with you, and when I hear forks and knives clinking on plates, I'll take my seat."

Fighting back a smile, Cheyenne nodded and headed into the hall. "Sounds good to me."

The sound of low muttered conversation rose up the stairwell as the drow made her way carefully down the steps. When she reached the bottom, she stared at the last three stairs where she'd sat, jumped up, and been laid out flat by Ember's magic. *So, I lost control but still remember the whole thing, huh? How the fuck is that fair?*

She flipped a middle finger at the stairs as she stepped down the last of them before turning around the banister to head to the back of the house. If Eleanor saw it, she didn't say a word.

Even before Cheyenne passed the sitting area to enter the open room where the dining table sat under the wide staircase, L'zar heard her coming.

"I think we got what we wanted," L'zar said. "Bianca, I have to say that housekeeper of yours is a gem. Where did you find her?"

"That's none of your business. And if you think so highly of her, I can't imagine why you insist on continuing to terrorize her."

"Terrorize?" He chuckled. "That's a little overstated, don't you think?"

Bianca didn't give him a reply, and when Cheyenne rounded the corner, she expected to see her mom staring at the drow thief, her eyebrow raised in as much contempt as Bianca Summerlin was apt to show outwardly.

"And here she is." L'zar sat back in his chair and spread his arms, grinning at his daughter. "You look well, Cheyenne. How do you feel?"

Cheyenne glanced at Ember, who was staring at her with her lips pressed tightly together. The fae looked away and lifted her drink to her lips. "Better."

"That's good news." Maleshi sat back in her chair at the head of the table closest to L'zar and nodded. "I'm glad to hear it."

"Yeah." The only two available seats at the table were on opposite sides, one next to Ember, the other beside L'zar. *I can't force Eleanor to sit next to him.* Gritting her teeth, Cheyenne took the chair beside her dad and nodded at Ember. "Eleanor's coming, but she said we should start without her."

"And now we can." L'zar grinned at the four different dishes laid out on the table. "What do we start with?"

"Whatever's closest." Ember reached for the platter of lamb and served herself. "You know how to pass food around a table, right?"

He eyed the fae in amusement. "Why, yes, Ember. I believe I have an acceptable level of experience."

Ember glanced at Cheyenne and raised an eyebrow but didn't say anything.

Cheyenne grabbed the salad bowl and dropped a pile of it on her plate with the tongs. She passed it to L'zar, then turned to look at Bianca. Her mom sat as primly as usual in the dining chair, supported by the cushion she'd used on the veranda. She met Cheyenne's gaze and offered a small nod as Eleanor stepped slowly around the corner past the sitting area.

"Oh, good." The housekeeper approached the last empty chair between Ember and Bianca. "I hope our guests are pleased with dinner."

Bianca pursed her lips in not-quite-a-smile and looked at her friend. "Anything else would be impossible, Eleanor. Thank you."

"Hmm." Eleanor looked sharply at Cheyenne, then brushed down the sides of her teal cardigan and nodded. "You're welcome."

When Ember passed along the lamb, Eleanor remained standing to serve Bianca, loaded her own plate next, then walked around her employer to hand Cheyenne the platter.

"Thanks." Cheyenne tried not to frown as she set the platter on the table between her and L'zar. *Since when does Mom not serve herself?*

As dishes were passed around and no one bothered to start the conversation they all knew was coming, Cheyenne studied the place settings. *No one's drinking, either. Not even Mom. Weird, but I'll call it a good sign, I guess.*

Bianca leaned forward to lightly pinch the straw sticking up out of her water glass before placing it between her lips. When she lifted her fork to start eating with agonizing slowness, her forearm didn't touch the table once.

Cheyenne took a long drink of her own water and stared at her mom. *That explains the straw. How can she sit here in that much pain and not even wince?*

"You're staring, Cheyenne." Even as she said it, Bianca didn't look away from the gilded centerpiece. Her fork slipped slowly into her mouth.

"Sorry." Cheyenne set her water down and reached across the table to take the asparagus dish from Eleanor.

"And you're reaching across the table?"

"Mom, I'm not gonna make Eleanor play musical chairs all night. She's already done enough."

Eleanor blinked furiously. "I have no problem with it."

"Well, I do." Cheyenne spooned the asparagus onto her plate, set down the dish, and looked at her mom again. This time, Bianca had turned her intense gaze on her daughter. "How bad is it?"

"It's manageable, Cheyenne. That's all I'm willing to say right now. This isn't a conversation to have at the dinner table."

Shit. It's bad.

"Fine."

"Then let's have a different conversation, shall we?" L'zar stuck a huge bite of lamb into his mouth, hummed in delight, and wiggled his eyebrows at Eleanor. "Scrumptious."

The housekeeper grabbed a dinner roll out of the basket and dropped it unceremoniously on her plate before muttering, "You know, I considered making something with an extra kick for you specifically."

"Ooh. Like what? I do love a bit of heat in my food."

"Like arsenic."

Maleshi snorted and quickly took a drink of her water. Ember shot the housekeeper a sidelong glance, then looked at Cheyenne and cleared her throat.

Bianca slowly stabbed another bite of lamb with a barely discernible smile. "No need to give him special treatment, Eleanor. He'll have to satisfy himself with what's acceptable for the rest of us."

L'zar laughed. "And I'm sure you've already discovered the impressive fortitude of a drow's constitution, having spent so much time with Cheyenne over the years. As lovely as the idea may seem, Eleanor, I can assure you arsenic would have added nothing more than a light, nutty flavor."

Eleanor glared at him. "You can't taste arsenic."

"I can."

"If no one has any objections," Maleshi said, "I'd like to change the subject."

Bianca looked at the human-illusioned nightstalker at the other end of the table and cocked her head. "By all means. And I don't believe we've been properly introduced."

Cheyenne focused intently on her plate. Maleshi's laying the etiquette on thick today. Wait 'til Mom sees what she really looks like.

"That was an unconscionable oversight on my part." L'zar gestured at Maleshi. "Bianca, this is General—"

"Call me Maleshi, please."

"General?" Bianca raised her eyebrows. "I wouldn't have guessed."

With a polite smile, Maleshi dug into her food. "Well, my military days are behind me."

L'zar chuckled. "Not entirely."

The general cast him a warning glance, her green eyes narrowing, and the drow thief smiled right back at her. "You never had any say in my decisions, L'zar. That hasn't changed."

"When it concerns my daughter, General, I believe I have a say in most of your decisions."

"Well, you're mistaken." Maleshi cocked her head at him. "Seeing as you won't be making the crossing again anytime soon, with Cheyenne or without her."

"That's hardly relevant."

"I'm here for her. Not you." Maleshi grabbed her water glass and raised it to him in a mocking toast. "And Corian's not here to placate your ego."

L'zar stared at her, then slowly turned back to his plate and scooped another forkful into his mouth. "Or to stop me from reminding you of your place."

"My place." Maleshi snorted. "In case you haven't noticed, I now outrank you, too."

Bianca's closed-lipped smile widened as she watched the composed display of animosity battling it out at the opposite end of the table. "Well, I, for one, very much appreciate your company, Maleshi."

"Thank you." The general nodded at her with a pert smile. "And I appreciate the hospitality."

Cheyenne held back a laugh and kept eating. *They're bonding over a fondness for politely telling L'zar to eat shit. Could be worse.*

Maleshi cleared her throat and set her fork delicately on her plate. "Cheyenne."

"Yeah." The drow looked slowly at the general.

"I know you don't want to talk about it, but we have to."

"Yeah, I know." Cheyenne glanced at Ember, who'd lowered her fork to her plate too, and waited for the conversation to take its inevitably weird turn. *And we can't move forward if I don't tell them what's up.* "It worked. Mostly."

"The potion." L'zar raised an eyebrow.

Cheyenne forced herself to ignore her mom's stillness and the wide-eyed look of trepidation Eleanor focused on her own plate. "Yeah. So I guess Inolu delivered."

"Hmm. Whatever this Underman brings to her equation, it must be a hell of a lot more knowledge than a bane-breaker could possess on her own." L'zar shrugged, took another bite, and spoke around a mouthful. "The only time I've ever gotten anything from a bane-breaker for free is when I stole it."

Cheyenne shook her head. "Okay."

"When you say 'mostly,'" Maleshi added, "what does that mean?"

Cheyenne thumped her hand lightly against the opposite shoulder with only a small grimace. "It means I can do that and not fall over, but they're not healed."

"That's definitely an improvement."

"So we're trusting Inolu's information, then." It wasn't a question from Ember, but she still looked at Cheyenne like she expected the drow to deny it again.

"I guess we have to, right?" Cheyenne frowned at the centerpiece. "Obviously, I'm not the only one who doesn't want to believe it, but we don't have another choice." She stopped herself both from going too deep into details and from turning to look at her mom. "It got really bad today. I don't wanna run the risk of it getting that bad again for anyone else."

"We're right there with you, kid." Maleshi nodded. "And I think it's best if we move now."

"Now?" L'zar glared at her.

"Well, tonight."

His fist thumped on the table, making the dishes and silverware and Eleanor jump. "That's too soon."

"It's not." Maleshi nodded at Cheyenne. "You're not the first to say you need more time, and we saw what happened when your daughter thought she needed more."

"This is different." L'zar dipped his head and leaned toward the general with wide eyes. "This is not my daughter, and there's no precedent for this kind of thing."

"The blight had no precedent either, and the bane-breaker's potion healed Cheyenne better than anything either Venga or Ember could come up with." Maleshi leaned over to L'zar and narrowed her eyes. "I'm much more inclined now to trust a magical who's stayed hidden from both of us on this world and delivered results when you and I had run out of options."

L'zar swallowed and sat back in his chair. "It's not right."

"That never used to stop you."

"This is different," he protested, turning to look at Bianca, who'd abandoned her dinner to try to piece together this not-for-humans conversation. She narrowed her eyes at him, and he looked down at the table. "It's just different."

Maleshi ignored Bianca's blatant glare aimed at the drow thief. "What makes it different is that you have a stake in this. Something you didn't read in the Weave because you were too preoccupied with what you did see."

"I should have seen it," L'zar hissed. "Then I could have stopped it."

His fists clenched in his lap, and Cheyenne leaned forward in her chair, ready to stand if she had to. *If he loses it now with this little pity party, I'm not holding back.*

"There still has to be another way," L'zar muttered.

"There isn't."

"Cheyenne got worse, but Bianca hasn't."

Bianca straightened even more in her chair. "Excuse me?"

L'zar ignored her. "That could be the window we need. There's still time."

"You want to risk both worlds for your screwed-up sentimentality?" Maleshi hissed.

"They're not connected!"

"The woman has O'gúl runes on her flesh, L'zar."

"Enough!" Bianca's uncharacteristic shout cut the conversation short, and everyone turned to look at her. She stared at Cheyenne, quickly regaining her composure before continuing, "You're all excused from this table. My daughter and I need to discuss things in private."

CHAPTER SIXTY-SEVEN

Eleanor immediately scooted her chair away from the table and stood. "I'll be in the kitchen."

"Thank you, Eleanor."

None of the other magicals around the table moved as the house-keeper made herself scarce.

Bianca turned slowly to glare at L'zar. "That includes everyone but Cheyenne."

"Of course." After wiping his mouth with the cloth napkin, L'zar stood and placed the cloth on the table beside his plate. He took one quick look at Bianca, changed his mind about saying anything else, and headed to the opposite side of the house.

Maleshi nodded at Ember. "I'd like to take a look at that other vial."

"Sure." Ember floated to her feet and met Cheyenne's gaze. "You need anything?"

"I'm good, Em. Thanks."

"Right." With a confused frown, Ember headed after Maleshi.

Cheyenne took a deep breath and watched her friend disappear around the staircase too. *I gotta clear the air with her later. Not sure how to do that when I lost my mind and she force-fed me a healing potion.*

Bianca shifted slightly on her cushion to face her daughter, still taking great care not to brush any other parts of her body against anything around her. "Well."

"I know, Mom. You don't like talking about this otherworld stuff. It shouldn't have been over dinner. I'm sorry."

"Cheyenne, your father has been squatting in my house for days. Ember's feet don't touch the floor. No one's eyes glow like that Maleshi woman's, so she's obviously hiding something." Bianca blinked slowly. "I have undecipherable symbols burned into my flesh. I think we're past the point of not talking about magic in my presence."

"Oh." Cheyenne swallowed. *First time for everything, I guess.*

"Despite how much I detest that particular subject, I have even less tolerance for being discussed by those whatever-they-ares without the courtesy of an explanation." Bianca dipped her chin and raised her eyebrows. "So I want you to tell me what all this is about. Clearly and succinctly."

"Right." Cheyenne took another deep breath. "The problem with this is that there isn't a clear and succinct answer."

"Well, when we're dealing with reason and logic and reality, Cheyenne, that would indeed be frustrating, but whatever's going on right now is clearly not any of those."

A small, humorless chuckle escaped the drow. "That's an understatement. Just try to keep an open mind about all this, okay? It's not something I wanted to believe until about half an hour ago."

Bianca nodded slowly.

"Okay." *Well, if her sanity doesn't shatter at the end of this, she's gonna let me have it. And I'll just have to take it before handing her a potion and dragging her through a portal. Fuck, this is insane.*

Cheyenne slowly gave her mom as much background information as she could about Ba'rael Verdys the Spider, the blight, and everything she'd seen in both worlds that forewarned of what would happen if they didn't fix this. She showed her mom one of her shoulder wounds again, talking about the blight and the potions. She left out her short-lived reign as the O'gúl Crown, her cousin Neros and her dreams, the Sorren Gán's suggestions, and both Inolu and the Underman's warnings.

I'm trying to help her understand how she's a part of this, not send her running from the room.

"There's a lot more to all this, generally speaking."

"That's fine." Bianca tilted her head. "Just get to the part you're so terrified of telling me, Cheyenne. The fear is always worse than the facing of it."

Cheyenne almost laughed. As far as pep-talks from Bianca Summerlin went, that was a real winner.

"Okay. The newest symbol. The one on your chest."

"Yes. I heard. It means 'vessel.'"

"Right. And I've been hearing things from a lot of different sources that I have to bring the vessel back to Ambar'ogúl. To heal the blight and keep everything else from spilling over into our world."

"So, what is this vessel?"

Cheyenne wrinkled her nose. *Fuck. If I say it out loud, it's true.*

Bianca widened her eyes in as much encouragement as she knew how to offer.

"It's you, Mom."

"Me."

Cheyenne's bottom lip trembled as she sucked in a shuddering breath. "Yeah. Or at least, that's what all the signs are pointing to. The biggest sign is the potions I got from the bane-breaker. One's for me, a healing potion, and I didn't want to believe that's what it was until I couldn't *not* take it. It helped with this poison. It worked like it was supposed to."

"Good."

"And the other one's for you."

"A healing potion?"

Cheyenne swallowed. "No. It's to help you make the crossing into Ambar'ogúl so we can finally finish all this, and then yeah, we can heal you after that. You need to take it to get you there 'cause humans don't make this trip as a general rule. I don't want you to, but I…"

Tears welled in the drow's eyes, and she sniffed. *If I don't keep it together, no way in hell will she agree to this.*

"Mom, I tried to keep all this shit away from you. I know you don't want anything to do with it, and I never meant for it all to fall on you. I can handle my part fine, but you're not…" She glanced at the ceiling and forced the tears back where they belonged. "Apparently this is what always needed to happen, and I was an ass for thinking I could change it and keep you out of it. I literally don't see any other way. We'll both get worse if you don't come with me across the Border. And everyone else doesn't have a chance otherwise. I should've brought this to you sooner. I'm so sorry."

She sniffed and hung her head, leaning over her lap with her forearms propped up on her thighs. *There. Now it's all fucking true, and she's gonna lose it. Jesus, I seriously screwed this up. I should've listened to Ember from the beginning.*

Cheyenne almost lurched away when her mom's cool fingers pressed the underside of her chin. Blinking back even more tears, she didn't try to resist Bianca slowly lifting her face so mother and daughter could look each other in the eyes.

"Thank you for telling me."

A weak laugh escaped the drow. "Well, I think the other option was to tie you up and carry you across."

Bianca didn't smile at the poorly timed joke, but she did study her daughter's gaze and gently removed her hand. "Will he be coming with us?"

"L'zar? No." Cheyenne sniffed again and quickly wiped beneath her nose. "No, he was banished from Ambar'ogúl for life the last time I went over there with him. He'll die if he tries to go back."

"Hmm." Bianca's gaze moved from her daughter's face to the wall of windows looking out onto the veranda and the valley behind the estate. "As tempting as that notion is, I assume convincing him to ignore those consequences will be nearly impossible."

"Yeah." Cheyenne forced back a laugh. "He values his life quite a bit."

"Yes, I've noticed." When Bianca looked back down at her daughter, a small smile flickered across her lips. "You won't have to kidnap your own mother, Cheyenne. I'll go with you."

The drow blinked fiercely and sat fully up in her chair. "Did you just say yes?"

"If L'zar won't be accompanying us, then fuck it."

A laugh of disbelief burst from Cheyenne's mouth. *She said his name and cursed in the same sentence. Maybe I did just break her.*

Bianca's eyes widened. "I'll go with you and whoever else to Amber Mogul."

"Ambar'ogúl."

"Fine. And I'll be this vessel if that's what's required of me. But I have to ask if doing this will give me my body back." A humming laugh rose from Bianca as she glanced down at her lap. "This isn't my preferred state, you understand."

"Better than you know." Cheyenne nodded slowly. "I can't promise anything, Mom. But I hope that'll happen when all this is over."

Bianca blinked slowly and seemed to finally let out a breath of relief. "For now, I believe that's as much reassurance as I need."

"Okay." Cheyenne stared at her mom. *What the fuck? Is this really happening?* "And you're sure?"

"Cheyenne, you know I don't agree to anything on a whim. Don't ask me again."

"No problem." Forcing back another laugh, Cheyenne sat all the way back in her chair and stared at her mom. Bianca was gazing through the windows at the sprawling landscape colored with bright sunset hues.

She said she's willing to step into another world she's been pretending doesn't exist for the last twenty-one years. Now we're literally unstoppable.

CHAPTER SIXTY-EIGHT

Eleanor tsked and shook her head, scowling at the table as she cleared the half-full plates.

Bianca eyed her housekeeper. "You don't have to take care of all this right now, Eleanor."

"It's been sitting out for an hour already. If no one's hungry enough to appreciate a full meal, I might as well put the leftovers away." Eleanor scoffed. "We haven't had leftovers in decades."

"I'm sure it'll taste even better the second time," L'zar offered with a grin.

Eleanor looked sharply up at him and turned away from the table with her arms full of dishes. "Well, if there is a second time, you can get it yourself."

Cheyenne and Ember glanced at each other across the table, and both tried to hide their smiles.

L'zar chuckled and sat back in his chair.

Maleshi folded her hands on the table and leaned forward. "Ms. Summerlin, I want to say how—"

"Bianca. Please." The woman nodded. "Unless you'd prefer to be addressed as General."

The nightstalker smiled. "Fair enough. I want to thank you for being open to this. I've been in your world for a long time, and it's rare to meet a human who rolls with the punches like you have."

"Well." Bianca raised her eyebrows. "The fate of two worlds is on the line, isn't it? How could I say no?"

"Oh, jeez," Cheyenne whispered, dipping her forehead to cover it with a hand. "Mom, you don't have to!"

"What? Don't tell me I got it wrong."

Maleshi laughed. "No, that's absolutely correct. And it's rare to hear someone say that in casual conversation, but okay. Time to lay out the next steps, huh?"

"You need a portal," L'zar offered.

"Oh, look. The Weaver found the hole in our unformed plan."

He folded his arms and shot the general a wide grin. "That's not all I can do."

"Yeah, but you've done enough," Cheyenne added. "Unless you have anything helpful to add."

"Well, if I knew where to find another portal that wasn't either defective, destroyed, or swarming with those pitiful magicals calling themselves agents, Cheyenne, I would have suggested it."

"Good thing you're not the one calling the shots right now." Maleshi shot L'zar the same feral, mocking grin when he looked at her with wide eyes. "We'll take the portal at Colonial Williamsburg. Won't that be fun?"

"I'm sorry, where?" Bianca asked.

"Colonial Williamsburg." Ember shrugged. "You know, the tourist place that's like stepping back in time."

"Thank you, Ember. I am familiar with the location. Isn't that a rather public place for this crossover?"

"Crossing," Cheyenne muttered.

"Yes. That."

"We'll go tonight after dark." Maleshi nodded. "Employees and tourists will be snuggled up in their beds, and the barn will be empty."

"The barn." Bianca blinked quickly. "Is there a specific reason for the involvement of horses?"

"That's where it popped up, Mom. Nothing to do with horses or cows."

"I see."

L'zar cleared his throat. "You'll need to take precautions for when you get to the other side. We don't know how far the blight has spread since we've all been over here."

"I'm pretty sure the blight hasn't spread all the way to Hangivol yet," Ember said.

"What?" L'zar stared at the fae. "A portal into Hangivol?"

"Yeah. Cheyenne, wanna tell him how it got there?"

The halfling closed her eyes. "Not really."

Maleshi didn't bother to wipe the smug satisfaction off her face. "The Sorren Gán was kind enough to create a new one just for us, L'zar. How thoughtful, right?"

The drow thief raised his eyebrows, his nostrils flaring, but said nothing.

"I didn't go chasing it down, in case you were wondering," Cheyenne added. "It was already passed out at the fellfire pits. So at least we know the thing keeps its promises."

"Oh, I know it keeps its promises," L'zar hissed. "What I don't know is why the hell you would ever want to talk to it."

"Actually, it wanted to talk to me." Cheyenne shrugged. "I didn't have a choice." *I'm choosing not to tell him that the only thing he's afraid of pulled me across the city like a kite on a string.*

Bianca tapped a finger on her lips. "Would someone please explain to me what this Sorren… What is it?"

Cheyenne leaned over to her. "Sorren Gán. You know what, though? We can go over the specific names later."

"Yes. Better yet, you could make me a list."

Cheyenne and Ember both snorted.

"I don't see the humor in any of this." L'zar's careless, joking demeanor had disappeared beneath his irritation. "And I don't understand why this crossing has to happen tonight."

"You of all magicals shouldn't need an explanation," Maleshi said.

"But I understand the value of options. You're the one who told me we had to explore every avenue."

Cheyenne leaned forward to catch his attention. "L'zar, there isn't any other avenue at this point."

"There's the bane-breaker." His nostrils flared as his gaze flickered back and forth across the tabletop. "That's another option. Yeah. I'll go pay her a visit. There's bound to be more information there than she bothered giving you, Cheyenne."

"I'm not sure that's how it works."

"I couldn't care how it works." L'zar slapped a hand on the table and stood. "If you all insist on making this move tonight, I insist on ensuring we haven't missed anything. And you can't stop me."

Cheyenne folded her arms and raised an eyebrow at her dad on the verge of a full-blown drow fit. *He's pissed he can't be a part of the plan and that we know more than him.* "Go ahead, then. You know where she lives?"

L'zar's golden eyes narrowed at his daughter, and he lifted his chin. "I don't."

"Huh. Too bad. She doesn't take new customers past nine at night anyway."

Ember's eyes widened. "Oh, that's why. Because of the demon."

Bianca choked on her water and delicately pulled the straw out of her mouth. "I'm sorry, what?"

Cheyenne shook her head. "That one we can forget about."

Maleshi stood from her chair and walked to the open area between the dining table and the wall of windows. "Any other day, L'zar, I'd agree with you, but I don't think we have the time for a detour to the Earthside bane-breaker. I know Cheyenne doesn't."

L'zar glanced at his daughter. "Is it worse already?"

"Not yet. But the way this crap works, if it didn't heal, it'll get worse."

"I only used about a third of the vial," Ember muttered. "You know, just in case."

Cheyenne gave her friend a small smile. "Good thinking."

"Then it sounds like we have everything we need. Almost." Maleshi cleared her throat and opened a portal in front of the wall of windows.

Bianca frowned at the nightstalker. "What is that? What's she doing?"

Cheyenne forced herself not to smile. *She's like a kid at Disneyland all of a sudden.*

"It's a portal, Mom."

"Surely not like the one outside."

"No, it doesn't go between worlds."

The dark window of Maleshi's portal bloomed to full size, and the general chuckled. "That would solve so many of our problems, wouldn't it? But alas. I can only bridge the gap in one world at a time."

"Alas? Did you just fucking say alas?" Lumil stomped through the portal with her arms spread, frowning at the nightstalker. "Who the hell are you?"

"I kinda like it. Alas." Byrd emerged from the portal behind the goblin woman, nodding. "Sounds fancy."

"Oh, yeah? What the fuck kinda reason do any of us have for needing to sound fancy?"

L'zar stared at Maleshi with a tight grimace and clasped his hands behind his back. "Do we need them here for this?"

The goblins both turned to him. "L'zar! Where the hell have you been, man? We got the whole warehouse to ourselves, and you disappeared."

"I've been here."

Lumil gazed around the room and nodded. "Yeah, it's a nice place, huh? I don't blame you."

When the goblin woman grinned and pointed at Bianca, the woman leaned toward Cheyenne. "What's happening?"

"Check it out, man." Lumil slapped the back of her hand against Byrd's gut before stalking to the table. Byrd doubled over with a wheeze, then shook it off with a frustrated grunt and followed her. "You're awake. I'll tell you what, magical or not, anyone who gave birth to Cheyenne and stuck around to raise her definitely has what it takes to break through a curse, huh? Good for you."

"Cheyenne."

Huffing a sigh, Cheyenne stood and gestured at the goblins. "Mom, this is Lumil. And Byrd."

Byrd raised a hand. "Hiya."

"And they know about our situation?"

"Oh, yeah." Lumil folded her arms. "We were here when you went all human-statue by the portal. Then it was lights out, and we had to take off to break a scaleback necromancer out of Chateau D'rahl, so, you know, we couldn't stick around for too long."

Bianca slowly licked her lips. "Perhaps I shouldn't have asked."

"But it's great to see you up and moving around." The goblin woman nodded. "Congrats."

Byrd shot Bianca the guns with both hands. "Ditto."

"Ditto?" Lumil frowned at him. "What are you, seven?"

"What? I'm agreeing with you."

"You can't just take someone else's compliments and slap a 'ditto' on top. That doesn't give you shit for credit."

"Dude, I'm just sayin'."

"Moving on." Maleshi clapped her hands together and nodded. "Here's the deal. We're taking the portal in the barn tonight. Bianca is coming with us."

Lumil snorted. "Good one."

"It's not a joke," Bianca said, lifting her chin. "I'm making the crossing with you."

Byrd's mouth dropped open.

"Say what, now?" Lumil scratched the back of her head, her yellow hair flopping over her forehead. "Hey, it's okay. I get it. You just woke up from a curse. Makes sense if your brains are still a little scrambled, lady. That's not exactly something we do."

Bianca didn't miss a beat. "It is now."

The goblin woman whirled to stare at Maleshi. "Why the fuck are we smuggling humans into Hangivol all of a sudden?"

Maleshi offered Bianca a tight smile and spread her arms. "I didn't have a chance to fully explain the situation to my associates."

"Associates?" Byrd scoffed. "That's new."

"I understand," Bianca replied.

"Wait, so she's not insane?" Lumil turned back to Cheyenne and her mom. "And you're cool with this, halfling?"

Cheyenne shrugged. "It's something we have to do. I'm gonna need you to step it up and keep an eye on my mom in the in-between, right? 'Cause we're all going together."

"Except for L'zar," Byrd added.

"Yes." L'zar sneered at him. "Except for L'zar."

"Yeesh. Talking about himself in the third person." Lumil rolled her eyes. "Someone's pissed."

Byrd chuckled. "Guess that's what happens when the Crown banishes you for all eternity, huh? Hey, at least she didn't banish you only to the warehouse. The place is starting to fall apart without Persh'al."

"Who knew the troll was so good at keeping things clean, huh?" Lumil snorted and pointed at L'zar. "You should see what he's done with Hangivol. You ever see that *Flip That House* show? It's like that, but, you know, way more badass."

"Yeah, but what's with all the white?" Byrd shook his head. "I never got that."

L'zar's golden eyes widened. "What *Persh'al's* done?"

"Yeah. He's pullin' his own weight around there, that's for damn sure." Lumil stuck her thumb behind her at Cheyenne. "I think I can speak for everyone when I say it didn't seem like the best choice, but I tell you what, L'zar. Your kid knows how to pick 'em."

The drow thief turned slowly to his daughter and cocked his head. "You handed the throne to Persh'al?"

"Oh, whoa." Byrd exaggerated a grimace and blinked at Cheyenne. "You didn't tell him, huh?"

"Oh, shit." Lumil wrinkled her nose. "I just spilled your magical beans. Sorry, kid."

Cheyenne folded her arms and ignored the goblins. "I didn't just hand it over, L'zar. I offered it to him, and he accepted. I think I made a pretty damn good choice."

Maleshi nodded. "She did."

"It's not official yet, is it?"

"It's entirely official." Cheyenne watched him carefully. Even as she spoke, her dad's anger swelled visibly behind his blazing golden eyes. "Sworn in and everything. Right there under the tree."

"He's a troll!"

"It doesn't matter." She gestured at the general. "Maleshi and Corian figured out how to bind Persh'al with the Nimlothar. And yeah, I helped. The Crown doesn't have to be a drow, and in case you missed it, everyone in this room agrees that he's the right magical for the job."

L'zar glanced at Bianca, who closed her eyes and shook her head, lifting a hand to exempt herself from the conversation. "Cheyenne, I should have been consulted."

"You weren't there, and that's not my fault."

"No." His nostrils flared, and one eye twitched briefly. "I merely helped you seize your birthright and was banished because of it."

Cheyenne shook her head. "Don't try to turn this around on me. You hate Ambar'ogúl. And you know what? I don't know why we're having this conversation. I don't need to explain my decision to you. It's done. Persh'al's the O'gúl Crown, I came home for Bianca, and now we're going back to clean up the mess you and your sister left by fucking around with the natural laws of your own world."

L'zar didn't blink.

"She's right." Maleshi nodded. "Persh'al was the best choice. You know he'll do whatever it takes to steer things back in the right direction."

Lumil snorted. "Yeah. Especially now that he and Elarit finally got their *myrein.*"

L'zar hissed and whirled on the goblin woman. "Elarit?"

"Shit, you're steppin' in it today," Byrd muttered.

Lumil gave the drow a sheepish grin. "Come on, man. You had to see that coming, right?"

L'zar sucked a sharp breath through his clenched teeth, then growled and stormed around the table before disappearing beyond the staircase.

"Whoa." Lumil sniffed and shoved her hands in her pockets. "I was tellin' the truth."

"And he'll have to learn how to handle the truth without being able to change it." Maleshi glanced at the front of the house, then dusted off her hands and returned to the table. "It's almost eight-thirty. I suggest we call it a night right now and try to get as much rest as we can. I want everybody ready to go at two. Got it?"

"Yep." Lumil raised her eyebrows at Bianca, then strolled casually to the sitting area. "Ooh, yeah. I call that weird couch without any sides."

"Wait, what?" Byrd hurried after her. "You should take that other one. I'm taller."

"Yeah, by like a centimeter. Fat fucking chance, man. You snooze, you lose. And I'll be snoozin' on this fancy bench."

Bianca looked at her daughter with a surprisingly calm expression. "They don't know what a settee is."

"I guess not. And I don't think they care."

"What are they, exactly?"

Cheyenne fought back a laugh. "Goblins."

"Hmm. What a horrid-sounding word."

Maleshi chuckled. "Most of what comes out of those two's mouths is almost as bad. But the important thing is that we can trust them, and they know what they're doing when it counts."

Bianca lifted her chin toward the general. "Which is?"

"We'll save that for tomorrow."

A blood-curdling screech came from the hallway beside the sitting area.

"What the…whoa, lady. Hey!" Lumil shouted. "Hey, what are you doing with that tray?"

"Get off the furniture, you green…" There was a loud grunt, followed by a metallic clang. Then Byrd burst out laughing.

Maleshi gazed around the dining area with a grin. "I didn't realize Eleanor was so protective of the upholstery."

"When there are goblins sitting on it, yes." Bianca could only turn so far in her chair before the pain made her stop. "I suppose she is."

"You too. Off!" Eleanor hit Byrd with the serving tray, and the goblin man yelped.

"Hey! I took off my shoes!"

"I'll take off your head if you don't get off this instant!"

"Eleanor?" Cheyenne called.

"I'm handling it!"

Byrd and Lumil stomped back into the dining area, rubbing the backs of their heads. "We didn't do anything, man."

"I thought she'd recognize us. It hasn't been that long."

"Just because I recognize you, it doesn't mean I approve." Eleanor bustled in after them, her face flushed and her hair falling loose from its bun. "Why you think you can waltz right into this house and kick your feet up wherever you want is beyond me."

"Eleanor."

"Yes?"

Bianca reached out with one hand, still unable to turn all the way around to look at the housekeeper. "If you don't mind, I'd like to lie down for a moment."

"Of course." Scowling at the goblins, Eleanor set the tray on the table and gingerly helped Bianca to her feet. "I'm sorry about the furniture. It won't happen again."

"It's fine." Bianca nodded at her daughter as Eleanor supported her away from the table. "They're staying the night, so you needn't whack the sleeping goblins if you should find them anywhere else. I think they've learned their lesson."

"Huh." Eleanor barked a surprised laugh. "Yeah, I think they did."

When the softly laughing women disappeared around the staircase, Cheyenne looked at Maleshi and shrugged. "Could be worse, right?"

"Absolutely." The general sat in her chair at the head of the table, stretched her legs out in front of her, and crossed her ankles. "Honestly, she's taking all this a lot better than I expected."

"Yeah, me too, but that's her thing. Constantly exceeds expectations." With a wry chuckle, Cheyenne headed after her mom and Eleanor. "I'm gonna make sure she's got everything. Obviously, make yourselves at home. I guess."

Lumil scoffed. "Just not on the giant bench, huh?"

"Apparently." Cheyenne pointed to the other end of the house. "Or her study. That's on the other side of the house. If you think Eleanor lost it over the settee, I wouldn't risk letting her catch you in the study. So anywhere else, I guess."

Byrd eyed the bottom of the staircase above them. "What's upstairs?"

"Oh, no. The guest bed's already taken." Ember shook her head. "By me."

"Damnit." He pounded a fist into his other hand. "Any other comfy places up there?"

"I mean, there are armchairs in the breakfast room."

"All right, fae. You show me where."

Lumil wrinkled her nose. "What the fuck's a settee?"

CHAPTER SIXTY-NINE

"What about at night?" Eleanor spun away from the large walk-in closet in Bianca's master bedroom and shook her head at Cheyenne. "Does it get as cold there as it does here? Because I don't think she should risk being out in the cold in her condition."

Cheyenne dipped her head. "Well, we'll mostly be inside."

"Without electricity, though, right?" Clicking her tongue, Eleanor stepped back into the closet and rummaged through her employer's wardrobe, wooden hangers clacking together. "Of course not. Anyone who puts their dirty boots up on the furniture has no concept of civilized behavior. You'll need at least a pullover, and I'll pack a set of long underwear. The silk ones."

When Cheyenne opened her mouth to protest, Bianca whispered, "It's how she processes."

"Oh. Okay." The drow folded her arms and watched the empty doorway of the walk-in closet as Eleanor mumbled to herself.

"Jeans are practical. No, they chafe. What am I thinking?"

"Cheyenne." Bianca patted the edge of the bed beside her, and her daughter slowly sat down. "You look worried."

Cheyenne took a deep breath. "I'd call it nerves."

"Ah. Understandable. No one enjoys letting their mother tag along in their personal life. I know I didn't."

"You took Grandma across a magical Border into another world with you too?"

Bianca's rare chuckle filled the room, and Cheyenne couldn't decide whether to be proud of the achievement or flinch from it. *Nothing's gonna be the same after this. Not even Mom.*

"No magic, Cheyenne." Bianca's small smile widened the tiniest bit. "But there were times she insisted she accompany me to one function or another, most notably during my first campaign tour with Senator Brystol. That was a memorable evening, to say the least. We got into quite the argument."

"Really?"

"Oh, don't look so surprised. We rarely got along. She'd be rolling in her grave right now if she knew about this." Bianca squinted at the ceiling. "Hmm."

Cheyenne stared at her mom and waited for the rest of the story. *If she wants to tell me, she will. Asking won't make a difference.*

The woman reached out and gently patted Cheyenne's thigh before gingerly returning her hand to her lap. "You know, I never told you the full truth behind this place."

"You're not admitting that you lied to me, are you?"

Bianca shot her daughter a sidelong glance. "Please. I withheld irrelevant information. You know the difference."

Cheyenne grinned and looked down at her lap. "Not as well as you do."

"Oh, I'd say you've come a long way in the last few years." Taking a deep breath, Bianca studied the wide space between the bed and the closet. Eleanor grunted, and two light jackets flew through the doorway to land in the middle of the room. Bianca tilted her head and stared at the crumpled clothing. "She's taking longer than usual."

"To process or to pack?"

"Both." Bianca cleared her throat. "Earlier, I was about to say your grandmother would have done everything in her power to keep us from having the life we have now if she'd known certain facts about my personal life before she passed. And your grandfather would have gone along with it, just like he always did."

I can't believe she's talking to me about them. Cheyenne ran a hand through her black-dyed hair and waited.

"The full truth is that, fortunately, they passed before I could no longer hide my pregnancy."

Cheyenne frowned. "What?"

"It would have made more sense if you were born a century ago, or even sixty years. The Summerlins have always taken great pains to avoid scandal whenever necessary. However necessary."

"You never told them."

Bianca raised her eyebrows. "Of course not, and they left this life believing their daughter would continue going up the ladders they'd bred her to climb. I might even go so far as to say they were proud."

"Why wouldn't they be?" Cheyenne ran her hands up and down her thighs. "I mean, you did keep climbing."

"Indeed. Just not in the way they anticipated. So, I'm sorry to say, they did not know they were grandparents. I still believe it was better that way."

Ouch. Cheyenne swallowed. "Yeah, not a lot of people can handle raising a halfling, so you have that under your belt."

Her mom smiled again. "Not better for them, Cheyenne. Better for you."

"Oh." Frowning at the pristincly polished hardwood floor, Cheyenne couldn't think of anything to say or do after that.

"That's it." Eleanor grunted and poked her head out of the walk-in closet. "The overnight bag isn't big enough. I'm going with the small duffel."

"That's fine, Eleanor. Whatever you think is best."

The housekeeper glanced at the Summerlin women, nodded, then disappeared again into the closet. "And maybe an extra pair of shoes. Would slippers be going overboard?"

The clacks of hangers and thumps of bags and shoes being set aside returned to fill the silence.

Cheyenne drummed her fingers on her thighs. No idea they were grandparents, huh? What kind of scary did they have to be to make Mom hide something like that?

Her mom didn't offer any more information, but an even more relevant question popped into her daughter's head.

"Not that I'm saying this is the most important thing, but if they didn't know you were pregnant, how did they sign off on the trust fund?"

Bianca slowly turned her head as far as she comfortably could to meet her daughter's gaze. Her lips pursed in and out of a knowing smile. "You're not the only one with experience in amending legal documents."

"What?" Cheyenne let out a small, disbelieving laugh. "You forged the whole thing?"

"And backdated the signatures, yes." Bianca shrugged slightly. "A Notary Public owed me favors at the time."

"Wow. I can't believe you're telling me this."

"It's not *that* impossible to believe, is it?" This time, the woman's eyebrows flickered together in the kind of concerned frown Cheyenne had only seen maybe twice. "Cheyenne, I'm well aware of my deficiencies when it comes to motherly instincts."

"No, Mom, it's not."

"Don't insult me by trying to argue. We both know it's true. I realized by the time I was twelve that I wasn't cut out to be a parent, and it was not something I built my future around. Not in the cards, as your grandfather would have said, until suddenly it was. I had absolutely no idea what to do." Bianca dipped her chin and gazed intently at her daughter. "But from the moment I knew you existed, I have done everything in my power to give you the best chance possible. The best of everything I had to give. And honestly, I would do it all over again, given the choice. I know it seems as if Bianca Summerlin stands against all storms, but I wouldn't have been able to survive nearly as many of them without you."

Cheyenne's eyes widened, and she held her breath against the sharp sting in her nose before her vision blurred. *What the fuck is happening right now?*

"So, yes." Bianca returned her attention to the crumpled jackets on the floor, which had since been joined by a pair of flats and the silk long underwear set. "I forged your grandparents' signatures for your trust fund. I paid private doctors for more undocumented house calls than I can count. For both of us. I amended their wills as well."

"Wait." Cheyenne blinked the tears away, and they disappeared quickly under her surprise. "What kind of amendments are we talking about here?"

"This estate was originally intended to be mine after I turned thirty, but I wanted it before then." Bianca's smile returned. "We faced enough challenges in this house as it is. Imagine trying to tackle them in a waterfront studio apartment?"

Cheyenne snorted. "I'm not sure I want to."

"Exactly."

"Where in the world would *I* have slept?" Eleanor lugged the half-full duffel bag out of the closet and thumped it on the floor beside the other loose articles. Huffing a breath, she swiped away the loose gray curls dangling in her eyes, then stuck her hands on her hips. "No, I very much like the space we have, thank you."

"I'd assumed you were too preoccupied to overhear our conversation," Bianca replied.

"Oh, please. You know I can't help myself any time you start talking about forgeries."

"What, like, more than one?" Cheyenne frowned at her mom, unable to keep the surprised smile off her face. "Is that what she means?"

"I don't discuss business with my family, Cheyenne. You know that. And especially not in my bedroom."

"Oh, my God." Cheyenne stared at Eleanor instead. "And you've known all this since when?"

"The day she hired me." Eleanor nodded and hunkered down with a grunt to rearrange the clothing in the duffel bag. "Each day's been as exciting as the last ever since, and it's not just because we had you running around causing all sorts of trouble."

"I didn't cause that much trouble." When both women stared at Cheyenne, she shrugged. "Okay, maybe things were a little wild for a few years."

"Or eighteen."

Bianca chuckled. "The first two and the last two weren't all that bad."

Eleanor laughed. "Speak for yourself."

"Yeah, okay." Cheyenne shook her head. "I know you guys aren't looking for a pat on the back or anything, but you did okay."

"Just okay, huh?" Eleanor pretended to consider the semi-compliment. "I suppose it's not the worst thing you've ever said about us."

Bianca tilted her head. "Not the best, either."

Both women laughed again, and Cheyenne playfully rolled her eyes. *Laughing it up like we're packing for a week in the Bahamas together. Which would never happen.*

"Well, given however much trouble I got into," she said, turning to her mom, "I promise I'll keep us both out of it from now on."

The smile faded from both Bianca's and Eleanor's faces. Cheyenne's mom nodded. "I'm not sure you can separate yourself from trouble, Cheyenne. It seems to find you."

"Maybe, but after this, I'll make sure it stays away from you. Both of you. And I won't let anything happen to you while we're over there, Mom. We have Maleshi and the goblins coming with us. Ember's one of the best magicals to have around, and then when we get there, Persh'al and Corian will do whatever they have to to make sure you're safe."

"Beyond the general traveling aspect, are there more specific dangers in our immediate future?"

Only every local O'gúleesh feeling about humans the same way we feel about cockroaches over here. "No. No specific dangers, Mom. I don't want you to worry. That's all."

"I'm not worried."

"You're not?"

"Not in the slightest." Bianca shook her head. "Believe it or not, I'm looking forward to getting out. It's been a while."

"I'm worried." Eleanor pushed to her feet. "This isn't a weekend getaway in the Adirondacks."

"Are you still upset about that?"

"No. I'm not still upset. I've put it behind me." Eleanor looked at Cheyenne. "You just make sure she comes back in one piece."

"I will."

"Because I won't know what to do with myself in this house on my own. And no, I'm not letting that white-haired buffoon stay here with me, either."

Cheyenne smirked. "I'll tell him to leave."

"You do that. So will I." Eleanor glanced at the half-packed duffel bag and let out a choked whimper. "Can't forget the toiletries."

"I'll let you get some rest." Cheyenne stood from the edge of the bed and nodded at her mom. "Want me to wake you up when it's time?"

"I know how to set an alarm, Cheyenne, but thank you. I'll see you in a few hours."

"Yeah. Okay." She looked for Eleanor, but the woman had disappeared into the master bathroom. *She's apparently still processing, and there's definitely something wrong with Mom if she's looking forward to this.*

CHAPTER SEVENTY

Cheyenne gently closed the doors to her mom's bedroom and headed down the upstairs hall. When she passed the open door of the breakfast room at the back of the house, she found Ember sitting in one of the armchairs facing the windows. "Hey. You going to sleep in here?"

Ember turned in the slightly angled armchair facing the curving bay window and offered a weak smile. "Doesn't matter where I am. I don't think I'm gonna be sleeping tonight."

"Yeah, it does kinda seem impossible." Cheyenne crossed the room and sat in the other cream-colored wingback armchair beside her friend. The valley behind the Summerlin estate and the forest stretching far below were now shrouded in darkness. She saw more of her own reflection in the window than anything else outside. "We should talk about what happened earlier."

"Probably, yeah," Ember snorted. "I'm not sorry I did it."

"I don't want you to be." Cheyenne drummed her fingers on the upholstered armrests. "I'm sorry. I shouldn't have let it get that far."

"No, you shouldn't have."

Nodding, Cheyenne stared at the floor in front of them. "I remember the whole thing, Em. Me being a serious asshole. Trying to fight you. And your spell. Which, by the way, was pretty badass if I ignore the part about you casting it on me."

A humorless chuckle escaped the fae. "Well, thanks, I guess. Maleshi and L'zar thought you were already gone. You know, that the blight had taken over."

"Seriously?"

"Yeah." Ember smoothed her hair away from her face and shook her head. "I knew you weren't. They weren't going to do anything, so I had to."

"I was there the whole time, only I couldn't do anything about it." Cheyenne kicked off her black Vans one at a time and pulled her legs up onto the armchair. "Like, I split into two different people, one who was seriously confused, and the other one who was taking over and wanted to rip all three of you apart."

"That's the one I tied up with magic and tossed on the stairs." Slowly, Ember turned to look at her friend, her eyes wide beneath a concerned frown. "The poison spread all the way to your eyes, Cheyenne. All black. Not like when you break out the black fire and go full-on drow, but like that skaxen village by the transport station. It was fucked up."

"I know."

"It's not like I enjoyed attacking my best friend and forcing a healing potion down her throat, by the way."

"Yeah, I figured that went without saying."

"But you're still pissed at me for doing it." Ember raised her eyebrows. "I can tell."

"I'm not pissed at you. I mean, I didn't enjoy it, but I know you did what you had to do."

The room was silent for a moment, then Ember took a deep breath. "Look, I don't think I've tried to tell you what to do or how to do it. At least, not when you're thinking clearly. When I do say something, it's because I know you're not in the right place to think things through on your own. When that happens, I need you to shut up and trust me. Okay?"

"I will, Em."

"Good."

"On the bright side, I can't think of anything worse than having to accept the fact that my mom's the vessel we need to take across the

Border to heal a magical world she hates. So it'll be a lot easier to shut up and trust you with anything else that comes up."

Ember snorted. "Well, don't jinx it."

Cheyenne reached over to the tall, round wooden side table between the armchairs and knocked on it twice.

With a small, confused smile, Ember frowned at the side table. "I didn't peg you for a superstitious drow."

"I'm not. Generally." Cheyenne shrugged. "But at this point, I'll take all the help I can get."

"Not a bad plan."

They sat there for a few minutes without saying anything else. Cheyenne thought, *Feels like we got it figured out. Definitely a bad idea to make the crossing with all that hanging between us.*

"Shit. I'm supposed to teach tomorrow."

Ember shrugged. "I doubt anyone will have an issue with another canceled class, especially if being on that part of campus makes every-body forget what they're doing there."

"Right. The blight seeping out into the air. One more thing on the list." Cheyenne stood from the armchair. "I'm gonna go pull another marginally believable excuse out of thin air and hope the undergrads buy it, at least. I'm pretty sure the rest of the program faculty won't, but whatever."

"You'll figure it out. Trust me, it's not so bad, stepping away from school for a while to take care of slightly more important things that are way more exciting."

Cheyenne said, "Thanks, Em. I'm probably headed that way anyway."

"Well, good luck. See you at two, I guess."

"Yeah." Cheyenne left the breakfast room and headed down the stairs to a surprisingly quiet main floor. Wherever L'zar, Maleshi, and the goblins were, no one made a sound. *Not like I'm trying to talk to any of them right now anyway.*

She went straight to her mom's study and the next set of French doors to close behind her before she found herself sitting in Bianca's executive desk chair and turning on the computer. *She has to know how many times I used to sneak in here to do this. Well, not exactly this.*

As Cheyenne logged on and pulled up the extra VPN she'd

connected to her mom's computer years ago, she smiled. *I wonder what kinda gear she used to hack into her parents' wills?*

First, she weaseled her way into the VCU Medical Center database, and her activator helped her find the template she wanted for a doctor's note. If any of the VCU program faculty ended up calling Dr. Andrews to follow up, Cheyenne had a feeling the guy would cover for her. He hadn't said anything about her first shoulder wound or the FRoE tracker he'd removed from it what felt like forever ago. The man could handle covering for her.

On Dr. Andrews's electronic letterhead, she typed a quick explanation of the condition she didn't have, some kind of septic blood infection, followed by an assertion that Cheyenne Summerlin required at least the next week free from external stressors, including working and teaching.

When she finished, she found an image of his signature, slapped it at the bottom, and read it one more time. *Good enough. Ordering myself to be on bed rest might be taking it a little too far.*

The note got emailed to each of her graduate professors, including Maleshi, then Cheyenne pulled up her VCU email account and typed another version of the story she was sticking with.

Professors Bergmann, LePlant, Beckwith, Dawley, and Hersh,

As you are all aware, I've been struggling with personal issues over the last week. I was able to make it in for class yesterday, but I've recently become ill, and I am in need of recovery time. My physician, Dr. Andrews, should be forwarding each of you written communication he was kind enough to draw up on my behalf. I won't be able to return to campus to teach the Advanced Programming class at least until Wednesday of next week, but it may be longer, depending on how long it takes me to recover. Should I need more time, Dr. Andrews will reach out again to verify this need.

I highly value my position as an undergraduate instructor and greatly appreciate all of your willingness to provide an alternative route through the graduate program this year to accommodate my schedule and my skillsets. I also want to apologize for not having been as available to teach this course as I would have liked, and I do hope this doesn't affect the future of my academic studies at Virginia Commonwealth University or within the graduate program.

However, if changes need to be made or you as my professors conclude that this temporary leave of absence is unacceptable, I understand. Hopefully, I can recover quickly without any other obstacles getting between me and my pursuit of higher education and earning my master's degree. 2021 has been one heck of a year.

Thank you for your time and understanding.

Cheyenne Summerlin

When she finished typing the email, she sat back in her mom's executive desk chair of mahogany and chocolate-brown leather and read it one more time. *Fifty-fifty chance they'll believe I wrote this. Maybe Maleshi can put in a good word after the fact.*

CC-ing all her professors, Cheyenne sent the email and typed another one to her undergrad students that was a lot shorter and sounded a lot more like the instructor they'd come to know over the last few weeks.

Advanced Programming Students,

I won't be in for tomorrow's class, Friday's, or Monday's. If I have to stay home longer than that, I'll let you know. Apparently, doctors still write notes for grad students and undergrad instructors. Just because I'm taking sick days, it doesn't mean you don't have to show up for class. Either you'll have a sub, or the program will contact you to let you know if and when the classes are canceled.

Don't hang around the quad too long on your way to the Computer Sciences building. I think there's some kind of gas leak (and no, that's not why I'm sick).

See you next week. Probably.

Cheyenne

The email was sent to her dozen students, then she clicked out of everything, shut down the VPN, and put everything back into place before shutting off her mom's computer.

Then she sat back in the chair and stared at the black monitor with a grimace. Probably won't even be getting my master's now, at least not when and where I planned. It sucks, but that's not even on the priority list.

The chair rolled smoothly and silently away from the desk as she stood, and Cheyenne wheeled it perfectly back into place before gazing around her mom's study. The room was neat and tidy, everything made of wood and leather in dark, intimidating colors. Bianca's usual smell of vanilla and sandalwood filled the space and made her want to go check on her mom again.

No, she's fine. Despite the amount of sleep she'd gotten in the last twenty-four hours, all of it forced on her by either a bane-breaker's magic or a potion poured down her throat, Cheyenne couldn't hold back a massive yawn. Blinking quickly against the welling tears it brought, she sniffed and headed back across the study. *And I need to lie down.*

Before she reached the doors, a framed photograph she'd seen a million times on the built-in bookshelf on her right made her stop. She stared at it for a moment, then slowly approached the bookshelf to take down the dust-free frame for a closer look.

Cheyenne's grandfather grinned, his eyes narrowed so much they nearly disappeared within the laugh lines and wrinkles around the corners. Her grandmother stood on his left, her smile thin, composed, and dutifully prim. On the man's right, a much younger Bianca echoed the same thin smile, her hands clasped in front of her. All three of them stood on the steps of the H. Carl Moultrie Courthouse on a gorgeous spring day, the cherry trees in full blossom in the background.

I never asked when this was taken.

Frowning, Cheyenne turned the frame over and undid the clasps to open the back. Sure enough, there was her mom's neat, looping handwriting across the back of the picture in thick black ink: *Moultrie Courthouse March 4th, 2000.*

"Holy shit." It sighed out of the drow as a whisper, and she quickly replaced the frame's backing before setting it exactly the way it had been on the shelf.

Bianca would have been eight weeks pregnant the day this picture was taken. *They never knew. Did she even know that day?*

For some reason, deep in her gut, Cheyenne knew the answer was yes.

CHAPTER SEVENTY-ONE

Even in the eerily quiet house with nothing to distract her for the next four hours, Cheyenne couldn't get past the first stages of slipping into unconsciousness before her brain kicked her awake again. She tossed and turned in the twin-sized bed, and her poor sleep this time had nothing to do with how much she hated being in her childhood bedroom.

Finally, after being jolted awake one more time by her subconscious, she tossed the covers aside and sat up with a grunt. Her eyes ached under the bright light when she grabbed her phone and turned on the lock screen. *One forty-two. Great. Three minutes before the alarm, and now I get to cross into Ambar'ogúl on zero sleep.*

Running her fingers through her hair, she set the phone in her lap and stared at the dark shapes in her room. *Mom needs extra guest rooms.*

She turned on the bedside lamp, grabbed her activator off the nightstand, and picked her trenchcoat up off the floor before shrugging into it. The lack of searing pain in her still-sore shoulders this time brought a small smile to her lips. *Improvement. Better than becoming a blighted zombie-drow, that's for damn sure.*

By the time she went back into the breakfast room for her Vans, Ember was already floating down the wide central staircase. The fae stopped halfway down to wait, then gave Cheyenne a sympathetic smile and descended the rest of the way with her.

"You're looking a little rough."

"Really?" Cheyenne snorted. "After being drugged by a healing potion and deciding to escort my mom across the Border, I figured I'd be glowing."

Ember let out a wry chuckle. "Didn't sleep, huh?"

"I almost slept about a dozen times. Does that count?"

"Probably not."

They reached the bottom of the stairs and turned to head to the back of the house and the low drone of voices coming from the dining area. "What about you?"

Ember shrugged. "Four hours of sleep in an armchair might not be any better. It was super comfy, though."

"Yeah, I know."

When they reached the dining area beneath the stairs, L'zar, Maleshi, and the goblins sat at the table. They all looked at Cheyenne and Ember, the conversation on hold, and nodded grimly.

Maleshi spread her arms. "Just another day in the life, huh, kid?"

"I guess." Cheyenne stuck her hands in her pockets. "I'm hoping we never have a repeat of this day."

"We won't." Ember nodded. "After what we we need to on the other side, Bianca won't ever have to make the crossing again."

"Speaking of Bianca, has she come down yet?"

Lumil shook her head. "Nope. It's almost two, right?"

"Hey." Byrd's eyes widened. "You don't think she, like, got worse all of a sudden and can't even walk down the stairs?"

Lumil slapped the back of his head and scowled at him. "What the fuck's wrong with you?"

"Ow. What? It's a fair question."

"Even if that were the case," Bianca said as she came into the sitting area, her hand firmly clenched around Eleanor's forearm, "I make a habit of always providing myself with alternatives. That includes getting from one floor of my home to another."

L'zar stood immediately from the table and clasped his hands behind his back, looking Bianca over with barely concealed concern. Maleshi frowned at him but got to her feet as well.

Byrd rubbed the back of his head and studied the woman, who was dressed in loose, charcoal gray joggers and a matching zip-up sweater. "You mean, like another staircase?"

"Like an elevator," Cheyenne muttered.

"No way." Lumil's yellow eyes widened. "You have a fucking elevator in this place? Of course you do. Why am I even surprised?"

Cheyenne approached her mom and the grim-faced Eleanor. "How are you feeling?"

"Like a pincushion, Cheyenne." Bianca gave her daughter a thin-lipped smile and stopped at the head of the dining table. She stood as stiffly as she'd walked and didn't move when Eleanor plunked the small duffel bag onto the table. The thing was stuffed almost to bursting.

"Now, I packed everything she could possibly need for something like this. Extra clothes, toiletries, a heavier pair of shoes. You know, for more difficult terrain." Eleanor patted the top of the bag and stared at it. "A light jacket. A heavier jacket. Oh, and there's a hunting knife and a can of Mace."

"You think that's what she needs to make the crossing?" Lumil blurted.

The housekeeper looked quickly at her. "We don't know how long she'll be gone."

"Well, she sure as shit won't need Mace."

"Nobody asked you," Eleanor hissed. "Now, if you don't mind, I'll kindly ask you to mind your own damn business, gobbler."

Byrd barked a laugh. "We're goblins."

"I honestly couldn't care less."

"Eleanor." Bianca shot the woman a sidelong glance. "Until we depart, these magicals are still our guests. And they're here to help."

Cheyenne and Ember exchanged quick, surprised looks. More proof she's losing it. She's trying to catch on to the magical world's lingo.

Eleanor glared at the goblins, then turned to Bianca with tears in her eyes. "I'm doing everything I can to make sure you have what you need. This nonsense from the green peanut gallery over here doesn't help anyone."

"Oh, come on." Byrd spread his arms. "She doesn't need a bag like that. You think Hangivol doesn't have way better stuff than whatever you packed up for a trip that'll take us twenty minutes?"

"I have no idea what that is," Eleanor muttered.

"The city, lady."

"I got it." Cheyenne grabbed the strap of the duffel bag and slipped it over her head and shoulder. "Thanks, Eleanor."

"Yes. Well. It's not like I'll be particularly useful here after you all take off." Blinking quickly, the woman wiped away the tears leaking from the corners of her eyes and sniffed.

"I still need you." Bianca reached out and took her friend's wrist. "You're the only person I trust to keep things running smoothly while I'm gone, Eleanor, and I will most certainly need you when I return."

"I know." Eleanor gently patted the back of her employer's hand before Bianca let go.

"We'll come back as soon as we can." Cheyenne stepped over to the housekeeper and opened her arms for a hug.

"You'd better." Eleanor practically threw herself at the drow, sniffling, but she was aware enough not to crush Cheyenne in her embrace as usual. When they drew apart, the woman swallowed thickly and tucked the drow's hair behind her ear. "Be careful, sweetheart. I know I don't need to tell you to take care of her. I've been the one doing it for so long."

"Made an excellent example for her." Bianca nodded. "We'll be fine."

"You've both been excellent hosts under the circumstances, especially on such short notice." Maleshi stepped away from the table and over to the windows to cast a portal. "It's time for us to go."

As Ember and Eleanor hugged and said their goodbyes, the goblins headed after Maleshi to wait for the portal. L'zar headed to Cheyenne, his hands still clasped behind his back. His golden eyes widened as he dipped his head toward her. "I don't agree with every decision you've made since we set out on this path together, Cheyenne."

"Wow." She raised her eyebrows. "The feeling's totally mutual, and you still need to work on your pep talks."

"But I know you will succeed in every endeavor you undertake. Just like you always have."

"Okay. Thanks, I guess."

His eyebrows drew together, and he glanced briefly at Bianca, who had focused intently on the dark window of light opening on the other side of her dining area. "I didn't anticipate this, and it's not entirely comfortable to say it, but I do wish I could go with you."

"Better not try your luck on this one though, huh?" Cheyenne jerked her head at her mom. "And I don't think she'd do this willingly if you could."

"What does that mean?"

"It means we're all exactly where we need to be, L'zar. We're making the crossing to undo everything Ba'rael screwed up, and you're staying here." *Where he can't fuck with our plans and make an even bigger shitshow out of the whole thing.*

L'zar cocked his head, frowning at something only he could see behind his daughter's head. "I don't enjoy having no choice in the part I play."

Cheyenne reached out to give his shoulder a quick pat, half-reassuring, half-condescending. "You'll get used to it like I did."

She turned away from him and headed over to Maleshi, the goblins, and the now-open portal into the barn at Colonial Williamsburg. Ember floated quickly across the floor behind her, giving L'zar a brief nod as a goodbye.

The drow thief strode briskly toward Bianca and Eleanor, who were saying their private farewells in low voices. "Bianca."

She turned slowly to look up at him and took a step back when he leaned toward her.

"It would have been quite the adventure to accompany you on your first journey into my world." L'zar studied her face before a frown of L'zar-style remorse wrinkled his eyebrows. "I never intended for any of this to happen. You must know that."

"Your intentions apparently had no effect on the end results."

"No. Indeed, they didn't." He cleared his throat, at a loss for words and clearly confused by it. "I'm so sorry I can't accompany you."

Bianca lifted her chin and raised her eyebrows, assessing him with the calculated apathy she'd honed over a lifetime. "I'm not."

She stepped around him and headed over to the group of magicals standing in front of Maleshi's open portal.

"Bianca, wait."

Despite the obvious pain it caused her, Bianca moved a lot more quickly than Cheyenne expected. "Is this thing ready for us, General?"

Maleshi blinked in surprise and fought back a laugh. "We just walk right through."

"Excellent."

L'zar headed after them. "Bianca. Please."

She ignored him and stepped boldly through her first nightstalker portal without hesitation.

"Oh, shit." Byrd grimaced at L'zar and shrugged. "Better luck next time, man."

Lumil chuckled as she followed the other goblin through the portal.

L'zar clenched his fists at his sides and gazed at Cheyenne. "I can't do anything."

"I know. But we will." She and Ember both stepped through the dark window.

Maleshi lifted her hand to the drow thief and shook her head. "Whatever it is can wait."

"What am I supposed to do until then, General?"

"That's up to you. Done any meditating lately?"

L'zar glared at the general as she stepped through the portal, then the whole thing closed with a soft pop. He spun to face Eleanor and smoothed his white hair away from his face. "Well, then. It looks like it's just the two of us."

"Oh, no, it's not." With one hand on her hip and the other pointed to the front of the house, Eleanor scowled at him. "This is the part where you leave this house. Immediately."

He chuckled and spread his arms. "It's two o'clock in the morning, Eleanor."

"Exactly. And I won't be able to go back to sleep, knowing you're skulking around this house doing God knows what. You know where the door is."

Eyeing her, L'zar dipped his head. "I can recognize when I'm no longer welcome."

"Good. I've made it quite obvious."

The corners of his mouth twitched, and he walked halfway to the hall before pausing. "Could you spare a meal before I go?"

"Out!"

"Fine." He rolled his eyes and stomped to the front of the house.

Eleanor hurried close on his heels to make sure she saw him step through the front door before it slammed shut behind him.

CHAPTER SEVENTY-TWO

Cheyenne stared at her mom's outline, silhouetted against the dim moonlight in the barn. The first time she's left home in what, almost ten years? And it's not even for a political function. Jesus.

Ember leaned over to her and muttered, "Is it just me, or does your mom look weirdly at home here?"

"Bianca looks weirdly at home everywhere she goes." Cheyenne met her friend's gaze and shrugged. "One of her superpowers."

"I bet her clients hated it."

"Yep. They stopped complaining about having to drive out to the estate."

"All right." Maleshi pointed at the far wall of the barn, and a flash of silver light illuminated a shimmering wall at the back. "There it is."

Bianca studied the Border portal with nothing but curiosity. "Refracted light."

"I'm sorry?"

Cheyenne's mom turned to look at the general. "Like sunlight on a pool."

"Ah. That's temporary." Maleshi nodded. "You'll have to excuse me, Bianca. What you see right now isn't truly me. I just want you to have fair warning. You understand."

"Well, I'm trying."

With a sympathetic smile, the nightstalker snapped her fingers. Her body shimmered silver, and her human illusion fell away to reveal the black fur, glowing silver eyes, and feline features of General Maleshi Hi'et, Ambar'ogúl's Blade of the Untouched Eye.

Bianca's only reaction was a slight widening of her eyes. "I see."

Ember released her illusion too, and her hair regained the streaks that were the same color as her large, luminous purple eyes. A faint pink glow rose around her inhumanly pink skin, and she pulled the brown glass potion vial from her pocket to uncork it. "This is for you."

"Ah." The woman reached gingerly for the vial and gave it a hesitant sniff. "How unfortunate."

"Mom?" Cheyenne studied her mom's slight disappointment. "What's wrong?"

"You know I'm not a fan of anise." Without hesitation, she lifted the vial to her lips and tilted her head back, draining the whole thing in three seconds. Pursing her lips, she handed the vial back to Ember and delicately wiped the corner of her mouth. "I suppose I shouldn't have expected it to be pleasant."

Ember pocketed the empty vial. "How do you feel?"

"No different, Ember. Thank you. Shall we?"

Cheyenne glanced at Maleshi, who returned her gaze with a small smile and a brief nod. *This is so weird.*

She slipped into her drow form and pulled the thick silver cuff from the pocket of her trenchcoat to slide it onto her wrist. Bianca gave her a quick once-over but didn't say a word.

"The important thing to remember, Bianca," Maleshi said, "is to always keep moving once we're through. We'll take care of the rest."

"Well, that sounds simple enough."

"Ember and I will go through first. You'll follow. Cheyenne, Lumil, and Byrd will take the rear."

"Ambar'ogúl will have its first human," Lumil said with a nod. "That's fucking weird."

Byrd sniggered.

The general eyed the goblin woman for a moment, then gestured at the shimmering window of the Border portal. "Ready?"

"Lead the way, General." Bianca lifted her chin and watched Maleshi and Ember disappear through the shimmering light. Pressing her lips together, she walked stiffly through after them and vanished.

Cheyenne gritted her teeth. *Here goes nothing.*

The sharp, burning pressure in her lungs hit her immediately when she stepped into the in-between. Doubling over, she waited for the sensation to pass and was almost knocked over by Lumil barreling into her from behind.

The goblin woman sucked in a wheezing breath and waved the drow off when Cheyenne glanced at her. "Sorry, kid. Just a sec."

Byrd thumped a fist on his chest and cleared his throat. "Worst fucking part."

Ember and Maleshi recovered quickly as well, and everyone looked at Bianca to gauge the woman's reaction.

Cheyenne's mom stood erect in the thick, soupy blackness of the in-between, which was now infected with the blight. She seemed more surprised by the magicals' discomfort during the first stage of the crossing than by her new surroundings. "Did I miss something?"

"It's a little rough, stepping through," Cheyenne muttered. "It doesn't last very long."

"Hmm."

Ember swallowed and took a deep breath to compose herself. "You didn't feel that?"

"I'm not sure what I should have felt, Ember." Bianca gazed around the in-between at the thick, sludgy black smoke moving like soup through the unnatural air. "This is certainly different."

"Let's move." Maleshi waved them all forward, then turned to lead the way, studying the slow-swimming shadows as she stepped through the black ooze covering the ground none of them could see. "Stay sharp."

They moved single file through the gray non-light of the in-between, and Cheyenne found herself searching every moving shadow and trailing wisp of syrupy black smoke with more caution than any other time she'd made the crossing. *If she keeps it together like this when the monsters show up, I'll know she's officially lost her mind.*

"Just let the bastards try to take us," Lumil muttered. "I'll send 'em right back where they belong."

"You mean here?" Byrd frowned at the goblin woman and shook his head. "Where else are they gonna go?"

"It's a figure of speech, moron. Shut up."

Cheyenne flexed her hands as they moved, and a slight wind whistled through the nothingness around them. She swept her gaze across the blackness, pausing briefly to look at her mom's rigid back in front of her. A cloud of particularly thick black smoke glided toward them, and she gritted her teeth. "Just keep moving, Mom. No matter what, okay?"

"I heard the warning the first time, Cheyenne." Bianca turned to look over her shoulder and gestured ahead of her, and her hand floated through the thick cloud passing in front of her. "It's hardly a complicated directive."

The second the woman's hand entered the cloud, the black smoke burst aside and filtered out into nothing, moving swiftly away from her.

What the hell?

"Maleshi." Cheyenne nodded at her mom when the general turned. "Do you see this?"

"You'll have to be a little more specific, kid."

"Mom, do that again. Wave your hand."

"Cheyenne, this hardly seems like the time."

"Hold on." Maleshi's silver eyes widened when she saw the next thick puff of black smoke redirect itself away from Bianca at the last second. "Everyone keep moving. Bianca, come up here with me if you would."

"All right." Bianca stepped quickly toward the general, and puffs of disintegrating black sludge cleared away from her footsteps, leaving a trail of clear gray space behind her. When Maleshi's eyes narrowed, Bianca raised her eyebrows and kept walking. "I don't see what all the fuss is about, honestly."

"Is she for real?" Byrd asked.

"Man, look at that." Lumil thrust a hand at the smoke clearing in a widening circle around Bianca. "Like fucking oil and water. What the hell is this?"

Maleshi didn't say anything when Bianca stepped past her and kept walking. "I think we'll follow her."

The other magicals exchanged confused glances and quickly stepped through the trail of cleared space after Cheyenne's mom.

No way this would happen for every human.

Cheyenne frowned at her mom, who picked up the pace in a direct line through the hazy darkness.

Bianca hardly moved her head as she walked, lifting her arm now and then to gingerly wave aside a thick cloud of darkness. The roiling sludge spewed away from her feet to reveal perfectly gray ground beneath her. Shadows rose and fell on either side of their party, but the dark creatures that called the in-between home stayed well away from the human woman leading a group of magicals across the Border.

Ember looked over her shoulder at the drow and raised her eyebrows. "You think it's the potion?"

"I hope so, Em." *If it's not, then it's Bianca Summerlin's presence. This is insane.*

They walked for what felt like another five minutes until Bianca pointed ahead. "That light up there?"

"Yes, that's where we're headed." Maleshi nodded, staring with wide eyes not at the opposite doorway but at Bianca. "Just head that way."

"I was under the impression that this was a dangerous undertaking, General."

"Well, we're not through yet." Maleshi shot Cheyenne another surprised look and shook her head.

Yeah, I'm right there with you.

The slowly flickering tendrils of in-between blackness shuddered and withdrew when Bianca approached the doorway, shrinking into themselves and disappearing around the rectangle of light. "And we step through this one just like the last?"

"That's right." Maleshi scanned the thickening shadows around them with a deep frown. "Just keep going."

"Simple enough." Just as Bianca reached the doorway, her body pulsed with orange light. The runes etched into her skin illuminated all at once, the orange light showing through her clothing. With a gasp, she threw her head back and faltered before her next step.

"Mom?"

The runes pulsed brighter, and Bianca screamed.

She crumpled to the ground, sending up sprays of disintegrating black smoke. The screaming didn't stop.

"Shit." Cheyenne raced to her mom, gritting her teeth against the earsplitting screams and the howling wind kicking up around them. "Mom! Hey, I'm here. Can you hear me?"

She reached out to touch Bianca's shoulder, and the woman flinched away from her with a shriek.

"Move." Maleshi's hands crackled with silver light as she scanned the dark shadows closing in on them.

"Fuck. Mom, I'm sorry."

"Now, Cheyenne!" Maleshi snarled as a huge black tentacle wove toward them.

Cheyenne scooped her mom up in her arms, gritting her teeth against the ache in her shoulders, and carried Bianca through the doorway. The woman continued to scream, writhing and flailing in her daughter's arms. The rest of their group darted through the doorway after her, and Cheyenne sucked in a sharp breath when Bianca's hand smacked her face.

They stood outside the fellfire pits where the Sorren Gán had created the portal. Hangivol's lights filled the darkness in front of them, and Bianca wouldn't stop screaming.

"What's wrong with her?" Lumil tossed her hair out of her eyes.

"Mom. Mom, it's okay." Cheyenne struggled to keep her hold of Bianca's jerking body, which was growing hotter in her arms by the second.

"What happened?" Maleshi asked.

"I don't know." Cheyenne crouched and tightened her hold on her mom before the woman could throw herself to the ground. "Shit. Ember, grab my activator."

"Pocket?"

"Yeah. This one. On the right!"

Ember floated over to her and shoved a hand into Cheyenne's pocket. Her head jerked sideways when Bianca's flailing hand caught her in the temple, but she finally wrenched out the activator and had to brush Bianca's arms aside to stick the thing behind Cheyenne's ear.

The drow's eyelids fluttered, and she almost dropped Bianca again before the activator synced with her magic.

"Cheyenne, she needs to—"

"Don't tell me what she needs," Cheyenne growled. She brushed past Maleshi and stormed across the fellfire pits, which sent an occasional plume of green flames into the night sky.

Bianca bucked and flailed in her arms, letting out shriek after agonized shriek, but Cheyenne moved swiftly up the tunnel to the walkway around the city's outer wall. *I need to move faster.*

CHAPTER SEVENTY-THREE

"Cheyenne, wait!" Ember called, racing after her friend through the tunnel. "We're coming with you."

Cheyenne barely heard the fae's shout, focused only on not dropping Bianca as she scanned the scrolling lines of code racing along the metal of Hangivol's walls and the walkway beneath her feet. *She's not gonna make it.*

Her activator pulled up prompts she barely acknowledged, but her magic and urgency worked for her automatically. Line after line of code in the walls lit up in her vision without her having to choose or even read them. She didn't need to find a programmed door in the city's walls. All she had to do was keep walking, and Hangivol responded to the true O'gúl Crown without hesitation.

The wall opened in front of her, metal segments sliding back and folding in on themselves. Cheyenne picked up the pace, moving steadily as Bianca screamed and flailed. The drow hardly felt her mother's uncontrolled slaps to her face and neck or the growing heat of the woman's body.

The city groaned around her and came to life, moving and rearranging in anticipation of where Cheyenne wanted to go even before she knew. A staircase materialized in front of her, and when she stepped onto the first stair, the metal lifted her and rearranged again.

She could see through the city walls now, the multiple layers of Hangivol's district levels racing through her vision like the entire world was written in two-dimensional code. *I need to be in the Heart. I have to get her there.*

Without thinking about it, she stepped forward, and the lines of code racing across the O'gúl capital exploded. She carried her mom through them like they were smoke on the wind, the walls racing past her and shrinking, melting away. Two steps later, she was in the Heart, starlight spilling through the central courtyard from the open ceiling.

"Anyone here?" she shouted. "Help! I need help!"

Bianca kept screaming, and one of her flailing legs hit Cheyenne's wounded hip. The drow cried out in pain and dropped to one knee.

"Anybody!" She gently lowered her mom to the white stone of the Heart's floor beside the gnarled, twisted trunk of the last Nimlothar. Bianca bucked and squirmed, seizing on the ground as the glowing runes burning through her skin lit the courtyard with a blazing orange glow. "Help!"

Two windows of dark light opened in front of her. Maleshi and Corian raced through their portals at the same time and hurried to Bianca.

"What happened?" Corian growled, his silver eyes blazing.

"I don't know. We made the crossing, and she just—" Bianca's knee came up into Cheyenne's stomach and she grunted, doubling over. "Help her. I don't know what to do."

"Be careful with her," Maleshi warned as Corian dropped to one knee on the other side of Bianca and reached toward the woman.

The general's voice and Bianca's screams faded to nothing as purple light raced up the Nimlothar's trunk and illuminated every branch and the few leaves still clinging to their perches.

Now, Cheyenne.

"What?" She turned to the tree, breathing heavily and supporting herself with a hand on the stone floor.

Purple and black light raced up and down the tree's trunk, glowing brighter.

Now you may fulfill your promise. It must be now.

Cheyenne was vaguely aware of Corian lifting Bianca into his arms. Maleshi shouted something at him as she opened another portal out of the Heart, but no sound emerged. Cheyenne couldn't take her gaze away from the glowing Nimlothar the nightstalkers didn't seem to notice.

"I can't do anything yet," she muttered.

The tree flashed again, and all the strength seeped out of the drow. She fell forward, her jaw striking the stones with a muted crack, and she couldn't move, but she felt herself rising from the floor again, pulled by the force of the Nimlothar's magic. She looked down at her body, still lying sprawled on the white stone, and although the sight sent a brief panic racing through her, she couldn't control any of it.

What is this? What the fuck's happening?

You promised, Cheyenne. Now you have everything you need to finish what you started.

She gasped at the visions bombarding her mind as she rose. She saw the deadened Nimlothar forest in the mountains, every not-quite-dead tree ablaze, not with the black fire she'd seen in the last warning vision, but with green flames. A burst of healing energy raced through her and the forest and every tree tied to drow magic. The lifeforce of Ambar'ogúl seemed to squeeze into Cheyenne's body, not the one lying on the ground but the one floating above the stone of the Heart's courtyard.

Cheyenne screamed.

No sound emerged.

The vessel is here. You must use it to heal us all. While the Black Flame reigns, the vessel will undo what has been made to rot.

The vessel. Cheyenne could hardly hear herself think when another vision burst through her head of Bianca standing in a dark room, the runes on her skin glowing bright without the pain that had incapacitated her. She saw herself beside her mom, her body flickering with green and black flames like the rest of the world.

I thought I was the one who had to fix everything.

You cannot do it alone. The tree pulsed with purple and black light again as Cheyenne floated over to it. *We need you both.*

Her translucent hand reached out to the shimmering bark of the last Nimlothar standing to deliver the messages no one else could hear.

The second her finger brushed the withered tree, Cheyenne was shoved back down into her body. A weight unlike anything she'd ever felt pressed against her, crushing her, and she couldn't move. Everything went dark. She tried to move, but it was impossible.

Do it now.

Her lungs burned, but she couldn't breathe. Then the need for air was gone. All Cheyenne could feel was a weightless nothingness, and she joined it.

Cheyenne's body jerked on the stone floor, and she drew in a raw, gasping breath. A fit of coughing overtook her, dust and small flecks of stone being blown away from her as she fought to pull more air into her searing lungs.

"Oh, my God. Cheyenne." Ember knelt on the ground beside her friend and reached out to help the drow up off the ground. Her luminous violet eyes shone even brighter with brimming tears. "Are you okay?"

"Fuck." Cheyenne groaned and let her friend help her up before pressing a hand against her head. "What the hell was that?"

"You tell me." Ember sat back on her heels and took a shuddering breath. "I didn't know what to do. Maleshi tried to get you up, but none of us could touch you."

Cheyenne glanced quickly around the courtyard and tried to push to her feet. "Where's Bianca?"

"She's fine, Cheyenne."

"I have to find her. Corian got her, right?" Stumbling across the stone, Cheyenne had to brace herself with her hands before she could finally stand. "She needs help, Em."

"Hey, slow down." Ember rose with a flash of violet light and grabbed Cheyenne's arm to keep the drow from dropping to the floor again. "She has help. The runes stopped glowing, and she's feeling better, okay? She's fine."

"What made them stop?"

"I don't know. Time, I guess." Ember gently released the drow's arm and shrugged. "I haven't seen her in a while. I didn't want to leave you here by yourself. Someone had to watch you."

Cheyenne gazed up at the Nimlothar. The tree wasn't flashing anymore, but it seemed to loom over her. Then she realized how bright everything was and looked at the open ceiling and the daylight spilling down into the Heart. "How long was I out?"

"A long time. I don't know. Ten, maybe twelve hours."

"Jesus." Letting out a slow, heavy sigh, Cheyenne scanned the arches leading out of the courtyard. "I have to go see her, Em. Make sure she's okay. Where is she?"

Ember wrinkled her nose. "She's with Venga."

"Fuck. Are you kidding me?" Cheyenne staggered to the arch on her left, her activator lighting the quickest path to the necromancer's lab.

"But she's fine. Hey, slow down. You can't even walk straight."

"Why would you leave her alone with him, Em?" Cheyenne stumbled and caught herself against the walkway.

"Why would I? Cheyenne, I've been sitting with you. Corian had taken her up there by the time I finally got here." Ember floated quickly after her, reaching out every time her friend wobbled, but she didn't have to support Cheyenne. The drow quickly regained her strength and moved through the corridor leading to the closest staircase. "You left us outside the city. You know that, right?"

"You should've tried harder to keep up."

"Hold on." Ember grabbed the drow's wrist and pulled her aside at the bottom of the staircase. "It's not like you left a clear path for any of us to race after you."

"What are you talking about?"

"You just walked through everything." The fae frowned. "You don't remember?"

"I had to get her here, Em. You saw what happened to her."

"Yeah, and I saw the entire city shift around you in, like, five seconds. How the hell did you do that?"

Cheyenne blinked quickly and stared at the lines of code scrolling across the walls that now looked like off-white stone. "I don't know. I just did it."

"Okay."

Cheyenne stumbled against the wall, reeling from the residual flash of the Nimlothar's vision of the entire forest blazing with green fire.

"What just happened?"

The drow shook her head and swallowed. "I'm fine. I think we're running out of time."

"Well, that's not exactly new," Ember said when Cheyenne pushed up the staircase, "But you don't have to worry about your mom right now."

"She's with the necromancer who created the blight and shoved a surprise potion into my chest, Em. Are you seriously telling me to trust the asshole with my mom?"

They reached the top of the staircase, and Cheyenne followed the illuminating lines of code down the last corridor to Venga's lab.

"It's not like he's gonna hurt her. She's the—"

"Please don't say it." They emerged into the wide passageway leading to the massive iron doors of Venga's lab. "Not right now, Em."

"Okay."

Cheyenne shoved the doors open with a slam and stumbled into the lab. "I swear on the old laws, Venga, if you so much as touch her—"

"Cheyenne."

She froze.

Bianca sat on a massive chaise covered in a dark mauve material that looked like velvet. Her back was perfectly straight, the runes no longer glowing, and she looked much healthier than before they'd left the estate. A metal tray filled with O'gúleesh fruit and this world's version of bread rested on the chaise beside her. She popped a small black berry into her mouth and studied her daughter. "There's no reason to barge in here like the world's about to end."

"Mom." Cheyenne hurried to Bianca, staggering over to her mother. "Are you okay?"

"I'm perfectly fine. Thanks to your friend."

"My friend." Cheyenne spun away from the chaise to see Venga in full scaleback form, his four arms spread out to the side with either a vial or some experimental tool in each hand. His black eyes glittered at her as his scaly lips drew back in a mocking smile.

"Indeed." Bianca nodded. "Venga's been quite attentive, and I feel much improved. Well, beyond the obvious, of course."

Venga chuckled. "Easy to accomplish with such a well-mannered patient."

"Cheyenne, I was just telling the…forgive me, what was it you called yourself?"

"Necromancer," Cheyenne muttered.

"Yes, necromancer. Interesting choice of professional title." Bianca popped another berry into her mouth and gazed around. "From the look of this room, I would have expected doctor or healer or something of the sort."

"No, that would be me." Ember slowly looked away from the woman to stare at Venga. The scaleback switched one of his implements into another hand to free one of the four up for a grating scratch on his dry, scaly head that sounded like sandpaper on cement.

"I had heard something about fae and healing, Ember." Bianca nodded. "It suits you."

"Thanks." Ember raised an eyebrow at Venga and pointed at the black berries Bianca was popping into her mouth one at a time. "Those are the regular kind, right?"

The necromancer shrugged with only two shoulders. "Why wouldn't they be?"

"No reason."

Now that her urgency was gone, Cheyenne had time to take in the full transformation of Venga's lab. The massive metal tanks Ba'rael had used to torture her victims for their magic had been removed. Apparently, Persh'al's rearrangement of Hangivol's aesthetic had extended even into this room, and where the shelves of dark implements and the necromancer's rage-fueled messes had once been, everything was now neatly in its place. Two more O'gúleesh armchairs, these decorated with small bones and yellow-amber gemstones, joined the chaise in replacing the sludge tanks. Soft, warm light radiated from conjured lanterns hovering below the ceiling.

Okay, sure. Maybe it's a lot more like a doctor's office. Or a naturopath's. Does it fucking matter?

Cheyenne shook off the thought and bent down to her mom. "But you're okay?"

"Everyone's been perfectly hospitable, Cheyenne. I'm a lot more comfortable than I expected."

"Yeah, I can tell." The drow shot Venga another quick glance. "He didn't give you anything, did he? Potions or treatments?"

"Nothing beyond a bit of refreshment and thoroughly enjoyable conversation."

Venga pointed at Bianca with a clawed finger and grinned. "One of the many things we seem to agree on."

"He's told me quite a bit about this world," Bianca continued. "And his work. I find it fascinating."

Though she was relieved to find her mom doing so well, Cheyenne hadn't managed to let go of her resentment for the necromancer. "Did he tell you how he got back here to his work?"

Bianca lifted a copper cup of water to her lips and didn't make a sound as she drank. "You mean, the bit about everyone breaking him out of that prison?"

Cheyenne blinked. "Yeah. That."

"Well, it's in the past, and we're here now." Bianca shrugged. "You of all people know what a waste of time and energy it is to dwell on past mistakes. The intentions behind improving one's aims are what counts."

The woman raised her cup to Venga with a curt nod.

"Right." Cheyenne glanced between them. *If I hadn't just had an out-of-body experience with a damn tree, I'd be convinced I'm hallucinating right now.* She cleared her throat. "Good to see you're getting along with the locals. I guess."

"Your mother is a remarkable creature, Cheyenne." Venga chuckled and turned back to his workbench. "For a human. The first one I've seen in Ambar'ogúl. Possibly the first ever."

"Why, thank you." Bianca sipped her water again, staring at Cheyenne over the copper rim the whole time.

"I'm glad you're okay, Mom."

"As am I. Now, can anyone tell me what this oddly shaped blue item is?"

"Oh, yeah." Ember floated to the chaise and bent to study the tray of O'gúleesh fruit. "Yeah, that one's safe to eat. It's the blue stuff that glows and sometimes moves that you want to stay away from."

"It moves? What a novel concept for produce."

CHAPTER SEVENTY-FOUR

Knowing Ember could handle whatever might come up in conversation with Bianca, and it could be anything at this point, Cheyenne crossed the lab to join Venga at the workbench. She folded her arms and watched him work. The necromancer busied himself laying out various instruments beside a group of crystals and metal shards arranged in an intricate pattern on the bench. *At least he's not mixing anything that explodes.*

"Seriously," she muttered, "what did you do to her?"

Venga didn't look away from his work, though he moved with a much slower and more exact manner than the last time she'd been here. "Nothing. Not yet, at any rate."

"When we crossed over, she was out of her mind with pain."

"And that lasted for a full five minutes after Corian delivered her into my care."

Cheyenne snorted. "That's what I mean. What kind of care?"

The necromancer finally turned his scaly bald head to look at her with glistening, all-black eyes. "Patience. Observation. And she did mention thoroughly enjoyable conversation, did she not?"

He's still mocking me. She ignored the comment and watched his clawed hands delicately lifting another implement or stone or metal shard and place them exactly where he wanted. "What made it stop?"

"The same thing that started it, I imagine."

"Venga, we can't do what we have to do by imagining the answers."

"Hand me that frequency scale, will you?"

Cheyenne scanned the workbench. "I don't know what that is."

Without looking away from his work, the necromancer pointed at the end of the workbench. "The coil, Cheyenne. Red."

She found it and dropped it into his open hand before folding her arms again. "So she erupts with burning runes all over her body the second before we pass through the second doorway, settles down a few minutes after she reaches your lab, and you have no idea why?"

"Oh, I have an idea." Venga delicately lowered a dark-purple crystal into the center of the design on his workbench and tapped it once with the tip of his claw, then turned to face her. "The vessel has arrived. It returned to its natural state within the physical body of your mother, but that natural state was always meant to exist here."

"No, she's human."

"Ah. But you are not." He chuckled. "There are far more layers to conceptualize than I originally anticipated, but it can be done."

"What are you going to do to her?"

"I need to study her. For the rest of the evening, I suspect, possibly into the night. Preliminary testing will follow."

"Testing?" Cheyenne shook her head. "It better not be the kind of test you ran on me the last time. She can't handle that kind of manipulative abuse."

"Oh, spare me." He waved her off and gazed at Bianca and Ember, who were engaged in a perfectly civil conversation about the different types of magical fruit. "I performed that trial on you because I knew you could handle it. You can't honestly expect me to repeat the process with a new and still-undiscovered set of variables."

"I don't know what the hell to expect from you."

"Bianca's not a drow. Not even half-drow, if we're technical." Venga glanced at his symbol creation one more time, then nodded and gave her his full attention. "I can't tell you what will or will not be required of her to do what must be done, but I can say I will treat her like the fragile being she is. Physically speaking, of course."

Cheyenne took a deep breath and let it out in a long, resigned sigh. "No preliminary tests without me here."

"As I said, I need the rest of the evening to study the vessel. Otherwise, I won't know what we're dealing with."

"Venga." She widened her eyes at him. "Not without me here."

The necromancer touched a clawed hand to his chest, then tossed it flippantly in the air. "You have my word."

"Thank you. And if anything else that's not supposed to happen happens, you let me know."

"Yes, Cheyenne. I'll engage the messaging system in your domicile. But you have nothing to worry about for the time being."

Yeah. He knows where I live.

"Okay."

With a widening grin showing rows of stained razor-sharp teeth, the scaleback leaned toward her and widened his all-black eyes. "This is the next step toward victory, Cheyenne. I'm pleased to see you've finally managed something useful in that regard."

She gave him a deadpan stare, then spun and headed back across the lab. *Fuck this guy.*

Venga let out a low, rumbling laugh and returned to whatever he was doing with crystals and metal.

Not like I can entirely trust the word of a necromancer, especially not the one who created the blight. I need something better.

Cheyenne stopped in front of the huge double doors and watched Bianca and Ember.

"I'm serious. Those same berries." The fae pointed at the tiny black fruit and laughed in disbelief. "I mean, they were delicious."

"And more than that, it seems." Bianca plucked a handful of berries off the sprig and handed them over.

"Yeah. Delicious and psychedelic, or whatever they call that over here." Ember dropped all the berries into her mouth and closed her eyes as she chewed. "But it gave me my magic back, and then some."

"I'll just say that that is an experience I'd rather leave to the non-humans."

Both women chuckled and continued picking through the fruit tray.

Cheyenne studied the lines of code scrolling across this new, brighter, far more inviting version of Venga's lab. Before she realized she'd had the thought, her activator prompted her with a spell it translated as "Communication." Her fingers flickered at her side as she opened the command path to read through it to the end.

Yeah, okay. I guess that's good enough.

When she confirmed the selection, her hands worked seamlessly with her magic in casting the spell she couldn't have explained even if she'd tried. The floor beneath her moved in dozens of segmented parts, much like they had on the roof of her Hangivol apartment building, and she pulled a series of metal pieces from the floor of Venga's lab to float in front of her.

The necromancer turned at the sound of metal pieces clinking against each other. His eyes narrowed when he saw bits of his lab swirling in the air around Cheyenne's raised hands. "What are you doing?"

"Calling in backup. Or whatever." She focused on letting the activator and her magic do the rest, and when she was finished, a three-dimensional four-pointed star the size of her palm spun slowly in front of her. It flashed with deep-purple light when she plucked it from the air, and she took a moment to study the lines of code moving in every direction along its surface.

I guess that's it.

When she turned to her mom, Bianca and Ember had stopped talking. Both stared at her in surprise.

"That's something I haven't seen before."

Cheyenne gave a dry laugh and approached the chaise. "It won't be the last time while you're here, either. Here."

"What is this?" Bianca accepted the four-pointed star, which flashed again when Cheyenne released it.

"Just in case. If you need me for anything," she said, studying the scrolling runes translating into English around her mom's fingers. "Just hold it with both hands and say my name. I'll find you."

"Where are you going?"

Cheyenne glanced at Ember, who cluelessly shook her head. "I have an apartment here, Mom."

"I see."

"And I need to lie down."

"You don't have to explain yourself to me, Cheyenne. By all means, take the time you need. I have no issue with staying here however long Venga needs me."

Cheyenne snorted. "Okay, well, don't get too comfortable."

Bianca glanced briefly at the red burn scars on her wrists peeking out of the bottoms of her sweater sleeves. "That won't be difficult."

"Right."

As the drow turned to the door, Ember cleared her throat. "Is this a 'leave me alone' moment?"

"I mean, it's your place too, Em." Cheyenne pulled one massive door open and glanced at Venga. "Your word."

"I gave it, and you have it." The necromancer waved her off. "Quit breathing down my neck."

Rolling her eyes, Cheyenne jerked the door open wider and hurried into the hall.

"Bianca." Ember pointed at the four-pointed star in the woman's hand. "Don't be afraid to use that if you have to."

"I'm well aware of what happens when I doubt Cheyenne's abilities, Ember. Thank you."

"Okay." Giving Bianca a final attempt at a reassuring smile, Ember slipped through the door after Cheyenne and floated quickly down the wide corridor beyond to catch up with her. "Hey. Everything okay?"

Cheyenne sighed. "I mean, if we forget that Bianca's in Ambar'ogúl and I just got blindsided by visions from a tree reminding me to keep my promise to it, sure, Em. I'm good."

"And you're going to lie down? You were out for, like, half a day in the courtyard."

"Just because I've been unconscious for an entire day in the last three, it doesn't mean I've gotten any sleep."

"Huh."

Quick footsteps echoed toward them, and Maleshi rounded the corner. She slowed when she saw Cheyenne, her silver eyes narrowed. "Finally snapped out of it, huh?"

"I wouldn't say that, exactly."

The general approached them and folded her arms, glancing at the drow and her fae *Nós Aní*. "Judging by the mix of every emotion I'd expect to see on both your faces, I'm guessing you just paid the necromancer a visit."

"Yeah." Cheyenne blew a heavy breath. "He didn't do anything to her?"

"Not as far as I know. Why? Does she not seem herself?"

"No, she does. That's what's weird." Cheyenne looked over her shoulder and frowned at the huge doors into Venga's lab. "I'm going to the apartment, which is still weird to say. Keep an eye on her for me, yeah? Don't let him do anything without me."

"Deal." Maleshi nodded, then eyed the drow again. "Still feeling better?"

"The blight wounds, yeah. I'll have to get back to you on the rest."

"Go get some sleep, kid. Corian and I are taking shifts checking on Bianca. We'll find you when it's time."

"Thanks." Cheyenne couldn't look the general in the eye any longer and brushed past her to continue down the hall.

Ember and Maleshi exchanged knowing glances but didn't comment on what they were both thinking. Whatever Cheyenne was going through, she hadn't bothered telling anyone the full extent of it. Hopefully, she would.

CHAPTER SEVENTY-FIVE

Cheyenne and Ember exited the Crown's fortress at an unmarked place in the wall with a wave of Cheyenne's hand. Ember stayed close behind her friend, looking over her shoulder to shoot the fortress' outer wall a surprised glance as the segments unfolded and replaced the makeshift doorway behind her.

Hangivol's drow inner circle was quiet and empty-feeling, only a handful of drow passing across the main avenue taking care of whatever business kept them on this level of the city. Cheyenne didn't say a word on the way to their apartment building or during the trip up the floating circular platform to their floor.

Ember didn't push her. She had serious shit to sort out before she was ready to talk about it. The fae could wait.

The door to the apartment next to theirs flashed in a pattern of different-colored lights spilling across the floor when they passed. Low chanting by at least three different voices carried through the hall, but Cheyenne didn't stop to listen in on whatever drow ritual was taking place on the other side.

The apartment door slid into the wall the second she approached it, moving seamlessly so she didn't even have to slow down before stepping into the sparsely decorated space made of harsh lines and little comfort. The door slid shut again behind Ember, and Cheyenne stopped halfway to the room she'd claimed on the right.

"What's wrong?"

Cheyenne gave a half-hearted shrug and approached the bare, seemingly empty wall that served as their kitchen. "I should probably eat something."

"Hey, if you're hungry, I'll make something."

"I'm not." Cheyenne frowned and stared blankly at the wall. "But I should be, right?"

Ember chewed the inside of her cheek. *She's got L'zar-style space-out written all over her. Not a good sign.*

"I mean, food's important, whether or not you feel like it." The fae approached her friend and put a gentle hand on Cheyenne's shoulder.

The halfling twitched and pulled slightly away from Ember's touch. "Sorry."

"Don't be. How about you go sit down on the couch that might as well be a concrete slab, and I'll pull something out of the wall."

"Yeah. Sure." Cheyenne turned slowly and practically staggered across the mostly empty space before lowering herself gingerly onto the boxy black couch. She propped her feet up on the equally boxy ottoman, her hands falling limp beside her on the alleged cushion, and closed her eyes.

Ember selected something from the kitchen wall's coded menu that looked and smelled safe, as close to baked chicken as they were likely to get, and her less-advanced activator had what it took to help her program the kitchen to heat up their meal. While she waited, she scanned the menu and found a bottle of Bloodshine listed beneath the fellwine and something the activator translated as *uruni* milk. She narrowed her eyes at the wall and shrugged. What the hell.

Her fingers swiped the coded lines, and a refrigerated drawer slid out of the wall to present an unopened bottle of Bloodshine and two copper cups. By the time she brought them to the couch, Cheyenne looked like she'd already fallen asleep.

"I can hear you watching me," Cheyenne muttered. "Or feel it. One or the other."

Ember snorted. "You know how creepy that is, right?"

"Why do you think I told you?" The drow opened one golden eye to study her *Nós Aní*, then smiled and pushed herself up straighter on the couch. "At least you brought booze."

"There is that." A soft, chiming alarm came from the kitchen wall. "And the food is ready."

Cheyenne poured their drinks while Ember lifted the tray of chicken-smelling something out of the wall. A wave of the drow's hand brought a thick black coffee table up out of the floor, and they ate.

The apartment remained unusually quiet until Ember finally had to say something about it. "So, what's really going on? And yes, I do mean besides the obvious."

Cheyenne peeled away a strip of meat with a slight orange tinge and popped it into her mouth on autopilot. "Lack of sleep. Bianca getting super cozy with Venga."

"Yeah, that was weird." Ember raised the cup of bubbling golden liquid to her lips and washed down the O'gúleesh "chicken." The instant buzz of the Bloodshine racing to her head and bubbling in her nose made her set the cup aside. "None of this fazes her even a little. It's like she's been around magicals her entire life."

"Well, she's spent the last twenty-one years with one." Cheyenne shook her head. "I expected her to freak out, or at least look scared. Unsure. I think maybe she snapped."

"Like, mentally?"

The drow stared at her friend and raised an eyebrow. "Kinda the only way at this point. Only she hasn't."

"I mean, it supports the whole 'Bianca as the vessel' thing, right?"

"Maybe." Cheyenne sat back on the couch. "And that stupid tree."

Ember scooped up another bite with her fingers and ate slowly. "Yeah, you haven't gone into detail about that."

"I know. When Persh'al swore in, I talked to it, I guess. Promised I'd heal the dead Nimlothar forest that isn't dead, only I have absolutely no idea how to do that. And today when Bianca and I were in the Heart—"

Ember quietly sucked the spiced sauce off her fingers. "Visions, right?"

"The thing pulled me out of my body, Em. I was just floating there. I could see myself lying on the ground, and the tree told me I had to keep my promise basically right then. That the vessel's here, so now my mom and I have to heal everything. Including the forest. What the hell am I supposed to do with that information?"

"Use it, I guess." Ember shrugged. "You know, just be who you are, and let Bianca be who she is."

"I guess." Cheyenne lifted the cup of Bloodshine to her nose and gave it a curious sniff. She only drank a little of it, then set it down on the table again and shook her head. "My head keeps spinning in circles about the whole thing. It wasn't supposed to happen like this, but then I keep thinking about all the crap the Sorren Gán said about what I still have left to do with the vessel. That I'm only one part of the whole. I guess I kept assuming I was the only one who could do any of this, you know? Getting rid of Ba'rael and healing the blight and turning this whole world inside out so nobody fucks it up like this again. But it hasn't only been on me."

"Right. Neros magicked his mom right out of here. Persh'al's the Crown. And Bianca's the vessel."

"So why does everything center around me, then? Huh?" Cheyenne ran a hand through her hair. "If it doesn't fall only to me to get all this done, I don't see why I have to be at the head of it."

"Hmm." Ember took another sip of Bloodshine, thought she was about to sneeze, then shook her head. "Well, look at what happened when everyone else tried to do it on their own. L'zar had who knows how many kids who didn't make it. Ba'rael screwed over an entire world and almost brought the same thing to Earth, and your mom raised you all on her own and tried to keep you safe by doing what she thought was right."

"Yeah, and it didn't exactly turn out the way she wanted."

"That's my point." Ember leaned forward and stared at her friend until Cheyenne finally looked at her. "Shit doesn't work out the way we think it's supposed to when we try to keep everyone else out of it and do it all on our own. I don't think you're an exception to that."

"Oh, thanks."

Ember laughed. "No, I mean, I think the point is something different from what everyone thought it was. Sure, you're the Crown under the surface. The Black Flame, right? Persh'al wouldn't be able to do anything he's doing if you hadn't turned the new Cycle. But you're not the be-all-end-all here, just the catalyst."

"There. Right there." Cheyenne pointed at her friend. "That's it. Feels like everything I touch these days bursts into flame, and I can't figure out how to put out the damn fire."

"You could think about it a little differently." With a small smile, Ember shrugged. "L'zar said it when we walked out of the Heart after you put your coin on that altar, right?"

The drow rolled her eyes. "L'zar says a lot of shit that isn't worth paying attention to."

"He said you're the bridge between worlds."

Cheyenne frowned and slowly met her friend's gaze again.

"Think about it. A bridge might be the only thing connecting two sides. It holds itself up, and it makes it safe for whoever to cross back and forth, right?"

"You're saying I should let everyone walk all over me to get wherever they need to go?"

"Now you're being an ass about it." They both laughed, and Ember shook her head. "No, I'm saying a bridge's purpose is to help everyone else get where they need to be. If it's not supported the right way, shit hits the fan. Without it, trying to get across is a hell of a lot more dangerous. Maybe even impossible."

Cheyenne frowned at the metal plate holding their pseudo-chicken dinner and cocked her head. *How can she make this much sense when everything's falling apart?* "I get it, Em."

"You don't look convinced."

"I think this bridge needs some real sleep." The drow pushed to her feet and tried to give her friend a reassuring smile. "If any messages come through that stupid box by the door, wake me up. Even if you have to slap me, okay?" Cheyenne's eyelids drooped. "Whatever it takes. I can't be passed out whenever Venga decides it's the right time to get a move on with his tests."

"Deal."

"Thanks, Em."

"Yeah. Oh, hey." Ember pulled the vial of Inolu's healing potion, still two-thirds full, and handed it over. "Maybe just take a little this time. At the very least, it'll probably help you get to sleep."

"At the very least." Cheyenne took the vial and nodded. "Gotta stay on top of the poison, right?"

"Exactly." The fae watched her best friend move slowly across the apartment to her bedroom. Even after the door slid back into place behind Cheyenne, Ember kept staring. She lifted the copper cup to her mouth again and took a bigger sip this time. *Venga better hurry the hell up. I don't know how much longer she's gonna keep getting back up on her feet.*

CHAPTER SEVENTY-SIX

Cheyenne kicked off her black Vans and shrugged out of her trenchcoat before staggering to the raised platform of her bed in Hangivol. *I'm so fucking tired of being tired.*

Once she'd crawled onto the surprisingly comfortable mattress, not bothering to turn back the sheets, she pulled the cork out of the vial and took a small sip. The healing potion worked almost as quickly as the last time, filling her body with a heavy warmth spreading into her fingers and toes and the tips of her pointed drow ears. She had just enough time to stopper the vial again before it dropped from her fingers, then she sank down onto the pillow and closed her eyes.

Just a little sleep. That's all I need right now. Then I can keep being the goddamn bridge that has to hold everybody else up.

It felt like mere seconds later that she slipped into another dream. In this one, she rose out of her body as she had in the Heart's central courtyard, only this time, when she got off the bed and stared at her own body curled up on the mattress, she wasn't translucent and didn't float away. Cheyenne felt her lightened weight stepping firmly down on the stairs below the platform bed and her fingers trailing across the edge of the platform before she turned to the bedroom door.

Apparently, I'm lucid-dreaming. Kinda defeats the point of getting real sleep, right?

Still, she couldn't help but feel like there was something outside her bedroom, beyond the walls of her Hangivol apartment, that she had to see.

"It's good to see you, Cheyenne."

She whirled and found Neros standing at the foot of her bed. Her cousin's washed-out drow skin and bone-white hair looked solid, and his pale blue eyes with their faint golden glow focused intently on her.

"I'm totally dreaming, right?"

Neros dipped his head. "You might say that."

"Because I need sleep."

"Your body is resting, cousin." He stepped over to her and gestured at the bedroom door. "For now, your mind is free. Walk with me."

With a small, knowing smile, Neros passed her and disappeared through the solid door of her bedroom.

Right. Walk with him. She snorted. I guess this is what's happening right now.

Cheyenne waved her hand at the bedroom door, but it didn't move. "No magic in dreams, right?"

She rolled her eyes and stepped through the closed door to find Neros waiting for her in the empty living room.

He smiled and waved her forward. "Things are different in this realm, Cheyenne, but you are the same. I want to show you."

"Show me what?"

His pale eyes widened above a knowing smile, and he stepped across the apartment before disappearing through the front door again.

Even in my dreams, there are no straight answers. Awesome.

Cheyenne passed through the front door after him without feeling even a hint of physical resistance, and she emerged on the other side, not in the hallway outside the apartment but on the wide avenue of the drow inner circle.

The clean, light-colored streets of the highest city level cast an orange reflection beneath the sunset over the capital. Neros clasped his hands behind his back and stared up at the glowing sky, his white hair fluttering away from his face that was turned into the breeze. Cheyenne couldn't feel the wind, but it was easy to imagine when she saw it playing through her cousin's hair and ruffling his loose white tunic and trousers.

"Any chance you will tell me what we're doing here?"

"You will see." Neros turned to her and gestured down the main avenue. "But it's not here."

"Okay, I get it. I'll walk with you." Cheyenne fell in step beside him, wanting to stick her hands in her pockets but finding her trenchcoat left behind in the dream.

Nothing moved around them as they crossed the inner circle. The only sounds were a soft whistle of wind from far away and Neros' footsteps padding softly across the ground. Cheyenne's own steps didn't make any noise, though she spent a moment studying the way her feet half-floated, half-pressed against the metal surface.

"So, if you won't tell me where you're going," she said, "can you at least tell me where you are right now?"

Her cousin chuckled. "I'm with you."

"Well, yeah. In a dream. I mean for real. Where did you go after you and Ba'rael disappeared?"

"Ah. Sometimes Nor'ieth. Sometimes elsewhere." He turned to her with a reassuring smile. "One place is not so different from the other."

"But you're still alive. Right?"

Neros dipped his head.

"Is she?"

"In a sense, yes."

Cheyenne shook her head. "That's not an answer."

"Ba'rael is in existence, Cheyenne. For now, she cannot return to stand in your way, if that's what concerns you."

"I'm not concerned."

Neros raised his eyebrows slightly and turned to scan the edge of the city's highest level as they approached. "Perhaps you should be."

"Because she might come back."

"Only if you do not succeed in time." The warning was at odds with Neros' playful smile. "Do not let your thoughts linger on the Spider, cousin. Focus on where you need to be."

"Yeah, I wish it was that simple." Cheyenne gazed out at the rest of Hangivol stretching below them. "I don't even know where that is."

Neros turned to stare at her and pointed straight ahead. The next second, they were standing not at the edge of the inner circle but far below the city's surface. The orange sunset was gone. The sky and all the tall, glittering buildings were gone. And in their place was the dark stone wall at the end of the passageway Cheyenne instantly recognized. "You know this place."

"The darkseller bazaar?" She frowned at him. "How is this where I'm supposed to be?"

"Everywhere you are is where you belong, Cheyenne. Do not forget that."

"Okay."

Neros disappeared through the stone wall Mirl had opened the first time she'd been led down here.

Cheyenne glanced at the dark ceiling of the passageway and shook her head. "That's gonna get old."

She passed through the wall to rejoin her cousin on the other side. The darkseller bazaar of her dream glowed with a dark light seeping from every shadowy corner, like a photo negative. Everything was lit in reverse, the magical lights hanging from the curved underground ceiling casting the darkest shadows while the places that should have been the eeriest and hardest to see flared the brightest with shimmering light.

"Why are we here?"

"The darkness is part of you." Neros' footsteps whispered across the stone floor as he strolled casually down the alley in Hangivol's most avoided marketplace. "As it is a part of me. Of all drow."

She stared at the body of a sleeping magical curled up in the open doorway of a shop as they passed. "The darkness."

"The pieces of yourself you have yet to accept." Neros nodded, turning his head slowly left and right to take in the quiet stillness of the dreamscape bazaar. "Surely you know by now there is no light without the darkness."

"Now you're feeding me clichés. Awesome." She moved smoothly after her cousin, not quite walking and not quite floating. *Venga said I'd be back here. Sorry to disappoint, but I'm not that kinda drow. The darkness will have to do without me.*

"You've been fighting for too long to be something you're not," Neros added.

"Okay, that's where I have to stop you." Cheyenne stopped moving, and her cousin turned to face her with that same knowing smile. "I'm not pretending. Everything I am is out in the open for everyone to see."

She spread her arms, and Neros chuckled. "On the outside, yes. That is only part of it."

"I'm not following in Ba'rael's footsteps if that's what you're trying to tell me."

"Not at all." For the first time, the pale-skinned drow frowned and seemed at a loss for the words he wanted. "Ba'rael is lost. She always has been. But you have known from the beginning who you are. What you show the world of yourself is exactly who you must become to alleviate the plague the Spider set loose on both your worlds. It started within her, Cheyenne. And within L'zar. The time has come for you to return to what our race has forgotten. What we have abandoned for the pursuit of this power that consumes everything it touches."

Cheyenne narrowed her eyes. "Can you read my mind?"

"I can see your heart, cousin. Now you are here to see it for yourself."

A shadow passed across the avenue of the bazaar, and Cheyenne spun to search the strangely glowing darkness. "What was that?"

"Your next journey."

"You know, you haven't gotten the hang of laying it all out there on the table." When she turned back to him, Neros was gone. "Neros? Hello?"

The clack of hollow bones and beads rustling came from behind her, and she whirled again to search the dark recesses of the open shop doorways and the displays of darkseller wares she'd rather not explore. A shadow moved again, then a form took shape in the darkness, a humanoid figure outlined in sharp spikes, sprouting feathers, claws, and stacked bones.

What the fuck? You're dreaming, Cheyenne. Get a grip.

"Whatever you are, we're in my dream. Got it?"

The figure lifted two clawed hands to its misshapen head and pulled back an outer layer of the dark, feathered hood. Dark light shimmered on the slate-gray skin and bone-white hair of yet another drow, one she recognized.

Great. Now I've got the damn bone drow showing up in my dreams. Cheyenne scowled at him. "What are you doing here?"

R'leer's kohl-blackened eyes roamed over her face, and the briefest hint of a smile flickered across his lips. "I knew I'd see you again."

This is the last thing I need right now.

Bones and beads clacked again when R'leer circled her, crouching like a predator about to strike. Then he straightened and reached toward her with both hands.

"What are you doing?"

A dark flash of light exploded from his hands, and he clapped them together before jerking them back to him.

The world shimmered around her. Cheyenne felt her body moving from somewhere far away, rushing through space to meet her here in her dream. Then her body and her dream-self slammed back together and threw her forward. She gasped and stumbled, coughing uncontrollably as the natural differentiation of light and movement returned to her. Everything that had been illuminated with the glow of her dream now darkened into shadow again, and the darkseller bazaar returned to its dull, dirty self.

"What the fuck?" she wheezed, fighting to catch her breath.

She stomped her foot on the ground, sending a jolt through her leg with a muted thump.

I'm actually here. Like, for real.

She even felt more solid as she patted down her sides and turned in a circle to view the rest of the bazaar.

"I knew I'd see you again."

Cheyenne turned back to the creepy bone drow eyeing her with hungry amusement and scowled. "What the hell am I doing here?"

R'leer raised an eyebrow. "You tell me."

She spun again, searching for Neros despite knowing he'd disappeared. *Not a dream, though. What? Astral projection or whatever the hell we're calling it?* "I wasn't really here."

"I saw your energy." R'leer shrugged. "You were here."

"You saw my energy. Great." Cheyenne staggered to the closest shop doorway and braced herself against the wall. All the weight and exhaustion she'd left behind in her sleeping body had caught up to her and was now dragging her back down. "I need to sit for a second."

"Suit yourself." R'leer stepped quietly past her through the doorway, which happened to belong to his shop. He did stop to hold the curtain of strung bones aside for her. "You came here for a reason."

Rolling her eyes, Cheyenne followed him through the bone-strung curtain and stepped inside his shop. R'leer went straight to a counter along the left-hand wall and took a small drawstring bag of some scaly hide out of the folds of his feather-covered jacket before dumping it out on the counter.

Cheyenne's legs nearly gave out, but she lowered herself quickly to the floor to avoid falling and slumped against a shelf. *Okay. Get a grip. I was dreaming. Or projecting or whatever. And now I'm here. How fucked up does shit have to get before I finally get a break?*

CHAPTER SEVENTY-SEVEN

The clink and rustle of R'leer sorting through whatever he'd deposited on the counter filled the front of the shop as he worked. He cast her a quick sidelong glance but said nothing.

Yeah. I can pretend to ignore you too, buddy.

She smoothed her hair back from her face and took a deep breath. *There's no way Neros brought me here for no reason, so I have to ask.*

She sucked in a sharp breath when her fingers flared with burning heat. Cheyenne lifted her hand to see the tips of her fingers pulsing with dark-purple light. "What the hell?"

R'leer stopped whatever he was doing and turned to her. His golden eyes widened when he saw her glowing fingertips, and he hunched again like a curious animal sniffing danger. "How did you get that?"

"You mean, radioactive fingers?" Grimacing, she stretched out her hand, and the pulsing glow faded, along with the heat. "You're the one dealing in dark magic."

"Drow magic." R'leer stepped cautiously over to her, staring at her fingers. Then he pointed at her hand. "The Nimlothar marked you."

"What?" Rubbing her fingers, Cheyenne frowned at him. The bone drow's glowing golden eyes seemed that much brighter surrounded by the dark, smudged kohl lining them. *He'd fit right in with the Goth crowd if we were anywhere else.*

R'leer cocked his head. "Tell me."

"Tell you what? I don't even know how the hell I got here or why any of this is your business."

He dropped into a squat beside her, beads and bones rustling and clicking when he draped his forearms over his knees. His eyes roamed her face again, then he looked her dead in the eye and didn't blink once. "The Nimlothar marked you."

"Yeah, you said that already."

"Right here." He grabbed her wrist and jerked her hand up so it hovered between them. The fingers of his other hand brushed hers, and he nodded. "I saw it. You felt it. Tell me how it happened."

Rolling her shoulder back, Cheyenne pulled her hand out of his and searched his gaze. "I'm not into holding hands. Or touching. Don't do that again."

R'leer's mouth twitched into a smile, and he raised an eyebrow. "But you touched the Nimlothar."

The tree's visions came back to her, along with that first out-of-body experience. *I touched it but didn't touch it. And now the tree's reminding me of this stupid promise by making my fingers burn purple?*

Cheyenne sighed. "If I told you, would you know what to do with that information?"

R'leer tilted his head in the opposite direction and looked her over. "That depends on what it said to you."

"What it said to me." She snorted. "You know trees can't talk, right?"

"You know that's not true." He glanced at her hand again. "The Nimlothar have not spoken to drow in centuries, but I've been listening. And you bear the mark. Tell me."

For some reason, Cheyenne couldn't make herself look away from him. *He's a drow, and he knows old-school drow shit, right? That's why he's down here.*

"Okay, fine. But this is only because I'm out of ideas right now. Maybe you can help."

"Maybe."

When R'leer didn't straighten from his crouch or give any indication that he'd stop hovering over her, Cheyenne scooted away from him, grimacing at the renewed throbbing of her hip and shoulders. *Not nearly as bad as it used to be. I can take it.* "I'm guessing at this point you know why I was in the Heart, right?"

The bone drow's eyes narrowed. "May the Black Flame reign."

"Yeah, okay." *I'm never gonna live that down.* "When Persh'al Tenishi swore in as the O'gúl Crown, I was there with him. The Nimlothar showed me a vision of the dead forest. And it's not dead."

"Correct."

Okay, well, he gets points for not batting an eye at that one. Maybe he's more than a creepily pretty face. Who's still way too close. Cheyenne dipped her head and leaned away from him.

"I promised it I'd help heal the rest of the Nimlothar. And then today," she said, glancing at her hand again, "I guess it wanted to remind me that I still haven't held up my end of the deal."

"And it marked you."

"Seriously, that's three times now. You got your point across fine the first time."

R'leer rubbed a long, slender finger back and forth across his lips and stared at her. "I don't have the tools to help you fulfill that promise."

"Great." Cheyenne closed her eyes with another heavy sigh. "I shouldn't have expected it to be this easy."

"But I know who does."

"Really?"

R'leer stood, his over-the-top ornaments rustling and clicking as he strolled across his shop. "We'll go together."

"Oh, jeez." She rolled her eyes. "Look, if you're about to tell me there's an Oracle who can answer all my questions, forget it. And the Sorren Gán can suck it too, okay? Once was enough, and I got even more than that."

He turned swiftly to look at her over his shoulder. "You spoke to a Sorren Gán?"

"Among other things, yeah."

R'leer's golden eyes flickered across his shop, studying the dark corners. Then he nodded at the back. "I promise this is nothing you've seen before. Few drow have."

"Great." Cheyenne gritted her teeth and tried to push herself off the floor. Her arms shook beneath her, her eyelids were heavy with exhaustion, and she thumped her head back against the shelf again. "Any chance we can put a hold on this for like a few hours?" *Something tells me I got way less than the recommended hours of sleep.*

The bone drow moved in a blurry streak of gray, black, and white and slipped out of enhanced speed right in front of her.

"Jesus." Cheyenne leaned away from the slight breeze brought by his movement and the small pebbles tossed across the floor of his shop in its wake. "Could you not right now?"

R'leer offered her his hand and dipped his head. "If you want to see, Cheyenne, it must be now."

So he does remember my name. Guess I'm still good with first impressions.

She stared at him for a moment, then reached up to take his hand. He helped her swiftly to her feet and took a lot longer than necessary to release her. He didn't bother to back out of her personal space, either.

"This is what we've all been waiting for."

Cheyenne swallowed. "What is?"

He leaned sideways, studying her like she was a prized work of art instead of a half-drow with personal boundaries. Taking a deep breath through his nose, reminding her a lot of the way Neros had first examined her, R'leer gestured at the back of his shop again. "Come."

He turned away from her and headed in that direction, the bones and beads on his weirdly feathered jacket and headdress clicking with every step.

Right. Get all up close in my face but don't give me a straight answer. Maybe I'm the only drow who thinks that's an issue.

Cheyenne followed him through the shop, gazing at the darkseller's wares with a mix of hesitation and amused curiosity. The ogre woman who was apparently R'leer's assistant wasn't anywhere to be seen, and the shop was empty of other magicals. At least until they reached the back room.

She smelled the sharp, pungent odor before R'leer led her around the corner. Thick tendrils of white smoke wafted up from the closest corner of the next room, slightly obscuring the figure cloaked in black rags and huddling there in the darkness. The smoke rose from the burning top of a hookah in front of the hunched figure, and when the thick white smog cleared as R'leer strode past, Cheyenne recognized the Oracle Ur'syth.

The crone's black-painted eyes were closed, and a thin stream of dried red trickled from the corner of her wrinkled mouth. She breathed slowly and steadily but didn't open her eyes or move an inch.

Cheyenne stopped and stared at Ur'syth. *Just because her eyes are closed, it doesn't mean she's sleeping. Guess now I know where she disappeared to.*

"I said, no Oracles," she muttered.

R'leer turned and glanced at the motionless crone. "Ignore her. Where we're going, she can't follow."

Cheyenne frowned at him. "What's that supposed to mean?"

He met her gaze with his golden eyes. "You'll see."

As he continued to the other side of the back room, he reached up to stroke a lantern of red glass hanging from the ceiling. The magical light inside that was casting the entire room in an obnoxious red glow winked out, and the smoke trailing to the ceiling streamed away from the lantern as if R'leer had blown out a huge candle.

Blinking in the darkness, Cheyenne moved cautiously after him, avoiding the piled metal plates of half-eaten rotting food and a metal pot that smelled even worse. *Jesus. If he's gonna keep the Oracle down here, he should at least dump out the chamber pot.*

"Why is she here, anyway?"

R'leer stopped at the top of an even darker staircase and turned back to study the smoke-filled room. "Sanctuary."

"From what?"

"More than even I know."

Cheyenne wrinkled her nose. "You could use a maid in here or something."

R'leer looked her over again, and that small smile returned. "Trust me, I've tried. Her hovel is worse."

When he disappeared down the stairwell, Cheyenne found herself imagining the inside of the crone Oracle's hut in the dark courtyard where she'd given Cheyenne that last vague, interrupted prophecy. *Someone needs to set some serious boundaries for his guests.*

The bone drow's footsteps echoed up the dark stairwell toward her, and Cheyenne braced herself with a hand against the wall before descending after him.

Another soft light illuminated beneath R'leer's hand as he brushed his fingers against the glass lantern at the base of the stairs. This one was made of black glass and shed enough light to see the stone wall less than five feet from the last step. Cheyenne stopped before reaching the landing and searched the small space. *Dead end. I need to stop giving drow the benefit of the doubt.*

Beneath the dark light, R'leer pressed his finger against five different points in the stone, then drew lines between them and twisted his hand on the wall. Everywhere his finger touched, a thin purple glow trailed behind and faded again. Only after he'd finished the spell did Cheyenne's activator pull up some flickering lines of code in her vision.

So the tech still works this far underground.

When she tried to read the coded lines, she found a different data stream she hadn't seen moving through the rest of the city. The code faded before she could zero in on what it meant, and the stone wall let out a muted whir of gears, followed by a series of heavy thumps. The wall shivered and drew apart like elevator doors, revealing a metal contraption behind it, dozens of tiny metal gears covered in a thin layer of rust still moving.

"What is this?" The question slipped out of her before she could stop herself. *Great. Now I'm putting out the clueless-drow vibe.*

R'leer studied the whirring metal contraption that looked kind of like a door and delicately tapped a finger against the moving parts when they reached the desired location. "A portal."

Cheyenne squinted at the dark-purple light that flashed every time the bone drow touched the metal. "Not over the Border, though."

"Part of me wants to pity you," he muttered.

"Excuse me?"

"But the rest of me realizes you haven't had the right guides to show you what's truly important through your journey."

She snorted. "You don't know anything about my journey. Or my guides."

R'leer didn't turn to look at her, too intent on tapping the right metal gears and sliding bars moving over the pseudo-door's surface. "Most drow have forgotten what we all used to know. What used to drive us. I don't blame you."

"You don't get points for that after saying you pity me."

"I said I want to, but I don't." With a final tap, R'leer stepped back to the bottom of the staircase. The door's spinning mechanisms slowed and clicked into place before a small lens opened in the center. It let off a red flash, followed by a dark window of light opening between the bone drow and the strange half-tech contraption.

Cheyenne frowned at the portal and the jagged stone walls on the other side. "You forgot to mention it's a nightstalker portal."

"Oh, good. You know that much, at least."

Is he throwing my sarcasm back at me? She folded her arms. "Whose blood did you take for this one?"

"Blood?" Grinning, R'leer turned. "Drow will always be drow, but we didn't use to be so barbaric. There's no blood for this portal."

"Then I'd love to know how a non-nightstalker opened a night-stalker portal under the city. If you don't mind."

R'leer gestured at the window of dark light and tilted his head. "This was created during the birth of Hangivol. One drow who wanted access to the nexus. One nightstalker willing to create the means to do so. I don't expect any of the O'gúleesh you call your mentors know about the way things used to be."

My mentors. He better not be including L'zar in that mashup. She eyed the portal again and leaned sideways to peer around it at the mechanical contraption that now only let out a soft click every five seconds. "But you know, is that it?"

"I haven't strayed from the path laid out for me, Cheyenne. I've been walking it since the beginning."

"Okay, wait. How old are you, exactly?"

R'leer turned back to the portal. "Not as old as L'zar."

She glared at his back and muttered, "Mentioning the Weaver isn't gonna get you on my good side."

There was no way the bone drow didn't hear her, but he ignored the comment and stepped through the portal.

Everyone knows everything about me, huh? Including the guy who thinks he's so special that I'll follow him through a portal without asking any more questions.

She followed R'leer through the portal and couldn't think of any more questions to ask.

CHAPTER SEVENTY-EIGHT

As soon as she stepped through, Cheyenne expected to hear the portal closing behind her with that telltale pop, but it didn't. She turned to see the bottom of the staircase beneath R'leer's shop and heard the soft click of the metal contraption. *This better be our way back too. Or I'm stranded in who the hell knows where with a drow who thinks he's fucking smart.*

R'leer stepped slowly through the cavern stretching out in front of them. A dim light illuminated at his fingertips and rose high above their heads, disseminating across the vast darkness to fill the cave with a glow that reminded Cheyenne of the in-between's gray non-light.

"This is the nexus," he said, not bothering to turn back and make sure she was following him. "Beneath the heart of the northern mountains beyond Ki'uali."

"Wait, we're out by Hirúl Breach?"

"Farther."

Shit. What did I get myself into? I can't be all the way out here with half-healed poison wounds and the blight moving through the Outers.

"Hey, maybe you've been cooped up in your creepy shop this whole time and haven't noticed, but it's not the safest place."

R'leer spun to face her and darted through drow speed again until he stood mere inches from her. His eyes narrowed above a curious smile. "Creepy?"

"That's what I said." *Just like how close he's standing right now.* For some reason, she couldn't bring herself to tell him that, but she lifted her chin and stood her ground against yet another violation of her personal space.

"You have a fascinating view of things, Cheyenne."

"That's one way to put it."

R'leer leaned closer to her, dipping his head slightly because of all four extra inches he had on her height. His golden eyes flickered from her eyes to her lips and chin and back up again. "My shop is a necessity, or you would not have found yourself there without knowing your own intentions."

The tips of her ears burned. *Good thing it's dark in here.* "Maybe I don't know why I projected myself to the bazaar, or whatever I did, but don't try to convince me you know more about my intentions than I do. I have a lot on my plate."

"Yes, you do. And I don't think you'd be nearly as ready for this if you hadn't been carrying it all with you the way you have."

Cheyenne narrowed her eyes. *Not the time or place for psychoanalysis, buddy.*

A low, rumbling chuckle rose from behind R'leer's closed lips and echoed softly through the cavern. "Time to let the walls down, Cheyenne. We need you."

He turned swiftly away from her and continued across the cave. She closed her eyes and fought not to clench her fists at her sides.

You made a promise. To a tree, sure, but it's still a promise. And right now, this weirdo you might've had a thing for in another life is the only shot you have of figuring out how to keep it. Get moving.

When she opened her eyes again, R'leer was staring at her from six feet ahead.

"Quit looking at me like that. I'm coming."

The cavern narrowed when they reached the far side, where a narrower passageway twisted off to the left. R'leer's summoned light followed them as he led her down the tunnel of roughhewn stone. Somewhere up ahead, Cheyenne heard the steady trickle of water and the accompanying echo of an occasional drip into a deep pool. *If it's another lake of fire, I'm out.*

The passage opened again into a much smaller cavern with a lower ceiling hanging maybe a foot above R'leer's head. The stone floor dipped into a sharp drop at the back of the cavern, and a dark slumped shape rested against the wall only a yard from the narrow chasm.

"Come." R'leer beckoned her forward as he slowly approached the dark shape.

Cheyenne glanced around the cavern and took note of the shriveled roots poking down through cracks in the ceiling. *One minor earthquake and this whole place will come down on top of us.*

She headed to R'leer, who now knelt in front of the bent, misshapen thing against the wall. His golden eyes glowed in the darkness as he looked over his shoulder at her and watched her approach. When he pointed at the stone floor beside him, she gritted her teeth and forced herself not to make another smartass comment as she knelt. Then she looked at the dark shape in front of them, and the shadows moved just enough beneath the conjured light around them that she could finally see what this was. An ancient, shriveled drow face was barely visible within the pile of black rags, clods of dirt, and small dead vines crawling from the wall of the cavern to stretch across the figure. Snarled, tangled hair that looked more brown than white sprouted from the withered head in clumps.

"Whoa," she breathed.

R'leer stared at the old drow as he dipped his head in a respectful bow. Despite how softly he spoke, his voice echoed around them. "This is Agalyse."

"And you brought me to her tomb," Cheyenne whispered.

The bone drow slowly shook his head. "She's not dead."

"What?"

"Agalyse still lives. The only one among us in Ambar'ogúl who was here to see Sylra Nightflame take the throne."

"Wait, you mean she was alive before Hangivol was built?"

"For quite some time already, yes."

So this is what L'zar's gonna look like in a million years, huh? Not much to look forward to.

Cheyenne frowned and slowly shook her head, trying to wrap her mind around the fact that this shrunken, root-covered thing was a living drow. "Why is she down here?"

"To protect herself." R'leer shot her a sidelong glance, his lips twitching in amusement. "I may have spent most of my time beneath Hangivol, but I've seen the darkness spreading across this world. Agalyse sees it too. She sees more than either of us can imagine."

"But she's practically attached to the wall."

"She draws strength from the life vein of Ambar'ogúl." He nodded. "A slow, steady trickle these days, but she's still here, sleeping to preserve what remains of her and her wisdom."

"Sleeping." Cheyenne stared at the decrepit drow woman, whose eyes were sunken above her hollow, washed-out cheeks and hidden in dry wrinkles found more often in mummified humans than living magicals. "Why are we here?"

R'leer's eyes widened. "To see if I was right."

"You know, this would be a whole lot easier if you offered up more than vague one-liners."

"Agalyse withdrew beneath the mountains when the Cycle turned for K'laht the Everbrite. She saw the Weave unfolding far before its time. Ba'rael's rule. How she would rape the land and those sustained by it. How much of Ambar'ogúl would fall to that darkness." The drow turned his golden eyes on the huddled mass of paper-thin flesh and loose bones in front of them. "Then she came here to commune with the lifeforce veins running through this world and to strengthen the connection between her and the drow who trusted in her wisdom. She is well cared for, Cheyenne. I believe she'll know what is required to fulfill your promise."

The oldest living drow. Might as well be the three-eyed raven from *Game of Thrones*, and we all know how well that worked out for everyone.

"I'm flattered that you brought me here," Cheyenne whispered. "Really. I had no idea this place existed, so thanks for the drow history lesson. But I don't see how someone this old who's been sleeping for this long—"

Agalyse's sunken eyes flew open, sending a spray of centuries-old dust puffing away from her face.

"Jesus." Cheyenne jolted back and couldn't look away from the deep, almost orange glow of the ancient's drow's eyes as they flicked between her and R'leer.

A low, scratchy wheeze emanated from the drow woman's chest, followed by a rattling breath that filled her lungs for the first time in who knew how long. Bones and dry roots and stone creaked and groaned when Agalyse turned her head by an inch to face Cheyenne. A muffled croak escaped her shriveled lips with another puff of dust.

"*Majiya*," R'leer whispered and bowed low. "She's here."

"I know she's here," Cheyenne muttered and stopped when Agalyse wheezed out another breath. The decaying rags covering the drow woman's body cracked and snapped as her frail chest rose again beneath them.

"Cheyenne."

What the fuck?

R'leer lifted his head with a grin, his eyes wide and blazing with eagerness. "I knew it."

Agalyse drew another rattling breath and stared at the halfling as if L'zar's daughter sat at the ancient one's deathbed to hear her last dying wish.

I seriously hope that's not what's happening right now.

"How does she know my name?"

"I told you she sees much." The bones strung on R'leer's weird head-dress and through his hair and across his jacket clicked together when he straightened. "I've said it more than once."

Agalyse's lips whispered against each other before a strangled, croaking voice rose between them. She didn't look away from Cheyenne, staring intently at the young drow in her presence as her dry rags cracked and sent more clumps of dust and dirt to the cavern floor. A dark, wrinkled hand lifted slowly to point at Cheyenne with a crooked finger that might as well have been nothing but bone.

Cheyenne shook her head. "I can't understand her. What's she saying?"

R'leer stared at her too, grinning as he translated Agalyse's ancient O'gúleesh words into the message Cheyenne was meant to hear. "You've finally come. Now the Black Flame will burn away the afflic-tion, and Ambar'ogúl will rejoice."

You gotta be kidding me. More prophecies?

Cheyenne shook her head. "That's just a name. I promised the Nimlothar I would do this."

Agalyse's whispering voice continued, and R'leer spoke over her almost as if he already knew what she would say. "I've seen you in the Weave. Your father's daughter, and your mother's. The bridge and the bane. You will fulfill your promise made in the Heart above the lifeforce vein. To restore the balance this world has distorted. We must remember, Cheyenne. The *mór edhil* wither as the Nimlothar cry out for justice. Restore us before we all fall into the ruin of our own making."

The old drow's eyes narrowed at Cheyenne, her chest rising and falling in long, shallow breaths.

Glancing quickly at R'leer, Cheyenne shook her head. "I know what I promised and what's at stake. How the hell am I supposed to do it?"

Agalyse gasped, her eyelids fluttering as a trembling shiver wracked the body that hadn't moved in centuries. "Take the drow of Hangivol to the forest. They must lend their lives to the trees."

"What?" Cheyenne glared at R'leer. "That doesn't save anyone."

He shrugged and gestured at Agalyse, licking his lips in consideration. "I'm merely the messenger."

She turned back to the ancient drow and leaned forward. "What do you mean, 'lend their lives'? That sounds a lot like suicide to me."

Agalyse stared at her, unblinking, and drew another harsh, ragged breath before speaking again.

"None will die," R'leer translated. "We will all live. If you fail to do what must be done, the *mór edhil* will not survive the purging of this world without the Nimlothar. And the last of them is closer to death than I."

Fuck.

The shriveled drow's raised hand returned to its place at her side within the nearly fossilized folds of her black rags. Then Agalyse stopped moving. A whistling breath escaped her cracked, slightly parted lips, and after her eyes closed again, she didn't take another.

The cavern fell intensely silent, with only the constant trickle and drip of water as proof that Cheyenne could still hear anything.

She stared at the ancient drow woman, waiting for another long breath or a final word, but there was nothing. "Is she…"

"Sleeping again." R'leer bowed to Agalyse, then straightened and cast Cheyenne a sidelong glance. "Believe me, when the final deathflame calls the *Majiya*, we will all know."

For a moment, Cheyenne couldn't find the words she wanted. She pressed her lips together and pushed away all the questions and the doubt seeping into her mind. "She made it sound like the drow are on the verge of extinction or something."

"In a way, perhaps we are." With a final glance at Agalyse, R'leer rose fluidly to his feet and offered Cheyenne his hand.

She took it and couldn't stop staring at the ancient drow's face. *She looks dead to me.* Pulling her hand slowly out of his grip, she muttered, "That portal back to Hangivol's still open, right?"

"It is."

"Good. I'm going back."

"Cheyenne, wait." R'leer grabbed her wrist as she turned away, the beads and bones clicking with the same urgency she found in his eyes. He released her and dipped his head. "I want to show you one more thing."

"Is it gonna come back from the dead to give me even more riddles in O'gúleesh?"

"If that was a riddle, it was more straightforward than any I've heard."

True. She told me exactly what to do. Just not how.

"It won't take long. Please."

Cheyenne blew a long, heavy sigh through loose lips and gave Agalyse one more hesitant glance. "Fine."

R'leer's smile widened, then he turned and headed to the sharp drop in the cavern floor. Lowering himself to the stone, he slid his feet and legs over the edge of the chasm and looked at her. "You can climb, can't you?"

"Yeah, I can climb." *On a full night of sleep and after a decent meal, I could climb all day. We'll see how far I make it like this.*

The bone drow slowly lowered himself into the darkness. As his summoned light floated across the cavern and down after him like glowing fog, Cheyenne stepped to the edge of the drop and peered into the void. R'leer half-climbed, half-shinnied down a space barely wide enough to fit a drow, his back pressed against one side as his feet walked slowly down the other.

Cheyenne lowered herself into the crevice after him, making sure to climb down at least three feet over from the path he'd taken. *If I get more visions or pass out again, at least one of us won't end up in a pile at the bottom of this thing. Wherever that is.*

CHAPTER SEVENTY-NINE

The climb took at least ten minutes, and Cheyenne's entire body ached with the effort of pressing against both sides of the chimney. Then she heard R'leer's feet softly thump on the ground below her. *Finally.*

She lowered herself as far as she could until the wall in front of her dropped away six feet from the ground. Turning awkwardly, she scrambled for the last few hand- and footholds to descend the rest of the wall and jumped down the last three feet. A jolt of pain shot through her wounded hip, but she gritted her teeth and ignored it before turning around.

R'leer's head barely cleared the ceiling of the tunnel below Agalyse's chamber, so he hunched his shoulders and motioned for Cheyenne to follow.

They walked under the claustrophobically low ceiling beneath the northern mountains for another five minutes, then the ceiling opened into another pitch-black cavern of unknown size. His golden eyes settled on Cheyenne again as he reached up and brushed a hand over the edge of the low ceiling.

Great. I bet this is the part where he tells me his plan to take the Crown and tries to kill me. I'm only half-joking.

As soon as he removed his fingers from the ceiling, shuddering green light raced over the stone walls, spreading quickly from his touch to the walls of the huge chamber beyond. The green streak branched off over and over, illuminating an intricate root system running farther ahead of them than Cheyenne could see.

Every few yards, the green-glowing veins gave way to clumps of purple light. Once they lit up, they pulsed slowly the same way the last Nimlothar had pulsed with its own living light. A plume of green flame shot from a crevasse in the wall, followed by another, and another farther down the cavern. The green fire flickered in and out of existence from one geyser after the next, along the ceiling, then on her right, then from the cavern floor twenty feet away.

Cheyenne pressed her lips together to make sure her mouth hadn't fallen open. "What is this?"

"You know what it is."

"I don't."

R'leer pointed at the stone floor at her feet. "Watch yourself."

She stepped aside before a plume of green flame leaped into the air as high as her waist and settled back down. Cheyenne stared at the ground, searching for a hole in the stone that didn't exist. R'leer's soft chuckle made her look quickly up at him with a scowl. "That's funny, huh?"

"A little." Clasping his hands behind his back in a way that reminded her way too much of L'zar, R'leer gazed at the ceiling illuminated by veins of green and purple that no longer required his conjured light to see. "I don't think you give yourself enough credit for what you already understand, Cheyenne. It is not my responsibility to explain it all to you, nor does that appeal to me."

Oh, sure. He thinks I give a shit what appeals to him.

With a deep breath, she studied the pulsing purple veins stretching across the cavern walls between sprays of green fire. "If we're farther from the capital than Hirúl Breach, this magic isn't coming from the Nimlothar forest."

R'leer reached out to brush his fingers along the closest purple vein. It shuddered under his hand and flashed brighter before dimming again. "The Nimlothar are not relegated to one place."

"Are you telling me the trees can move?"

"At one time they did, yes." He narrowed his eyes. "Does that surprise you?"

She snorted. "Not really, I guess."

"Their residual magic still runs through the heart of these mountains. And the Outers. And the plains of Lefhaim. Through Hangivol as well."

"Leftover Nimlothar magic." Cheyenne swept her gaze over the cavern again and blinked when a particularly large column of fire sprayed straight out from the wall. "Why is there fellfire under the mountain right next to what's left of it?"

"Not fellfire." R'leer took a deep breath through his nose, his golden eyes reflecting the intermittent bursts of green. "This is the deathflame running beneath the world. Through it. And we'll use it to heal the forest."

"Wait a minute." She spun quickly toward him. "This wasn't a 'we' kind of deal, R'leer."

"Ah." He grinned and didn't bother looking at her. "So I took time out of my night to bring you here without purpose. Because of course, you would have found your way to the portal and to Agalyse's side without my guidance. And you do speak O'gúleesh."

She grimaced and shook her head. "You don't have to say it like that."

"Like what?" He stepped slowly over to her, eyeing her with an appraising smile that made the tips of her pointed ears burn hot. "Does it anger you to consider that you may need me, Cheyenne?"

Jesus Christ, he's laying it on thick.

"I don't even know you." She lifted her chin again to stare him down as he got closer. "And you don't know me. Not well enough to tell me what I need."

"But enough to tell you that you cannot fulfill your promise to the Nimlothar in the Heart on your own." R'leer leaned toward her, tilting his head to study her like some kind of specimen again. "You've taken on so much, thinking the entire burden had to be yours alone. It doesn't."

"Maybe." Half of her wanted to shove him away, and the other half wanted to see what he meant to do by standing so goddamn close.

"I said you haven't had the right guides to show you what's truly important, did I not?"

"Yeah, I remember."

"In this, I can show you."

Cheyenne narrowed her eyes, ignoring the stuttering bursts of green deathflame shooting up around them at all angles. "So, what? We go back to Hangivol, gather all the drow, and take everyone out to the Nimlothar forest with a bunch of deathflame torches?"

"Something like that." R'leer bit his bottom lip and glanced at hers. "Ambar'ogúl must burn to free itself from what it has become."

"See, that's what I've been trying to avoid this whole time." She'd meant to turn away from him, but for some reason, she couldn't move. Instead, she lifted her chin even higher and leaned forward until only inches of space existed between them. "I'm not burning down anything."

"Then you'll be consumed with the rest of us." He shrugged slowly. "That is your choice."

Then he stepped past her, his fingers brushing hers, and headed to the other wall of the cavern to study the pulsing Nimlothar magic that hadn't been destroyed with the trees.

Cheyenne blinked furiously, and a hot and cold flush washed over her. *What the fuck?*

"If the Nimlothar are not restored, Cheyenne, our race will perish. Not immediately, but we drow tend to take our time, don't we?"

She turned and tried not to look as confused as she felt. "Is there some kind of hidden message in there or what?"

R'leer ran his hand along the wall, trailing pulsing purple light behind his fingers. "Do you know how many drow in Ambar'ogúl have yet to pass their trials?"

The sudden turn in the conversation made her frown, and she thought of the girl Ki'zi and how badly the young drow wanted to step into her power. *And her parents are holding her back, with good fucking reason now.* "No, I don't."

"It used to be only the young, those with hundreds of years of preparation ahead of them." R'leer turned to face her again, and his smile was gone. "Now, it's more than half. Drow who spent their formative years under the Spider's rule have lived far past the time of their trials and still cannot fully tap into who they are. The younger ones are fortunate. They don't remember the days of Ba'rael's treacherous grasp on what makes us *mór edhil*. They never knew what it was to stand before her in the Heart, desperate to draw strength from the Nimlothar seed they were given that had less than what was required to complete their trials. They didn't see their kin fall beneath her spiteful control. Many of us perished because of what was made of our union with the Nimlothar. A deadly farce, Cheyenne. Nothing more."

Cheyenne swallowed and clenched her fists at her sides. *I don't need to hear this.*

"If the Nimlothar fall, if *we* fail, no drow will pass their trials. Our entire race will come crashing down on itself with nothing and no one left to raise us up again. You may believe healing this world from the poison Ba'rael created is the final step, but can you honestly say you'll be satisfied with that victory if there are no more drow to celebrate it?"

Fuck. Why does it have to be this guy?

"I get it, okay?" She gazed at the seemingly endless expanse of cavern in front of them, flickering with green and purple magic. "We need the blight gone and the forest saved. I need to figure out how to get both those things done with what I've got."

R'leer spread his arms. "You have me."

She cocked her head and shot him a sidelong glance. "Fantastic."

Ember was totally right. I'm the bridge to get magical A to location B, and now it looks like I'll be running around Ambar'ogúl with a pyromaniac drow who may or may not be seriously into me.

"Fine. You can help me."

R'leer grinned. "Yes, I can."

"Under one condition."

"Name it."

Cheyenne pointed at him. "Don't lie to me about what has to happen. That includes giving me straightforward answers I don't have to dance around to find out what they mean. Deal?"

"Agreed. Ask me anything, Cheyenne." He looked at her again and blinked slowly. "Even if I wanted to lie to you, I'm not sure I could."

"Right. First, do we have to climb all the way back up that hole in the wall, or is there another way out of here?"

His chuckle echoed through the cavern as he turned back the way they'd come. "You told me you could climb."

Cheyenne said, "Yeah, I can climb."

CHAPTER EIGHTY

Agalyse hadn't moved an inch when they shinnied up the crevasse and hauled themselves back up over the edge. Cheyenne dusted her hands off and studied the pile of ancient drow as they walked, her footsteps whispering across the dusty stone floor in rhythm with R'leer's. *At this point, I should always expect something to jump out at me at any minute.*

But the sleeping drow remained still and silent even after R'leer led Cheyenne back down the twisting corridor and into the much larger cavern on the other side. The portal powered by some nightstalker's magic from a bajillion years ago still shimmered at the far end, waiting for their return. Cheyenne forced herself to keep up with R'leer's swift gait when they stepped through and returned to the dark staircase beneath the darkseller's shop.

With a quickly cast spell and a series of taps on the contraption built into the wall, R'leer closed the portal. The machine of old-school O'gúl tech whirred and spun, hundreds of parts shifting and clicking into place before the stone walls slid closed in front of it again. The sound cut off abruptly, and Cheyenne cocked her head.

That's gotta be a seriously powerful sound-proofing spell if I can't hear what's behind those doors.

R'leer headed back up the staircase without a word.

Cheyenne pushed her exhausted body to follow him, steadying herself once again with a hand against the wall. "Okay. I have another question."

He looked over his shoulder with a tiny smile. "You're more curious than I realized."

Yeah, not that curious. "Why are you down here in the bazaar? With your shop and all this dark stuff that no one else wants to dirty their hands with?"

The other drow didn't say anything as they climbed the staircase.

Cheyenne gritted her teeth. "We made a deal. Straightforward answers or I'm burning down the forest to save it by myself."

R'leer spun around on the top step, and Cheyenne nearly launched herself back down the stairs as she reeled in surprise. She caught herself, hissing in frustration, and glared up at him.

"Our agreement didn't include a timeline for forming my answers."

"Oh, great. You know, I didn't have enough extra-literal drow in my life as it was." She raised her eyebrows and waited for him to step aside so she could finish hauling herself up the last few steps.

R'leer took off through the smoky back room, where Ur'syth the wrinkled old Oracle hadn't moved either since their last encounter. Cheyenne's nostrils flared, and she forced herself not to breathe through her nose until they were moving through the main part of his shop again.

"In case you weren't aware, I'm one of those drow who took Agalyse's words to heart when she told us what was coming." He stopped beside one of the display counters to pick up a glowing lump of fossilized something, studying it as if he were a browsing customer instead of the shop's owner.

"You mean, random drow don't find their way down to that portal and into the caves?"

He ignored her sarcasm and continued along the closest shelf, running his hands over the displayed items. "When the Cycle turned for Ba'rael, many things changed in this world. Hangivol specifically. I merely chose to rely on what allowed our race to thrive at no expense to others."

"Drow used to be the only darksellers. I know."

With a surprised hum, R'leer turned to her. "Then why are you trying so hard to fight what you are?"

Cheyenne cocked her head. *Not sure how much I can say without causing a whole different kind of shitstorm.* "If you knew what I am, I don't think you'd have to ask that question."

"Because your mother is human?"

A lump formed in her throat, and she forced it back down with a rough swallow. "Would it make a difference if she was?"

"Hardly." He walked slowly over to her again and pulled a long strand of clicking beads and bones on his weird headdress away from his hair, then snapped off one of the bottom bones and turned it over and over in his fingers. "I think our agreement should go both ways, Cheyenne. Straight answers. No lies."

So, either everyone in this world knows I'm a halfling, or I've got some kinda stalker. I guess Ur'syth could've told him.

"Okay." Cheyenne nodded. "I can do that."

"Great. How's your mother?"

She almost choked on her next breath, and R'leer chuckled. "I'm not standing here in your shop to talk about my mom. Got it?"

"You agreed."

A growl of frustration burst from her throat before she had the chance to pull it back. "She's fine, okay? Doing much better, so thanks for fucking asking. How did you even know?"

"L'zar isn't the only drow who can read the Weave." R'leer shrugged. "I may not see it as clearly or succinctly as he does, but I see it."

"Huh. And you didn't run off to a Sorren Gán for that kinda thing, right?"

A surprised laugh escaped him. "Is that what he did?"

"Yep." *Not like L'zar's coming back anytime soon to find his secret's out.*

"Leave it to the Weaver to walk the most treacherous path." R'leer glanced down at the bone in his hand and shook his head. "I hope his daughter doesn't follow too closely in his footsteps."

"I'm working on it."

"Take this." He extended the bone to her, and she wrinkled her nose at it.

"Not 'til you tell me what it's for."

"I'll need more time to prepare for our mass drow exodus to the forest." R'leer jerked his head at the back of his shop and held her gaze. "I could walk straight into the fortress of the Ironbreak and fetch you, but I'd rather not."

She snorted. "Smart move."

"I know. Take it, Cheyenne. When it's time, you'll know where to find me."

Cheyenne slowly accepted the hollow yellowed bone and studied the runes engraved on the side. She looked at him and tilted her head. "So, which poor bastard's fingers are you wearing in your hair?"

He gave her a crooked smile and leaned toward her. "My father's."

"Damn." With a surprised chuckle, she stuck the bone in her pocket and didn't try particularly hard to wipe away the quick image of her wearing L'zar's bones like this. "I have to make sure my mom's taken care of before we can do whatever this is. Probably a few days."

"I may be ready sooner."

Cheyenne frowned. "Well, I might not be. I know what we have to do, and thanks for the help, but I'm putting her first."

"Suit yourself." R'leer stepped back and raised both hands.

"What are you doing?"

"Until you can accept that you belong exactly where you are, I don't see any reason for you to stay here."

Everywhere you are is exactly where you belong, Cheyenne.

Those were Neros' words, and only now did they make the first hint of sense.

"Wait. R'leer!"

Violet light burst from his hands as he clapped them together with an echoing smack. Then he thrust them at her, and all the wind was knocked out of her without the darkseller making contact. She felt her body separate from the rest of her again, the part that could think and still see R'leer grinning at her as her incorporeal form rose three inches from the floor.

Cheyenne glared at him and spread her arms. "Are you fucking serious?"

The darkseller winked, then whatever spell he'd cast on both her forms jerked her across Hangivol, through countless walls and floors and ceilings, and blasted her back into her body lying curled up on the raised mattress in her O'gúleesh apartment.

A heavy weight pressed her down into unconsciousness, and across the entire city and far below it, she thought she could hear R'leer laughing.

CHAPTER EIGHTY-ONE

Cheyenne woke with a pounding headache and a disturbingly dry mouth. With a groan, she pushed herself up off the mattress and almost dropped to the floor five feet below her before remembering the platform bed had stairs. *Okay, not the worst dream I've had in the last few months, but definitely the weirdest.*

The muscles of her arms and legs ached, but she brushed the pain aside and went to the far side of the bedroom to pull up something reminiscent of a sink with her activator and a brief swipe on the metal wall. Two metal panels slid aside to reveal a shallow basin and a spray of cold water from a hidden faucet. "Sure. That works."

She splashed water on her face, then held her hair back and stuck her mouth under the gushing stream for a long drink. Without a handle to turn, she had to swipe the wall again in the prompted sequence to turn the whole thing off before the basin disappeared. Then she walked stiffly out of her room and found Ember sitting on the boxy couch.

"Morning." The fae smiled at her friend, then cocked her head. "You know, for someone who just slept for fifteen hours, I'd expect you to look at least a little better."

"Thanks." Cheyenne ran a hand through her hair and blinked heavily as she scanned their empty living room. "Fifteen hours, huh?"

"Something like that. I'm not sure, but I think this world runs on closer to thirty-hour days."

"You found a clock, huh?"

"Nope. Just looked through the system a little. Not everything translates very well from O'gúleesh."

Cheyenne headed to the alleged kitchen. "Tell me about it." It'd be great if activators translated speech too, but of course, that would make things too easy. *Wait. What was I just thinking about?*

Ember raised her eyebrows when the drow shook her head and paused four feet from the wall. "Everything okay?"

"Yeah. I'm still feeling a little off, I guess." Cheyenne focused on the coded menu scrolling across the wall and selected something that might or might not have been a breakfast sandwich. The kitchen went to work heating up her small breakfast, and she stood there to wait for the chiming alarm. *I'd kill for eggs Benedict with real toast. When was the last time I even had breakfast?*

"Maybe you need more sleep," Ember offered. "You know, since being knocked out cold by a bane-breaker and potions and a Nimlothar doesn't count as decent rest."

"Yeah, trust me, Em, it doesn't count. Heard from Corian or Maleshi while I was out?"

"Nope, but we can probably assume no news is good news."

"It better be." She stuck her hands in her pockets and watched the timer counting down on the wall. "If Venga hasn't finished studying Bianca by now, I don't know what else we can do."

She froze and almost jerked her hand out of her pocket.

"Cheyenne?" Ember floated off the couch in a flash of purple light. "What's going on?"

"No fucking way." Slowly, the drow pulled her fist out of her pocket and opened it. The small bone rolled in her palm, revealing the runes etched into the side. "It wasn't a dream."

"Okay." Ember let out a nervous chuckle and approached her friend. "I'd love to know what you're talking about with this one."

"Last night," Cheyenne said, turning slowly to her and staring at the bone, "I had this crazy dream, Em."

"You said it wasn't."

"No, it was. At least at first. I think, but then I was back in the dark-seller bazaar, and R'leer woke me up."

"Wait, the bone drow?" Ember stopped and glanced down at the darkseller's talisman. "Holy shit. You sleepwalked all the way down there?"

"What? No. I don't even know how to explain it. Neros was there with me, then he wasn't, and R'leer summoned my body to meet up with the rest of me, and I…ah!"

The bone dropped out of her hand, which she brought instinctively up to her shoulder. That was where the intensely flaring pain started at least, but it quickly spread to the rest of her until she doubled over and gritted her teeth.

"Whoa." Ember spread her arms, reaching out to the drow to try to support her but unsure if touching was an option. "Hey, what's going on?"

"No idea." Cheyenne grunted, feeling like her whole body was on fire again and trying to get a grip on herself. A ripple of pain coursed down her back when she straightened, wave after wave of searing heat racing across her skin like bursts of flame. "What the hell is this?"

"You tell me." Ember shook her head and floated backward a foot or two. "I don't see anything. Is it the poison or what?"

The chiming alarm of the O'gúleesh microwave sounded, and neither of them noticed.

Cheyenne stared at her friend with wide eyes, her vision blurring, then jerked down the collar of her shirt to take a look at the blight wound. The black streaks were spreading again, but that hardly seemed impor-tant at this point because faintly glowing echoes of the orange runes burned into Bianca's flesh now covered her daughter's. "What the fuck?"

"The healing potion's in your room, right?" Ember headed that way. "I mean, it doesn't look nearly as bad as before, but if it's hurting you this much, you should take a little. Cheyenne."

Hastily whipping up the hem of her shirt, Cheyenne stared at her stomach and the ghostly glow of even more runes. They spread along her ribcage as well, and when she turned her hand over, she found them on the back of it too and spreading up her forearm. "It's not the poison, Em. Look at this."

"I don't know what I'm supposed to be looking at." Ember shook her head. "But you're freaking me out."

"You don't see the runes?"

"Am I supposed to?"

"Shit. Something's wrong." Cheyenne darted past her friend and waved her bedroom door open to jam her feet into her shoes. With everything she needed already on her, she left her trenchcoat where it was and staggered back into the living room in her haste.

"You gotta tell me what's going on, Cheyenne." Ember blinked, her violet eyes wide with concern.

"I don't know if it's an echo or some kinda spell or what." Cheyenne stooped to snatch up R'leer's small bone gift and stuck it in her pocket. "It's Bianca."

"What's Bianca?"

"I don't know."

"We didn't get any messages. I know. I've been checking."

"Doesn't matter." Cheyenne waved the front door open and darted into the hall.

Ember hurried after her. "Then how do you know there's something wrong?"

"I just know, Em!" The drow booked it to the end of the hall and cursed having to wait for the damn circular lift to rise all the way up to their floor. *All this tech, and no one could make a better way to get up and down a building?*

The apartment door closed behind Ember when she swiped the sequence on the wall, and she hurried to Cheyenne. "So, what? Do you think Venga already started? Maleshi said she'd keep an eye on him."

"I don't know." Cheyenne gritted her teeth and stared down the dark hole where the platform lift should've appeared by now. She sucked in a sharp breath when the flaring heat returned to her body and fought not to scratch her own skin and the runes that obviously didn't exist. "I swear, if he did anything without waiting for me, I'll rip his head off all four of his scaly fucking shoulders."

Ember eyed her friend and shrugged. "Well, I totally agree with you, so I'm not gonna slap you out of it this time."

Cheyenne shook out her hands and hissed impatiently. "Fuck this. Step back."

"What?" The fae did as she was told, grimacing when Cheyenne raised both hands in front of her to cast a spell with gestures neither of them recognized. "Just please tell me you're not trying to blow a hole through fourteen stories of…whoa."

The metal floor responded to Cheyenne's spell in an instant, segmenting and folded back in on itself to reveal a brand-new lift platform where they'd been standing. Cheyenne stepped onto it with a scowl, and Ember barely made it on before the whole circle of metal dropped through one floor after another. The halls opened to let them through and rippled back together with echoing clangs of metal slamming against metal.

Ember gasped and grabbed Cheyenne's arm in surprise, eliciting a snarl of pain from the drow. She quickly released her grip and forced out a mumbled apology through the sharp drop in her stomach at their descent.

When the platform hit the ground floor with a sharp clang, Cheyenne stumbled forward and took off running down the hall.

Ember gazed up at the disappearing hole in the ceiling, then turned in a slow, surprised circle to study the walls around them before floating after the drow. "Cheyenne!"

The apartment building's front door burst open. Cheyenne barreled through it, then another wave of burning ripples pulsed across her flesh. She cried out and staggered sideways. *Hold on, Mom.*

A second after the drow slipped into enhanced speed with a crack and a burst of wind, the side door to the fortress all the way across the inner circle's main avenue flew off its hinges and clattered to the ground. Ember slowed down. "First it's moving the whole city around her, and now she's tearing it apart at the speed of light. I swear, if she starts teleporting after this, we're gonna have a serious talk."

She pushed herself to hurry across the avenue, ignoring the strange looks aimed her way as Hangivol's drow watched the fae float with perfect balance and not nearly as much speed as she wanted toward the fortress. *When the hell are my goddamn legs gonna work again?*

CHAPTER EIGHTY-TWO

Cheyenne didn't drop out of enhanced speed until she reached the huge iron doors of Venga's lab. When she did stop, the shockwave hit the doors with a bang, followed by another bang when she shoved them open with both hands. "Mom!"

Bianca writhed soundlessly on the chaise, her body jerking and bucking as her eyes rolled back in her head. Cheyenne raced to her and spun around when a glass beaker shattered on the floor. Venga stared at the mess on the ground, then glared at the drow with an angry hiss.

"What did you do?" she shouted, crouching beside her mom.

"I did nothing." Venga returned to his hasty work on the bench, growling. "We had an agreement."

"So then, what's wrong with her?"

"You tell me, Cheyenne! You two are the only living things in this world with human blood running through your veins." The scaleback hissed again and mumbled unintelligibly as he worked.

"*Mom*. Mom, can you hear me?" The second Cheyenne reached out to steady Bianca's flailing body, the blazing runes on the woman's skin flared to life again. This time, they did the same on Cheyenne's flesh too, and both women cried out in pain.

Another glass vessel shattered on the ground, followed by a series of metal parts clanging and bouncing around beneath the workbench.

"Endaru's balls, drow!" Venga whirled and chucked a round metal ball at Cheyenne's head, missing her by less than an inch. "Hold her down!"

"I'll hurt her even more!"

"Do it, *dae'bruj*!"

Cheyenne's chest heaved as she fought the pain that wasn't really hers, her hands hovering over her mom. "I'm sorry. I have to. I'm sorry."

When she pressed her hands down on her mom's shoulders, Bianca screamed and bucked even harder. Cheyenne's hands burned furiously, and thin lines of smoke rose from beneath them. Snarling, she pulled her hands away and stared at the fresh burns on her palms. *Fuck.*

Corian ported into the lab, his silver eyes blazing as he took in the sight of the Summerlin women on and beside the chaise. Then he snarled at Venga and stormed to the scaleback. "You were not to touch her, necromancer."

"I did no such thing."

"Then what is this?"

"An unexpected variable. Now shut up and let me work!"

"Corian, I can't hold her down." Cheyenne stared up at him, her seared palms upturned as her mom thrashed around on the chaise.

"She needs to be held down." If the nightstalker noticed her burned hands, he didn't put two and two together. He hurried over to them and reached out to Bianca. "She'll hurt herself even more if we can't get her to stop."

A bright-orange light flashed around Bianca's body and sent the nightstalker flying across the lab. He crashed into the shelves on the wall beside the doors and roared. "This again?"

Maleshi ported into the lab as the doors flew open and nearly bashed Corian against the shelf again. Ember floated through and froze when she saw the chaos. "Oh, shit."

The general raced to the chaise. "Cheyenne, we need to hold her down."

"No, don't!" Cheyenne pointed at Corian, who was steady on his feet again and brushing off bits of broken glass and a coil of blue thread that had toppled onto his light-brown hair.

"We can't touch her," he growled.

Maleshi snarled at Venga. "What did you do?"

The necromancer roared and chucked a large metal box at the general.

Bianca's hand whipped out and slapped Cheyenne's face, and the woman started to slide off the side of the chaise. Grimacing against the pain of touching her mother, Cheyenne lifted her off the furniture to put her gently on the floor, where at least she couldn't fall. More smoke rose from the drow's singeing flesh, and she backed away from her mom. "Somebody do something. This has to stop."

"If that's the result of touching her, kid, we might have to let this run its course."

"Run its course?" Cheyenne whirled on the general. "She's having a magical seizure!"

"It would seem so."

"Does anybody in this world know what the fuck they're doing?"

With a final gasping choke, Bianca fell still on the floor. Her head rolled to one side, her arms and legs splayed, and she didn't move.

"Mom?" Cheyenne knelt beside her, relieved to see her still breathing. Fortunately, Bianca was now unconscious. "Venga, what were you doing before this happened?"

"Running tests. I told you it was the case, though it took longer than I expected it to."

"What tests?"

"Nothing even remotely harmful! I drew blood to test its interaction with various artifacts. She was perfectly fine when I extracted a sample, and when I administered it to the items, she started doing that." The necromancer tossed a hand at Bianca without turning around from his workbench. His other three arms moved ceaselessly, mixing and pouring and crushing.

"What artifacts?" Cheyenne pressed the backs of her hands into the floor to push to her feet and staggered across the lab to him.

"Do you want me to talk about it, or do you want me to find a solution?"

"Venga!" Maleshi barked.

"Fine. Fine. These, right here. They're harmless artifacts meant to trace magical afflictions to the source. I was trying to find a possible remedy for the curse so I could remove it before we did anything useful, but that seems like a particularly stubborn obstacle at this point."

Cheyenne scanned the items on the workbench, which was half-covered with glass pieces or random bits of metal and crystals tossed around by the necromancer's anger. Then she caught sight of a purple pulse of light from beneath a toppled clay jar and moved the jar aside. "Jesus. You forgot to mention the Nimlothar leaf."

"The what?" Venga turned his glistening black eyes on the jar in Cheyenne's hand and snatched it away. "You're mad if you think I'd—"

He nearly smashed the jar when he slammed it on the bench and stared at the purple-glowing Nimlothar leaf. A smeared trail of blood covered the edge, and he gingerly lifted the thing between two claws to sniff it. "Well."

Cheyenne glared at him. "That wasn't part of your tests, was it?"

"Of course not." He waved the leaf in her face. "Does this look like the necessary precision required to formulate any sort of hypothesis?"

The drow summoned a churning sphere of black energy in her hand and raised it as a warning between them. The fresh burn in her palm blazed in protest, but she ignored it. "No. It looks like you were being sloppy and fucked up."

"Hold on." Corian glanced at the unconscious Bianca, then stormed across the room, hissing when he stepped on a fallen metal canister. "Her blood on a Nimlothar leaf."

"I can verify one-hundred-percent that's what this is, yes."

Corian shot the scaleback a warning glance, then looked down at the blood-smeared leaf. "This is the one L'zar gave you."

"I certainly didn't climb that ancient relic in the Heart and pluck a new one."

The nightstalker thrust his hand at Venga's throat, the air ringing with the sound of his four-inch silver claws extending. Their deadly tips made three small divots in the thin, scaly skin below the necromancer's chin. "My patience has run its course with you, scaleback. Understand?"

Venga slowly raised all four arms in surrender, his black eyes twitching as they held the nightstalker's silver gaze. "This was an accident."

"Accidents get magicals killed," Corian hissed. "And humans."

"Accidents are responsible for some of the greatest alchemical discoveries." The necromancer grunted and rolled his eyes when Corian's claws pressed deeper into his flesh.

"Try again."

"We now know of one reaction, at the very least." Venga lifted the Nimlothar leaf in front of Corian's bared teeth and twirled it between his claws by the stem. "What is the significance of this particular specimen?"

"If you don't know the answer to that one, your usefulness has run its course."

"I mean to us, you imbecile." Venga leaned away from the glinting points of Corian's claws when the nightstalker hissed and slipped a sharp tip beneath one of the necromancer's scales. "To L'zar! Why did L'zar have this on him? He traded it to me, but we didn't go over the specifics of how and why it was in his possession. There must be some other significance."

"There is." Cheyenne swallowed and stared at the purple leaf. Venga and Corian turned slowly to look at her, though the nightstalker's claws still pressed threateningly against the scaleback's throat. "It came through the portal Ba'rael destroyed."

"She destroyed a portal." Venga raised a scaly, hairless cyebrow. "That's hardly significant."

"Yeah, well, Earthside, that portal led right to my mom's backyard. The same one that leaked out all the extra curse meant for L'zar."

Venga turned away from Corian's claws and lifted the Nimlothar leaf closer to the elongated nostrils of his reptilian face for another sniff. "That information would have been useful beforehand."

"There's no way to know what's useful to you," Cheyenne muttered. She glanced at Corian, who retracted his claws with a grimace but eyed the necromancer warily all the same. "It's not like any of us had a clue what would happen if you accidentally spilled her blood on a leaf."

"As I said, accidents are responsible for some of the greatest alchemical discoveries."

"Oh, enough with the excuses," Maleshi snarled. "You had no idea what you were doing with that human's blood, and this only happened because you're too careless to pay attention to—"

"Uh, guys?" Ember's voice squeaked, and she cleared her throat.

Venga snorted. "No, fae. You still will not be able to heal the human from her affliction. When it becomes an option, I'll let you know."

"Well, then I seriously hope you have an explanation for this."

Cheyenne, Venga, and both nightstalkers turned to look at the fae. Ember pointed at the ground and swallowed thickly.

Bianca Summerlin rose slowly off the floor of the lab, not on her own two feet but pulled by some invisible force connected to the center of her chest. Her arms and legs dangled below her, and her head hung limply. Orange light surrounded her, and a wind that didn't exist whipped her hair away from her head. Hovering five feet in the air, Bianca tilted forward until she hung upright, suspended by the magic flowing through her. Her eyes flew open, and a darker orange light blazed behind them with blinding intensity.

Corian bared his teeth and growled. "Shit."

CHAPTER EIGHTY-THREE

"That's seriously all you have to say right now?" Cheyenne clenched her fists, then hissed at the pain of the raw burns and opened them again. "What's going on?"

"Hmm." Venga tapped the Nimlothar leaf on his scaly lips, realized what he was doing, and quickly lowered it. "It would seem we've breached the next level in the vessel's purpose."

"Dumb it down, necromancer," Maleshi growled.

"The vessel has been activated."

"Are you kidding me?" Cheyenne glared at him. "You know what? Put the leaf down and don't touch it again, okay?"

Corian thrust an open hand under the scaleback's nose but didn't take his eyes off Bianca. Venga hissed and slapped the Nimlothar leaf into the nightstalker's hand. "I think I understand what must be done."

"Just a guess this time too, or do you finally know what you're doing?"

"We shall see." Grinning, the necromancer turned back to his workbench, his four arms flying into action again as he searched through the mess for whatever he thought he needed. "Keep an eye on her, yes?"

"What the hell else would we do?" Cheyenne stared at her mom, who didn't look like Bianca anymore as she floated in the air, the runes on her flesh blazing brightly through her clothes and her eyes open in an unblinking orange stare.

"Just do what you can to avoid any distractions."

"Like what?" Ember asked, her mouth falling open.

Bianca's arms lifted from where they'd hung limply at her sides, and her palms flashed with more orange light. The ground trembled.

"Ah." Venga pointed at her before snatching a small tin box off the shelf beside him. "Like that."

"What's she doing?" Cheyenne asked.

Maleshi leaned backward and shook her head. "I don't know."

Bianca screamed.

The fortress at the center of Hangivol rocked on its foundations. What little real stone existed crumbled under the magical force, and the metal made to look like stone groaned. Sparks flew where the ceiling met the walls, and the floor bucked beneath them, sending fractured metal segments flying away from Bianca in all directions.

"Fuck." Cheyenne stumbled sideways, then shoved herself away from the workbench and headed to Bianca. "Mom?"

"She can't hear you, drow," Venga shouted. In the courtyard on the other side of the lab, a huge slab of stone broke away from the wall and crashed to the ground. "Don't let her tear the place apart, or we'll have to start all over."

"Then that's what we have to do." Maleshi marched toward Bianca, and Cheyenne spun to head her off.

"Don't."

"Don't what, Cheyenne?"

The next ripple pulsing away from Bianca along the metal floor sent all the magicals staggering backward.

"She hasn't done anything."

"But she will." The general gestured at the floating human in the center of the room. "Look at her!"

"Not until we have to." Cheyenne dodged a flying shard of metal ripped from the floor. "And I do it."

"Fine. You can't hesitate."

"You don't know what she'll do!"

"If you can hold her off long enough," Venga shouted over the trembling roar of the fortress slowly coming apart at the seams, "I should be able to prepare what we need."

A huge section of the metal wall ripped apart with a screech and sailed across the room. Corian's claws were out in half a second, slicing the projectile in half before it had a chance to crash into him. "Is that a guarantee?" he shouted.

"It's good enough!"

The orange light around Bianca burst outward, ripping metal infused with O'gúl magi-tech out of the floor and walls and ceiling. Shrapnel and thick chunks of metal spun around the room, with Cheyenne's cursed human vessel at its center.

The halfling blasted a flying shard aside with a telekinetic wave and ducked another hurtling toward her head from the other direction. "Why is she doing this?"

"Built-up pressure," Venga shouted, then sniggered. "She needs to let off some steam."

Ember dodged more shrapnel and raised a shield of purple light in front of herself. "Not funny."

A wind kicked up beneath the spinning, hurtling pieces of metal and picked up the tools and supplies from Venga's workbench. The necromancer snarled in frustration as he tried to block his work from the growing vortex behind him.

"Cheyenne, if this gets too far out of hand," Maleshi called above the roaring tremble beneath them and the howling gale building in the lab, "you know we can't hold back."

"That won't happen." Cheyenne stared at Bianca, who was harder to see by the second with all the flying objects spinning around her.

Bianca threw her head back and jerked in the air before every floating thing in the lab closed in on her.

"Mom!" Cheyenne darted toward the compressing wall of junk.

"Cheyenne, wait!" Corian leaped after her, then the room exploded with orange light.

Shrapnel and tools, books, and sheets of the metal wall were flung away in a massive shockwave. Cheyenne and Corian were blown backward by it. The halfling managed to raise a shield in front of them both before the sharpened pieces hit it. Ember floated across the floor, her fae shield protecting her even as she bumped into the wall and was pinned there by the blast. Maleshi darted into enhanced speed and knocked aside the worst of the explosion, slamming huge chunks of metal to the ground between bursts of crackling silver light. Venga gripped the workbench with two hands to steady himself and kept working with the other two.

With a low growl, Cheyenne glanced down at the curved end of what looked like a pair of scissors sticking out of her thigh. She jerked it out and tossed it to the floor, then headed for Bianca again. "Mom. Can you hear me? You can fight this."

"You don't know that," Maleshi spat.

"Hey, I'm the only other one directly affected by this curse." Cheyenne flashed her burned palms at the general. "So unless you have any better ideas, I'm gonna go with—"

A streak of orange light slammed into her chest and knocked her to the floor. Cheyenne sucked in a gasping breath against the pressure in her lungs and blinked. More streams of orange light burst from Bianca's palms and feet, crashing into the walls and shelves of Venga's supplies without any real purpose. The chaise exploded under another attack, sending a spray of turquoise feathers into the air.

Cheyenne pushed to her feet and took a deep breath. *I can't believe I'm about to fight my mom right now. With magic. What the fuck?*

"Venga, hurry up!" She dodged another blast of orange light as Bianca spun slowly in the air, glowing brighter with each passing second. Another magical explosion cracked the wall and sent a spray of metal shards raining down on the workbench.

Ember floated over to Bianca and hesitantly turned to look at Cheyenne. "Anything I can do?"

More vessel than Bianca Summerlin now, the floating woman spun in the air and launched an orange attack at Ember. Cheyenne threw a shield up in front of her friend, and the orange blast ricocheted off the dark wall of her magic before crashing into the sparsely filled shelves above Venga's workbench.

"Yeah, Em." Cheyenne nodded at her friend. "Maybe don't draw any more attention to yourself."

Venga swiped the scattered bits of broken glass and metal fragments out of his way and kept working.

"Got it." Ember raised a shield again and didn't move.

Corian and Maleshi prowled back and forth across the lab behind Venga, watching Bianca becoming more and more unhinged as they ducked the messier bursts of warded curse magic and darted into enhanced speed to avoid the others.

The ground trembled again, more particles of dust and finely ground metal sifted down from the ceiling, and Cheyenne saw cracks growing from one side of the lab to the other. *She's gonna bring this whole place down on top of us.*

"Mom!"

Bianca spun in the air, shooting orange attacks in all directions.

"Mom, look. Come on. I'm right here."

"What are you doing, kid?" Maleshi growled.

"Trying to get through." Cheyenne stepped over to her mother, whose eyes were unfocused orbs of uncontrollable magic. *How the hell does she have all that inside her?* "It's me. You have to focus."

A small whimper came from the woman's lips.

Corian cocked his head. "Huh. Didn't expect that to work."

The flashing orange lights slowed, though the walls of Hangivol's fortress still trembled around them in a pulsing rhythm.

"You're here for a reason, remember? And it's not this, Mom. We're not ready yet."

Bianca slowly lowered from her hovering vantage point in the center of the room, orange eyes maybe focused on her daughter, maybe seeing something else.

Cheyenne thought, *I have no idea what she's thinking in there, if she's even thinking anything. But I guess being vague enough has its uses.*

When her mom's feet came within a foot of the trembling ground, Venga slammed a fist on his workbench and whirled, thrusting a black circlet into the air that looked like it was made of dark light and nothing else. "Got it!"

Bianca spun toward the necromancer and roared, reaching out with both hands to pelt Venga with streams of orange attack magic.

"Mom, stop!"

Venga raised the black circlet, and the vessel's searing magic bounced off it in waves, redirecting it at the walls and the ceiling.

Maleshi looked at the growing cracks and hissed. "Get her to stop, kid."

"I don't know how!"

"If you don't, I will."

Cheyenne looked between her mom and Venga, who laughed as the circlet protected him but quickly destroyed what remained of his lab. *I can't. I can't just take her out. I almost had her back.*

The cracks in the ceiling widened, and one end dropped before stopping, barely hanging on by secured metal panels.

"Time's up." Maleshi darted to Bianca, her silver claws flashing in the glow of the orange light and magic and sparks flying around.

"No!" Cheyenne darted into enhanced speed and raced after the general. Lashing black tendrils shot from her fingertips and wrapped around Maleshi's wrists before she pulled. The general slipped into enhanced speed with her as she was jerked backward and sliced Cheyenne's magic with her claws.

The drow cried out, and Maleshi crouched with a hiss. "You said you could do it."

"We're not there yet!"

"We'll find some other way, kid, but if your mom can't pull it together, we're all going down with her."

Cheyenne gestured at Venga in suspended animation, the black circlet he'd created raised in front of him to block Bianca's slowed attack. "He said he has it. Whatever it is, it works against this vessel magic. I'll get her to stop, and Venga gets the chance to use it. We still have time."

Maleshi stared at the cracked ceiling and half the room slowly caving in on itself as time moved much slower everywhere but within their conversation.

"What if you're wrong?"

"I get it."

The flash of blinding white light bursting from the circlet in Venga's hands overwhelmed them. It knocked them both out of enhanced speed, and Cheyenne watched everything else happen as if the rest of the world were still frozen.

She saw Venga's newest invention spew a stream of crackling white magic at her mom. She saw the cracked ceiling cave in the rest of the way. She saw Maleshi running toward Bianca, not to hurt the woman but to get her out of the way.

Cheyenne's drow magic took over in an instant. Black flames burst to life on her flesh and raced over every part of her as she darted between Venga's attack and her mom. The white stream of fiery light struck close enough to one of her wounded shoulders to make her roar in pain. It knocked her against Maleshi, who barreled into Bianca and was thrown aside by whatever wards surrounded the vessel.

Bianca and Cheyenne fell to the ground as Maleshi crashed against the far wall of the lab. The drow had just enough time to see the ceiling drop toward her and her mom.

"Cheyenne!" Ember raced toward her friend as the fortress' ceiling crashed down on the drow and her human mother. Dust and sparks and screeching strips of metal pelted the rest of the lab, but Ember raced forward behind her violet-tinted fae shield.

"No, no, no. Get...*hey!*" She spun toward a stunned Corian. "Help me!"

He blinked quickly, looking confused as he stared at the massive pile of rubble where Cheyenne and Bianca had been.

"Corian!"

"Yeah." He shook off his bafflement and ran to the ruins to haul a massive chunk of metal and crumbling stone off the top of the pile.

Ember's hands spewed purple light as her magic tossed one broken bit of ceiling after another across the lab.

Venga still held the wavering black circlet tightly with two hands, his all-black eyes shimmering as he searched the wreckage for movement. "This was not part of the design," he muttered. "If the vessel is destroyed, we're all fucked."

"Shut up and do something useful, will you?" Maleshi peeled herself off the floor with a grunt and staggered over to the caved-in mess. She joined the others in trying to unbury Cheyenne and Bianca, baring her teeth and growling with every toss of metal rubble.

They got halfway through the huge mound before the rest of it shifted and trembled. Corian and Maleshi saw the movement at the same time, and he reached tentatively to Ember. "Stop."

"No! She could still be okay!" Ember's purple magic flickered as she tossed more rubble aside.

"Ember." Maleshi walked quickly to her and grabbed the fae's wrist. "Just stop!"

Ember's elbow swung into the general's nose with a sharp crack. Maleshi shouted and staggered back. The fae spun to see what she'd done but didn't apologize. "I'm not giving up."

Maleshi wiped the trickle of blood out from under her nose and sniffed. "You don't have to. Just look."

The pile of rubble trembled and groaned, metal screeching and clanging as hundreds of pounds of Hangivol's fortress' ceiling bucked and lifted bit by bit. Ember stared and slowly backed across the rubble-strewn floor. "What?"

The debris rose into the air and slowly started spinning like it had around the vessel. Corian grimaced. "What if the human starts shooting warded blasts again?"

"It's not Bianca," Ember muttered.

"Are you seeing something I'm not, fae?"

"Yeah." Ember pointed at the center of the swirling metal pieces.

The only thing visible in the center of the clanking, spinning storm was a thick ball of black flame—no Cheyenne, no Bianca, just the drow black fire. Then the shards and crumpled bits and dented plates of metal sparked with blue light racing across them like an electrical charge. Every destroyed piece returned to its place in the ceiling, walls, and floors, the metal tech and magic working together to shift and reform into flat surfaces. Small segments unfolded and reattached themselves in seconds, sealing all the cracks and whisking every metal speck back into place.

Venga hissed and staggered sideways when a broken piece beneath his clawed foot jerked out from under him and slammed into the wall above his workbench.

The ground finally stopped trembling. They all stared at the massive ball of black flame roiling in the center of the lab.

"Is she in there?" Maleshi asked.

Ember shook her head. "I don't know."

The ball of fire grew, filling the air with a frigid burst of air. Then the flames sucked back into the center and shrank until they were flickering across Cheyenne's flesh.

The drow was on her hands and knees, one leg on either side of Bianca's body and her hands pressed to the floor on either side of her mom's head. The runes all over Bianca's skin still burned with furious orange light, but her eyes had lost the fierce glow of the ward magic held by the vessel. Instead, black flames burst from the woman's eyes, echoing the black fire in her daughter's as Cheyenne stared at her mom and held her gaze. Both of them were breathing heavily.

"Venga!" Cheyenne growled.

"By Yelv'iyt's fell-damn foreskin," the necromancer muttered.

"If you still have whatever the fuck that thing is, use it now. I'm running on empty."

CHAPTER EIGHTY-FOUR

"Oh, my God." Ember stared at her best friend who wasn't crushed by the cave-in and most of the now-restored fortress and slowly sank to her knees.

Venga sucked in a sharp breath and hurried to the drow, who was holding her vessel mother at bay with a fiery gaze. His clawed feet scraped the ground and his thick tail whipped out behind him as he crouched beside Bianca's head. The shimmering circlet of black light in his hands opened with a click. "Would you like to do the honors, or shall I?"

"Just fucking do it!"

"Agreed." He hastily slipped the open device around Bianca's neck, and the thing sealed on its own.

Bianca drew in a raw, gasping breath. The burning runes blazing on her flesh flickered and faded back into angry red scars again. The woman blinked furiously at the vaguely recognizable outline of her daughter's face beneath the black flames. Her mouth worked soundlessly for a moment, then she croaked, "Cheyenne, I believe you're on fire."

Maleshi snorted. Corian clapped a hand to his head before turning away in relief.

Cheyenne swallowed, and the black flames racing across her body snuffed out. With a groan, she rolled onto her back and lay beside her mom, staring at the reconstructed ceiling. "Jesus."

"Ha! That's it!" Venga leaped away from them, clapping two hands together and throwing the other two into the air. "It worked!"

"Congratulations," Cheyenne muttered. "You were almost too late."

"Ah, but the timing was perfect." A low, rumbling chuckle escaped the necromancer, his scaly lips peeled back to reveal a stained row of razor-sharp teeth. "There is so much more to discover after this. Yes. I should run more tests."

"No!" Cheyenne coughed and groaned as she sat up and glared at the scaleback. "For fuck's sake, give it a rest with the tests. Just for a minute."

He scowled at her and stormed back to his workbench. "No appreciation for the process. No gratitude. Everyone loves a fell-damn drow who can rebuild an entire room by thinking it, sure, but I'm the one who thought quickly and worked even faster." He thumped a fist on his chest and snarled. "You're welcome, by the way."

Cheyenne couldn't hold herself up any longer and thumped down on her back again. *I had to black-fire my own mom into submission. We're in way over our heads.*

Cold fingers nudged Cheyenne's hand, and she turned her head on the floor to look at her mom. Bianca stared at her with wide eyes, the flames now gone from them and her breath coming slowly and steadily again. The woman took a tighter grip on her daughter's hand and swallowed.

Cheyenne studied her mom's face, then glanced at the shimmering circlet of black light that looked like a collar. "Are you okay?"

Bianca squeezed her hand and whispered, "Thank you."

The drow couldn't say anything. *If we talk about it, I'm gonna fall apart.* She nodded slowly, her hair whispering against the ground.

Her mom took a sharp breath. "I love you."

Cheyenne's nose burned, the onset of tears blurring her vision, and she squeezed her mom's hand back and whispered, "I love you too."

"Well." Maleshi cleared her throat and grimaced as she stepped over to the Summerlin women, pressing a hand against her side. She extended the other hand toward Bianca and nodded. "Let's get you off the floor, huh?"

"Thank you." Bianca took the general's hand and accepted a gentle lift to her feet. When Maleshi released her, the woman frowned down at her hand. "Which of us is bleeding?"

"Me," Maleshi replied.

At the same time, Cheyenne muttered, "I am."

"Huh." The general glanced at the blood on the hand she'd used to help Bianca up and chuckled. "But this isn't mine."

Bianca wiped her bloody hand on her joggers in an uncharacteristic attempt to clean it off.

Ember scrambled across the floor on her hands and knees as Cheyenne sat up. "Jesus Christ, Cheyenne. I thought you were dead."

"I know. I guess I should've thrown an 'I'm okay' in there, huh?"

The fae let out a weak laugh of disbelief and reached out for her friend's hands. "Damn. Looks like someone filleted your palms open."

"Just burns, and a little scraped off on the floor. Oh, and some scissors stabbed my thigh."

"Yeah, I can at least do something about all that." As the golden glow of Ember's healing magic pulsed above each of the drow's hands, then her thigh, Cheyenne looked at her mom.

Bianca stared at the general's abdomen and pointed at Corian. "Mr. Nightcreature?"

Cheyenne would have laughed if she hadn't been concerned with the crimson stain growing through Maleshi's shirt beneath her hand. "Corian."

"Hmm?" As he turned to look at them, Maleshi grunted and staggered to the wall. He was at her side in a flash of silver light, shushing her and holding her up with one hand as he peeled her hand away from her side with the other.

Maleshi grimaced and gazed at him through fluttering eyelids. "Not as bad as Karu Ga'abil, eh, *ma gairín?*"

Corian shook his head. "Almost."

The general's legs wobbled and gave out beneath her, but Corian gripped her tighter to keep her upright. "Maleshi. Look at me. Stay here."

"I just need some rest. Maybe a bottle of Bloodshine." She started to chuckle but cut off in a groan. "Or two."

"No, what you need is a healer." Ember slapped Cheyenne's healed palms, then pushed to her feet and trudged across the lab to the nightstalkers. Her footsteps echoed softly across the floor, and the fae was the only magical in the room not looking at the lack of space between the soles of her shoes and the ground. "All right. There's nothing special I need to know about healing a nightstalker, is there?"

Maleshi and Corian exchanged wide-eyed glances. "I certainly hope not."

"Right. Just let me know if anything feels weird." Ember studied the massive stain below the general's ribcage, then lifted the hem of Maleshi's shirt and winced. "Ouch."

"Yep." Maleshi grunted and stared at the ceiling, "Any time would be great, Ember. I'm not made of blood."

"I mean, technically, you are."

"Just do it."

"Yeah, yeah. I got it." Ember closed her eyes and took a deep breath before her healing golden light grew between her palm and the massive, gaping slice on the general's side. A thoughtful hum escaped her, and her eyebrows flickered together. When the healing was finished, she stepped away from the nightstalkers and let out a surprised chuckle. "Wow. That was more than I expected."

Maleshi lifted her shirt again and raised an eyebrow at the perfectly healed wound, still slick with her blood. "Takes a lot outta you, huh?"

"I mean, nothing I can't handle." Ember swiped her hair out of her face. "You might wanna sit down for a while, though. Just in case."

Corian chuckled. "Yeah, you too."

"What? No, I'm fine."

"Apparently so." He looked down at her feet and raised his eyebrows.

Ember followed his gaze and let out a strangled gasp when she saw her feet touching the ground. Then her knees buckled.

Maleshi's hand shot out to grab Ember's arm, and she hauled the fae back to her feet. "You obviously haven't forgotten how to use them, so do it."

Ember blinked at the nightstalkers, then spun to stare at Cheyenne. "Tell me what's happening right now."

"Exactly what it looks like, Em." Cheyenne nodded. "You're back."

"Fuck. I mean, fuck, yeah!" Ember swallowed and dropped to the floor, steadying herself with a hand against the end of the shelf. Her legs spread out in front of her, and she thumped her fists down harshly on both thighs. "Ow, shit. Ha!"

Bianca sniffed, and Cheyenne looked at her. "Mom? Are you okay?"

"Just something in my eye, Cheyenne. You know." The woman wiped her eyes and stepped to the far end of the lab to pretend to look at Venga's unorganized supplies on the long shelves.

What the fuck? She cries for Ember's legs, and that's it? A sharp laugh burst from Cheyenne's mouth, and when everyone glanced at her, she lost it. She threw her head back and howled with laughter, rocking as she tried to push to her feet.

Corian leaned toward Maleshi and muttered, "Remind you of anyone?"

"She just got buried beneath the ceiling, trying to save and incapacitate her mother at the same time." Maleshi smacked the back of her hand against his chest and shook her head. "Don't jump to conclusions just yet."

"True. That is a uniquely Cheyenne combination."

Wiping tears from her eyes, Cheyenne gasped several times and finally got hold of herself. "I'm fine. I'm good." She chuckled again, then cleared her throat. "Totally fine."

Ember accepted the drow's hand up and stomped her feet on the floor. "Damn, that feels good."

Bianca turned, one hand on the wavering black collar around her throat. "Would anyone mind telling me why I seem to have been shackled around the neck?"

Every magical in the room turned expectantly to Venga. The lab fell silent, then the necromancer slammed a clawed hand on his worktable. "Oh, now you want my opinion, do you?"

He whirled, and his tail thumped the wall.

Cheyenne glanced at her mom. "How about just the facts?"

"Fine. I made an educated guess after the reaction between Bianca's blood and the Nimlothar leaf. As it turns out, I was correct."

"What about?" Maleshi asked, folding her arms.

"About Bianca's adverse reaction to the Undoing. And vice versa, of course." The necromancer pointed a claw at Bianca. "That device is powered by a small dose of the Undoing's organic composition, plus extra viable and quite powerful combinations."

"Wait a minute." Cheyenne blinked. "You put a necklace made out of the blight around my mom's neck?"

"If that's what you want to call it, Cheyenne, I suppose that will do."

"No. Take it off her. Right now."

"Absolutely not."

She stormed across the lab to him and summoned a churning sphere of black energy. "Now."

The necromancer didn't flinch. "So, you want a second round of the debacle in my lab, is that it?" Venga hissed and nodded at Bianca. "Because that's what will happen if I remove the device before we have everything in position for the vessel to fulfill its purpose."

"Her."

"What's that?"

Cheyenne forced her anger back down and swallowed. "Bianca is a human woman. You know, my mother. Not 'it' or 'the vessel.'"

"Yes. Anyway." Venga peered around her to get a glimpse of his invention again, which pulsed around Bianca's neck. "If anyone else were to endure prolonged exposure to even that much of the Undoing, I'd say they'd have three to four days before the infection would spread."

"You're not making a very strong case for yourself, scaleback."

"But your mother is the vessel, Cheyenne. She repels that particular poison, and that device keeps her activated abilities, if you will, dormant. Until, of course, the time comes when we are fully prepared to heal Ba'rael's bastardization of the Undoing from Ambar'ogúl, et cetera, et cetera. It's perfectly safe. For her."

The energy sphere snuffed out in Cheyenne's hand, and she turned to stare at her mom. "You feel weird from wearing that thing, say something, okay?"

"Of course." Bianca tilted her head and tugged lightly on the circlet. "Though I will say the mere fact that this exists on my person is weird."

"Wait." Ember took a sharp breath and pointed at Venga. "How did you get the idea that the blight triggered the vessel? Her blood was on the Nimlothar leaf."

"Ah, yes." Venga scratched his scaly head with a clawed hand, sending a rain of dry skin and dirt to the ground. "Well, that's simple. The Undoing—and we should stop calling it anything but what it is— has reached the last Nimlothar in the Heart, so I suppose we're working on a bit of a faster timetable."

Cheyenne and Ember looked at each other, and the drow's shoulders drooped. "Shit."

CHAPTER EIGHTY-FIVE

After that, Cheyenne had no choice but to tell them about her dream from the night before that had, in fact, become her waking reality: seeing Neros, finding R'leer in the bazaar, their visit to Agalyse, and what the darkseller drow had told her they needed to do. The discussion after that was more of a unanimous decision. Cheyenne had to take R'leer up on his offer to help heal the forest because after what they'd learned about the way Bianca and the blight interacted, it sounded a lot like this mass drow exodus out of Hangivol and into the mountains was a one-solution-fixes-all-problems kind of deal.

For now, Bianca was safe, Cheyenne was being poisoned to death, and all they needed was the okay from R'leer that he was ready to head out to the Nimlothar forest for a good old-fashioned deathflame bonfire. Whatever that was supposed to look like.

With Bianca resting in a private room in the Crown's fortress and Ember off on her own two legs for a solo walk around the city, Cheyenne headed out that night to find R'leer one more time and get a status update. When she reached the bazaar, the darkseller was in the middle of tossing a scrawny orc dripping with brown sludge out of his shop and into the already dirty underground alley.

"I don't want to see your face for at least another three hundred years, Zur."

The orc stumbled across the avenue, wiping slime off his face and flicking it onto the cobbled stones at his feet. "Greedy fucking drow. You have any idea what I had to go through to get that?"

R'leer's draping strands of beads and bones clacked when he lifted his hand and pointed down the avenue. "Better make it four hundred. Go clean yourself up."

Cheyenne turned to watch the orc sloshing off with a trail of reeking muck in his wake, then nodded at R'leer when he noticed her approach. "Looks like fun."

He smirked. "For me. Why are you here?"

She stopped. "What?"

"I haven't sent for you yet."

"Oh, I'm sorry. I didn't realize this was invite-only." Cheyenne glared at him, and the corner of the darkseller's mouth twitched in amusement.

"Well. That was my next order of business anyway."

"Really?"

"Yes. It seems you've beaten me to it."

She tried to peer around him and through the curtain of strung bones into his shop, but it was impossible. "You're ready?"

"We are ready." Raising his eyebrows, R'leer gestured at his shop. "Though there are still some steps left before we head out for all the action. Care to join me?"

"For what?"

He dipped his head and flashed her a crooked smile. "The last steps, Cheyenne. Having trouble listening?"

"It's been a day." Shooting him a sarcastic smile, she brushed past him and slipped through the curtain of bones into his shop.

R'leer peered up and down the avenue of the darkseller bazaar, then turned to follow her inside. "Indeed. I have to ask, was that little event in the Heart earlier today your doing?"

Cheyenne stopped in front of the counter cutting through the center of the shop and pretending to study the items there. *Of course he knows about that.* "No. That was a sloppy necromancer."

"Ah. Understandable." The darkseller clasped his hands behind his back and stopped on the other side of the counter to stare at her.

When he didn't say anything, she stepped farther down the display and glanced at him. "What?"

"Nothing."

"Then stop staring at me like that."

R'leer smiled. "As you wish."

His intent gaze made her temples and the tips of her ears flush hot. "You can't say, 'As you wish,' and then not do as the other party wishes."

"Then what do you want me to say?"

She stared at him for a moment longer, then stepped farther down the counter and picked up what looked like a hardened glittering peanut shell before tossing it back into a woven basket filled with the same. "You could start by telling me what the next steps are."

"Hmm." He kept staring at her until she'd had enough and turned to fake-peruse the items on the opposite counter, her back facing the darkseller. R'leer chuckled. "It's only one more step. I've done what I could to make the process as easy as possible for you, but admittedly, you'll have to do most of the heavy lifting. Being the Black Flame and all."

"Well, I can climb and take care of the heavy lifting, so it shouldn't be a problem." Cheyenne looked over her shoulder at him. "What do I have to do?"

"Send a message to every drow in Hangivol and tell them we leave for the northern mountains. Tonight."

She snorted. "So that's the big plan, huh? Just shoot out a mass memo, like, 'Hey, drow. The dead Nimlothar aren't dead and need our help, so rally your pitchforks and torches, 'cause we're gonna burn down the whole damn thing and save ourselves. Oh, yeah, and you have to give up your life to heal a bunch of magical trees.'"

R'leer eyed her as she moved along the counters. "Agalyse said we must lend them our lives, not hand them over."

"Right. Well, until I have proof that it's anything else, I'm gonna keep calling this a suicide mission. That way, we won't be disappointed if something goes wrong." *Which it usually does.*

"You still don't understand your part in this, do you?"

"Oh, no. I do." Cheyenne turned and spread her arms. "I'm the bridge between worlds, darkseller. The only way to get from point A to point B, and there aren't any other options because I'm pretty sure I'm Plan B also."

R'leer tilted his head and watched her stroll casually around his shop, highly amused by her half-sarcastic, half-serious performance.

"So fine, I'll send this damn message. And I'll sign it, 'By Order of the Black Flame' too. How does that sound?"

"I suppose that will do." Grinning, the darkseller headed to the counter on the other side of his shop. "Come. I'll help you make sure you say everything that needs to be said."

"You mean, what I spelled out isn't up to par for drow-wide messaging?"

R'leer ignored her and opened a metal box on the counter, turning it around so the contraption inside faced Cheyenne when she approached. "One of the only working message boxes down here. They come in so handy, I couldn't bring myself to get rid of it with all the other tech."

"Right. You are prepared." Cheyenne widened her eyes at the old-world messaging system with a snort, and her activator pulled up the thin lines of code and prompts for inputting whatever the hell she wanted and sending it to every drow in Hangivol.

Thinking about how she'd start this kind of message, she paused when R'leer stepped closer and leaned toward her. "You know, I am looking forward to meeting your mother."

She burst out laughing. "Why the hell would you say something like that right now?"

"Because she'll be there with us, will she not?"

"Yeah. She'll be there."

Cheyenne ran a finger along the edge of the message box. Bianca Summerlin in the woods, surrounded by hundreds of drow trying to heal a bunch of Nimlothar as she zaps the blight out of existence. L'zar's gonna lose his shit when he hears about this one.

The story isn't over quite yet. Join Cheyenne and her friends in the epic conclusion to the Goth Drow Series in *The Drow Will Leave*

Get sneak peeks, exclusive giveaways, behind the scenes content, and more.
PLUS you'll be notified of special **one day only fan pricing** on new releases.

Sign up today to get free stories.

or visit: https://marthacarr.com/read-free-stories/

Have you ever heard of the <u>10Q</u> project? It's free and was started by a non-profit to celebrate the Jewish New Year and everyone is welcome to take part.

I've been doing it for about five years now. Each year in early September, I get one question a day that asks me to think about who I want to be in the coming year. It's not like resolutions, which often have to do with outer goals. Lose weight, earn more money, clean out closets.

These questions are designed to get us to look at the inner workings.

Well, it's about that time and because this is 2020, they're adding 10 additional questions that are related to what's happening this year.

For example, describe an experience from before the COVID-19 pandemic that may now feel like it belongs to another world entirely. When you think about it, how do you feel?

Or, as society reopens and you reemerge, how would you like to see society shifting in the coming months? Or would you like it simply to go back to the way it was pre-COVID-19 pandemic?

Those are great questions. There's still nine days till the vault opens on September 18th and I think it's going to take me all that time to know the answer. Till then I'll contemplate some thoughts when I take my morning runs.

There are no wrong answers because they're all yours and no one else will see them except you – one year from now. Ten days after the experiment begins anew, the thousands of answers that are collected from thousands of people are stored away until one year later. Then they will all be returned to us to give us a brief glimpse backward into who we thought we were and where we thought we were going.

Provocative even in normal times and kind of fun.

But add in the year 2020 and it rises to something completely different, weird and maybe even better. I know I've lost a lot of the distractions I used to have that made it easier not to think too hard about a lot of things. Over the six months (I know... six months) that we've been struggling with everything I haven't been trying to find answers so much as relaxing into it and letting answers find me. I've become more willing to listen and to change.

And something has changed.

I'm less fearful in general and believe more easily that things will work out. Not only work out but grow and thrive. I'm more willing to stand out front and lead, instead of follow and see where the journey takes me. I've learned that leading doesn't mean you have all the answers. It means being willing to go and get up the next day and go again without waiting for permission from someone else.

A lot of low-level anger has burned off. Anger I didn't even know I possessed but was there. It was like I was mad at myself for not just doing what I wanted to be doing. Hard to explain if you're not in my skin.

So, back to the questions. I can't wait to see what I wrote last year before this year began. Maybe some general optimism and hopes and dreams. This year, it will all be replaced with a more grounded sense that all I've ever been asked to do by that inner voice was try and then I'll hang on to see where I just know I will soar. More adventures to follow.

AUTHOR NOTES - MICHAEL ANDERLE

OCTOBER 13, 2020

Thank you for not only reading this story (technically three stories) but also to our *Author Notes* in the back!

So, in 2019 I started an effort to test whether putting out three books as one (basically a box set) first was a better choice than releasing them as regular-sized books and eventually boxing them up.

The short answer is, "it depends."

For some of you, super-long books are fantastic. You felt like you really got into the meat of each story as we moved along instead of the short (60-70k) books we usually release.

However, some never started the books because they want to be into it and finished (or they read slower) and feel that 500+ pages is a bit much for them.

Finally, what happened to the company (that I have to admit I didn't foresee) is what happens when you commit to six megabooks. It takes forever to finish the series!

Six megabooks (like *Goth Drow*) are actually eighteen regular books. For normal release schedules, that is over four years of releases at four books a year.

Well, I got ahead of myself and LMBPN was doing a few of these types of series such that many of them were finishing in September of 2020—and all of a sudden, we had NO new series coming online.

Oops.

Actually, the answer was "Oh, crap" when our Editing Guru Walking™ Lynne mentioned it to me. I might have actually said, "Oh @#%@!#!!!." But you know, I don't remember.

(*Editor's Note: He did.*)

So, now we aim for books in the 80-120k range (occasionally going under or over that), but we have eighteen books for *Goth Drow* that will start releasing next year, after the megabook *Goth Drow* 6 is released on or about December 16th, 2020.

Which means we have eighteen covers to create. Nothing like knocking on our cover artists' virtual doors and asking, "So, got room for eighteen covers?"

They love it. Trust me. Kelly (who handles the author management for LMBPN), maybe not so much.

Because it wasn't just *Goth Drow*, but also *Witch of the Federation* and *Steel Dragon* and *S. Beaufont* and…. (Actually, I forget this one.)

Something like 80+ covers we dropped on our artists in a couple of days.

SIGH… So, that's a moment in Indie Publishing. Nothing like lining up that many covers and then thinking…

Wow, those are going to be hella-large invoices!

I'll talk later. For now, I think I need to go take some TUMS.

Ad Aeternitatem,

Michael Anderle

CONNECT WITH THE AUTHORS

Martha Carr Social

Website:
http://www.marthacarr.com

Facebook:
https://www.facebook.com/groups/MarthaCarrFans/

Michael Anderle Social

Website:
http://www.lmbpn.com

Email List:
http://lmbpn.com/email/

Facebook
https://twitter.com/lmbpn

Instagram
https://www.instagram.com/lmbpn_publishing/

BookBub
https://www.bookbub.com/authors/michael-anderle

OTHER BOOKS BY MARTHA CARR

Series in the Oriceran Universe:

THE LEIRA CHRONICLES
THE FAIRHAVEN CHRONICLES
MIDWEST MAGIC CHRONICLES
SOUL STONE MAGE
THE KACY CHRONICLES
THE DANIEL CODEX SERIES
I FEAR NO EVIL
SCHOOL OF NECESSARY MAGIC
THE UNBELIEVABLE MR. BROWNSTONE
SCHOOL OF NECESSARY MAGIC: RAINE CAMPBELL
ALISON BROWNSTONE
FEDERAL AGENTS OF MAGIC
SCIONS OF MAGIC

Series in The Terranavis Universe:

The Adventures of Maggie Parker Series
The Witches of Pressler Street
The Adventures of Finnegan Dragonbender